W9-AWL-092

...has its price.

By Kim Harrison

Books of the Hollows

A PERFECT BLOOD
PALE DEMON
BLACK MAGIC SANCTION
WHITE WITCH, BLACK CURSE
THE OUTLAW DEMON WAILS
FOR A FEW DEMONS MORE
A FISTFUL OF CHARMS
EVERY WHICH WAY BUT DEAD
THE GOOD, THE BAD, AND THE UNDEAD
DEAD WITCH WALKING

Short Story Collection

INTO THE WOODS

World Guide

THE HOLLOWS INSIDER

And Don't Miss

UNBOUND
ONCE DEAD, TWICE SHY
HOLIDAYS ARE HELL
DATES FROM HELL
HOTTER THAN HELL

And Forthcoming in Hardcover

EVER AFTER

A PERFECT BLOOD

KIM HARRISON

HARPER Voyager

An Imprint of HarperCollinsPublishers

This book is a work of fiction. The characters, incidents, and dialogue are drawn from the author's imagination and are not to be construed as real. Any resemblance to actual events or persons, living or dead, is entirely coincidental.

HARPER Voyager
An Imprint of HarperCollins*Publishers*
10 East 53rd Street
New York, New York 10022-5299

Copyright © 2010 by Kim Harrison
Bonus chapter copyright © 2012 by Kim Harrison
Excerpt from *Ever After* copyright © 2013 by Kim Harrison
Cover art by Larry Rostant
Author photograph by Kate Thornton
ISBN 978-0-06-195790-1
www.harpervoyagerbooks.com

First Harper Voyager mass market printing: October 2012
First Harper Voyager hardcover printing: March 2012

Harper Voyager and) is a trademark of HCP LLC.

Printed in the U.S.A.

10 9 8 7 6 5 4 3 2 1

To the guy who likes remodeling even more than I do

Acknowledgments

I'd like to thank my agent, Richard Curtis, and my editor, Diana Gill, without whom the Hollows would be but a small dream.

A PERFECT
BLOOD

One

The woman across from me barely sniffed when I slammed the pen down on the counter. She didn't care that I was furious, that I'd been standing in this stupid line for over an hour, that I couldn't get my license renewed or my car registered in my name. I was tired of doing everything through Jenks or Ivy, but DEMON wasn't a species option on the form. Friday morning at the DMV office. God! What had I been thinking?

"Look," I said, waving a faded photocopied piece of paper. "I have my birth certificate, my high school diploma, my old license, and a library card. I'm standing right in front of you. I am a person, and I need a new driver's license and my car registered!"

The woman gestured for the next guy in line, her bedraggled graying hair and lack of makeup only adding to her bored disinterest. I glared at the tidy Were in a business suit who had moved to stand too close behind me, and nervous, he dropped back.

The clerk looked at me over her glasses and sucked at her teeth. "I'm sorry," she finally said, tapping at her keyboard and bringing up a new screen. "You're not in the system under witch or even other." She squinted at me. "You're listed as dead. You're not dead, are you?"

Crap on toast, can this get any worse? Frustrated, I

tugged my shoulder bag up higher. "No, but can I get a dead-vamp sticker and get on with my life?" I asked, and the Were behind me cleared his throat impatiently.

She pushed her thick glasses back where they belonged. "*Are* you a vampire?" she asked dryly, and I slumped.

No, I was obviously not a vampire. From all accounts, I looked like a witch. Long, frizzy red hair; average build; average height; with a propensity for wearing leather when the situation demanded it and sometimes when it didn't. Until a few months ago I'd called myself a witch, too, but when the choice was between becoming a lobotomized witch or a free demon . . . I took the demon status. I didn't know they were going to take everything else, too. Demons were legal non-entities on this side of the ley lines. God help me if I should land in jail for jaywalking—I apparently had fewer rights than a pixy, and I was tired of it.

"I can't help you, Ms. Morgan," the woman said, beckoning the man behind me forward, and he shoved me aside as he handed her his form and old driver's license.

"Please!" I said as she ignored me, leaning toward her screen. Beside me, the man grew nervous, the spicy scent of agitated Were rising up.

"I just bought the car," I said, but it was obvious this date was over. "I need to get it registered. And my license renewed. I gotta drive home!"

I didn't—I had Wayde for that—but the lie wouldn't hurt anyone.

The woman eyed me with a bored expression as the man took a moment to write his check. "You are listed as dead, Ms. Morgan. You need to go down to the social security office and straighten it out there. I can't help you here."

"I tried that." My teeth clenched, and the man in front of the counter fidgeted as we both vied for the scrap of worn carpet. "They told me I needed a valid driver's license from you, a certified copy of life from my insurance company, and a court-documented form of species status before they'd even talk to me, and the courts won't let me make an appointment because I'm listed as dead!" I was shouting, and I lowered my voice.

"I can't help you," she said as the man pushed me out of his space. "Come back when you have the right forms."

Shoved to the side, I closed my eyes and counted to ten, very conscious of Wayde sitting in one of the faded orange plastic chairs under the windows as he waited for me to realize the inevitable. The twentysomething Were was one of Takata's security people, having more muscles than tattoos showing from around his casual jeans and black T-shirt, and the small, stocky man had a lot of tattoos. He'd shown up on my doorstep the last week of July, moving into the belfry despite my protests, a "birthday gift" from my mom and birth father/pop-star dad. Apparently they didn't think I could keep myself safe anymore—which bothered me a lot. Sort of. Wayde had been on my mom's payroll for nearly four months, and the anger had dulled.

My eyes opened, and seeing that I was still in this nightmare, I gave up. Head down, I gripped my birth certificate tighter and stomped to the bank of orange plastic chairs. Sure enough, Wayde was carefully staring at the ceiling, his feet spread wide and his arms over his chest as he snapped his gum and waited. He looked like a biker dude with his short, carefully trimmed orange-red beard and no mustache. Wayde hadn't told me this was a lost cause, but his opinion was obvious. The man got paid whether he was playing chauffeur for me or camped out in the church's belfry talking to the pixies.

Seeing me approach, Wayde smiled infuriatingly, his biceps bulging as his arms crossed over his wide chest. "No good?" he asked in his Midwestern accent, as if he hadn't heard the entire painful conversation.

Silent, I fumed as I wondered how the woman could treat me like I was just some jerk-ass nobody. I was a demon, damn it! I could flatten this place with one curse, burn it to nothing, give her warts or turn her dog inside out. If . . .

Hands clenched in fists, I gazed at the decorative band of

charmed silver on my wrist, glinting in the electric light like a pretty bauble. If . . . If I hadn't wanted to cut off all contact with my adopted kin. If I wasn't such a good person to begin with. If I wanted to act like a demon in truth. I'd devoted my life to fighting injustice, and being jerked around like this wasn't fair! But no one messes with a civil servant. Not even a demon.

"No good," I echoed him as I tried and failed to get rid of my tension. Wayde took a deep breath as he stood. He was small for a man, but big for a Were, coming to my five foot eight exactly, with a thin waist, wide shoulders, and small feet. I hadn't seen him as a wolf yet, but I bet he made a big one.

"You mind driving home?" I asked, handing him my keys. Crap, I'd had them in my hand for only the hour it had taken to get to the front of the line. I'd never get to drive my car legally.

Introspective, Wayde fingered the lucky rabbit's foot key chain, the metal clinking softly. There wasn't much on it these days—just the key to a car I couldn't drive and the key to Ivy's lockbox. "I'm sorry, Rachel," he said, and I looked up at his low, sincere voice. "Maybe your dad can fix something."

I knew he meant Takata, not the man who had actually raised me, and I grimaced. I was tired of going to other people for help. Hands in the pockets of my little red leather jacket, I turned to the door, and Wayde slipped ahead of me to open the milky glass. I'd get the car registered to Jenks tomorrow. Maybe Glenn could help get my license pushed through—they liked me down there at the human-run Federal Inderland Bureau.

"Ms. Morgan?" crackled and popped over the ancient PA, and I turned, a stab of hope rising in me even as I wondered at the hint of worry in the woman's voice. "Please come to window G."

I glanced at Wayde, who'd frozen with his hand on the door. His brown eyes were scanning the room behind me, and his usually easygoing expression was professionally wary. The switch surprised me. I hadn't seen it before, but then, it had been pretty quiet around the church since I'd officially switched my species to demon. Very few people knew the band of silver around my wrist truncated about half my magic arsenal. It was basically a Möbius strip, the charm's invocation phrase never ending, never beginning, holding the spell, and therefore me, in an in-between space where it was real yet not completely invoked and barred any contact with the demon collective. Long story short, it hid me from demons. My inability to do ley-line magic was an unfortunate side effect.

"Ms. Morgan, window G?" the worried voice came again.

We turned our backs on the bright, windy day beyond the cloudy glass. "Maybe they found another form," I said, and Wayde slid into my personal space, making me stifle a shiver.

"If you'd give the I.S. and the FIB the lists they want, you'd get your citizenship faster," he said, and I frowned. This didn't feel good. There was way too much whispering behind the counter among the no-longer-bored clerks. People were looking at us, and not in a good way.

"I'm not going to write out every single demon curse so they can decide which ones are legal and which ones aren't," I said as I found the hand-lettered, dilapidated G hanging over a small window at the end of the room. "Talk about a waste of time."

"And this morning wasn't?" he asked dryly.

I ignored that, hopeful as I approached the woman waiting for me. She was dressed like a supervisor, and the flush on her face ratcheted my worry tighter. "Ah, I'm Rachel Morgan," I said, but she was already lifting the counter to let me into the back area.

Eyes bright, she glanced at Wayde. "If you could come with me, Ms. Morgan. Both of you, if you like. Someone would like to speak to you."

"If it's about—" I started.

"Just please come back," she said, standing aside and ushering me through in excitement.

My gut tightened, but I wasn't helpless, even lacking half my magic, and Wayde was with me. Again my eyes touched on the band of charmed silver. I didn't like being without ley-line magic, but I'd rather that than the demons knowing I was alive. I'd made a few mistakes during the last year, the least of which had caused a leak in the ever-after. The entire alternate reality was shrinking, and as soon as the demons realized it, they'd probably take turns at me.

The woman sighed in relief as she closed the partition behind us, her low heels clacking fast as she led us to the back offices. An elated, frazzled living vampire in a black dress suit sat behind a cluttered desk in one, her face flushed and her eyes bright. She was young, professional, and probably bored out of her mind with working in an office day in and day out if the photos of her skydiving and running zip lines that were posted to her three-by-two calendar on the wall meant anything. Her office was overflowing with stacked folders and files in a weird mix of organized clutter. She probably took on more than she could handle. Trying to prove herself at the office, maybe as she clearly liked doing on her weekends?

I'd guess her human heritage was Hispanic, with her long dark hair pulled back in a simple clip and her dusky complexion, dark eyes, oval face, very red lips, white teeth, and pretty eyelashes. Her fingers tucking in her blah-brown blouse were long and slender, her nails painted a dull red. I could sense her confidence as she looked up at our entrance, a strong thread of self that ran through her. She was a living vampire, but clearly not high on her master's favorites list. I thought it odd that the more favored a living vampire was, the more emotionally damaged she was. This woman was clearly one of the forgotten. Lucky her. Being forgotten meant you lived longer, and having been forgotten, she'd probably lack most of the darker abilities that Ivy, my roommate, had developed in order to survive.

"Nina," the supervisor said, and the young woman stood, by all appearances not interested in me as she stacked the papers on her desk in a vain attempt to tidy up. "This is Ms. Morgan, and, ah . . ."

Wayde stepped into the hesitation, extending his hand as he moved both of us into the small, cluttered room. "Mr. Benson," the Were said. "I'm Ms. Morgan's security. Pleasure to meet you, Ms. Ninotchka Romana Ledesma."

The elaborate name rolled off his lips as if he'd grown up in the south of Spain, and surprised, I looked at the nameplate on the desk and decided I'd stick to Nina.

Nina blinked, her gaze going from him to me as if seeing me for the first time. "Ah, good to meet you," she said as she confidently shook Wayde's hand. She turned to me, hesitating as she saw my hands deep in the pockets of my red coat. "Sit if you want."

I glanced at Wayde. Nina was excited, yes, but not about us. *Was someone else coming?* I thought, looking at the only open chair in the cramped office.

"Uh," I started, blinking when Nina shifted her bra strap and took a peek down to make sure everything was where it was supposed to be. "Do we need another chair?"

"No," she said abruptly as the woman who had brought us back here left, closing the door behind her. "Unless your security wants one. But don't they usually stand?"

"I'm fine," Wayde said as he took up a position just inside the closed door. "Ma'am, just what is it you want with Ms. Morgan?"

Tense, the young woman ran a hand down her hip and sat behind her desk, hiding her hands when she noticed her fingers trembling. "*I* don't want anything. It's not me, it's *him*," she said, and the tang of excited vampire reached out and smacked me. God, she smelled good, and I felt a tingle from the vampire bites under my perfect skin. "I've never done this before. I didn't even know he knew I was alive, and now this!"

"Ah, all I want is my license renewed and my car registered in my own name," I said, shaken from the surge of pheromones. I'd been right. She lacked control, but if she had been forgotten, it didn't matter much. "If you can't help me, I'm leaving."

Alarm flashed over the living vampire, and she almost stood. "Someone in the I.S. would like to talk to you," she said, her eyes wide. "I'm the only one here he wants to work through. My cousin is in the I.S., and well . . ." Flashing me a nervous smile, she suddenly looked scared. "It's an honor to be asked to channel a master."

I felt for the chair behind me and sat down. "A dead vamp wants to talk to me?" I gingerly perched on the edge of the seat. Sure, it was daylight, but the dead ones were still awake, deep underground. Apparently one wanted to talk to me, one so old that slipping into an unfamiliar living vampire was possible. *Not good.* But maybe he could get my car registered for me . . .

Uneasy, I glanced at Wayde. He shrugged and fell into parade rest. "Fine," I said. "But make it quick. I've got to ask Jenks to register my car since you won't do it through me."

Ignoring my sarcasm, she shivered violently, jerking once as her eyes became unfocused and she reached for the stability of the desk with a white-knuckled strength. Her breath came in with a slow, sensual sound, her hair falling forward as her head bowed. She sighed, her red lips closing and her gaze sharpening on her hands gripping the edge of the desk. Slowly her fingers let go and her hands dropped into her lap. She seemed to grow taller as she pulled herself straight and looked at me—smiling to show her pointy little canines. I shivered at the new glint in her pupil-black eyes. I couldn't help it, and her smile grew wider still as she took in the shape of my face in a decidedly masculine fashion. It wasn't Nina anymore.

I stiffened as she breathed in deeply, shifting her shoulders back as she tasted my unease, something Nina probably wasn't skilled enough to read on the air currents. The slight grimace as she looked down at her clothes made me wonder if she was uncomfortable with being in a skirt, or because of the cheap fabric. Her confidence before had been within herself. Now it was the assurance that she could do anything she wanted and no one would think twice. From the door, Wayde whistled, his arms loose at his sides.

"You've never seen this before?" I asked, and he shook his head. I watched "Nina" look over the room, placing herself, hearing things I could only guess at, sensing things I'd seen on the way in. "I once saw Piscary take over Kisten," I said softly. "Ivy hated it when Piscary took her over."

Across from me, Nina smiled. "She enjoyed it," she said, her voice sounding deeper, richer, more sophisticated. "Don't doubt that."

Realizing I had crossed my knees submissively, I put my feet square on the floor and leaned back in my chair as if relaxed—but I wasn't. This was eerie, seeing a man in a woman's body, and I was sure the undead vamp was a man. Someone's phone was vibrating, probably mine, and I ignored it.

Nina stood, gracefully catching her balance and frowning down at the scuffed heels she was wearing. Her hand came out to me in invitation, and I cursed myself when I found my hand rising to hers against my will, shivering as she breathed deeply over it, sensing what he/she was doing to me. "It's good to see you again, Ms. Morgan," she said slyly, and I reclaimed my hand before she tried to kiss it. God, I hated dealing with the old ones.

I glanced at Wayde, standing stiffly by the door. "You were the driver in San Francisco," I guessed, remembering that the driver had been channeling an undead vamp of some importance, eavesdropping on coven business as he drove me out to take care of someone they couldn't.

Smiling to hide her teeth, Nina inclined her head, looking devilish and seductive both as she took up a slightly wide-footed stance. It was really weird. This was not the flustered vampire who had been here when I walked in. And it wasn't what Nina would become when she died her first death. It was someone else entirely, someone old.

"I don't like not knowing who I'm talking with," I said, trying for annoyed but hearing it come out as petulant.

"Today I look like Nina," she said, settling back in her chair and grimacing at the dirty corners of the office and the lack of a window. "You may call me that."

"Who *are* you?" I said more firmly, and she just smiled, steepling her fingers.

"Someone who can help you," she said, and I rolled my eyes as Wayde coughed. From my bag on the floor, a tiny ping told me someone had left a voice mail. "If you're willing to make an effort, that is," Nina continued, ignoring Wayde. "We failed in recognizing you. We let you slip from us. You've done well, but you could do even better—with a little . . . structure."

"I'm not coming back to Inderland Security," I interrupted, flushing. Crap, if that's what this was about, I might be in trouble. Saying no to them could shorten your life span. But all Nina did was send her pupil-black gaze to a paper on her desk. It was a copy of my license. Under it was a blank registration form. I sighed, remembering the world we lived in. Damn it, my phone was ringing again, too, but anyone important like Ivy or Jenks would know to call Wayde.

"I might work a job for you, though," I added grudgingly. Still Nina said nothing, her black eyes making me fidget. If the dead vampire had really been here, he could have tempted me into anything, but Nina was a young, forgotten vampire, and she didn't have the right hormones turned on for the vampire she was channeling to use. Yet.

"What is the job?" I prompted, wanting to get out of here before I asked to have her baby.

The light in her eyes speaking of a possessive strength, Nina smiled, showing enough teeth to make me stifle a shiver. "Right to the point," she said as if it pleased her, and

I stared when she tried to put a foot on one knee, checking her motion at the last moment when her skirt caught. She reclined instead to look even more masculine, more in control, not caring that she was showing a healthy portion of leg. "You do know the only reason I didn't notice you was because Piscary saw you first?"

Piscary was dead now, but I liked this even less. "What do you want?"

Nina tilted her head, dangerously suave as she eyed me from under her thick eyelashes. Ivy had given me that look before, and I stifled a flash of libido, knowing it was coming from the pheromones Nina was kicking out.

"I want you and Ivy Tamwood to help us find a group of Inderlanders committing demonlike crimes in and around the Cincinnati area. We have three sites to look at."

I sat up, shocked. "Three! How long has this been going on?" There'd been nothing in the papers, but then, if the I.S. didn't want it in the news, it wouldn't be.

"Several weeks," Nina said in regret, her gaze falling from mine for the first time, "which would be evident once you looked at the data, so listen as I tell you what you won't find there."

My eyes squinted. But ticked off was better than being turned on. "You should have come to me right away," I said. "It will be harder now."

"We thought it was *you,* Ms. Morgan. We had to make sure it wasn't. Now that we know for sure, we wish to engage your services."

Engage my services. How old is this guy? "You've been following me," I said, remembering that itchy feeling between my shoulder blades whenever I was out: the grocery store, the shoe mall, the movies. I had thought it was Wayde, but maybe not. Crap, how long had they been shadowing me?

"Three weeks," Wayde said, answering my unspoken question. "I didn't know it was the I.S. or I would have told you."

I turned to him, appalled. "You knew someone was following me and didn't think I needed to know? Isn't that your job?" I snapped, and Nina chuckled.

His expression closed, Wayde looked first at Nina, then at me. "It's *my* job, and *my* call."

"We believe there's more than one person responsible for the crimes," Nina broke in, and my attention was recaptured by his/her silken, aged voice. It was still Nina's, but the self-assurance was mesmerizing. "There seem to be two modes of operation, harvesting, then dumping. Witches. All the bodies were those of witches."

My expression twisted. I didn't like the sound of that. "Harvesting? That's ugly."

Nina took a deep breath, almost as if she'd forgotten to breathe—which was a distinct possibility. "It's the dumping that's disturbing us the most. Nina will escort you through the newest site, and by the time you're done, a courier will have delivered to your church the information we have on the earlier crimes. I'd rather you not come into the I.S. tower, if you don't mind."

"Not a problem," I said softly, thinking it over. De-monlike crime, not demon crime. I didn't want to risk the demons knowing that I was still alive. But if it was truly demonic work, it would be all over the airways. Demons are not subtle. No, it was probably a group of wannabe witches dabbling in black magic, giving demons a bad name. Taking them out would not only make me feel good but it might help me get my citizenship pushed through.

"Okay," I said, and her soft, pleased sigh slipped over my skin like a silk scarf, raising gooseflesh. "I have to make a call. And that's even assuming I take the job. What does it pay?"

Nina reclined in her chair as if she owned the entire building. "What do you want?" she asked, her slim fingers gesturing gracefully, the red-painted nails catching the light. "Money?"

The word held a badly hidden disdain, but no, I didn't need money. My purse was plenty fat. Literally. My credit cards had been canceled, my bank account, my phone plan, everything. I was unwillingly off the grid and carrying cash thanks to the money Trent Kalamack had given me, money originally from the Withons, a small (by his standards, not mine) token amount he'd demanded as an apology for their trying to kill him. Good thing I had a bodyguard.

"A valid driver's license would be nice," I said, fighting not to look at the form on the desk. With that, I might get my bank account back. "And my car registered in my name." The independence would do wonders for my self-esteem.

Leaning forward with a masculine huff of air, Nina brushed her long fingers through the forms between us, making me wonder what it would feel like to have those sensitive fingertips on me, and I shivered again. It wasn't her/him, it was the vamp pheromones rising in here, and I leaned past Wayde to crack the door. Office chatter, loud and excited, drifted in, and the undead vampire smiled, knowing why I had cracked it, though Nina wouldn't have had a clue.

"I'd appreciate a list of the curses and how they're performed so we can decide which are legal and which are not," she said, and I caught back a bitter laugh.

"You have a library card, right?" I said flippantly. "It's all in there."

Nina cocked her head and eyed me from around her long, beautiful eyelashes, making my heart thump. "Not all of it," she said softly, her words like an old jazz song down my spine.

I licked my lips and sat straighter, knees pressed together and hands clasped in my lap. "I don't deal with my legal kin—Nina," I said tightly, not liking the undead playing on my libido, and not through a young, innocent woman. Raising my hand, I jiggled the band of silver preventing me from tapping a line. He knew I had it. They all did. "I'm a limited-magic demon. Give me my car registration and my license, and I'll find them for you. That's my offer."

"Done," Nina said so quickly that I wished I'd asked for more.

Nina leaned forward, her long hand extended. I took it, and as we shook, the undead vampire left and I was suddenly shaking Nina the DMV worker's hand.

Nina's eyes widened as she gasped and pulled away. The scent of sweat rose, thick, and she fell back into her chair, her head lolling as her legs splayed awkwardly under the desk. "Wow," she gasped to the ceiling, her lungs heaving as she struggled to catch up on the air her guest had probably forgotten to take in. Her face was pale and her fingers were trembling, but her eyes were so bright it was as if electricity was arcing through her. "What a rush!"

I looked at Wayde, who seemed nonplussed, and Nina suddenly sat up as if remembering that we were still in here. "Ah, thank you, Ms. Morgan," she said, rising to her feet, full of energy. "I'll get your registration started and give you the address to the cemetery. I'd take you there myself, but I have to do something for him first and will meet you there. I have to go." Eyes wide, she caught her breath, and I swear I saw her shiver.

The paper was a soft rustle as she darted for the door, her speed edging into that eerie vampire quickness that Ivy, at least, took great pains to hide from me. I jerked, staring at Wayde as Nina's exuberant voice echoed in the outer offices. "My God! I could hear everything!"

Exhaling, I unclenched my fists. Track down some bad witches. I could do that. Like *Nina* had said. All it would take would be some detective work—which I sucked at—and some earth charms—which I could still do. "I should call Ivy," I said softly.

Looking uncomfortable, Wayde handed me my bag, and I slipped a hand inside to find my cell phone. I frowned at the missed-call number. *Trent? What does he want?*

"That's probably a good idea, Ms. Morgan," Wayde said, leaning over to look out the office door, but I was having second, third, and fourth thoughts.

Good idea? Right. That was the last thing this was.

Two

Friday traffic was thick this time of day in downtown Cincinnati, and I huffed as I stopped at yet another red light, my head tilted as I held my cell phone to my ear. The woman had put me on hold to check the appointment books, and I was ready to hang up on her.

Just getting across the city had been trying. The little blue sticky note Nina had given me two hours ago had only a street name and number. I didn't remember a cemetery on Washington Street, and I wondered if she'd meant the old potters' field where they'd built the music hall. God, I hoped not. Dead people gave me the willies.

Wayde sat beside me, his legs flopped open and taking up the entire passenger seat, trying not to look uneasy as I slipped my little car through traffic—I'd shaved at least five minutes off our travel time. I hadn't had the chance to try the Mini Cooper out in traffic until today, and the new-to-me vehicle was fantastic for turning on a dime.

"Miss?" the young voice on the other end of the line said, and the light turned green.

"Yes!" I said, glad I had an automatic as I crept forward through the intersection and tried to aim the heat vents at the same time. "I can't make it. Not today, and probably not this weekend."

My hair blew in the warm draft, and the woman sighed.

In the background I could hear some progressive alternative rock. Takata's latest, maybe? "I can take you off the books, but Emojin isn't going to be happy."

"I've got a job this week," I explained loudly as I took a quick look behind me and swerved to the right to get around some old guy in a blue Buick. Sure, the run didn't pay money, but getting my license and car registration back made me more than happy. Baby steps. I could do this.

Wayde grabbed the chicken strap, swinging with the momentum. "Ticking off your tattoo artist isn't prudent."

Frowning, I snapped, "Like saying no to the I.S. is any better?"

He shrugged, and I turned back to the road, slowing down. We were close to Fountain Square, and they usually had a cop on a horse somewhere. "When can you come in?" Emojin's assistant asked. "These specialty dyes don't hold their qualities forever."

I slowed more, my bumper almost on the car ahead of me. Crap, I could almost read the print on the tube of lipstick the driver was applying in the rearview mirror. "I'm sorry," I said, feeling a touch of guilt. "I'll be busy all this weekend and probably next week. I'll call when I can come in. Okay?"

The light had turned green, but the woman ahead of me wasn't moving. "Watch it!" Wayde shouted as I crept forward, and thinking we must be closer than I thought, I stomped on the brake. Our heads swung forward and back, and I grimaced. "You're going to lose your license the same day you get it if you're not careful," he said; letting go of the strap and sitting straighter.

"There's a good ten inches there," I grumbled. "It looks closer because the car is small."

From the phone came a faint "I'll put you down for Monday, midnight."

Is she not listening to me? "I won't be there!" I exclaimed. "I wouldn't have to keep canceling if you wouldn't keep making appointments I can't keep.

"Hey!" I yelped when Wayde snatched the phone.

"Give me this before you crack us up against a wall," he said darkly, his eyes pinched and his expression cross, his red beard making him look like a Viking.

"I can drive and talk at the same time," I said, indignant, then hit the gas to make the next light before it turned and we were stuck behind Miss-America-Wannabe again. Rearview mirrors are for seeing who's behind you, not for putting on makeup.

"Not well, you can't." Wayde put the phone to his right ear. "Mary Jo? This is Wayde. Give Rachel my next appointment. I'll get her there."

I looked askance at him, and from the tiny receiver came a relieved "Thanks, Wayde. She's a pain in the ass."

Wayde and I exchanged a long, slow look over the small space between us, and my fingers on the wheel tightened. "Really?" Wayde said, his face deadpan. "I've never had any trouble with her."

He hung up with a flick of the wrist, and my pink phone looked funny in his hand. "Would you mind if I put this in your purse?" he asked, and my irritation tightened. *Get me there?*

"Go ahead," I said, glancing at his tattoos as he gingerly opened my bag and dropped the phone in. He wasn't wearing a coat, and he looked cold. "You have an appointment at Emojin's? I didn't think you had a scrap of skin left to ink."

Smiling now, Wayde rolled up his left sleeve, making a fist and showing me his well-muscled biceps. *Damn.* An Asian dragon wound around it, its mouth open to show a flicking, forked tongue. Some of the scales were glinting gold, others were drab and blurry.

"Emojin is touching up my dragon. Giving it a little shine. I was stupid back when I got it, not caring who inked me. Emojin is one of the reasons I agreed to take this job."

Traffic eased the farther we got from the city center, and I risked another look at him, surprised by his eagerness. "Excuse me?"

Wayde rolled his sleeve down. "Emojin is one of the best inkers this side of the Mississippi, if not in the entire U.S.," he said. "I wanted to be a part of what she does, and if I'm here . . ." He shrugged, resettling himself in his seat.

I thought about that as I turned onto Washington. My heart gave a tiny thump, and I shifted my grip on the wheel, finally warming up in the car's heat. November was cold in Cincinnati.

"Standing her up is disrespectful," Wayde said softly. "She's an artist. If you don't respect the art, at least respect the artist."

My breath came fast. "I don't want a tattoo. I would've thought that was clear by now."

Wayde made a rude sound. "It is," he said sharply. "Put your big girl panties on and do it already. It's been ages, and you're being disrespectful to your pack. David—damn, if you were my alpha, I'd pin you by your throat and make you behave."

"Yeah, well, that's why you're not an alpha," I said, then wished I hadn't. My tight shoulders eased and my head throbbed. "You're right, though," I admitted, and he stopped tapping the armrest. "I need to do this." But it was going to hurt!

God, I was such a baby. At least I knew Wayde didn't have a day off until next Friday. I'd have until then to screw my courage to the sticking point.

We had to be getting close, and the street was almost empty compared to the last street we'd been on. I slowed, looking for addresses. Maybe it was a church. A lot of the little ones had small cemeteries beside them.

"There," Wayde said, and I followed his pointing finger to the I.S. van stopped at the curbside parking of a small city park. The music hall was across the street, but that wasn't where the cluster of vehicles was. I didn't see anyone among the trees and benches, but it was a six-acre park.

"Look, Ivy's car," I said, turning in to park beside her. I'd been hoping that she'd get here before me, wherever here was. If I didn't know better, I'd say the hour and a half it had taken to get my license and registration had been an excuse to keep me away until the real work was done.

Deep in thought, I put the car into park and pulled my bag onto my lap. The charmed silver around my wrist thumped down. I missed the protection that being able to set a circle had given me, and I didn't like crime scenes to begin with. Everyone made me feel stupid, and I always seemed to do something wrong. But I'd stand beside Ivy with my hands in my pockets and watch her work. She was great at crime scenes. She'd been the I.S.'s darling before she bought out her contract to go independent with me. I think it had saved her sanity. My thoughts darted to Nina, and I hoped that core of self she had would survive now that her master knew she was alive.

Wayde didn't move as I opened my door. The cool air rushing in smelled faintly like garbage. I looked into the park and saw nothing but trees and the top of a large gazebo in the distance. "There's no FIB here," I said softly, still inside the car. Unusual. Nina had said that they'd been working on this for a couple of weeks. Perhaps the crime had been labeled as strictly Inderlander, no human involvement.

Wayde stretched out as much as a Were could stretch out in a compact car. "You need me, just whistle," he said as he arranged his ball cap over his eyes against the sun leaking through the frost-emptied branches.

After weeks of him accompanying me and my hating it, I hesitated. "You're not coming?"

Lifting the brim of his cap, he eyed me. "You want me to?" he asked blandly.

"Not really, no."

He dropped the brim and laced his hands over his middle. "Then why are you bitching? It's a crime scene, not a grocery store. No one's going to bother you, and they won't let me in."

There *was* that. Nodding, I got out, hitched my bag back

up on my shoulder, slammed the door shut, and started up the sidewalk snaking into the park, hearing the radio chatter coming from the gazebo. My boot heels clicked, and I hesitated at a confident hail from the open I.S. van as I passed it. There wasn't any tape strung up, but with all the official vehicles, it was obvious the park might be closed.

"Excuse me, ma'am?" It came again, and I turned back around, fluffing my hair and smiling. I had a bent and dilapidated FIB sign under my car seat that I could put in the window when I was at crime scenes, but that wouldn't help me today. At least I had my *license*.

"Hi!" I said brightly, waiting until he asked for it before I dug it out. "I'm Rachel Morgan. From Vampiric Charms? Nina, uh, one of your bosses, told me to come out and take a look." I had stopped in a spot of light, and squinting at the thin, overly aggressive witch in an I.S. uniform coming toward me, I tucked my hair back. "I should be on the list."

"Identification?" he said, the word nasty and sharp. He was ticked that he'd been relegated to the parking lot when he wanted to be at the scene. I knew how he felt.

"Sure." I handed it to him, my cold fingers fumbling. "I'm with Ivy Tamwood and the pixy?" God! What was it with me making everything a question? I'd been asked here.

The man's confusion cleared, but he didn't hand me my license back, looking down at it with mistrust. "Oh! You're the, uh . . ."

My eyes narrowed at the derision that had crept into his voice. "Demon," I finished for him, snatching my license. "Yes, that's me." My charmed silver felt cold as I shoved my license away. Sure, be mean to the demon when she's got no magic. "They're over there, huh?"

I turned away, teeth clenching when he called after me, "Ma'am, if you could wait a moment? You need an escort."

Since when? I thought, my heels clumping to a stop. Behind him, at my car, Wayde made a bunny-eared kiss-kiss at me and went back to sleep. Irate, I leaned against a tree growing into the sidewalk. The trunk was still wet from last night's rain, and I crossed my arms and gestured to the cop that I wouldn't go anywhere.

He gave me a warning look and actually touched his wand, but when I pushed myself away from the tree, he turned and paced quickly to the van. Satisfied, I slumped back. Stupid ass. Now my mood was thoroughly ruined.

Sighing, I strained to hear the radio chatter, but it was too far for anything but background gibberish. Jenks would have been able to hear it from here. Ivy, too. My gaze went to the nearby music hall, and I shivered. The building had gorgeous architecture, but there was something wrong with it. Even the gargoyles avoided it.

A faint, familiar voice pricked at my awareness, and my face, screwed up in a squint from the sun, slowly became a frown as I turned to the park. The masculine sound rose and fell in a politically practiced wave designed to soothe, assure, and convince. It brushed against me with the warmth the November breeze lacked, and my pulse jumped. *Trent?* What was he doing out here?

The sidewalk was still empty, and I pushed away from the tree again, concerned as I remembered his missed call an hour and a half ago. If it had been important, wouldn't he have called Ivy or Jenks? But they were already out here. Damn it, I'd missing something, and I took a step forward when he and Nina came around a bend, their pace holding a businesslike quickness.

Jerking to a halt, I hesitated. Nina looked about the same. By all appearances she was channeling that undead vampire as she slapped Trent on the shoulder and pulled them to a stop when she noticed me waiting. They were too far away to hear what they were saying, but it was obvious that Trent wasn't happy.

I hadn't seen him in months, apart from visiting Ceri when her little girl, Ray, had been born. He looked good, if a bit preoccupied with hiding his anger behind a pleasant, fake smile—better than good, actually, and I fidgeted, remembering the passionate kiss that I'd promised to forget.

His fair hair moving in the breeze caught the light, and I could tell the movement bothered him when he tucked it behind his ear. He was clean shaven, ready for the office as he stood in a patch of sun in his thousand-dollar shoes and a wool overcoat that came down to his knees. It hid his athletic physique, but I'd had a pretty good idea of what was under it—every wonderfully toned, tan inch of him—thanks to having burst in on him in the shower once. Oh my God, seeing him with a towel around his shower-wet hips had been worth the entire twenty-three hundred miles stuck in a Buick with a carsick pixy.

He was about my age, my height, and way out of my tax bracket, even if he had given up on his bid for mayor and was no longer even a city council member. The illegal bio-drug lord, murderer, and real-time businessman blamed it on wanting to devote time to his new family, but I knew that coming out of the closet as an elf had hurt him politically. I felt no sympathy.

The thought of his silky hair in my fingertips as my lips moved against his rose through me, and I looked away as he and Nina clasped hands. The woman shook like a man, firm and aggressive, with a men's club air about her. *Why is Trent out here?* I probably should've used that hour and a half and called him, but I'd been afraid of what he wanted.

My eyes were squinting again when I looked up. Nina was bent over Trent's hand, probably commenting on the missing digits. Al, the demon I was hiding from, had taken them. He'd been well on his way to killing Trent at the time until Pierce had taken the blame for my being brain dead—which I hadn't been. My soul had just been trapped in a bottle until my aura could heal.

Cold, I tugged my coat closer as Trent jerked his hand back and said something terse. I left wreckage like a hurricane among those I knew. No wonder I didn't have very many friends. His pace fast and angry, Trent strode across the grass and to the nearby curb, clearly avoiding me. It was unusual that he wouldn't try to hide his anger, but what was the point if you were talking to a vampire older than the Constitution who could read your emotions on the wind?

"Trent!" I called out, hating the snubbed feeling creeping into me.

He tilted his head to acknowledge my presence without slowing, and my next words died at the look of what might be betrayal in the slant of his lips. "Next time, answer your phone," he said curtly from almost twenty yards away, his beautiful voice a study in contrasts. "I don't call unless it's important."

"I'm not on your payroll." Realizing how bitchy that had sounded, I took my hands out of my pockets. "I was in a meeting, sorry."

Frowning, he looked away, his back hunched slightly and his shoulders about his ears as he went to a small black sports car and slipped behind the wheel with notable grace. The door shut with a soft thump. If taste and sophistication had a sound, that was it, and I dropped back to the tree and watched him check behind, then drive away, the engine a low, soft thrum of gathering power, hesitating as he took a turn and was gone.

Nicely handled, Rachel, I thought sourly, glancing at my own little Cooper and seeing Wayde watching the entire incident. Nina was coming to me, her pace slow and provocative. I could tell the second that the dead vamp left her. Her heels began to click, changing from a confident, sedate pace to a fast cadence, her arms beginning to swing and her hips to sway. Her eyes, too, were no longer intense with sly dominance, but sparkled with the emotion of having been recognized by someone she respected. Her entire posture shifted from lionlike satiation to one brimming with tense excitement.

I didn't like that they had Trent out here. What had me most concerned, though, was that Trent was here on his own. *Curious.* Seeing my mistrust, she slowed her pace. "You got here fast," she said by way of greeting, her smile fading as she took in my unease.

I uncrossed my arms, trying not to broadcast my wariness. The DMV office had called her to say that I was on my way? Perhaps I wasn't supposed to know that they had Trent out here, too. *Curiouser and curiouser.*

"I made the lights," I said as she eased to a halt beside me, looking me up and down with a soft grimace, as if seeing me through her own eyes for the first time. Smiling, I extended my hand and the young woman took it, her expression questioning when I said, "Hi. I don't think we've really met."

"Um, it's not like that," she said, her voice a little faster, a little higher, and a lot more positive than just a few hours ago in the DMV office. "It's still me. It's always me, and then . . . him, too."

"Right." I put my hands back in my pockets. She was all bouncy and excited now, but I had a feeling that something was going to go wrong with this arrangement despite her obvious enthusiasm. There was a reason the undead didn't do this all the time, and it was probably going to leave Ms. DMV Worker in a padded cell when the undead master didn't need her anymore. "I'm supposed to wait for an escort," I said, and she gestured for me to accompany her.

"So, you working for the I.S. now?" I asked, trying to keep the anger out of my voice as I swung into step beside her, and she shook her head, a faint intake of breath telling me that she'd had an interesting ninety minutes while I'd been getting my temporary license.

"Not officially, no," she said, pulling herself straight. "I'm his temporary assistant."

Is that what they're calling blood whores these days? I thought, then quashed it. This wasn't her fault. She was the victim, even if she was willing. "So you won't mind telling me why Trent Kalamack was out here?" I asked, and she laughed.

"*He* wanted to meet him," she said, her tone somewhere between sly and derisive.

She was having way too much fun in this arrangement with the undead, and I made sure our feet hit the sidewalk at exactly the same time, adjusting my steps to be a little shorter since she was still in heels and I had on comfy boots. Recalling the almost betrayed look Trent had given me before driving off, I said, "That's why walkie-talkie man was out here, not why Trent was."

Nina's breath hissed in angrily. My pulse hammered, and I sidestepped from her before I even knew what was happening, finding my balance as she turned to me, her posture bent and aggressive. My hands were out of my pockets, but Nina was already relaxing, a sullen expression on her face as she refused to meet my eyes. "Walkie-talkie man?" she said, her tone sharp with accusation. "It's a good thing he likes that, or I'd have to teach you otherwise."

We started walking again, a good three feet between us now—and it was her pace that adjusted to my longer step. "I'd like to see you try," I muttered, and Nina jumped as if having been rebuked. It seemed as if her master vampire was listening in and didn't like her attitude. That was nice, in a creepy, somewhat uneasy way. Still, prudence had me exhaling slowly, trying to relax before Nina tried to jump my jugular. The woman was getting a huge unexpected eddy of sensory input thanks to the vampire possessing her, input that she hadn't had time to learn how to deal with. If walkie-talkie man wasn't there to pull in the reins, there might be accidents. Sure, it was nice now, but eventually there would be running and screaming and blood on the floor.

"I thought the crime scene was at a cemetery," I said cautiously.

Nina nodded as she looking intently into the park, toward the unseen crackle of radios. "It used to be one," she said, her voice distant, as if she was listening to the dead vamp in her head, "until they moved the bodies."

I'd never understood that, but I suppose it was better than having cemeteries taking up prime property when a small town grew into a larger metropolis. "Did they miss any?" I said as I paced beside her, her heels now clacking in harsh discord with my boots. Nina was still looking into the park as if trying to place herself, though I'd be surprised if she'd ever been here before. I was starting to feel like something was creeping up on me, and my shoulders itched.

From behind us, the little cop who had stopped me shouted, "Hey! I told you to wait!"

Nina turned with the suddenness of a cracked whip, every inch of her demanding obedience. "Do. Your. Paper. Work." The man backed up, his face white. I jerked, stifling a shiver as I looked at her, her teeth showing in a pleasant but frightening smile. The powerful dead vamp was back.

"Y-yes, sir," the officer stammered, almost falling as he backed his way to the van. The smooth sound of plastic wheels on metal broke the stillness as he slammed the door shut, and Nina turned, her hand lightly on the small of my back as she calmly ushered me forward with the grace of another age, not caring that the man had called her sir.

"I believe the reasoning behind depositing the body here was because it had once been a cemetery," the undead vamp said softly, continuing the conversation as if I'd been talking to him all the time.

I remembered to breathe after about three steps. "I'll give you one thing, Nina. You're a handy man to have around."

"I've been told that before," she said with an honest, companionable warmth that raised just about every warning flag I had. Even so, the hint of amusement in her voice was soothing, and I relaxed, knowing that—oddly enough—I'd be safe now. *He* was back and in control, and I thought it strange that I'd feel safer with a monster in control of himself than with a woman struggling to find it.

"You're going to handle this investigation personally? Why?" I said, tugging my bag onto my shoulder again to disguise the wrong feeling her hand was making on my back.

Nina smiled and shifted her hand from my back to take my arm as naturally as if she already owned it. It wasn't as possessive, and my unease loosened, even as I disliked the fact that the undead vampire in Nina had been reading my emotions and was trying to ingratiate himself with me. "I want to get to know you better," she said, her high voice taking on the hues of fine cigar smoke, rich and multilayered.

Swell. Nina's steps beside mine had become silent next to the soft thumps of my boots. "The last vampire who wanted to 'get to know me better' ended up beaned by a chair leg," I warned, but I didn't pull away. There was a delicious tingle rising where she touched me, and I liked playing with fire.

"I'll be careful," Nina said, and I shocked myself when I looked up and saw her long black hair and delicate face, not one wrinkled and leathered, wise in the ways to screw over the world. "You are a demon, Ms. Morgan," she said, leaning her head toward me as we walked as if we were close friends sharing a secret. "I want to know who you are so I can recognize your kind when it comes again. Who knows? Perhaps the I.S. is riddled with witches on the threshold of becoming demons."

"Sure, okay," I said, knowing I was the only witch besides Lee Saladan that Trent's dad had saved, modifying our mitochondria to produce an enzyme that allowed us to survive the naturally occurring demon enzymes in our blood. I could pass the cure on, but Lee couldn't.

"Oh dear," Nina said around a sigh, somehow injecting the soft oath with a world of disappointment. "There are no more of you?" she asked, having sensed in my last words that there were not. "Are you sure? Pity. I think I will stay nevertheless. You amuse me, and so little does anymore."

Better and better. With a solid effort, I pulled my arm from hers as we stepped from the sidewalk and walked on the frost-burnt grass. I still wanted to know why Trent had been out here, but didn't think I'd be willing to pay the price for it. Besides, Jenks and Ivy would probably know, seeing that they were out here already.

Nina's eyes were full of a delicious delight at my rebellion as we headed for the crackling radios. The older dead vampires got, the more human they became, and seeing such an old presence in a young body unnerved me more than seeing a masculine presence in a feminine one.

"I kind of like Nina, you know," I said, not knowing why but feeling I had to stick up for the woman being used so callously. I'd lived long enough with Ivy to know that those who attracted the undead's attention were abused and warped, and Nina had no clue to the depth of misery she was in for.

Nina sniffed, shifting her shoulders to look at the sky through the branches. "She's a sweet girl, but poor."

Ire pricked through me, and the last of his charisma shredded. "Being poor is not an indication of potential or worth. It's a lack of resources."

Nina turned, her dark eyebrows high in surprise. The delicious tang of experienced, confident living vampire was growing more complex and stronger the longer the undead vamp was in her, and I felt my expression freeze as I remembered Kisten. A fairy tale of a wish slipped through me that this might be Kisten, undead and reaching out to me, but no. I'd seen him dead twice. Nothing remained of him but memories and a box of ash under Ivy's bed. Besides, this guy was really old.

"You've loved one of us before," Nina breathed, as if the undead vampire in her shared my pain.

Blinking, I pulled myself out of my brief misery, finding that I'd put a hand on my neck to hide the scar that could no longer be seen. "I don't want to talk about it."

"This way," Nina said, making me take a small detour around a patch of grass. I could see nothing different about it as we passed, and Nina sniffed. "There are bones there," she said, her low voice having the hint of old emotion.

Curious, I looked back at the earth again. "Must be icky knowing where everything is buried," I said, thinking she was better than a metal detector.

"She was about eight," Nina said. "Died of cholera in the 1800s. They missed her grave when they moved them because someone stole her marker."

We were nearing the gazebo, wreathed with people and noise, but I turned to look behind me again even as I continued forward. "You can tell that from walking over a grave?"

"No. I helped bury her."

"Oh." I shut my mouth, wondering if the missing marker was under this guy's coffin. The undead did not love, but they remembered love with a savage loyalty. Uneasy with all the people, I looked to find Ivy, standing with two I.S. agents in suits, going over a stapled printout. The sparkle of light on her shoulder was probably Jenks, the pixy making a burst of bright dust to acknowledge me but not leaving the warmth of Ivy's shoulder as they studied a clipboard.

Behind them stood the gazebo bandstand, brightly painted and open. It would have been pretty except for the bloody, contorted body hanging from the center of the ceiling like a rag doll, spread-eagled, with filthy cords holding the limbs out. I felt myself pale as I realized the body had hooves instead of feet, and the brown I'd thought was a pair of sweats was actually a blood-soaked pelt of tightly curled fur. Blood had dripped from the corpse to puddle underneath, but there wasn't nearly enough there to drain a body, and by the gray skin visible above the waist, he was drained, the blood either somewhere else or leaked through the cracks to the earth below.

My pace slowing, I swallowed hard and wished I had an amulet to soothe my gut. At first glance, I'd say that it looked like a misaligned curse had hit him and he'd been strung up as a warning—sort of a perverted public announcement against the dangers of black magic.

Then I saw the letters scrawled on the steps in blood. Stopping dead in my tracks, I felt Nina hesitate, evaluating me for signs of guilt as I took in the single word.

EVULGO, it said. It was the word that the demons used to publicly acknowledge and register a curse, and very few people would know it.

Someone was calling me out.

Three

My head hurt, my heart was pounding so hard. Had Nina brought me out here to shake a confession from me? Was the I.S. blaming me for this . . . this *atrocity*?

Scared, I backed up, but she was a vampire, and with walkie-talkie man in her, it would take eight feet to give me any measure of security. Nina watched me, her expression more one of sour disappointment than the excited thrill of making a tag. Looked like I had passed the "let's surprise Rachel" test.

"You thought I did that?" I said, shaking as I gestured at the body hanging spread-eagled from the roof of the bandstand. "You thought I did that perverted . . . thing!" My God, the body had been utterly deformed. Whoever had done this was either seriously disturbed or utterly lacking in compassion. Demonic? Perhaps, but I didn't think a demon had done it.

Ivy looked up from the clipboard, and Jenks rose high, a silver dust slipping from the pixy. Feeling braver, I faced Nina, outrage filling me as I tried to push out the horror. This was why Trent had been here. As the man who had successfully banished me to the ever-after, they probably figured he'd know better than anyone if I'd done it.

"You brought me out here thinking I did this and that I was going to give something away!" I shouted, my back to the hanging corpse. Everyone was watching now, and Jenks darted to me with a sparkle of dust. I leaned in, furious. "What does your sniffer tell you? Did I do it?" I said bitterly. Jenks hovered before the dead vampire, his garden sword drawn. The pixy was clearly cold but ready to defend me, his tiny, angular features bunched in anger.

"No, not anymore." Nina's suddenly black eyes squinted as she looked past me to the hanging corpse. "But if you so much as scratch me, pixy, I will prosecute. I take care of those I borrow."

Jenks's sword drooped, and when I backed up a sullen step, he put it away and flitted to my shoulder, his dragonfly-like wings clattering angrily. Borrow. Sure. I suppose there were legal ramifications to letting the body you were controlling die. If anyone could kill a living vampire, Jenks had the reflexes to do it. Though pixies were generally a peaceful, garden-loving people, they fought fiercely for those they gave their loyalty to, and Jenks and I went back a long way. He looked about eighteen in his black, double-layered, skin-tight cold-weather gear, the only softness to him a decorative red sash his deceased wife had made for him. The color would keep any pixies not yet in hibernation from slaughtering him for being on their turf.

"Hi, Rache," Jenks said as the four-inch man landed on my shoulder, bringing the scent of dandelions and oiled steel to me. "This vampire flunky giving you trouble?"

Nina grimaced at the slur. Behind her, Ivy made her slow way to us, scuffing her boots on the sidewalk so there'd be no misunderstanding of her intentions. She looked relaxed in her black jeans and leather coat, open to show her tucked-in T-shirt, but I'd lived across the hall from her for over two years, and I could see her tension in the tightness of her eyes. Some of it was a lingering jealousy she couldn't help, because I was talking to another vampire—one stronger and more influential than she was—but most of it was concern as she prepared to stand up to a dead vampire. Her mother's Asian heritage made her slim, her father's European background made her tall. Straight black hair hung almost down to her midback again. It was in a ponytail right now, swaying as she came closer. Confident, she nevertheless had a healthy respect for her undead kin, and I dropped back a couple of steps to make room for her.

"Hi, Rachel," she said, letting a soft, sultry tone into her voice to help cement her high political standing in Nina's mind. Ivy was still alive, but she came from a very powerful family. "Are they not letting you on the crime site again?"

Feeling better with my friends around me, I uncrossed my arms. Nina was silent, and the surrounding I.S. officers were drifting into scoffing groups, probably making bets. "I don't know yet," I said tightly. "Walkie-talkie man here only gave us the job to find out if I did it."

Jenks's laughter sounded like angry wind chimes, and Ivy tilted her head as she took in Nina's off-the-rack dress suit, scuffed heels, and a warm but clearly last year's style coat, knowing in an instant that she was channeling a dead vampire. "Another stellar decision from the I.S. basement," Ivy said, smiling to let her slightly pointy canines show.

My anger slid three points to unease when Nina smiled back at Ivy with an obvious attraction, clearly liking her strong will and defiant attitude. Yeah, that was about right for the old ones. The more you defied them, the more you relieved their boredom and the more they tried to break you.

Jenks recognized Nina's sultry look as one of the slow hunt, and his wings clattered in warning. Ivy recognized it, too, and grimacing, she rolled her eyes and blandly offered her hand to Nina. "I'm Ivy Tamwood," she said without emotion as she tried to repair the damage and distance herself. "But you already know that."

Nina became almost coy, formally taking her hand and kissing the top of it in an overdone show that looked really odd with the dead body strung up behind them. Jenks and I exchanged looks as the game of cat-and-mouse chess continued.

"I worked with your mother before she retired from the

I.S.," Nina said, her voice as gray and silky as holy dust. "You have her strength and your father's humor. Piscary was a fool for mishandling you."

Ivy yanked her hand back. "Piscary was my life. Now he's dead and I have a new one."

Ivy glanced at me, and I couldn't meet anyone's eyes as Jenks harrumphed. My scar was tingling at the vamp pheromones the two of them were kicking out, and I was struggling not to hide my neck when a ping of sensation snaked its way down to my groin. *Vampires* . . .

I took a slow breath, knowing by Ivy's widening pupils that she was feeling it, too. Nina was getting better at channeling her undead master. Either that, or new hormones were being turned on the longer the master was inside her brain. I was betting it was the latter, and probably part of the perks of putting up with someone being inside you.

A faint yelp from the parking lot turned me around, and I wasn't surprised to see Wayde jogging up the sidewalk, the I.S. officer from the van limping behind him. Nina made a small noise when he ran right over that patch of holy ground, clearly not pleased.

"I thought you were staying in the car!" I shouted as Nina sourly gestured to the surrounding I.S. officers to let him pass.

Giving them space warily, Wayde slowed as he approached, his eyes widening as he glanced at the body, then did a double take. "You yelled," he explained, then looked again and swore under his breath. "I came. That's my job. What the hell is that?"

"Someone's mistake," I said. "They asked me out here because they thought I did it. I got mad."

"Sir," Nina started, and I wondered why he/she used any term of respect at all.

"He's my bodyguard," I said tightly. "You know that. I don't trust you. I should walk away from this, but I'm here, and I'm going to take a look. He stays. Got a problem, take it up with my mom."

Jenks laughed as the undead vampire looked through Nina's eyes, assessed the situation, then nodded, Nina's stance taking on a faint swagger at odds with her slim figure. "He may stay if his talents include keeping his mouth shut."

Wayde exhaled, seeming to lose body mass and tension, but it all came back when he glanced at the body again. "Uh, sorry it took me so long to get here," he said to me. "I had to get around limp dick there."

I looked behind Wayde to the retreating I.S. officer. He had his hand on his nose, and I think he was bleeding if Nina's sharp eyes on him meant anything. Fresh blood and the scent of a fight were like champagne to the undead, and my estimation of Wayde wavered. A good bodyguard could have gotten by the I.S. officer without drawing blood.

"Don't worry about it," I said as I glanced at Ivy and she shrugged almost imperceptibly. "I appreciate it." And despite my doubts, I did. Regardless of having broken the cop's nose, he'd clearly been doing his job if the I.S. had been shadowing me and all I'd gotten was a faint feeling of unease. I wasn't helpless, but another pair of eyes and fists usually kept incidents from ever happening. The best body-guard was one who didn't have to do anything but be there.

Jenks's wings clattered as he took off from my shoulder, clearly struggling from the weight of his extra clothes. November was the cusp for pixies. Most were hibernating by now, but Jenks and his family would winter in the church, and if the day was warm enough, Jenks would brave the cold.

"We gonna watch walkie-talkie vamp have a blood orgy, or are we going to look at someone else's?" he said snidely, and Nina gestured to the pair of I.S. officers who had been nervously lurking nearby. The better-dressed one jogged forward with the printout and handed it to Nina before back-ing up. I'd be cautious, too, if my superior had been lusting after someone's nosebleed.

"I've sent a copy to your church of the information we've already gathered," Nina said as she handed it in turn to Ivy. "I want this back. It's my copy."

Ivy took it, her lips tight with repressed anger. Something was bothering her, something more than the body. I looked past Nina to the body again, repulsed and yet riveted. My God, the man had only one hand left. It was thick and malformed, bending in as if cramped, with a thick, horny, inflexible skin. The fingers looked as if they were made of dough and just stuck on. The other hand and both his feet were perfect cloven hooves. If anything, he looked like a faun, only everything was perverted and disproportionate. There were no such things as fauns, never had been, but perhaps mutilations such as this were where the fable had gotten started.

Feeling ill, I looked away, noticing that the blood-drawn pentagram under him was one made to gather power from an external source. Jeez, I hoped this had nothing to do with me. The man looked as if he'd been in his midtwenties, fit apart from the half-goat thing.

"How many have there been?" I asked. They might only have asked me out here to see if I had done it, but now that I was here, I was going to find out who had. Ivy, too, was studiously looking through the packet of information, clearly eager to take the run. There were a lot of papers. The I.S. wasn't known for being meticulous about data gathering, meaning this had been going on for a while. They should have come to me sooner.

Spinning gracefully, Nina turned to the body, looking at it as if it were a painting on a wall. "This is the third incident. His name was Thomas Siskton, and he was a university student, missing since last week."

Jenks whistled by rubbing his wings together, and then he darted to the railing, standing on it and facing the body. "There hasn't been anything in the news. You'd think a hoofed university student with horns would make the papers."

"Keep your mouth shut," Ivy said, knowing how hard it was for the pixy to keep a secret.

Nina looked between me and Wayde, clearly not happy

with the Were being here. She probably didn't know Jenks was the higher risk for blabbing despite pixies being noncitizens. "We've kept it quiet. It needs to stay that way."

"Don't worry about me," Wayde said, dropping back and putting a hand in the air as he looked down submissively. "I'm a professional."

I grimaced, hearing what the undead vampire was saying. You don't just keep something like this quiet without illegal memory charms. Great. I hated memory charms.

Nina saw my understanding and smiled with her new, confident, sexy eyes and turned to Ivy, a hand out as if to escort her up the stairs. "The site is open for your inspection," she said as she walked over the blood-painted word of Latin as if it meant nothing. "We've already gathered what we need."

"Good." Ivy casually sidestepped Nina's guiding hand and walked up the stairs by herself. "I'll let you know what you missed."

Her attitude was surprisingly belligerent, and I wondered why she was letting her emotions show like this. She knew it would attract the undead's attention all the more, and clearly she didn't like him. Concerned, I went to follow Ivy up, and Wayde touched my elbow. "Hey, uh, I'll stay here if you don't mind," he said, his face pale as he looked up at the body.

Jenks snickered, which I thought totally unfair, following it up with a "Not used to the blood, wolfman?"

Wayde's expression sharpened on the pixy. "He's half turned into something. You know how many nightmares I've had about that?"

Yes, I suppose being able to turn into a wolf, painfully, might give one a new kind of nightmare, and I smiled as I gave his arm a squeeze, feeling the hard muscle under his shirt. "You can wait at the car if you want. I'll be fine."

"No, I'll stay. Just not up there," Wayde said, and Nina cleared her throat for me to hurry up, even as Wayde looked past me to the body and shivered.

"Rache . . ." Jenks complained, and I headed up the stairs,

hands in my pockets and giving the Latin a wide berth, reminded of how Nina had skirted the dead child under the ground.

"This is the third," Nina said, and I blanched as I now had nothing else to look at other than the blood-soaked, softly pelted, cloven-hoofed, disfigured man before me. Jenks was right; he even had tiny horns, and his skin was gray and softly textured like a gargoyle's. What in hell had they done to him? And why?

Please, God, may it have nothing to do with me. But I was the first demon this side of the ley lines, and I was getting a really bad feeling.

"We found the oldest one just last week," Nina added, almost as an afterthought, her voice telling me the vampire speaking through her was deep in thought.

"You didn't find them in order?" Jenks had parked himself upwind of the corpse. It smelled, but the cold had suppressed most of the stench. Actually the body had a distinctive meadow scent under all the decaying blood, and I wondered if that was part of the faun thing that it had going.

Nina gave Jenks a dry look. "All the dump sites are similar to this one, but the first involved three teenagers from three different schools, missing since the fourth of November. Two were contorted like this one, the other died from heart failure. Her medical history shows she had heart issues, and we think she died from fright."

I breathed deep, trying to get beyond the atrocity so I could think. The scent of wine and salt tickled a memory. Electricity, ozone, old books: it all added up to demons, except for the fact that there wasn't the faintest hint of burnt amber. Demons stank of it. Jenks had assured me that I didn't smell like the ever-after, but I think he was lying.

I'd been born a witch, but my blood kindled demon magic and the way the coven of moral and ethical standards saw it was that if it looked like a demon, did magic like a demon, and could be summoned like a demon, it was a demon. I couldn't find fault with them. It had been a shock when I realized my blood didn't invoke every witch charm, failing at the most complex because of the demon enzymes in it. Al, my demon teacher, was the same. I *was* a demon, like it or not. The first of a new generation thanks to Trent's father. How nice was that?

The soft sound of pixy wings pulled me from my sour musings, and Jenks landed on my shoulder, his wings tinted blue from the cold. He knew where my thoughts had gone just by looking at me. "I don't smell any burnt amber," I said, and Nina nodded. Her canny gaze looked wrong on someone so young.

"It wasn't at any other sites, either," she said. "That's why we thought of you."

Ivy cleared her throat in reproach, and Nina broke eye contact with me to stare at her for a long, slow moment, the smaller woman quietly asserting her dominance until Ivy looked away. "All the victims had a large quantity of their blood drained from them, as you see here," Nina said, turning back to the body. "The first victims showed evidence of being held against their wills: split fingernails, bondage marks, bruises, cuts, contusions. They resisted their capture and restraint. Evidence points to one to six days' worth of torture. The moulage was old, but we're fairly confident that none of the victims was killed where we found them."

The man before me looked worn, in the dry air his dead eyes starting to sink back. The moulage here was clean, too, or Ivy would have said something. I couldn't see emotion imprinted on the world, but vampires could. Most moulages faded with the sun, but murder left a stronger impression that could last weeks or even centuries if the crime was heinous enough and the spirit desperate to continue life. It was the source of ghosts—most times.

"Where were the others found?" Ivy asked, and Nina aggressively took the packet of papers from her, handing them back with a page of photos flipped open.

"The first victims were at an abandoned school," Nina said as she looked down at the page, her jaw tense at Ivy's subtle refusal to accept her authority. "It had been built on property that had once been a cemetery. Like this," she said, her gaze lifting to the surrounding bare trees as if seeing it in another time. "It's one of the ties between the crimes. The second victim, who we found first, was in the driveway of a museum."

"Let me guess," Jenks said snidely. "It was built on an old grave site."

Nina inclined her head, smiling with her teeth hidden. "Cincinnati is riddled with abandoned churchyards. Bodies were moved a lot, and not always back into the ground."

Brow furrowed, I thought of our own graveyard, attached to the church. I didn't want a body showing up there, especially not one with hooves and horns.

I didn't even know this man's name, and I carefully stepped over a blood-soaked cord holding his, ah, hoof so I could see his back, forcing myself to look closer to try and make sense of this. A hint of a tail made my stomach clench. I'd caught a glimpse of the school photo before Ivy turned away, and it made me even more uneasy. The pentagram surrounding the body here was the same they'd used at the school. It was fairly common in the higher charms, but drawing it in blood wasn't. Someone was playing at being a demon.

"The victims at the school were decomposing badly when we found them," Nina said, distracting me, "but they had clearly been restrained. The second victim had been kept sedated. We don't know about this man. The tests haven't been run yet, but he's clearly been held against his will."

Jenks took off from my shoulder, his wings clattering in anger. "Decomposed!" he exclaimed, clearly disgusted. "In this weather? Just how long had they been dead?"

Nina ignored his anger. "The three at the school had been dead somewhere between eight and ten days. We know they went missing on the fourth, but we aren't sure how long they were dead before we found them Tuesday."

Tuesday? Like three days ago Tuesday?

"Tink loves a duck!" Jenks exclaimed. "What have you been doing? Sitting on your thumb and spinning?"

"Jenks!" I exclaimed, and the undead vampire let some of his anger show, Nina's eyes squinting. The anger wasn't directed at us, telling me he wasn't happy with how the investigation had been handled, either.

"The best we can tell, they probably died between the eighth and the tenth," Nina said.

I really wanted off this bandstand, but I didn't want to look squeamish.

"Magic killed them, not blood loss," she added, holding her breath when the wind blew and the man's blood-caked hair moved in the breeze. "That came afterward. Apart from the girl at the school, they died from a transforming spell that wasn't done properly. We can't be sure until the necropsy, but if this man follows the pattern, his insides will be as deformed as his outsides. They died because their bodies couldn't function."

Jenks was a tight hum at my ear, and he was slipping a green dust. "Hey, Rache, you mind if I check the sitch with the local pixies? They aren't hibernating yet."

Nina stiffened. It was a slight movement that probably would have escaped my detection if I hadn't been looking for it. The dead vampire thought it was a waste of time, but not breaking our eye contact I nodded. "Good idea, Jenks."

"Back in a sec," he said, and in a flash, he was gone. I wished I could fly away, too.

"Whose blood made the spells that did this?" I asked, starting to get a bad feeling. Three teenagers killed, then a few days later, a second victim, then a few more days, and then Thomas.

"What an interesting question." Nina backed up to lean against the railing. "We didn't catch on that fast—Ms. Morgan."

Her stance said I knew too much. Maybe she was right. Maybe it just took a demon to catch a demon. "Whose blood twisted the spells that killed them?" I asked again, jaw clenching.

"At the school, they died from their own. The second victim died from a spell kindled with blood from one of the teenagers. We don't know yet whose blood this man died from."

My shoulders slumped as I exhaled, and Ivy, who was looking from the bloody floor to one of the photos to compare the glyphs, met my eyes, reading my worry. Crap, they were leapfrogging. Taking the blood from the last victim to capture and experiment on the next. I put a hand to my middle and looked at the pentagram around me, wishing I had enough guts to take my charmed silver off and see where the nearest ley line was. Close, I bet. Graveyards were often built on them. If Jenks were here, I could ask him.

"Our working theory is once the perpetrators harvest sufficient blood to play with, they simply use the blood of the previous victim to experiment on and torture the next," Nina said.

Play. That was a good word. It was what I'd already figured out, but hearing it made me more nauseated yet. At least there'd probably be no bodies older than the ones found at the school.

"Experiment?" Ivy looked up from her pages.

Nina drew herself up into a lecturing pose, and I wondered if the vampire inside her had been a professor. "In each case, the blood has been modified. To what end, we don't yet know."

I didn't know, either, and I looked at the body so I wouldn't have to look at Nina. This man's death had been painful, his body spending several days twisted somewhere between a human and a goat as his captors played with his blood. But why? This was just nasty. Whoever had done this had dumped him to create a sensation and get noticed. A perverted warning against black magic . . . or a way to get my attention?

"How about the circle?" I said, my hands in my coat pockets. "Whose blood made it?"

Nina drifted closer to me, her posture having a relaxed tension as she passed the body with barely a flicker of acknowledgment. "We're having difficulty finding that out. Our standard, magic-based tests are coming back inconclusive, and we're having some trouble duplicating the FIB's barely legal tissue-typing techniques. We think it's from the second victim as well. He died only a week ago. A businessman in town for a convention."

"Let me guess," I said, doing the math in my head. "Thomas went missing exactly five days after the businessman died."

"Exactly . . ." Nina whispered, her voice drawing through me to make me shiver and Ivy frown. *Was she jealous?* "How did you know?"

Knees wobbly, I sat down on the top step, my feet just shy of the word written in blood. The man's cloven feet were at my eye level, and I turned away, breathing shallowly. "Because if you know how, and have the right equipment, you can keep witch blood active for that long. After five days, they'd need a new source of blood." I looked up, my gaze flicking to Wayde, at the foot of the stairs. "Anyone file a claim for missing lab equipment?" I asked Nina, and her eyes narrowed.

"I'll find out."

"Good idea," I said sarcastically. God, vampires were clueless sometimes, so secure in their superiority that they didn't ask the right questions.

"So let me get this straight," Ivy said, the papers hanging from her hand as she stood beside and above me, her hip cocked and clearly not impressed. "You found body number two before you found the earlier crime with the kids?"

Nina flushed. "The location of the first bodies was remote. Whoever did this was unhappy that we missed the first one and so left the next one in a more public space."

The better to tease you with, my dear, I thought as I held my breath and looked at the floor. A drop of coagulated blood dangled at the tip of the man's hoof, suspended forever. Why couldn't I have just taken the blue pill and gone home? Taking a deep breath, I stood, gripping the railing until I was sure I wouldn't fall over. *Someone was torturing witches. Why?* "Ivy, what do you think?"

She shrugged. "Lots of IV marks. He reeks of antiseptic. They tried to keep him alive."

"They were successful for about a week," Nina interrupted.

Seeing me again upright, Ivy slid herself up to sit on the railing and leaf through the packet of information. Her ankles were crossed, and she smiled at me as she saw me catch my mental balance. Shrugging, I turned back to the body hanging before us. Yes, it was ugly, but if I couldn't get past it, I'd never find out who had done it so I could pound his or her head into the pavement.

"The businessman," I said as I finished my circuit of the man and carefully stepped between the cords keeping his legs spread-eagled. I was at his face, and I dropped my eyes. His skull looked malformed, the brow heavy. "Was he contorted like this?"

"Fairly close, but he still had his hands. Obviously they're working toward a specific body type. There was no sign of a fight from him. Stress levels recorded in the body say he was kept alive for several days under a sleep charm after he was subjected to the malfunctioning spell. They probably woke him only to try a new charm or feed him. The change in SOP was either to extend his life after the failed spell or because their new facility was somewhere public and they couldn't risk someone hearing him. We're not sure."

Whoever did this was insane, but I was willing to bet it wasn't a demon. A demon curse would have worked, and this obviously hadn't.

Ivy perked up as she found something she liked in her paperwork, her feet swinging as she sat balanced on the railing. "They kept moving their base?" she said, not looking from the pages. "Odd."

"Agreed." Nina rocked from her heels to her toes and back again, her hands clasped behind her in a decidedly masculine gesture. Behind her, the I.S. officers were getting impatient, wanting to cut the body down and get on with it. "Microscopic evidence from all the victims is different: dust samples, pollen, residual ley-line orientation at the time of death."

Ley-line orientation at the time of death? I'd been out of the I.S. for a little over two years, and I'd already missed hearing about new technology.

"We'll try to locate where they held this man, but they've probably moved already," Nina said, glancing at the I.S. officers and the radio chatter below us. Two geeky living vampires at the bottom of the stairs with a gurney and a body bag fidgeted in the cold as they waited for us.

"We found enough evidence on the businessman's body to sensitize an amulet. It led to an abandoned site, thoroughly cleaned, but they left the cage so we'd know it was them."

Ivy slid from the railing with the papers securely bundled in her arms. I could tell she was not going to give them back. "They're laughing at you," she said mockingly as she started for the stairs, her motions slow and provocative. Crap on toast, she was intentionally goading the undead vampire, knowing he'd screwed up this run and rubbing his nose in his mistake. Either that or she just wanted to talk to the waiting techs.

"I know they're laughing at us," Nina almost growled, but she was watching Ivy's ass as she took the stairs, and Ivy knew it. Jenks flew in to land on Ivy's shoulder when she reached the sidewalk. He'd probably finished his investigation a while ago and simply hadn't wanted to get near the body again. I could understand. It was probably like being next to the rotting carcass of a blue whale.

"Can we see the previous sites?" I asked just to get the undead vampire's eyes off Ivy.

"If you like," Nina said, annoyed as she brought her attention back to me. "All the information you need is in the reports.

There's evidence of at least four people involved in holding the victims." She looked at the hanging man and frowned, her fingers twitching, grasping for something unseen—a nervous tic belonging to an undead vampire. Curious.

I exhaled as I took in what Nina was saying. If they'd moved and dumped the body, then we had five days to find the next victim. *Damn it all to hell, this is ugly.* Somewhere in the city a terrified man or woman was being experimented on, turned into this . . . halfway thing.

Jenks left Ivy to make irritating yo-yo motions in front of me, his color high. "One guy and two women dumped this guy," he said proudly, and Nina's expression showed stark amazement. "That is, if you trust pixies," Jenks added snidely. "They came at four thirty-five in the morning, strung the guy up, finger-painted with blood from a bag, and left in a blue car. The local pixies didn't pay much attention to them. A guy with a dog found him thirty-seven minutes later, and the I.S. flunky responding hit him with a forget charm and sent him on his way. He's fine, but the dog is going to need massive amounts of therapy."

Nina looked livid, but I was delighted. It was probably the best intel we'd get, and more than the I.S. had gotten in over two weeks—if they were being honest with us, that is. Forget charms. I hated them, and I made a mental note to see if I could find anything in my earth-magic spell books that would counter one. I didn't want to take this run only to be charmed into forgetting everything when the I.S. had what it wanted.

"Nice going, Jenks," I said, unable to resist the dig. "We'll give you that for free, Nina."

The two vampires with the gurney and the folded body bag had started forward, and feeling a little better, I asked, "How long until the new tracking amulets made from the evidence here are ready?" I wanted to nail this coffin shut like yesterday.

Head down, Nina rubbed her chin. "Twelve hours," she said sourly, looking startled when she found her skin smooth and unstubbled. "I don't expect to get a ping from any of them. Ms. Morgan, is there a curse that you can perform to track them down faster?"

I lingered at the top of the stairs, the body hanging, ugly, behind me, the forbidding walls of the music hall peeping through the bare trees. Ivy was with one of the techs on the sidewalk, their heads close as they talked shop. Between us, radio chatter and the dull murmur of anxious cops filled the air. I'd had my look. I'd seen enough to get sick, scared, and now angry.

"Curse? No," I said, feeling cold as I gripped my shoulder bag tighter and took the stairs. I couldn't do a curse to save my life while wearing this band of charmed silver. "But if they're using this man's blood to stir spells to torture the next, you can find them with that using any old earth or ley-line charm."

I started down, and Wayde edged toward me, that same uneasy expression on his face. "It's a big city," Nina said, almost under her breath as she followed me down the stairs, her steps silent in her scratched knock-off heels. "Profilers think there are at least five people involved. Witches."

Witches killing witches? Not impossible, but something felt wrong to me. Jenks was dripping an angry red. "You can't find five psychotic witches?" he said caustically.

"It's a big city," Nina said again tightly. "Do you realize how many witches are in Cincinnati?"

Wayde glanced up at the body as he joined us, sliding close as the gurney vamps brushed past. "Uh, witches didn't do this," he said.

I turned to him as the gurney vamps stood before the body, discussing the best way to get the body down as they put on their protective gear. "But it *is* witch magic that did this," I said, and the pixy bobbed up and down.

"Witches did this," Nina said, her voice iron hard. "End of story."

Wayde's weight landed solidly on his front foot. "Witches would not use HAPA hate knots to tie him up."

What?

Nina spun to him, and Wayde jumped back at the snarl she wore, her pretty features drawing up into what was almost a hiss. Hunched, she glared at the nearby techs, who were suddenly white faced and apologetic, as if they were supposed to have removed the knots. Ivy was a blur between us, taking the steps two at a time to see for herself, Jenks right beside her, dropping swear words like red sparkles. I stayed where I was on the lowest step, suddenly a lot more scared as I looked at the cords and paled. Damn, he was right. I hadn't even noticed, but the ropes holding him up and spread-eagled *were* tied with the complex knots that HAPA had been known for, used for hanging witches, tying dead vampires in the sun, and quartering Weres in the nightmare four years of the Turn.

Slowly I sat on the lowest stair again, my back to the body. HAPA: Humans Against Paranormals Association. It was the fear of being dragged out into the street and burned by your neighbors made real, an extremist hate group that had gained a brief foothold during the Turn and advocated genocide for the very same people they'd lived next to and who'd taken great personal risks to keep them alive. It was believed HAPA had vanished years ago, but perhaps that's only what the I.S. had wanted everyone to think. By Nina's pissed attitude, I had the ugly feeling that the I.S. not only knew HAPA was alive and well but had been covering up its activity so they could take care of them the old-fashioned way.

Sickened, I wrapped my arms around my middle. I didn't know which was uglier: the body hanging behind me, or the I.S. hiding the crime so they could quietly murder those responsible for it. "It's coincidence," Nina said, but though the knot had been around for centuries, the knowledge that HAPA exclusively used it was not. After that little display of temper, I doubted very much that it was a coincidence here.

Beside me, Wayde was clearly not buying it, either.

"Before I got my security license, I worked large crowds. That's a HAPA knot. We kick two or three haters out of every show. Why are you hiding this?"

Ivy looked up from her crouch where she had been examining the knot. "Maybe it's a copycat organization trying to blame HAPA."

"HAPA would never use magic," I said, agreeing with her. "Not in a million years." Witches had suffered the most from HAPA. Weres were naturally reticent, and vampires were better at hiding. Witches, though, were easy to spot if you knew what to look for.

Jenks hovered between Ivy and me as if torn. "What better way to get rid of a group of people than to use their individual magic to sow distrust among them?"

I stood up, frustrated. "HAPA doesn't use magic!"

Ivy's brow furrowed. "They used to, until they decided that even magic-using humans were tainted. What has me scared is why now? Why start using magic again?"

Something evil was crawling over my shoulder, and I looked up to see that Nina's entire posture had shifted. Anger had made her eyes hard. She wasn't talking, but clearly Ivy was right. "HAPA has been using magic for the last two years," Nina said, looking as if she had eaten something sour. "We think it's because they have something they think can wipe us out once and for all. Now you know, and you have a choice," she said as she gestured roughly and a nervous agent edged his way up the stairs and handed her an evidence bag. Smiling without mirth, she held it up so I'd be sure to see the curly red hair in it before she tucked it in an inner pocket. "You can either quietly help us find and 'reeducate' the people responsible for this, or you, Rachel Morgan, will take the blame for it, because as everyone knows HAPA does not use magic."

"What the hell?" Jenks exclaimed, spilling red dust as he got between me and Nina, his sword out and pointed. Ivy was aghast, and Wayde's hand clenched on my shoulder until I shrugged it off. Reeducate? They meant catching and killing them without a trial in a back basement somewhere. If I didn't help the I.S., that curl of red hair was going to make me responsible for it. All they'd have to do was drop it at one of the sites, and standard magic detection would lead them right back to me.

Son of a bitch.

"I am *not* taking the blame for this," I said hotly.

Nina tucked the bag in an inner coat pocket. "Good. I'm looking forward to seeing how you work," she said calmly. "I want a list of the curses you can do on my desk by tomorrow night. Early."

They thought I was going to *work* for them? Fuming, I stood on the sidewalk. Ivy's eyes were black, and Jenks almost dripped sparks. I was not going to do this. I was not going to become one of the I.S.'s elite hit squad—as flattering as that was. "There's always option three," I said tightly, and Jenks hesitated. Ivy, too. They'd been sending hand signals to each other, planning something that would probably end with me in the hospital or in jail.

Nina's benevolent smile pissed me off. "Option three?"

I sent Jenks the signal to stand down and fumbled in my bag, not taking my eyes off the woman. Behind her, I.S. agents were slowly dropping back. Finding my cell, I flipped it open and scrolled through the numbers-called list. The one I wanted was at the bottom. I hadn't realized it had been that long. "A HAPA hate crime is the FIB's jurisdiction, not yours," I said as I texted HAPA @ WASHINGTON PARK to Glenn, thumbs moving fast, and Nina sucked in her breath, her eyes going black.

"You wouldn't dare," Nina said, and I fought to not back up as I hit send. "The FIB can't find their asses in a chair! They don't even *want* these people caught!"

"I think they do," I said, and she stepped toward me, her hands rising in wicked claws.

Ivy shifted forward and Jenks's wings clattered. I shut my phone, heart pounding as I took up a stance, smelling the spicy, complex scent of Were behind me. The vampire stopped, her jaw clenched as she evaluated us and her own people quietly retreating. Ivy shook her head at the incensed vampire. If the head of the I.S. had been here in person, we could be in trouble, but here, in the sun in a body he wasn't familiar with and had a responsibility to keep unmarked, he was at a disadvantage—and we all knew it.

"Too late," I said, and Nina's hands shook. "I don't like being blackmailed," I said, not knowing how we were going to get out of here without setting her off. "Didn't watching the coven teach you anything?"

Must be calm and controlled. Relaxed and matter of fact, I thought as my stomach knotted. I was used to dealing with out-of-control vampires. I could do this. "Hey! Leave the body," I said to the gurney guys still in the gazebo, trying to distract Nina by doing something not focused on her. "The FIB will want a look at it first."

I turned to Nina. "You should stick around. I'm sure the FIB's Inderland specialist will want to talk to you. Get your take on the situation. Detective Glenn's a very reasonable guy."

"Do you have any idea what you have done?" she nearly spat at me as she halted an unsafe four feet away, anger flowing from her like a wave. "Any show that HAPA is still active will increase their numbers. They're like a pestilence. Given the right conditions, they bloom like fireweed. You've just destroyed the facade of decades of peace between us and them!"

Us and them? I felt sick. I knew the unrest existed. We all did. I saw and ignored it all the time, wanting to live in a world that accepted us as we were, hoping that if I believed in it hard enough, it would happen. There was a reason most of Inderland lived in the Hollows, away from humans, and it wasn't the lower property taxes. But the disfigured form of a tortured man hanging six feet away was too much to pretend away. "Your fake peace is making the right conditions, not me," I said, heart pounding. "A cooperative venture between the I.S. and the FIB to take down a hate group is better than a decade of your fake peace. You should just go with it, Nina. Make lemonade."

It wasn't the best thing I could have said. She jerked into motion and I found myself yanked out of her reach by Wayde. I gasped as I stumbled and then found my balance, but Nina was walking away from me and back to the street, her hands clenched and her stride showing her anger.

I gave Wayde a weak smile and pulled away from him, thankful for his quick reaction. It could have been me she had been going for just as easily. Maybe he was better than I thought. Fuming, Nina stormed across the park, I.S. officers fleeing her path. "Thanks," I whispered, and he winced.

"I should've kept my mouth shut," he said, shooting a quick glance at the knots, and I shrugged. Perhaps, but there was no sense in crying over squished tomatoes.

Ivy's steps were slow as she came down from the gazebo, the I.S. gurney guys thumping behind her. Jenks was laughing, but I was more than worried. I was still going to have to find and catch these guys, but with the FIB involved, I might survive being successful.

"Don't worry about it," I said to Wayde as my phone hummed and I saw it was Glenn. Smiling weakly, I showed Ivy the screen and flipped the phone open. He was either going to be really happy or really pissed. I just hoped the I.S. wouldn't take my license away.

Four

Someone had left the kitchen window over the sink open a crack, and after turning the water off, I leaned over and shut the old wooden frame with a thump, sealing out the chilly, damp air. It was closing in on midnight, but the kitchen, bright with electric lights, was soothing. Turning, I dried my fingers on a dish towel as I leaned against the stainless-steel counter and listened to the sound of pixies at play in the front of the church. They'd moved in last week, shunning my old desk that held memories of their mother, and instead finding individual hidey-holes all over the church. The separation seemed to be doing them good, and I'd already noticed a marked decrease from last year in the amount of noise they made. Maybe they were simply getting older.

Smiling faintly, I draped the dish towel to dry and began wiping down the counters with a saltwater-soaked rag. I loved my kitchen with its center island, hanging rack, and two stoves so I didn't have to cook and stir spells on the same surface. One might think that my herbs and prepped amulets, hanging in the cabinet from mug hooks, would made an odd statement given the modern feel of the rest of it, but somehow their dried simplicity blended in with the gleaming counters and shiny cooking utensils. Ivy had updated the original congregation kitchen before I'd moved in, and she had good taste and deep pockets.

Ivy was across the kitchen at the big farm table shoved up against an interior wall, the report she'd taken from Nina un-stapled and set in careful piles so she could see everything at a glance. The table was Ivy's, the rest of the kitchen was mine, and right now, I was getting ready to use every last inch of it to prep some earth-magic, scattershot detection charms. I hadn't wanted to get involved in this, but now that I was, I'd go all out. I didn't need to tap a line to do earth magic.

Ivy was sleek and sexy as she stood leaning over the table, her long hair, no longer in a ponytail, falling to hide her face. Rain spotted her boots, and she moved with a marked grace as she tried to piece together three weeks of shoddy inves-tigation. The I.S. relied on scare tactics and brute strength to get things done—not like the FIB, who used data. Lots of data.

"You sure know how to attract the powerful dead, Rachel." Taking a pencil from between her teeth, she straightened, head still angled to the table as she added, "God help me, he's old." Turning a photo sideways, she tilted her head to evaluate the difference.

I dropped the rag on the counter and reached for my second-to-smallest spell pot from the rack over the center island counter, setting it on the rag so it wouldn't wobble. "Walkie-talkie man?" I asked idly since I knew she wasn't talking about Nina. I liked it when we were both working in the kitchen, her with her computer and maps, and me with my magic. Separate but together, and Jenks's kids as a noisy backdrop.

Giving me a coy look, Ivy said, "Mmm-hmm. Walkie-talkie man. Who do you think he really is?"

"Besides psychotic?" I lifted a shoulder and let it fall, then hesitated as I looked at my spell library on the open shelves under the counter. Locator charms were out. They worked by finding auras, which existed only on living bodies. An earth-magic detection charm was an option, but all the ones the I.S. had on the street were coming up blank. I was going to try a scattershot detection charm. They were normally used to find lost people when there wasn't a good focusing object, pinging on minuscule bits of stuff that we left behind when we stayed somewhere, things too small to wipe down and clean out. It was a very complex spell, and I was worried it might not kindle from my blood, seeing that it contained higher than normal amounts of the demon enzyme that tended to interfere with the more complex witch charms.

"You're not liking him, are you?" I said as I pulled one of my spell books out and dropped it on the counter.

Ivy was silent, and I looked up, blinking. "He's going to make me take the blame for this if we can't find them, and you like him?" I asked again, and she winced. The more dangerous a vampire was, the more Ivy liked him or her, and Nina was channeling a very old, very powerful one. "Ivy . . ." I prompted, and her sigh made my brow furrow. "I'm the one who makes bad life choices, not you."

"No, I'm not interested," she said as our gazes touched and she looked away. "It's just been a while, that's all. Nina, though . . ." Lip twitching in a rare show of unease, Ivy sat at her keyboard. "The woman is in trouble and she doesn't know it," Ivy said softly, her long pianist's hands shifting papers as she concentrated. "She reminds me of Skimmer, in a lot of ways, but she's utterly oblivious and unprepared for what he is doing to her, to her body. Helping her survive it isn't my job. She'll figure it out, or die trying." Her head came up and she stared at the wall, probably remembering something she would never share with me. "But I feel bad for her. The highs let you touch the sky, and the lows give you no way out."

Concerned, I ran my finger down the index, searching. Been a while . . . What she meant was that it had been a while since she'd been with a master vampire. Her master, Rynn Cormel, didn't touch her. It wasn't a matter of lack of desire, but that he'd rather his "adopted daughter" find blood with me. Yeah. Like that was *ever* going to happen . . . again.

"Why do you think they had Trent out there?" I said. *Page 442. Got it.*

Ivy looked up, her pencil provocatively between her teeth. "I think they were considering him as a scapegoat in case they can't find HAPA. You're a better one, though."

She was right, which didn't bode well for me, and I began shifting pages for the correct charm. What I really wanted was some sort of spell to prevent an I.S. memory charm from making me forget that the I.S. owed me a big thank-you for taking care of their mess, because I would take care of it, and I didn't want to find myself wandering in the park wondering what I was doing out there. Besides, it looked bad when a demon couldn't remember who owed her what.

Trent might have one. The thought came unbidden, and I shoved it away, not trusting his wild magic. A memory rose up to replace it, even worse: me and Trent trapped in my subconscious, baking cookies at this very counter as he tried to untwist the elven magic he'd done to save my life. Saving me had taken a kiss. A rather . . . hot and heavy one that had prompted me to slap him when I woke up. *I shouldn't have done that. At least I apologized.* Eyes closing briefly, I quashed the memory.

The kitchen became quiet as I leafed through the spell book, knowing I wouldn't find anything as complex as a memory-retention charm in it. Ivy typed something from her papers into a search engine and began scrolling. I had hated Trent for a long time, and letting that go made me feel good. Lately, though, he had scared the crap out of me with his dabbling in wild magic, and my gaze became distant as I recalled Trent, ashen faced and wearing a cap and a ribbon of intent as the world fell down around us. He'd been afraid, but he'd done it. *To help me?* To help himself. I should stop being stupid and just call him. He probably didn't want to wake up not remembering this week, either.

My fingers turning pages slowed as I found the detecting charm's recipe, and I bent my head over the book, trying to decide if I could do it or not. It wasn't a matter of skill, but tools. Anything that required tapping a line was out, given my bracelet. Fortunately most earth magic was simply putting things into a pot, mixing, heating, and adding three drops of blood to kindle it, and then invoking it—and a knot of tension eased when I decided that I could do the scattershot charm. It called for a circle, but only as a precaution to keep undesirables out of the pot. I'd risk it.

Nodding sharply, I started moving from drawer to cupboard looking for my empty amulets, tick seeds, sticktights, and fairy-wing scales. The last made me flush, and I hoped Belle wasn't around. The de-winged fairy had moved in with the pixies, physically unable to hibernate or fly anymore to escape the cold.

"Jenks?" I shouted, knowing that if he didn't hear me, one of his kids would relay the message. "Do you have any sticktights and tick seed in that stash of yours?"

"Tink's tampons, Rache!" he called back, sounding like he was in the back living room. "It's raining!"

"Really? I hadn't noticed. Where else am I going to get them? Wally World?"

There was a small thump, and I smirked at Ivy in the following silence. He'd probably gone out the fireplace's flue. Bis, our resident gargoyle, kept it clean, claiming that the creosote tasted like burnt caramel. I wasn't going to question the teenager on his dietary needs, and he was cheaper than a chimney sweep.

"You're making a locator charm?" Ivy said as she went back to her Web search. "I didn't think you could invoke those."

"I can't," I said as I got out one of her bottled spring waters from the fridge. "I'm going to make a scattershot detection charm since the I.S.'s regular detection charms aren't turning up anything. Looking for scattered evidence of the man in the park might get better results." I cracked the bottle's cap and nuked it for a minute to take off the chill. Chances were good I might spend all night on these only to find I couldn't kindle them and I'd have to find a witch to

invoke them for me. It wasn't as if I had many witch friends
. . . anymore.

The microwave dinged and I took out the water, suddenly
melancholy. Not that I'd ever had many species-specific
friends. I'd always thought it was my personality, but now I
was wondering if my "fellow" witches had known I was different on some basic level and had kept their distance, like
chickens pecking the unhealthy bird to death.

I set the warmed water next to the tiny clip of hair that
Jenks had swiped from the corpse before we'd left the park.
I didn't like having to prep this without a protection circle,
but I didn't have much choice.

A ping of guilt hit me as I shook the blood-caked hair
out of the fold of paper I'd stored it in. How do you explain
to the next of kin that your loved one had been tortured
and drained for someone's political message? That HAPA
was involved was still being kept out of the papers, but the
FIB had released the information that a body with demonic
symbols had been found in the park. They were hoping it
would slow the perpetrators down, but I knew HAPA was
on a schedule that couldn't be tweaked. *Days.* We had days.
I wanted to believe that the I.S. and the FIB could work together on this, but I knew the reality was going to be difficult, if not impossible.

I heard Jenks before I saw him, his wings a harsh clatter,
getting rid of the rain as he flew into the kitchen shedding
water drops everywhere. I dove for the assembled ingredients, waving my hands to keep him back. "Watch it, Jenks!"
I exclaimed. "I'm working without a circle!"

"All right, all right!" he crabbed at me, landing on the far
side of the island. "I got your tick seed and sticktights. Tink
loves a duck!" he exclaimed as he tried to open his jacket
only to find that the prickly seeds had caught on the natural
fibers. "Look at me! I hope you're happy, Rache. It's going
to take me hours to get all this unhooked. Couldn't you have
done this *before* it started to rain?"

"Thanks, Jenks," I said as I turned the oven on to give

him a place to warm up, and three giggling pixy kids came in to play in the updraft. "I couldn't do this without you."

"Yeah, yeah, yeah," he said sourly, clearly pleased as he plucked one of the seeds from his chest with a sudden pull of motion. "I'll leave them here for you. Jrixibell! Get the Turn out of the oven! What if someone shut you in there!"

Her eyes on her monitor, Ivy clicked a few keys with the sound of finality. "They will have switched bases before you can find them," she predicted, then closed out her window and stood, stretching to show a glimpse of her belly-button ring. "Gone before you get there."

I carefully measured out the right amount of water and put it in my second-to-largest spell pot. My smallest had a dent in it from who knew what. "Probably," I said as the water went chattering in and the bowl rocked. "But I'd like to see what the FIB can pull from a crime scene that the I.S. can't."

Ivy smiled with her lips closed, and we watched as the three pixy kids in the kitchen rose up in a noisy swirl of silk and darted into the hall. "Me too," she said as she began to tidy her papers. "The I.S. is way outclassed when it comes to the detective work."

Her smile became wicked, and I wondered whom she was thinking about as my neck started to tingle, but then one of Jenks's kids flew in with an exuberant "Detective Glenn is here!"

Jenks rose up on his dragonfly-like wings and hovered a moment in the open archway to the hall. "I'll let him in," he said, proud that he could work the system of pulleys to open the heavy wooden doors. The two of them buzzed out, and I heard a small uproar in the sanctuary.

Ah, I thought as I made sure I hadn't gotten Jenks's stick-tights on my shirt. *That's why Ivy is tidying up her papers.* Her hearing was better than mine. She'd probably heard him drive up in that big-ass SUV he had.

"About time. I'm starving," Ivy muttered as the distant

sound of the door opening filtered back, and Glenn's cheerful "Hello in the church" came to us. I took in Ivy's soft flush of anticipation, making me wonder if she was simply talking about the pizza he was supposed to be bringing over—or something more earthy.

I reached for an apron as I recalled finding Glenn's coat last spring smelling like Ivy. They'd been out on more than a few dates. Normally I'd be worried if a human tried to keep up with Ivy—she was a living vampire who'd been warped by her previous master into not being able to love without physically hurting her partner—but Ivy was learning new patterns and Glenn was not your average guy.

Glenn was ex-military, not overly large but powerful, having the grace of a slow jazz song, the sure momentum of an ocean wave, and the need to raise a person to the best of her abilities. He was nothing if not steady, and Ivy needed steady. I thought it telling that the first time they'd met, he'd asked me why I risked living with her, calling her unreliable, dangerous, and a psychopath, none of which I had been able to deny at that point. But she was also loyal, strong, determined, and a damn good person trying to overcome her past.

I looked up from tying on Ivy's COOK THE STEAK, DON'T STAKE THE COOK apron as Glenn breezed into the kitchen from the dark hallway, a box of pizza in one hand, Jenks on his shoulder, and pixy kids wreathing his head, all of them talking at once. I smiled. So much for first impressions.

"Still working?" the tidy man said as he noted Ivy's papers and my spelling equipment. Rain spotted the short leather jacket that showed off his narrow waist and wide shoulders. He was a shade taller than Ivy, one ear having a diamond stud and his curly black hair in a flattop, making him look more military than usual.

"You too, I see," I said, my smile faltering as he dropped the pizza box next to my spelling supplies and a tuft of dandelion fuzz took to the air. The pixies were on it in an instant, and with a squeal of excitement, a bright-cheeked, excited boy who looked about four darted out of the kitchen with it, six of his siblings in hot pursuit.

"Come back with that!" Jenks shouted, almost as fast as he zipped after them.

Ivy leaned in to give Glenn a quick kiss on the cheek, and in a smooth motion, she shifted the pizza box to the kitchen table as she stood. There wasn't a mark on the man's beautifully dark skin, and as he took his coat off and draped it over a nearby chair, I couldn't help but wonder where Ivy had been biting him. Then I wished I hadn't.

"I'm off the clock, but who really stops working?" Glenn said as he shifted his shoulders to make his shirt fit better. He liked to dress the part of an FIB detective, especially when he was mingling with his I.S. counterparts, and he made it look good. "There's a lot of information to go over and only a short time to catch these maniacs."

"Besides," Jenks said as he brought me my dandelion fluff, "coming over here gave him an excuse to eat pizza."

"Thanks, Jenks," I said, wondering if the spell was ruined even before I'd lit the Sterno can. My stomach grumbled at the smell of the pizza. I hadn't eaten yet, but mixing spell prep and food was a *very* bad idea. I'd eat later.

Ivy turned from the cupboards with three plates. "You brought your copy, right?" she asked. "You're not using mine."

Grinning to show his very white teeth, Glenn pulled a creased, copied version of the I.S.'s information, still stapled together and showing signs of having been worked with. "I know better than to write on your paper." He smacked her on the butt with it, and Ivy turned, growling at him as she opened the pizza box. It was obvious she was enjoying the attention. I'd seen Ivy and Glenn interact before, but it still kind of freaked me out. Wiping my hands on the apron, I put myself behind the center counter where I could work, stay out of their way, and yet keep an eye on them. Jenks, too, looked uncomfortable, and together we pretended to read my recipe.

Sighing happily, Glenn sat in Ivy's chair before her computer, leaning forward to take a piece of pizza. He was the only human I knew who'd eat it, and he'd become quite the tomato junkie. I'd pimped ketchup to him in exchange for handcuffs until he got tired of the blackmail and admitted to his dad that he ate tomatoes. Most humans wouldn't since a bio weapon had accidentally slipped into a genetically modified tomato and killed a quarter of the world's human population about forty years ago.

Humanity owed its continued existence to us Inderlanders coming out of the closet to keep society intact as plague swept through their genome, killing everyone who had eaten the lethal fruit. It hadn't affected us, and they were understandably skittish about tomatoes even now. But Glenn . . . I smiled as he groaned in pleasure, a long string of cheese running from his mouth to his piece of pizza. Glenn had risked it when cornered in an Inderland eatery and the choice had been to eat it or admit to a room full of vampires that he was chicken.

"Mmm," he said, chewing slowly and savoring every morsel until he swallowed. "Ivy, I wanted to go over the distance between the dump sites and where the victims were held. See if we can narrow the search. The I.S. has their amulets all over the city, but if we can zero in on one borough, it will be faster."

I lit the Sterno can from the stove's pilot light and set the spell pot on the tripod. Competition between the I.S. and the FIB was good. I didn't trust the I.S. amulets, which was why I was making my own. That standard magic-based tests were not working normally also didn't sit well. They were usually as reliable and a great deal faster than the pre-Turn techniques of genetic comparisons, which were now barely legal.

"Besides," Glenn added, his voice a dark mutter, "I don't think they'll tell us immediately when they find the latest base of operations."

Ivy had sat down kitty-corner to him, angling her chair

so that her back wasn't to me. "You think the I.S. will keep information from you now that you've got jurisdiction?" she said, her voice mocking and high. "Glenn, we're all in this together." Leaning over the pizza on her lap, she patted him on the cheek a little too hard.

Jenks and I exchanged a look, and his wings hummed nervously. I set the spring water to boil, hoping I wasn't going to have to watch them flirt all night.

"You know I won't withhold information," Glenn said, a smidgen of his usual business attitude showing. "I don't like that they managed to keep three HAPA crimes quiet for almost two weeks." Glenn's eyes narrowed suspiciously, and his pizza dangled, forgotten, from his thick hands. "That's almost too hard to believe."

I tended to agree with him. *Memory charms.* I was starting to have a real problem with them. My motions to grind the seeds up grew rougher, and I leaned into the job, taking my anger out on the dandelion fluff, tick seed, and stick-tights. "They thought I was the one doing it," I said when I backed off to add the corn pollen.

Glenn looked first at me, then Ivy to see if I was joking. His expression was a mix of amazement and anger. "You?" he almost barked when she nodded.

Seeing that Ivy had quit tweaking the man's libido, Jenks darted to the open pizza box. "Rache set them straight," he said proudly as he hovered over the crust. "In loud words," he added, using a pair of chopsticks from his back pocket to help himself to the sauce.

"I'll bet." Glenn set his pizza down, reaching for the paper towels we kept out and tearing one off. "I'm sorry, Rachel. If I'd known that, I wouldn't have been so nice to them."

I shrugged, then cracked an egg, shifting the yolk from eggshell to eggshell to separate it from the white. Not many earth charms used eggs, but this one did to bind the dry ingredients to the wet. "I'm getting used to it," I said sourly, hoping we'd seen the last of Nina. "At least I got my license back and my car registered in my name." Until they wiped my memory. Damn it, those things were illegal for a reason! I knew the demons had a curse that would block memory charms, but that was out. Maybe the elves had one. Trent could make a Pandora charm, which was basically a spell that repaired the damage from one. I simply wanted to prevent it.

Frustrated, I promised myself I'd call Trent as soon as I had ten minutes to myself. He'd sounded mad at me, but that was all the more reason to talk to him. I wasn't going to let misunderstandings fester anymore, especially with Trent. The man was starting to scare me.

"Jenks, you want this?" I asked the pixy as I held up the yolk still in the shell half, and he shook his head. Eggs gave me migraines, so I dumped it down the sink, dusting my hands as I turned around. Almost done.

Glenn finished his first piece of pizza, and after a longing look at the rest of the pie, he moved his plate to the center counter. "'Scuse me," he said as he reached across Ivy for one of her maps, intentionally brushing her. Ivy almost hit his jaw as she went for a pencil next to her keyboard, and I looked away when they put their heads together and began talking of walking speeds and the problems inherent in analyzing rapid transit.

Jenks took one look at them and flew back to me in disgust. "Jealous?" he asked me as he landed on the open spell book, and I frowned.

"No. Get off the spell book."

He was laughing as I shooed him away, landing on Glenn's plate instead, just about the only place I'd let him alight at this point. The water was boiling, and after checking the recipe, I carefully brushed the crushed seeds into it. It fizzed and foamed, and I blew out the flame. I'd add the egg white and fairy dust along with the focusing object after it cooled. In this case, I'd be using the man's hair. This was sympathetic magic, meaning it worked by making a connection between the amulet and whatever it was sensitized to.

Sticktights, tick seed, and egg white were for binding. Corn pollen, fairy dust, and dandelion seed were for drifting on the ether to search, and my blood would be the catalyst to make it work. The man's blood would have made a better focusing object, but there wasn't a clean enough sample. Hair was a good substitute.

So why did I feel so weird using it?

I glanced at Ivy and Glenn, happy with maps and colored markers, then teased a hair from the bundle Jenks had snatched for me. It was black and fine, from his head and not the curse-modified pelt he'd had from the waist down.

Ivy laughed, low and throaty, and I looked up to see them absorbed in whatever point of contention they had deemed worthy of arguing over. Jenks snickered, and I glared at him. "Shut up," I muttered, my shoulders shifting uncomfortably. Damn vampire. It was starting to smell good in here, what with the pizza and the pheromones. And the scent of . . . wine and salt?

It was coming from the bundle of hair that Jenks had snitched for me, and with a sudden burst of connection, I brought it to my nose. As Glenn's deep voice murmured about property values and crime rates, I closed my eyes and breathed deeply, smelling sweat and fear. Deeper was shampoo, and lightly, lacing it like a perfume that he'd once walked through, was the hint of wine and salt. I'd smelled it at the crime scene, too.

My eyes opened. "Jenks, come sniff this."

Jenks's wings clattered, but he didn't move from where he was licking his chopsticks clean. "Tink's panties, Rache. You're starting to sound like my kids." Turning his voice mocking and high, he said, "Dad! Come smell this! It stinks!" Shaking his head, he dropped his voice and added, "Why the hell would I want to smell something if it stinks?"

I put my forearms on the counter and loomed over him. "Seriously. Wine and salt?"

Eyeing me, he stood, walking over and making a big

show of smelling it. "Yeah," he finally said, and my heart gave a thump. "Once you get past the meadow."

"Thanks," I said, and he went back to his dinner, his attitude cautious. *Wine and salt . . .* Motions slow, I set the hair aside and dropped one strand into the cooled liquid before adding the egg white and the fairy dust. All that was left was my blood to kindle it. I was afraid to try. It might not work, and it wasn't as if I could do the demon equivalent anymore.

My gaze dropped to the counter, as if I could see through it to the shelf where I kept my demon books next to my missing scrying mirror. I'd lost it and never replaced it since I didn't need the interdimensional chat charm if I was playing dead to the demons.

That's when it clicked.

Scrying mirror. Someone was trying to make a scrying mirror into a calling glyph. But to do that, they'd need demon blood.

Shit.

I gripped the counter, feeling my face go cold and wavering, as if I'd moved too quickly. That's what HAPA was doing. This wasn't merely a scare tactic and hate crime. They were trying to duplicate demon blood in order to perform curses. The mutilated corpses the I.S. had found were their attempts to turn a witch into a demon.

"Oh my God . . ." I whispered, and Ivy and Glenn both looked up, their expressions holding curiosity as well as banked heat. HAPA wanted a little magic of its own, and since demons were considered tools, they didn't have a problem using demon magic.

"You want to share with the class, Rache?" Jenks said, and I tried to find my voice.

"The blood analysis," I said softly, holding the counter to keep from swaying. "Ivy, what does it say about the magic-enzyme levels?"

Ivy shifted a few inches from Glenn as she reached for it, crossing her knees as she rocked back in the chair. " 'Blood composition in all the victims show elevated levels, progressively worse with each victim.'" She slowly blinked, her eyes going blacker as she sensed my dread. "Is that important?"

I nodded. "If they started from someone with naturally high levels of those enzymes, everything would go faster. Does it say if they are carriers for the Rosewood syndrome?"

Jenks made a high-pitched noise, and Ivy shook her head, her lower lip between her teeth as she double-checked. "You think . . ." she said, her words trailing off as I nodded.

Rosewood syndrome. I wasn't a carrier. I was a survivor. I had twice the enzymes they were playing with now. *Crap on toast.*

Glenn's chair creaked as he leaned back, concern pinching his usually smooth brow. "Aren't you—" he started.

"Rache!" Jenks shrilled, darting into the air to leave a puddle of yellow dust that dripped over the edge of the counter and to the floor. "You can't take this run! I don't care if you said you would. They're calling you out. They want your blood! If they get it, they're going to have what they need and . . . Crap, Rache! What are we going to do?"

My grip on the counter tightened until my knuckles were white. My head was bowed, and I could see the little spell pot with its uninvoked potion. "You think you could check and see if the victims had a history of Rosewood syndrome in their families, Glenn?" I finally said.

Ivy stood, and I tried to shove my unease aside so I could get on with what I had to do, but I knew, given her expression of concern, I must look sick.

Glenn too had stood, and he was taking a slim cell phone from his belt. "I'll get that started right now," he said. "Excuse me a moment." Punching numbers, he stepped across the hall and flicked on the light in the back living room, several pixy kids going with him.

Jenks landed on my shoulder, the cold draft from his wings making me shiver. "Everyone knows you're a demon."

"True," I said sourly as I smacked my empty amulets around, arranging them on the counter in a straight row. "But if they wanted me, they would've taken me by now.

Bodyguard or not," I added. "Besides, I have a vested interest in seeing that this gets done right," I said as I carefully mixed the wet ingredients with the dry and poured the finished, but not invoked, brew onto the seven discs. It soaked in without a hint of redwood scent, but then, there wouldn't be any until they were invoked.

Damn it, what if they did try to snatch me? I didn't want to have to take the bracelet off, and I looked at it, around my wrist like a security band. I did *not* want Al to know I was alive. He'd risked everything he had to keep me alive, and in return I'd broken the ever-after, dropped a demon psychopath into his living room, and saved the elves from extinction after the demons had been trying to exterminate them for five thousand years. Al was broke and trying to pay for everything I'd done. Not only would he be pissed if he found out I was alive, but he'd make me leave reality forever. I had nothing with which to bargain this time. I'd never see Ivy or Jenks or my mom again.

I looked up at the silence. Ivy had her arms over her middle as she stood with the counter between us. "Jenks is right. It wouldn't hurt you to sit this one out."

Frowning, I jabbed my finger with a finger stick, massaging three drops of blood onto one of the finished amulets. Trying not to look like I was, I breathed deep for the telltale scent of redwood, but there was nothing. It just smelled like wet wood. Damn it, either I'd done them wrong or my blood was too far from the witch norm to invoke it.

In a pique of bad temper, I threw the now-contaminated charm into my salt vat, sending a splash of water up to spot the cabinets. I'd have to ask someone else to invoke the rest.

Jenks landed close, his expression as worried as Ivy's. "Glenn won't mind handling this on his own."

"I'm not sitting this out," I said dully, wiping the tiny spot of blood from my finger into nothing. "The I.S. will pin it on me if the FIB doesn't catch them."

"No they won't," Jenks whined, but he'd seen the bag with my hair in it, too.

"It's a demonic crime," I said, head down. "I'm a demon. Perfect fit. Why blame a hate group they don't want to admit is still active when they can blame me?" I looked up, seeing Ivy frowning. "No offense to Glenn, but the FIB can't bring in a magic-using human *or* HAPA without help, and the I.S. would rather have me take the blame than admit HAPA even exists."

"True," Ivy said, Glenn's muted conversation sounding loud from the other room.

"I can find them without much risk," I said, looking down for something to do. "If they'd really wanted me, they would've taken me already. I think they're scared." I brought my head up and gestured flamboyantly in the air. "Look who they've snatched. Teenagers, a businessman, and some college kid. None of them had a lick of real magic."

"Yeah, but your magic sucks right now," Jenks said, glancing at the vat of dissolution saltwater, and Ivy frowned at him to shut up. From the living room, Glenn's voice continued.

I moved the empty potion bowl into the sink and closed my eyes. If I didn't find these jokers, they were going to keep killing innocents by twisting them into that goat thing. *Is that what Al really is?*

"Rachel?"

My eyes opened, and I remembered Algaliarept sitting at a table, his skin almost black and a fuzz of red fur on him as he tried to remember what he used to look like.

I took a deep breath and let it out. The worry in Ivy's and Jenks's eyes shook me, and I forced myself to smile. "Yeah, I mean, yes," I said softly. "I'm okay. We have to find them. Fast. I'll be careful in the meantime. It's time for Wayde to earn his keep."

"You got that right." Jenks dropped down to the finished amulets, easily handling a wooden-nickel-size disk of wood and stacking it on the next. "Who you going to get to invoke these little babies?"

I turned my back on them as I untied my apron and hung

it up. "I don't know. Maybe walkie-talkie man has a witch for a secretary." Neither one of them said anything, but Ivy was frowning when I turned back. I didn't trust the undead vampire, either. "Now that Keasley is gone, the only witch I know who isn't in jail, dead, or on the West Coast is Marshal. You want me to call him?"

"Not really," she said softly, then shifted to make room for Glenn, coming back in. He was smiling, but it wasn't a happy expression.

"I'll have an answer for you about the medical records in an hour," he said, taking a slice of pizza and dropping it on his plate. "What'd I miss?"

Jenks's wings clattered. "Rache overcompensating for you two lovebirds cooing in the corner by going through her little black book."

My brow furrowed. "I am not!" I said, and Glenn and Ivy put space between themselves without a word. "I'm not trusting the I.S. to invoke them. Marshal is the only witch I know well enough to ask to do this for me," I said as I moved the dirty spelling equipment to the sink. "You could have these invoked before the next shift, or you can wait until the I.S. gets around to it. What's your choice, Glenn?" I wasn't looking to rekindle anything between Marshal and me. *But now that I wasn't shunned, it was a real possibility.*

Even as the idea appeared, I dismissed it. I'd been in trouble, and Marshal had left. I didn't blame him. Dating a shunned witch would get you shunned in turn. I'd told him I had control of the situation. He'd believed me. I hadn't and things had gone wrong. He had left. No hard feelings on either side. But to go back now? No. I didn't blame him, but he *had* left.

Jenks hovered before me as I rinsed out the pot, a devilish smile on his sharply angular features. The chrysalis that Al had given me last New Year's lay behind him on the sill, safe under an overturned brandy sifter. "Methinks she doth protest too much," he said, and I threatened to squirt him.

"Knock it off," I said as I dunked the rinsed pot in the dissolution vat to get rid of any lingering charm. "I'm good with Ivy dating Glenn, biting Glenn, whatever with Glenn."

"And Daryl?" the pixy needled me. "You good with Daryl, Rache?"

I stiffened, and from behind me, Ivy said, "Where's the glue? And your cat, Jenks?"

Jenks snorted. "Like you or that orange fuzz ball could catch me," he said, but he was going for altitude.

Glenn looked awkward when I turned back around, shifting from foot to foot, slightly flushed. I gathered up the dried amulets. "I'll see what I can do about having these delivered to the FIB as soon as possible. It might take me a day, but as Ivy keeps pointing out, they're only going to take you to an empty building by now."

Glenn's attention flicked from the charms to me. "Uh, whenever you can get to it, that'd be great," he said, actually dropping back a step. "Thanks. Rachel, I want you to stay here—"

Stay here? My temper popped, and I smacked my hand down onto the counter. Jenks darted up, surprised, but Ivy chuckled, going to the fridge to give me space while I vented. "You are *not* turning me into the chief cook who never gets off the boat," I exclaimed. "I'm going to be an active member in this run!"

Ivy came out from behind the fridge door, raising a bottle of orange juice in a show of solidarity. "We've already been over it."

"So don't even try telling her to stay home," Jenks added, grinning as I glared at the FIB detective frowning right back at me, his chest puffed out. *Puff all you want, FIB detective. You're not turning me into the librarian.*

Ivy had her back to us as she poured out a glass. I knew she wasn't thirsty. She was trying to cloud her senses as I filled the air with my anger. "We're good at watching her."

Glenn took a step back so he could see Jenks better. "Against wackos abducting Rosewood syndrome carriers, to try to create synthetic demon blood? Rachel, I know you have a bodyguard and all, but how smart is it to put yourself where they can grab you?"

"She said she'll be careful." Ivy leaned back against the counter with her ankles crossed, looking like sex incarnate as she drank her juice, her long, pale throat moving slowly.

Stifling a shiver, I looked away. "I'll only go to secure sites," I said under my breath as I snapped up my spell book and crouched to put it away. This was a mess, and I wasn't talking about the kitchen. The I.S. had asked for my help. The FIB desperately needed it. HAPA was stringing their victims up to taunt me into finding them. They knew I had what they wanted—what they were mutilating people to find. "Promise."

I shoved the book into its spot, then hesitated, growing angrier as I looked at the demon curse books right next to it. Suddenly I was twice as set on not giving the FIB or the I.S. a list of what I could do. They could hire an intern and get it from the library—I wasn't going to give them the rope to hang me with.

Never would I have guessed making it public knowledge that I could kindle demon magic would lead to this. It was no longer a secret that witches were stunted demons, so far removed from their original species that they were a species unto themselves—and clearly someone had made the correct assumption that the Rosewood syndrome had something to do with it. As one of the two people to survive the deadly but common genetic abnormality, I'd made myself a target.

"I have to call Lee," I whispered, then straightened, my fingers trailing from the demon books reluctantly. I couldn't feel anything from them anymore, and it sort of hurt. "Glenn, can you make me a list of the Rosewood carriers in the city? Maybe watch them?"

Immediately he uncrossed his arms, his belligerence at my resistance turning into concern for the masses. "Seriously? There has to be a couple hundred at least."

The number was probably closer to a thousand. The genetic abnormality wasn't that uncommon, and it was only when the recessive genes doubled up that there was a problem. "You don't have to watch all of them," I said. "Just the high risk. The young, the stupid." My thoughts went to the man in the gazebo. He hadn't been stupid. Careless, maybe. "Telling the general public might be a mistake," I said softly. "No need to start a panic."

His reluctance was clear as he ran a hand over his short haircut. "I'll see what I can do."

That didn't sound promising, and I began to get angry again. No, it was frustration, and he didn't deserve it since it was mostly at myself. I exhaled. "Can you at least have the vulnerable people on a list so that when they're reported missing they get attention?"

Glenn nodded, looking at his phone for the right number. "That I can do," he said, and Jenks hovered over his shoulder, probably memorizing the number for future use, until Glenn snapped his phone closed.

Call Trent about a memory charm blocker. Call Lee to warn him about a possible abduction. Talk to Wayde and tell him I'm a target. My mind was swirling, and jaw clenched, I loosened my grip on the counter, not having realized that I'd grabbed it. Ivy had, though, and she watched me in concern from across the kitchen, her orange juice in a grip just as tight. "Excuse me," I said as I started for the hallway. "I need to talk to Wayde."

"First smart thing she's done all week," Jenks said, and I squinted at him.

"Alone," I added, and he made a face at me before darting to Ivy's shoulder to sulk. The last thing I wanted was Jenks making smart-ass remarks as I asked Wayde to step it up.

"Uh, before you go, have you given any more thought to making that list of, ah, curses?" Glenn asked hesitantly.

I came to an abrupt halt six inches in front of him, since he wasn't moving out of the doorway. "I've thought about it, and I'm not doing it," I said, trying to be calm and reasonable, but I'd just about had it.

"Rache is not making you no list," Jenks said hotly, making Ivy brush his dust from her.

"Why not?" Glenn asked, and Ivy cleared her throat in warning. "No, really," Glenn asked again, appearing truly at a loss. "If it's common knowledge, what's the big deal?"

I refused to back up, and my face flushed as I put my hands on my hips. "It's not all common knowledge," I finally said, "and what they don't know, I don't want to tell them. Move, will you? I have to talk to my bodyguard about upping his surveillance."

Glenn glanced at Ivy, then said to me, "Rachel, I'm under a lot of pressure here."

"Oh, for the love of Tink!" Jenks said.

"Why is everyone afraid of what I can do all of a sudden?" I exclaimed, backing up to the center counter.

Again glancing at Ivy to gauge her control, Glenn caught his own rising temper, calmly saying, "Because there's a goat man strung up in a city park, surrounded by demon symbols and marked with the demon word to make it public. The sooner you give them the list, the sooner you can get on with your life."

My lips pressed together as I remembered the DMV office. I didn't want to give up that part of myself. Not to the I.S. or the FIB, where anything or anyone would have access to it.

Jenks darted into the air when Ivy jerked into motion, but she was only going to the window, jamming it all the way open to get a better airflow. The autumn-night rain slipped in with the scent of decaying leaves, and my shoulders lost most of their tension.

"People are scared," Glenn said, calm again and not simply masking his anger. "You say you can do demon magic but won't. You have demon books you won't share the contents of. You're registered in their database."

"That wasn't my idea," I muttered. "And I've got almost no magic anymore. See? I neutered myself!" Angry, I shifted my weight to my other foot and glared up at him. "There's nothing to be afraid of," I finished, depression starting to take hold.

"Rachel, I'm sorry," he said when he saw my mood shift. "I'm not afraid of you, but it's easy to be scared. Understanding is harder. Just make the list. I don't care if it's complete. I'll take it in, and then you can get your life back."

I looked at Ivy, my gut saying no even if it sounded easy. I was getting tired of having to bargain for every little thing I deserved, like a license or the ability to make a plane reservation. But still . . . "And when they find out I didn't tell them everything, they'll use that against me," I said softly. "No."

"What is the problem?" Glenn said. "Don't get mad. I'm trying to understand!"

He really was, and Ivy moved from the window to tug him out of my way and back to his chair. "She's right," she whispered in his ear, and I felt my own neck start to tingle. "If anything ever comes across an I.S. desk that looks like something Rachel admits she can do, they'll say it's her even if she's wearing charmed silver, because she's an easy target."

Glenn slumped, looking beaten as he stared at the floor. "Okay," he said, then looked at me. "I see where you're coming from, but I don't agree with it. I'll stall them. Asking you for it wasn't my idea."

Finally I could smile. "I know. I'll be right back. Save me a slice of pizza, okay?"

"Let me know if Wayde needs anything from me," Glenn said, but I was already in the hall, headed for the stairway. Ivy had been kicking out I'm-hungry pheromones for at least an hour, and I had to get out of there for a while.

"Will do!" I shouted over my shoulder, making my sure way through the dark. There was no way I was going to make a list for the FIB or the I.S. I'd rather live off the grid.

Driving was overrated, and maybe I wouldn't have to pay taxes this year.

I couldn't help but wonder, though, if what I was really fleeing was seeing Glenn and Ivy—happy together—and knowing it could have been me.

Five

Arms swinging, I entered the sanctuary, dimly lit by the TV, on in the corner where the new furniture set was. Pixies perched on the backs of the chairs in rows, cheering when the crocodile took down the zebra. Pixies and nature shows went hand in hand. Who knew?

I wasn't in the best of moods. I knew Wayde was going to take whatever I said as me telling him he wasn't good at his job. He was, but he needed to be better than good until this was over. The sight of my desk, unused and gathering dust, didn't help. Ivy's piano, seldom played but utterly dust free, didn't help, either. Kisten's pool table, the felt still burned and charred from a "white" charm a coven member had thrown at me, slid my mood clear back into depressed.

"I'm sorry, Kisten," I whispered, touching it as I passed it on the way to the foyer and the narrow staircase to the belfry. I had meant to get it refelted a long time ago, but life kept interfering. *I'll call the rec place right after I call Marshal,* I thought, feeling a pang of guilt. Marshal probably wouldn't return my call, but it was either him or trusting the I.S.

I entered the dark foyer, still lacking a light and pitch-black. How long had I been promising myself to wire one in? I wondered, counting it in years now.

I can do better than this, I thought as I pulled the narrow door to the stairway open with a soft creak, and a faint *tap,*

tap, tap echoed down in the slightly cooler air smelling of wet shingles. Wayde was working on his room again, and I started up, thinking there had been too many things I wanted to do, and none of them was getting done. *I've got to start taking care of things,* I thought, vowing to do something this time.

"Hi, Ms. Morgan!" a high, resonant voice called out, and I jumped, nearly falling backward down the stairs.

"Holy crap, Bis!" I exclaimed, looking up to see the cat-size gargoyle clinging to the sloping ceiling like a weird bat. "You startled me!"

The small teenager grinned to show his black teeth, his red eyes glowing slightly in the dim light of the stairway. He had lightened his pebble-gray skin to match the raw wood brown of the walls, and his clawed hands and feet dug in as he wheezed/laughed at me. As I watched, his skin shifted color again, and he swished his lionlike tail. It even had a tuft on the end that matched the long hair on his ears. It helped him balance in flight, apparently.

"Sorry," he said, his pushed-in, almost ugly face turned up in a smile. Leathery wings spread, he jumped to my shoulder and wrapped his warm tail around my neck. I braced for the sensory overload that never came . . . and sighed. Before my bracelet, his touch had sent every ley line in Cincinnati singing in my mind. Now there was nothing, and I breathed in his odd scent, a mix of old iron and feathers from the pigeons he ate.

"I don't think you're sorry at all," I said mildly as I started back up, and his tail tightened. Immediately, I forgave him. Bis was a good kid. He'd been living in the belfry for almost a year now, having been kicked off the basilica for spitting on people. Jenks thought that was just fine, and Bis paid his rent by watching the church and grounds the four hours around midnight that Jenks liked to sleep. Where else was the little guy going to go?

"Wayde is decent, right?" I asked, again hearing the faint *tap, tap, tap* come again.

"Decent?"

I could understand Bis's confusion. He usually didn't wear clothes—they interfered with his ability to go chameleon.

"Uh, maybe you could just warn him that I'm coming?" I said, slowing as I neared the top, the steady glow of light coming through the wide crack under the door.

But then Wayde's easygoing voice echoed down. "I'm decent. Come on in."

The *tap, tap, tap* started again, and I continued up the stairs, trying to decide how I was going to do this without hurting his feelings. Wayde had been fixing up the belfry—he liked the space better than camping out in the back living room. I hadn't been up there yet to see what he'd done. There'd been lumber deliveries and several furniture vans, and I was curious. Last time I'd seen it, the room had been an empty hexagon with the church's bell hanging over it and no insulation. It had been a nice place to sit and watch the rain, but not to live in.

"Wait until you see," Bis said proudly. "Wayde made a shelf for me in the steeple."

I smiled as I ascended the last of the stairs. "I didn't know you wanted one. Sorry, Bis."

Again his tail tightened, and I almost choked. "It just kind of happened," he said, and I could breathe again. "You know, extra wood and stuff."

Electric light? I thought, looking at the slice of warm yellow glow coming through the crack under the door as I neared the last steps.

Bis jumped from my shoulder and my hair flew as he landed on the door to swing it open. Another wing pulse, and he was in the air again, darting up past the huge bell making a false ceiling. Light had spilled out, and I heard the thump of a hammer being set down. "Come on in. What do you think?"

Head swiveling, I came in as Wayde turned from the window he'd been working on. The old slatted frame was out, propped up against the wall beside him, and the dark square of the rainy night was beyond him. A new, stickered window was next to him, ready to go in. His shirt was off and his lightly tanned skin glistened from either sweat or the mist coming in off the roof. I blinked, taking in his tattoos. I'd seen only a fraction before, but the man was covered in them. They moved as his muscles did, and he had a lot of those, too. He looked good over there with his tools and stuff. Really good.

"Nice," I said softly, and Wayde ducked his head, smiling slightly.

"I meant, what do you think of the room?"

I stood in the doorway and eyed him. "What did you think I was commenting on?" But when I actually looked at the room, my lips parted. It *was* nice. The original oak floor still needed to be finished, but a large circular rug added softness and warmth. Wallboard had gone up, already mudded and with insulation behind it, I was sure, from the rolls I'd seen in the sanctuary last week. The cathedral ceiling around the bell was finished, but the original heavy beams still showed. The metal rings that held the rope to ring the bell had been polished of rust, and they gleamed dully.

Amazed, I craned my neck until I spotted Bis on his shelf. It ran along the entire interior of the steeple, and it looked cozy. "I didn't know there was electricity up here."

"I ran a line up through the walls," Bis said proudly, shifting his wings in a leathery hush.

Wayde exhaled as he sat on the sill, his back to the night, one booted foot dangling, one touching the worn floorboards. The rain on the roof sounded nice—it smelled even better. "That kid is better than a snake," he said, and I didn't think he meant the living kind. "Three minutes, and he had it to me."

"Wow, you guys do good work. This looks great!" I said. There was a single camp-style bed in the corner, almost hidden behind the antique marble-top dresser that had been here when we bought the place. A small electric heater sat across the room, humming faintly. The faded fainting couch was beside it, and the shelf where I'd once had my demon curse books. I felt warm as I remembered what Marshal and I had done on the couch, then shifted awkwardly.

"It's small," Wayde said, eyes on the huge bell acting like a fake ceiling. "But I like it. It's the first time I've been in any one place longer than a month. It feels good to settle, I guess."

I came farther in, fidgeting inside as I tried to find a graceful way to bring up his work habits. My old folding chair was set beside the bed, the one I used to sit on when I'd come up here to get away from everyone and just watch the rain. "I've never lived anywhere other than Cincinnati. Long term, that is."

Wayde had gone back to his work, and he picked up his hammer, ripping the last bit of molding out. "You name it, I've been there."

"Detroit," I said, thinking his back looked strong, from running probably, since his muscles were smooth, not chunky from weights.

I flushed when he turned, catching me ogling him, but he was pointing to a skid-mark tattoo on his arm. "Detroit," he said in challenge.

Okay. I like games. "Atlanta?"

Hammer still in his hand, he pointed to a blue star on his shoulder. It was sending sparks out, one of which was setting the tail of a snaking dragon on fire.

"New Orleans?" I asked next, and Wayde's ears went red.

"Uh, trust me on that one," he said, then swore under his breath as he looked at the clock on the dresser and set his hammer down.

"It's on his butt," Bis volunteered. "A naked woman with a saxophone."

Wayde reached for his shirt and frowned at Bis. "That was privileged information."

Bis laughed and wheezed, and I watched him shake out a big pillow and settle on it. There was a bowl up there, too, and the shirt that Jenks had gotten him last June, right next to a vase of plastic flowers and a picture he'd once asked for of the garden. Jeez, I should've asked if he had what he wanted.

"Thanks for being so nice to Bis," I said softly, the guilt running high. He just seemed so independent.

"Don't worry about me, Ms. Morgan," Bis said. "It was only scraps of wood. If I was at home, I'd be out on the roof with my parents. I don't need all this stuff."

But he clearly appreciated it. He had a real space, and I couldn't help but feel that I'd let him down. One more thing that had fallen by the wayside.

"I think it's turning out good," Wayde was saying as he stuffed his shirt into his jeans. "I don't get a chance to use my hands much."

"Are you cold, Ms. Morgan?" Bis said, his wings opening up. "I can warm this place up better than that heater."

Waving my hand for him to stay there, I shook my head. "I'm good," I said, pushing up to my feet. "I, ah, just came to talk to Wayde for a moment."

Wayde hesitated. "I usually only hear that from a woman who wants to break up with me." He faced me squarely, pulling to his full height. "What?"

Heart pounding, I forced myself to stop fidgeting. "Don't take this the wrong way . . ."

He squinted at me, his stance becoming aggressive. "Too late. What?" he repeated.

I took a deep breath. Why was this so hard? "HAPA is calling me out," I said, my attention following the grain of the floor. "They're after my blood, literally, and I wanted to ask if you needed help or anything from the FIB until we get them."

"You don't think I'm good enough to keep you safe," he said blandly, and my head came up. Damn it, I was trying to be grown up here, and he was going to get touchy.

"No," I insisted, but I sounded insincere even to me. "You're great at your job. I'm not helpless, so I don't think round-the-clock protection is needed, but I'm on HAPA's hit list and—"

"Let me tell you something, witch," he said, taking a step forward and pointing at me with a stiff finger. But then he hesitated and looked at his watch. "Shit, we're going to be late. I've a better idea. Let me *show* you something."

My air came in fast and I pulled away, but I was too slow, and with a gasp and a yank, I found myself caught in a submission hold, my back to Wayde's front, held tight. "Hey!" I yelped, wiggling and finding I was really caught. Damn, he was fast. "What are you doing?"

"We have to meet David for your appointment, and since you think I'm not good enough, I'm going to prove it to you."

Appointment? My tattoo? I didn't think that was until Friday! "Prove what?" I said, my heart pounding and my breath fast. "That you're a bully? Let me go," I insisted, not caring so much about the damn tattoo as him thinking he could manhandle me like this.

"You've been looking down on me since I got here," he said, his words a warm breath on me. "Don't think I can't tell. I'm a patient man, but I'm tired of it, and if you're going to survive, you have to trust me. You're the kind of person that show means more then tell, so we're going to have it out, right here, right now. You and me."

Is he nuts? "Wayde, this is *not* how to convince me you're good at your job," I said, trying to twist from him, but he had me firmly and my skin burned. "Let go before I hurt you!" I exclaimed, then gasped when he spun me around, sending me almost crashing into the new window.

I found my balance and settled into a ready pose with my hands in fists. He rocked to a halt between me and the door, and I thought about his work as a bouncer, thought about those muscles covered with tattoos. "What the hell is wrong with you?" I said, spitting mad. "I said I'd get the tattoo, and I will!" If he touched me again, I was going to smack him a good one.

Wayde crossed his arms over his chest, looking like a

rock between me and the door. "This isn't about the tattoo. I've been watching your back for three weeks, and you are oblivious to everything. Oblivious!" he said, waving a thick arm. "And you think I'm not capable of my job?"

"What in hell do you want?" I said, just as mad. "A citation of merit? I didn't ask you here, and if you can't do your job, you need to leave!"

His chin lifted. "That's what I thought," he said. "You really think I'm shit. Fine. If I get you downstairs and in your car, you stop doubting me. If I can't, I'll pack up and be on the next vamp flight out."

I thought about that, steaming in anger and feeling his fingers on me, though he was across the room. Bis's eyes were wide as he silently watched, his tail twitching in excitement. Okay, maybe I had been harboring a sliver of doubt that he was up to it, because I eagerly settled into a fighting stance, light and balanced on my feet—and nodded. He wasn't getting me in that car.

Wayde looked up at Bis, who was watching with breathless anticipation. "Finally," he said, and calmly came at me.

I swung a foot at him, teeth clenched when it hit his offered arm with nothing to show for it. He ducked my next swing with the speed of a wolf, then dodged another kick. My eyes widened, and I backed up until I found the wall, having forgotten how fast Weres were. "Wayde!" I shrieked, but he had grabbed me around the waist and flung me over his shoulder.

"Put me down!" I yelled, hitting his back. "Damn it, I don't want to hurt you!" I said, jamming my elbow into the soft muscle between his neck and shoulder to no effect.

"Whatever," he said, having to raise his voice because the air was suddenly full of pixy kids and the draft from Bis's wings. "Jumoke," the Were said calmly as I wiggled and squirmed. "Go tell your dad I'm taking her in, and if he wants to go, he'd better hurry."

"Put me down! Wayde, I swear I'm going to smack you!" I said, though I'd smacked him a couple of times already.

"Bis, will you get the lights?"

"Sure!" the gargoyle said, and it went dark. I could suddenly smell Wayde all the more, his scent lifting from his canvas coat like sweet water, smelling of damp woods and moss. Why did Weres have to smell so good?

"Hey!" I yelped when he jumped, settling me firmly on his shoulder before he started down the stairs, his boots making a harsh, hurting pace. "Let me go!" There were pixies in my hair, and I'd about had it. There were probably three ways I could get out of this, but all of them would seriously hurt him. With the loss of my magic came the loss of finesse. It was all or nothing, and I was starting to get mad at myself. God help me, I was stupid. I was relying on Wayde when one splat ball would have ended it.

"I'll let you go as soon as you're in the car," Wayde said. "Your alpha asked me to bring you to him, so shut your yap, okay?"

"You son of a bitch!" I yelled, furious that David was in on this.

"Like that's a surprise?" Wayde said, laughing as he found the bottom of the stairs and waited for the pixies to open the door for him. Ivy and Jenks were nowhere to be seen, and my face burned. They knew full well what was going on, were probably willing to let us work it out on our own. "Face it, Rachel. I'm better than you think I am. You owe me an apology."

"We're not in the car yet!" I exclaimed, not wanting to be carried out the door like this, but not wanting to hurt him, either. "Put me down, you son of a bitch!"

But he didn't, and I kicked and squirmed, unable to take a clean breath of air with his shoulder shoved into my gut. His grip on me was tight, unbreakable—the strength of a wolf pinning his prey. All right. He was good. But this wasn't encouraging me to trust his abilities. It was pissing me off. "I'm warning you, Wayde!" I exclaimed as the door creaked open and a cool wash of damp air blew in.

"Yeah, yeah, yeah," he said, and he shifted my weight until my breath huffed out.

"Put me down!" I shouted, and Wayde jerked to a halt at the soft scuffing on the stairs.

"Ah, this isn't what it looks like," Wayde said to someone, and I squirmed, twisting awkwardly, and saw Trent standing on the steps, his car running at the curb in the rainy night. Trent's eyes were as wide as mine, and in a sudden burst of motion, he flung out his hand.

"*Obstupesco!*" he exclaimed, turning from businessman to assassin as he crouched on the stairs, his long coat furling, and I shrieked, covering my head with my arms and ducking back behind Wayde.

The spell hit Wayde square on, and I cried out again when he shuddered—and then dropped like a stone.

The world spun. I felt Trent *almost* catch me, dragging me from Wayde in such a way that only my hip hit the cement stoop. Pain shot all the way to my skull.

"Trent! Don't hurt him!" I said, dazed, as I spit the hair out of my mouth, Trent's arms under my armpits as he struggled to lift me. Wayde was out cold, and I found I didn't care as much as I thought I would. "He's my bodyguard!"

Trent's weight shifted wildly as I struggled to get my feet under me, the smell of wine and cinnamon becoming strong as he grappled for control, his dress shoes slipping on the wet cement. "My God, I forgot how heavy you are," he said, practically shoving me up and away. "I know he's your bodyguard. What is he doing carting you out of your church over his shoulder?" Glancing down at Wayde, he tugged his long coat straight, grimacing. "Oh, I'm sorry. Did I interrupt some sort of dominance foreplay?"

His tone was rude, and I leaned against the church's open door and caught my breath. "No," I said, frowning at the pixies giggling out of sight. "What are you doing here?"

Shifting from foot to foot, he tugged his coat straight, trying to find his usual aplomb, but after three days in a car with him, I could see right through to his creased brow and finger twitch. "HAPA is harvesting witches with elevated levels of Rosewood enzymes," he said, appearing oblivious to Wayde. "Excuse me for being concerned. I thought you should know before you try to apprehend them. Maybe if you returned my calls I wouldn't have to drive out here."

Guilt pricked at me, and I bit back my next tart reply. Whispers of pixies drifted at my back, and the damp night brushed my cheek. Two steps away, Trent stood awkwardly in the mist, rubbing his hand and waiting for my response. It was the one that Al had ripped the fingers from, and it probably hurt when he used it to spell with. He looked angry, and I thought back to seeing him earlier today at the park, upset, frustrated, and altogether appealing.

Seeing me silent, he nodded as if not surprised. Expression becoming dark, he spun on his heel. Panic slid through me, and I didn't know why. "I'm sorry. I should have taken your call. I don't know why I didn't," I blurted out. "The I.S. already said as much, that they're going to use me as a scapegoat if I can't find HAPA, so I think you'll be okay."

He hesitated, his foot reaching to find the next step down. Slowly he turned back, the tension in his shoulders easing. The motion was slight, but I caught it in the dim light from the sign above the door. "I thought that's why I was out there," he said guardedly, shifting his weight to his back foot as he found the top of the stoop again. "Though they told me they wanted my opinion as to the possibility that you did it. I told them you didn't. I was hoping to get to you before they took you out there."

"It wouldn't have made any difference," I whispered.

Trent took a steadying breath, glancing down at Wayde as he stepped closer. "That's not the only reason I came over. Rachel, have you given any thought to taking the bracelet off?"

I backed up, feeling sick. The church loomed behind me, safe and secure, and yet fear coursed through me like a red ribbon. "No."

His jaw tightened as he came closer. "Whatever trouble you're in with the demons, I can help. I gave the bracelet to you so you could have a choice, but you aren't choosing anything. You're letting your fear make your decision for you."

"Fear!" I exclaimed, stiffening, and the last of the pixies vanished deeper into the church.

His head dropped for a moment. When it came up, in the streetlight I could see his anger clearly. I could tell I wasn't going to like whatever was going to come out of his mouth next. "You aren't being a demon," he said, actually stepping over Wayde. "You aren't being a witch. You're hiding, and that's not why I gave you the bracelet."

Peeved because he was right, I jerked away from him, the silver glinting between us like a guilty secret. "I'm trying to be me, okay? But they won't let me. I had to take this stupid job just to get my license back."

Behind him, Wayde's breathing quickened, and Trent's expression became frustrated. "That's great, Rachel, but do you want to live the rest of your life doing crap jobs to win what is your god-given right?"

Damn it, I hated it when he was right, but I hated admitting it to his face even more. I did have my pride. "If I take this off, I'm in the ever-after," I said as I shook the bracelet at him, sure now that Jenks and Ivy were listening. "I'm in the ever-after washing dishes and fending off demon advances for the rest of my life. I don't like it there, okay?"

"I said I'd help you," he said quickly, his frustration probably because I wasn't being reasonable, but I couldn't help it. The man was scaring me, and I didn't know why. He never had before. *Help me? Why would he help me? And could I trust that?*

"You need to consider the risk that you're putting yourself and those around you in by choosing to sever your ability to do quick, adaptive magic," he finished softly, persuasively, his beautiful voice coaxing me to just . . . listen.

My head drooped, and I looked past Trent to Wayde, his face down and his hand reaching for nothing. "I can't,

Trent," I whispered. "If I start hurting people, then I start killing them. I don't want to be that person."

I looked up and was shocked by his understanding. I blinked, and he hid it by rubbing his hand over the cup of his ear and ducking his head. "I understand where you're coming from," he said. "I really do, but this?" He gestured behind him to Wayde. "This isn't safe for you or anyone else. One good charm could have prevented this altogether."

"I know that," I said, feeling the sting of guilt, but he only came closer, his expression softening more.

"Instead, you did nothing, letting it escalate until someone else had to step in, and now instead of a sprained wrist, he might have a concussion."

"I am not going to kill people!" I said, and he winced as my voice echoed in the rain-emptied street.

"I'm not asking you to," he said, his eyes finally meeting mine. "But you *are* a demon."

Arms wrapped around my middle, I looked up into the misty rain.

"That comes with responsibilities and expectations, but it also gives you a way out," Trent was saying, but my gut hurt. "My God, Rachel, you have an arsenal of abilities you're ignoring, weapons that can be used to minimize the damage your existence creates. You're forcing others to pick up your slack. It's time to grow up."

He had me until his last words, and my head snapped down. "Stop it. Just stop," I said, and his shoulders slumped as he realized he'd gone too far. "Thank you for coming over here and rescuing me from my *bodyguard*."

Trent's posture shifted to one of belligerence, his hair dark in the misty rain. "Tell me that again when you mean it, and I'll buy you dinner," he said, and my jaw tightened.

"I appreciate that you want to help me screw up my life even more," I said, heart pounding, "but with all due respect, Mr. Kalamack, when I want the damn bracelet off, I'll ask you."

"Is that so?"

His words were clipped, and I desperately wanted to say something different, but he was right and I was scared. And when I got scared, I got stubborn. "Yes," I said, chin lifted.

For a long moment he looked at me, unknown thoughts making his own jaw clench and a dangerous light catch in his eyes. "Mr. Benson can't keep you safe from HAPA."

I stood up straighter, hoping he didn't see me shaking. "I'm only going out to secure sites. I'm making up some earth-magic charms later. If I'm prepared, I'll be okay. It's not as if I've never been under a death threat before."

Trent's lips lost their hard slant, and he almost smiled. Head dropping, he stepped closer to say something, but behind him, Wayde moved, his knee scraping on the cement as he sat up.

"Damn," the Were breathed, his head still bowed as he felt his chest. "What the hell hit me?"

I'd never find out what Trent was going to say because he bent to help Wayde to his feet. "Sorry about that," he said, and I swear I saw a faint glow as he did some healing magic and Wayde blinked fast. "I thought you were taking Rachel against her will."

"He was," I said, ignored by both men as I fidgeted at the open door.

Wayde squinted up at me in the dark before he dropped his head again and rubbed the back of his neck. He was wet from having been on the cement, and still dazed. "I was trying to prove a point."

Trent nodded, that same tight look about his jaw. "It would have worked except for one thing," he said, and Wayde looked up.

"What's that?" he asked blearily.

Silent, Trent stared at me while my heart hammered, once, twice, three times. "She's got friends," he finally said. His head cocked in challenge, Trent turned his back on me and paced quickly to his car, his steps light and almost silent.

Wayde groaned softly, hunched over as he felt his middle. "Are you okay?" I asked him as I put a hand on his back, then watched as Trent drove away, his wipers going and his brake lights shining on the damp pavement.

"Yeah. Can we go now?"

I nodded, taking his elbow to steady him as we went down the steps. Sure. We could go now. Damn it, I was going to get a tattoo. Swell.

Six

David put his heater-stuffy, gray sports car into park in front of a deserted shop front, and I stared out the front window, the misty black adding to my stellar mood. Even the familiar, pleasant scent of Were mixing with David's expensive cologne didn't help. There were no cars here, no pedestrian activity, the rain having emptied the usually busy Inderland neighborhood. It was one in the morning in a bad part of town, but seeing that I was sitting next to an alpha Were with an angry bodyguard in the back, I'd probably be okay, even if David's car was likely on three chop-shop lists. I'd been in worse neighborhoods on my own.

David looked across the street to a trashy storefront, its windows plastered with old band posters. It looked like a cross between a beauty parlor and a motorcycle outlet, and I suddenly realized that it wasn't abandoned, but closed. EMOJIN'S was stenciled in faded gold letters on the door. *They're closed,* I thought, seeing the dark windows. *Thank you, God.*

"Thanks, Rachel. I appreciate this," David said, and Wayde, in the back and nursing a massive headache, snorted.

"They look closed," I muttered, not looking at either of them.

David opened his door and got out, and the faint scent of old garbage and wet pavement slipped in. "This is the fifth appointment you've missed. They don't expect you to show. Wait here until I know if they'll see you."

Wayde lurched out of the backseat, groaning as he found the pavement, and carefully stretched. "I'll check," he said. "If I don't keep moving, I'm going to stiffen up."

David settled back in the soft leather. "I'll wait here with Rachel," he said, and Wayde shut the door, a shade harder than necessary. I knew he was ticked about the bruised ribs, but he shouldn't have tried to carry me out of the church over his shoulder.

Wayde tapped on the glass, glaring at me. "You're being an ass. Apologize."

Sneering, I almost flipped him off.

Wayde, hiding a faint limp, crossed the road to the tattoo parlor. Angling his hand through the wide bars, he knocked on the thick glass. He looked right at home on the street, hunched against the misty rain in his rough canvas coat, faded jeans, and thick army boots. A light came on in the back and I turned away. Great. Someone was still there.

"I mean it," David said earnestly as he turned the heat down, and I sighed. "I appreciate you doing this, but if you don't want to, that's okay. I understand."

But it wasn't okay, and I frowned. *Wayde was right.* I was being an ass, not to mention childish. "I want to do this," I said, unable to look at the man, my voice sullen. "I'm sorry for being such a pain. I'm excited about it. Really."

David laughed, then sobered. "I try to steer clear of your affairs . . ." he started.

"I know," I said, meeting his eyes. "I appreciate it."

"But I'll feel better once you have your pack tattoo," he finished, his dark eyes even darker in the soft rain spotting the windows. His wipers squeaked back and forth, and he turned them off. "You're vulnerable without all your magic. One man with a van and another with a wad of ether, and you're gone."

"It's not that bad," I said, uneasy as I remembered Trent saying the same thing in different words.

"Yes, it is," he said, his brow furrowed. "Especially now that you've lost the one thing you had going for you, your anonymity. You're a demon with little magic, a prize for every self-styled magic slinger this side of the Mississippi who wants to make a name for himself. I'm not about to curtail your freedom, because when you chain someone up to be safe, they're still chained, but if you don't take steps to protect yourself, I will, and you will accept it."

Ashamed, I fiddled with the lip of my shoulder bag.

"Glenn told me what you, Jenks, and Ivy are working on with him," he added, and I turned to him.

"He told you?"

David nodded, watching Wayde talk through the barred door to an irate woman in jeans and a sweater. "Not a lot," David said, "but enough to be able to read between the lines of the official statements." His gaze went to mine, locking on my eyes and holding them. "Be careful," he said, and I almost shivered. "These people are calling you out. Having a visible tie to someone will make it easier for me to let you go about your business. Especially now that your magic is limited."

"Ye-e-e-es," I said slowly, fingering the bracelet. I said I was a demon, but was I really if I couldn't walk the walk?

Looking at the shop, David said, "You have friends and allies out there. With a tattoo, they'll recognize you. You deserve it. Accept it with grace."

Confused, I winced. Trent was telling me to stand on my own, that I had to accept magic as both my downfall and my saving grace. David was telling me to rely on my friends, that doing so was the "grown-up" thing to do. I didn't know what to think anymore. Maybe I could do both. "Thank you," I said softly. "I'm sorry. I shouldn't have come out of the closet."

"Oh no," David said, and my head came up at the amusement in his voice. "I'm glad you did. It invoked the demon clause. Between Trent and me, we almost have you solvent again."

"Demon clause?" I asked sourly, sure the smile quirking his lips was at my expense.

"Demon clause," he echoed, nodding sharply. "Any action caused by a demon cannot be held accountable to any person and is considered an act of nature. It's in most boiler-plates, and what it means is that all the lawsuits against you have no validity."

My lips parted, and I sat up straighter. I'd known that David and Trent had been working together to both put laws into place to give me back my rights as a citizen and minimize the damage that me being me wrought, but this was new. "I wasn't legally a demon when most of those suits were brought against me," I said, and David smacked a hand on my knee, clearly in a good mood.

"Yes, you were. You were born a demon. The miracle is that you survived it." I began to smile, and he added, "My lawyer is having a field day making a name for himself. I think he should be paying us to retain him."

I snorted, relieved that something good had come out of it. "Glad I could help," I said sarcastically. The woman talking to Wayde was looking at me. Her expression wasn't eager, and I waved at her. That went over really well by all accounts as she frowned at Wayde, and I watched her say, "I'll ask her. Wait here." The glass door shut, and Wayde turned, shrugging.

"Come on," David said as he opened his door again, clearly in a much better mood. "Let's see if she'll let you in."

A shiver of excitement tempered with dread sifted through me, and I got out, almost tripping on the curb, David had parked so close. Bag high on my shoulder, I shut the car door behind me with a thump that echoed in the rain-wet streets. I looked at the damp, world-weary buildings around me, able to tell that the river wasn't that far away.

"I'm sorry, David," I said, and he smiled at me over the hood of his car. "I should have done this a long time ago. Thanks for putting up with me." Why could I admit I was wrong to David, and not to Trent?

"Not a problem," he said, then gestured to the store. "Shall we go?"

I nodded and started across the road. There were more lights on now. My head down to watch for the potholes, I made my way to the front door, David beside me. Upon reaching the chipped curb, I peered past the old posters and into the shop, avoiding Wayde's disgruntled stare. The windows were so thickly covered with colored images that it was hard to see in.

"I'm not going to run away," I said when Wayde leaned over, almost pinning me to the door.

"Good," he said shortly, not backing up. "Emojin is on her way down. She's not sure anymore that she wants to ink you. Way to go, Rachel."

"Not ink her?" David dropped back a step. "I already paid for it!"

Wayde's expression was hard. "Then you should have gotten her here before she stood Emojin up five times."

"I'm sorry about that!" I said loudly, hearing my voice echo in the deserted street. "I wasn't ready, and I don't like being pushed!"

The door was being opened, and Wayde turned to face it. "Then I suggest you tell her."

Inside, a shadow moved, outlined with a sudden light when an interior door opened. There was a glimpse of a stairway up, and then the door shut. David dropped back, and the outer door was opened by a barefoot, heavy woman in a blue-and-green sari-like garment.

I froze. The woman was absolutely gorgeous. I'd never seen a woman this large who carried herself with so much elegance and dignity. Her skin was a pale cream with absolutely no blemishes or marks from a tattoo needle, looking as soft and supple as a newborn's. Her hair was a silvery white, braided up off her neck. She had comfortable folds of wrinkles that said she smiled a lot, but she wasn't smiling now. Native American and French, perhaps? I didn't know.

"Emojin," David said through the bars. "Thank you. We finally cornered her."

"I haven't said I'd do it," she said, and I stepped on Wayde's foot. He backed up, and I felt better. "Rachel Morgan?"

I felt trapped as her brown eyes hit me. "Uh, I'm sorry," I said, feeling like I was back in kindergarten. "I was an ass for standing you up, but I wasn't ready, and I don't like being pushed. Will you accept my apologies?"

She took a deep breath, holding it as she looked me up and down again. "Maybe. Come on in and let me hear you talk some."

Hear me talk? I mused, but she had unlocked the wrought-iron door and turned away, moving her bulk with grace as she went deeper into the store.

David opened the door for me, and feeling like I was being coddled, I went inside. Wayde came in behind me, and finally David. They shut the door with a soft thunk, sealing us inside. I took a slow breath, letting the place seep into me.

The first thing I noticed was a lack of echo. It was warm, too, almost eighty, I guess, and I immediately relaxed. The cement floor had been painted with a fantastic array of colors, mimicking a tattoo. Most of it was faded. The walls were covered in sketches, clearly several layers deep. There was a seating arrangement up front made from old bus seats and a hairdresser's chair, a huge, stained microwave and coffee urn beside it. Three separate rooms that would have been offices anywhere else took up one side of the store. They didn't have any doors, but the ceiling-to-waist-high windows had blinds, and they were closed.

Emojin had shifted her bulk behind a U-shaped, businesslike counter in the center of the store. The scratched glass cabinets held jewelry for body piercing. Behind her were deep shelves with sketchbooks of all sizes, the largest thicker than a wallpaper book.

Seeing David and me making our way to the counter, Wayde put his thumbs into his pockets and sauntered over to the young woman who'd answered the door. Mary Jo, maybe? She looked up from the invoices she was going over and smiled, and I rolled my eyes.

"So you're David's alpha?" Emojin said as I halted before her. She was eyeing me pensively as she settled herself on a high stool before a state-of-the-art monitor and keyboard. "You're nothing like the other girls."

Pulling myself straight, I extended my hand over the counter to her. "I'm Rachel," I said, feeling her smooth, un-worked hand slip coolly into mine. "I don't want to be a bother," I said, looking over the clearly closed store.

Emojin's pale eyebrows rose. "Too late for that," she said sourly. "Well, you're here, but I'm not going to do this if you don't want it." She crossed her arms over her chest and looked from David to me. "I know he dragged you here. Let me hear it."

I was so embarrassed. "I want this," I said, then glanced up, seeing her tight expression of disapproval. "Really. I've been unconscionably rude to you and to David. And the rest of the pack. I was unprofessional in standing you up, and I'm sorry. I was just scared."

The big woman grunted in surprise, and her arms un-crossed. "Still scared?" she asked, the first hints of her mood softening starting to show.

I looked at David, then Wayde, who had rolled up his sleeve to show off one of his tattoos to the young woman, and then back to Emojin. "Yes," I blurted out, and David winced. "But I'm scared about a lot of things that I do. I want this more than I'm scared." The skin around my eyes tightened as I looked at Wayde. "If I had really wanted to get away, I would have."

Exhaling heavily, Emojin nodded. "I can't believe I'm saying this, but okay. I'll do it. *And* I accept your apology."

I sighed, not realizing until now how much this meant to me. "Thank you. I'm really sorry. I do some of the stupidest things sometimes."

Emojin glanced up. "You think this is one of them?"

"No," I said quickly. "I meant ignoring this was. I should have handled it better."

"Well, it's done," the big woman said. Beside me, David had regained his excitement, and was leaning on the glass counter until Emojin tapped a hand-lettered sign taped to the top telling him not to.

"You're a witch, right?" Emojin muttered as her fingers clicked over the keyboard. She had a beautiful voice, as soft and full as the rest of her. Her perfume was nice. Sort of a powdery coolness. "We have David's basic design on file."

David ducked his head, tugging his coat straight as he looked up eagerly again. "I'd like to add to it to show her higher status."

Emojin stared at her monitor as one finger kept tapping a key, scrolling. "Not a problem. I thought you might."

Something special? For me? "Really?" I said, then warmed at the eagerness in my voice.

David smiled, showing his teeth, taking my hand and giving it a quick squeeze before letting go. "Of course. This is important to me."

And here I'd been avoiding it. God! I was such a jerk.

Behind Emojin, Wayde was following the younger woman to one of the "offices." She flicked on the light and put her hand on the Were's chest, stopping him at the archway. Telling him to stay outside, she started to clean everything. The smell of antiseptic tickled my nose, and Emojin lit a stick of incense, waving it briefly before dropping it into a dusky bottle to smoke to nothing.

"Here's your registered design," she said as she spun the screen to David and me, and we both leaned closer, being careful to not put our weight on the glass. The basic tattoo was a simple dandelion flower gone to seed, the fluffy parachutes being black instead of white, and the green stem coming from a small cluster of leaves. The moon was behind it. It was nice, I guess, but David clearly wanted something special. To be honest, it wasn't doing anything for me. I was just happy the other ladies hadn't wanted broomsticks and bats.

"I'll do the draw myself," Emojin said, and I blinked in surprise. She had put on a pair of round-rimmed glasses, reminding me of Al as she looked over them at me. "But Mary Jo will color you in. She's my daughter and almost as good as me."

"Okay," I said, glancing at Wayde and Mary Jo. She was pushing him out of her way, firmly pointing a finger to the front waiting area. The guy didn't have a chance, but they both looked like they were enjoying the game.

"A tattoo should have meaning beyond its individual art," Emojin was saying as she tapped the design. "What can you bring to this that is entirely you?"

Wincing, I tilted my head. "I don't know. What do you think, David?" I asked, seeing that he'd clearly given this a lot more thought than I had. I was such a bad alpha.

"More flowers on Rachel's tattoo," he said immediately. "And the moon behind it."

Emojin was nodding, her gaze distant as she saw it in her mind. "To match yours?"

"Yes, but we're not a couple, so they should be different," he said. "Make hers full to show her completeness."

Complete? Was he kidding? I was about as unfinished as one could be and still survive.

"Let me think." Emojin hit a few buttons on her keyboard, and a huge, outdated printer behind her hummed to life. "I gave you black fluffs. Let's keep that element the same between you to show unity."

This was getting more complicated by the moment, but I didn't want the two of them to come up with something that was going to take more than a day to complete and cover my entire back. "Um . . ." I said hesitantly as a piece of paper slid from the printer. "Sometimes less is more. Maybe we could stick with just three flowers. Make one yellow, one that's closed and ready to change, and the last one with the black dandelion fluff?"

Emojin leaned to take the printout. Her eyes were sharp on mine when she came back and set it before her. "Change," she said, looking me up and down with the same evaluating air she'd had when I first met her. "That's what you're all about, isn't it? David, she's right. Give me a second."

"Only three flowers?" he said, clearly thinking that I should have more, and I smiled nervously. I didn't want a bouquet. I wanted something simple.

Emojin had a black pencil in one hand and another in her teeth. Almost oblivious to us, she began sketching a new drawing beside the original print. She was a true artist, and as I watched the tattoo start to take shape, I decided I liked the idea of wearing something that this woman created.

"This is good," she said as she added a few floating seeds from the open seed head. "Simple, elegant, easy to do, and rich in symbolism. What do you think?"

She spun the drawing to us, and I took in a breath, loving it. "Oh, this is beautiful," I said as I picked it up, and Emojin beamed. Even David seemed happy despite there being just three flowers and only two actually looking pretty. The third was in an ugly in-between stage, like me, I suppose. My God, she had somehow made the angles on the leaves look like wolf heads, and with the moon highlighting it, it was a true piece of art. And it was mine—if I wanted it.

"Okay," I said, handing it back. "I'll do it. I don't care how much it hurts."

Emojin smiled, all her wrinkles folding in, making her beautiful. "I knew you would."

From the front of the store, Wayde made a rude bark of laughter, and I turned to him. "What are you laughing at?" I demanded, and David put a calming hand on me.

"You." Wayde slouched in his chair. "God, Rachel. It's not going to hurt that bad. The way I hear it, you've had worse."

"Not intentionally," I said, stifling a shiver. "You're just sulking because you got pwned by an elf."

David gave my arm a squeeze as Emojin slid from her

stool. "Thank you," he said earnestly. "I know this means more to me than you."

Uncomfortable, I winced. "I'm sorry it took me so long, but at least now I know it will last." I shook my arm with the silver band, and a hint of worry crossed his expression.

Moving slowly, Emojin joined us. "So, all I need to know is where you want it."

I blinked, remembering a demon asking me the same thing. "Uh . . ." I said intelligently. "Where would you suggest?"

She exhaled, tired. "You've not given this any thought."

Wayde had started our way, and he pulled his collar aside, saying, "A real Were would put it here, where everyone could see it, but since you don't want to show affiliation—"

"Mr. Benson," David growled, facing him with his hands clenched.

"That's not it at all!" I said, angry as well. "I just didn't want to get one only to have it vanish after some stupid demon transformation curse! They don't last through that, you know."

Wayde stopped a good eight feet back, slumped with his weight on one foot in a maybe-show of submissiveness, but his jaw was still clenched defiantly. Smirking, Emojin stepped between them. "I'd suggest an arm or an ankle," she said as if the two weren't ready to face off. Training or not, Wayde would lose badly. The only reason David had asked for Wayde's help was because David had a problem forcing me, his alpha, into anything.

Emojin shook the paper to get David and me to look at it. "You're going to want to show this off on request. Putting it on your ass might be a bad idea."

I laughed to help defuse the tension, and both men turned from each other. "The ladies have put theirs on their front shoulders," David said. "It's very showy."

But I didn't want showy. I wanted subtle, and my stomach started to hurt.

"With your fair skin, this is going to look fabulous,"

Emojin said, seeing my hesitation. "I may ink this myself. Can you hold still when something hurts?"

I nodded, remembering the needles from when I was a child. God, I hated needles. "Yes," I said, trying to find a way to meld my desire for subtlety with David's wish for show. If it wasn't where someone could see it, there wasn't much point to it as far as he was concerned.

"I'd like this on the back of my neck, high and almost behind my ear so my hair covers it most of the time," I said, taking the drawing from Emojin. "And the detached fluffs coming around the front somewhat. One on my neck by the main piece, one on my collarbone where everyone can see it, and a third where you think appropriate."

I looked up, fixing on David's eyes. "If someone knows it's a pack tattoo, they'll recognize it flat out. And if they don't, then they won't need to see the larger one."

David thought about that, and Emojin took the paper back. "Like an open secret," she said, pleased. "Rachel, this is good. I'm so pleased that you came in. This is going to be one of my more satisfying pieces."

"Why?" Wayde asked, his stance belligerent. "Because she's been such an ass about it?"

Emojin stopped, turned, and nailed him with her glare. "Because she's making this one piece all she'll ever need to show the world who she is instead of coloring her body with random images and needing thirty expressions to show her soul."

My lips parted, and I stared as she paced to him, looking as if she wanted to smack him.

"She might have come in sooner if she had had something to mull over other than you men telling her it isn't going to hurt, because she knows it is, and to believe otherwise is stupid."

Wayde backed up another alarmed step as the shorter woman faced him. "I told you to bring her by for a drawing session first," she said. "Rachel may have been an ass for standing me up, but she did come in." Turning, she made a last huff, then smiled at me. "Men," she said as she took my arm and led me to the brightly lit room. "They forget we need to see the outcome of pain before we willingly put ourselves through it. How else would we suffer nine months to have a beautiful child? We already know we have guts. Getting a tattoo to prove it means little. You're going to like this. I know it."

She patted my arm again, inviting me to follow her into her small/big world of ink and needles and expression of soul. And this time, trusting her, I went.

Seven

I squinted, trying to tilt Ivy's hand mirror just so and keep the damp hair off my shoulder as I stood with my back to the bathroom mirror so I could see my tattoo. It was a sunny afternoon, but not much light made it into the old men's room that had been converted into a laundry and bath. Exhaling loudly, I dropped my hair to turn on the light.

"Hey!" Jenks complained as he darted out of the way, but I wanted to see it, too.

"What do you think?" I asked as the bright fluorescent light flickered on, and I pulled my hair back again. The mirror was foggy from my shower, and it took me a second to get the hand mirror lined up with the cleared spot, but then I eyed the back of my neck in the small mirror. Jenks's wings were a cool draft, and he hovered behind me spilling a silver dust. His hands were on his hips, a garden sword on his belt, and a dirty jacket on his back. He'd been in the garden all morning strengthening the security lines and was probably trying to get his afternoon nap in. He'd finally cut his hair, and I felt better knowing he'd gotten over that stumbling block. It had grown long in the months that Matalina had been gone, and it was nice seeing him getting back to normal.

"I suppose it's okay," he said, being of the mind that no one should subject themselves to injury for vanity's sake, though in my case, it hadn't been vanity, but a real need to show affiliation. "If you like that kind of thing."

"Okay?" I shifted to get a better look at it. "I love it. I shouldn't have waited so long."

"Sure, it looks good now." He cocked his head and tugged his garden jacket up where it belonged. "But it's going to peel soon. And what about when you're a hundred and sixty? Those flowers are going to look u-u-u-u-ugl-y-y-y when your skin gets all saggy." I frowned at him through my reflection, and he added, "Did it hurt?"

Dropping my damp hair, slick with detangler, I turned to face him. My eyes were drawn to the tuft on my collarbone. The shower water had burned, but I didn't think that's what he'd meant. "It hurt like hell," I said, meeting his gaze. "I passed out."

"You?" Jenks hovered backward until there were twin pixies in my mirror.

Nodding, I set Ivy's mirror on the dryer and looked through my drawer for my comb. "It was weird. I could take the pain okay. I could've taken more, but I passed out." Finding one, I tried working the detangler through my hair some more. "David panicked. Emojin told him that it only meant my mind was stronger than my body." Which was about par for me. It had always been that way. I was tired of people overreacting when I had a minor problem that would work itself through. So I had passed out. So what?

Jenks snickered, wings clattering as he dropped down to take a closer look at the seed tufts.

"I'm glad you got your hair cut. Did Jhi do it?" I asked.

Darting back, Jenks's face was aghast. "Jhi?" he yelped. "No. It was, uh—"

He hesitated, and I winced as I found a knot in my hair. "Who? Bis?" I guessed, the thought of the somewhat clumsy gargoyle near Jenks's head with a pair of scissors kind of scary.

"It was Belle," he admitted, his feet landing on the faucet's knob.

I looked at him, surprised. "Belle?" I thought he hated the fairy.

Jenks's wings were a bright red, fanning into motion though he didn't move at all. "She cut it for me when I got it tangled in some burrs. She said that only babies have short hair, but if I was clumsy enough to catch it on something, I needed to cut it."

"Short is probably a good idea," I said. "Fairies can't move as fast as pixies, so they don't have to be worried about snagging it. Personally, I like the way men look with long hair."

"Really?"

I glanced at him, thinking about Trent's wispy hair. His wasn't curly like Jenks's, but it had been oh-my-God silky as I had run it through my fingers. *Stop it, Rachel.*

"Short looks better on you, though," I said, shaking away the memory.

He squinted at me in mistrust, probably wondering why I wouldn't meet his eyes. "It won't tangle in the garden now," he said cautiously. "I don't know how the girls deal with it, but theirs isn't curly."

I switched sides, carefully going through my hair as I tried to plan my day, thinking that seeing Jenks get back to normal was a quiet relief. The tasks that Matalina had performed were slowly being picked up by Jenks's kids, and now Belle, apparently. I never would have guessed that that would happen, but maybe because she was a fairy, she could do the matronly things Matalina had done without threatening Matalina's place in Jenks's mind.

I didn't quite know what to do with myself today. It was Saturday, and usually I'd be in the ever-after. The amulets that the I.S. had were either not working or they weren't telling us what they'd found. We'd probably hear nothing new until I got the amulets I'd made yesterday invoked and out to the FIB. Setting down the comb, I picked up the cream that Emojin had sent me home with and dabbed a bit on, starting with the little fluffs at my throat. Weres would recognize even this small bit as part of a pack tattoo, and humans wouldn't care. It was perfect.

Jenks noticed my wince, and he rose, wings clattering. "Does it still hurt? You want a pain amulet?"

I squeezed a small amount onto my fingertips and reached for the fluff in back. "No. I wouldn't use one anyway. Pain is apparently part of the mystique. That's why vampires don't get tattoos."

"Yeah, okay. I still think it's stupid." Jenks looked to the front of the church when the front door opened with a creak. "Scarring yourself to show you belong to something."

The familiar clicking of boot heels on the worn wooden floor echoed in the sanctuary, and I recapped the ointment. "Ivy?" I asked, and Jenks nodded. Most of his kids were still asleep, but someone was always on sentry duty, and if it had been anyone else, they would have raised the alarm.

"She was out all night," I said as I grabbed a T-shirt from the dryer and shrugged it on over my chemise. Ivy had been out when I'd come back from Emojin's. I figured she'd gone into the FIB with Glenn to check on something, and I wasn't surprised she had decided to spend the night, or morning rather, with him. *I'm glad she's happy—my new motto.*

Ivy's feet sounded loud in the hall, and knowing I was in the bathroom from the closed door and the scent of soap, she said, "Hi, Rachel. Is there coffee?"

Her feet continued on, and I shouted, "Just made it. Help yourself!"

A silver dust slipped heavily from Jenks, and he hovered before me, a devious smile on his face. "Excuse me."

He slipped out through the crack under the door, and I heard him exclaim loudly, "Sweet mother of Tink. Where have you been, Ivy? You stink!"

"Glenn's," she said, clearly weary. "And I showered."

"Yeah, I can tell. So tell me . . ." he started in, his voice becoming faint as they went into the kitchen. There was a thunk of something hitting the wall, and I heard him swear at her. Smiling, I opened the door, knowing that she was probably in a good mood if Jenks was needling her enough that she was taking potshots at him she knew would never land.

My pulse quickened as I padded barefoot down the dim corridor to the kitchen. I'll admit I was more than a little nervous about showing Ivy my tattoo. Weres wouldn't ink vampires since vampires turned pain into pleasure. Every so often, a vampire would start a parlor to give tattoos to their kin. It usually lasted a week before the place was torched—by vampires, not Weres. The old ones didn't like scars on their chosen that they didn't give them. I honestly didn't know where Ivy fell on the tattoo side of things. Not that it mattered, but I'd like it if she thought it was cool.

Squinting in the brighter light, I hesitated in the doorway. Ivy was standing stiffly at the sink, looking out into the garden, Jenks sitting on the overturned brandy snifter on the sill. It used to hold Mr. Fish, my betta, but had since been relegated to imprisoning the blue chrysalis that Al gave me on New Year's. I thought it had to be dead, but Jenks insisted it wasn't. I suppose he'd know.

Ivy looked good, even if she was irate: slim, comfortable, sated, and in the same clothes she'd had on last night. "I've got this under control!" she said, hushed but strident, clearly peeved at having let go of her ironclad hold on her emotions. Jenks looked at me and Ivy stiffened, not having realized that I was there.

She turned, a faint flush on her cheeks, and tugged her short jacket closer, as if cold. "Hi," I said, wondering about the sudden flash of guilt that crossed her face. Ivy knew I didn't care how or when she took care of business. And by looking at her swift reactions I knew she had. It was pretty obvious, in hindsight, what with my leaving, her and Glenn here, and then coming back to an empty church. I was glad they got along so well. It made living with her easier.

"Hi," she echoed, giving Jenks a sharp look to shut up before she picked up a glass of orange juice. "Is that it?" she said, the glass almost to her lips.

Her eyes were on the tuft showing above the neck of my T-shirt, and I pushed myself into motion.

"Part of it," Jenks said as he rose up off the brandy snifter. "Most of it's on her neck."

Gathering my wet hair, I turned my back to her and tugged my hair clear of the tattoo. "See?" I said, head down as I looked at the amulets out on the counter, still waiting for Marshal to come over to invoke them. I'd wanted them done and out by now, but Wayde and David had sort of blown my night for me, and Marshal was on a human clock. "What do you think?"

I heard her steps come close, and then her soft touch on my skin. "It looks red," she said, and I stifled a shiver. "Did it hurt?"

"She passed out!" Jenks said, and I grimaced. But then I froze, the scent of honey and gold lifting from her like a memory. I'd smelled it before on Glenn. My neck tingled, and suddenly, I realized why Ivy was acting funny. Honey and gold and Old Spice. It all added up to one thing.

I spun, dropping my hair and staring at Ivy. She flushed and took a step back. "You . . ." I said as my hair fell into place, and she took a deep breath and turned away. *Holy crap. Ivy, Glenn, and Daryl?*

But by Ivy's discomfort, I knew I was right. The nymph was probably used to threesomes, being a nymph. And threesomes were common in vamp society where a savage vampire might use another person to help even things out or act like a spotter of sorts to make sure everyone made it out alive. Glenn, though . . . This was a surprise.

I couldn't help my smile. Jenks hovered between us, trying to figure out why I was almost laughing and Ivy was avoiding my eye. But what Ivy did was Ivy's business.

"Um, it's okay," I said, hoping Jenks thought I was talking about having passed out, not that Ivy had moved her relationships with Daryl *and* Glenn to a new level. Holy crap, what was I going to say to Glenn the next time I saw him? But I suppose if I could survive the embarrassment of Ivy and Jenks seeing my tongue halfway down Trent's throat, Glenn would survive my knowing that he and my roommate were exploring their options with a nymph.

Her back to me, Ivy looked out the window. Jenks finally landed on the counter, looking from one of us to the other. "Hey, uh, what am I missing?"

"Nothing," I said, touching Ivy's elbow to make her look at me. "Is everything okay?"

Blinking fast, she tried to smile. "Yes," she said, that same guilty look crossing her face. "It was comfortable."

I gave her elbow a quick squeeze and let go. "Good," I said, hoping she knew I was okay with this. "I'm glad."

And I was. Ivy and I had come to terms with the fact that there was never going to be anything between us other than an ironclad friendship. Ivy making ties outside me was a good thing. It was what we both wanted, and I was proud of her for moving on. And yet . . . even though I didn't want blood or sex with Ivy, much less a threesome with two of my colleagues, I couldn't help but feel ditched. Both Ivy and Jenks were moving on with their lives, and I wasn't. I was alone. Again. Right when I thought I'd finally gotten everything together.

"Comfortable?" Jenks's features concentrated as he figured it out. With a burst of gold dust, he shot up into the air. "Tink's diaphragm!" he shouted, waving his arms as he figured it out. "I don't want to know. Oh my God! Ivy! You're worse than Rache!"

Ivy leaned against the counter and crossed her ankles. "You want to can it, Jenks? Put it on a shelf for later?"

"No!" the pixy exclaimed. "I want to burn it out of my brain! Is Glenn all right?"

My back to them, I poured myself a cup of coffee. "Jeez, Jenks. It was just a little threesome. Grow up. It's what vampires and nymphs do. Glenn can handle himself. He's a big boy."

"He'd have to be!" Jenks shrilled as I turned.

"He is," Ivy said, a weird half smile on her face as she held her glass of orange juice and stared off into space.

"Shut up! Just shut up!" Jenks yelled, and I chuckled.

The front doorbell rang, and I straightened, my untasted coffee in my hand. Great. Now Jenks's kids would be up again. But before I could move, Jenks was headed for the hallway. "Thank God," he muttered, a blue dust sifting from him and looking like a weird sunbeam on the floor. "I'll get it."

"It's probably Marshal," I called after him, then looked at Ivy and shrugged. I still had six uninvoked charms to get to the FIB. If they hadn't tracked HAPA down by now, my amulets would help. Nervous, I pulled a strand of damp hair over my collarbone.

"I like your tattoo," Ivy said as she noticed me trying to hide it.

"Thanks," I said, feeling a tingle where her eyes had been as I poured Marshal a cup of coffee in the most masculine mug we had. "Me too."

I heard the *clump, clump, clump* of Marshal's boots, and something in me fluttered. I had liked Marshal. He was a fun man to be around. I'd never expected to ever see him again when we'd parted, and I didn't know why I'd asked him to help me except for the fact that he was the only witch I knew on the East Coast.

"Just don't ask Ivy about her morning," Jenks said as the two of them entered.

Marshal stopped short, took off his knitted hat, showing his skull, hair clipped short for the swimming pool. Looking uncomfortable, his eyes went from me to Ivy, and then back again. "Uh, hi, Rachel. Ivy," he said, and Jenks left Marshal's shoulder to get a few drips of coffee from the coffeepot.

He looked almost the same as when I'd last seen him. His waist was just as slim, and his shoulders as wide. He still carried himself with that athletic grace that had attracted me to him in the first place. Clean shaven and wearing jeans and a sweater, he stood there with most of his weight on one foot, his hands in his coat pockets. He looked like he was in his midtwenties, but I knew he'd passed that almost ten years ago. Marshal was a ley-line witch in his prime with a good job, a good life, and it showed.

Why had I asked him to come over? Someone at the I.S. could have invoked them, even if I'd have had to stand in the lobby and beg. This had been a stupid idea. *Why had he come?*

Rolling her eyes, Ivy saluted him with her empty glass. "Hi, Marshal. If you'll excuse me, I need to wash my hair," she said dryly. Pushing herself forward, she headed right for him.

Marshal sidestepped, frowning as Ivy stalked into the hall and her door shut a little too hard. God, he looked good standing in my kitchen, not afraid of her. Not afraid of anything. Mostly. His hands were clenched as he glanced down the hallway after Ivy, and I remembered how they'd felt on me, the waves of sensation that crested from his touch as he drew a line through me and made me come alive.

What are you doing, Rachel?

Jenks's wings clattered in warning as he landed on my shoulder. "Rache?"

"Don't you have something to do?" I said, then smiled at Marshal. "It's good to see you. How are you doing?"

Shaking himself free from his dark thoughts about Ivy, Marshal smiled and came into the kitchen. "I'm doing great," he said, his hand out in what might have been a handshake, but it might have been half a hug, too.

I hesitated, and after a confusing moment, he awkwardly gave me a hug. I leaned into him, breathing the chlorine/red-wood scent he had mixing with the damp dead-leaf smell of a cold November morning. Why had I asked him over? I wasn't looking for a boyfriend. They always tried to change me.

"You look good" rumbled through me, and I pushed backward. Jenks was scowling at me from the top of the door frame to the hall, and I ignored him.

The rims of Marshal's ears were red, and he rocked back, his hands in a fig leaf. "I can't tell you how glad I am you got your shunning rescinded," he said, his words too fast, his eyes too reluctant to meet mine. "I read all about it. I knew you could."

Then why did you leave? But I didn't say it. He'd left when I'd been almost at my lowest point. I didn't blame him, but to take up where we'd left off was stupid. He'd left once; he'd leave again.

My chest hurt, and I forced myself to keep smiling as I went to the coffeemaker. "How's the job going?" I said, my back to him as I tried to make my voice even. This had been a mistake. A huge, friggin' mistake.

"Okay. I'm not in the pool as much as I'd like to be. Too much paperwork."

I nodded, and from the door Jenks said, "Yeah, that'll kill you."

I sighed, knowing why Jenks was being rude, but unable to fault it, either.

The soft tinkling of the bell Jenks had put on his orange cat jingled, and I looked to see Rex come in. I wasn't surprised. The feline had liked Marshal. What surprised me was Belle astride the animal like a furry horse. I'd seen the wingless fairy using the cat as transportation before, but it still startled me.

Marshal's lips parted at the sight, and I handed him his cup of coffee, saying, "Belle? This is Marshal, an old friend. Marshal, this is Belle. She's staying with us now."

"Um, hi?" he said, at a complete loss. Fairies and humans didn't get along very well. Okay, fairies and *any* people didn't get along very well, but Belle and I got along just fine. Maybe it was because we were both damaged and trying to make our way the best we could.

The six-inch fierce woman gave Marshal a quick look, probably assessing the chances of his stepping on her by mistake. Sliding from Rex, she came forward with a bundle of fabric over her arm. "Nic-ce to meet you," she said, her voice hissing over the vowels. Her teeth were more savage than a vampire's, given her carnivore diet. Standing two inches taller than Jenks, she looked odd wearing pixy silk in what was clearly a fairy style, the blue cloth draped about her to resemble a shroud. The effect of death-warmed-over was heightened by her sallow, gaunt face. Her hair, too, was thin and pale, coming to her midback in ragged strands. If they were people size, they'd be the scariest Inderlanders I'd ever seen. At six inches and wearing a scowl that would rock Ivy back, she was still pretty scary.

"Jenks-s-s," she said, her lisp obvious. "I'm tired of waiting on you. Try it on. I have things to do."

As one, Marshal and I looked at Jenks, and the pixy rose up on a column of red sparkles.

"Belle!" he exclaimed, flushed. "I was just coming. I'll try it on in the hall."

Her black eyes bored into him, and I heard his wings falter. "Get down here and fold your wings-s," she demanded as the cat behind her fell over on her side and started to purr. "It will only take a moment."

"Yeah, but—" he started, and she bared her teeth at him.

Making a little hiccup of sound, Jenks dropped to the floor. "Belle," he pleaded. "Can't we do this later?"

"Fold your wings!" she demanded, and I made a soft sound of appreciation when she shook out the fabric and it unfolded into a vibrant, extravagantly embroidered jacket. It looked small in her hands, but I could tell it would fit Jenks perfectly.

"Oh, try it on!" I exclaimed, handing Marshal my cup and dropping to sit on the floor before them. "Belle, did you make that?"

"I did!" she said angrily. "The pixy turd won't try it on so I can size it properly!"

Jenks shrank into himself, and his wings drooped. "Aww, Belle," he complained, and Marshal hid a laugh behind a cough when the taller fairy spun Jenks around and pretty much dressed him like a sullen little boy.

"Turn," she demanded, and Jenks showed her his back, lifting his wings so she could do the ties in the back. "How does that feel?"

"Belle, it's beautiful!" I said, seeing the golds and reds swirling in unfamiliar patterns. Clearly she'd woven the cloth herself.

"It feels fine," Jenks grumbled, glancing at me like it was all my fault.

"Too tight?" she asked, and when he muttered that it wasn't, she put a foot on his backside and yanked the ties again.

"Now it is!" Jenks shrilled, struggling to reach behind him and spinning in circles. "Damn it, woman! I can't put my wings down!"

Belle was smirking, and I bit my lip so I wouldn't smile as she caught his shoulder and loosened them again. "The goddess-s-s help you," she said as she undid the ties altogether and Jenks shrugged out of it, throwing it back at her like it was a rag. "What is it with men and clothes? You think you'd rather go to war naked."

"I don't plan on going to war at all!" Jenks said, rising up an inch or so until he was looking her right in the eye. Behind him, Rex patted at his dangling feet, her eyes full and black. "And I can't go to war in that. The tails are too long."

"The tails are appropriate." Belle shook it out and draped it carefully over her arm. "That is not a suit for going to war. It's for celebrating. You won't wear it until I say you can. I can tell you're not *planning* on war. The lines are full of holes. I don't know how you ever survived without me."

Jenks spilled a red dust and sputtered, "I just spent all morning tending the lines. There's nothing wrong with them. Rex, knock it off!"

But Belle only smiled. "If you like it, I'll put the final trim on it and hang it in your clos-s-set. Thank you for allowing Jezabel to teach me that stitching for the wings. It's more complicated than I'm used to, but it gives wonderfully where you need it. Would you take offense if I s-sshow my sister when I s-see her again?"

"Tink's titties, I don't care," Jenks said sullenly. Belle stood there, waiting, and when I cleared my throat, he added, "Thanks. It's nice."

My mouth dropped open, and even Marshal shifted his feet uncomfortably. "Nic-c-ce?" Belle said, a pale green coming to color her face, a fairy's version of a flush, perhaps. "You think this is nic-c-ce?" She squinted at him for a moment with her lips closed over her long teeth. "Thank you," she said stiffly, knocking into him as she walked past the purring cat, her back stiff and her pace slow. With a little trill of sound, Rex got to her feet and padded after her.

I looked at Jenks, his feet on the linoleum as he watched her leave, then up at Marshal. "Wow, Jenks," I said as I got up. "You're a bigger ass than even me sometimes. Nice? That wasn't nice. That was exquisite."

His expression twisted up in annoyance and guilt, Jenks flew up to my eye level. "She keeps making me stuff," he said plaintively. "And she keeps trying to plant things. Nothing has even come up. The kids are laughing at her."

"Then maybe you should stop giving her bad seeds. She's trying," I said, not wanting to be too hard on him, but honestly, that had been a beautiful coat. "It must have taken her at least two weeks to make that, and you call it nice?"

Jenks looked at the hall when the cat door squeaked shut. "Actually, it was twice that if you count dyeing the thread. Um." His altitude shifted up and down. "Could you excuse me?"

I nodded, and Jenks darted off. "Belle?" I heard him shout, and my frown eased. Her kin had killed Matalina. I had destroyed their wings. And now we were all learning to get along. What was wrong with me?

"Rachel," Marshal said, and I looked up at the pure delight in his voice. "I'd forgotten how much fun you are to be around. That was a fairy, right? Why is she making Jenks clothes?"

I swallowed back a heavy sigh before it came out, wondering how this new wrinkle was going to iron out. No one could take Matalina's place, but Belle had begun to see where there was a need and did what she could. "She's keeping an eye on me," I said. "She'll murder me in my sleep if she thinks I'm going to betray her or her surviving family, now living with Trent."

Still laughing, Marshal set his cup down. Slowly his smile faltered as he realized I was serious. "Is this them?" He looked at the charms, obvious on the counter between us.

I pushed myself from the counter, feeling more space fall between us. "Yup. Let me get you a finger stick. I really appreciate this."

"Not a problem." Marshal took the tiny blade as I held it out, and he broke the safety seal with his thumb in a practiced motion. "How is Jenks doing? I talked to Glenn yesterday, and he said his wife died. Is that why Belle is here?"

The scent of redwood blossomed as Marshal massaged his finger and three drops of blood soaked into the first disk. A feeling of relief swept over me, and a slight headache I hadn't realized I was fighting began to dissipate. I'd spelled the charms right, and now I had something to use to find these bastards.

"Jenks is doing okay," I said. "He has his ups and downs, but he smiles a lot more."

"Good." Marshal looked at me, then back down at the next amulet. "How about you?"

Me? "The shunning?" I said, flustered. "Okay. It's been nice not having to go to the ever-after every week. Kind of weird. The demons think I'm dead, and I want to keep it that way." I shook my arm to show off my charmed silver, adding, "I don't even mind that I can't do ley-line magic." But I did, if I was honest.

Marshal's eyes were outraged as he straightened from over the amulets. "The coven of moral and ethical standards is making you wear that?"

"This? No. I put this on myself. You think I liked going

to the ever-after every weekend?" Al would friggin' kill me if he knew I was alive. If the demon hated one thing, it was being broke.

Marshal's eyes became worried, and he looked back at the amulets. He invoked two more, and I started putting them in my shoulder bag, one by one.

"Thanks again," I said, not liking the silence. If Marshal was silent, Marshal was thinking, and that made me uneasy. "I can still do earth magic. The higher spells can tell the difference in my blood and don't invoke, is all."

He looked up as he finished the last, his expression brightening with understanding. "Oh! That's why the ones you made last year . . ."

I nodded. "Yes. I thought I'd done them wrong . . . but it's my blood."

Marshal knew I wasn't a witch—he was there the week I figured it out for myself—but I could tell by his suddenly sick expression that he hadn't really believed it. He thought that I'd taken a label to get the coven to back off. "Then you really are . . ."

His words faltered, and I slumped, tired beyond belief. "I'm a demon," I said, looking away. A demon with no demon magic. "Well, thanks," I said as understanding, and even worse, pity, cascaded over him. "I don't know any other witches I could have asked to do this. Isn't that stupid?" I tried to laugh, but it came out wrong, and the silence afterward was worse.

The amulets were invoked, and still he stood there, four feet and an entire chasm of unspoken thought between us. "No," he said softly, and I looked up, seeing his pity, his fear, and his reluctance all wrapped up in one terrible expression. "Rachel, I'm sorry this happened. And I'm glad you got your shunning removed. I didn't like the way things ended."

"Me neither," I said, backing slowly away. My stomach hurt. This was such a bad idea. I couldn't go back—this proved it—but what hurt wasn't Marshal as much as it was me grieving, letting go of the hope that I could be the person

I'd always thought I was. It was going to be harder now that I couldn't pretend.

"That's why I came over today," he said, but I didn't know if I believed him. "Not because I wanted to start dating again or anything. I just wanted to see that you were really okay and not just surviving."

I leaned against the sink, wishing he would go away. I hadn't invited him over here to see if he was available, but now I felt even more alone. "I'm doing okay," I said, wishing I could say it louder.

"You're doing great!" he said, but it sounded flat. I jumped when he touched my elbow, and his hand fell away. "You're doing great," he said again, softer this time. "I'm glad that no one is telling me I can't talk to you anymore, because you are a very special woman."

My gut hurt, and I made a fist, jamming it into my side. "Thanks. You're not so bad yourself." I was not going to cry, damn it.

"You deserve good things," Marshal said, but he was still wearing that damn pitying smile. "There's someone out there for you. I really believe that."

"Me, too," I lied, then swallowed the pain down where it could fester. "I'm glad you're doing okay, too. And thanks again. For the amulets." I was never going to call him again.

Marshal reached out and I shook my head, unable to look at him. The soft slap of his hand meeting his leg was loud. "Bye, Rachel," he said, and I closed my eyes so I wouldn't cry when he leaned in and gave me a chaste kiss on the cheek.

"Bye, Marshal," I said, my voice surprisingly firm, though my chest felt like it was caving in. It wasn't Marshal, it was everything else.

"I'll let myself out."

"Thank you," I said softly, and I looked up as he walked away. I took a deep breath, gazing at the ceiling as I shook my hair out. It was almost dry. I wasn't looking for someone to complete me, but having someone to do stuff with would be nice. And I didn't think I could even have that anymore.

"I have to get out of here," I said softly, feeling the walls close in on me. If I didn't do something, I'd explode in a puff of self-absorbed pity. But not with Wayde watching me. Yes, he was right that I was vulnerable without my ley-line magic. Yes, Trent was right that I was putting those I cared about at risk by not accepting my full abilities. But I was *not* helpless. I had survived an I.S. death threat, banshees, Weres with guns, and political witches—all without demon magic. It would've been an entirely different story last night if I had been prepared and had had my splat gun. Perhaps Wayde needed to know that.

I heard the front door shut, then stuffed the last of the amulets into my bag, sliding them next to my restocked splat gun. I was so out of here. Wayde still had my keys after driving me home last night, but I could take the bus to the FIB. He kept telling me he could keep me safe, but he wasn't taking this seriously if someone he'd never met had come into the church and left without Wayde checking him out. The Were needed a wake-up call, and I was frustrated enough to give it to him.

"Ivy?" I called out, knowing she had probably been listening to the entire conversation. "I'm going to take the bus to the FIB. I've got my splat gun and phone."

There was a hesitation, then through the walls came, "What about Wayde?"

"I think he's still sleeping," I said loudly, knowing he couldn't hear us, and not caring if he did. I'd been afraid to hurt him last night. The stakes hadn't been high enough, and I'd been showing restraint, not cowardice. Today it would be a different story.

Again the hesitation, followed by "Call me when you get there!"

I felt a surge of gratitude. Ivy knew I wasn't helpless. Feeling better, I grabbed my jacket, shuffling into it while slinging my bag over my shoulder. Phone in my pocket, I strode through the back living room to the porch door. I'd spent almost an entire year taking public transportation, and

I knew the schedule. If I hurried, I could catch the next bus into Cincy—easy.

Catch me if you can, big boy, I thought as I scuffed my garden shoes on and opened the back door. I owed him a little grief for last night if nothing else.

Eight

Garden shoes did not make the best getaway attire, and I was leaving little clumps of dirt as I eased the door shut behind me. Exhaling, I turned, taking in the sunny but wet garden. The trees had lost most of their leaves, but the sun was warm. All the vegetation looked tired and worn, kind of like how I felt, and I tugged my jacket closer. The soft hush of a passing car disturbed the Sunday afternoon, then silence.

"Some bodyguard," I said sourly, thinking he should have been on to me by now. It wasn't as if I was trying to sneak out. I was prepared for trouble and would be fine.

The church sat on an entire city block, the graveyard taking up the lion's share of it. A shoulder-high stone-and-wrought-iron wall encompassed the property, helping separate the living from the dead. A low stone wall divided the mundane witches' garden from the gravestones, but I used almost every inch of the place for my plants. From where I stood on the porch, I could see over it to the homes and cars on the street behind the church. There was a bus stop, too. That was where I was headed.

Arms wrapped around myself, I stomped down the wooden steps and into the witches' garden. Ivy's grill was covered, and the picnic table, scarred by a past curse, was soggy from last night's rain. Rex, Jenks's cat, was sitting on the knee-high stone wall where Jenks had made his new summer bachelor home. Her tail was twitching, and figuring that her tiny master was inside the wall, I gave her a wide berth. But the stupid cat stood, her back arched and her tail crooked as she minced along the top of the wall to me, and I waved for her to stay. Rex had avoided me like the plague for our first year together, but now, when I wanted her to stay, I was her favorite toy. Figures.

"Stay there, you stupid cat," I whispered, then froze when I heard Jenks's voice, faint on the still air. "It's a beautiful coat, Belle," I heard him plead. "I'm sorry. No one has ever made me anything except my mother and my wife, and I didn't know what to say when you gave it to me. Let me see it again."

"No," Belle said, her lisping voice harder to distinguish above the whispering of the leaves. "I have my pride. I'll give it to my brother. Oh, that's right. *You killed him.*"

"You killed my wife," Jenks replied. "Let me see the damn coat! I want to wear the Tink-blasted thing!"

I couldn't help my smile, deciding that as long as Ivy knew where I was there was no need to bother him. Besides, he didn't have his winter clothes on, and it was cold. Giving Rex a scratch under her chin, I stepped over the low wall, starting through the tombstones for the distant wall. There were two bars in the rusted car gate that had been wedged apart just enough for a size eight tall to squeeze through.

A feeling of excitement began to push out my melancholy. I hadn't been on a run in ages. Not a run run—I ran regularly at the zoo before they opened, Wayde in tow. I meant a bad-guy run, where the adrenaline flowed and both the brain and the body got a workout. Ivy had been trying to include me in her work, but I'd not had much business since I'd been labeled a demon, and I missed it. But now, as I slunk through the graveyard, the hair on the back of my neck prickling from being in sight of Wayde's windows, I felt a thrill down to my dew-wet toes. If he didn't see me, then my gut feeling that he wasn't up to this was right, and I needed to stop depending on him.

The bus stop was about thirty yards away—and right in Wayde's line of sight should he be looking. I thought it inexcusable that I could have gotten this far without him knowing it, and a feeling of justifiable anger suffused me.

The choking gurgle of the bus brought my head up, and I peered down the street, heart pounding. It was early. Smiling, I ran for the fence, the bus passing me as I slipped between the rusty bars. "Wait!" I shouted, the bars leaving a long red stain on my jacket as I shoved my way through, waving my arm as I ran. Man . . . I hoped they'd pick me up. Sometimes they didn't. You take the hair off the first three rows with a misfired charm and they never forget. "Hey! I'm running here!" I shouted, garden shoes squishing.

I pounded after it, and the bus finally stopped. "Rachel!" I heard Wayde bellow, and I, grinning, didn't turn. It was about time. I knew I should stop, but I was burning with the need to rub his nose in something. "Rachel! You wicked little witch! Get back here!"

The bus's door was open, and I grabbed the handle, swinging myself in. "Thanks," I said breathlessly to the driver, then turned to wave at Wayde as I stood on the lowest step. He was in his boxers and a white T-shirt, standing on the porch steps with his hair wild and his beard matted. Clearly he had expected me to be a good little girl after yesterday's show of masculine strength. He was still in his jammies.

Wayde just about lost it, stomping down the stairs and heading across the wet grass in his bare feet. *Crap, I had to get out of here.*

Skittering up the steps, I dug a couple of dollars out of my bag and dropped it into the plastic piggy bank. "Thanks again," I said to the sour-looking man driving the bus. He frowned, which made his deeply wrinkled face even more crevassed.

"Is he after you, miss?" he asked, and I smiled and nodded.

"Yep. Mind making this thing move? He's a bastard before his first cup of coffee."

With a tired sigh, the man closed the door and revved the

engine. He put it into motion, and I swayed my way to the very back seat so I could watch Wayde skitter through the graveyard, trying not to walk on anyone's grave. "You have to move faster than that if you want to keep up with me, wolfman," I said under my breath, my mood much improved as I plunked myself down.

From the other side of the bus came a soft masculine throat clearing. "Boyfriend?"

My hand smacked into my shoulder bag and the reassuring presence of my splat gun. Startled, I turned to the other back seat and saw a young man in a short brown coat. By the tattoo peeking out of his collar, he was a Were. His tousled hair was black and wavy. A thick stubble was on his face, jet black and sexy. His smile was sly, and it went right to my gut and twisted.

I resettled myself, glad I had my jacket even if I was right over the heater. "Boyfriend? No. But he acts like it sometimes." I looked out the back window, seeing Wayde making his way back to the church, his head down and his arms swinging. Yeah, he was mad. "I need some time alone," I said as the bus turned the corner and he was gone.

"Oh, sorry," the man said as he shifted his body angle away from me.

"Not from everyone," I said, realizing what I'd sounded like. "Just . . . everyone at home. You know?"

He turned back to face me, his smile warming me through my thin jacket. "Trex," he said, extending his hand across the aisle.

Oh my God, I probably looked a mess, but I reached for his hand, hoping my fingers had warmed up as I took it. "Hi, Trex. I'm Rachel."

Trex's eyes went from my tattoo to the bracelet of charmed silver peeping out of my cuff, then back to the tattoo fluff on my neck. "You're Rachel Morgan? Black dandelion pack? Let's have a squint at it."

Wow, word gets around fast. Flustered, I turned and yanked my shirt aside to show him.

Trex drew close for an instant, then pulled back; whistling in appreciation. "That's new," he said, and I spun back around. "Emojin?"

I nodded, propping myself against the back of the next seat up when we hit a bump. We were heading into Cincy over the bridge. There wasn't much traffic on a Saturday afternoon, and we'd be right downtown in a matter of minutes if we didn't have to stop for anyone. That was cool. I could get a coffee before I headed to the FIB. My own first cup was still sitting untouched on the kitchen counter. "Yes. She inked me last night."

"Quality." His eyes fixed on mine, he pulled his coat and shirt aside to show an hourglass broken by a thorny rose vine. Red sand spilled out like blood. "Blood sand," he said. "Good to meet you."

"It's a pleasure," I said, deciding that it was. I was never going to see this man again, but that was part of the joy. He was here, I was here, we were sharing a moment, and it wouldn't impact my future one bit.

My phone began ringing in my back pocket. It was on vibrate, but I think Trex could hear it, since his eyes went to it. I ignored it, smiling at him. "Your phone is ringing," Trex finally said, and I sighed, reaching around to my back pocket and slumping in the seat when I saw the church's number.

"It's Wayde," I said glumly as I dropped it into my shoulder bag, wondering if he knew how to track me with a live phone. "The guy in boxers."

"You need some help ditching him?"

Just the offer meant the world to me, and I gave him a bright smile. We were already among Cincy's tall buildings. I could run my errand and be back in a few hours, easy. "Thanks, but no," I said as I stood, seeing Junior's just down the block. "I'm good. It was a pleasure."

He nodded, his lips still curved up, but with disappointment in his eyes. He had no idea how much that meant to me, and I could have hugged him. I'd been shunned and reviled for so long that even this harmless flirting felt great. I could not go back, but I could go forward. David was right. A show of pack membership had rubbed out the stigma of being a demon. At least for Trex here.

"Have a good run," he said as the bus came to a stop and I headed for the door.

I didn't think he meant my errand to the FIB, but rather a run run. He knew what I was doing. I got off the bus, wishing I'd worn a heavier coat as I stood in the cool wind coming off the river. The door shut, and the bus took off. I resisted the urge to wave to Trex, but barely. I smiled up at the bright sky, enjoying being alone while surrounded by thousands. Maybe I could grab a late breakfast somewhere after dumping off the amulets.

I walked away, feeling sassy despite my garden shoes squishing. *Coffee. Yeah. That sounded good.*

The chimes on the handle reminded me of Jenks's kids' laughter as I pushed the glass door open. Warm air smelling of coffee and ginger enveloped me, and I immediately felt warmer. I paused just past the threshold to take in the familiar tables and booths, and the weird pictures of babies dressed up as fruit and flowers. I still didn't get it.

I was leaving mud behind as I went to place my order. Junior's had only recently opened a drive-through window, and though it was busy outside, the tables held only a few people. Most of them looked like they were drumming up business, their advertising logos prominently showing as they interviewed potential acolytes.

Rubbing the cold from my arms, I went to the pastry shelves, deciding I'd treat myself. I hadn't had breakfast yet, much less my first coffee.

"Hi, what can I get for you today?"

I looked up to see Junior—or Mark, rather—with a bright red manager tag on his apron. He was smiling professionally at me, and I smiled back, but then his expression clouded. "What are you doing here?" he barked as he recognized me.

My smile faded. "Getting a coffee." I pulled myself to

my full height in my soggy, muddy garden shoes. "I'm not shunned anymore. Okay?" The patrons looked up, and I lifted my chin. Squinting at him, I put my palm on the counter, making sure my band of charmed silver hit it with a small clink.

Mark looked at it. He was a witch—I'd seen him make a circle before—and he knew what it was. But like everyone else, he probably thought that the coven of moral and ethical standards had put it on me to keep me from doing any magic.

"I can take it off if it bothers you," I said lightly, running a finger along the inside.

Mark frowned and backed up a step. I figured he'd put himself in an uninvoked circle—having them behind the counter was standard practice in case of attempted armed robberies. My good mood was falling apart.

"What do you want?"

It was flat and hostile, but I couldn't blame him—much. Last year, I'd almost trashed the place trying to catch a banshee and her psychotic serial-killer husband. Then just a few months ago, my ex-boyfriend Nick had caused a scene to give me time to escape a member of the coven. Mark hadn't known it was me then, but the papers had made it public. It made me wonder if Junior's had been built on some kind of "galactic time-warp continuum." Everything seemed to start or end here.

"I'd like two of the mini scones," I said, then added, "No, make that three." I'd take one back to Jenks and the kids. "And a grande latte, double espresso, Italian blend. Light on the froth, skim milk." Whole milk would have been better, but the scones were rich.

Mark was writing this all on the side of a cup, which he then tossed to another barista. "You want your scones warmed up?" he asked, his tone stiff, but at least he was civil.

Smiling insincerely, I said, "Yes, please," then handed him the ten I had waiting.

He took my money and gave me my change. I hesitated, then decided against the tip.

Watching to be sure he didn't hex my food, I slid down the counter. From the other end of the coffeehouse came a cheerful "Double espresso, low froth, low cal. Grande. On the counter!"

That had to be mine, but Mark was taking my scones out of the oven and shoving them in a bag. His brow was furrowed as he folded the bag over and extended it to me.

"I got that banshee, by the way," I said.

His expression darkened. "I heard someone died."

I yanked the bag out of his grip. "Tom Bansen," I said, since the papers hadn't given out his name. "He was a black witch, working in the I.S. as a mole. The nice lady banshee who was sitting in your coffeehouse sucking in everyone's aura killed him, not me. It took me a week to recover from her myself. You have a great day—Mark."

I turned to the tables, my good mood trashed. Yeah, that might have been a little sarcastic, but the fading adrenaline was making me depressed. Leaving chunks of dirt behind, I went back to the pickup counter for my coffee. I'd been thinking about taking it outside and into the cold sunshine, but staying in here might tick Mark off. My thoughts went back to Trent once saying that I made decisions based on what would irritate people, and I frowned.

"Cinnamon," I muttered, turning my back on the door to sprinkle a heavy layer on the light foam. Crap, I'd forgotten to put raspberry in it.

Sighing, I turned back around to find a chair where I could sit and glare at Mark for a while. But then I blinked, smiled, and walked slowly to Wayde, sitting nice as you please at one of the small round tables with his back to the wall. He was scowling, and his hairy legs showed above his biker boots. He was still in his boxers, too, and he looked like a crazy man in the T-shirt that he'd slept in. Outside I could see Ivy's bike, her helmet on the seat.

Clearly cold, he rubbed a hand over his beard, untidy and

flat on one side. I hadn't known you could have bed beard, but that's what it was. When he didn't take the time to clean up, he was a raggedy man.

Mark had noticed him, too, and was talking to the barista as if ready to call the cops. Whatever. The man had had worse in his store before than an angry Were in his pajamas.

I set my cup down and smiled at Wayde, feeling vastly better. "Nice boots."

Wayde's expression became even more sour. "You done running?" he said tightly. "Have fun this morning?"

I sat across from him so we both could look out the window. "I wasn't running away from you, and yes, I did have fun this morning. It felt good to get out by myself."

He snorted, and I tore open my bag of warm scones and set it between us. "You want one?" I asked, and he eyed me in disbelief, sitting up and looking even more uncomfortable and unkempt. "Here, you look colder than me," I added, and I slid my coffee to him. If truth be told, I was feeling kind of guilty. I had *not* snuck out, but I hadn't let him know, either.

The coffee he accepted, and I watched him take a careful sip, easing back when he decided it was good. "You are an *ass,*" he said, shoulders hunched as he glared at me from over his cup. "No wonder your mother is crazy."

My first feeling of goodwill died, but I calmly took a bite of my scone, enjoying the tart lemon icing. "My mother isn't crazy," I said as I chewed. "She simply has a harder time than most reconciling her reality with everyone else's reality. You sure you don't want one of these? I got three."

He only glared, and kept glaring, his brown eyes hard. "I should throw you over my shoulder and take you home right now. I can't believe you left without telling me."

"Okay," I said, head tilting. "Let's talk about that."

"Didn't last night teach you anything?" he barked at me, and my resolve stiffened.

"Other than you're a bully? No, not really."

Wayde jabbed a short, powerful finger at me. "If you want to go out, fine, but give me ten minutes to get dressed."

"It was eleven in the morning!" I said, not caring that people were looking at us. "You never did get me in the car last night. You tell me you can keep me alive, but you aren't dressed like you're supposed to be, or paying attention like my dad is paying you to do. I had people over and you never came down. Never woke up as far as I could tell! You aren't taking this seriously, and yes, I've got a problem with it."

"Is that what you think?" he said sharply. "That I'm lazing about? Ignorant of everything that's going on?"

"If the bone fits, chew it," I said, heart pounding but voice calm. "The only reason I'm alive is because of my friends. I know I'm vulnerable, but I'm not helpless, and I *don't* like being manhandled. The only reason you got me over your shoulder and down those stairs last night without a broken nose and a fractured wrist is because I didn't want to hurt you!"

"Is that so?"

"Yes. That is so, you big douche bag. As far as I'm concerned, you can walk out of here and explain to my mom why you're not cashing her checks—bud-dy."

I sat back, ticked. Damn it, I still hadn't gotten any coffee. Now I was going to have to drink whatever the FIB had in their back offices.

Frowning, Wayde looked at my bag. He knew I'd made up some new charms, knew I was prepared this time, knew that he might end up on the floor, unconscious, with no ID and in his underwear, the I.S. responding. Growling something it was probably just as well I didn't hear, he pulled his coffee closer, almost spilling it.

"I'm going to finish my coffee," he muttered. "If you aren't on the back of that bike when I walk out of here, I quit—I will quit, Rachel. I have *never* worked with a more annoying, self-centered—"

"I am not self-centered," I interrupted. "I gave you my coffee, didn't I?"

"—irritating flake of a woman in my entire life," Wayde finished. "And trust me, I've seen some fool women while working your dad's shows. You think I'm fixing up that belfry because I like heights? I knew Marshal was on the church's grounds a good three minutes before you did. I also knew *exactly* who he was, having looked him up the night before after you mentioned having him over. The license numbers matched, and though you are right that I probably should have come down, I thought the risk less than your need to have the illusion of not being watched all the time."

Excuse me?

"I am *good* at what I do," he said, pointing a finger at me. "So good that it looks like I'm not. You think your dad would send some jerk-ass wannabe to protect his only daughter?"

My face was cold. Embarrassed, I scrunched down in the seat. I needed a crowbar to get my foot out of my mouth, I'd jammed it so far down. I had no idea he had moved into the belfry for that reason, much less that he was screening people. "But you keep making newbie mistakes," I offered lamely. "Breaking that guy's nose yesterday. Running after me in your boxers."

Wayde smirked, coffee in hand as he leaned back, his eyes scanning, still scanning. "I broke that guy's nose because he disrespected you and it pissed me off," he said, making me feel about three inches tall. "That, and to get that undead vampire's eyes off Ivy. She's come too far out of her addiction to be pulled back in by a bored lamprey. The boxers, though . . ." He hesitated, the rims of his ears going as red as his straggly beard. "You got me there. That was a mistake. I should have been dressed. I never imagined you would leave. Without telling me."

His accusation was clear, and I winced. "I'm really sorry," I said, meaning it. "I am an oblivious ass, and I don't blame you if you leave. Please stay. I won't doubt you again."

My eyes flicked up as Wayde leaned forward over the table. He was smiling. That was one of the things I loved about Weres. You didn't have to say much, but you had to mean it. "Apology accepted," he said, scratching his stubble like a dorm student after an all-nighter. "If you're ready to work with me now, I have just one question."

I waited, cringing. He could ask me anything right now, and with me feeling the way I did, I'd answer him with self-humiliating honesty. I'd been wrong, so wrong, and yet he sat there ready to let it go. I owed my dad a huge thank-you and Wayde a great deal more respect.

"Tell me why you walked off this morning," he said, and I blinked, caught off guard.

Wayde put one arm on the table. "Walking out like that was stupid." I took an angry breath, and he added, "All right. You're not as helpless as I've been making out . . . obviously." He frowned at my shoulder bag. "But what you did was the out-of-the-ordinary crap that smart people die from. I want to know why. I can't fill in the gaps of your security if I don't know how you're going to react."

My shoulders slumped. *Shit.*

Wayde leaned closer. "What happened?"

Avoiding him, I sought out Mark, on the floor arranging shiny bags of coffee. "Hey, can you make another one of these?" I asked him when our eyes met. "And put a shot of raspberry in it?"

Saying nothing, Mark frowned and stiffly went behind the counter. I looked at Wayde across from me, startled by the expression of sympathy in his eyes. "I, ah, had to get out of there," I said, and Wayde leaned back, waiting.

"To prove you could after I got the best of you last night," he said, and I shook my head.

"Yes. No. I left because everyone is moving forward in their lives. Without me."

Wayde rolled his eyes. "You left because your roommate is sharing blood and having sex with someone besides you?" he mocked. "She's a vampire! You don't want that. What's really bothering you?"

"Just forget I said anything," I said, feeling hurt as Mark approached with a grande. Both Wayde and I were silent as he set the cup down and I handed the guy a five. "Thanks,

Mark. Keep the change," I said, miserable as I took a sip of my wonderful raspberry coffee, feeling it go all the way down. It sat in my stomach like lead.

Wayde waited with the patience of a wolf, his arms across his chest and a tightness to his lips. I fiddled with my coffee cup, finally saying, "Ivy came home smelling like a friend. She came home happy," I said louder when he started making noises of disbelief again. "And I'm glad for that. She deserves it. And Jenks."

I looked at the table and pushed my cup around some more. "Jenks is never going to find another person like Matalina to share his life with, but seeing him and Belle together . . . They fit, you know?" I said, not caring if he didn't get it. "I used to be in there with them. I'm seeing me starting to slide out. It needs to happen, but I don't like it."

Unfortunately, that was the truth. They were growing, and I wasn't. Or rather, I wasn't growing in the direction I wanted.

"People change," Wayde offered hesitantly, but it was obvious that he didn't get it.

"Tell me about it." I took another sip of coffee, feeling sorry for myself even as I enjoyed the rich, sweet caffeine. "I used to be the one changing and they were the ones trying to keep up. Now I'm sitting still and they're the ones moving on. Without me."

"Waah, waah, waah." Wayde reached for a scone, the bag crackling.

The Turn take it, I'd opened up to him, and he thought I was being self-centered. "Forget I said anything, okay?" I said, wishing I had kept my mouth shut and let him believe I'd left because I was mad about last night. "I'm not going to shrink down and be a pixy, and I'm not going to sign my will over to a vampire, even if I do love her. It would destroy both of us."

Wayde's chewing stopped.

"This is good," I insisted, my eyes on the torn bag as I folded it up around Jenks's scone. "All of it. Jenks and Ivy.

It's good. They will live longer, happier lives without me, and I'm glad." *I just wish it didn't hurt so much.*

"I understand." Wayde put his hand on mine, stopping me from crushing Jenks's scone. "I grew up surrounded by big egos, Rachel, and I get it."

I pulled away from him, shoving Jenks's scone into my bag. "I do not have a big ego."

"Yes you do," he said, wiping the crumbs from his beard and chuckling. "It's probably how you survived living with Ivy. Get over it. You've got a big heart to match, and your dad is just as bad. But as you say, they're getting on with their lives and you aren't. Why do you suppose that is?"

Staring at him, I flopped back against the seat. "If I knew that, I wouldn't be sitting here with you in your pj's, drinking coffee."

And still he smiled, looking far too disorganized to be giving me advice. "Jenks and Ivy know their lives are going to be here. Right now and today," he said, tapping the tip of his finger on the table. "They're making decisions to move forward. Ivy is letting go of her past—that means you—and finding partners who fulfill her emotional, intellectual, and physical needs. Jenks is doing the same. You aren't, because you know in your gut that you won't find what you need here."

The sweet coffee in me seemed to go sour, and I stiffened. "Beg pardon?"

He shrugged and leaned back out of easy reach, looking grungy and disheveled. "For a smart woman, you are clueless sometimes. You're a demon."

Frowning, I glanced over the coffeehouse to make sure no one had heard him. "You want to say that a little louder, maybe?"

His teeth showing in a quick grin, he took a sip of coffee, clearly thinking he had the upper hand again. "I don't blame you for fighting it at first, but you're a demon and you need to accept that. All this about Kalamack giving you a *choice* that really isn't one aside. It's all you got, woman. Be the demon. The more you try to make the demon a witch, the more you hurt yourself. Why not try it the other way around? See what happens. If it doesn't work, they'll still be here. Waiting for you."

His attention was on my charmed silver bracelet, and I covered it up. It sounded so simple. Maybe he was right.

Wayde let a hand hit the table, making me jump. "Never mind," he said in a tired voice. "Don't listen to me. I'm just pissed you snuck out. You belong here with Ivy and Jenks. Maybe all you need is some new friends. Some who you can just . . . hang with for a while with no strings attached."

My lips quirked. No strings attached wasn't how I worked. "But not you, obviously," I said, and Wayde took another sip of coffee.

"Obviously. Rachel, you are one crazy bitch. But I like you. Your loyalty impresses me. It makes putting up with the rest of your crap worth it."

"Gee, thanks, Wayde." I lifted my cup to him in a salute. "From you, I'll take that as a compliment." Again the coffee slipped into me, and the tightness in my shoulders finally started to ease. "So, ah, how did you find me?"

Wayde snorted. "I have the bus schedules and routes memorized, and you left your coffee on the counter. There was only one place you'd be," he said, and I sighed. When I read a person wrong, I really get it wrong. "Your phone is ringing."

Yes, it was ringing, humming at the bottom of my bag. It had been for the last couple of minutes. It was probably Jenks, ticked that I'd gone out without him. For crying out loud, Ivy knew where I was.

"Yup," I said, my expression bland as I tugged my bag closer and reached in to get the phone, the multiple flashes of green from the amulets catching my attention as my aura touched them. I glanced at the incoming number, then froze. It was the church, but what gave me pause were the amulets.

They were active—and pinging on something.

"Oh my God!" I said as I dropped the humming phone

into my lap and snatched up an amulet, not believing it when the green held steady. "It's my scatter-detection amulet," I said, pulse racing as I pulled it out, thrilled. "Holy crap, it's working! Wayde, it's working! Here, hold it!"

"What, me?" he exclaimed as I shoved the amulet at him, almost knocking over his coffee. "I don't know how to work this thing."

"Just hold it," I said as I fumbled for the phone and flipped it open. "If you have an aura, it works. Damn! I can't believe it's working! Somewhere within a mile or two is something linked to that poor man they strung up in Washington Park."

From behind the counter, Mark slammed something shut, clearly having heard me.

Wayde was looking at the amulet as if it were a chunk of rotting flesh, gingerly cradling it in two hands as I flipped the phone open. "You said you weren't going to go out to any sites unless they were secure."

"The I.S. and the FIB will be there," I said, excited. "Besides, HAPA is long gone. We're going to find an empty room unless we're really lucky." The receiver clicked open. "Ivy?"

"No, it's me," Jenks said, his tone sounding tinny over the phone lines. "What the hell do you think you're doing going out without Wayde? He's more ticked than a shaved cat."

"I know," I said, looking at the uncomfortable Were sitting across from me. "He's with me. We're cool. Ivy knew where I was, so what's the big deal?"

"You ditched me!" he accused, and I winced.

"You didn't have your winter clothes on, and I had to catch the bus!" I said, then lowered my voice. "Wake up Ivy, will you? And get your working blacks on. The scatter-detection charms went active. I'm at Junior's with Wayde."

"Tink's little red panties, Rache! You ditching us?"

No more than everyone seems to be ditching me, I thought, then shoved my mini pity party away. "Did I not just say put your working clothes on? Get Ivy and get out here. I'm calling Glenn next, and then Nina." I glanced at

Wayde. "Could you bring out a pair of jeans and a shirt for Wayde while you're at it?"

Jenks's snort told me we were okay. "Yeah, I got it," he said, his kids shrieking in the background. "I'll ask Belle to watch my kids."

"I'll wait for you here as long as I can, but if the FIB or the I.S. gets here first, I'll be with them," I said, wondering if I should try Glenn at home. He might be off shift, but he'd come in for this, long night or not.

"Gotcha, Rache!" he said cheerfully, and hung up.

I cleared the phone and started scrolling for Glenn's home number. I'd try there first. I looked up when Wayde chuckled. "What?" I said, blinking at him.

"You're funny," he said, draping the amulet over my neck and tweaking my nose. "I'm going to see if they have a disposable shaver in the bathroom. Think about what I said, okay?"

He stood, and I stared at him.

"About having casual friends?" he added, looking back at me. "They don't make the pain any less when you move on, but they help cover it up." He hesitated, but I didn't know what to say.

"Don't run off, okay?" he finally added, looking good as he made his confident, casual, and scruffy way to the men's room, exchanging a masculine greeting with the barista as he went. And what did he mean by think "about having casual friends"? That hadn't been an invitation . . .

Had it?

Nine

Even at a slow thirty mph on the back of Ivy's bike, the wind was frigid, and I pressed my head into Wayde's shoulder, shivering. He was still in his boxers and T-shirt, and if he could take it, I could, too. The feelings of dread and anticipation had tightened my gut until I felt ill. The sweet coffee wasn't sitting right, and the rumble of Ivy's bike under me, usually soothing, only wound my tension tighter.

We were down by the waterfront, the Cincy side of things, and when our momentum shifted, I looked up through the cloudy goggles that Ivy kept in her side bag for unexpected riders. We were at a stop sign, and whereas I knew Wayde would probably not have stopped under most circumstances, he did now.

I put down a foot to help keep us balanced. The smell of soap and Were drifted back, and I breathed it in as I pushed my goggles up and looked at the amulet in my hand. This was why he'd stopped, not the sleek black new-model Lexus following us.

"Keep going," I said loudly, seeing no change in the amulet's glow, and Wayde nodded.

The heat from the Lexus's engine hit the back of my calves, and my foot rose to the rest as we accelerated. Nina was driving it. I suppose I could have done this from the comfort of her borrowed front seat instead of freezing my ass off out here behind Wayde with no real coat, no leather, and garden shoes instead of my boots, but I wasn't willingly going to put myself alone in a car with her, even if she had been polite at the coffeehouse. It was obvious she still wasn't happy about my forcing them to give primary jurisdiction to the FIB, even if I had agreed to see the run through. If I didn't finish this quietly and to their satisfaction, they were going to frame me or wipe my memory, or both.

Mental note. Call Trent about a possible elf-magic-based spell to block memory charms. There'd been nothing about one in my spell books, nothing from a quick Internet search. I was sure the demons had something, but that didn't help me.

Nina had shown up almost immediately after my call from Junior's, making me wonder if she'd been waiting for it. Ivy and Jenks would join us when they could, and Glenn was probably on his way. I longingly thought of my coffee, left behind when I said I'd ride with Wayde. He'd had time to shave, but he was still in his jammies. We must look quite the pair, creeping down the service road with a Lexus twenty yards behind and two I.S. vehicles after that.

God, he smells good, I thought as I hugged Wayde. I lied to myself that I was just trying to stay out of the wind, but the reality was, this was the closest I'd gotten to another human being in months, and I wasn't above teasing myself. My thoughts strayed to our conversation at Junior's, and my focus blurred. It sure had sounded like the hint of an offer to hang with him for a while. True, he was kind of straggly looking right now, but I'd seen him out of his shirt and had been duly impressed. Unfortunately, though I knew that it might start with no strings attached, it would turn into something more. I couldn't do that, as pleasant as it sounded.

Why again was I on this bike? Oh yeah. Avoiding Nina.

I pulled my head up as Wayde went by the two empty stadiums. Squinting, I pushed back from him enough to look at the amulet. "Keep going!" I shouted, and he motored on.

The wind increased as we slipped from the lee, and I

hunched into him again. I was more than a little relieved that whatever my amulet had pinged on wasn't at the stadiums. There wasn't a game today, but I'd been banned, and if Mrs. Sarong found me poking around, it would strain our delicate relationship. Finding a mutilated body or the magic to turn a witch into a monster would have been the icing that made the camel trip . . . or whatever.

I shivered, not knowing what we'd find, other than it probably wouldn't be pleasant. The sites that the I.S. had found had contained little more than a heavy moulage coating, a cage, and washed-down walls.

My eyes glanced at the amulet and my pulse quickened. It was getting fainter. "Turn around!" I said, squeezing his middle. "We passed it!"

But what had we passed? Nothing obvious. I'd swear that the amulet was focused on something between the expressway and the river, and there wasn't much between them. Maybe there was an entrance to the forgotten Cincy tunnels down here.

Wayde flicked his turn signal on and made a smooth, probably illegal U-bangy and started back the other way. There were a few low buildings between us and the stadiums, and letting go of Wayde's middle, I pointed at the buildings as we passed Nina and the two I.S. cruisers. No Glenn yet, and while Wayde took a left onto the service road, I tucked the amulet away and tried to get my phone out.

"What are you doing?" Wayde asked as my weight shifted and the bike swerved.

"Calling Glenn," I said loudly as I put one arm back around his waist and punched numbers with my thumb. I could barely hear the dial tone over the wind, and I eyed the low building as we approached it. It looked like an old office complex turned museum. Museum? I didn't like the sound of that, and my head started to hurt.

"Rachel?" Glenn's voice came over the phone, and I leaned into Wayde to get out of the wind. "Where are you? I'm at the coffeehouse. Are Ivy and Jenks with you?"

I frowned. *Coffeehouse? What is he doing still there?* "I was kind of hoping they were with you," I said. "I'm down by the stadiums. Nina was supposed to call you. I'm sorry." I looked up as we slowed, idling into a circular drop-off at the front of the building. "We're at the Underground Railroad Museum. Huh. I didn't know this was here." *Pierce would like it,* I thought, then squashed it. I doubted Pierce was still alive. He'd taken responsibility for my "death" so Al would take him into the ever-after instead of Trent. Pierce hated Trent, but Trent had been the only one who knew how to move my soul back into my body. There was no doubt that Pierce had loved me, but ultimately I hadn't trusted him, his loose morals, or his questionable black magic. It bothered me, and a flash of guilt rose and died.

I was so messed up.

Glenn hadn't said anything, and I pressed the phone closer. "Glenn?"

"I'm here," he said, and my foot went down when Wayde stopped the bike at the museum. "I'll be there in five minutes. Don't let Nina go in there without me, okay?"

I could hear the tension in his voice, his anger. "You got it," I said, turning where I sat to glare at Nina, now pulling up behind us. I'd be willing to bet she hadn't called Glenn. The Turn take it, what was it with them? The important thing was that we stopped these wackos, not who got the credit for the tag. Besides, there probably wasn't going to be anything here that Nina hadn't seen before. Unless this was a cover-up? They hadn't wanted the FIB involved at all until I forced the issue. What was a high-ranking I.S. vampire doing on a run anyway?

"Stop it, Rachel," I muttered as I swung myself off the bike. Nina was here because I'd jerked primary jurisdiction away from her, not because they were covering up anything.

Wayde tugged his shirt back down where it belonged, a strange look in his eyes when he took his helmet off and set it on the back of the bike. "You okay?" he asked, surprising me.

"Nina didn't call Glenn," I said, handing him the goggles.

"And you're surprised because . . ."

I gathered my hair in a thick, tangled ponytail, then let it go in dismay. I'd never get through the tangles. My front was cold from where I'd been pressed up against Wayde, and we watched Nina get out of her fancy borrowed car, shutting the door carefully, using two hands, actually polishing her fingerprints off with the cuff of her long coat. Clearly it was hers only for right now.

She'd taken the time to go shopping since I'd last seen her, and was now in a tailored pantsuit, purchased, I was sure, with the dead vampire's funds. Her hair, too, had been styled, falling in professional, attractive waves. New, very expensive shoes finished the look, stylish yet comfortable enough to run in. They matched her handbag and new watch. *Nice that he is making her descent into hell so pleasant.*

Holding her hair against the wind, she talked for a moment with one of the officers from another car. A family came up from the nearby underground garage, the parents giving us a wide berth as they went inside with their kids protectively close.

My back stiffened when the officer talking to Nina turned, crossed the road, and went up the wide stairs to the big glass doors. "Hey, wait a minute!" I called, and Nina waved him on.

Jaw clenched, I strode up to Nina. "The FIB has jurisdiction," I said, pointing at the officer vanishing inside. "We *wait* for Glenn. Get your man back out here. And why didn't you call Glenn? I just got off the phone and he had no idea where we were." Eye to eye with the woman, I glared at her. "Think he's better than you? Worried you need the advantage to look good? You should be. The FIB is better than you want to admit."

Nina reached for my hand, and I took a quick step back, sobering fast as her undead companion slipped in behind the woman's eyes. I could tell, not only because they flashed pupil black, but because her entire posture now had the relaxed tension of the undead, sort of a satiated-lion look.

"Afraid? I am nothing of the kind," she said, her voice smooth and confident. Still very womanly, she now exuded a feeling of control and power, an intoxicating mix of masculine and feminine, yin and yang. She gave Wayde a long up-and-down look, taking in his army boots and thin T, then dismissed him. "My message surely got lost in his voice mail. When did you have the time to get that marvelous tattoo, Rachel? It suits you. Does it go all the way around your neck? May I see?"

Blinking, I took another step away, forcing my hand down. Hiding one's neck only made it look that much more appetizing to a vampire.

"Your tattoo?" Nina prompted, showing her small, pointy teeth, and I backed into Wayde. Sure, she was smiling, but I knew better. The vampire inside her was still peeved about yesterday. That my amulets worked when theirs hadn't probably hadn't gone down well, either.

"Yesterday," I said, more nervous yet. "Get your man out."

My voice didn't tremble at all. Go me. Where in hell was Glenn?

"My officer is simply speaking with the curator," Nina said, and I breathed easier when she looked away. "You can't have two I.S. cruisers pull up to your establishment and not explain yourself." Expression blank, she looked me up and down, and I suddenly felt grossly underdressed in my jeans and garden shoes. "How sure are you that this is the place?" she said with a sniff, her taking a wider stance, her hand straying to her waist where I'm sure the dead vampire kept his phone.

I looked at the amulet around my neck, glowing green. "Pretty sure. If you want, we can do a triangulation with the rest of the amulets before we go in with guns blazing."

Nina laughed, and I watched Wayde hide a shudder by scuffing his feet. "We aren't going in with 'guns blazing,'" Nina said. "If they're holding to their usual pattern, the people who committed these crimes are long gone. If this is indeed where they were." Her eyebrows rose. "It hardly looks like the area where one would go to perform acts of demonic magic," she said softly, squinting into the wind and bright autumn light as she looked up at the roofline.

"Yes, well, looks can be deceptive," I said. The more suave Nina became, the less I liked it. Living vampires considered it an honor to let their undead kin see through their eyes, speak through their mouths, and it was obvious that Nina the DMV worker was getting a great deal out of the arrangement, but I couldn't help pitying her for the emotional fall when the dead guy left her for good and she went back to being just herself again. And that was if she was lucky.

I watched her from out of the corner of my eye, trying not to be obvious about it as I searched for something, anything, that belonged to the living Nina, but it was as if she was entirely gone, reduced to an elegant pantsuit and a pair of Prada shoes. Ivy could have been something like this. Had been, perhaps, before she stood up to Piscary. No wonder she'd wanted out.

As I watched, Nina frowned and brought her gaze back from the city. A second later, Wayde breathed a relieved "There he is." I followed his gaze across the interstate to the city to see the flashing lights of an FIB vehicle.

"Finally," I said, and Nina chuckled.

"We could have gone in to wait," she said as she extended her arm to invite me to cross the informal drive to the front steps. "It would have been warmer."

"I'm fine," I said, cursing under my breath as I found myself automatically moving and jerked myself to a stop before I'd gone more than a step. This guy was good. "How old are you?" I asked sourly, and Nina smiled.

"Old enough to know better, and young enough not to care."

That wasn't the answer I was hoping for, and I slid two more feet away from her as Glenn pulled up behind the last I.S. car and got out. In the distance, another car followed. "You made good time!" I shouted before he was close, and we all crossed the wide, informal drive to the shallow steps leading to the front door, Wayde lagging behind and looking uncomfortable around all the suits.

Glenn seemed pissed, his arms swinging as he joined us. He looked a little tired, too. No surprise after a morning with Ivy. Blinking at Wayde's less-than-professional dress, he turned to me. "Thanks for the call. Apparently the one that Nina made got stuck in my voice mail."

It was a thinly veiled rebuke, and Nina smiled. "My apologies?"

Nina didn't look sorry, and Glenn's expression became even tighter when the I.S. agent Nina had sent in came out with a bookish-looking man, wire glasses on his nose and wearing a polyester suit, the hem of the jacket whipping in the wind off the river. His shoes were shiny, and it looked like he didn't get out much as he awkwardly followed the I.S. cop down the stairs to meet us somewhere in the middle.

"What was he doing in there?" Glenn asked, and Nina pleasantly inclined her head.

"I simply sent a man in to inform the curator of why we were parked on his drive. Relax, Detective Glenn. No one is trying to hide anything from you." Her eyes turning black, she turned to the short man looking at us from a step up. "We can go in now?"

The officer stiffened. "Mr. Ohem—"

Nina raised a hand to stop him. "It's Nina," she said calmly, but it was obvious he wasn't pleased about the slip— which made me all the more curious as to what his name was.

"Sir," the officer tried again, flushing. "This is Mr. Calaway, the curator on duty."

Mr. Calaway, oblivious to the blunder, stuck his thin hand out, and he and Nina shook. "Pleasure to meet you," he said enthusiastically, his narrow face beaming at the woman. It was obvious he didn't have a clue that he was shaking hands with a vampire, much less one channeling a dead one, and I exchanged a quick look with Glenn. His eyes were as bright as I figured mine must be. Mr. Calaway was human. That put him as a suspect, perhaps? How could he not know there was demon magic being practiced in his building? The screams would give it away. It was always the quiet ones who were the ax murderers.

"Detective Glenn," Glenn said as he gave me a twist of his lips to acknowledge my suspicions. He took a breath to introduce me, hesitating when he saw the tattoo of the dandelion tuft on my collarbone. "Ah, this is Ms. Morgan, who is helping us with the magic, and Mr. Benson," he said, a faint smile quirking his lips, "her security."

Mr. Calaway nodded at me, then did a double take at Wayde, his hairy legs showing between his army boots and his boxers. "I hope we can take care of this quickly," he said, his eyes squinting in worry at the official cars and the young family with a stroller giving them a wide berth. "We haven't had any trouble for a long time. It's a museum. Nothing much changes here except the interns."

I forced a smile as I leaned forward and shook his hand. "We will be as unobtrusive as possible," I promised, but it was as if I didn't exist for him, and it kind of rankled. I wasn't dressed as nicely as the people around me—except for Wayde, and he had dropped back to run a hand over his face as he looked out over the river, his untucked thin shirt flapping in the wind.

Nina gestured toward the door, and we all began moving. "You okay?" I asked Glenn, and he gave me a sharp look.

"Why shouldn't I be?" he asked, and I warmed, resolving to keep my mouth shut.

"Come on in," the curator was saying. "I can't imagine anyone's been here, but we don't go down into the lower levels much. It's damp down there. Low water table."

Mr. Calaway opened the door, and all the men hesitated, looking at me. I knew I had promised Jenks and Ivy that I'd go to only secure sites, but this was a museum lobby, not the bad guys' lair. Besides, it was cold, so I hunched my shoulders and went in, appreciating the lack of wind as I took in the tall-ceilinged entryway with its placards explaining what the museum was about. There was an official-looking desk for buying tickets and arranging for self-guided audio tours, and the eyes of the woman manning it widened as the rest filed in behind me, Mr. Calaway's mouth never stopping.

"There's a tour going through right now. Is there any way you can avoid them?" he asked in worry. He still didn't get it, but the I.S. officer probably hadn't told him we were tracking down a militant human fringe group that was deforming witches with black magic.

Glenn brought his attention back from the artifact case. "We will be as circumspect as possible. We don't need to do a room by room since we have a detection charm."

"Oh." The human looked at me doubtfully, and I smiled sarcastically.

"It's a super-duper murderer finder," I said, holding up the glowing amulet as I remembered him dissing me on the front steps. "I made it in my kitchen last night. Don't you worry, Mr. Calaway. We'll find those serial killers and get them out for you."

"S-serial killers?" the curator stammered, his dark complexion lightening considerably.

"Rachel . . ." Glenn growled, but Wayde had turned his back on us, laughing, I guess.

"Didn't they tell you?" I said, making my eyes wide and enjoying jerking the stiff man's chain. "What did the I.S. officer say we were here for? Inspecting for fire-code violations?"

Nina frowned, and Glenn pinched my elbow. "You like causing trouble, don't you?" Glenn insisted, and I stopped. Maybe being ignored on the front steps bothered me more than I'd realized, but that had felt good, and now I was pretty sure that Mr. Calaway wasn't a suspect. I didn't want to walk around a museum with a serial killer. I had promised to be careful, right?

Glenn stepped nearly in front of me, taking the upset man by the shoulder and all but leading him to the turnstiles. "We only need a few people until we know for sure if what we're looking for is here, Mr. Calaway," he said, giving me a glare to keep my mouth shut. "There's no need to be alarmed, and we're grateful that you're letting us look around without a *warrant*. Ms. Morgan is *exaggerating* the situation."

I sighed, but got what Glenn was saying and resolved to shut up. If Mr. Calaway refused to let us in, we could lose a day in the courts getting a warrant. The thing was, though, I wasn't exaggerating, and Glenn knew it.

"Um, I'll get the keys," the curator said, his focus distant as he reached over the counter and brought out a ring of them. "I've got a key for everything."

Right at the front desk, I thought, thinking security was pretty lax. But who was going to run off with any of this stuff?

Mr. Calaway started for the museum's entrance, his pace fast and jerky. Glenn grabbed my elbow and propelled me forward, his grip a shade too tight and his shoulders tense. He wasn't happy with me, but I didn't care. Wayde was behind me, and Nina ahead, her eyes scanning, evaluating, searching, her motions both graceful and tense. I don't think the vampire she was channeling had ever been in here before. It was like watching a cat, furtive and sleekly sexy at the same time.

"This is our main room," the man was saying as we took our turns going through the turnstile and entered the large four-story room. Tours fanned out from here, but it was the log cabin my eyes lingered on. As the curator started in on his memorized spiel as if we were tourists, I stared at the building, wondering why it drew my attention—other than its being a building inside another.

"That is creepy," I said to Wayde when I read the placard and found the log cabin had once been hidden inside someone's barn and was a holding pen for slaves being moved and sold. "Something doesn't look right," I added as I continued reading, finding that it had been painstakingly reassembled here for instructional reasons. Kids ran in and out of it as if it was a playhouse, while serious adults tried to take in the atrocity it represented, and yet . . . something felt off.

Nina rocked toward me. "It's a fake," she said softly, her eyes on the roofline.

I looked at her, as did Wayde, leaving Glenn patiently listening to the curator and trying to wedge a word in and get this train moving.

Nina shrugged, her hands loose at her sides. "There's no moulage on it," the vampire said, still not having looked away from the thick, dark timbers. "It's a fake, a replica."

"But moulages fade with time and sun," I said. "This thing is ancient."

"Ancient? No." Nina reached out to touch the timbers, apparently blackened artificially, and not with the blood the sign said they were. "But something like this—something built to hold people against their will, to imprison lives, souls, and fears—tends to soak up emotion and hold it like a sponge." Scrunching up her face, Nina looked at the chimney. "It will hold its emotion for a long time, and this has none."

A banshee might have soaked it up, I thought, but dismissed it. "A fake?" I asked, thinking it was unfair that they would try to pass it off as an original.

Nina's eyes flicked behind my shoulder, and I jumped when Glenn touched me, asking, "Rachel? Which way?"

I took a deep breath and exhaled. Oh yeah. Fumbling for the amulet, I held it even with my chest and walked in a circle. There was only one direction where the glow strengthened, and I stopped, staring at a service-oriented area with no displays. An oversize door with no window and painted the same color as the walls was obvious, and I pointed. "There."

Mr. Calaway bustled past me looking positively relieved. "That leads to the research area," he said as he fumbled with the keys, finally bringing one up to his face and peering at it. "This one, I think." He slid it into the lock and opened the door, flicking the lights on as he held it for us. It looked like your average hallway, with white tile and boring painted walls. A little wider than most, perhaps, but bland. "Sue!" he shouted, his voice echoing. "We're going downstairs. I'll be back in a moment! Lock the doors and let the place empty naturally."

The woman from the front desk peeked around a wall. "Yes, sir."

"What about Ivy and Jenks?" I asked, not wanting to leave them out, but wanting to see what the amulet had pinged on. What was taking them so long anyway?

Glenn turned to Mr. Calaway, looking as anxious as I was to get moving. "Two more people are coming. A Ms. Tamwood and a pixy named Jenks. Could someone bring them down when they arrive?"

Sue smiled. "Yes, sir. I'll let them in and send them down."

Wayde shifted from foot to foot, clearly uncomfortable. "I'll stay here," he said, and I gave him a questioning look. "Technically, I'm not allowed to be at a crime scene without prior arrangements." He turned to me, his gaze intent as he touched my elbow. "I think you should stay with me. This isn't a secure site. Someone else can work the charm."

My breath came in slowly, and I forced my jaw not to clench. He was just doing his job. "I have my splat gun," I said patiently. "I'll be careful. Besides, there's no one here."

"You don't know that," he said, and in my peripheral vision, I saw Glenn chafing at the delay. *Yeah. Me, too.*

"Cautious?" Nina mocked in her expensive pantsuit, crisp and pressed, her voice like silk. "That's not like you, Ms. Morgan."

"Maybe I'm getting smarter," I said dryly. "I'm working the amulet until there's reason to believe they're still here," I added, wedging Wayde's fingers off me. "I'll be smart about it."

"Smart is staying here until you know for sure," Wayde said.

"My job puts me at risk. I said I'll be careful, and I will," I said loudly, then locked my knees as the heady scent of excited vampire cascaded over me like water. It was Nina, and I sidestepped her so she wouldn't link her arm in mine.

"I'll see to Rachel's safety personally," the woman said gracefully, not at all upset that I'd avoided her. "I can smell them, you see," Nina said, and she touched her nose as she smiled coyly. "Nasty little humans with mischief on their brains. I'm sure Ms. Morgan will be most careful, but I will restrain her from entering any room that's unsafe. Physically . . . if necessary."

"There, you see?" I said brusquely, my heart pounding as I made a mental promise that Nina wasn't *ever* going to lay a hand on me. "You should stay here, though. You're right about the legal thing. You might get hurt and sue the city."

"I would not," Wayde said with a scowl, but Glenn was pointing at one of his men to stay behind with him. "Fine. I'll stay," he said with bad grace, arms over his chest and his feet spread wide. "I'm starting to see why you don't have many friends."

I probably deserved that, but with only the faintest tug of guilt, I followed the curator into the wide hallway, the rest of the men behind me, and Nina behind them. The wide door shut behind us with a solid thump, and I stifled my shiver. Almost immediately we found a set of stairs, and Mr. Calaway started down, turning on big industrial lights as he went. It was cold, and the air smelled stale. My feet in my soggy garden shoes didn't make a sound. Neither did Nina's, and it was giving me the creeps. I could feel her behind me, lurking. Maybe leaving Wayde behind hadn't been such a good idea, but I was surrounded by men with guns looking for an empty room. What did he think was going to happen?

I checked my cell phone when we reached the bottom of the stairs, not liking that there was no signal. The amulet still worked, meaning we weren't too deep to reach a ley line. Small comfort, since I wasn't going to.

"Which way?" Glenn asked when we came to an intersection. He was tense, and I could see Nina enjoying the mild temptation Glenn was making himself into. It probably didn't help that he smelled like Ivy.

"Give me a moment," I said. Head down over the amulet,

I left them, half on the stairs, half in the lower hallway, and went a few paces to the left, watching the amulet's color.

"That leads to storage," Mr. Calaway offered. He was starting to fidget, and Nina smiled, basking in it.

"What do you store here?" Nina almost purred, clearly happy belowground. "Brochures?"

I turned at Mr. Calaway's scoff, but then he hesitated and backed up several steps when he saw her almost lascivious expression. "Mostly artifacts that we haven't gotten prepped for display or those that we don't want to make available to the general public."

Glenn spun on a heel, his face creased in irritation. "Why wouldn't you want them on display?" he asked belligerently.

The curator adopted a stiff posture, one step up from Nina. "Slavery was an ugly business, Officer Glenn. It became more so when given a high monetary value and people took inhuman steps to protect their *investments*."

Clearly this was a sore subject for the man, but Glenn had turned to face him squarely, just as upset. "It's Detective Glenn. And what right do you have to determine who gets to see it?"

Mr. Calaway squinted at the larger man, not backing down an inch. "I'll arrange a private tour for you if you like, and if you still feel the same way, I'll be very much surprised."

Eyes down, I walked past them in the other direction. My pulse jumped when the amulet glowed a brighter green. Nina must have sensed it because she came down the last few steps, her eyes alight. "I think it's this way," I said, and Mr. Calaway waved his hands in protest.

"There's nothing down there," he claimed, but my amulet said differently, and we all strode forward to find it ended in . . . nothing. No stairway, no door. Nothing.

"I don't understand," I said, staring at the empty wall as I remembered doing almost the same thing in Trent's labs a few months ago. There'd been a door that I had needed to use a ley line to walk through to the room beyond. I couldn't do that now, and I looked from my band of charmed silver to Glenn, feeling ill.

"What's behind this wall?" Glenn asked, his hand skating over the smooth paint.

Mr. Calaway thought for a moment. "That's the storage area for the holding pen."

Glenn stiffened. "The one upstairs is a fake?"

"Absolutely!" the man exclaimed.

"What are you afraid of?" Glenn pressed.

I looked down the hallway to Nina, leaning casually against the wall and wedging something from under her fingernails. It was a very masculine gesture that looked odd with her carefully manicured nails. This was not going well, and Mr. Calaway flushed.

"I'm not afraid of anything," he said, flustered. "The holding pen is behind this wall, yes, but we have access to it through the elevator. If you had told me that's where you wanted to go, I would have taken you there in the first place. Follow me."

Glenn clenched his jaw, and Nina closed her eyes, soaking in his anger. I turned and trudged after Mr. Calaway as he backtracked to a set of huge silver doors. He keyed it to life with a flourish, glaring at us as the machinery rumbled and whined. I shivered as the doors opened to show a huge elevator that looked big enough to hold an elephant.

"It's not right that you're hiding a piece of history down here where no one can see it," Glenn grumbled as he filed in after me.

Mr. Calaway entered last, and he used a second key to light up the panel. "We don't have the original holding pen up for display for several reasons, Detective Glenn," he said stiffly as we waited for the lights to quit flashing and the panel to warm up. "Preserving the priceless art created by the people confined within it for one, maintaining people's sanity for another."

Sanity?

"The truth should never be hidden," Glenn insisted.

Nina covered a smile as the smaller man fumed. "It's not hidden," Mr. Calaway barked. "It's simply not on public display! The original inscriptions on the interior of the structure are as priceless as they are heartbreaking, but there are magics associated with the structure itself, and that's what we are keeping from the public. Black magics."

My gut tightened, and I exchanged a look with Nina, who was suddenly a lot more alert. Black magic under the museum? Maybe there was a method to the madness after all.

The angry, smaller man punched a button, and we started to descend. "It was deemed better to have a small lie that the public could touch, sit in, and connect with on a physical level than a harsh truth behind glass that would divorce them from experiencing anything," Mr. Calaway said, the rims of his ears red. "You'll see."

Glenn shifted from foot to foot and faced the front. "It can't be that bad."

Something was crawling up my back, and I turned to see that it was Nina's attention.

"You are such a delight to watch," she murmured, but everyone in the elevator could hear the seduction the dead vampire was putting into Nina's voice. "Every thought you have passes over your face."

"Y-yeah . . ." I drawled, trying to remember who had told me that before.

"Do you always fight crime in dirty shoes?" she asked, and Glenn, in the back of the elevator, cleared his throat.

"Give me a break," I said, trying to hide the wrinkles in my shirt. "I was having coffee with my bodyguard. I didn't expect to be hunting bad guys until later. Leather before sundown is tacky."

"Besides," Mr. Calaway muttered, "if we had the pen upstairs, it would fall apart in twenty years. We have it in the biggest temperature-controlled room in an eight-hundred-mile area," he said proudly. "That's why the museum was set here in the first place. It was originally university property."

My eyebrows went high. *Do tell?*

Oblivious to my sudden interest, Mr. Calaway said, "Some of their machines are still down here, and we let university people in occasionally to use them. The room has its own heating and cooling system, and battery backup in case the electricity goes down."

Machines? I thought, forcing myself to be still, but inside I was fidgeting. "Mr. Calaway? Just what kind of machines do you have here?"

The man's enthusiasm vanished, and he winced. "Uh, they tell me they're used to identify genetic markers," he said, and Glenn grunted. "It's all perfectly legal," Mr. Calaway said as the doors opened to show a hallway almost identical to the one above, with the exception of a huge double door facing us from across a wide hallway. "Nothing unsavory," the curator insisted. "We use it occasionally to find out who used an artifact, owner or slave. It's old technology, and they need the cooler room to run it in."

Airtight room. Black magic. Genetic, borderline technology. I wasn't liking what this was adding up to, and I followed Glenn to the locked door. My amulet was a bright green. Clearly this was it, and the tension grew.

"There, huh?" Mr. Calaway said, disappointed as he glanced at the amulet and then his massive key ring. The first key he tried didn't work, and Glenn became impatient. The second one didn't, either, and when he tried the first one again, Glenn just about lost it.

"Open the door," he demanded. "Or I'll call in for a warrant and sit here until it arrives. Rachel, go stand over there."

"I'm trying!" the curator insisted as I obediently moved to where Glenn wanted me, knowing it was going to be an empty room but wanting to prove that I could be a team player as well as the next person. "My key isn't working," he said, bringing the key right up to his nose and squinting at it. "Either the key has been changed or the lock has."

Glenn squatted before it, breathing gently on the lock with his hands unmoving before him as he looked it over. "It's the lock," he said softly as he stood. "You can see the new scratches in the paint. We need to get a team down here for fingerprints."

"They can't do that!" Mr. Calaway exclaimed, affronted. "I'm the curator!"

"I don't have time for this," Nina said impatiently. "Excuse me."

She moved vampire fast, and both Glenn and Mr. Calaway backed up when she grasped the knob and simply yanked the mechanism out of the door. It gave way with a terrible shriek of twisted metal and, looking satisfied, Nina threw it into the open elevator.

"Shall we?" she said as she tugged down the hint of lace at the hem of her sleeves.

Glenn was outraged, sputtering at the loss of fingerprints. Mr. Calaway looked at the waiting vampire, then the broken lock in the elevator, and finally the door. "Sure," he said weakly. I think he'd only just realized she was a vampire.

My skin prickled as Glenn pushed the door open, tense and straining for sound as he slipped into the darkness past the threshold. Nina was next, straight and upright as she casually strolled in and turned on the lights. Thinking about the mutated, twisted body in Washington Park, I hesitated where I was with Mr. Calaway. "We're good," Glenn's voice echoed out, and I lurched to get in before Mr. Calaway.

The room was at least two stories high, lit with fluorescent lights still flickering and ringed with banks of cupboards and counter space. At the center of the room was the holding pen in a huge snow-globe-like affair, all blackened timbers and broken chimney. The windows were mere slits, and the walls had fallen apart in places. It was ugly, awful, and I was glad it was behind glass. Maybe Mr. Calaway was right to hide this. The emotion coming from it was almost too much to bear.

Shivering, I went in farther. Mr. Calaway was staring, aghast, at the twin empty spaces against the opposite wall. I could see why. There were scrape marks, and in one place, the wall had been busted and a thick cable had been pulled out. The end was raw and looked like it had been connected to something, hardwired in, and just cut out.

There were no bodies, no blood, and it looked barren. *Perhaps too barren,* I thought as Mr. Calaway began a high-pitched cry, his hands over his mouth.

"They're gone!" he shouted, pointing at the broken wall with a trembling finger, and Glenn turned from where he'd been staring at the holding pen.

"Who?" the FIB detective asked, his voice suddenly aggressive.

"The machines!" Mr. Calaway said, pointing again. "Someone took the machines! They're gone!"

Ten

The come-and-go chatter of the FIB guys was pleasant, much like the audible equivalent of the hot chocolate I was sipping: warm, comfortable, and soothing. I watched the FIB officers with half my attention as they finished up, having vacuumed, photographed, measured, and taken samples within an inch of being ridiculous. They hadn't strung up their yellow tape except for the door, and after I had promised that I'd stay sitting on the counter, they'd left me alone. I was being a good girl, and I think they'd forgotten I was here. It had been almost four hours.

My eyes strayed to a square of concrete that was lighter than the rest, and I couldn't help but wonder why no one had commented on it. Even Ivy and Jenks—who had been allowed to help gather information—ignored it.

Setting my paper cup of powdered fat, sugar, and cocoa down, I pulled my knees to my chest and wrapped my arms around my legs. I couldn't help my sigh. Ivy took to data collection like a duckling to water, and Jenks, with his ability to see the smallest thing and wedge into the narrowest place without leaving anything but dust, was equally as welcome. Even the two I.S. personnel, standing on the outskirts and watching, were more accepted than I was. Somehow, between the investigation at Trent's stables a few summers ago and the house where a banshee and her psychotic husband killed a young couple and stole their identities, I'd gained the reputation of being a disruptive force at a crime scene.

"But they can't be replaced!" Mr. Calaway exclaimed as an FIB officer tried to lead him back out into the hallway. Smiling, I rested my cheek on my knees. The guy was having a very bad day, and his tidy state had slowly decayed. His small temper tantrum of frustration at Glenn's estimation of his chances of recovering his property had been entertaining. I thought it odd that Mr. Calaway was more upset that his machines had been stolen than the fact that there had been six people living down here for almost a week without his knowledge, but I agreed with his assessment that even though the machines had been insured, replacing them would be impossible. They didn't make equipment and software that revolved around identification of the genetic markers anymore.

Trent probably had one, I thought. I'd ask him if he was missing any sensitive machinery when I talked to him about the memory-charm blocker.

A soft prickling of the skin on my neck brought my head up, and I looked across the wide room to see Nina making a slow beeline for me. Her expression was one of surprise that I'd felt her attention, and I shifted my legs to a more professional position, dangling them over the sides of the counter and a good foot off the floor.

"May I join you?" she asked formally, and I nodded, feeling uncomfortable. She'd been here as long as I had, going upstairs once to make a call before returning to sit on the outskirts and watch. I didn't think she was waiting her turn like I was, but rather learning firsthand how extensive FIB data gathering was.

She sighed heavily as she leaned a hip against the counter, sounding so alive that I stared at her. "Not mad at me anymore?" I said, and she chuckled.

"Mildly annoyed," she drawled, her hands holding her biceps. "Losing jurisdiction was a small concession for the chance to see you work." Looking sideways at me, she all but smirked. "If the FIB fails to apprehend the people responsible and to keep HAPA out of the headlines, you will still take the blame."

It was what I figured, and peeved, I thumped my heels into the cupboard I was sitting on. "Getting settled?" I said sourly, meaning him into Nina, and her expression flashed, dark.

But then she smiled to show her little living-vampire teeth. "Nina is most appreciative," she said, her voice lower than one would expect. "She was destined to be no one, and now she will walk away from this with myriad coping techniques and little wisdoms that other vampires will recognize and acknowledge. I've furthered her evolution tremendously, and her chances of living past the crucial forty-year ceiling after death have increased as well."

I was talking directly to the undead vampire, and it gave me the creeps. "Okay, so why don't you do this all the time? There's got to be a downside."

Nina shifted her body away. "How right you are, Ms. Morgan."

I waited for more, but he/she wasn't telling, instead watching the FIB personnel examining the bags of dust they'd sucked up in the vacuum. "Tell me yours, and I'll tell you mine," I mocked.

Nina stiffened. She slowly turned back, still leaning casually against the counter but with a new wariness tightening her features. "Why should I?"

I was dealing with the devil, and my heart hammered. "Rynn Cormel believes that I can save her soul after death." I glanced at Ivy, who was studying a printout with Jenks. "He believes I'll find a way to keep her soul intact after she dies, and with that, she won't need the blood anymore. The information might help me figure out how." I licked my lips. It was the first time I'd openly admitted to anyone not my friend why the city-wide master vampire and former U.S. president had put me and my roommate off-limits to everyone.

Apparently my "show" was enough for a "tell," and Nina turned her attention to Ivy, saying, "Borrowing Nina this long isn't healthy. I'm feeling a great lack in myself, a longing. I've had to almost double my blood consumption to combat it. Feeling her emotion, even filtered through my thoughts, has taxed my ability to maintain my balance."

It went with what Ivy had said earlier, and I shivered when Nina's eyes suddenly became a hungry-vampire black and her reclining posture became a threat.

"I am quite hungry," she said casually. "But it's not for blood. I want to feel the sun on my face, not feel it through Nina. It grows harder to not give up and simply . . . rise into the sunlight. It might be worth ending it all for that exquisite moment of joy." Her eyes fixed on mine. "What do you think?"

I put my palms on the counter, wanting to inch away from her. "I think you need to stay where you are, in the dark."

The undead vampire thought about that for a moment, then nodded, all the rising tension washing out in a soft sigh. "Perhaps you're correct," Nina said, and I breathed easier when she looked across the room to Glenn, peering up at Jenks, who was standing in a heating duct. "This Detective Glenn. My information says he's been working with you for some time. Do you find him . . . trustworthy? Unbiased?"

I appreciated the change of topic, and I eased when she shifted her position so we were more side to side than facing each other. Unbiased. What he/she meant was unprejudiced. It was an understandable question. "I've worked with him off and on for a couple of years," I said, remembering Jenks pixing the man for all but kidnapping me that first day. I chuckled, then explained, "He wasn't afraid of me when we met. He still isn't, but he learned respect quickly."

Nina made a small sound of agreement. "Respect can't always save you. He's been with a skilled vampire," she said, her eyes on Glenn in a way that made me feel decidedly protective. "A dead one, by the look of it."

Concerned, I brought my knees back up to my chin. It

was cold down here. "Glenn? No. He's dating Ivy. He knows better than to get involved with a dead vampire."

"Her?"

I frowned at the disbelief in Nina's voice, and brought my attention from where Ivy and Glenn were discussing something with Jenks. Jenks wasn't happy, and red dust was pooling under him. "Yes, her," I said. Ivy's old master had made Ivy into something just this side of the undead, while still living, to satisfy his own depraved longings. "And you will leave her alone," I added, "or I'll track you down, Mr. Ohem-whatever-your-name-is, and I and my little pixy friend will do something permanent."

Nina smiled ingratiatingly, and my face burned. I fingered the charmed silver on my wrist, feeling my tension rise. Would I take it off to save Ivy? Probably, though it would mess up my life. Nina suddenly sobered. "You are serious," she said, her brown eyes wide. "Then I apologize. I will leave her alone."

"Good," I said tightly, unkinking my fingers from around my shins. *Why is he being so chummy? It was almost as if yesterday hadn't happened.*

Ivy, too, had smelled my anger, and she swung her hair from her face and looked at me, her gaze flicking questioningly to Nina. I gave her a sour bunny-eared kiss-kiss to tell her we were okay, and she said something to Jenks, who then laughed like wind chimes.

"She knows you're talking about her," Nina said, sounding almost wistful.

"Yup." I didn't want to think about how close a tie we had for her to be able to do that. Ignorance was bliss.

Jenks darted up and down like a yo-yo, and I tossed my nasty, snarled hair off my shoulder as he approached, but it was my knee he landed on. His wings looked gray with cold, and they were rattling. They'd been getting progressively louder the longer he stayed down here.

"You okay?" I said as he landed, huffing a little. "Want them to turn up the heat?"

"Nah, I'm okay," he said, but he sat down to take advantage of the heat coming up off my knee. "The people who strung up that witch in the park were here, all right. The air ducts are closed, but you can tell they were opened recently and the filters changed. Hardly a day's worth of dust on them. The ductwork has been cleaned, too. Only a pixy could tell." He glanced at Nina, listening intently. "Or one of those optic lines, maybe.

"And the computers?" the pixy added, his wings shivering to up his core temperature. "I got into the history files of the ones they didn't take. All of them say they haven't been used recently, but the trash was wiped last Thursday, so it's my guess that that's when they left."

Nina tapped her fingers and pushed herself away from the counter. "The day before they dumped the man in the park."

Jenks nodded. He looked about as cold as I felt, and I promised myself I'd make cookies tonight to get the kitchen warm and cozy for him. "I don't even know why they used them," Jenks said. "They're so old that a laptop would have more power."

"Not the same programs, though," I said, wondering if he'd accept the unused tissue I had jammed in my shoulder bag as a blanket.

"Right," Jenks said. Arms wrapped around himself, he looked up at me, an odd look of both revulsion and attraction on his face. "The curator said the computers down here were for doing genetic stuff."

I nodded. "Helpful when you're making witches capable of invoking demon magic," I said. God! What were they doing? This was crazy. Who would want to be like me? My life sucked.

"Like you," Jenks said, his voice thick with warning.

"Yes, like me," I said, then sighed. "I'll be fine, Jenks." I glanced at Nina, who had heard my theory in the coffeehouse about what these wackos were doing. "They know better than to go after me, or they would've done it by now."

"Maybe they would have except for Wayde," he said.

"He's a lot better at this than you give him credit for. You need to get off his case."

"I know. I apologized," I said, and he made a satisfied noise.

"You need to stay away from Ivy, too, Mr. Walkie-Talkie Man," Jenks said suddenly.

My head came up to see Jenks standing, still on my knee, with his hands on his hips and staring at Nina. "Ah, Jenks?"

Nina slowly slouched until she was reclining against the counter again, her attention on the FIB as they began packing up their gear. On a man, her posture would have looked casual and attractive, but on Nina, it was untidy and at odds with her expensive pantsuit. "I know. I apologized," she said, mimicking me to sound mocking.

"I know your type," Jenks said, unconvinced. "You see something, and you want to know if you can eat it. You're worse than my youngest daughter. Stay away from Ivy or I'll find where you sleep and send my gargoyle in to carve out your heart."

"I'm staying away from Ivy," she said flatly, and Jenks hummed his wings.

"Good. See that you do."

"Oh, thank God," I whispered as Glenn started our way, and Jenks took to the air when I dropped my feet back over the edge of the counter. "Maybe I'll get out of here before the sun sets."

"Agreed," Nina said sourly, standing to tug her cuffs down. "I have things to do tonight."

I didn't want to know. Really. The FIB personnel were starting to leave, dipping under the yellow tape and talking loudly in the hall as they made their way back to the elevator. Glenn was taking off a pair of blue plastic gloves as he approached, cataloging my weary acceptance and Nina's bored apathy as he shoved them in a back pocket. "Thanks for staying out of the way," he said as he halted before me, and I winced.

"No problem."

"The room is remarkably clean," he said, ignoring my sarcasm. "No fibers, no small particles. Nothing. They wiped it down, meaning they knew we'd find it."

"It's unusual for serial killers to move like that," Nina said, and Glenn shrugged.

"The stain in the corner is coolant from the machine they moved. Jenks told you about the ductwork?"

I nodded. "Cleaned out. He told me the computers were wiped, too. It might be nice to know what programs were on them. And the ones that were stolen."

"Already have a call in to the university," Glenn said.

Ivy had finished with the lab guys, and Glenn shifted to make room for her before he could possibly have heard her coming. Nina made a small noise as she noted it. "There was a lot of fear here," Ivy said as she scuffed to a stop. "I'm not registered to do a court-rated moulage, but you can tell what's coming from the cabin and what isn't, and there's a lot to be accounted for."

Nina closed her eyes and breathed deep. "I taste it, too," she said, and I shivered when her eyes opened, black as sin. "Perhaps that was why they chose to be here. Someone passing in the hall wouldn't be as likely to notice. My God, it smells good."

Camping here because of the cabin's moulage was a good theory, but I was betting the computers they took were the real reason.

Ivy's attention flicked to Nina, worry pinching her brow as the dead vampire struggled to bring Nina back under control. As I watched, Ivy suddenly frowned and turned away, as if refusing to acknowledge the incident. Ivy had a tremendous—and usually hidden—need to nurture, and I knew the risk that the master was putting Nina through was bothering her.

"So," I said as I slid from the counter in an effort to put more space between me and Nina, quietly vamping out. It was a longer drop than I had counted on, and my ankles, stiff from the cold, hurt. "You ready to let me move around, Glenn? I've been waiting hours."

Jenks laughed, and the tension eased even more. "Face it, Rache," he said, slipping gold dust as he warmed up. "You and crime scenes don't mix. You should have seen the mess she made of one last year."

"Which one was that?" Ivy dropped back a few steps to make room for me, worry for Nina showing in her slow movements. "Getting her fingerprints on the sticky silk at Kisten's boat, or touching things at the house with the banshees?"

"Hey! I'm being good," I said, not as upset about the ribbing as I thought I'd be. Must have been the cocoa—or that the laughter at my expense was giving Nina's master something to hook his control on to and calm her down. "I'm sitting here waiting my turn until everyone else gets what they want. And if you remember, *I* found the information that turned the entire case around. *Both* times." My mood became suddenly melancholic as I remembered Kisten. *Sorry, Kisten,* I thought, my gaze down on my damp, dirty shoes. Damn memory charms. No wonder Newt was nuts.

Recognizing my mood and knowing its source, Glenn tapped his clipboard against his palm. "We're almost done, yes."

"Then you want to know what the amulet pinged on?" I said as I pulled it from underneath my shirt. "I do."

Jenks's wings hummed in anticipation as he moved to my shoulder where he could watch better, but Glenn looked betrayed. "You mean—"

Nina put a hand on my other shoulder, and I stiffened. "There's more, yes," she said, her voice low, rich, and rolling with her master's accent. Jenks had taken off when I shuddered, and I slipped out from under Nina's grip.

"No touching," I said, glaring at her. "Okay? Them's the rules."

Ivy, too, wasn't happy, and Jenks was nearly beside himself, sifting a bright red dust as he hovered with his hands on his hips. Nina ignored them both, hands behind her back. "Rachel, you've developed your timing to the point of exquisite delayed gratification," she said. "Use your amulet. I'm dying to know what drew us here."

"You mean it wasn't the ambient residual evidence?" Glenn said, and I filed that away for future use. Ambient residual evidence. Nice.

"No." I frowned as I pointed at the patch of new concrete behind him. "I've got a bad feeling about that."

"That what?" Jenks asked as I went to stand over it, watching the amulet more than my feet clinging damply to my garden shoes.

"That this," I said flatly, pointing at the new cement.

Glenn came over and looked down. "That what?"

"This," I said more stridently. "The floor. Where they poured the new concrete?"

Glenn's brow furrowed. "Uh, the floor looks fine to me," the FIB detective said.

"No friggin' way!" I exclaimed as the last of the FIB crew left. "You can't see the patch of new concrete? It's right there!"

Ivy and Nina came over and looked down, but I could tell they couldn't see it, even when Jenks walked right over the seam, spilling a faint hint of dust. "There's a patch of new concrete!" I said, pointing down. "Right there! It's about three by four. You can't see it?"

Glenn crouched and ran a hand over the floor. "I can't even feel it."

"No fairy-assed way!" Jenks strutted over the floor, looking for but not seeing what I was. Scared, I backed up. Nina was waiting for me when my head came up, and I froze at the anger in her expression.

"Maybe Ms. Morgan can see it because she poured it?" the vampire suggested.

Ivy's hands clenched, and Jenks rose up, his fingers on his garden sword. "You take that back!" he shouted. "Rachel can see it because it's a curse, and she's in the demon collective," he exclaimed, and I winced. I had a feeling I could see it because I *wasn't* in the collective, not because I had been.

"Will you take it easy!" I exclaimed, and Jenks zipped back to me, leaving a slowly falling cloud of silver dust. "I've never been down here, Nina, and you know it. You smell me down here? Huh? Do you?"

"No," she said, clearly reserving judgment.

Disgusted, I turned my back on her, not wanting to know what was under the floor but knowing we'd have to find out. I didn't like the fact that I was the only one who could see it.

Jenks hovered close, then landed on my shoulder. "How come we can't see it, Rache?"

Taking a breath, I brought my head up. "I don't know," I lied, figuring it was a demon curse that required the collective to work. Curses stored and doled out from the collective didn't recognize me because of my complete lack of connection to the lines, a basic, living connection to the source of all energy that even the undead and humans had. I was special, and I hated it, even if it was a good thing in this instance.

"Maybe we should open it." I looked up, reading worry in Ivy, doubt in Glenn, and mistrust in Nina. "I'm telling you, something is buried under the floor."

Glenn put one hand on his hip and stared down at the floor. "Where are the outlines?"

My pulse hammered. I went back to my bag on the counter and dug in it until I found my magnetic chalk under my splat gun. Breath held, I carefully crouched over the floor, moving awkwardly so Jenks wouldn't lose his balance and have to fly from my shoulder as I ran a line next to the seam.

Nina bent over the lines when I stood, a young, manicured hand feeling the line as the old presence in her analyzed what it might mean. "I still don't see it." Stretching, she snagged a metal rod from a pile. There were others inside the glass box propping up the pen, and she tapped it experimentally on the floor, her back hunched, making her look old. I retreated to stand beside Ivy as Nina continued tapping, her expression shifting when the tone changed as she worked her way off the new floor and onto the old.

Nina looked up, her eyes fixing on mine with such ferocity I could almost see the undead vampire in them. "There is something under here," she said, and I shivered.

"Yeah, we know, dirt nap," Jenks said. "Rachel already told us."

"Chill, Jenks," I said, and he clattered his wings, cold when they brushed my neck.

"Can we get a saw here?" Glenn shouted, but everyone was gone.

"Back up," Nina said as she took a firmer stance, feet spread wide. "It's hollow. I'll open it up."

I was getting a really bad feeling. Whatever was under the floor was close to but not quite identical to the man in the park. Ivy yanked me out of the way, and I stumbled. My eyes were fixed on the new concrete, hidden by a curse tied to the collective. Someone had made a deal with a demon. Or, even worse, they had succeeded in duplicating demon blood and twisted the curse on their own. Watching Nina lift the bar over her head, I wasn't sure which one scared me the most.

Nina sent the butt of the support bar crashing into the floor with a grunt. The cement cracked at the blow, and Jenks left me in excitement. Again the vampire swung. This time, the pole went right through, the resounding crack of cement seeming to shake me to my bones. Nina stumbled to catch her balance, and Glenn reached out to stop her fall before she could tread on the broken slab.

"I can see it!" Ivy exclaimed, and I jerked my attention from Nina, staring at Glenn's hand on her arm.

"Well, if that doesn't beat all creation," Nina said, and I stiffened at the old-world phrase. I must have heard it a dozen times from Pierce, and it would make the vampire in Nina at least 150 years old.

Cold, I leaned forward over the hole. "You must have broken the charm," I said, not wanting to call it a curse.

Jenks flew down to the dark hole, rising almost immediately with his hand over his face and gagging. I found out why when he brought the scent of burnt amber to me. "Tink's titties!" he exclaimed as he landed on Ivy's shoulder, grasping a swath of her hair and hiding his face in it. "Rache, it stinks more than you when you get back from the ever-after."

"Thanks," I muttered, trying to see in as everyone else backed up. The smell didn't bother me much—anymore.

"That's burnt amber," Ivy said, her hand over her nose. Wincing, she looked over the patched floor to Nina. "Can you open it up more?"

"What the hell is wrong with you Inderlanders!" Glenn protested. "You can't just bust it open! Give me ten minutes, and I'll have a saw in here!"

But Nina was already hammering at it with the regularity of a metronome. Cement chips flew and we all backed up and let her go, dust and dirt layering her new pantsuit. Glenn looked as angry as if Nina were beating up his little sister, but finally Nina set her pole down and wiped her forehead. Rust-smeared hands on her dusty knees, she peered past the chunks of head-size concrete and dust to the small cavern below. The scent of burnt amber was obvious, thinner but somehow more pervasive as it was diluted out.

As one, Glenn, Ivy, Jenks, and myself crept forward and peered down to the burlap bag holding a shape about the size of a large dog. It was tied with a HAPA knot.

"You all see that, right?" I asked, and Glenn nodded, not looking up. "Better open it then," I said as I backed up, and he reached for the blue gloves jammed in his back pocket.

Nina fidgeted at the delay as Glenn put his gloves on again and knelt over the bag, cement chips popping under his shoes. His fingers worked the knot, and I clenched my teeth when it opened to show another mutilated body, curled up as if sleeping, under four inches of concrete. She was wrapped in a sheet. I don't think clothes would have fit her anymore, her limbs were so twisted.

"Please tell me she was dead before she was cemented in," I said, seeing the hoofed feet and curly pelt.

Dropping the sheet to the side, Glenn carefully shifted a wrist, red and swollen. "She was restrained," he said in a flat voice.

"For only a few hours," Nina said, and she shrugged when she met Ivy's gaze. "If it were longer, there'd be more damage."

"And you'd know all about that, huh?" Jenks asked. Yeah, the dead vampire would.

Glenn turned the corpse's face and lifted a lid. Red, demon-slitted eyes stared up, cloudy in death, and I shuddered, making Nina suck in her breath to gain control. Or perhaps she/he was responding to the corpse's teeth, pointed like a living vampire's. The skin was ruddy like Al's, but bubbled and pebbled like a gargoyle. It was hard to see with her curled up, but the arms looked wiry and strong, as if she could haul nets over the side of a boat all day. *Wings?* I thought, and I backed up fast. What were they doing to these people?

"Okay," Glenn said as he stood. "We need to get this back to the . . . ah, forensics lab. I want to know how long the body was stressed before she died."

"An hour. That's all. Perhaps less." We all looked at Nina, and she shrugged, dust and rust marring her makeup like dried blood. "But by all means, do your scientific poking and prodding. She's suffered so much, what's one more indignity?"

Hands over my middle, I turned my back on one monstrosity to face another that society had deemed too uncomfortable to put on public display. My vision grew blurry, and I wiped a hand under my eye. Damn it, she'd been conscious when they'd done that to her, I could tell by the pain in her face. And it was a her. Something gut deep told me it was a woman, something more than her pointy facial features landing somewhere between a pixy and a buffalo.

I could hear the soft sound of sliding fabric as Glenn opened the shroud farther, and the creak of his shoe's leather as he shifted his weight. "A body under the floor doesn't match anything you've found at the earlier sites. We need to revisit them for a spell-hidden body."

I nodded, stiffening when Ivy touched my shoulder. "You'll be okay for a moment?" she asked. There was pity in her eyes, and I tightened my resolve even more. "I'm going up to make a call. The reception down here sucks like a dry socket. You'll be okay until I get back?"

"Yes," I whispered, and she strode to the hallway, the sound of her feet vanishing almost immediately. The whining of the elevator replaced it, and I closed my eyes. This might be the last time I had a chance to look at the body, and unclenching my teeth, I opened my eyes and turned around.

Nina noted my pain and said nothing, probably cataloging it as something to be used against me at a later date. "Apart from the young woman whose heart gave out, this is the first female victim we've found," she said. "She's also the most deformed. Even more than the newest victim."

"Meaning?" Jenks prompted harshly as he sat on Glenn's shoulder.

"Meaning perhaps what they're doing is more effective on the female gender," Nina said as she shifted the shards of broken cement around with the tip of her metal rod. "I don't think they expected what happened here. This woman lived for a day. They buried her instead of putting her on display. They weren't ready to move yet, and couldn't risk her being found."

I put a hand to my middle again, sick from the cocoa. I'd grown up with experimental practices and wild theories as my parents struggled to keep me alive, and this was hitting close to home.

"I know this woman," Glenn said, and Nina looked sharply at him. The FIB detective was carefully examining the woman's clenched hand and didn't notice the vampire's dilating pupils. "Not personally, but from the missing persons' files. I looked them over last night."

"The I.S. files?" Nina asked, and Glenn glanced up, blanching at Nina's black stare.

"Yes. I don't remember her name, but her ring matches the description of one worn by a witch who went missing last Friday."

Glenn dropped her hand, and the deformed fist fell against the corpse with a soft sound.

Numb, I stood over her and forced myself to look. "Did you notice if she was a carrier for Rosewood?" But I already knew the answer.

The skin around Glenn's eyes gave away his distress. "Yes. They all were."

Nina squinted at me as if we had been holding out on her. "Rosewood? The blood disease? They were all carriers? When were you going to tell me this?"

"I confirmed it this morning," Glenn griped back. "When were you going to tell me Rachel had found a new site?"

Jenks was a darting blur of silk and glowing dust. "Rache," he said, trying to get into my line of sight. "What more do you need? God to send a telegram? I know you think you're safe, but you need to go into hiding, and you need to do it *now*!"

"I'm fine," I breathed, my eyes on the woman's hand, the skin red and cracked, as if it was trying to turn into a hoof and she had held the change off by her will alone. "She has something in her grip."

Glenn hesitated, sighed at Nina's gesture, then gave up on protocol and pried her hand open. Jenks flew down and darted back to me, something shiny in his arms. "Hey!" Glenn protested, but I wouldn't let him land, and he finally dropped it right into the collection bag that Glenn had hastily opened.

"It's a piece of mirror!" he said as Glenn zipped the bag shut and wrote on the label.

"Now you can see it," he grumbled as he handed it over, and Jenks landed on my wrist as I took it. I'd seen evidence through a bag before, and together we peered down at the thumb-size piece of rose-tinted glass. My heart sank.

"I think it's a chunk of a scrying mirror," I said, and Jenks hummed his wings.

"No fairy-assed way!" he said, clearly not seeing what that meant.

Demon magic, hidden bodies deformed into increasingly familiar shapes, blood slowly being changed into something else. The scattershot amulet I'd used was keyed to the man's hair. Clearly he wasn't under the floor, which meant the man's structure had been changed right down to the genetic level enough to match the woman and to ping on a scatter-shot charm. They really *were* trying to make a demon. They were trying to make a demon out of a witch by using the questionable success of each previous victim and layering it on the next. And by the looks of this corpse, they might be getting close.

"There's blood on it," I said, my fingers trembling as I handed it back. "If it's not hers, it belongs to one of her captors. We can use it to make a locator charm and find them instead of an empty room."

Glenn shifted in excitement, but I felt awful as I looked down at the woman and silently thanked her. She'd been forcibly abducted, experimented on, and tortured. Yet she had given us a clue, hiding it with her body and hoping we were clever enough to find it, recognize it, and then use it.

"Let me smell," Nina said. "I can tell you what species it is."

There were voices in the hall, and, grimacing, Glenn quickly broke the seal and held it under her nose. Nina jumped as the scent hit her, and Jenks and I watched as the two consciousnesses fought for control, eyes closing and hands trembling. It was the elder vampire who looked out at us when Nina's eyes opened again. "Human," the undead vampire said through Nina, a ribbon of excitement in her voice. "It belongs to one of the captors. We have a chance. Finally we have a chance."

I looked at the ruined woman under our feet and silently thanked her again. A chance. That was all I needed.

Eleven

The kitchen was overly warm and smelling of chili, the black square of night past the blue-curtained window dark, clear, and frigid. The waning moon had a harsh crystal clarity to it that matched my mood, cold and hard. A waning moon wasn't the best time to be making spells, but I didn't have much choice. That I'd gotten them done before midnight made me feel better.

Bis and Belle were on top of the fridge having an impromptu reading lesson, Jenks was in the garden, and Wayde was upstairs getting some wolfsbane to spike the chili with. With all that, I should've been in a good mood, but the memory of what we'd found under the floor of the museum kept my motions quick and my shoulders tense.

I'd been in the kitchen since getting home from the museum. My feet hurt from being on them all day, but the new set of scattershot amulets was already at the FIB and I.S. Glenn, who had brought us home, had waited for them. I'd also made more batches of sleepy-time charms.

The cookies I'd wanted to bake had turned into flicking the oven on and cracking it to warm the space. Not efficient, I know, but Jenks had been nearly blue with cold by the time we'd gotten back from the museum basement. I wasn't going to risk him getting chilled and possibly slipping into a stupor he might not wake from until spring. His kids had enjoyed the updraft until their papa had warmed up enough to yell at them from the salt and pepper shakers on the back of the stove. I could hear them in the back living room, arguing over a moth one of them had dug out of a crack. Jenks's kids were kind of like cats, playing things to death.

The kitchen was warm, but I was cold as I finished injecting the last of the splat balls with the sleepy-time potion. It wasn't the night seeping in around the kitchen window frame, but the cold from the memory of the woman curled up in the fetal position, twisted and broken, buried under a slab of cement and a demon curse. What they'd done to her was so horrific that they'd tried to bury it—and yet I'd found her.

My jaw clenched, I held the tiny, empty blue ball up to the light as I injected another portion of potion into the specially designed paintballs. Slowly the ball inflated, and I pulled the needle out, being careful not to get any potion on me despite my plastic gloves. Waking up to a bath of saltwater and Jenks laughing at me was not my idea of a good time.

It had been the last, and setting the empty syringe down, I wiped the ball off on a saltwater-soaked rag before I dried it and dropped it with the rest in Ceri's delicate teacup. It was overflowing with little blue balls. Maybe I'd gone overboard, but I wanted to nail these bastards, and thanks to the two would-be assassin elves last year, I now had two splat guns to fill.

Taking off the gloves, I crouched before the open cupboard under the center island counter and pulled out the one I hadn't filled yet. When not in my shoulder bag, I kept my splat guns at ankle height in a set of nested bowls. The smooth, heavy metal filled my hand, and I stood, enjoying the weight in my palm. It was modeled after a Glock, which was why it was cherry red. The coven of moral and ethical standards had worked hard to keep these from needing to be licensed. Sometimes, what humans didn't know saved us a lot of trouble.

"Can I help?" Bis said from behind me and atop the

fridge, and I turned from throwing away the old charms still in the hopper.

"No, but thanks," I said, seeing him there with Belle, a sheet of Ivy's paper, and a pencil. The fairy was too embarrassed to tell Jenks she didn't know how to read, so Bis was helping her.

The tight sound of Jenks's wings prompted a flurry of motion, and I watched Bis jam the wad of paper into his mouth and Belle yank a hand of homemade cards from under her leg. Bis suddenly had a hand of cards, too—looking tiny in his craggy fist—and I rolled my eyes when he threw a card down on the pile as Jenks flew in.

"Hey, I got the last of the toad-lily flowers you wanted," Jenks said as he dropped a bundle of them on the counter. "The best of the lot. They're done. Trust me."

"Thanks," I said, tapping the hopper on the counter to get the balls to settle. "Here's hoping I won't need any more before spring."

"The Turn take it, it's colder than Tink's titties out there!" he exclaimed as he made the hop-flight to the stove. "Think we're going to have snow early this year?"

Belle tossed her cards down as if having lost, and Bis began shuffling. "I've never s-seen snow," the fairy hissed dubiously. "Are you sure it's safe? We've always wintered in Mexico."

"It's safe." Jenks strutted to the edge of the oven, and his hair rose in the heat. "My kids even have snowball fights."

I chuckled, remembering it. They'd gone after me, and I'd nearly fried them, thinking they were assassins. It was funny now, but I'd been furious at the time.

The larger fairy frowned as she picked up the cards Bis dealt her. "You're making it up," she said, and Bis shook his head.

"It's true!" he said, his red eyes wide. "You can bring the snow inside and play with it before it melts."

I finished filling the hopper, replaced it in the gun, removed the air canister, and took up a firing position, my feet spread wide and my elbows locked. Holding the gun up as if I was going to shoot, I aimed it into the dark hall. Maybe someday we'd actually get lights put in. I glanced at Jenks doing warm-up exercises with his feet an inch off the warm porcelain. *Maybe not.*

A sudden soft scuffing in the hall turned into Wayde, and he stopped short as he saw the gun pointed at him, his eyes wide as he put his hands up in mock surrender. "All right, all right. I'll tone the chili down!"

My arms dropped, and he smiled. "Sorry," I said, then held up the empty air cartridge in explanation. "No propellant."

He made a growl of a response, shuffling in and edging to the bubbling pot of chili. A fragrant wash of steam rose when he took the cover off and sprinkled in some wolfs-bane. He was still grumpy because I'd gone down into the museum basement, but he, Ivy, and Jenks had since had a private conversation, and we seemed okay again, especially now that I was taking him seriously.

"You know that stuff is toxic, right?" I said.

Wayde snorted, looking comfortable in my kitchen. "I know what I'm doing."

My gaze slid to Jenks, at the sink getting the mud off his boots, and I confined my answer to a slow "Uh-huh." Wayde had been raised in a band tour bus by his older sister. I didn't want to know where he'd gotten his empirical knowledge of toxic drugs.

"Not that spoon!" I exclaimed when he took a ceramic one from the counter, but it was too late, and he'd already dunked it in his chili and given it a quick stir. "I've been spelling with that one," I said as I took it from him and dropped it in the sink. Jeez, I'd have to wash it twice, first to get the grease off it, then any residual charm.

"It looked clean to me," Wayde said as he took the wooden one I gave him.

"You haven't been using that one, have you?" I asked.

"Uh, no?" he said, telling me he had, and I sighed, my eyes closing in a long blink as I looked out the kitchen window at the night, vowing that he was going to taste it before anyone else. The worst it would do to him would make him go to sleep. Maybe.

I opened my eyes when Jenks flew to the fridge. "Whatcha playing?"

"Pixy sticks," Belle said, then slammed her hand down on the pile and yelled, "Squish!"

"Aw, pigeon poop!" Bis said, throwing his cards down. "Are you cheating?"

"If I was-s, I wouldn't tell you."

Wayde was smiling. It had been his idea for Bis to teach her how to read, and he knew the game was just a subterfuge to hide what they were really doing. "Any word yet on the amulets you sent out?"

I watched him blow on a spoonful of chili, and when he didn't fall down after tasting it, I pushed myself from the counter and started cleaning up my mess. "No. Nothing from either the FIB or the I.S." I looked at the clock on the stove behind him, then moved a dirty pot to the sink. It hit with a clang, and Wayde jumped.

"Why are you doing this?" he asked suddenly. "You're going in angry, and you shouldn't be going in at all."

"Dude!" Jenks exclaimed from the fridge, a hand of cards half his size in his awkward grip. "We talked about this!"

Wayde was standing before the oven, that spoon in his hand like it was a baton. "No," he said. "I think I'm within my rights here. I want to hear from Rachel why she thinks the I.S. and FIB can't do this without her. She made the charms. Enough already." He dropped the spoon back in the pot and turned to face me, his stance awkward and belligerent. "It's as if you're taking this personally. It's not your mother out there."

Taking a deep breath, I leaned my elbows against the counter, almost the entire length of the kitchen between us, glancing at Jenks to tell him that it was okay and to chill. "No, it's not my mother. But she was someone's daughter. She had hooves, Wayde. And fur." Pushing up from the counter, I ran a hand over it to brush the fir needles into my palm. Calm. Cool. Collected.

Faced with my nonchalance, Wayde lost some of his bluster, and he replaced the lid with hardly a sound. "It's dangerous going in already vulnerable."

"You should have seen Hot Stuff a year ago," Jenks said. "At least now she takes the time to plan things out."

A soft tapping of boots in the corridor, then Ivy breezed in with a clipboard of several color-coded pages. "Any word yet?" she said as she sat before her computer. She took a deep breath, read the tension in the air, and looked at me, her eyes starting to go black and her posture suddenly very still.

"Or at least she lets Ivy plan it," Jenks said snidely.

"Splat!" Belle shouted, and Bis slammed his hand down, barely beating her.

"You guys keep changing the rules!" Jenks exclaimed. Dropping his cards, he flew to Ivy, circling her in an annoying pattern until she flicked a long finger at him.

"What are we talking about?" the sultry vamp said as she leaned back and stuck the end of a pen between her teeth. I was pretty sure she'd sated her hunger yesterday, but the crime scene had probably put her on edge.

Jenks landed on the top of her monitor, and I turned my back on them to rinse out my rag. "Rachel taking an active part in this run," the pixy said. "Going in angry."

"It's how the woman rolls," she said, and I tried to ignore the ribbing as I wiped the counter down. "She shouldn't be going in at all, but she is. We'll adapt."

"Yeah, the angrier she gets, the more the bad guys suffer," Jenks said, his pride obvious. "And they are going to suffer this time, baby!"

I frowned, unable to meet Wayde's disapproving eyes as I tucked Jenks's toad-lily flowers in a cupboard to dry. I wasn't proud of that part of my personality—especially since I didn't have much magic anymore to back up what came out of my mouth. "I'm not angry," I said, shutting the cupboard with a thump.

"Yes, you are."

"I am not angry!" I shouted.

Bis made a small noise from the fridge, and Ivy looked up from her computer. Her eyes going to Jenks, she clicked her security back on, stood, and stretched. "Excuse me," she said, and left. Bis followed, clinging to the ceiling like a chagrined bat, Belle in a crook of his tail.

"Jenks!" Ivy shouted from the hall.

"What?" he shouted, hands on his hips. "She says she's not angry!"

Damn it, I hadn't meant to push Ivy's buttons. "Look," I said as I brought my attention up to find Wayde waiting. "You haven't really given this much thought, have you?" I said softly. "What's really going on here."

"Now you're in for it," Jenks said, hovering backward, enjoying this.

Wayde's posture shifted, and somewhat uneasy, he said, "I saw the man at the park. You need to back off and let someone else do this."

More tired than angry, I shook my head. Weres were not known for looking at the big picture, focused more on the here and now. They made great bodyguards and crime scene techs, but not so much so when it came to extrapolating. "HAPA is trying to make a source of demon blood so they can have their own magic. What do you think will happen if they're successful and humans can do demon magic at will? With a cost they don't believe in and a risk they can't see?"

Wayde made a "so what" face at me, but I could see him thinking, and when he seemed to sober, I backed off, satisfied.

"Who is going to control them if they're successful?" I said, tossing the rag into the soapy water to make it splash. "Who's going to keep them from wiping us out species by species? Not me. We aren't prepared for a new demographic of magic-using humans who are sadistic, power hungry, don't like Inderlanders, and see genocide as an acceptable form of communication." My head hurt, and I put a damp hand to it, smelling the fresh scent of soap. "At least demons have some sense of fair play."

I couldn't believe the words coming out of my mouth, but it was true. Their morals might not match ours, but demons did have them. *Demons had them . . . These humans did not. What is wrong with this picture?*

"Demons enslave people," Wayde said. He was taking bowls out of an adjacent cupboard, but hungry was the last thing I was.

"Not as many as you think. And they don't snatch innocents, only people who have made themselves available." My head hurt, and I opened my charm cupboard for a pain amulet. "I need to call Trent."

Jenks flew over from Ivy's monitor, and his sparkles seemed to make my headache worse. "Why? You think he might side with you?"

My headache eased as my fingers touched the amulet, and I shut the cabinet, Jenks darting out of the way with time to spare. "Yes, I do, actually," I said calmly as I tucked the amulet underneath my shirt. Trent played in the genetic pool like a lifeguard. He might be able to shed a little light on the situation, maybe give me an idea as to how close HAPA might be. Besides, I wanted to know if he was missing any equipment and if he had an antimemory charm.

Wayde shoved a bowl of chili at me, his eyes down and his back hunched. "Here," he said as I fumbled to take it. "If you're going to fight bad guys, you might want to eat."

I looked down at the bowl, then up at him, reading his distress. He wasn't happy about me working this run—hell, I wasn't happy about working this run—but he'd help me now instead of hindering me. "Chili? On a stakeout? I'm going to smell like—"

"The back side of a fairy's outhouse?" Jenks supplied, and I shifted my fingers on the warm porcelain so I could take the spoon Wayde was handing me.

"Thanks," I said, grateful that Wayde finally understood. He shrugged, and I wrangled the phone into the hand already holding the spoon. Chili in the other, I crossed the dark hallway to the dimly lit, pixy-noisy living room. Ivy had decorated it, apart from the holes in the couch from Belle's family trying to kill me last summer. The entire room was in soothing shades of gray and slate, the occasional splash of color keeping it from being bland and depressing. Someone had lit the fire and it was pleasant, even with the shredded pieces of toilet paper drifting down like snow.

"Okay, everyone out!" I said loudly over the pixy shrieks. "Take your fake snow and go! I've got to make a call."

They were good kids, and one of Jenks's eldest girls corralled the youngest, ushering them out the door. I set the bowl of chili down and plopped morosely into the overstuffed chair. Vampire incense and bits of toilet paper snowflakes rose up. A pixy buck darted in, gathered them up before they could move more than an inch . . . and was gone.

"You going with her?" I heard Jenks say from the kitchen, and I put my heels up on the coffee table and made myself comfortable.

"As far as the parking lot," Wayde said. "They won't let me accompany her on an official action, though I might sneak in. You want some of this?"

"Does Tink wear little red panties?"

I smiled at Jenks's enthusiasm, and I wasn't surprised when a streaming flood of pixy kids flowed past the living room and into the kitchen at Jenks's wing whistle. Punching in Trent's number, I listened to it ring as I ate a bite of chili. "Oh God, this is good!" I shouted around my full mouth, then swallowed when someone picked up the other line.

"Hello, Rachel," Trent's voice eased out, sounding both professional and annoyed.

I could hear the sound of babies in the background, and a high-pitched, angry wailing. They were still awake? It was almost midnight. Elves napped around midnight and noon.

"Trent?" I said, surprised. "Since when do you answer your own phone?"

"Since we got a new switchboard," he said tiredly, and I think he almost dropped the phone. "It recognizes your number and shunts you to whatever phone I cleared you for."

"Really?" I sat up straighter, surprised again. Trent irritated me like no other person on either side of the ley lines, but I trusted him—most days. Seeing him casual like this meant a lot to me. It was so rare he showed anyone anything other than a professional veneer. Two baby girls in his house were doing him worlds of good.

There was an expectant pause, and Trent said in a bored, formal voice, "You ready to take the bracelet off?"

"And have Al take off my head three seconds later? No." Though truthfully, I was more worried about Al forcing me to stay in the ever-after than anything physical he might do to me. In the background, someone started to cry. "Did I get you at a bad time? I'm sorry, but this is important. Ah, is this a secure line?"

Immediately I felt his entire mood shift, even through the phone line.

"Ceri," I heard him say over the receiver. "Could you . . . thank you. It's Rachel. She's fine, amazingly enough. At least I think she is."

I brought my knees to my chin, enjoying the little bit of his home life coming over the line. It seemed weird that Trent was a dad. Clearly he was taking his duties seriously, but after seeing the love in his eyes for his daughter, I wasn't surprised.

"You *are* okay?" Trent asked, repeating off the phone that I was when I said yes.

There was another moment of rustling and baby complaints, and then it grew quiet. "So what's not making the news?" Trent asked. "My usual sources are not saying anything."

Interesting, I thought as I tucked the phone between my ear and shoulder. "We found another body hidden at the Underground Railroad Museum," I said. "She was even worse than the one at the park. Lasted an hour maybe." The chili wasn't sitting well, and I set the bowl on the table at my feet, my knees bent. "She looked halfway to what I think the demons might have originally looked like," I added, and Trent made a small noise. "Glenn tells me that all the victims were carriers for the Rosewood syndrome."

Trent made another deep-thought sound. "They have some rare computers down there."

"Not anymore, they don't. The curator almost had kittens. Trent, the victim's hair at the park pinged on the body at the museum with a scattershot detection charm. They had it hidden under a demon curse I could see through because I'm disconnected from the lines."

The phone at my ear beeped, and I jerked my attention from the band of silver around my wrist, glinting in the firelight. "Ah, I've got another call coming in."

"Don't switch over," Trent said, his voice rushed. "You'll compromise the security. Your amulet pinged on a body unrelated to the one you took the sample from?"

"Yes," I said, feeling uneasy. "That's what worries me. I think they layered the woman's modified genetic structure over the man to change him down to his genetic level, enough so that a charm designed to detect minute amounts of a person found her. She was a mess," I said, unable to keep the distress from my voice. "If the genetic mutilations didn't kill her, she might have died from Rosewood. She lasted only a few hours by the look of it, but the men so far have lasted nearly a week. I think HAPA is trying to make demon blood."

There. I'd said it again, and it still made me queasy. "I thought you ought to know."

"This isn't good," he finally said, having followed my thoughts to the ugly conclusion faster than Wayde had, and I laughed mirthlessly.

"You think?"

"Two of my more sensitive machines went missing last week." Trent's words were clipped and short. "Apparently they're more portable than I thought."

"What did they take?" He didn't say anything, and I stared at the wall, waiting. "What did they take, Trent?"

"Two machines my father programmed for a branch of genetic research that has been outlawed. This is the second time I've been broken into in less than a year. Damn."

I could count on one hand the number of times I'd heard him swear. In the background, Ceri called faintly for Trent. "She's okay," Trent said, his voice muffled. "I'll tell you in a moment." When he came back to me, concern was heavy in his voice. "Rachel, maybe you should sit this one out," he said, and I flopped my head back against the top of the chair. "Let the I.S. and FIB handle it."

"Not you too," I almost moaned. "I thought you of all people would understand why I have to stop these guys!"

"If they're trying to duplicate demon blood, where is the sense in putting yourself within their reach? Let me put Quen on it. Actually, I'm going to do that anyway, so . . . wait, will you?"

I exhaled, tired, then jumped when my cell phone began humming from my back pocket. "Good. If anyone can help, it's Quen," I said as I twisted, trying to reach my cell. "But I can't sit here when Nina has promised to make me the scapegoat. We both know the FIB is in over their heads. I have to be there. Me, Ivy, and Jenks."

"You'd be more effective without that band of silver around your wrist," he said, and my lips pressed. I hated it when he was right.

"I'm the only person this side of the ley lines who knows anything about demon magic," I said as I put my feet on the floor and used two fingers to wiggle out my cell phone. My eyes went to the screen and my shoulders tightened. "Crap on toast. Trent? Glenn is on my cell."

"Rachel, we need to talk."

I couldn't wait anymore, and I flipped my cell phone up. "Glenn?" I said before it went to voice mail. "Hey, can you hold on a sec? I'm on the phone with Trent."

Glenn made a choking cough. "Mr. Kalamack? Rachel,

leave the man alone. He's not responsible for HAPA's activities."

"I know!" I said, trying to talk to both men at the same time. "Can you hold on a sec?"

From my other ear, Trent cleared his throat. "As entertaining as this is, Ceri and I would like you to come to tea tomorrow," he said dryly. "I'd like to talk further with you about the safeguards I've developed to make taking that charmed silver off your wrist safer."

I took a breath to say no, then exhaled, rubbing my forehead. "You think we can overpower Al? Find a way to keep him from taking me to the ever-after? Trent, I can't live there. I can't!"

"And I know Ceri would love to see you. The girls as well," he continued as if I hadn't said anything, but I'd rescued him from the hell of the ever-after, and he of all people would understand my fear.

"Rachel!" Glenn shouted into my other ear. "This is important."

"Tomorrow, say three?" Trent asked. "They'll be fresh from their naps."

It was more likely that he'd have the charms he wanted to contain Al prepped by then. I stifled a shudder. Maybe together we could keep Al off us long enough to explain, but caging him would only piss the demon off even more. "Tomorrow at three. I'd like to talk to you about a block for memory charms, too. And, Trent? I'm sorry about the park."

He grumbled softly. "Don't worry about it. Watch yourself in the meantime. Everyone knows who you are."

I couldn't help my smile. I might almost think he cared. "See you then," I said, and I clicked off the phone.

"Glenn?" I said, setting the landline phone down and shifting the cell phone to my ear. "Why didn't you call Ivy on her cell?"

"You are unbelievable," the man said, his irritation obvious. "Get your good boots on. I don't want to see you in garden shoes and grubby jeans anymore. Now Nina thinks we don't pay you enough. The amulets you gave me pinged. We've found their current base."

I sat up, adrenaline flowing. "Ivy! Jenks!" I shouted, then turned back to Glenn. "Where are you?"

"Five minutes from the church," he said, and I heard a background of radio chatter. "We have them triangulated at an abandoned industrial park. FIB and I.S. We're waiting for you."

They were waiting for me. I almost friggin' cried.

Jenks darted in. "We're on?" he asked, a bright silver dust slipping from him.

I eyed him, worried. He was flying well, and his winter clothes from last year were over his arm. "We're on. You'll need those. And anything else Belle has come up with for the cold."

"Tink's little pink dildo!" the pixy shouted, and he darted out, as excited as I was.

"We'll be ready," I said into the phone. "Thanks, Glenn."

"Don't thank me until it's over," he muttered. "You're staying in the car."

I snapped my phone shut and sank back into the cushions. *Car? I doubt it.* My eyes touched upon my band of charmed silver, and a flash of worry went through me. "That's why I've got the sleepy-time charms," I whispered as I stood. I was going to kick some serious ass, and I didn't need demon magic to do it.

Twelve

I stood from my crouch beside the warm, ticking car and handed Ivy the night binoculars. The brisk wind tugged at a strand of hair that had escaped my ponytail, and I tucked it behind an ear as I looked at the industrial building across the parking lot. The lights of Cincy were distant, and no moon lit the spaces in between. Deserted for forty years, the industrial area had been left to rot when the world fell apart. Trains still ran through here, but they didn't stop anymore.

I felt akin to the empty tracks and vacant buildings, abandoned when things went wrong while others thrived. Frowning, I fingered the band of silver around my wrist, thinking. Simply cutting it off would send a burst of ley-line force through me large enough to fry my brain. It was, after all, a piece of the elves' and demons' historic war, designed to make demons almost useless. Being able to cut it off wouldn't be very effective. It had to be disenchanted first. That meant Trent.

His offer to help me pacify Al long enough to explain had me more than nervous. I wasn't so sure that *anything* we could do or say would keep me on this side of the ley lines once Al knew I was alive. The ever-after was a hellhole, and despite my earlier thoughts that demons were more moral than HAPA, they were only when they felt like it. It was like trying to play cards with five-year-olds who kept changing the rules and lying. If you didn't have the clout to make them hold to their rules, they wouldn't.

I'm going to talk to Trent about the options. That's all, I thought, and stomach tight, I blew on my cold hands and shoved the thought away to worry about later. It was above forty-three degrees, so Jenks would be okay, but it was going to get colder the longer this took. Glenn had driven us here, taking the last road with his lights off and the car barely moving, his excitement pushing Ivy's buttons to the breaking point. Wayde had thought it was amusing, but I didn't see anything funny about it.

That had been about fifteen minutes ago, and I was getting antsy myself as I watched car after car show up and the slow deployment of people and equipment. Wayde was fidgeting by the I.S. van specially designed to hold magic-using criminals. He shouldn't even be out here, but they were cutting him lots of slack. Jenks was somewhere on the other side of the building. I didn't like him being gone this long, especially when it was so cold.

I grimaced, my low boots grinding into the grit. The parking lot was laced with cracks that allowed grass as tall as my thigh to grow, and the entire area reminded me of the tomato cannery that Ivy and I had once stormed when I'd been interning at the I.S. with her. A Were had died that night—one we'd been trying to save. I hoped it wasn't a premonition. The other Were, though, we'd saved. It bothered me that I couldn't remember her name.

I half turned when Glenn broke from the FIB officer he was talking to, his motions sharp as he stomped our way, dress shoes kicking up tiny pebbles and his suit jacket open. Ivy stood, exhaling as she handed me the binoculars. "Please tell me that's not the tomato cannery," I said.

"It's not," she said as Glenn stopped between us. His mood was tense, and I could smell his aftershave on the cool night air. There were two yellow FIB vests in his hand, and I eyed them suspiciously. They were probably ACG, but I still didn't want to wear one.

"You've been here before?" he asked as he handed one to me, and sure enough, my fingers felt the somewhat slimy feel of material coated with an anticharm spray. Maybe if I put it on they wouldn't give me any crap about being part of the team storming HAPA's hold.

Shaking my head no, I put the vest on over my thin leather coat. I wasn't wearing leather as a matter of style—though it did look good—but as a matter of my not wanting to leave skin grafts on the pavement. Chances were good I'd go down at least once before the sun rose. "No," I said flatly, not wanting to explain. "Is everyone *finally* ready to move?"

His motions holding an excited quickness, Glenn looked at his wrist, the dial softly glowing a faint blue. "No," he said, and Wayde rubbed his beard and edged closer, his hands in his pockets and his shoulders up about his ears. "Someone from the FIB wants to observe. We wait until she gets here."

Ivy rolled her eyes, black in the dim light. "Are they questioning your methods?"

"I've no idea," Glenn said, his low voice going lower. "They've never done this before."

A soft "mmm" came from Ivy, and she touched his shoulder. "You've never worked this closely with the I.S. before."

Wayde's posture said he wanted to argue with me again, and I turned my back on him, relieved when I spotted Nina striding in from the distant parking area at the head of about six people. "Excuse me," I said softly, then started her way. I could tell even from this distance and in the dark that it was Nina the DMV clerk, not Nina the dead vamp, and I wanted to talk to her.

Behind me, I heard Ivy say, "I'm not wearing that," and Wayde's nervous laugh.

Finding a smile somewhere, I pasted it on my face, extending my hand as I approached. The young woman took it, looking a little more unsure than that afternoon in the DMV office. A jumpy wariness had taken the place of her eager, confident excitement, and she looked somewhat wan, even in the dark, her attractive features tight and drawn. Nina the DMV clerk wasn't looking healthy anymore, even if she was better dressed and had a bevy of people looking to her.

"How are you doing?" I asked, and her eyes jerked to mine, probably catching the wisp of pity that had arisen from nowhere.

Her hand pulled from mine, and the positive smile returned—barely hiding a flash of fear. "I'm fine, of course," she said, her entourage coming to a halt behind her. "Why would I be otherwise?"

I shrugged, rocking back to get a glimpse of Ivy and Glenn. "I've seen how hard it is to have a god inside you," I said, and her eyes flashed a frightened black. Her hands trembled, and my old vampire scar tingled as she suppressed a rising hunger, a hunger *he* had instilled in her, one she didn't have the practice to contain on her own.

Crap, Ivy hadn't been kidding, and I stifled a surge of fear. This woman wasn't safe anymore. "I'm surprised he's not here himself. It being dark and all," I added, trying to say something to take her mind off her needs while she tried to get a grip on them.

Nina breathed slow and deep, standing stiffly as she regained control. She looked scared. She should be. "He doesn't come out of the basement much, actually," she said as she pulled her shoulders back to find a stronger posture. "He was—"

I looked up when her words cut off. Nina shivered, and like magic, I watched the I.S. boss slip in behind her eyes, shake the reins, so to speak, and take control.

" . . . waiting for you to arrive," she said, her voice now low and soothing as she eyed my leather with a much darker thought behind her appraisal. She blinked in appreciation, and I felt myself flush.

"Hi," I said dryly, and she shook her head.

"I already said hello," she said as she waved her people off and took my elbow to direct me back to Glenn, Wayde, and Ivy. "Are you not listening?"

"Don't touch me," I said as I pulled out of her grip. "Or aren't you listening to me? I don't like what you're doing to Nina. You need to spend some time helping her gain control of the crap you've been turning on in her brain before she hurts someone."

"Nina is fine," she said, smiling even more beautifully as she tugged the lace hem of Nina's shirt out where it belonged to make a more feminine statement in the otherwise business-looking attire. "I've not been at an actual tag for decades," she said as she watched Ivy and Glenn, still arguing over the FIB vest, then turned her attention to the dark building. "You've no idea how odd it feels to be able to use magic openly like this. You will participate?"

In the tag? I patted my hip, and then my back where my splat guns were. "Don't see why not." *And by God, they were going to let me,* I thought, glancing at Wayde.

The soft popping of gravel under tires became obvious. Ivy, too, looked up, shoving the vest back at Glenn, her posture becoming somewhat hesitant as she took Nina in, evaluating her, perhaps.

"About bloody time. I think they might be ready," I said when the FIB car swung around to park beside Glenn's, and Nina and I started toward it. "Ivy, have you heard from Jenks?" I asked, and she shook her head, clearly as worried as I was.

"Ahh," Nina said as she gazed at the sleek black car and rubbed her hands together as we walked. "Have you met Teresa Cordova, Ms. Morgan? She's the woman that Detective Glenn probably told you about. She wants to talk to you. Something about . . . a list?"

My pace bobbled, and Nina smoothly put a hand to the small of my back, propelling me forward. The scent of vampire incense rolled over me, and my pulse hammered as I was reminded of Kisten. "Uh," I said, halting ten feet from the still closed car.

Nina leaned close, laughter in her voice as she said, "That's what I told her you told me when I brought it up.

I don't trust her any deeper than I can bury her. Watch her face when she realizes who I am. She's fun."

The car door opened, and Jenks darted out, his dust a bright silver, telling me he was fine. "I could have made better time if I'd flown!" he exclaimed, making bright circles around me. "Tink's panties, Rache, the guns they got over there! You ready? Seen the plan?"

I held my breath until his dust settled. I had seen the plans—several times, actually. And "fun" wasn't the right word to describe the older woman getting out of the car.

Impatience colored her motions, making her look jerky as she tugged on her gray business skirt to get rid of the wrinkles. She looked about fifty-something, a very unhappy fifty-something in low heels and hose. It was hard to tell in the dark, but it looked like her hair was an attractive mix of hard black and silver that only a lucky few women get as they grow older. A lined face, narrow chin, and no makeup made her look even more severe. She sent her gaze over the assembled team, her expression looking as if she smelled something bad.

An aide had his head near hers, and the woman's eyes flicked to mine and held when he said something. Putting a small hand on his arm, she brushed by him, headed for me.

"Watch now," Nina said as she took a deferential step backward to leave me all alone. "She doesn't know it's me," she said into my ear, leaning forward to whisper it. "You can't pay for entertainment like this."

Curious, I thought, feeling vulnerable until Jenks landed on my shoulder. A vampire with a sense of humor? Perhaps the fun-loving, skydiving Nina was rubbing off on him.

"Teresa," Nina said suddenly, her voice pointedly cheerful, "have you had the pleasure of meeting Rachel and her team yet? They're one of the biggest assets this city has. Look, she brought her own spell pistols. Grand little weapons, those. I wish we'd had them when I was still in the field. They're powered by compressed air and don't need to be licensed!"

The woman's hand extending toward me faltered, and then she grimaced, reaching out to take mine in a firm grip, warm from the glove she was wearing against the chill. "I see you've met Felix," she said, her aide standing an irritating three feet behind her, talking into a cell phone.

Nina laughed at her sour expression, and I wondered. Felix? I thought he hadn't wanted me knowing who he was. "Pleasure," I said, wincing when my band of charmed silver slipped down to thunk into my wrist.

"I've explained this, Teresa," Nina said as our hands parted. "Call me Nina now. That is who I am." Leaning conspiratorially to me, she whispered loudly, "Felix was the name of the man I did my daylight work through when we first met. I guess that sort of thing sticks with the living. I miss him," she said, and I leaned away as Jenks buzzed a warning that she was too close. "He was very small, but quick. Died of an infected tooth, poor boy."

"You don't get out much, huh?" I said as I stood between Cincinnati's head of the I.S. and the head of the FIB, wondering why they were here. Really. Why were they here?

Nina smiled deviously, and something in me twisted. She looked like a woman, but the arrogant eyes raking over me were very male. "Not that anyone can prove, no."

Lips pressed, Teresa brought her attention back from Glenn, waiting a respectful distance away. "Thank you for your help today, Ms. Morgan," she said, a big "however" in her tone.

From my shoulder, Jenks coughed, saying, "Lame!"

Her eyes tightened at the corners. "And your help in the past as well," she said, her eye twitching as she saw the tattoo fluff visible on my collarbone. "It's the future that concerns me."

I kept my hands in my pockets as my tension rose. "We get the bad guys and go home. What's more to know?" This was taking forever. If it had been just Ivy, Jenks, and me, we would have been in and out by now.

The woman sighed, and Nina shifted, smiling as if waiting for the expected punch line. "Ms. Morgan, we would appreciate a list of the magic you can do as a demon," she said, and Jenks made a weird, almost unheard whine. "For your own protection."

"That's a cap of toad shit!" Jenks said, and I raised my hand as if to cover his mouth.

"Ms. Cordova," I said firmly.

"Doctor, actually."

Well, la-di-da. "Dr. Cordova," I started again. "If you want to know what demons can do, then go to the library and look it up. Then subtract ninety percent of it and you'll be close. I'm not going to give you a list so you can blame every demonic act on me."

The woman glanced at Nina as if for support, but the vampire was stifling a laugh, badly. Dr. Cordova's finger and thumb rubbed together, the fabric of her glove scratching, and I thought she ought to lose that particular tell. It made her look like a bad movie villain. "We're concerned that—"

"No."

Nina made a dramatic sigh. "She won't give me one, either," she lamented, and I tugged out of her grip when she tried to lay claim to me. What was it with vampires anyway? No sense of personal space.

Dr. Cordova's eyes squinted, and seeming to give up for the moment, she turned to Glenn. "Detective, I'm anxious to see how you work a team. I suggest you get to it."

Jenks hummed his wings as he stood on my shoulder, whispering a delighted, "Ohh, she's pissed, Rache. You made her look bad in front of walkie-talkie man."

"Then she shouldn't have asked for something I didn't want to give," I said, but I was starting to fidget, and I wished I could slip out from under her sharp gaze. You don't get to the head of Cincy's FIB division by being nice and working well with others.

Glenn had shifted closer, his uncomfortable stance melting into determination. "Jenks," he said, and the pixy took off from my shoulder, leaving a softly glowing dust. "We're under radio silence. Will you tell team two six minutes from . . . mark?"

"Gotcha," he said, and he was gone, his dust dissolving to nothing in time and distance.

Glenn's dark eyes took in Ivy, not wearing her vest, and me in my stylish, sulfur-coated nylon. Beside the car, Wayde stood in frustrated silence. He wanted me to stay with him at the transport van. It wasn't going to happen. Glenn clapped his hands together once. "Everyone's set. Let's go. Rachel, stay with Wayde."

Like hell I am. I shook my head at Wayde, making him grimace. My pulse jerked into a faster pace, and after checking my splat guns, I broke into a slow jog after Glenn, now headed for the building. Ivy was behind me, her footfalls almost unheard over my come-and-go breaths.

"I am *not* going to run over there." Teresa's voice came faintly. "Get in the car, we'll follow at a discreet distance and time."

"Rachel . . ." Glenn all but growled, and I smiled slightly at him as I jogged. Dr. Cordova's car door thumped shut, and he winced at the noise.

Looking back, I was surprised to find Nina tagging along with us, looking especially trim in her suit as she effortlessly loped along. "Storming HAPA with two dozen guns is safer than sitting in a parked car with Dr. Cordova," she said.

"Yeah!" Jenks was on Ivy's shoulder so his dust wouldn't give us away. "That woman is a pterodactyl."

"There," Glenn said, and we angled to the service door I'd seen earlier with the binoculars. There was an FIB man decked out head to toe in anticharm gear beside it, complete with a helmet, night goggles, and a weapon as long as my arm that looked like it should be in the armed forces, not a residential arsenal.

We came to a stop, none of us breathing hard. "Did you know he was coming?" I whispered to Glenn, and his eyes flicked to Nina behind him.

"I didn't know *you* were coming," he said sourly, looking

at the red-glowing screen the FIB officer held out to him. It was a breakdown of where everyone was. I hadn't known the FIB had such technology. Neither had Nina, if her high-eyebrow expression meant anything. The vampire had put on an I.S. armband during our jog here. It looked vaguely like something I'd seen in an old '40s movie, and again I wondered how old this guy was.

"Rachel, I appreciate your zeal. Go back to the car," Glenn said as he studied the screen, the information electronic, not magic, and Jenks snorted.

"The pixy is right," Nina said, and Glenn's eyes fixed on hers with a hard intensity. "Rachel is safer surrounded by the I.S. and FIB than sitting in a car, even if she is in close proximity to the very people who would like to see her captured. I'll keep an eye on her."

Glenn glanced at his watch, then dropped his head, tired. "You good with that?" he asked me, and as Jenks hummed his approval, I nodded, even as I edged away from Nina. I'd go with a chaperone if it got me inside. Once the fur started flying, it wouldn't matter, and I felt the bumps of saltwater vials I had in my belt pack, nervously counting them.

For another long moment, Glenn looked at me, his brow furrowed. "You stay behind us," he finally said, and I nodded. "Okay, let's go," he added, and eased to the door, already open and waiting for us. I slipped in after him, immediately sliding to the side and out of the small patch of lighter darkness. Ivy and Nina followed, and the FIB guy eased the door shut and remained outside to keep our retreat open.

I was in. Elated, I breathed the smell of moldy oil and decayed sawdust. It was a single large room with the ceiling girders glinting softly in the skylights. In the corner came a flash of a penlight, one, two, three.

"The primary entrance to the lower floor is over there," Glenn whispered in my ear. "Stairs. That's what we'll take. There's a service elevator outside against the far wall where the majority of the men will come in."

Ivy took off, loping toward the light when it blinked again. Clearly it was another FIB guy. They had this place stocked with them. I followed her, Nina taking the position behind me, and Glenn bringing up the rear. We said nothing as we passed the man at the top of the stairs. He was suited up head to toe in ACG like the one outside, making me feel naked with only my vest, but Glenn was wearing only a suit. And a pistol. And a really big grudge that Dr. Cordova was here.

The stairway was painted cement block, and the round pipe railings on either side were cold as I followed Ivy belowground, the air becoming chill and stale as we descended. Another man waited at the bottom. This one was an I.S. cop, which surprised me until I remembered living vampires could see in the dark better than the best night goggles. It was a joint effort in the truest sense of the word, which made me feel good.

The man respectfully inclined his head at Nina before gesturing Glenn closer. Apparently word of top I.S. brass possessing DMV workers got around. "There's an air shaft not on the plans," the living vampire said softly to Glenn, pointing behind him into the dark. "It vents out into the parking lot. They, however, are over there." He pointed in the other direction to a hazy light showing the low ceiling, and my teeth clenched.

Glenn nodded, and we crept farther into the dark. I wasn't used to having this much vanguard on my runs, but there was no such thing as being too careful when it came to black magic and HAPA. My pulse quickened at the growing light, and we slowed. The area downstairs appeared bigger than the area upstairs, a mere eight feet above our heads with thick pylons holding up the ceiling. It looked as if they'd stored huge tooling machines down here at one time, but the space was mostly empty now. My heart hammered when I heard a feminine voice call out, but it wasn't in anger or surprise. It was *them*.

We stopped at a thick ceiling support where another I.S.

officer waited. His small pistol was holstered, but the look in his black eyes said he was ready for anything. "There," he said as he pointed, and I leaned around him to look. My mouth went dry, and I felt for my splat guns.

The suspects had hung milky plastic sheets from the ceiling to the floor to make an indistinct thirty-by-thirty room. Fuzzy shadows moved in the bright light behind it. It looked as if the plastic was two layers thick to help retain heat. I could hear the soft droning of a machine, and the easy talk of two people who hadn't a care in the world—and it pissed me off.

Glenn pulled back into the shadow, and we clustered around him. He glanced at his watch, grimacing. "We have two minutes before they come in the far end through the elevator shaft on the other side. How many people are there?"

"Two males," the I.S. guy said, glancing first to Nina, and then Glenn. "Three females, one in a modified dog cage. We can't tell if she's conscious, but we're getting good aura impressions from her. We might be in time for this one."

God, I hoped so. I thought it odd that vampires preyed on people and yet had a huge drive to protect, but that's the way it was.

Glenn checked his watch again, and I wiped my hands off on my leather pants. Ivy retied her hair back out of the way. Nina cracked her knuckles and took off her coat.

Ivy stared at her. "You're not coming any farther," she said flatly. "I'll watch Rachel."

Nina stiffened. Silent, she handed her coat to the I.S. officer and commandeered his pistol.

"You don't have the practice resisting your instincts in a high-stress environment," Ivy said, her voice low but intent. "Felix, listen to me. *You will lose control.*"

"You overstep yourself, girl."

Nina/Felix's voice was angry, tight, and threatening, and I edged back. Glenn was getting huffy, but the I.S. officer had retreated, too, his eyes going dark as he read the emotions flowing between the two vampires, one dead for at least a hundred years, and the other living, but the epitome of vampiric lust, desire, and restraint all rolled up into my roommate.

"With all due respect," Ivy said, not backing down an inch, "you've been out of the field too long, and the child you're in has *no experience at all*. Stay here. Otherwise, I'll be watching you so you don't kill your host and you'll be more of a hindrance than a help. You're more of a liability than Rachel."

Glenn's frown deepened, and he turned his back on the room glowing with light and warmth just a few yards away. "If your presence is going to jeopardize a safe acquisition, you will remain here. Sir."

Yeah, like that was going to happen.

Nina sighted along the pistol at nothing. "I'm older than all of you together. I have control."

"Your host doesn't," Ivy insisted. "Felix, please. You know who I am. You know I understand what I'm talking about."

I held my breath as Nina finally looked at her, eyes squinted in thought. "Aye, you might at that. I'm thinking Nina is tired of her desk job and is impinging upon me more than I'm wont to accept. She's enjoying the adrenaline far too much. You're correct. I will stay and observe."

My exhaled breath slipped from me in a slow sound of relief as Nina gave the I.S. officer his gun back. But then Nina's head came up, and I watched her eyes dilate.

I spun when a high-pitched beeping came from the glowing rectangle of light. It was followed by harsh, feminine swearing, and behind the milky plastic, people moved. Someone had tripped an alarm, and I didn't think it was us.

"No!" Ivy hissed, her hand outstretched as Nina darted into the dark for the quickly moving shapes behind the plastic.

"Go! Go! Go!" Glenn exclaimed, and we followed.

Something had given us away before we were all in position, and if we didn't catch them in the next thirty seconds, there wasn't going to be anything left to catch.

Reaching them long before us, Nina tore a sheet from the ceiling, her trim, feminine outline suddenly sharp against the backdrop of silver machines, lab equipment, and people scrambling. A blond woman in a lab coat sitting on a rolling chair stared at Nina as she ran an arm over a countertop, sending glassware, papers, and samples into a sink. *"Accendere!"* she shouted, and a ball of flame rose up in it, incinerating everything.

Magic. *HAPA was using magic.*

Nina shouted her outrage and leapt at a military-looking man wearing a beret and a necklace of amber nuggets fumbling at the woman's cage.

"Ivy! They're hot!" I shouted as I burst in, meaning they were magic users, but she'd probably figured that out. Gasping in fear, a second dark-haired woman in high heels and jeans ran for a desk, and with tiny puffs of smoke, more evidence vanished.

"Felix, no!" I yelped when Nina yanked the man away from the cage, wrapped her hands around his neck—and squeezed. Ivy ran forward, and I drew my gun, hesitating when she got in my way.

"Get the women!" Ivy shouted, and I turned back to the blonde, who was laughing manically as she threw everything in the cupboard onto the floor and started another bonfire.

"Everyone freeze!" Glenn shouted, his stance domineering and his voice hard as he slid in with the I.S. guy behind him, screaming into the radio.

Dropping the radio in disgust, the I.S. officer ran for a second man in a pair of overalls trying to get that terrified woman out of her cage, and I heard a soggy thump of fists into flesh as they met. The alarm was still beeping. Where was the second team? Were they deaf?

"Too late, you putrid corrs!" the blonde in the lab coat sang out, smacking her hand into a big button set, then pushing off the counter, rolling her chair to a distant desk and the last set of papers. I shot at her, missing, then dove for the floor when she threw a spell at me, laughing merrily. My arms took most of my fall, and my teeth clicked, just missing my tongue. Why the hell was HAPA using magic?

Fall number one, I thought as I tossed my head to get a strand of hair out of my eyes.

His gun holstered, Glenn went for her, and my eyes widened. "I said freeze!" he shouted, his expression ugly with frustration. The scent of acid blossomed, sharp enough to make my eyes water, and the irritating beeping emitted a sad wail and died. That last button she'd pushed had fried the computers in a very permanent way.

"Don't touch her, Glenn!" I shouted from the floor. The plastic behind me was melting. Where was the other team?

But with a gleeful *"Doleo!"* the woman met Glenn's extended hand with her own.

Glenn choked, trying to pull his hand back from what would have been a submission hold, but it was too late, and he dropped to his knees, his mouth open in a silent scream. Holy crap, the woman was packing! That had been a black ley-line charm. I remembered Ceri using it on Quen once.

Glenn collapsed, and the woman ran for a second desk, littered with papers.

"You son of a bitch!" I shouted, shooting at her as she laughed and flashed a bubble in place to deflect it.

"Follow the drill!" the woman said as she stood over the desk, her arms full of notes as the I.S. officer, grappling with the man at the cage, crashed into a machine, out cold. The thick man in the overalls turned back to the cage, yanking the door open. And still, Nina choked the first man despite Ivy desperately trying to pry off her fingers.

The woman in the cage screamed when she was pulled out, babbling and begging him to let her go. Sitting up, I swung my pistol around. Maybe he didn't know how to set a circle. My eyes were tearing from the bonfire, and I held my breath at the twin puffs of air. "Damn it!" I shouted as they missed, and the man swung the woman over his shoulder and ran to the small row of cots. The alignment was off. This was the last time I trusted assassin weapons.

"Please! Help me!" the woman screamed, her arm reaching back for me.

I took aim, but the I.S. officer had regained his wits and darted after them, getting in my way. Glenn was still out cold, and that blonde in the lab coat was still burning everything she touched and laughing. As soon as she was done with the papers, she might start in on us.

The captive woman screamed again as the man flung open a panel in the floor, and in an instant, they were down it and gone. An I.S. officer followed.

"Damn it!" I shouted, not knowing who to shoot.

"Rache!" Jenks exclaimed, and I puffed a strand of hair out of my eyes as he hovered beside me, dripping a bright red dust.

"Where is everyone?" I griped, then shot at the brown-haired woman chucking paperwork on the bonfire, and she ducked, swearing at me. "This is insane!"

"Elevator jammed. Someone cut the power before they got out."

Swell.

Nina howled, and Ivy flew through the air, crashing into a pylon, then slumping to the floor.

Jenks darted to her, and my eyes squinted. I'd had enough. I should've come down here by myself, all quiet like, and just put them all to sleep. "Take a chill pill, Nina!" I shouted, and with everyone out of my way, I sat on the floor, aimed a little to the right, and plugged Nina. Twice.

The vampire spun: her fingers savagely bent, eyes black, hunched to attack. I could see Felix behind the out-of-control DMV clerk, and with a silent "Thank you," Nina collapsed with a sigh. The man she'd been choking fell beside her without a sound.

"Damned bug!" a high-pitched voice shouted, and I looked at the brown-haired woman swinging wildly at Jenks. She was bleeding from several scratches, and Jenks was easily staying out of her reach.

"Just flick the switch and let's get out of here!" the blonde said, standing with a cardboard box of papers on her hip as if I wasn't still in here and it was over. Maybe it was. Ivy was out, Glenn was down. I didn't know what had happened to the I.S. guy in the tunnel. And where was the rest of the team? Taking a friggin' coffee break?

Head down and one hand waving about as if at random, the brown-haired woman flicked a lever and a hiss filled the air, accompanied by the lightest touch of mist. "Tink's a Disney whore!" Jenks shouted, and dropped.

Sticky silk, I thought when my eyelashes became clingy, then panicked when the woman in the lab coat started for him. "This is how you take care of bugs," she said, her foot raised.

Jenks looked up at her, terrified, as he tried to get himself unstuck from the floor. Anger was a hot wash through me, and I shot at her. She froze, a bubble flashing into existence around her, but the air in my gun just hissed and nothing came out. *No wonder those assassins hadn't been able to hit anything,* I thought as I flung the gun aside and reached for the other one.

"It's that witch!" the woman shouted, her eyes going wide. "I told you putting the corr on display would get her attention. Get her!"

My jaw dropped. *Get her?* I shared a panicked look with Jenks, then lunged to the side as a ball of who-knew-what went hissing past me.

Suddenly I was dodging spells as the two women ganged up on me. I grabbed a still warm tray from the dying bonfire, trying to use it as a shield. It took a spell, then another. My anticharm vest would go only so far. The blonde came at me, and I spun, kicking her in the middle when she reached for me. She flew back into the labware she'd thrown on the floor, shrieking as she went down.

Grinning, I looked at the younger brown-haired woman, who abruptly looked scared. I didn't have time for any finesse, and I slammed the tray on her head.

"Way to go, Rache!" Jenks cheered as the woman dropped.

I turned, heart pounding at a soft click, but it was only the panel on the trapdoor clicking shut. The blonde had run. She'd left her friend out cold and just run. The sound of excited men grew loud, and I realized why. *Finally.*

Jenks rose up, his wings moving fitfully as he continued to dust heavily to get the silk off. "Son of a Disney whore," he swore, face red and head down as he worked at it. "What a bitch! Sticky silk? Who uses sticky silk?"

I looked at the brown-haired woman, and nudged her with a toe, not caring if she had a concussion. "People who know we might have pixy backup," I said. "Is Ivy okay?"

"I'll survive," she said softly, and I turned as she sat up with a hand to the back of her head. "How's Nina?"

Relief was a heavy sigh, and I looked at the downed vampire, slumped over the unmoving man. I thought she'd killed him. "She's fine," I said, glancing at my splat gun. "I'm sorry, but I spelled her. She was out of control."

"Tell me about it." Ivy rubbed her arm, looking up as the first of the FIB guys tore in, their guns out and screaming at us to freeze.

"We're good!" I shouted, hands high and gun dangling from a finger. "It's over! Don't shoot me, for God's sake! I'm wearing one of your lame-ass vests!"

Someone took my gun anyway, which I couldn't have cared less about, and after I glared at him for even suggesting I was one of the bad guys, I yanked the vest off and went to Glenn. Jenks was on my shoulder, and we peered down at him as Ivy stumbled closer. The charm he'd been hit with was bad, but it wasn't lethal.

Around us, the FIB guys were putting out the fire and securing what evidence was left. Someone had gone down the hole in the floor and an unconscious I.S. man was being hoisted up. Shoving aside the FIB guy shouting for a medic, Ivy knelt beside Glenn, gingerly lifted his lids and felt for his pulse. Shrugging, she looked up at me. "He's stable."

"Maybe he stepped in some of your potion?" Jenks suggested, and not knowing what else to do, I dumped a vial of saltwater on him to simply shock him awake.

Sputtering, Glenn came to. Ivy leaned back on her heels, and I sighed in relief. Wiping his face, he lay on the floor and looked up at us, then sat with Ivy's help. Looking angry, he watched Nina being dragged off the body of the unidentified man and the FIB crew yammering. The brunette had regained consciousness, and she was screaming about her lawyer as they cuffed her to that rolling chair. Yeah. Right. Insults were falling from her like prom-date promises, and my gut tightened. I hated the C word.

"I missed the fun," Glenn said, his breathing shallow as he glanced at her raving in the chair.

"You're all right," Ivy breathed, and Jenks and I exchanged a look at her worry.

"I'll live," he said, and we backed up as he got to his feet. "What did she hit me with? It felt like I was going to die."

"Pain charm," I said. "You passed out, which was probably the best thing you could have done," I said loudly when Dr. Cordova click-clacked in, her eyes cataloging everything and her lips curled in disapproval. She'd gotten here too fast. Maybe she'd tripped something.

"Let me go!" the brunette screamed, making the rolling chair jump up and down as she struggled. "I'm a scientist, you rutters! You're nothing but a bunch of four-flusher scabs, working with chubies and corrs! We're going to sweep the world clean of these filthy animals!"

"My God, the woman has a mouth worse than yours, Jenks," I said, and the pixy darted to her, his hands on his hips.

"Yeah? Well, you look like toad shit right now, Suzie-Q," he said, and she howled, lunging at him, making the officers laugh when her rolling chair moved a few inches and her hair fell into her face, which made her look even crazier.

"Uh, you did cuff her with charmed silver, right?" I asked, relieved when Glenn nodded.

"Goddamn scuppers! Let me go! You don't know who you're dealing with!" she yelled.

My jaw clenched at the insult. Glenn leaned toward her, eyed her up and down, and whispered, "We're going to find out. I promise you that."

The brunette stared at him, her chin quivering in anger. What was this woman on? She looked about twenty-something, but seemed to think she ruled the world.

Dr. Cordova smacked her gloves together before handing them to an aide, and Glenn straightened, turning on a heel to face her. "We'll be lucky if we get anything we can use in court from this," she said disparagingly, her gaze dropping to the char that was once evidence.

"Someone broke early," I said before Glenn could say anything. "An alarm went off. We were lucky we even got this much."

"Especially when some jack-crap lunker cut the power to the elevators *before* the doors opened!" Jenks added, and I swear I saw Dr. Cordova's eye twitch.

"Get a team in the escape tunnel," she said shortly, and the FIB officer looked past her at Glenn for direction. That time, I know I saw her eye twitch, and when Glenn gave the man a slight nod, the officer spun away, calling out names and converging on the hole with flashlights.

The suspects were long gone, though. Their departure had been executed with too much precision, too much . . . polished talent. I'd heard that HAPA had bases hidden in the Smoky Mountains, training areas and breeding grounds for hate cells. They knew what they were doing. *And they were using magic?*

Turning my back on Dr. Cordova's ongoing harangue, I dropped the wad of my FIB vest and looked past the dead man and Nina, still unconscious but arranged to look like she was sleeping. In the corner, as yet untouched and hopefully a source of fingerprints, was a makeshift kitchen and five cots.

Ivy sighed as she eased up beside me. "Better wake up

Nina," she said as she rubbed her scraped elbow. There was an ugly handprint on her neck that I was sure was going to bruise.

Dr. Cordova's voice cut off in midthreat, and she barked out, "Why?"

I looked her up and down. "Because it's polite," I said, pulling out one of my vials and dousing Nina with it.

"Give her room," Ivy said, pulling me back as the young vampire gasped, her eyes flashing open wide to show they were utterly black.

"No!" she cried out in a frightened, high-pitched voice.

The click of safeties going off was scary as people fell into defensive postures, but Ivy put a hand up. "Wait," she said sadly, and Nina's pupils shrank.

Nina sat up, her expression becoming frightened as she saw everyone looking at her. Her roving eyes landed on the body, and her lips parted in horror. "No, no, no!" she cried out, clearly Nina and not Felix, hunching into herself as she sat on the cold floor. "I couldn't . . . stop." Her face wet with tears, she looked at Ivy. "Please. Make it stop," she whispered. "I didn't mean to. It was too much. *I couldn't stop!*"

The last had been an anguished cry of heartache, and I felt a wash of pity. Ivy brushed past me. Kneeling beside Nina, she took her in her arms and held her as she wept. The FIB officers turned away, uncomfortable and not knowing what to do. Hell, I didn't know what to do. I had a bad feeling that Nina had overpowered Felix, even as the dead vampire had tried to stop her from killing that man. The power had been too much, and she'd lost it, exactly as Ivy had said.

Glenn crouched beside Ivy and Nina, his hand going out in a show of support. "Let me help you upstairs," he said softly, and Nina jumped, shrinking back as he touched her.

"Don't touch me!" she shouted, cutting through the softer conversations. Her voice was panicked, and my sympathy deepened.

Dr. Cordova cleared her throat. "Detective, can I speak with you a moment. You and your . . . team?"

It wasn't a question. Glenn and Ivy exchanged knowing looks over the huddled, shaking woman, and he drew back, standing with a resigned air. Behind him, Dr. Cordova waited, clearly eager to punch him a new one. Behind her, a mix of Inderland and human cops all reluctantly gathered closer.

"I'll take her upstairs," Ivy said. Jenks landed on my shoulder, and we watched Ivy lead the stumbling woman past the plastic sheets still hanging and to the elevator, presumably. If anyone could help Nina, it would be Ivy—and Nina was going to need help.

"Put her in the van," Dr. Cordova said. "She's going into custody for the murder of that man."

"What?" I shouted, spinning around so fast that Jenks took off, startled.

"She murdered Kenny!" the woman tied to the chair screeched, moving the chair as she all but jumped up and down in it. "That clot murdered Kenny! I saw her do it! You all did!"

"You've got to be joking!" I said, aghast, but Glenn was wincing, his head down. Ivy kept moving, her stance at once aggressive, protective, and defiant with her arm over the broken woman's shoulder. Wherever she was taking her, I doubted very much that it was going to be the waiting suspects van. She was going to be halfway to a safe house three minutes after reaching the surface. Nina was going to suffer enough emotional trauma. Putting her in jail wasn't going to help. *Was I as corrupt as Trent?*

"You're letting her walk away!" the brunette shouted at their vanishing shadows. "Damn clot suckers! You're not going to get away with this," she yelled, spittle flying as she leaned forward against her bonds and raved. "I'll track her down myself and—"

"Will you shut up!" I shouted, having enough of her to last a lifetime.

The woman grinned at me, her mascara running from her sweat. "What's the matter with you, you little chubi?" she mocked, and my breath sucked in.

Jenks's wings clattered, and the murmured conversations suddenly ceased as my face paled.

"What did you call me?" I said, my voice quavering in anger at the crude, vulgar insult aimed at witches that had evolved during the Turn.

"Chubi, rhymes with booby, which you don't have, or doodie, which is what your face looks like," she said smugly, leaning back and making her chair squeak.

Appalled, I could do nothing as the men and women behind Glenn retreated farther into the shadows. "Get her out of here," Glenn said harshly, and two men hastened forward to volunteer, living vampires by the look of it, wheeling the woman past the still-standing milky plastic sheets to the distant elevator, eager to get out of Dr. Cordova's sight.

"Get your fucking hands off me, you bloody clots!" the woman was shouting, and Glenn's face darkened.

"If I may speak to you, Detective?" Dr. Cordova intruded smoothly.

Glenn briefly acknowledged her, then turned to me instead, making her angrier. "I, ah, need to tie off a few ends here," he said, ignoring Dr. Cordova for a moment more. "I'll see you upstairs. You did good, Rachel, despite not staying at the car."

I smirked, and Jenks snorted from my shoulder. "Yeah, we all did good," Jenks said tartly. "Can we get out of here? Rache, I'll show you the way to the elevator."

He darted into the dark, and I shook hands with Glenn. Pulling him into me, I whispered, "I don't care what she says, getting a HAPA member alive is more than the I.S. or the FIB has done in forty years."

"That's what I'm afraid of," he muttered back. "I have to keep that foul woman alive."

"Now, Detective!"

Our hands parted, and I gave him one last look before smiling at Dr. Cordova's anger. The adrenaline sparkling through me was wearing off, leaving a pleasant feeling of satisfaction. Past the remaining sheets of plastic, the air was cooler and didn't stink of vampire. Breathing deep, I followed Jenks's fading trail of dust and the distant sound of the woman's continual threats. I'd take the stairs. If I was stuck in an elevator with her, one of us wasn't going to come out alive.

"I've seen you, chubi!" the woman screamed at me, seeing me through the closed doors as I walked into the puddle of light spilling out onto the concrete floor from the huge industrial-size elevator. "We're going to get you. Your clot and rotter can't protect you!"

One of the vampires with her stopped the door from closing so I could ride up with them, and I rocked back with my thumbs in my pockets. "You're kidding, right?" I said, and he shrugged, letting the door go.

"There are more of us than you!" the woman howled as the doors began closing again. "We're everywhere! You're dead."

Jenks landed on my shoulder. "Can't they shut her up?"

"Dead!" she shouted through the metal doors, and the elevator hummed to life, rising.

Behind me, I could hear Dr. Cordova reaming Glenn out. No one would be coming up anytime soon, and I reached for the fire door to the nearby stairway. The stairwell was dark and unlit, but Jenks was dusting heavily enough to see by. The walls were cold and damp, and I wrapped my arms around myself for the first couple of flights, letting go when my exertions warmed me.

"Don't let it get to you, Rache. She's just an ignorant lunker," Jenks said as he rested at one of the turns.

"Person," I said, head down to watch my footing. "She's a person. Scared and ignorant. She doesn't know better." That's what I kept telling myself, but I'd never been called a chubi before, even at school, not even by the mean girls.

The elevator was open and empty when I got to the top of the stairs and left the stairway. It was just as dark in the empty warehouse, but the lighter square of darkness showed clearly where the wide double doors were now flung open.

The silhouettes of the two vampires with the woman still handcuffed to her rolling chair showed clearly, and then I jumped at the twin pops of a gun.

"What the hell?" Jenks said softly, banking his dust.

The vampire pushing the handcuffed woman dropped. My eyes widened, and I put a hand to my mouth, my pulse jumping as the remaining one turned to a new figure in a long coat. It was the blonde. I could tell from here.

"Get Glenn!" I shouted at Jenks, and I started running.

The pop of a gun went off again, missing the remaining vampire as he dodged it and the glowing ball of magic the blond woman threw at him. It was her. She was trying to rescue her friend! And nearly everyone was downstairs listening to Dr. Cordova yell at Glenn!

That woman was gleefully throwing spells like it was a carnival game, making me wonder again at HAPA's new acceptance of magic even as they tried to wipe us out. Maybe she wasn't HAPA at all.

Jenks's wings were a clatter by my ear as I pounded to the open door, and I glanced at him. "Go get Glenn!" I told him again, and not waiting for his answer as I spilled out into the lighter darkness and cracked cement.

The vampire ducked another gunshot, then lunged at the woman, his hands outstretched to grab her.

"No!" I shouted in warning, and the woman still tied to the chair spun to me, her expression ugly as she struggled to free herself. But the vampire had touched the blond woman in the lab coat, who laughed maniacally as she coated him in a hazy green glow. He pulled back too late, clawing at his throat and screaming as he went down.

The sound was chilling, his shriek of pain in the black night. "Stop!" I shouted as I ran forward, my hand reaching to the small of my back to find . . . nothing. *Damn it all to hell, the I.S. guy took my gun!*

Both vampires were down, one still, the other writhing madly, clawing at his throat and leaving bleeding gouges. I hesitated over him, unable to do a thing as he died. The blond woman was kneeling behind the woman in the chair, the keys to the cuffs from the first vampire catching the faint starlight. "You stupid bitch!" I shouted as I lunged for them. The blonde was still working the cuffs. I had seconds.

"Turn me!" the woman in the chair screamed, and I jerked back as she kicked out at me, her tiny feet thumping harmlessly into my leg. I drew back and pulled myself together to give her a quick front kick and snapped her head back, but with a howl of revenge, she exploded out of her chair before I could recoup, her little fists flailing. She was out. I couldn't bring them both down unless I moved fast.

"Rache! Look out!" Jenks shrilled.

Shocked, I spun to him, then cried out as the rolling chair Suzie-Q had been in hit me square on. It took my knees out from under me, and I fell, hitting the cold pavement and yelping as soft body parts met hard, angular chair bits. *Fall number two,* I thought, holding my elbow as I sat up and kicked the chair away. Great.

"Where did they go?" I whispered, then jumped when someone grabbed my arms and shoved me down, face-first, onto the cement—again.

"Hey!" I yelped when my arms were yanked behind me and someone else jammed a sweet-smelling rag in my mouth.

I bit down hard, and a woman hissed as the rag was yanked away. "You Inderlander bitch!" the blond woman said, then smacked my face.

"Jenks! Get help!" I shrieked, then winced when something hit my head. I think it was a size 6 shoe, brown leather with a little rhinestone bow. More pissed than hurt, I wiggled, snarling up at the woman.

"Try her gut, Jenn," the blonde said, and my eyes widened as the brunette wound up and kicked me right in the solar plexus.

My air puffed out, and I curled in on myself, face grinding into the pavement. I couldn't breathe. Oh God. It hurt, and I struggled to hold on to my lunch, my arms pulled behind my back and my face bruised. My splat gun was long gone, and there was a wet spot on my thigh that I think was my broken vials.

"Get the bug," I heard the blond woman say matter-of-factly, and her lab coat came and went before my eyes. "Damn it, get the bug before he scratches my fucking eyes out, Jennifer!" she said again, louder.

Jennifer? That crazy woman in the chair was named Jennifer?

"Sons of bitches!" Jenks shrilled. "You friggin' sons of bitches!"

I had no magic. I was down. Despite all my preparations, I was helpless. Wayde was right. Trent was right. I was wrong, and now I was going to pay dearly for it. The blonde held my hands behind my back, and the familiar feeling of plastic went around my wrists. "Stop," I gasped as my air finally came back, and my fingers cramped when the strip was tightened too far.

The smell of propellant hissed into the air. Jenks hit the ground, struggling to run so they wouldn't step on him. His wings were glued shut. *Oh God. Run, Jenks!*

A car was coming from the distant parking lot, its headlights shining on me. Hope leapt in me. They'd heard the noise and were coming. "Over here!" I shouted, then grunted when *Jennifer* kicked me again. I squinted as the car pulled up to the warehouse door, its tires screeching. But my hope vanished when the window was rolled down and the man who'd run out with the woman who'd been in the cage shouted for the women to get in. Oh God. I was in trouble. From the trunk, thumps and screaming sounded.

Bobbing flashlights were coming closer from deep within the warehouse, and I frantically kicked out, fighting. If I could keep from being put in that car, I'd be okay. "Over here!" I shouted, squirming. "We're over here!"

In the glow of the headlights, the blond woman stood confidently, her fingers moving in a charm I recognized. Panic filled me. "Down! Everyone get down!" I shouted, but it was too late, and with a victorious glint in her eyes in the bright light from the car's headlights, the woman clapped her hands.

"Dilatare!" she shouted, and I cowered as a boom of sound pushed from her. The officers cried out and the lights fell and rolled as the force hit them. My eyes clamped shut, and my ears began to ring.

"That should do it," the woman said in satisfaction, her voice muffled to my spell-stunned ears; then she turned to me. "This is for hitting Jennifer," the blond woman said, her foot pulling back.

Her boot met my head, and I felt myself move, my body sliding across the cement a few inches. My head felt like it was exploding, and my breath eased from me in a soft sigh. A pair of masculine arms went under my arms, shortly followed by the pinch of being lifted and half dragged to the running car. I barely recognized the wonderful smell of fine leather car upholstery as my face hit it, and then the car light went off as the doors thumped shut.

"Suck it up, Gerald! I'm not going to sit in the back with that animal!" the woman said. "Drive!"

The engine thrummed, and my eyes shut, and I felt unconsciousness, creeping out from the pain, take me. But before I passed out completely, I had one last thought.

Five cots. But we had seen only four captors.

Thirteen

My forehead was pressed into something small and cold, and it hurt. My outstretched arm was tingling, as if something was wrapped tight around my biceps. The floor was equally cold and hard, and it smelled like bleach-washed stone. I could hear a series of soft noises that could only be described as a shuffling clatter. Behind that was a soft weeping.

A woman's high-pitched voice said, "Hurry up, will you? I've almost got this thing calibrated," and my eyes flashed open.

I was on the floor with my arm stretched through a narrow gap in the mesh of a cage, my head pressed into the wires. A syringe was stuck in me, and Jennifer was reaching to undo the tourniquet. Her eyes opened wide when they met mine, and her little mouth dropped into an *O*.

"Hey!" I shouted, painfully yanking my arm back through the mesh and sitting up. Jennifer's grip slipped from my wrist, but her hold on the syringe was tighter, and it pulled out of me, leaving a long, throbbing scratch.

Jennifer fell back on her butt, her round, baby-doll face showing fear. In a corner, a man in overalls, on his hands and knees, glanced up from wiring a TV monitor to a panel, then went back to work. I recognized him as the man who had been driving the car. The woman from the cage was in here with me, and she hid her face and sobbed, scrunching deeper into her corner.

"Holy shit!" Jennifer breathed, looking behind her to the blond woman in the lab coat. "You see that?" she said, scooting back to stand up. "You see how fast the chubi came to?"

"Maybe I should've kicked her harder," the blonde said, then turned back to the tabletop machine she was fiddling with.

"You call me that one more time, Jennifer, and I'm going to choke you in your sleep," I said, unwinding the tourniquet and dropping it beside me. "You're not getting any of my blood. Got it?" Oh my God. I was stuck in a cage who knew where? At least Jenks was okay.

Jennifer went white. "She . . . she knows my name!" she said, her face ashen and her grip on the syringe going white-knuckled. "How do you know my name?" she shouted, totally freaking out. "He was right! You're a demon!"

The woman trapped with me sobbed harder, her hands now over her head as if I were going to beat her. Yeah, that was a laugh. I was just as scared as she was. Where in the hell was I? It looked like one of those basement lockups they use to keep expensive equipment from wandering away, the painted mesh going from ceiling to floor on three sides, the fourth being the basement wall made of mortared stone.

My head hurt, and I rubbed at the new hole in my arm and scooted back. The cage wasn't very big. Maybe ten by eight, and just under six feet tall. We were definitely in a basement, one being used for storage by the amount of clutter stacked at the edges—no windows, low ceiling, thick stone walls by the absence of any other sound. The floor was old cement, and I could see a faint light from a bare bulb in the distance past the clutter. The light here was from floor lamps that looked like they belonged in the '50s.

"Chris! The witch knows my name!" Jennifer babbled, her pretty little size 6 shoes backing up on the poured cement floor.

Chris turned from the machine she was working with,

her expression cross, as if things were clearly not going well in calibration land. "Will you shut up!" she said harshly, the scratches Jenks had given her looking red and sore. "She probably heard it before she woke up, the same way you just told her mine, you idiot!"

Jennifer caught back her fear, her dark eyes squinting in anger from under her long eyelashes. "Fool," Chris muttered, jotting down a number before fiddling with a dial and dropping a vial of clear liquid into the machine's hopper and pushing a big black button.

The machine started humming, and Chris turned, stretching for a metal folding chair. Snapping it open, she sat in it, her back to me as she waited for the machine to cycle through. The man at the monitors grunted happily. Getting off the floor, he flicked a switch. One of the monitors blossomed to life to show a narrow empty stairway, a bare bulb with its paint worn away from the tread. Satisfied, he began working with another camera.

Jennifer hesitated, then sneered and flipped me off as if it was my fault. I didn't get this. Chris was clearly the power-hungry bitch, but what was the gutter-mouthed china doll doing here? She'd been freaky scary when we caught her, but fringe organizations promoting species eradication usually didn't mesh with women named Jennifer who had rhinestones on their shoes.

"I got enough to run a sample," Jennifer said, setting the syringe beside Chris. "When we need more, I'll just dart her."

Like an animal? Not good. Not good at all. This wasn't the first time I'd been locked up: Alcatraz, demon jail, Trent's ferret cage, a hospital bed. If I could escape that one twenty years ago, then this one was only a matter of time. But as I looked over the bleak surroundings, warm and damp, I wondered. This was bad. *Really bad.*

"I'm Rachel," I said to the lump in the corner.

"Winona," the woman said, lifting her head from her seated fetal position just enough to see me. Her brown eyes were terrified. "Don't touch me. Please."

She sounded frantic, and I stopped moving closer. Her tasteful pair of slacks and a blouse were wrinkled by several days' use, but expensive. Her low heels were functional. She was an office professional by the looks of it. Someone who would be missed right away. Either they were confident no one would find us, or she had something they needed that was worth the risk.

My head hurt, and I felt it carefully and found three sore spots. I only remembered being kicked hard enough to hurt once. My gut hurt, too, and I lifted my shirt and saw an ugly bruise just shy of my kidneys. A little higher, and Chris would have cracked a rib. Bitch. I reached to push my hair out of my eyes, finding someone had tied a knot it in. My face screwed up in anger as I realized it was a HAPA knot. Real funny.

My band of charmed silver slipped down as I worked the knot free, and my anger grew. I supposed I could break my hand and slip it off—and fry my brain in the process. I was a day late and a dollar short in talking to Trent.

Winona was crying, her brown hair falling over her drawn-up knees, and after I got rid of the knot, I inched closer. "Hey, are you okay?"

"Why do they want us?" she quavered.

The answer wouldn't make her feel any better. "I don't know," I lied.

In the corner outside our cage were five rolled-up sleeping bags and several bags from a chain grocery store. Two locked army green boxes were stacked near them. There was no kitchen, but a beaker of soup was warming up on a Bunsen burner on a makeshift counter. My stomach growled, and I took that as a good sign. It was obvious they hadn't been here long, but it was equally obvious that much of it had been waiting for them.

Someone likes to plan, I thought, and I rubbed my head.

The tabletop machine made a clattering of noise and spit out a small strip of curling paper. Chris tore it off and looked at it. "Spectrometer is good to go," she said, popping open the little drawer and tossing in the empty vial. "Where's her sample?"

"Here." Jennifer took the needle off and handed her the end of the syringe with my blood in it. "Be careful."

Chris's eyebrows were mockingly high. She looked from the blood to me before turning her back on me. "I don't think she's really a demon, charmed silver or not."

Jennifer leaned back against the card-table counter, crossing her ankles and trying to look nonchalant. "Me neither," she said, her flippant voice giving her lie away. "We caught her easy enough. She didn't do one demonic thing."

My eyes narrowed and I leaned forward, curving my fingers through the mesh. "Let me out, we'll see how demonic I can be."

Ignoring my threat, Chris popped another vial into the machine and hit the button. "I think it more likely that Captain America is wrong about her."

"What about the coven?" Jennifer's shoulders stiffened. "They called her one. They put *that* on her."

She was looking at my bracelet, and I sneered at her pretty little face, wanting to smash it.

"Propaganda," Chris said simply, busy with the machine.

"Yes, but he was right about us needing to move." Bending down with her hands on her knees, Jennifer looked at Winona as if she was an animal in a zoo, interesting but easily forgotten.

Chris grimaced. "I think he was the one who gave us away," she muttered as she went back to her work.

Jennifer stood. "Maybe we shouldn't have strung that guy up in the park. They weren't looking so hard for us before that."

"If we hadn't, Morgan would never have become involved," Chris said, preoccupied.

The man at the monitors, almost forgotten, made a noise of disagreement. "Eloy didn't give us away," he almost growled, his thick fingers manipulating one of the cameras. "Staying was a bad decision. *Your* bad decision, Chris. I'm not so convinced taking *her* was a good idea, either." He glanced at me. "Even if she's not a demon, she's too violent and we're not set up to hold two people."

Chris never moved, focused on the machine. "I didn't ask for your opinion, Gerald."

The man's eyes narrowed, deepening his few wrinkles as he scowled. "That putrid clot in the suit killed Kenny."

Taking a deep breath, Chris turned, spinning smoothly on the metal chair. Her expression was mocking, and her hair was starting to float. She was tapping a line. Jennifer flicked her attention between them, clearly nervous. "Don't you have more cameras to install?" the distasteful woman said harshly.

In a noisy motion, the man stood, his cameras tucked in the crook of his elbow as he stiffly walked toward the edge of the clutter. "You are a cold, unfeeling bitch." I heard him hit something out of my sight with a grunt, and Chris smiled.

Looking smug, she spun back to the machine. "I don't think Morgan's blood is going to be any different from any other corrs we've taken," she said, and I became more uneasy. They knew my name. They knew the coven had labeled me a demon. I'd thought that I could ride this wild horse, but it was running away with me and I couldn't get the bit out from between its teeth.

The machine whined harshly and spit out another curling bit of paper. Jennifer grabbed for it, taking a step back out of Chris's reach. Her eyes widened, and an awestruck "Dudes!" slipped past her lips.

"Give it to me," Chris snapped, lurching to her feet to take it. Frowning, she dropped back into her chair, sitting sideways so that she only had to turn her head to see me. I could tell it was bad news for me by the way Jennifer was shifting from foot to foot.

"Look at her Rosewood levels," the younger woman said, pointing down over Chris's shoulder. "My God! She should be dead!"

Exhaling, Chris handed the strip to Jennifer. "I've never seen such a narrow spike. Hold off on pasting it in the data book. I'm going to run it again."

But Jennifer had already pulled a worn theme book from a cardboard box and was leafing through it. I recognized it as one of the books Chris had saved from the industrial park, and I was wondering about their backgrounds when Jennifer taped the strip in, then signed and dated it.

Her brow furrowed, Jennifer studied the page. I could see about eight strips pasted in. Eight people, six of whom were probably dead. Her careful data taking was going to land her in jail for murder. "You should be dead," Jennifer said when she looked up.

"That makes two of us," I snarled, and Chris chuckled as she popped in a new vial and hit the go button.

"A Rosewood spike doesn't mean she is a demon." Chris stood and stretched, going to stir the soup with a glass rod. "It means she's a freak of nature."

"But it's the increased level of the Rosewood enzyme that's killing them," Jennifer said, her finger on my printout. "Not necessarily the transformations themselves. She should be dead with what she has. Clearly she's got something, maybe another antigen, that's counteracting the first, allowing her to survive. If we can find out what it is, then we can keep them *all* alive—"

"Why?" Chris interrupted her. "We're not a hotel."

"No, you're a butcher," I said, ignored, and Winona trembled in the corner. "Oh, crap, I'm sorry," I whispered, and she drew back from me.

"Keeping them alive isn't the goal," Chris said, making me angrier yet. "Getting closer to the ideal is. As far as I'm concerned, the shortened life expectancy is a boon. What would we do with them otherwise? Stack them up like wood?"

My God, this woman was unbelievable.

Jennifer dropped her eyes, looking uneasy as she leaned against the counter and hugged herself. Clearly she had some smarts if she was spouting off about antigens. Maybe I could work on her guilt and convince her to let us go.

The machine spit out another strip of paper, and after Chris read it, she set it on fire using the Bunsen burner. "I have a better way to find out·if she's a demon or not," she said, watching the paper go up with a weird green flame from the ink.

"What?"

Jennifer's voice sounded scared. Hell, I knew I was, and I scooted forward to the front of the cage, getting into the light. "Yeah, what?" I said boldly, but I wasn't. They had at least three drops of my blood left in that syringe.

Chris sauntered to me, crouching until the hem of her lab coat brushed the dirty floor. It was demeaning, being looked at like that, and I stiffly got to my feet, trying to hide where I hurt.

"The coven put charmed silver on her," Chris said as she rose as well, her eyes going to my wrist. "She can't do ley-line magic, but her blood is still good. I'm going to try one of those curses again—using her blood to invoke it."

Oh. Shit.

I looked at Winona, my thoughts zinging back to that monstrosity of a broken body found in the basement of the Underground Railroad Museum. That had been done with witch blood. Using mine might have even worse consequences. "Don't do this," I said, retreating from the wire mesh. "Please."

Seeing my fear, Chris smiled. "If it works properly, then Morgan is a demon and we have a good source of blood to pattern the synthetic stuff on."

"Don't do this!" I said, then jumped when Chris smacked the cage and Winona cried out.

"And if it doesn't work," the woman continued as she held the syringe with my blood in it up to the light to estimate how much was left, "we can use Morgan to shift the tolerance for the Rosewood antigens forward that much more." Chris set the syringe aside and smiled. "Like every other chubi we've had."

I pressed into the fieldstone wall, fingering my band of silver. This was bad. Really bad.

"Um," Jennifer said, shifting nervously as she slid from the table. "He said not to do anything until he gets back."

"The hell with him." Motions stiff, Chris strode to a cardboard box and began digging through it. "I'm not going to sit on my ass and wait. I'm the one doing the science, not him. If she's a demon, I want to know. Where's that damned book? The one with no title?"

Book? With no title? *Oh, no,* I thought, fear sliding into me when Chris made a happy sound and lifted out an old leather-bound book with frayed pages and a broken binding. It was a demon text, filled with demon curses. I could tell from here.

"Uh, ladies?" I said when Chris dropped the book on an open space and pulled her folding chair up to it. "I know you're all excited about thinking you're the superior species and all, but you seriously need to rethink this."

Chris's lips pursed. "Oh, that's interesting." I stared as she whispered Latin, practicing. "I need a strand of hair," she said, and I pressed deeper into my corner. Jennifer came to stand before the mesh door, and I growled at her, "Come in here, and you'll find out how it feels to have my foot in your face." But she only plucked a strand from the mesh, handing it to Chris and wiping her hand on her pants.

"I don't like using magic," she said, glancing at me. "Eloy says it's evil."

"Eloy is old school who calls blowing things up progress." Chris held the strand up between two fingers. "He has his place, but it's not making decisions. Magic isn't what makes them animals. It's that they prey on sentient beings."

"Kind of like what you're doing here, eh?" I said, but I was trembling inside. I had no idea what she was going to do, but it was going to be nasty.

Chris's attention flicked to me, then back to the book. "Anoint the hair, and break it while you say *Separare.* It's a communal curse, already twisted and just needing to be invoked."

Separare. That was Latin for sunder, wasn't it? Crap, what was she going to do? I pushed forward. "Don't do this," I said, gripping the mesh of the cage and giving it a shake. "I'm warning you!"

But what could I do, caged like a dog?

My pulse thundered and Winona looked up, scared, as Chris took a drop of my blood from the syringe and pulled my hair through it. *"Separare!"*

I braced for anything, staring as Chris's eyes grew wide. With a howl of pain, she shoved the demon book off the counter. It hit the floor as Jennifer gasped in fear, a few pages coming loose from the binding and drifting almost within reach.

"Chris!" Jennifer cried out as the woman gasped and hunched over in pain. "What's wrong?" she said, holding on to Chris's shoulders and trying to keep her from falling off the chair.

Was it the imbalance? I thought, feeling myself as if looking for a gunshot wound, but nothing felt different, nothing hurt. I heard Winona shift, watching now.

"Bitch . . ." Chris rasped, still hunched in pain as she glared at me.

"What happened?" Jennifer asked, bending over her in concern.

Chris shoved Jennifer away. "I'm fine!" she snapped, finally able to straighten up. Her eyes were bloodshot as she glared at me, her skin pale. "Not so helpless after all. Demon. Demon whore!" Taking a breath, she looked at her hands. They were trembling. "The bitch bounced the curse back at me."

Jennifer looked confused, but I wasn't. "Uh, if that band of charmed silver prevents her from doing magic, then how could she bounce it back at you?"

"I don't know!" Shaking, Chris stood up, bending to snatch the pages that had fallen out and shoving them into the front of the book before turning to glare at me, reminding me of Jenks with her hands on her hips like that. "Maybe curses don't work on demons. Maybe that's why the last woman died so fast."

Winona caught her breath, terror making her eyes wide.

I edged back from the front of the cage, relieved. The curse hadn't bounced back because I was a demon. Like Trent had said, if the curse worked through the demon collective, it wouldn't recognize me and would bounce back. I was safe. But Winona wasn't.

"I'm going to try it on the other one," Chris said, and a drop of ice ran down my spine. Winona had gone white, her fingers gripping her knees stiff and clawlike.

"No, you're not!" I shouted.

But Chris was drawing a long brown hair through her fingers, coating it with blood. I looked at Winona. Oh God. I couldn't stop this. "Winona," I whispered, and the woman's eyes met mine, scared. "I'm sorry."

"Separare!" Chris shouted, and the strand of hair broke.

Winona's eyes bulged, and she stiffened. Her desperate, despairing cry of pain echoed in the small area. She pushed to her feet, and I lunged for her, grabbing her before she could run into the wire mesh. I felt helpless, but I tried to make the pain go away by just being there, giving her something to feel besides agony.

"It's okay," I whispered, tears coming from me as she screamed in pain, her entire body stiff with it. "It's okay. It will go away. I promise." I didn't know if she could hear me, but her screams turned to sobs as she shook.

"It worked!" Chris crowed. "Jenn! It worked perfectly! We have it! I can do anything!"

I brought my head up as I rocked Winona, the woman slowly starting to relax as the pain ebbed. The blond sadist was almost dancing, her finger and thumb red with my blood and the gluttonous light of power in her eyes.

"It's getting better," I said to Winona, wishing I could help her. "See, it's going away."

"I want to go home," she cried as she slipped from me to the floor and huddled, her hair hiding her face. "I just want to go *home*."

"Me too," I said, feeling helpless. She'd be okay until they decided to do something else. "I'm so sorry. You shouldn't be here."

Gerald shuffled in, his expression irate and the cameras gone from his hands. "Keep it down," he said, weaving past the woman in the lab coat doing a happy dance as if she'd made a touchdown. "I can hear you all the way to the stairway." He looked at Winona, huddled in the corner with me, glaring at all of them. "What did you do?"

"It worked!" Chris sang, and Jennifer made notations in a second workbook, her expression pulled up as if she was smelling something rank. I knew it was the idea that Chris had done magic, not that she'd caused someone great pain. "I did a curse, and it worked. Morgan's blood is demonic. We have working demon blood, and it didn't cost my soul to do it!"

Which sort of answered the question of how they'd gotten a curse to hide that woman in the basement of the Underground Railroad Museum. They'd tried to get blood from a demon and had to settle for a curse to hide their mistakes. Whoever had twisted it was probably either laughing his ass off at their efforts or cheering them on to their destruction. God, I hoped it wasn't Newt.

I'd had it, and I fingered my silver band, feeling long past stupid. I had been so blind, clueless. If I'd been a normal witch, not having magic wouldn't have been a problem, but what ran in my veins was unimaginable power. It came with the ability to protect that power—and I had thrown it away. This was my fault. All of it.

"You made a woman feel pain," I said sarcastically. "Congratulations. I can do the same thing with my foot and it doesn't take a curse to do it."

"She's not a woman, she's an animal," Chris said, and my face burned.

The man frowned, then settled himself at the monitors, turning them on to show three new angles of dark basement. "Just keep it down," he said, turning his back as if a woman sobbing in the corner was an everyday occurrence. "They have tours upstairs, you know."

And now I knew it, too.

Jennifer slid her notebook in front of Chris, and the blond woman initialed it with a happy flourish. "I still don't like you using magic," Jennifer said as she put the notebook with the rest in the cardboard box. "It's evil."

"Magic is what is going to win this war," Chris said as she returned to her demon text. "If all it took was men with guns, we would've won it already." The zeal of the stupid in her, Chris began turning pages as if it were the winter solstice gift catalog, earmarking pages and cooing in delight at the new possibilities.

I gave Winona a last touch on the shoulder, then stood at the door to the cage. It was solid, locked with a chunk of metal. "You're not going to survive this," I said, shaking. I meant it to the bottom of my soul. I hated bullies, and that was all Chris was. A magic-using bully who had a problem with not everyone thinking as she did.

"I already have," Chris said lightly. "Mmm. I've got her baselines. Let's try the mutation curse."

The mental vision of the woman buried in the basement rose up.

Jennifer turned from where she'd been arranging the sleeping bags. "To change her blood? Why? It's demonic already."

"Not Morgan," Chris said, and I felt a wash of fear for Winona. "But we'll use her blood, not the stuff from the previous corr. Since her blood can invoke demon magic, it will work and then we'll have two of them."

My lips parted, and I looked at Winona. She was as terrified as me, and she hadn't seen the ruin of that woman buried in the basement. Jennifer had, though, and she looked uneasy.

"No," I breathed, coming forward to hold the mesh and

give it a shake. "Jennifer, you saw what it did to the last woman. It hits them too hard. For the love of God! Don't do this!"

"Shut up!" Chris dropped the demon book on the table. More pages separated, leaking out like blood.

"He's not here," Gerald said, and Chris just about lost it.

"I don't care!" she shouted. "If I say we do it now, we do it now! He could be in an FIB lockup for all we know! Get the corr out of the box and put her in the circle!"

Oh God, they were going to do it.

"You're not touching her!" I shouted, heart hammering. Winona was behind me, pressed into the wall, but Gerald grabbed a forked stick and opened the door to the cage. I watched the key go back into his pocket, knowing I'd never get hold of it.

I jumped for the open door, only to find the fork on my neck. Choking, I found myself pushed to the wall, my fingers trying to make a gap to breathe. Winona was screaming, and someone reached in and pulled her out. I tried to stop them, but Gerald knew what he was doing, and he didn't let up until they had her out and on the floor in a terrified huddle.

He pulled the stick off me. I held on to it, hoping he'd pull me out, too, but I let go when his foot came at me. I should have taken the hit.

The mesh door rattled shut, and I howled in anger. "I am not an animal!" I screamed at them, rattling it some more. Winona was crying on the floor. Jennifer had sketched a modest circle around her in the open area, and Chris was looking at her notes, as calmly as if preparing a class lecture.

"Don't," I pleaded, my hands hurting, swelling where I'd hit the cage. "Please. Don't. You're going to kill her!"

"Not if your blood is as good as I think it is." Chris looked up from her notes. "Get her out of her clothes. The last time we tried shifting one in his clothes, they stuck to his skin."

Winona lunged for the gap in the boxes in a silent panic, only to be brought down by Gerald. I could do nothing as she fought him while he took off her clothes, and I screamed at them, crying at my helplessness. This was the ugliest thing I'd seen. I hated them. I hated that I was helpless. I hated that I was grateful the curse wouldn't work on me and I wasn't the one naked in that circle. "Why are you doing this?" I shouted, my voice harsh.

Winona sobbed, cowering in a pile of white skin and long brown hair in the middle of the circle, her skin red where Gerald had gripped her. Tears ran down my face. I swore I'd make them feel the same pain, the same hopelessness they were forcing on her. I didn't care if I burned in hell for it. It was my fault.

"Why?" Chris let three precious drops of blood fall into a small copper pot that had taken the soup's place over the Bunsen burner. The scent of burnt amber rose, and my gut clenched when Chris made an "mmm" of approval. "Your kind is unnatural. Your very existence is a blasphemy," she said as she added what looked like a bit of shed snake skin. "If I'm successful, I can give humans back their rightful place. Maybe remove you altogether."

"Do you even hear yourself? See what you're doing?"

Chris ignored me, but Jennifer looked disgusted.

"Making her into a demon doesn't help you!" I tried again, and Chris laughed.

"We're trying to make demon blood, stupid, not a demon. What she looks like is just a side effect of the process," she said as she donned her gloves. They were anticharm. I could tell by the maker embroidered on the cuff. "Just think. If this works, you've saved countless lives."

I could have screamed, it was all so stupid, and I fingered the band of charmed silver. If only I wasn't wearing it, I could freeze her with a word and Winona and I could go home. "You've got my blood," I said. "Let her go."

Gerald stood between Winona on the floor and the opening to the stairway. He looked at Jennifer, and then Chris, clearly willing to do just that, but Chris was lost in the throes of unimaginable power, and I felt something in me die as she shook her head.

"I have been inching forward forever," she said as she stood over Winona. "I've seen the effect of this curse change as the blood did, becoming closer to actually working. Maybe with real demon blood, we'll get a real demon. Maybe she'll look just like you."

Her smile was mocking, and I bowed my head. I knew that wouldn't happen. So did Chris. She wanted the twisting of limbs and the pain. She liked it. What was wrong with her?

"Chris . . ." Jennifer said uneasily, but it was too late. Chris had already stepped across the circle to join Winona, and a barrier of green and black had risen, preventing any interference.

"Winona!" I said loudly, hoping she could hear me. "I'm so sorry. Winona, listen to me! It will be okay. I'll get you back to normal. It will be okay!"

Oh God, let it be okay.

"You are such a liar," Chris said, and laughing she finished the curse. *"Ta na nevo doe tena!"* she said triumphantly, and I swear the shadows grew, daring to come out farther than the light confined them. It wasn't Latin. It sounded . . . elvish? Winona gasped, then screamed.

"God, let me be the one to stop them," I asked as Winona made a choking gurgle and clenched under a wash of green and black. I could do nothing as she writhed on the cold floor, Chris watching in delight as Winona's legs turned to spindles with hooves, and her head became heavy with two horns. A curly red pelt blossomed over her, and her long brown hair fell out in sheets. A black tail lashed, as long as her legs. She coughed, her voice harsh and as gray as her skin became. Tears streamed down her face, now hard with a too-strong jawbone and forehead. She was unrecognizable.

"I will undo this," I whispered to her, finding her goat-slit eyes and holding them with my gaze. "Just hold on. I promise," I said, weeping with her. "I promise."

I never made promises. But I did this time, and I meant to keep it.

The circle fell, and Chris clapped her hands. "Look! It worked!" she crowed, dancing out of the circle. "It was easy! So damn easy!"

Gerald looked down at the woman at his feet weeping on the floor. "She looks the same as the last woman did."

"But she's not *dying* like the other one did!" Chris said triumphantly. "I told you it would work!" She peered at Winona, her lips curling. "You are an ugly son of a bitch."

I was going to be sick. I knew it. "I promise," I mouthed to the woman, horrified as she touched her hair that had fallen out, and defiance sparked in her. Her lips pressed down until her new canines made them bleed. She tried to stand and make a run for the unseen stairway, but she was unbalanced, unable to stand on her new hooves, and she sprawled ungracefully, her thin black tail whipping about to send her lost hair flying.

"Get her!" Chris demanded, flushed, making the scratches Jenks had given her stand out. "Put her in the cage with the other one!"

Gerald gingerly grabbed Winona's shoulder and leg, and threw her into the cage when Jennifer opened it. Winona hit me in a tangle of bone and tail, and I scrambled to escape. I was too slow, and the door was shut by the time I got to it. Jennifer backed away, fear in her eyes.

I looked at Winona, huddled in the back of the cage again. I reached out and touched her shoulder, warm and fuzzy under my hand, and she shivered as a harsh croaking came from her while she tried to breathe through her sobs. "Give me her clothes," I said flatly. "We aren't dogs."

"No, you're demons," Chris said, and she turned her back on us, excited, as she went to her textbook.

"Give me a blanket!" I shouted, but no one listened.

A warning beep had started at the monitors, and Gerald turned. Jennifer froze, and Chris looked bothered. "It's just him," Gerald said as a dark shadow passed under the first of the cameras.

My head came up, and I tried to see around Gerald.

Someone had shot the two vampires when Chris was freeing Jennifer—Captain America, Eloy, who was apparently good with a sniper rifle. *You are mine, moss wipe.*

"Good," Chris said, standing tall and firm beside her new demon book, a hundred ugly possibilities at her fingertips. "I want to talk to him."

"Me too," I said as a man with a rifle and scope walked in.

Fourteen

I see you managed to get away," the man said, casually dropping an army-green satchel on the makeshift lab bench, right on Chris's notes. My eye twitched, and I shifted to stand in front of Winona as the woman shook in fear and shock. "Nice job fucking up a perfect exit plan, Chris. Where's Kenny?"

Interesting, I thought as I took in the spare, athletic, somewhat military-looking man as Chris ignored him. He was dressed in jeans and had an army surplus jacket with a pre-Turn logo, a black T-shirt underneath it. His boots were suspiciously clean, but I could see a hint of dried mud on them, telling me he'd wiped them down recently. His hair was brown and cut close to his head. Average build, average height, nothing to make him stand out except perhaps the hard determination in his eyes and his stance, which would make me believe he was an alpha Were if I didn't know better. No, this guy was HAPA, from his pre-Turn army boots tied with HAPA knots to the necklace of amber nuggets looking odd and out of place around his neck.

Gerald's face went red, and he shot me a glance. "A clot in a suit choked him to death. They almost had Jennifer."

"I saw. You left evidence of yourselves everywhere getting her free. Thirty more seconds, and I would have shot you both instead of the clots." He set his rifle atop the monitors and faced me. "*That* is a mistake," he said, meaning me.

Jennifer fidgeted, head down as she subserviently moved the man's satchel to the pile of sleeping bags in the corner and began to set up the camping cots. Gerald returned to his instruments, avoiding the rising tension between Eloy and Chris with a tired familiarity.

"I'm not going to take responsibility if you can't follow a simple order," Eloy said.

Chris looked up, pissed and still riding the high of having done that curse. "I'm in charge in the field. Not you."

"Sure." Turning his back on her, he came to stand before the cage. "Why are there two goats in the box?" he said as he crouched, looking at us. "I told you, one corr at a time. God, that is one ugly bitch." He hesitated, turning to Chris even as he crouched before us. "She's still alive?"

"It's Morgan. Her blood worked!" Jennifer said as she unrolled a bag on a cot, and Eloy's eyes flicked to mine, holding. There was no fear—it was worry laced with knowledge, and my heart pounded. He looked away first.

"She came after us, and well, why not take her?" Jennifer said cheerfully.

"*That's* Morgan?" he said, and I gave him a bunny-eared kiss-kiss. "Shit," he mouthed, and I smiled bitterly at him. Yep, that was the reaction I liked. "Taking her was a mistake," he said as he stood and strode to Chris. "I told you not to put that corr on display!" he exclaimed, his back stiff as she continued to ignore him, her neck becoming red. "This is *exactly* what I was trying to prevent. I told you—"

Chris looked up, slamming her pen down and cutting his tirade off in midstream. "Either you told me a deliberate lie or you're less informed than usual. I'm tending to go with the first because you have too much intel to not know the coven destroyed her magic."

"It's cut off, not destroyed," Eloy said, glancing at me. "She's dangerous, magic or not."

Chris shifted slightly, crossing her legs at her knees.

"Morgan is helpless." She sniffed. "Her blood is good, though."

Clearly unconvinced, Eloy bent over her, putting one hand on her paper to prevent her from continuing her notes. "You deliberately disobeyed a direct order."

"I don't work for you."

Eloy's jaw clenched, and he straightened, clearly trying to keep from losing it. "This is a military operation, not your personal in vitro experiment! They're going to double their efforts to find Morgan. That I can adjust for, but we are *not* equipped to move two people without losses. They shouldn't even be incarcerated together."

"Relax, goat girl can't even stand up," Chris said as she continued to write her notes.

Pissed, Eloy squinted at her as Gerald and Jennifer quietly went about their separate businesses. "You have seriously jeopardized the entire operation for the last time, Chris. You're out. Both you and Jennifer. You have five minutes."

"Me!" Jennifer said, aghast, as she shook out another sleeping bag. "I told her not to!"

Eloy had his hand on the butt of his pistol. "I'm calling it in, and you're going to go back to the hospital where you belong. Using magic is a *mistake*!"

Chris slammed her pen down, standing to stare at him, eye to eye. "Look at that goat in there with her," she said, pointing. "Use your eyes. She's not dying. The curse worked with Morgan's blood, you cretin. As soon as we can synthesize it in quantity, we can wipe every last Inderlander from the face of the earth with one curse, and you tell me I've jeopardized the operation? That I've made a mistake?"

One curse. That's what the demons had twisted to try to kill the elves, and look what happened.

"*I* am the science here," she said confidently. "*You* are the muscle to keep the FIB and the I.S. off my back. If you can't do that within the parameters *I* set, I'll send you home and get another one just like you." Her stance stiff, she dared him to say anything, confident she had the clout she needed. "We don't need your kind anymore, Captain America," she said, pushing him out of her way and sitting down. "And you know it. Military idiots who use machine guns to open a jar of pickles. We are fighting magic with magic, and for the first time we are *winning*."

Hands slowly unfisting, Eloy walked with a heel-toe sharpness on the dirty cement as he went to the cots and sat on one. He frowned, his feet spread wide as he rested his elbows on his knees and assessed me, thinking. His eyes were too bright, too clever for my liking as they traveled over me, lingering knowingly on the bit of tattoo that he could see.

On the other side of the room, Chris confidently went back to work. She may have thought she had won and was in charge, but she wasn't. Scientists never won over the military. When push came to shove, she'd do what he wanted or find herself dead in a hole. He knew it as well as I did, and he didn't mind letting her think otherwise until the last moment.

Winona was making a breathy hiccuping sound, and I took her hand, thinking it felt too thick and short. At least she had fingers. "You're okay," I said softly, not liking Eloy's stare on me. "I'll get you back to normal."

How am I going to do that? I thought, but she nodded, her head suddenly falling forward as she forgot her head was top heavy now.

Jennifer finished with the last cot, her motions more sure as she started unpacking a small box of journals rescued from the last site.

"What were her Rosewood levels?" Eloy asked suddenly, and Jennifer jumped.

"Look for yourself, you lazy ass," Chris muttered, head bent over her notes, and Eloy's eyes narrowed.

"Excuse me?"

"I said, all you have to do is ask," Chris said sarcastically, pulling the data book closer and tossing the black-and-white journal across the space.

Eloy deftly caught it, propping the book on one knee as he leafed through it. "Peaked the chart," he said as he thumbed to the last entry. "She shouldn't be alive."

"Neither should any of you," I said. "Tell you what. Let me out, and I can fix that."

Chris slammed her pen down and half turned to me. "My God, doesn't she ever shut up?" Getting to her feet, she went to stir the soup, which made me all the hungrier. Her mood was shifting now that Eloy wasn't barking at her.

"And the other woman's levels?" Eloy asked, giving me a glance as he stood, book splayed open on his palm as he came to sit in Chris's chair—still playing the dominance game.

Expression mocking, Chris leaned over to flip back a page. "Here are her initial levels," she said, pointing. "We haven't gotten the new levels since her adjustment."

Her eyes flicked to Winona, and it was all I could do to stay quiet. Adjustment? She called that an adjustment? How about I adjust her right out of existence?

Eloy closed the book fast enough to make Chris's short hair shift. "Why not?"

Chris picked up the hot beaker with a Kevlar mitt and poured some soup into a black mug. "She didn't die, for one," she said as she shook off the mitt and blew on her soup.

"Thank God," Gerald muttered, almost forgotten at the monitors.

"We'll get the sample somehow," Chris finished, looking at me and sighing as if I was an errant child.

"Way to think ahead, Einstein," Eloy said, and she frowned.

"You're not touching Winona," I muttered. I had the sudden urge to use the bathroom. This might be a problem if I kept threatening them, but I couldn't stop myself.

Jennifer slid the last book away and turned, smiling brightly. "Want me to dart them?" she asked, eyes going to a box on the counter.

"No," Eloy said, exhaling softly. I didn't like the way

he was looking at me, like I was an animal he wanted to study—but one too dangerous to keep for long.

"Yes," Chris said, immediately countermanding him. "At least she would shut up. I thought the whining and crying was bad, but this is worse."

"Let me try," Eloy said, and Chris leaned back on the narrow counter. The light from the single bulb in the center of the room made her expression hard to read. Eloy put his hand up as if asking for patience. "I'm sure I can reason with them," he said, the expression on his face empty as he looked at me.

"And I'm just as sure that Dorothy's flying monkeys are going to come out of your ass," I said, and Gerald rose with a stretch to get some soup, chuckling.

Eye twitching, Eloy stood before me, his hip cocked as if his feet were sore. He was inches from the cage. I could throttle him if I could get my hands through the mesh. "Will you let us get a blood sample from Winona?" Eloy asked calmly, as if he was reasonable and I was an idiot.

"No." I lifted my chin, feeling powerful though I was on the wrong side of the cage. They wanted something. Bad enough to give a little, maybe?

Gerald growled something, and Jennifer sniffed as Chris turned to watch, amused. "You really think asking her is going to work? Jenn, just dart them."

"Wait!" Eloy said, inching closer, his gaze becoming canny, as if he knew I'd been caged before and had escaped. I wasn't cowering in the back, but snapping at the lock, and he respected that even as he thought I ought to be exterminated.

"You stole Kalamack's machines," I said. Not a flicker of change marred Eloy's expression, but behind him, Jennifer's mouth dropped open in a sweet little *O* of surprise. Honestly, how had she gotten mixed up with these people? My lips quirked as I got my answer from her, and Eloy dropped back a step, clearly peeved by her lack of finesse.

"Will you ask her to stick out her arm so we can take a blood sample?" he asked again.

I edged closer to the mesh, mocking him. "You've been stealing machines and living off the back of civilization like the scum you are. Moving around like this isn't cheap, either. HAPA doesn't have that deep a pocket. You're a back-woods, ignorant fringe group that should have died out with the space program in the forties. Who's funding you?"

Eloy never dropped his gaze from my eyes, but I could see the tension in his shoulders. "HAPA is bigger than you think," he said. "Our people are everywhere." Behind him, Chris went back to her work and Jennifer took the second mug of soup, which Gerald had poured her. The hierarchy was being played out more clearly than if they had been lions on the savanna.

"Who is funding you?"

Eloy smirked. "If you don't convince her to let me take some blood, they'll put you to sleep."

Winona's breath caught. Put us to sleep, and then take more blood from both of us. "Why are you talking to me?" I said, disgusted. "She is her own person. Ask her yourself."

Eloy turned to her, his lip curling when he saw her face, but I hadn't won anything in our verbal pissing match. "Can we please have some blood?"

Winona awkwardly flipped him off with her thick fingers, and I almost applauded.

"Have it your way," Eloy said, and my heart pounded as he turned away. Jennifer made a happy sound, setting her cloverleaf mug down and starting for a box.

These people are nuts! I thought, then sighed when Winona scrambled in a crawl to the front and shoved a skinny, red-fuzzed arm through the wire mesh with frantic haste. "You don't have to do this," I said, but if I was honest with myself, I was relieved.

Winona shrugged. "Ah don' wan oo be spelled," she slurred, her face going almost black in embarrassment as she tried to speak. "Oh, dhit," she moaned, feeling her mouth. "Ah dink mih 'onge is 'orked."

I winced, drawing back from the door as a clearly disappointed Jennifer noisily dropped a dart gun back into the box. As Chris snorted, Jennifer got her blood-gathering stuff together and cautiously knelt before Winona to tie her arm off. Gerald, too, was watching, his back to the monitors and his arms crossed over his chest. Eloy's eyes never left me as he assessed the threat I posed. Maybe I should have cried in the corner like Winona.

"Thank you," he said, and Winona jumped when the needle slid in.

Jennifer undid the rubber band around Winona's arm, nervously sneaking glances at the woman's mutilated face. It really was horrific. Chris made a scoffing sound and dug her spoon for the last bits of soup. "Bloody waste of time. We should have just darted them."

"Got it," Jennifer said, and Winona pulled her arm back, her eyes widening as she discovered it was double jointed. She gingerly rubbed the spot since Jennifer hadn't thought to give her a cotton ball to stop the bleeding. I could see why. I might use it and the tourniquet I'd pulled off my arm earlier to escape with. *God!*

Jennifer got to her feet, and Chris set down her soup mug and met her at the machine.

"A few more blankets would be nice," I said. "You're down a man. We can use his."

Chris tossed the old vial out and dropped in a new one. "Don't open that cage, Eloy."

"Winona needs her clothes," I said softly. "And I have to go to the bathroom. You've got to have a way worked out by now. I'm what, the eighth person you've held?"

Winona gasped, and I mentally kicked myself. Chris hit the go button on the machine and turned, smiling beatifically at me.

"Wha appen oo da uhders?" Winona stammered, then took a breath and tried again. "What appened do da uh-thers?" she said more slowly, her brown, goat-slitted eyes showing fear.

I sat down beside her, my thoughts going to the woman

they'd buried in the basement of the museum. "They died from Rosewood syndrome," I said, unable to give her the entire truth.

"My sisder died of th-that when she was th-three months old," Winona said, and I nodded. Her speech was getting better.

"You're a carrier," I said, giving Eloy a disparaging glance as he got the last dregs of soup. "That's why they abducted you."

The machine dinged, and Chris reached for the tape. I held my breath, wondering if Winona would be able to do demon magic. But Chris frowned, handing the strip to Jennifer to paste in her lab book. I exhaled, relieved.

"That's good," I whispered. "You're not a demon, Winona."

The woman pulled her hand from mine and hid her face in her arms, now draped over her thick knees. "Whoopie friggin' do," she said to the cold cement. "If ah look like this, you'd . . . dink ah might have some of da perks."

Perks? I looked at my band of silver. I'd never thought of demon magic as being a perk and to having been labeled as one, but the madness I was now wallowing in wasn't working, either.

Chris methodically cleaned the machine and ran a clear sample through to recalibrate it. "So are we good here for a few days?" she asked Eloy.

Eloy had put himself half in the dark on one of the rolled-up sleeping bags, again watching me. "Should be. I contaminated everything the FIB and the I.S. had before it got back within city limits. All they have now is a sample of dog spit. If they use it to make a finding charm, they'll lose an entire day until they figure out they're following a stray," he added, watching me for my reaction.

I shrugged at him, wondering if we would get any of that soup.

Eloy took his eyes off me, and I stifled a shudder. "We should be good for four days. Maybe longer. They'll probably try to find us using Morgan's hair. Good thing I put you so far from the city center this time." Tilting his head back, his Adam's apple moved as he got the last swallow of soup.

Jennifer leaned over her lab book and tore a strip of tape from a dispenser. "I don't understand how they found us this last time. Too bad we can't transform her, too," she said as she taped Winona's results down. "Change her so far that the charms won't recognize her," she added, her head tilted as she assessed the latest addition to her scrapbook from hell.

Arts and crafts. Would the woman's talents never cease?

"Change her?" Eloy said, looking alarmed.

"I'm not risking changing her blood by mistake," Chris said, and Eloy looked concerned as he eased down on a cot and stared at the low ceiling, his hands laced behind his neck and his boots on the sleeping bag. His military training was showing, and I wondered how he'd gotten through the armed services with the same attitude that got him into HAPA.

"They'll find us," I said, as much for myself as for Winona, and I mentally marked where Jennifer slid the lab book away. I wanted it when I got out of this cage. The floor was cold, and I shifted uncomfortably.

"Doubt it," Eloy said to the ceiling. "You really don't have any contact with the lines, do you?"

My brow furrowed, and I was silent for a moment. "Why?"

Getting up, Eloy went to talk to Gerald.

"Why?" I shouted, and Winona winced. Fear slid through me, and I turned to her. "Winona, you're a witch. Can you see ley lines with your second sight?"

She nodded, catching her head before it snapped forward this time. "We're underground," she said, looking scared.

I totally understood—you never knew what you'd see when you used your second sight underground—but I gave her hand a squeeze and she finally nodded. Closing her eyes, she seemed to relax as she brought up her second sight. Then she tensed. "Dere are two lines crossing not twenty feet from 'ere," she said, her eyes opening.

I exhaled slowly, hopelessness soaking into me. Eloy had picked this place well. Two lines crossing so close would make it difficult for charms to find us. The searcher would have to be almost on top of us. Add to that the fact that they probably wouldn't widen the search outside of Cincy's city limits for a few days. We were on our own.

Eloy looked back at me, cocky and satisfied. He didn't have to say a word.

Winona was looking at her hooves, unaware of how deep in the crapper we were, and I wasn't going to tell her. "I always thought my feet were too big," she said, her voice raspy but her diction clearer. A heavy tear brimmed and fell, making a shiny line on her dark, almost leathery face.

I leaned over to give her a hug, feeling her changed bone structure. "It's going to be all right," I lied. "I will do everything I can to get us out of here." That had been the truth, but it was just as true that we were in big, big trouble. We were on our own and pretty much helpless unless I could get the bracelet off safely.

I was starting to wonder why I had put it on in the first place.

Fifteen

The last of the peanut butter was sticking to my teeth, as it always did, and I took a swallow of the tepid water. It was hard with minerals; we were on a well. *He wasn't lying when he said that we were out of the city,* I thought as I set the plastic glass down and pulled my knees to my chin. I'd been stuck in this cage for almost twenty-four hours, but there was a feeling in the air that I didn't trust. I'd been watching Eloy to try to figure out what was up. He'd come in early this morning, grumpy and stiff, making me think he had spent the night outside on sentry detail.

Jennifer had left an hour ago wearing a pair of nursing scrubs and a doppelgänger curse invoked with my blood. Chris had spent the morning getting twenty years of dust out of the workings of one of the older-looking machines, now glinting a dull silver. Gerald was on a bathroom break with Winona, serving as both her balance and jailer.

Winona was a good girl. She could use the bathroom any time she asked. They let me go only when both Eloy and Gerald were around, and Eloy was gone more often than not. Right now, he was fiddling with Gerald's security cameras, trying to get them to pan. He was somewhere in the basement, visible through one of the monitors as he stretched and sweated. A light flashed on the panel, and Eloy grimaced, reaching around to try again.

Sucking on my teeth, I leaned back against the wall as I sat on the cold floor, a stinky sleeping bag the only thing between me and the cement, watching the subtle flow of emotions and feeling of expectancy. Everything had changed earlier this morning after a hushed, intense argument between Eloy and Chris. It had taken place out of my hearing and almost out of my sight, at the edges of the light. Eloy got his way in the end, though, whatever it was.

The snap of Chris carefully closing the box of her vials drew my attention, and I sighed. She had been counting them again. God, she was worse than Ivy.

Ivy, I thought, feeling my chest clench. By now she must be worried to the point of tearing someone's throat out, but she and Jenks would find me—and get me out of this cage. I fingered my band of silver, thinking I'd been more than stupid about this. No wonder Trent thought I was brainless. He'd been trying to tell me, and I hadn't listened. I guess I hadn't watched the right movies to know that with ultimate power comes ultimate responsibility. My blood was power, and I had a responsibility to keep it safe—even if that meant I had to hurt someone in the short term.

I didn't like it. But it was a moot point if I couldn't get out of here and fix things, and my jaw clenched as I watched Eloy through one of the monitors, squinting as the camera panned back and forth. Nodding in satisfaction, the man walked out of the camera's range. He flashed up on a second monitor before vanishing behind the new camera in turn.

"Hey, how about a bathroom break?" I said loudly. Chris had left a screwdriver on the counter after replacing the back of the machine, and I wanted it.

"Use the bucket," Chris said, not bothering to turn around.

"Winona didn't have to use the bucket," I said, then looked at the monitor and the gray shape coming down the stairwell, one hand on the railing, one hand holding a shopping bag.

"Shut up, you stupid little chubi," Chris said, pushing back from her chair as if she'd been killing time up until now. Sure enough, she went to her cot and grabbed her thick, army-green coat, shrugging into it as she muttered under her breath.

"Bathroom?" I prompted, ignoring the slur.

Chris searched her pockets until she found a tissue and wiped her nose. "Hold it," she said as she threw it away. Not looking up, she yelled, "Gerald! Jenn's back! Let's get this over with!" Rolling her eyes, she turned to the monitors, now showing Eloy and Jennifer. He'd taken her shopping bag for her all polite like. The woman didn't look like herself, being about twenty pounds heavier and just as many years older. It had to be her, though, seeing that Eloy was talking to her and the matronly seeming woman looked right up at the camera and waved.

I fidgeted, balling up my napkin and throwing it at the bucket. My blood had made the doppelgänger curse work, and it bothered me, even though voluntarily giving them ten cc's of blood had gotten me a much-needed trip to the bathroom last night. I was an unwilling demon, doling out wishes to an insane practitioner. At least Al could say no. I suppose I could say no, too, and pee in a corner. Maybe I should have. But then they just would have darted me.

"You think you're part of this, but HAPA is going to kill you when they don't need you anymore," I said, and Chris stiffened. "Why do you think Eloy is here? To keep you safe? They're using you, and as soon as they don't need you, you're dead."

"You open your mouth one more time, and I'll dart you this shy of a coma," she snarled, but I'd seen her flash of fear. Maybe she was smarter than I'd given her credit for.

The fast-paced sound of heels on cement grew loud, and Jennifer click-clacked into the circle of light, looking refreshed and red cheeked if nothing like herself. Eloy set her bag on the floor and went to Gerald's security camera, making sure the joystick worked.

"Why are you bothering to fix those?" Chris said snidely. "They don't need to pan."

"Why are you opening the back panels of those old machines?" Eloy said dryly. "They aren't going to work any better with the dust out of them."

Chris leaned against the makeshift lab bench, the nylon of her coat scraping it as she looked him over. She was ugly with her short hair, no makeup, the scratches from Jenks healing—and the fear I had reminded her of. "You do your job, I do mine."

"Uh-huh," he muttered, still standing hunched over the equipment.

"Wow, it got cold out there!" Jennifer said, her gaze going over the small room and seeing that Winona and Gerald were absent and that Chris had her coat on. "I thought we were staying in tonight," she said, picking her bag up and setting it on the counter. A new name tag attached to the pocket of her scrubs peeped out past her unbuttoned coat.

"Captain America has plans," Chris said shortly. "Any problems getting the stuff?"

Jennifer glanced at me, and I gave her a bunny-eared kiss-kiss. "No," she said, her eyes darting away. "The charm worked great. In and out, no problem." She shifted her shoulders as if shaking off a chill. "I feel like I need to take a shower, though."

"It's a curse, not a charm," I said loudly, and a flash of fear crossed her as she took wrapped sterile syringes out of the bag. "You should see how black your soul is now."

"Your aura is fine," Chris said. "Don't listen to the corr bitch."

"Filthy," I mouthed at Jennifer, and she paled. Hey, I took my digs when I could get them.

Jennifer set a small bottle of injectable something beside the syringes. "Why are we getting a new subject already?" she said, clearly still uneasy. "We can't move three people if we have to bug out. Eloy says the next base isn't ready yet. If something goes wrong and we have to leave, we've nowhere to go."

Chris frowned, crossing her ankles and barking, "Break

that curse and put your bar clothes on." Turning to the dark, she shouted, "Gerald, get goat girl back in her cage! Let's go!"

Goat girl? Oh, I owed her some serious foot-in-gut for that one.

Jennifer didn't move, but the curse washed from her, leaving her in clothes too big and a very concerned expression on her face. "Four people can't move three."

I stifled a shiver when Chris smiled at me. "We'll burn that bridge when we come to it."

What she meant was, they'd take the most useful and kill who was left. I suddenly felt like I was on the *Titanic*.

Jennifer spun to Eloy. "You're going along with this?" she asked, and Eloy shrugged.

All my warning flags went up, and Chris noticed I was watching Jennifer intently. Her eyes never leaving mine, she said, "Can I talk to you for a moment, Jennifer?"

My eyes narrowed in suspicion as Chris put a hand on the woman's shoulder, whispering into her ear. Jennifer's eyes went wide, then she looked at Eloy as he stood and stretched, finally bending to check that his boots were tied. Frowning in thought, Jennifer went behind the curtain she'd hung last night between her cot and Gerald's, changing into her bar clothes, I expected.

Eloy stood beside the syringes and picked up the tiny bottle, squinting as he read what it contained. "You know this is toxic, right?" he said, jiggling it in his palm. "You'll have to wait twenty-four hours for it to work its way out of the subject's system before you can alter him."

Alter? My face burned, and I sat up, pulling my cold back from the stone. "Why not just say mutilate, Eloy? That's all it does."

"That's not for the next subject," Chris said, annoyed. "That's for *her* if she becomes a liability."

Eloy nodded, and he set the bottle down with a tap. Her frown deepening, Chris turned to the stacked clutter. "Come on, Gerald!" she shouted. "It doesn't take that long to use the can!"

"We're coming!" came back faintly. "She can't walk that fast, for God's sake!"

Jennifer pushed the curtain aside, dressed in some slinky black dress, high heels adding four inches to her height. She looked at me and beamed. I felt like the butt of a joke being told out of my earshot, and I touched the corner of my mouth to see if I had peanut butter on it. The awkward trip-trap of Winona's hooves became obvious, and my pulse quickened. The door to the cage was going to open.

Gerald's hunched form eased into the light, Winona looking small and frail on his arm as she wobbled, hanging on for dear life. They'd given her blouse back to her, and it looked odd with her thick thighs and cloven feet showing from under it. Balancing on her tiny feet with that heavy head must be hard. She looked okay, if having wrinkly gray skin, a curly red pelt, goat feet, and a tail somewhere between a monkey's and a stingray's was okay.

Winona gave me a smile, her oversize canines making her look like she was growling, but I smiled back, tensing to jump at the door.

Angry, Chris turned to Gerald. "Hurry up. I'm tired of smelling these stinking corrs!"

"All right, all right!" Gerald muttered, his head down as he wove Winona through the last of the boxes and toward our cell.

I got to my feet, eyes on the door. "Hey! What about my bathroom break?"

"Use the bucket," Chris said, arms crossed as Winona grabbed the wire mesh for balance while Gerald fished the key from his pocket. There was only one, and Gerald had it.

"On your knees, facing the wall," Gerald demanded, and shoulders slumping, I turned my back on them and dropped to my knees. I don't know what movie he'd been watching, but it was effective. *No big loss,* I thought as I heard the door open and Winona totter in. Even if I did manage to get out, I wouldn't get anywhere. Not with them standing around watching.

Hearing the door shut and lock, I stood and turned, reaching to take Winona's thick hand. Her eyes met mine in thanks, and I helped her to her side of the cell and supported her until she was down. They really didn't need to cage her. She could barely stand.

Chris put the bottle of sedative in her purse with a couple of syringes. "I doubt moving three people is going to come up," she said. "We've never had a subject live longer than three days." She looked at Winona. "This is what, day two?"

"Winona is healthy." *Why are they scaring her like this?*

"And that's why she was puking all night?" Chris gestured for Jennifer to get her coat.

My heart pounded as the distasteful woman sauntered closer until only a few feet, some twined wire, and a canyon of morals separated us. "If it should come down to it," Chris said, her words crisp and mocking, "your surly nature might outweigh your blood, and we'll take Winona instead. Maybe you should be nicer."

I jumped when she smacked the door, my face burning when she laughed. "The last person who hit my cage died under a pack of dogs," I said, but she'd already turned away.

"Okay, let's go," she said, and my anger turned to hope when Eloy stood up from the monitors. *They were* all *leaving?*

"Rachel?"

It was Winona, and I turned to her, almost impatient until I saw her fear. My thoughts jumped back to what Chris had said. After a moment of hesitation, I went to her. "It's okay," I said, sitting so I could see if they took the dart gun. "You're not going to die. You were just getting rid of something you couldn't digest anymore."

"Maybe I should die," she said, and I stiffened. "I mean, what good am I now?"

I shoved my first response down, and settled myself more certainly beside her, rubbing my legs, aching from disuse. "Don't talk like that," I said, watching them bundle up with hats and thick coats.

"You sure they can't escape?" Chris said as she tugged on her gloves, and Eloy rattled the door.

"I can lock them in the bathroom," Gerald said, and Chris snickered.

"At least then she would stop whining about potty breaks." Her head came up. "Okay, let's go. We have a small window and I want to use it. I've been stuck down here for two days."

She was halfway to the edge of the light, and Jennifer and Gerald fell into place behind her, talking between themselves, their tension rising. Eloy was last, and I wondered at the look he gave me as he left.

Slowly their voices became faint, and with a thump that seemed to shake the air, the lights went out. Winona sighed, and I looked at her in the glow from the TV monitors. I could see them on the monitors at the stairway. Then even that light went off and the monitors glowed a dull gray of nothing.

"Couldn't leave the light on, huh?" I said sarcastically.

Winona moaned as if in relief. "I'd rather have them off," she said, surprising me. "The light was hurting my eyes. That annoying humming stopped, too."

I wondered if she was hearing the electricity in the wires. Jenks said he could. It was how he'd found that worn spot in the church's wiring last year before it burned the place down.

My chest hurt. Damn it, I was going to get us out of here. Somehow.

Standing up, I squinted at the ceiling where the wire mesh met it, wondering if there was a weak spot. I hadn't looked yet, knowing I'd never be able to take advantage of it if they knew I'd found one. Fingers looping into the mesh as high as I could reach, I gave a tug. Nothing.

Winona sniffed, and I moved a foot down and gave it another shake. My thoughts kept going over the last half hour: the conversations being said without a word, that look Jennifer had given me when Chris whispered in her ear. What bothered me the most was that Eloy hadn't protested their going out and grabbing someone else. He knew that putting three people in this cage was a mistake. Someone would die if they had to move fast, probably Winona, seeing that she couldn't walk and they could make more of her with my blood. Not that they cared.

My head hurt, and I moved down another foot and shook the mesh. And what was HAPA, a military outfit, doing working with scientists and magic, the same people that HAPA blamed for the Turn to begin with? Maybe once they got their magic elixir, they were going to turn on them, make the scientists take the blame and wipe them out with the rest of Inderland. Sounded about right.

I moved another foot, to the corner. Giving it a shake, I frowned. It was even sturdier with that embedded pole. Perhaps it was a group of frustrated scientists who were backing HAPA. If they used genetic research to get rid of the Inderlanders, then maybe the genetic medicines that had saved so many human lives in the past might be considered safe again. I dropped back to my heels, rubbing my head. Maybe Chris was going to run off with her research when they were almost done, and sell it to the highest bidder? Yeah, that sounded like something she'd do.

"We're going to die," Winona whispered, and I slid down a foot to give the mesh a shake.

"No, we aren't."

She sniffed, her rough voice sounding almost normal. "You know what the stupid thing is? I'm going to die, and I'm worried about my cat."

I turned to her, a lump of a shadow on the floor. "That's not stupid," I said, then gave the mesh a kick. I was worried about Ivy and Jenks. And my mother.

"I wish it wasn't so dark," I said, giving the mesh another shake. "If I could touch a line, I could make a light and maybe find the weak spot in this cage."

My breath caught, and I turned around to Winona. "Hey, you're a witch," I said, and she made a barking cough of a laugh. "No, I mean you can touch a line, right?" I said, and the shadow she was nodded. Her little horns caught the dim light and gave me the shivers.

"I don't know any magic," she said. "Especially any as complicated as making a light."

I quit my testing of the wire mesh and came back to her. "I do," I said as I stood over her, the first hints of an idea making me jittery. "I can teach you." I sat down in sudden thought, remembering how thick and stubby her hands were now. Still, she had fingers, and a ley-line charm shouldn't be beyond her.

"Really?"

It was the hope in her voice that did it. Stubby fingers or not, we had to try. "Maybe we can use it to get out of here," I added, taking her hand in mine and studying it. "I know a spell that warms things, burns them up. If you heat up the wires . . ."

She pulled her hand from mine. "I'm scared."

"Winona—"

"What if we get out?" she said, her voice louder. "What happens then? Rachel, I'm a monster!"

My jaw hurt, and I forced myself to relax. "You are not a monster."

"Then I'm a freak!"

Frustrated, I took her shoulders in my hands, making her look at me. "You are not a freak. They cursed you. Curses can be untwisted."

There was a glint of light on her cheek, and she wiped a stubby hand under her eye. "Promise?" she whispered. "I don't think my cat will come back if he sees me like this."

I knew she was trying to be funny, and it made me all the more determined that she wasn't going to end her life like this. "I promise," I said, but inside I was cringing. *I promise? I can't promise her anything. What am I doing?*

"Okay." Taking a deep breath, Winona seemed to settle herself, as if taking on the burden of seeing a great task to the end. She hadn't merely agreed to try to get us out, but agreed that she'd try to escape, to risk others seeing her like this, and find a way to get back to normal.

I gave her a hug, proud of her. She smelled different now that she'd gotten that protein out of her system. Meadowy and sunny. Nice.

Pulling back, I nodded once. "Okay." I thought as I looked at the door, knowing the lock was the weakest spot. "I've never taught anyone, but I've got a white ley-line charm that I use to warm water. I don't know why it wouldn't work on metal, too. If we can get the lock or hinges hot enough, maybe we can break the latch." Stretching, I gave the door a shove, and it gave slightly under my foot. "I'll do it first, then you try. You sure you can see me?"

"I can see everything," she said, her big eyes blinking once. "I can see better now than when the lights are on."

Okay-y-y-y. "I'll give you the words and finger motions together," I said as I scooted closer, and her head tilted down. "From candles' burn and planets' spin, friction is how it ends and begins," I said, feeling silly, but the rhyme helped me remember the finger motions, and Winona tried to mimic me, her thin lips moving.

I clapped my hands, saying, *"Consimilis."*

She jumped, and I added, "Cold to hot, harness within, *calefacio!*"

Winona looked at me, hesitated, and said, "Was something supposed to happen?"

I rocked back from her a little. "It would have if I had been connected to a ley line," I said sourly. It had felt weird doing the charm without being connected, like walking up the stairs in the dark to find that the last step isn't there when your foot falls through space. "Let me show you the finger motions again," I said, and she nodded. "That's what's important. The rhyme is just to remember them. That and the Latin."

"What if I accidentally fry myself? Or you?"

I smiled, remembering thinking just about the same thing when Ceri had taught me. "It won't work on anything with an aura," I said, and then my smile faded. I'd used it once to burn Kisten's murderer to ash, but the vampire had been dead—really dead—for almost a year before I'd found him. "It's really simple. You connect to a ley line, do the finger moves, and then say the Latin. Oh! And you need a focusing object."

My eyes had adapted somewhat, and I saw her screw her face up. "A focusing object?"

I reached over to the mesh and wiggled a stray wire back and forth, trying to work it free. "Sometimes I use one, sometimes I don't. It depends on how, ah, focused you are."

The wire started moving more easily, and with a ping, it separated. The end was warm in my fingers, and I handed it to her, hesitating. It wasn't as if she could hold it while she was doing the finger moves, and putting it in her mouth like I did when I warmed water wasn't the best option.

"Uh, maybe you should just touch the bars with your foot," I said. "That's a connection of a sort."

Winona took it from me, and I stared, shocked when she lifted her blouse and tucked the wire behind a fold of skin at her middle. "I, uh, have a pouch," she said, and I gaped at her, remembering to shut my mouth only when she began to look embarrassed.

"Does Gerald know?" I said, and she grinned.

"Nope."

"Well, if this doesn't work, maybe you could smuggle something in here with us."

"Way ahead of you," she said, her head going down as she pulled out a paper clip and a sharp chunk of thin plastic. "Put these in your sock, will you? They're making me itch like crazy."

"Winona," I said as I tucked them away. "Did anyone ever tell you that you'd make one hell of a runner?"

"I went to school to act," she said, the faint light shining on her teeth as she grinned.

The paper clip was warm from her body, and the plastic hard, but the sensations soon vanished. "With the focusing object, all you need to do is simply look at where you want the heat to go, and the charm will act there."

"I just have to look at it?" she said, her tone bordering on disbelief.

"You've never done anything like this, have you?" I asked, and she squirmed. "It's not as hard as most witches make out. You can do this."

She nodded. "I forgot the words."

I stifled my sigh, wondering if I was going to make a more impatient teacher than Ceri. "We'll do it together," I said. "Fire burns and planets spin. Friction is how it ends and begins. *Consimilis!*"

She mimicked me, and we clapped together. "*Calefacio!*" we both said simultaneously, our fingers moving as one. Winona jumped as the energy flowed through her, and I stifled a yelp when sparks burst from the door lock.

"You did it!" I cried, scrambling up to push on the door only to find that it was still latched. Disappointment brought my shoulders down, but Winona was delighted.

"It worked!" she said, not upset that it hadn't snapped the lock. "It's like putting a spoon in the microwave. All sparks! I'm going to try again."

"Hold on a sec," I said as I gingerly touched the metal to find it was barely warm. "Give it twice what you did, and I'll kick it."

"What if it catches you on fire?" she said, and I balled up my hands and took a stance.

"Then put me out, but I'm kicking that lock the instant you say the last word."

Winona took a nervous breath, and I clenched my jaw, focusing on the door. This was really dumb. Why *in hell* had I ever abandoned my magic? Because I didn't want to live in the ever-after the rest of my life? Because Al would be mad enough to lock me in a box? Okay, they were really good reasons, but it was time I accepted that my magic came with an awful price and just pay it, even if it left me alone and apart.

"You can do this, Winona," I said, deciding to worry about it later—if I had a later. "You're a strong woman." That metal hadn't been very hot. Maybe she didn't have the fortitude to channel enough ley-line energy.

"Consimilis, calefacio!" Winona exclaimed, and I darted my foot out in a side kick. It hit the door the same time her charm did, and the mesh shook as the sparks flew. The scent of hot metal rose, but the door didn't move.

"Again!" I exclaimed, my pulse quickening.

"Consimilis, calefacio!" she shouted gleefully, and I flung my foot at the door, screaming along with her.

The door gave way, and I fell forward, my momentum propelling me into the center of the room. Exuberant, I caught myself and turned. The door was swinging shut again, the lock a glowing mess of melted metal. The stench of burning wire was choking, and I grinned as Winona stared, her mouth open and her eyes huge and black in the dim light from the monitors. "I did it . . ."

"That was fabulous!" I exclaimed. Lurching, I stuck my foot in front of the door before it could swing back and melt shut. No way would it hold either of us again. The air, even a foot away from the glowing wires, was hot, and I held the door open with one foot while I reached in to help Winona up.

"I can stand," she said, scrambling up and balancing with no problem.

"You can stand!" I echoed, my smile getting wider. "You can walk!" I exclaimed, backing up when she trotted toward me, little hooves clacking on the cement.

"I was faking." Winona trip-trapped to where they had put her clothes and her purse. "I played the part of a cripple one semester. Got to be good at it." Frowning, she held up a long coat. It had a masculine cut that went to the floor and would hide her feet. "I think this must have been Kenny's."

My heart pounded. She tossed my coat to me, and I caught it. The dart gun was next, right in the drawer that Eloy had put it into. "Let's go," I said, looking up at the gray monitors, then hissed, "Wait!" when I remembered the data book.

Winona hesitated, and I scanned the books on the shelf, impatient until I found the one with the names of everyone they'd killed. "Okay," I said, excited as I tucked it under an arm. "Now we can go."

I fell into place behind Winona, marveling at how quickly she could move, almost as fast as a vampire. I couldn't help but stare at that little slip of a tail showing from under her coat. She was almost like a ghost as she went before me, her eyes seeing the boxes and low-hanging baskets before I did. Things were starting to look familiar from the monitors, and looking behind me, I saw a tiny red light glowing from a camera. Not knowing if they were recording this, I gave it the one-fingered salute and followed Winona to the stairway.

This wasn't bad, it was almost too easy. Winona slowed, looking up the stairs in consideration. "You need some help?" I whispered, thinking of her oddly shaped legs. She was doing great on horizontal surfaces, but this was almost straight up and narrow.

"I don't know." She put a hand on the banister and turned to smile. "I think I can make it, but I'll need to go fast. Maybe if you could open the door at the top so I don't run into it?"

Nodding, I touched her shoulder and crept up the stairs, listening. The woman was strong, I'd give her that. At the top of the stairs, I hesitated, then slowly turned the dented brass knob. I had no idea where we were.

The door stuck for a second, then the old paint let go and it swung open. Cooler air slipped past my feet, somehow smelling mustier than the basement. It was dark, and I gave the narrow, tall-ceilinged hall a careful look before slipping out. One way led to an open room, the other dead-ended at a window. It was even darker outside, no moon at all.

"Okay!" I whispered down the stairs, then stood in the hall and held the door while Winona tried the first stair. She almost fell, but then she backed up, gathered her long coat, and took the stairs at a dead run.

My eyes widened as she barreled up, making enough noise for six goats. She was out of control at the top, and I grabbed her arm to keep her from hitting the wall. Behind us, the door eased shut. I held her arm until she found her balance, then let go. Both of us were breathing heavily, me from fear, Winona from exertion. "You okay?" I whispered, and she pulled the long coat aside to look at her impossibly thin ankles.

"I think so," she said, then smiled, her thick canines catching the faint light. "Let's go."

There was only one way, and she tried to walk softly, but her hooves clacked on the old wood floor. If anyone was here, they'd hear it. Wincing with each step, we tiptoed to the end of the hall and looked into what seemed like a restored living room from the 1800s, complete with placards and roped-off chairs. Tall windows let in the faint light and cold through thin panes of glass wavering with age. Soft emergency lights lit the space, and by a set of official-looking doors was a reception desk. *Thank God. There'd be a phone.*

"Where are we?" Winona asked, and I sent my eyes up to the ceiling where a mock-up of the solar system shifted in the draft from the heating ducts.

"The observatory," I said, hope making me jittery. Damn, we were like ten minutes from my mom's old house. "Stay here. I'll make a call, and we can just sit and wait."

"Rachel," she hissed, but I was already moving. We could be home in an hour, have the entire HAPA crew in custody in fifteen minutes.

I slid behind the desk, looking for the phone. Seeing it, I picked it up and punched in Glenn's number. The 911 service would take forever.

"Rachel!"

"What!" I whispered loudly, then frowned. Why wasn't I hearing a phone ring? Hell, I wasn't even hearing a dial tone.

"Look out!" Winona shouted, and I looked up at the dark shadow coming at me.

"Get down!" Eloy shouted, and I threw the phone at him.

It wasn't connected to the wall, and it sailed the thirty feet and crashed on the floor in a crack of plastic.

"Now!" Chris shouted from somewhere, and the lights flashed on, blinding me. Winona shrieked, and I heard Gerald grunt. Squinting, I saw him holding his middle and Winona running from him, those feet of hers easily outdistancing Jennifer, reaching for her.

"Son of a bitch," I snarled as I pulled the dart gun, aiming at Eloy and pulling the trigger.

Eloy slid to a stop five feet from me, the little dart with the red fletch hitting him right in the arm where I wanted it. His eyes went to it, and my bravado evaporated when he plucked it out and shook his head. *Blanks!* I thought, then threw the gun at him, pissed.

Eloy ducked, and the gun clattered next to the broken phone. In the background, Jennifer and Chris were trying to corral Winona. She skittered from them, her eyes almost shut from the light.

"Too easy," Eloy said as he reached for me. "I told them you could escape."

"Yeah? Well, you were right!" I said, and kicked at him. Or at least I would have if someone hadn't sucker-punched me in the head.

Stars exploded as pain reverberated from my ear to my nose and back again. I reeled backward, suddenly nauseated as the lights went gray and the world spun. I fell to one knee, caught by someone smelling like blue jeans. It was Gerald, and his eyes still held the pain from where Winona had kicked him.

"This was a bad idea!" Chris was yelling. "She made it to the phone!"

Eloy bent over me, and I tried to push his hand away when he peeled my eyelids back to make sure my pupils dilated right. "That's why I unplugged it. Hag."

"Will one of you help us with goat girl here!" Chris shouted, clearly frazzled.

"You are all going to rot in hell, even if I have to carry

you there on my back," I breathed. My eyes were shut, but I could hear Winona's hooves and hear her crying, trying to find a way out.

"Look, you ugly goat!" Eloy shouted, and I felt him grab my hair and pull my head up. "Either you stop running, or I'm going to kill her! Right now! And it will be your fault!"

"Go, Winona," I tried to shout, but it came out in a whisper. "Go . . ."

"I mean it!" Eloy shouted, and something cold touched my throat. "I'll cut her open right here, and she'll bleed out in front of you!"

I tried to open my eyes, failing.

"I'm sorry. I'm sorry!" Winona cried out, and then she yelped. I heard a skittering of hooves, and then her sobbing close by. The knife vanished from my neck, and Eloy let go of my hair. My head fell against Gerald, and I felt like crying, too. It had all been a setup. They'd wanted to know if we could escape, and we walked right into it, all the way down to the blanks in the dart gun and the disconnected phone. I was such an idiot.

My head lolled as Gerald flung me over his shoulder. The blood rushed to my spinning head, clearing it for an instant, and then it got fuzzy again.

"Hey!" Chris shouted, and I felt her take her notebook out of my back pocket. "You're stealing my research?" she shouted.

"It's evidence," I slurred. "Get it right . . . bitch."

"The chubi tried to take my research!" she exclaimed again, and I managed to get my eyes open, right when the lights went off again.

"Shut the hell up," Eloy grumbled, and we all started back to the stairway. "Lock it up next time."

"She's *not* going to get out *again*," Chris vowed, and somehow, as I was carried back downstairs and dumped on a cold floor, I couldn't argue with her.

I'd failed miserably. If I'd had my magic, I could have put up a circle and blocked that punch. I could have flooded

Gerald with ever-after and dropped him like a rock. I could have lit the dark with a light, melted the bars with a word, punched a hole through the walls of the basement itself! But without it . . . I was nothing. *Useless.*

It wasn't who I wanted to be.

Sixteen

I'd been in the stinking bathroom long enough that I couldn't smell it anymore, and that sort of bothered me. They'd tossed me in here hours ago to keep me away from Winona. The tiny four-by-six room was disgusting, but careful inspection had shown me a way out. I just needed some time by myself. After I'd threatened to anatomically change Jennifer and Gerald if they dared open that door to so much as give me my dinner, peace was what I got. Stupid. The last thing you want to do is lock your prisoner in a badly designed, poorly constructed basement bathroom and ignore her. Whoever built this thing hadn't made it to code. There were at least two feet between the studs.

Lower lip between my teeth, I pulled another chunk of wallboard from the growing hole I'd started with the chunk of plastic Winona had given me. The piece of wallboard was about the size of my hand, and I quietly set it in the water tank. I could take a larger chunk, but the bigger the piece, the more noise it made. I thought it was about three in the morning, but I didn't like how close I was to their *lair,* and I was going to err on the side of caution. We weren't going to get another chance after this. If I failed again, one of us was going to die, and it would probably be Winona. I couldn't live with myself if that happened.

Cold, I wiped the back of my hand under my nose and

carefully wiggled another piece back and forth until the paper gave way. I'd not heard a peep from anyone in hours, and I hoped Winona was okay. The hole was big enough on this side of the studs for me to slip out. All that was left was breaking the other side open.

Muscles protesting, I slowly got up, feeling everything ache from sitting for so long on the cold cement. Stretching to the bare bulb, I carefully untwisted it until the connection broke and the light went off. I didn't know where the switch was, but it wasn't in here with me.

I jogged in place to warm up as I waited for my eyes to adjust. It was cold, and I wanted to be able to move fast if I had to. Slowly the faintest glow of light from under the door started to show, and I knelt in front of my hole.

Taking that bit of plastic that Winona had given me, I bored a hole into the outer wall. My noise was as soft as a mouse, but if anyone was watching the door, they'd hear it. Breath held, I put my eye to the hole and looked out, seeing nothing but shadowy lumps and a glow where they were likely sleeping, boxes and old file cabinets between us.

So far, so good. Emboldened, I stuck my finger through the hole and pulled. Slowly, I widened the hole. The air got fresher, and I worked faster, trading off silence for speed. If I was lucky, Eloy was sleeping, not on patrol outside.

Eloy, I thought as I worked, my jaw clenching as I recalled his mocking expression when he'd caught us. He'd expected I'd try to escape, and I'd walked right into it.

My head hurt, the sulfites used to preserve the cheap food I'd been eating for the last twenty-four hours finally having built up to where they were hitting me hard. Frustrated, I yanked on a huge chunk of wallboard, cringing when it broke away with a pattering of dust. I stopped, deciding the hole was big enough to squeeze through—I couldn't stand being in this bathroom another second. Fingers curved under and hurting, I crawled through the hole in the wall. My back protested as the edges pinched me, and my muscles felt stiff.

My foot caught on a chunk of wallboard, scraping on the

floor when it tore free. Still on my hands and knees, I froze, hair in my face as I held my breath and gazed at the faint light coming from behind the file cabinets and what looked like an ancient furnace. Not a sound broke the stillness, and slowly my pulse returned to normal.

Moving carefully, I stood and flexed my cold hands, my band of silver thumping down into my wrist. Satisfaction, and a little pride, made me smile. I'd gotten out without using any magic. None. Regardless, it made me all the more determined that I was going to get this stupid-ass bracelet off. *Oh God. Al.* I had to come up with something really big to bribe him with. *Maybe if I made enough tulpas to buy his library back.* But I knew it wasn't enough. It would never be enough. I'd torn a hole in the ever-after, and it was collapsing slowly but surely.

"I'll be right back," I whispered to Winona, knowing she couldn't hear me, then set a dusty box to hide the hole I'd made in the wall.

The stairs were a sure way out, but I wasn't leaving without Winona, and she was too noisy on them. Not to mention that the front door upstairs would be locked, with an alarm attached. Attracting official attention would be great, but it would take fifteen minutes for anyone to get out here, plenty of time to be recaptured and relocated. HAPA was scum, but their people were well trained and efficient.

What I really wanted was a quiet, unalarmed basement window to sneak out of. Hesitating, I turned away from the slight glow and picked my way deeper into the basement. There probably wasn't an elevator or a second set of stairs, since Gerald hadn't set up any cameras in this direction, but maybe there was a window.

Ducking under an iron water pipe, I felt my way, looking for the faintest glimmer of starlight. Thick walls of old field-stone held up the ceiling, supplemented by modern pipe supports. File boxes, dingy office furniture, and old displays, getting older the farther I went, that had once been upstairs filled the space.

"That looks promising," I whispered when the concrete floor became dry, dusty tile, and I found what looked like an old shower stall. Squinting, I looked over the tattered shower curtain and a broken commode that looked as if it hadn't seen water since the Turn. Across from them were two tall lockers, dented and with the latches broken. *Janitors' shower?* My heart pounded when I saw the black-painted square surrounded by the rough stone walls of the original foundation. It had to be a window—right at my head level.

Excited, I went back into the mess behind me to find something to stand on. The rolling chair on casters was out, but the heavy wooden crate with PLANETS stenciled on it was ideal. *Ivy.* I missed her—she must be worried sick. Jenks, too. Wayde probably wasn't having a very good day, either, though my capture was not his fault. The heavy box scraped lightly on the tile as I dragged it backward, and I winced. The dust tickled my nose, and I made one of those prissy-girl sneezes, almost blowing out my ears.

I finally got the box in place and scrambled up. "Please move," I begged the gods of irony, and my breath slipped out when the thin panel of glass shifted upward, the strips of metal grinding on the tracks.

Cold air bathed my face. The night was calm, the hum of the interstate traffic faint and distant. There was a raggedy foundation bush in front of me, but I could see the empty parking lot to my left, and an open field and woods to my right. It would be a tight squeeze, but I was fairly sure both Winona and I could make it. Once outside, we could be half-way to somewhere before they knew we were gone.

I took one last breath of freedom, then pulled the window shut lest the fresher air give me away. As I stepped awkwardly from the crate, my cold ankles twinged. Time to get Winona.

My pace back through the dark, winding basement was faster, and I stopped at the umbrella stand holding a set of "planet poles," picking out the thickest, shortest one as an unbalanced club. It slid from the rest with a soft scrape, and my pulse quickened. I might not have any magic, but I could still knock heads, and I hefted it, feeling empowered.

More slowly, I moved in the brighter gloom, seeing the empty counters and softly glowing lights from the machines as I crept by the three lumps sleeping on low cots. Jennifer's curtain was gone. Gerald was on his back, set apart from the two women, his mouth hanging open and snoring slightly. My grip on my stick tightened. I had a thought to bean him one in his sleep, but then the rest would wake up. No telling what Chris would pull out of her magic book to hit us with. If we could do this with no one the wiser, then all the better.

Winona sat up from the floor as I hesitated over Gerald. Her eyes threw back the glow from the machines, like a cat's, and I froze. She was okay. Leaving the sleeping thugs behind, I crossed the room to her. Winona didn't stand, instead scooted to the door on her butt, and I wondered if they'd hurt her. "Are you okay?" I barely breathed as I crouched beside her.

"I'm fine," she said, and our fingers touched through the mesh. "My feet make so much damned noise, it's better if I don't get up." Her ugly face smiled, making me shiver. "I heard you get out. I thought you'd left me."

I gave her fingers a quick squeeze, then pulled back. "I was finding a way out." I looked behind me to the sleeping people. "You heard all that? How come they didn't?"

She shrugged. "I can hear everything."

Impatience slowly tightened from my toes to my aching head. "Eloy?" I asked.

Winona brought her eerie cat gaze back from the cots. "He left after they soldered a new lock on the cage. They put charmed silver on me, too. I can't tap a line now."

I exhaled in dismay, and I spun on my heel, still in a crouch as I looked at the empty counters. There was a bolt cutter somewhere, but it would be noisy to look. "Key?" I asked hopefully, and Winona made an ugly face.

"Chris has it."

"Dart gun?" I whispered, and she shook her head.

"Eloy."

I frowned. Figured. He was probably waiting in the bushes somewhere playing soldier. It might be better to get her out of her cage first, then worry about getting her charmed silver off.

"Okay," I said as I put my lips next to the mesh. "I'm going to pick the lock. The window is in the back at an old shower. Left is the parking lot, right is the woods. Once you're there, keep running. They'll never catch you."

"What about you?" she insisted, and I cringed, thinking she was too loud.

"I'll be right behind," I said, trying to smile. "But if things go wrong and I can't run—"

"I'll pick you up," she said, her head down as she scratched at her middle.

I took a breath to protest, then blinked when she appeared to push her entire hand inside herself. It was her pouch, and I stared when she pulled out a pair of wire clippers.

"Where did you get that?" I hissed, shocked, and she grinned her sharp-canine grin at me.

"They left it out," she said. "I fell on it and no one noticed. I wasn't going to take the zip strip off until I knew we were escaping."

She held the clippers out through the mesh, and I took them, thinking cutting the mesh would be easier than trying to jimmy the lock—provided that it wasn't noisy. Eager, I awkwardly angled the business end of the clippers back through the wires and around her wristband. It was only one of the cheap plastic-coated zip strips that the I.S. used, not like my industrial-strength band, and it wouldn't fry her brain when it came off. With a soft thump, the sharp metal pushed through, and Winona sighed in relief.

"Thanks," she said as she rubbed her wrist. "I never thought I'd miss being able to touch a ley line like that." Her eyes went past me, and determination made her fierce. "You came back for me. We leave together, or not at all."

Grateful, I reached my fingers through the bars and gave

her fingers a quick squeeze. She wasn't that ugly, once you got used to her. "Thanks. Keep watch, okay? Monitors, too."

She flicked her gaze over my shoulder and nodded.

The wire was the thinnest where the mesh was attached to the door frame, and starting at the bottom, I clipped the wires one by one, hesitating after each thumping click. It was almost absurdly easy, and it wasn't three minutes before I stood and passed the clippers back through to her and she tucked them away, not even making a lump on her middle. Grabbing the long edge of the L I'd cut, I leaned back and let my weight bend the mesh up so Winona could slip out.

Her hooves clicked, and I held my breath as she moved slowly and erratically, trying to give her pace an uneven sound. Shoulders tense, she slid out sideways, exhaling when she was finally free. Smiling, I eased the mesh back down and took a relieved breath. *Almost there.*

"Son of a bitch!" a feminine voice exclaimed.

Winona's eyes focused over my shoulder, then widened. I spun to see a shadowy figure sitting up on a cot. "Run!" I shouted, but they were between us and the window, and I didn't know if there was another, more circular way in between all the junk down here.

"Oh no!" Jennifer cried, and my chest clenched when Gerald snorted awake, rolling onto the floor and reaching for something under his cot.

I snatched the pipe and took up a stance. Beside me, Winona had her head down and her fingers in her pouch. *"Consimilis, calefacio!"* she shouted triumphantly as she held up a scrap of paper.

A boom of sound exploded with a burst of light, and I cowered as every scrap of paper within a six-foot radius burst into flame. Holy crap, the woman had power!

"Go! Go!" I shouted as the two women shrieked and Gerald stood in his underwear in openmouthed awe. The files were burning, the toilet paper was char, and smoke was coming from Chris's precious machine. We had three seconds to get by them, tops.

Winona lurched into motion, apparently as shocked as I was at what she'd done, and she scuttled out past the cots, her hooves clacking merrily.

"My research!" Chris screamed, her complexion red in the light from the flames as she reached for it. "Get my notes. No, get them!" she cried out, pointing at us as we ran for the darkness, but all Jennifer did was sit on her bed and wail, her hair mussed and her chest heaving, scared to death.

Gerald lumbered to his feet with a small rifle in his grip. Winona made a horrified squeal and ran for the dark as he lurched over Jennifer's cot and came at me.

My anger bubbled up, and I swung my pole like a golf club, connecting with his chin as he reached out. His head snapped back, and his eyes rolled up as blood splattered.

Like a downed tree, Gerald fell back on Jennifer, and her screams took on a shrill, panicked sound as he pinned her. Chris had finally gotten out of her sleeping bag and was at the rack of books, trying to pull them off the shelves and stomp out the individual fires. She didn't even look up, and I heard her cry out in pain as she touched her demon book and it burned her hand. It wasn't on fire, but it was hot enough to give first-degree burns.

"Rachel!" Winona cried from the darkness, and I bolted. I didn't like leaving the lab book I'd wanted burning with the rest, but getting away would be victory enough.

Winona was a whip-tailed shadow ahead of me as I ran. Behind us, Chris was screaming and Jennifer was crying. Gerald was apparently okay since he was the one Chris was yelling at, and I heard a crash as he started to follow.

"Low pipe," Winona warned, not even breathing hard, and I ducked, almost hitting it.

It was only by the sound of her feet that I knew where she was. Behind us, I heard a dull, clanging *thwap* and Gerald's bellow of pain. I couldn't help my grin, even as I gripped my pipe tighter. If Eloy was anywhere nearby, or Chris thought to call him, we'd be in trouble as soon as we got out, but right now, we were free, and it felt good.

I dashed around the last of the junk, my eyes adjusting to the dim light. Feet skidding on the dust, I slid to a halt in the washroom. Winona was already on the crate, trying to pull herself up through the window. She was decidedly too heavy now for her arms to lift her body weight. The cool night air was spilling in around my ankles, and my heart pounded. Gerald was coming. I could hear him. I'd hit him good. He was going to be pissed.

"I'll boost you out," I said as I propped up my pole and scrambled up beside her. "Then you reach back in and pull me out, okay?"

"Rachel," she started, but I bent to grab her around her thick thighs. My cheek pressed into her fuzzy red pelt and I held my breath as I lifted her. My God, she was heavy, and she gasped, her weight shifting wildly as she wiggled her way out of the window.

"Watch it!" I gasped as her hoof found my shoulder. Finally her weight vanished, and I spun when an alarm went off in the building above us. A second later, I jumped at the groaning clank of air in the sprinkler system as it hissed on, drenching me.

"Corr bitch!" Gerald threatened as he slid into the shower area, almost going down in the sudden slick mud made from the dust. His arms pinwheeled, and he caught himself. Blood dripped from his chin where I'd hit him, and his posture was hunched like a bear's. That squirrel rifle was still in his grip, and he was pissed, head lowered and glowering at me.

Scared, I spun to put the wall to my back, the window behind my head. Instinct made me reach for a line . . . and I found nothing. Anger at my own past ignorance pushed away my fear, and I squinted at Gerald, the salt from my sweat making my eyes sting.

The sprinklers had drenched us both, and rivulets ran down him, plastering his hair to his face and washing away his blood. My chest clenched when he slyly propped his gun to the side and carefully reached for my pole, his eyes never leaving mine.

"Shooting you is too easy," he said as he took one end up and dragged the other across the tile, bumping and scraping slowly. "I owe you some payback."

"Yeah, well, you put me in a cage," I whispered. *Block the first blow. Break my arm. Save my skull,* I thought, readying myself for a whole lot of pain. This guy was 250 pounds, bare minimum, and all of it wanted to hurt me.

The soft scrape on the window gave me an instant to prepare, and then Winona leaned in, shouting, *"Consimilis, calefacio!* You ass!"

Gerald stared at her, behind me, as she grasped my shoulders and tried to pull me up and out, and then he shrieked, patting his clothes as they steamed. The curse wouldn't work on anything with an aura, but apparently it worked on the water he was soaked in. She was boiling him from the outside in. Her control was improving, thank God, or I'd be boiling, too.

My heart raced, and turning my back on him as he danced and slapped at himself, I locked my arms with Winona, and she pulled me up and out. Halfway through, we fell back, and I landed on that foundation shrub, my feet still dangling inside. My eyes widened when Gerald grabbed my legs and began pulling me back in.

Looking determined, Winona tugged back, and frantic, I kicked wildly. He cried out a muffled oath as I hit something, and when he let go, I pulled my feet out, turned, and panted, dripping wet and dirty as I stared at the tiny basement window. Gerald was probably too big to fit, but that rifle of his wasn't.

"Thank you," I said as I scrambled up. Grabbing her hand, I ran for the woods, letting go almost immediately. Damn, the woman could move! In the time I took to go ten yards, she was halfway across the field. "Go!" I said, waving her on, and she slowed to a jog, waiting for me to catch up. "Go!" I said again, thinking of Eloy. He was out here. I knew it.

"He's trying to get out!" Winona shouted, and I ran faster. "I can hear him swearing."

"Yeah?" I said between huffs, then looked to the distant, glowing city. *Fire trucks?*

I finally caught up with her when we hit the tree line, and we stopped, turning to look down the winding road and toward the sirens. The fire alarm at the observatory must be tied in to the city system, and they were coming out, lights flashing. The easiest way to be rescued would be to wait here, flag them down, and tell them to call Glenn at the FIB. But as I looked at Winona with her gray skin, curly red pelt, hooves, wildly whipping tail, horns, huge canines, and undeniable demonic appearance, I decided it might not be the safest. Besides, Eloy was out here. He could pick us off as we sat in the squad car.

"Rachel, I'm scared."

"It's okay," I said as I held her elbows and looked her in the face. Damn it, she was crying. She'd done so well, and she was crying because of what they'd done to her and what people would think she was. I was the demon here, not her. "Winona, you're like the bravest person I've ever met," I said, thinking my own worries looked petty compared to hers. "Come on. We'll run until we find a place for you to stay while I find a phone. I'll explain what happened, and then we'll get you back to normal."

Her grip on my arms tightened, and she dropped her head, nodding. "Okay." But then her head came up, and she turned, letting go of me and dropping back a step in alarm.

"Move, and I'll shoot you," Eloy said from the dark, his silhouette black against the starlit observatory. "Move, and I'll shoot you both. Right here. Right now."

Damn. I watched, frozen, as he cocked the small rifle. He was head to toe in camouflage, looking both threatening and ridiculous against the background of Cincinnati. We weren't in a fucking war here—but maybe we were. He'd said he'd shoot us, and I believed him.

"Hell, I think I'll just shoot you anyway," he said, pulling the gun to his shoulder in a very fast, professional motion.

"Run!" I shouted, giving Winona a push. If he was going

to shoot at us, a moving target was harder to hit—especially with that little rifle he had.

The sound of the rifle going off hit me like a slap, and something thunked into my leg. It stung, and I stumbled, almost pulling Winona down. I wedged her arm off me and fell, turning to look up at Eloy. My leg was wet, and I held it, praying.

Eloy made a huff of success and brought his rifle up again, this time aiming for Winona. My pulse thundered in my ears. Behind him, the fire trucks got louder, the first of the lights flashing on the building. Oh God. I was going to be killed by a rifle-toting, HAPA redneck with a grudge against the supernatural.

"Go!" I shouted, and with a snarl, she jumped right at him. Eloy dodged, silently swinging his gun to hit her. She caught it with a smack to her palm, and she yanked it from him, throwing it to the damp grass. "Son of a bitch!" the man cried, and she jumped onto his back, her mouth wide in a primal scream as she tore chunks of his hair out and pounded on him. Her tail whipped his face, and he reached behind himself, grabbing her and throwing her over his shoulder.

Winona landed on her feet and jumped at him again. The man covered his face and dropped to the ground, curled up like he was being attacked by a bear. Winona stomped all over him, her tiny hooves having almost 150 pounds behind each inch.

I scooted back until I found a tree I could use to get to my feet. I wouldn't let go of my leg, and my hand was sticky. People were getting out of the fire trucks. Now that they weren't moving, they might be able to hear us. "Winona!" I hissed as a huge truck light swung over the nearby trees. "Winona! We've got to go!"

A clatter of pixy wings brought my heart into my mouth. *Jenks!* I thought as my gaze darted to the new sprinkling of pixy dust arrowing to us from deep in the woods. I leaned against the tree, my hope rising. Could I be that lucky?

"Rache! Holy crap!" Jenks shouted as he came to a short stop inches from my face, and I almost collapsed in relief. "We found you!" the exuberant pixy said, and I grinned, feeling faint. "Good thinking to set the place on fire! Glenn thought you were in some mobile home, but I stuck with Trent. The cookie maker needs someone to look out for him. He's worse than you in making bad decisions. He did six things wrong since leaving his house. Let's leave dust before that freaky-ass demon sees you!"

"That's not a demon, that's Winona," I said, wincing as she gave Eloy a last kick and howled her success at the stars.

"Who?" Jenks asked.

"Winona." I leaned against the tree and pressed my hand into my leg. It was starting to hurt. That was a good thing, right? "She's a nice woman they snatched. They did that to her. With my blood." Oh God, they used my blood, and I felt a tear leak out. I knew it was the trauma, but I couldn't stop it.

His dust shifting to an alarmed red, Jenks hovered beside me as I started breathing shallowly. "Is she still smart?"

"Yeah." I took a breath, but I couldn't tell if the lights were spinning because they were really spinning or if it was from blood loss. "She's got a few issues she's working out, is all. That's Eloy she's stomping on. He's a son . . . of a bastard. He put us in a cage, and Chris did that to her. It's HAPA, Jenks. They're going to wipe us all out if they can duplicate my blood."

Winona turned to us, looking demonic but justifiably proud of herself as she grinned. Behind her, Eloy was not moving. Somehow I didn't care.

"Trent!" Jenks shouted, rising up for an instant. "We're over here!"

Trent was out here? I thought, Jenks's earlier words taking on an entirely new meaning.

Dropping down to my knee, he noticed the blood. "Shit, you've been shot! Trent, I could use some muscle here! Why the Tink-blasted daisies do you think I brought you!"

"It's just a small caliber. Why is Trent here?" I whispered, leaning against the tree. It was getting harder to breathe. Ivy. Ivy should be here, not Trent.

The hair on the back of my neck started to prickle, and Jenks rose up. "Trent, no!" he cried out, and my eyes flashed open to see a dark shadow. "She's with us! She's with us!"

But it was too late, and a ball of magic hissed through the air, headed right for Winona. The woman didn't have a clue, staring transfixed at the hunched shadow, looking like Peter Pan, crouched in the nearby tree.

I lunged for Winona. Jenks darted up, and I landed on her, right when Trent's spell slammed into me.

My breath came in with a gasp as it felt like my skin exploded, shooting jagged daggers from the inside out. Groaning, I clenched my jaw and curled into a ball as I fell off Winona, shaking as my pounding heart pushed the pain deeper, finding my chi and then exploding again. I could do nothing but ride it out, and it was a hard one. *Stupid-ass elf!* Jenks was right. He jumped to conclusions worse than I did.

"What the hell are you doing!" Jenks shrilled, and the world spun as Winona picked me up and began backing away, managing my weight easily. "You hit Rachel, you idiot!"

"Put her down, demon!" Trent said, his beautiful voice hard with threat as he dropped from the trees, the come-and-go lights from the fire trucks playing over him. "I'll kill you where you stand. I am her Sa'han, and you will not have her."

"You are not," I breathed, trying to wave him off, and Jenks hovered over us, lighting Winona's scared expression with his own dust. "Knock it off, will you? She's my friend."

"She's with Rache!" Jenks shrilled. "God! You're dumb! Do you think I'd be hovering here with my thumb up my ass if Winona was going to hurt her?"

"Stay back," Winona said, her tears hitting me, heavy and warm. "Stay back! Oh God, Rachel. Please be all right!"

"Jenks?" I murmured, trying to focus, but Winona was backing into the trees, terrified. Elf magic sucked. I didn't think I could move. Even my heartbeat hurt. Damn! Trent packed a punch. Someone needed to muzzle him. Stupid-ass businessman trying to play runner.

The glow of a phone screen lit his face, and he quietly said, "I've got her. Right where I said she'd be." He hesitated, a new tightness to his lips. "Why do you think I'm out here, Quen? I'll see you in a few minutes." He hesitated, then added, "Then you should have listened to me," and shut the phone. The light cut off. "Please, we have to move," he said, and Winona's arms around me tightened. Her meadowy scent rose high where my wet clothes touched her, and I felt numb.

"It's okay, Winona," Jenks said, darting to hover over Trent as he walked forward, his hands in the air, but Winona kept going back, deeper into the woods and away from the lights of the fire trucks.

"HAPA is still out here," Trent said, his expression unseen as the fire trucks flashed behind him now. "I can take you somewhere safe, but you have to trust me. I'm sorry about the spell. I saw you and . . . I overreacted. Please. Don't run. I can't help if you don't let me."

No, he couldn't. It was something I was learning at long last. I hoped it wasn't too late.

Trent's voice had lost its edge, falling into the more familiar coaxing businessman I knew. Winona wasn't buying it, and Jenks hovered over her shoulder. Winona shook her head, her tears hitting me, and Trent made a noise of frustration. "Some help here, Rachel?"

I tried to take a deep breath, my lungs on fire. "Idiot . . ." I wheezed. "You shouldn't be throwing spells like that unless you know what you're doing!"

"You want me to leave?" he said, and Jenks's wings clattered in frustration.

"Can you guys save this for after we get in the car?" he said, and I tried to focus on his glittering sparkles. I was so glad to see him, I could just cry. No, wait, I was already doing that.

"Winona, please," I whispered as my eyes shut. "I know this guy. You can trust him." My eyes opened, and I looked at Winona, seeing her need to believe that there might be a way out of this. "He can help us both," I slurred, then clenched as a new wave of pain hit. Oh God, the spell wasn't dissipating fast enough. I was going to go into shock.

"You're Trent Kalamack?" she warbled, and Trent nodded. She shifted from foot to foot, but I think it was Jenks still hovering over him that did it, and I sighed when Trent put his hands on me and the pain lessened. I sagged in relief, and Winona stiffened.

"It's okay!" Jenks yelled before she ran off with me. "He just broke the pain charm."

"I still hurt," I said, my eyes opening. I smelled cinnamon and wine, and Trent's finger turned my face to his. He was smiling, a hint of guilt and embarrassment behind it, and I tried to smile back. "What are you doing out here? Shouldn't you be taking over a corporation or something?"

"Ah, sorry about that," he said, worry pinching his brow. "Better now?"

Sorry? He was sorry?

"She's been shot," Jenks said, and I felt a new wash of warmth as he dusted my leg again.

"I see that," he said, his gaze going up the hill to the fire trucks. "I would've found you sooner, but everyone was focused on a trailer park, and it wasn't until Quen left that I had the chance to do a finding spell." He grimaced as he took me from Winona and the soothing scent of cinnamon and wine flowed over me anew. His hand with the missing fingers pinched, the pressure needed to hold me channeled into fewer fingers. "Maybe next time, they'll listen to me."

"Happens to me all the time," I said, eyes closing as he started walking and my head thumped into his chest. Things were getting fuzzy again, and I felt like I was being rocked as he walked, Jenks shining ahead of us.

"I've a car a quarter mile up the road," Trent said, concern edging his voice. "I'll have you in a tub of water in half an hour." He glanced at Winona. "Both of you."

A tub of water sounded like heaven. "You'd better be nice to Winona," I said. "Or I'm going to kick your ass. Understand?"

"More than you know."

I was cold, and my head slumping into him, I breathed him in, giving myself up to whatever came next. I was going to be okay, and that was enough for now. Trent had been looking for me? How nice was that?

But my next thought woke me back up. *He thought he was my Sa'han? What the hell did that mean?*

Seventeen

A high-pitched child's wail cut through the thick walls as if they were paper, sliding between my sleep and reason and pricking me awake. A soft adult admonishment quickly followed, soothing the desperate demand into a pitiful whining that dulled to the inaudible. I smiled. Kids were great, but I was really glad not to have any right now.

My eyes opened, and I looked up at the high arched ceiling, bright with the sun leaking past the curtains. The ceiling was painted with a hunting scene, like you might find in a museum, with dogs and horses—and one running fox. Somehow it managed not to look overdone. The opulent surroundings helped.

In less than a day I'd gone from sleeping on a grimy floor to Egyptian cotton, silk pj's, and enough pillows to drown in. Thank God there'd been a shower in between. Not to mention a trip downstairs to Trent's surgery suite to get the bullet yanked out of my thigh. I'd be there still, but after they patched me up and made sure my kidneys were working, I had taken out the IV and demanded a real bed or I was going to call Ivy to pick me up that instant.

It felt good to be alive, clean, rested . . . and sleeping in Ellasbeth's old room. *Na, na. Na, na. Na-a-a-a, na.* It had been redecorated in soft, earthy colors, and I could see Ceri's hand everywhere from the lace draped over the top of the huge mirror to the elegant French provincial furnishings. The bathroom, though, looked the same as the night Ellasbeth had walked in on me while I'd been innocently soaking in her tub. She'd probably been pregnant with Lucy at the time, now that I think about it.

Ray, Ceri and Quen's child, was only five months old. Lucy was eight months, and from the sound of it, had learned how to communicate without words. She was a smart little kid, the product of East Coast and West Coast elves, the attempt at forging a union between the two that I helped break not just once, but twice, first by halting their marriage, and then by helping Trent steal Lucy from Ellasbeth in an arranged agreement to avoid a legal battle for the child. Lucy was his now, lock, stock, and barrel. Trent had made me her godmother—her demon godmother.

I stretched with a happy sigh, grunting in surprise when my leg twinged. *Oh, yeah.*

Ceri had apologized profusely, but all the magic she knew that could help was demonic and therefore wouldn't stick. Trent hadn't even offered, probably still stinging over my less-than-enthusiastic response to being beaned by his pain charm—which *had* stuck. Wild magic had weird side effects in the best of situations, and he was a dabbler, even if he had laid me out. Ceri wouldn't practice the ancient, unpredictable, elven magic. She was a smart woman.

My thoughts drifted from seeing Trent as a dangerous shadow crouched in that tree to the kiss we'd shared last summer. It hadn't been unpleasant by any stretch of the imagination, but to think that it would go any further was stupid. I trusted Trent with my life, not my heart.

A shadow by the curtain moved, and I sat up. "Winona!" I said, quashing my first initial panic at finding a horned, tailed, demonic creature smiling at me.

"Sorry," she said, her lisp almost gone. "I didn't mean to wake you. You feel okay?"

The pillows behind me were too soft to give any support, and I carefully propped myself up against the headboard.

Seeing Winona in a long, dark red skirt and shawl threw me. "Pretty much. I should be up now anyway. Ivy and Wayde are probably banging on Trent's gate."

I looked for a clock before remembering Ceri had taken it out of the room, telling me to sleep myself out. Scooting to the edge of the bed took some doing, and I threw back the covers and lifted the hem of my borrowed pj's to see a big ugly bruise spreading out from under the bandage on my leg. It could have been a lot worse—should have been from that distance. I was going to have an interesting scar at the very least.

"My leg hurts, but I'm okay," I said, and she trip-trapped over to me, the sound muted when she found the rug. I let my legs hang over the side for a moment, my bladder warring with my need to slow down and gauge my fatigue. There was a pain amulet around my neck, and it was working well despite the throbbing in my leg. Small favors.

Slowly, with Winona ready to help, I stood. Everything seemed to shift as my feet took my weight, settle a little lower, a little more uncomfortable. I exhaled, then shuffled my way to the bathroom, Winona holding tight to my arm.

"Thank you for pounding Eloy last night," I said. "I can't believe you set the basement on fire with just one charm."

Her ugly face smiled fiercely. "I would never have made it without you. Thank you."

I touched the bedpost in passing for support, but my pace was becoming more sure already. "I think you would have managed it," I said, then glanced at my charmed silver as it thunked from my elbow to my hand. "I bet I missed breakfast. What time is it anyway?"

"Almost noon."

"Good." I put a hand on the wall beside the closed bathroom door. "I promised Ivy I'd call by one." I had talked to her shortly after the yanking-of-the-IV incident. She wasn't happy about my sleeping over until I told her I wanted to talk to Trent about getting this bracelet off. Wayde wasn't happy, either. He thought he'd let me down. I needed to talk to him, too.

Seeing me standing on my own power, Winona opened the bathroom door for me. I hobbled in, a twinge of nausea rising at the pain leaking through the amulet, but I turned and made a solid front when she tried to come in with me. "I've got this," I said, and she snorted, giving me a look that I'd expect from a third-grade teacher, decidedly odd on her demonic face.

"Just thump the floor hard when you hit it, and I'll come in," she said, and I heard her sigh when I shut the door.

I leaned back against the closed door and simply breathed for a moment. I was so damn tired. "Here we go again," I said as I pushed myself into motion. If I couldn't get dressed by myself, Trent might insist I stay. Ivy would cart me out of here anyway, but I didn't want to push the new truce Trent and I seemed to have. Weird.

I didn't need another shower, but my brands of detangler and toothpaste were waiting for me on the counter along with a complexion charm. Trent would remember them from our cross-country excursion, but it still threw me. My clothes from yesterday were laid out, cleaned and pressed. The bullet hole in my leather pants had been mended so well I couldn't see the patch unless I ran my hand over it, but there was no way I'd be able to wear them—not with my leg swollen like it was. Beside them was a robe and a pair of black sweats. The robe wasn't happening, but the sweats I could manage, and I sat on the dressing couch and carefully put myself back together as if I was getting dressed for battle, somehow managing even the socks.

Finally I stood before the mirror, my pulse a little fast, my body a little dehydrated, and I tried to smile. Immediately my lips turned down and my shoulders slumped. Today was going to be long and hard. Wayde was never going to let me live it down that I got hurt. But I was alive. I had survived. I was going to take the damned bracelet off, and I was scared to death. "There must be an easier way to grow up," I said with a breathy exhalation as I turned to the door.

Winona wasn't there when I came out, but I gratefully

took the single crutch propped up against the wall by the door, hobbling to the main room. The door was open, and Jenks was talking to Ceri. Lucy, too, was noisy, and I hesitated at the threshold, taking in the changes that I'd missed on my way up here, doped up on whatever magic pill Trent had had me on.

The room was bright with light being piped in from who knew where and emerging from big skylights. The small open kitchen was to my right, the suite's common room to my left. A wide stairway leading from Trent's private quarters to his more public house was beyond that. The huge window/video screen showed the woods, gray and bare for the coming winter. The common room itself had a lot less bachelor and a lot more kid, toys and books scattered everywhere. The big wide-screen TV was still there, but the leather couch in the sunken area had been exchanged for something lower to the floor, the top of the back almost even with the floor in the upper level.

Ceri glanced at me from where she was sitting on the floor in front of the low couch with her two girls, only one of whom was truly hers. The petite, fair-haired woman smiled, then looked back at Winona, as if chatting with a malformed woman who looked like a monster was a common event. But for the ex-demon familiar, it might be.

Jenks was on her shoulder, a wash of golden sunbeam dust heavy on her white dress. He'd seen me, too, but he was having too much fun teasing Lucy to move. I swear, if the little girl got her chubby hands on him and ripped his wings off, he deserved it.

Winona sat on the floor next to Ceri, looking both embarrassed and grateful—as if she was ready to cry—and I wondered if Ceri was on the floor because Winona couldn't manage the couch easily. I think their easy acceptance meant a huge amount to the traumatized woman. The girls weren't afraid of her, and Lucy sat up by herself and babbled, determined to keep up. Ray, still too young to sit unaided, was cradled in Ceri's arms, watching with big, wide green eyes.

The two girls were being raised as sisters though they shared not a single drop of blood. Lucy had the fair hair and complexion of Trent and Ellasbeth, but Ray had Quen's darker hair, completely overpowering Ceri's light wisps. Ray's complexion, too, was darker, in sharp contrast to her older sister. But both of them had tiny, pointy ears, the first elves to keep their ears undocked in almost two thousand years. I thought they looked sweet.

I smiled, and at my sniff, Ceri tickled Lucy's chin, saying, "Your aunt Rachel is awake."

"Aunt Rachel?" Jenks said dryly, and Winona raised a single eyebrow.

"You'd rather she be the demon godmother?" Ceri said, and Winona's smile faded.

"I like Aunt Rachel," I said as I leaned heavily on the crutch and hobbled for the steps down into the sunken living room.

Lucy, busy with her one-sided conversation, kept babbling, patting at the bright squares in the book before her, but I would swear that Ray's green eyes searched the room until they found me, the little girl kicking at her blanket until Ceri tucked it back.

"Hello, my little ladies," I said as I hobbled down the shallow steps and just about collapsed into the soft leather. I didn't care that I wouldn't be able to find my feet again easily. Ceri lifted Ray and set her in my arms. I breathed deep of the clean scent of baby, and the worries of the world dropped away—if just for a moment—as I held the promise of good things. No wonder nothing seemed to bother Trent anymore.

"Hi, Ray," I said softly, and the somewhat spare little girl blinked solemnly at me, her hand slowly reaching out to grab my nose. It took all her concentration, and my eyes watered when she found it, her tiny nails pinching. She smiled and let go, and snap my broomstick if she didn't look at her sister and smile as if she'd won.

Upon seeing her sister being held by someone new, Lucy

got a determined look on her face, rocking back and forth until she fell forward. It was what she wanted, but she still cried, pushing Ceri's hands away when the woman lifted her up and away from her determined crawl in my direction.

"I swear," Ceri said, corralling the fussy baby who refused to be distracted. "Lucy is a love, but she wants all the attention."

"They keeping you busy?" I said, and Ceri smiled blissfully.

"Like a fairy's ass trapped in a bee's nest," Jenks smartmouthed, and I frowned at him. Lucy, too, was grimacing, her small, angular face pinched as she chafed at her mother's restraint. Though not able to walk or talk, she seemed to have far more going on upstairs for an eight-month-old than she should. Elves apparently had a short childhood. Not like witches, who seemed to take forever to grow up, according to Jenks.

"I like their ears," I said, resisting the urge to touch Ray's, tapping her on her nose instead, and the little girl squealed as if I'd done exactly what she wanted me to do.

Worry entered Ceri's loving gaze. "I do, too, but children can be cruel."

I made a small noise when Winona sighed. "Tell me about it," I whispered.

Jenks hummed his wings at the soft footsteps on the stairway leading up from Trent's great room, and I wasn't surprised when Trent rose into view. I shifted nervously, glancing at my bracelet. I wanted it off, but wasn't sure how to handle the demon aftermath. I was *not* going to let myself be taken to the ever-after, and I didn't know how I—or Trent—would be able to prevent it. The thought that Trent might lose more than his fingers trying to make good on his promise to help me was intolerable. Not that I'd worry about him as much as Ceri and the girls would.

It didn't help that Trent wasn't meeting my gaze. The man looked good in a casual suit, without a tie, and socks instead of dress shoes. His wispy blond hair was a perfect match to

Lucy's, as were his green eyes. His tan was fading. I didn't think he got out into his stables as much as he used to. He gave me and Winona a quick nod as he came in, but he had clearly heard the ear comment and wasn't happy.

"We are *not* mutilating their ears," Trent said, his voice holding the weight of a past argument as he came directly down into the pit by stepping on the couch cushions instead of using the stairs. The move shocked me—I'd never seen him do anything so casual before—and my chin dropped when he sat cross-legged right there on the floor beside Ceri and took Ray from me as if I might dock her ears right then and there.

The missing fingers of his right hand were obvious, and I was embarrassed that he'd lost them while saving me. Ray left me with a wiggle and a baby complaint, the absence of her weight giving me more of a feeling of loss than I would've expected. From nowhere the memory of our kiss, and then the feel of Trent's arms around me last night, layered itself over my thoughts. He was still a bachelor despite the two babies he shared his upstairs rooms with, but clearly he and Ceri were finding common ground. I didn't have any romantic feelings for Trent, but I'd hated him for a long time, and that kiss . . . even if it had been to invoke a spell that saved my life, had been very nice. I was still chalking my enthusiasm-of-the-moment up to having been trapped with him in a car for three days. Not to mention having seen him in a towel and shower-wet skin. I was only human, after all. Well, not really, but the thought was there.

Damn it, I was mentally babbling.

Grimacing, I forced away the memory of what Trent's hair felt like in my fingers and the feel of his lips on mine, pretty sure I knew why he was avoiding my eyes as well. Lucy babbled loudly until he leaned over to tousle her hair, whereupon she kicked her legs and squirmed until Ceri distracted her with that book of bright squares again. Ray snuggled deeper into Trent's lap, content when he whispered something elvish.

Seeing them together like this was a picture of domesticity and peace I knew I'd never have, and I squashed the rising jealousy. If anyone deserved this, it was Ceri.

"You're looking better," Trent said, his free hand taking the book Lucy was waving and gentling it before her, his long fingers moving the pages as if it were a song.

"Thank you for that," I said, and Jenks buzzed his wings in agreement. "For taking the bullet out and not making me go to the hospital, for coming out with Jenks to find me."

"Yeah," the pixy said, now sitting on Winona's shoulder. "The FIB and the I.S. couldn't find their ass in a windstorm."

Winona started, and I glanced at the little girls. Who knew what they were taking in?

Oblivious, Jenks waxed eloquently, "The dumbasses had all their people looking in the wrong places. Glenn was pissed. He wanted to expand the search, and the director wouldn't let him. That's when I called Trent and found out he had a better way to find you, if the fairy farts would listen to him. It was a good thing I went with him, seeing that he almost killed you."

"Jenks . . ." I pleaded, and when he looked at me, I tossed my head to Lucy, listening in rapt attention to the new vocabulary.

"Oh, sorry," he said, his wings flashing a bright red.

Trent turned a page in the book, and Lucy patted a black horse prancing on a green field until Trent murmured a word I didn't understand, his voice more musical than before. My shoulders slumped, remembering his voice rising and falling in the car on the way here, soothing and concerned as he talked with Winona, but laced with guilt for having hit me with his worst.

His eyes rising to mine, Trent's expression became hard. "How much did they get?"

Blinking, I stared. *How much what?* Then I figured it out, and my gut tightened. He meant how much of my demon-curse-invoking blood did they get.

The silence stretched, and with a small sigh, Ceri handed

Lucy to Winona, rising as she said, "I'll make some tea. Winona, can you help me settle the girls down for their naps? Jenks, I'd like a word with you concerning your vocabulary around my daughters."

Jenks let slip a burst of embarrassed red dust, then meekly followed Ceri into the kitchen as Winona stood with Lucy, looking like a demonic teacher/nursemaid as she literally trotted into one of the four rooms that opened up onto the main common room, taking the stairs out of the lowered living room pit with practiced ease. Lucy was still waving that book, babbling as she craned her neck to see Trent, her tiny features starting to twist up into dismay.

Frustration warred with anger, and I tried to keep my expression pleasant as Ray sat cradled in Trent's lap, silently, and perhaps smugly, watching Lucy being carted out. "They're sweet kids," I said, then shifted my eyes to Trent. "You've already had them on a horse, right?"

Trent smiled, turning from successful drug lord and city power to proud father. "More than once." Standing, he handed Ray to Winona as the woman came back out.

From the nursery, a loud complaint was gaining strength. Ceri was "chatting" with Jenks in the kitchen, the pixy sitting miserably on the coffeepot, a gray dust sifting from his drooped wings, and I suddenly felt uncomfortable facing Trent, a world of questions between us. There hadn't been much time when I'd come in between getting cleaned up and put back together.

"How did you find me?" I said as Trent simultaneously asked again, "How much did they get?"

I winced, and Trent sat down across from me, insisting, "Me first."

Pushing back into the cushions, I glanced into the nursery as Winona sang to distract the girls. Everyone I cared about was in danger because I'd let a power-hungry human hate group get my blood. I'd learned the catch-22 of being a demon too late. "Too much," I said, then met Trent's eyes in time to see his flash of worry. "They had ten cc's last night. There's a faction in HAPA that wants to use magic to eradicate us. As soon as they find that enzyme that suppresses the Rosewood enzyme, they're going to synthesize it and . . ." Words failed me, and I looked down. Trent knew what they would do—the same thing the elves had tried to do to the demons only to end up on the verge of extinction themselves.

"They know how to store it, too," I said softly. "It's going to last a good four days."

"I thought they might," Trent said, his beautiful voice going soft. "I have something I want to show you downstairs."

"Now?" I blurted out, and Ceri broke off from her harangue in the kitchen long enough to clear her throat in rebuke.

Trent shifted, the fabric of his shirt making a soft hush of sound as he smiled at her, accepting, tolerant, and in acknowledgment that she was right and he was being rude by taking me downstairs before I'd even had a cup of coffee. I couldn't help but wonder what kind of relationship theirs was evolving into. Ceri loved Quen, but she let the press believe she was Trent's lover because it was the political thing to do. Trent clearly loved both girls as if they were his own, but I was willing to bet Quen had a lot of say in Ray's upbringing.

Ceri had been raised with the idea that you could love one man and be politically attached to another, so a formal marriage between Trent and Ceri might be in the future, but I knew she'd never share his bed. Regardless, they clearly functioned with a great deal of parental unity. It was weird, but it worked, and this show of dry humor at his own expense was a good sign that they were getting along on something other than a professional level.

"After you've eaten, of course," Trent said, *almost* rolling his eyes at Ceri. "Your turn."

My turn. I had a handful of questions, but what came out of my mouth was "The machines I've seen aren't cheap. The research into placing their sites isn't easy to come by, either, seeing that they're located to passively hide them from magic. Spells and charms aren't going to find them easily anymore, but we might be able to track their backer down using the money trail. Get them from that angle."

"Yeah, cut off the money supply to the Tink-blasted lunkers, and HAPA will dry up like a fairy's fling-flan," Jenks said from the kitchen, and Ceri succinctly told him to shut his mouth, her eyes flashing with parental outrage as she prepared the tea.

I watched Trent's tells as he leaned back into the couch, his eyes distant in thought. You couldn't have four perfect places to hide from the I.S. and the FIB where you could plug your illegal genetic machines in without a lot of hush money. At least I knew Trent wasn't behind it.

"I agree," he finally said, crossing his knees, which told me he didn't like where his thoughts had gone. "It's more than disturbing that they got into the lower levels and lifted two of my machines." His focus sharpened on me. "It's someone with a lot of money, very good intel, or both. Very few people even know they existed, much less where they were."

Jenks settled on the coffee table as Ceri made her graceful way down into the seating area, a small tray in her hands. There were cookies along with the expected steaming pot and three delicate teacups, and my stomach rumbled. "Trenton, you interviewed the techs who worked the machines. I can't believe it was any of them," Ceri said.

He nodded, even as he frowned. "Again, I agree." His eyes met mine, a hint of worry in them. "My concern is that it was someone my father once helped with a pesky case of diabetes."

I sighed, leaning back and rubbing the edges of my wound to see how close I could get. It could be anyone. Anyone rich, that is. Back to square one.

"I'll go through my Christmas card list," Trent said, his tone soft in thought.

We were silent, Jenks's wings still. "Where are my manners?" Ceri said suddenly, the cookie plate scraping the table as she extended it to me. "Rachel, you must be starving. That IV you were on last night won't do a thing for your appetite. Please. Take a cookie."

The world is falling apart, and Ceri wants me to eat a cookie? "I'm fine," I said as I accepted the cup of tea she handed me—I was desperate for caffeine in any form—but when my stomach rumbled, I took a cookie, then another, then finally a third when she refused to offer them to Trent until I did.

Trent shook his head when Ceri offered him a cup of tea, and I started when he stood in a quick motion. "Could you excuse me a moment?"

Ceri frowned up at him. "Honestly, Trenton. Can't you stop working for even an hour?"

The polished man stopped short and beamed a genuine smile at her. "This is what I am," he said, inclining his head and making her twist her lips in acknowledgment. "Quen needs to know what's going on or HAPA will be right back in here stealing the newer replacements I had installed last week. That's what thieves do. Take the old, then return for the new."

"Ah, tell Quen that they probably have a doppelgänger curse," I said, then hid my chagrin behind my cup of tea. It was too hot to sip, but that way I wouldn't have to look at him. The hem of his slacks was shifting in agitation, and when I glanced up, he wiped the ire from his face.

"I'll be back in five minutes," he said as he stepped over the twin shallow stairs and started for the stairway to the ground floor. "Eat your cookies. I want to show you something."

Crap, I hadn't had the chance to ask him about taking off the bracelet, and I stiffened.

Misunderstanding my tension, Jenks rose, his wings humming. "Trent? You want to run by me what you're going to show Rache?" he said, and when I gave him a tiny finger motion to go, he buzzed over to the man. Trent jumped, startled, then accepted his presence.

"Quen!" Trent shouted as he jogged down the stairs, and Jenks darted to the main floor ahead of him. From the nursery, a fussing complaint rose, and the trip-trap of Winona's feet as she shut the nursery door but for a crack.

Concerned, I looked at Ceri. "What am I going to be looking at?"

Ceri snapped a cookie in two between her teeth. "I've no idea," she said around a sigh. "Probably the room that the equipment was taken from."

She looked so happily frazzled, so much a person and so little a dead-inside demon familiar, that I felt a warm glow. Not all my screwed-up choices ended up bad. "So how's life?" I said, and her entire face seemed to light up.

"I am so happy it should be illegal," she said as she touched my hand, then drew away. "The children alone," she sighed at the closed dayroom door. "I never thought any of this, any life at all, would be mine. I wake up every morning and pinch myself."

Pleased, I set my tea down and bit into a cookie. It had that lemon flavor that I knew was hiding the distinct tang of Brimstone. I took a breath to protest, then glumly shoved the rest in my mouth and chewed. I didn't like using the Inderland drug, illegal since the Turn, but seeing that Trent manufactured it, purified it to remove the stuff that the people on the street bought it for, and left only the metabolism boosters that the vamps wanted, I'd probably be okay. I might set the FIB's Brimstone dogs into canine throes of delight, though.

"That night I saw you with Al," Ceri was saying, her expression misty with memory, "when he was going to make you his familiar? I thought I was going to die and you were going to take my place. You looked so stupid, but you really did know what you were doing."

I cleared my throat and swallowed, reaching for the tea to wash it down. Yeah, caffeine on top of Brimstone was a great idea. "It was luck," I said, uncomfortable. The tea had a pleasant smoothness, and I leaned back and ran a finger under the bracelet, wanting it off. It was funny how things had turned out, but Ceri was giving me more credit than I deserved.

Ceri saw me looking at my charmed silver and, with her usual bluntness, said, "You should get rid of that. I'd be able to fix your leg if you did. And you could help Winona, too."

Feeling guilty for having been so selfishly clueless for the last five months, I jammed another cookie in my mouth. So many good things would come from taking off the bracelet. So many good things, and just one bad. "I know. That's why I'm still here," I said around my full mouth, nervously wiping the crumbs from the corner of my mouth as Ceri's eyes widened.

"It's about time," she said, sitting oh so straight and proper, as if she hadn't just thanked me for saving her life. "Does Trenton know? He's been fussing in his spelling hut for the last two days."

I shrugged. "I was supposed to come over and talk to him about it yesterday. After spending it in HAPA's cage instead, I think he knows I want it off." Oh God. How was I going to keep Al from blowing away every single safeguard Trent could come up with and just . . . taking me? He was a five-thousand-year-old demon, and I was *not* going to delude myself into thinking that Trent had *anything* that could prevent Al from doing exactly what he wanted.

Unaware of my panic, she patted my hand as Winona slipped from the nursery and went to the kitchen to wash a bottle. "Rachel, I'm proud of you."

Again, I couldn't meet her eyes. Again, she was giving me more credit than I deserved.

Sensing my embarrassment and not understanding it, Ceri let go of my hand. Trent was coming up the long stairs, talking to someone by phone, and I hunched into the cushions, hating this. I wanted the bracelet off, but it was looking harder all the time.

Pace almost . . . bouncy, Trent took the last of the stairs

and stood behind and over Ceri. He'd found a pair of shoes somewhere, and I disparagingly looked at my socks. "Ready, Rachel? I'd like your opinion on the lab that was broken into." His eyes flicked past us to the closed nursery door before coming back to us, his smile fading as he noticed Ceri's tension.

I was such a coward. "You want me to look at a crime scene? That's a switch," I said as I laboriously got to my feet. Ceri rose as well, helping me to the stairs before handing me back my crutch. She was still trying to figure out what was bothering me, and Trent's mistrust grew.

"How's that pain amulet holding up?" he asked as he tried to take my elbow and I jerked away, almost falling. He knew the amulet was fine. He was fishing for what was wrong, and I didn't want to talk about it.

"It's good," I said. "I'm fine."

"You are not fine." Ceri took my arm, pinching it painfully to keep me from pulling away from her. "And don't you let her walk the entire way," she admonished Trent.

"I'm not going to pick her up and carry her screaming to the basement," Trent said. "It's a workday. Besides, she has a crutch."

"Crutch or no, she's hurt!" Ceri protested.

"I mean," Trent said intently, "she can hit me with it if I do something she doesn't like."

Winona snickered from the kitchen, a weird sort of snuffling chuckle. I turned to her, and she had her hand over her mouth in mortification.

Exhaling heavily, I hobbled to the top of the long stairway alone and felt myself pale. Crap, it was a long way, and vertigo threatened. "Thanks," I whispered when Trent slipped a hand under my elbow, and we took our first step down, my feet silent in my new socks. I was reminded of the night I'd been his security and he'd taken me to a casino boat, me wearing one of Ellasbeth's slinkier dresses. We'd always looked good together, though clearly apart even when standing next to each other. That I was in a nasty pair of sweats and he was in a casual suit didn't dispel the feeling of alone-apartness I again felt. Always alone. Both of us.

"I'm glad the amulet is working," he said, stiff and closed even as he helped me, the scent of sour wine a hint between us. "At least you can't be cursed."

His voice carried a hint of mistrust, and my jaw tightened. "I'll tell you when we get to the elevator," I said, and his grip eased on my elbow.

"I have something I want to tell you, too, before we meet Quen and Jenks. We don't have a lot of time. Tell me now."

That's why Jenks was gone. "I want the bracelet off, but there are some complications."

"I told you I'd help," he said, and I took another slow step down, the crutch hurting my armpit. I must have winced, because Trent's grip on my elbow shifted.

"Good, because I'm really going to need it," I whispered, leaning on him even harder.

Eighteen

My grip on Trent's arm had gone white knuckled by the time we got downstairs and to the elevator at the back of the bar, just off the huge great room. I hated that he knew I was hurting, but it wasn't as if I could hide it. There was a wheelchair beside the lift's doors, but I leaned on the wall when Trent pried my fingers off him and pushed the down button.

"Would you rather sit?" he asked, his beautiful voice rising and falling like music, and I ignored him, almost panting through throbbing hurt slipping around my pain charm. The doors slid open, and I hobbled in, propping myself up in a corner of the opulent lift and blowing a strand of hair from my eyes. I hated wheelchairs almost as much as I hated needles.

Trent had the decency to hold his opinion to a raised eyebrow as he trundled the chair in and silently positioned it next to me, locking the wheels in case I wanted to sit. With a soft sigh, he jingled a wad of keys from his pocket and brought to life the entire lower half of the panel. The keys were unusual. Trent liked his gadgetry card system, and I wondered if the recent break-in might have something to do with it.

. The doors slid shut, but we didn't move as Trent punched buttons. "I'm glad you want to take the charm off," he said, his thoughts clearly on something else. "What complications?"

I glanced at the chair, wishing I didn't hurt so much. "You know I put a hole in the ever-after when I made that ley line. The demons' reality is shrinking, and if the ever-after goes, the source of magic goes with it. That's not even touching on how angry they are about me helping you fix the elves' genome. If I can't keep myself on this side of the ley lines, my life is going to be a living hell."

Trent turned from the panel as we started to descend. "Minor details. You won't have to worry about the shrinking ever-after for a generation. As for the other, you are not going to be taken, so don't worry about it."

I looked him up and down in disbelief, not liking his confidence when I was the one in trouble, not him. "Don't you dare belittle my fears!" I said, my eyes narrowing. Weight on my crutch, I held my arm up, showing him the bracelet. "I sat in a cage and watched them do that horrible thing to Winona. I was helpless. I don't want to be helpless anymore. I want to get this damn thing off, and it just keeps getting harder!"

Trent sighed, infuriating me. "Fine. After we look at the lab, we'll look at your options. It can't be that much of an issue. It's just a little imbalance. I won't let Al take you, Rachel. Trust me."

Right. I couldn't stand upright anymore, and I grabbed for the handle of the chair, sullen as I sat down, my entire right side aching. "I don't care what you have come up with to keep Al under control, he's going to blow through it like a pixy through tissue paper, and I will be stuck in the ever-after. Again." I looked up at his confidence. "And this time, there's nothing you can do to stop it. Thanks a hell of a lot, Trent."

His grip tightened on my crutch. "Why are you always angry with me?"

I looked up at him, aching everywhere, frustrated that I hadn't been able to stop what they'd done to Winona, embarrassed that I had to show my weakness in front of him by sitting down, angry with everything. "You want the short list or the long one?"

"I'm tired of it," he said calmly, but the rims of his ears were red and his motions to prop the crutch in a corner were too fast. "Ever since camp you've been picking at me and my ideas."

Picking at him? "*You* are the one doing stuff to irritate *me*," I said, heart pounding. "Shall I start with today and go backward? You hit me with a pain charm—"

"You got in the way. I apologized for that," he interrupted, his green eyes squinting.

"You put me in a cage. Made me fight for my life in the rat fights!"

He smacked a button on the panel, and the lift eased to a jerky halt. In the distance, a faint buzzer sounded. "Your life was never in danger, and I apologized for that, too." His eyes were virulent, and something in me liked it.

"You hunted me like an animal!" I said, his anger fueling my own.

Smelling of ozone and broken trees, Trent leaned over me, his hands on the arms of the chair and his suit coat open to show his trim waist. "You *broke* into my desk," he said tightly. "You *stole* something that could put me and my entire species in the ground. You think I'm going to ignore that? I wouldn't hunt you *now*."

The chair shook as he pushed himself up and away again, standing with a fist on his hip and his stance tight.

Fine. I could write that one off. But it was easy to come up with things about Trent that irritated me. "You kill people," I said, coming out with what really bothered me. "All the time. I hate it."

"And you can't." His voice was mocking, pissing me off as he turned to face me. "Someday you'll thank me for that particular skill. I'm not proud of that ability, but I'm glad I have it. And you're alive because of it. I'm not asking for gratitude, but stop rubbing my nose in the ugly things I do to help you that you are afraid to do yourself."

Oh. My. God. He thought the ability to kill people was a skill? "You murder your own associates!" I shouted, my stomach clenching as I leaned forward in the chair and gestured wildly. "Jonathan practically raised you! And you ran him down under a pack of dogs like a common thief! Ivy and Jenks kill people, too, but *never* those who trust them!"

"Jonathan isn't dead."

As if that ended the conversation, Trent smacked the button to make the elevator move. Shocked, I lurched out of the chair and hit the stop button again. The car swayed and settled as Trent backed away from me, his stance stiff. My heart pounded. "He-he isn't?" I stammered, remembering the awful cry at sunset, the horse under me prancing at the chilling sound. The horse had known what it was. I had, too.

Trent's eyes flicked to me. "I told you he wasn't dead. I've never lied to you. Well, once, maybe. Do I have to apologize for that, too?"

Stunned, I reached for the chair and slipped back into it. "Where is he? Vacation?"

Trent seemed to relax, the tension in his shoulders easing as I carefully lifted my leg, painfully putting my foot on the rest. "He's in the doghouse. Literally."

I looked askance at him, and Trent shrugged, a faint smile playing about his lips as he fastened my crutch to the back of the chair. "I asked Quen to turn him into a hound at the last possible moment. He got bitten in the confusion, but he survived—as I wanted. I would've done it myself, but you were squeamish, and making you understand your position was more important than making Jonathan understand his."

"Is that what you were going to do to me? Turn me into a dog? Put me in your kennel until I learned to sit and heel at your command?" I said, warming as I remembered the dogs singing for my blood as I ran, then later, those same dogs jumping at the fence to get at me even as I stood before them and watched them slaver.

Trent unlocked the chair and shifted it slightly. "He tried to kill you using my magic," he said, not answering me. "I could not let that go. I'll turn him back when his disposition improves. I like him better as a dog, though. He's one of my best trackers."

Stunned, I sat in the chair and tried to make sense of it. Jonathan was alive? I don't know why that was important to me, but it was. Trent was still a murdering bastard, but somehow it felt different. "I don't know if I'm impressed as all hell, or disgusted."

"Like I said," Trent said as he pushed the button to get the elevator moving again. "Always angry with me."

I was silent, feeling him standing behind me, remembering the dangerous determination in his voice when he thought Winona was trying to hurt me. He'd looked for me. Found me when others couldn't. That was important, too.

"I wish you'd stop it," Trent said, his tone distant, as if he was talking to himself. "I like working with you. And Jenks. Even if my judgment needs some fine tuning, apparently. Everyone else I work with is so damn . . . polite."

This was a long way from the cocky businessman who offered me a job I couldn't refuse but had two years ago. I didn't know what to think anymore. The scent of wine and cinnamon was drifting over my shoulder, becoming stronger, reminding me of our three days in a car, the passionate kiss we had shared, his arms around me not twenty-four hours ago. The doors started to open, and I felt a moment of panic. Beyond the elevator was a white hallway, Quen and Jenks turning to see us. Beyond the elevator also waited Trent's mask. He was putting it on already. I could feel his posture stiffening, his hands on the chair becoming relaxed, the strong emotion that I'd seen in him moments ago already hidden.

Heart pounding, I reached out and hit the button to close the door. Jenks rose from Quen's shoulder in a clatter of angry wings, and then the doors shut and we were alone. I was shaking, and I laboriously shifted the chair so I could face him.

"What did you want to tell me?" I said, my heart pounding as I searched his expression, finding a tightness to his eyes that spoke of an opportunity ill spent.

Then it was gone, and I felt alone.

He shrugged, reaching to take my chair and slowly move me to face the doors. "It doesn't matter," he said, and he reached past me to push the button to open the door, the complex scent of linen and starch a breath in me.

"It does to me," I said, but the doors were opening, and Trent took the key from the elevator panel, tucking it away in a pocket as he bumped me over the small gap and out into the hall. Damn it, what had I wasted?

Quen had moved a few steps down the hallway with Jenks. The lean, sinewy man had his back to us, but he'd turned at the noise of the doors opening again. Quen was Trent's long-time security officer, dark where Trent was light, but still looking like an elf. It was in their eyes. The older man's face had the pockmarks that some Inderlanders came away with from the Turn, and spoke of the taint of human blood. You wouldn't know it from his magic, both wickedly fast and powerful. He was wearing his usual loose-fitting uniform, but the black fabric had a tighter fit now that showed off his build, and I wondered if Ceri was the reason for the change. His expression wasn't happy. Neither was Jenks's.

"Rache, we got no time for your elevator fetish," Jenks complained as he swooped to land on the chair's arm. "David's going to be here in half an hour."

"David?" I looked up from trying to appear as if the ride down here had been uneventful, but Quen was eyeing us suspiciously. He knew Trent better than anyone, having raised him as much as, if not more than, Jonathan after both his parents had died. "I thought Ivy was going to pick me up."

"Your alpha called this morning," Trent said from behind me, his voice polished and having a professional, almost plastic sound as he pushed me forward, so different from the elevator. "And since we needed to talk . . ."

I didn't like Trent pushing me. I could feel his eyes on my

tattoo. David, though, had a cooler head than Ivy, and the ride home would be easier on my nerves, so I said nothing.

"Good thing you're in a chair," Jenks said, "or it would take you that long just to walk down the hallway."

"Sure. Okay." I felt vulnerable as Trent slid out from behind the chair and Quen seamlessly took over. "Quen is the only one allowed to push me. Got it?"

"Heaven should fall if I did," Trent muttered as he fell into step beside the chair.

Jenks hummed his wings for an explanation, and I ignored him. "So . . . we're going to look at an empty room?" I asked.

"Something like that." His manner distant, Trent walked beside me, his steps almost silent. "I want you to look at the replacements and tell me if you saw them during your captivity."

"Winona could have done that," Jenks said, and Trent flicked his gaze to him.

"It's a workday. There are people down here, and Winona isn't ready to face the world."

I stiffened, wishing I hadn't yelled at him in the elevator, but a young man in a lab coat with hair as red as mine was striding down the hall toward us, his pace intent and slightly anxious.

"Sir?" he called out as if there was any question that we were his goal. "Mr. Kalamack?"

Trent sighed, and the chair stopped when the man halted before us, glancing at me in curiosity, then going bug eyed when Jenks gave him a peace sign from the arm of the chair. "Sir, if you have a moment?" the man asked, and Trent forced a neutral smile.

"Donnelley, I'd like you to meet Ms. Rachel Morgan and Jenks of Oak Staff," Trent said as he shifted to make more of a circle.

"Jenks of Oak Staff," Jenks echoed, clearly pleased as he rose to dust his hello.

"Pleasure," Donnelley said, shifting his clipboard to shake my hand. "How do you do."

"The pleasure is mine, Darby," I said, and the head lab rat started as I used his first name.

Blinking, he looked from Trent and focused on me for the first time. "Have we met?"

Trent was making a really weird noise in the back of his throat, but I kept smiling. "No," I admitted, "but I was there when Trent decided you were going to take Faris's place two years ago." *Watched him kill your predecessor. Give his daughter a scholarship. Tell Jon to move you up.* "You're Trent's chief geneticist, right?"

Trent cleared his throat, and Quen shifted the chair slightly, probably when he let go of the handles. "Uh, I am, yes," Darby said, his eyes wide. "It's good to meet you." Nervous, he shifted from foot to foot, clipboard before him like a fig leaf. "Mr. Kalamack, I hate to interrupt you, but could I talk to you for a moment? The last batch has gone somewhat awry," he said, somehow looking both confident and embarrassed, his freckles giving him a careless mien. "If you could look at the numbers before our meeting tomorrow, it would be helpful. I say more time, less stimulation. Andrea wants to toss the batch entirely, but we'll lose three months. Won't take but a moment to go over the numbers."

I'll give Trent credit—he didn't even sigh as he looked over me to Quen.

"I'll show her the instruments, Sa'han," Quen said, and Jenks rose up from the chair.

"Yeah, we know our way around," the pixy said, his hands on his hips.

Trent turned halfway from where he had started down the hall with Darby. "I'll meet you there," he said, then strode briskly away with Darby almost jogging to keep up.

Quen started us forward, our pace slower but following their path until they took a sharp right down another corridor and vanished. "I didn't know Trent did anything but fund this merry-go-round," I said.

"He doesn't do the grunt work, no," Quen said softly from behind me. "But he enjoys analyzing the data. His new interests lately have been pulling him away from it, and it shows."

New interests. His sudden zeal in practicing wild magic, maybe?

We passed the corridor that Trent and Darby had turned into, and Jenks rose up to follow them. "Jenks, if you would stay with us, please?" Quen said, and Jenks buzzed back, giving me a shrug as he landed on my knee. No one said anything, and the silence became uncomfortable as Quen slowed, then stopped before a door that looked like any other—apart from the formidable lock, that is.

"In here," Quen said as he came from behind me and unlocked it using a mundane key instead of the card reader. It looked like the reader wasn't even powered up, and again I wondered if the latest break-in had been the end of Trent's love for gadgetry.

I felt like an invalid when Quen opened the door, then backed me in like a professional, swinging me around to face the silent but clearly in-use room. It was a good size, with the expected lab benches, counter space, and machines lining the walls. There was a desk in the corner, and a table used as a makeshift second desk. Charts and graphs took up a bulletin board, and a small, locked cabinet held books, visible behind the glass. It looked very professional and up front, not at all like a place where illegal bio drugs might be researched or prepared, the tools of Trent's blackmail and rise to power on the back of his father's legacy—the same one that had kept me alive.

"What instruments did you see at the sites?" Quen asked, bringing my awareness back to why I was here.

Sighing, I stood, reaching for the crutch that Quen handed me. I fitted it under my arm, and the sudden throb retreated to a dull ache under the pain amulet. Jenks had already gone over the room in three pixy seconds flat and was now getting a drink from the dripping faucet.

"That one," I said, pointing to a machine whose purpose I

couldn't begin to guess at, but it looked the same. "And they had an autoclave smaller than this one," I added, pointing to the tabletop version. "It had a lot of scratches on it. They also had a mini deep fridge, which I don't see here, a couple of battery backups, and a test-tube centrifuge almost identical to that one." I turned, seeing Quen still standing beside the door with my wheelchair. "Bunsen burners, data books, syringes, the usual lab stuff."

He nodded. "Thank you."

"Is this the room they stole them from?" Jenks asked, and Quen's mood became guarded.

"No," he admitted, and my instincts sang out at his reluctance. "That's across the hall."

Crutch swinging, I started for the door, almost pushing Quen out of my way. "Just over there, you say?" I said, and he backed up as Jenks nearly flew into his face.

"Rachel," Quen protested, but I got the door open despite the wheelchair's being in the way.

Triumphant in my small success, I hobbled out the door with Jenks, coming to a quick halt when I almost ran into Trent.

"Oh! Hi!" I said cheerfully as Jenks dropped in altitude, thinking we'd never get a look now. I knew better. Trent wouldn't have asked me down here to simply identify machines. I could have done that from a photograph. He wanted me to look at something more, and I was willing to bet it was the crime scene. "Does this tour include the crime scene?" I asked, and Trent glanced behind me at Quen.

"It does." Trent took my elbow, surprising me. "I was hoping you would, if it's not too much trouble."

His manner was his usual businessman facade, but that touch changed everything, and I squinted at him, wondering at the slant to his eyes, the hint of humor at his lips. Or was it just my imagination, and he simply didn't want me to fall down and sue him?

"Sir," Quen said, pained by the sound of it, and Jenks laughed.

"Lookie there, Rache!" the pixy said as he landed on my shoulder. "Someone's going to let you in before the vacuum guys."

"Actually, we've been through it thoroughly already," Trent said as he let go of me and sifted through his own wad of keys. "But I do want Rachel's opinion. She finds what others miss: sticky silk, class-book photos, curse-hidden graves, HAPA hate knots." He held up a key. "Or so I've heard. Ah. Here it is."

"Wayde found the knot," I admitted, still feeling the warmth on my elbow where he'd gripped me. "Thanks, Trent," I said as he got the door open and leaned over to push it wide for me.

"After you," he said, his smile holding real warmth, but it was Jenks who buzzed in first, my ever-vigilant vanguard.

Hobbling in, I first noticed the stuffiness, as if the vents had been sealed off. Other than that, it looked like a normal lab, almost a mirror image of the one across the hall, with the exception of a few conspicuous blanks. I step-hopped to the empty lab bench, leaning against it while Jenks flitted over everything. Quen was watching him closely, and I spun in a slow circle, trying to get a feel for the room.

"There were no prints, no sign of forced entry," Trent said, and I stared at the ceiling, not knowing why. "We think they used a card, which is why we've gone to a physical key for the time being. Everything is as we found it except for some of the books. They're across the hall."

"Along with the desks?" I asked, and his eyebrows went up. "There aren't any here," I added, and he nodded in understanding.

Jenks finished his circuit and landed on the sink's spigot. "You sure you don't have a mole? It's the easiest answer."

Quen shifted his feet, a move that wasn't missed by Trent. "That's always a possibility," Quen said, sounding insulted.

"We're not actively pursuing that avenue of entry," Trent added.

I frowned and turned away. Though easy, a mole seemed

unlikely to me, too. Trent paid everyone far too much to be easily bribed, but ignoring any prospect seemed risky. "I saw one of these over there, too," I said, pointing at a titrator, and I shivered. It was scary knowing that HAPA had been an elevator ride away from the girls. Eloy had been here, taken what he'd wanted, and left. Illegal machines used for illegal genetic research.

I shifted down the counter, moving slowly so my motions wouldn't break my amulet-to-skin contact. Everything here had probably been used to save me from the Rosewood syndrome. It was weird that I'd once tried so diligently to bring Trent down. He hadn't changed. I had.

Had I sold out? I wondered. *Or just gotten smarter?* My dad had worked with Trent's dad. But my dad was not the honest, upright man that I'd thought he was. Sighing, I ran a hand along a mundane dishwasher. *Maybe I was wrong . . .*

"Who am I dealing with?" Trent asked, the cold tone in his voice pulling my head up.

"Besides HAPA?" Jenks asked.

I hesitated, silent but not ignoring him while feeling my way down the counter as if trying to sense the people who had been here before me. Quen was wincing at my hands-on approach, but Trent wanted me to touch or he wouldn't have let me in. I really needed to start cutting the guy some slack. He understood how I worked, and he let me get the job done.

"Two human women," I said as I lifted the door to the freezer chest and a wave of stale, room-temp air rose up. "Chris is the driving force behind the science. She can tap a line, so she's got some elf in her somewhere. I think HAPA is going to ignore that until they don't have to, and then she's dead. In the meantime, she runs the science behind the plan," I said idly as I closed the fridge. "She's not much of a team player, more of a team yeller. Thinks she's in charge, but she's not. Did they take anything from the fridge?"

Trent looked inquiringly at Quen, and the man muttered, "Several cases of tissue-growth media."

Nodding, I leaned heavily on the counter as I retraced my

steps, not knowing why. My leg hurt, and Jenks watched, his dust becoming a concerned blue. "Chris has no problem treating people as a means to an end," I said, jaw clenched as the memory of Gerald forcing Winona's clothes off swam up, unwanted. "Really likes her black magic. If she was a witch, curiosity would have her dead by now. If she doesn't smarten up, I give her a month, but I think she's just clever enough to survive. They used a curse to hide one of their victims, and I'd be willing to bet she owes someone a favor."

Once again at the far end of the counter, I opened a drawer to see a plethora of plastic-wrapped instruments. I frowned, not knowing what they were for, then shut the drawer, looking up in exasperation at the large fluorescent lights. "Then there's Jennifer," I said, and Jenks laughed.

"Jennifer?" he scoffed, and I curled my fingers under so he wouldn't see them shaking. "HAPA takes in Jennifers?"

"Don't stereotype, Jenks. HAPA is an equal-opportunity hate group," I said. "She's the pretty face they use to catch their takes and procure their lab supplies. I think she's a nurse when she's not mutilating witches. She keeps the data books." Frowning, I rubbed my fingers over the counter, wondering if I could feel a faint tingle of magic in my memory. "Jennifer doesn't like the magic, but she's not as military as Eloy."

My pulse quickened, and I looked at the floor and an unusual pair of scuff marks—as if from a ladder. Again I looked at the light fixture. By the door, Quen shifted his weight, probably concerned that he'd missed something.

"Then there's Gerald," I said, shuffling to the counter against the wall to look at the scratches from a different angle. "Up until I tried to take his head off with a pipe, he didn't seem to be a bad egg—for a hypocritical, bigoted card-carrying HAPA member with a squirrel rifle under his bed. He's the muscle and security. Guns and cameras. Good old boy with a degree."

My leg hurt, and I straightened. "Last is Eloy. He's not there much, either working as a distant sentry or just making himself scarce. He's old-school HAPA. Military background. Planner. Finds and stocks their next location. He doesn't like magic. At all. I think he was the one who killed the vampires when they took me." I dropped my head and rubbed my brow, thinking I might need a new pain amulet. Everything was hurting. "He's in charge, but is letting Chris have enough latitude that she thinks she's running it, and there is clearly some question in her mind. He has the purse strings, but the real question is where HAPA is getting their funds."

"I agree," Trent said slowly, and I noticed that he hadn't moved from where he'd first come in. "What are the chances that HAPA has teamed up with another group whose aim is simply a return to old science?"

I quit rubbing my forehead. "I thought of that, too. Chris was adamant that she's HAPA."

Looking from Trent's concerned expression, my wandering eyes landed on the ceiling again. Jenks cleared his throat, his hands on his hips as he waited for me to tell him what was going on in my head. "Jenks, tell me what you think of that light," I finally said, and his wings hummed into invisibility as he rose. Quen was frowning, but something had been right under the light and in the traffic flow, and I was guessing it had been a ladder.

Sure enough, the pixy whistled. "It's clean!" he exclaimed, still out of sight between the ceiling and the top of the fixture. "Really clean. Someone wiped it. No dust at all."

Trent turned to Quen, and the man had the decency to look embarrassed. "I'll find a ladder," Quen said, looking awkward as he shifted past Trent to get to the door.

Jenks dropped from the ceiling, his dust a bright gold. "I'll come with you," he said, and after Trent's initial cringe, he nodded his agreement. Not that Trent could stop Jenks from doing whatever the hell he wanted without downing him with sticky silk.

Quen almost slunk out the door, clearly upset that we'd found something he'd missed, but I wasn't going to lie to save face for him. Jenks had put himself on the chagrined elf's shoulder, and just as the door shut, I heard him say, "Hey, don't sweat it. I didn't think to look up there, either. She's good like that."

The heavy door shut behind them, and the silence took hold. Trent's suit made a soft sound as he levered himself up onto a counter, looking at odds with the lab setting, more like the man I remembered from our cross-country trip, even if he was wearing dress shoes instead of stable boots.

Remembering the conversation in the elevator, I ran my hand across the top of the counter, leaning against it, the space of the room between us. My chair was across the hall, and I was too macho to ask him to get it for me. Propping my crutch up beside me, I covered my middle and met his eyes, refusing to let the silence get to me. We were alone again, and this time, I swore I wasn't going to yell at him.

"Why did you come out to find me?" I asked, and he rubbed his nose, ducking his head to avoid my gaze as he slowly slid from the counter.

"I was afraid you might try taking your charmed silver off without breaking the spell first," he said, his gaze going to it. "And kill yourself in the process." His eyes met mine. "I rescued you. Mmm. I've never done *that* before."

"You didn't rescue me," I said. "Winona and I got out on our own! She even stomped on the bad guy!"

"You got shot," he said, his voice suddenly bland as he looked at the ceiling. "You had no phone, no magic, no car. Your only mode of transportation was a scared woman who looked like a demon." His attention fell on me, and I felt stupid. "Still mad at me, I see . . ."

Damn it, I was doing it again. Frustrated, I forced myself to exhale slowly. "You're right," I said, swallowing hard. "You rescued me. Us. Thank you." My eyes narrowed. "You're not my Sa'han, though."

He blinked, arms falling from his middle as he stood upright. "Ah, you heard that?" he said, face crimson.

I'd never seen Trent blush, and I hesitated in my anger. "Oh yeah."

He winced. "See, there's more than one meaning to that honorific. It's not always a term of respect from a subordinate to a superior."

I nodded. "Uh-huh. You're not my Mal Sa'han, either." I'd heard him try to call Ceri that, and she wouldn't let him. I had a feeling it had a romantic overtone.

"God, no," he said, his flush making me even more sure of it. "I only meant that your safety was my responsibility." I cocked my head, and he added, "My responsibility not like a jailer or a parent, but as an equal. It was your idea."

Mine? My confusion must have shown, because he said, "The curse that emancipated me? 'I will come to your aid in a time of war'? Your idea, not mine, but an agreement is an agreement."

My head flopped to the other side of my shoulders as I eyed him from a different perspective, but he still looked like the same irritating man, his ankles crossed and his stance confident. "So you were out there perched in that tree looking for me because of some stupid Latin phrase?"

"Why do I even try?" he whispered to the ceiling. "Rachel. Listen to me for once. I helped get you into this situation with the demons, and I am standing beside you to get you out. Whatever it takes."

I thought of Ceri and the girls, what the loss of Trent would mean to them. My pulse thundered. I wanted to believe him, I wanted to be someone who wasn't afraid. His eyes were on my bracelet, and I hid it under my other hand. "Trent. I've got nothing to keep me on this side of the lines. He knows my summoning name, so even holy ground won't work this time. I don't care what you've done, what charms or spells you've made, but there is nothing on God's green earth that is going to stop that demon from taking me."

"So you made a hole in the ever-after," he said, and I threw my hand in the air—he still didn't get it. "You'll find a way to fix it. Al is broke, but only if you're dead, which you aren't. He's going to be angry you hid out from him for five months, but that was your choice—deal with it. You saved the elven species, but you also have the cure for the demons' infertility. What more do you need?"

"No, I don't," I said quickly. "I am *not* going to be a demon broodmare."

He touched his chin in thought. "Perhaps I should have said I have the cure for their infertility. If I can fix you, I can fix them. All they have to do is trust me."

Like that will ever happen. But my clenched jaw eased. "You'd do that? I thought you were at war with them."

Trent's toe scuffed the floor. "No one can remember *why* the war started," he said. "Maybe it's time to end it. It's what my father wanted. Yours too."

I looked at my bracelet, my heart hammering. The memory of being helpless rose up, not of simply being in a cage and watching Winona being tortured and knowing I might have been able to stop it if I hadn't been afraid. No, it was the feeling of helplessness I'd known all my life, of being too weak, betrayed by my own body. And then the helplessness because of a lack of skill until I learned what I could do. The helplessness brought on by my own people when they shunned me, then being afraid of what I was and of what I had done. *I wasn't going to be afraid anymore. I could fix Winona. I owed her her life back.*

Swallowing, I turned to Trent, but my next words died as the door opened and Quen came in, Jenks riding the ladder he was toting. My face was hot, and I knew I had a panicked look on it. Trent had something they wanted. Something they wanted so badly I might be able to bargain with Al for my continued freedom. *Trent could help me,* I thought. And this time I believed it. If we could hold Al off long enough for him to listen.

The clatter of the ladder being set up was harsh, and both Jenks and Quen looked up when neither Trent nor I said anything. "In the meantime," Trent said to fill the breach, "Winona is welcome to stay. We don't have a nanny, and the girls seem to like her."

Jenks's wings buzzed, and even Quen accepted that at

face value, but I dropped my head, trying to lower my pulse before Jenks sensed it racing. I had to talk to Trent. I didn't want to be afraid anymore. I didn't want Winona living her life as a monster. I didn't want anyone killing for me when I could use my magic and avoid bloodshed altogether. And if someone had to die, then . . . Oh God, I didn't know if I could do that.

But I wasn't going to be afraid anymore, and it was the scariest thing I'd ever decided. With a single-minded purpose, I hobbled forward, my hand reaching for the ladder in support.

"What the Tink-blasted hell do you think you're doing?" Jenks said, and I started, shocked. *How did he know?*

"You're not getting on the ladder," Quen said dryly. "I can tell if the light has been disturbed."

Oh! I took my hand off the ladder, flustered. Still leaning against the counter, Trent watched me pull back as if stung. Our eyes met over the length of the room, and when he saw my frightened, lost expression, his entire demeanor shifted. His lips parted and he pushed from the counter. Eyebrows high, he smiled faintly, a new excitement making his motions sharp. He knew. I was an open book to him. It had begun, my terrifying, I'm-not-afraid world.

"Um, I have to go," I said, and Jenks's wings clattered in sudden mistrust.

"What did you say to her, Trent?" the pixy demanded as Trent came forward and took my elbow, helping me to the door. "Where are you going? We just got the ladder. Don't you want to know if this is how they got in?"

Oh shit. *I was going to take the bracelet off.* My heart pounded, and I felt dizzy.

Trent's grip on my elbow tightened and he slipped his mutilated hand around my waist. "Now?" Trent murmured. The scent of wine and cinnamon filled me, and I closed my eyes, trying to stand upright, but it only made me dizzier. "Let me know what you find," he said loudly, his voice calm under a lifetime of business dealings, but I don't think he was fooling Quen. "Rachel has been on her feet too long. I can get her to her chair okay. Ceri will skin me alive if she passes out. I'm going to take her upstairs. Quen, a full report of what you find, on my desk ASAP."

"I'm fine," I said breathily, but I wasn't. I couldn't meet Jenks's eyes as I shuffled out, but he was more excited about helping Quen with the light than anything else. I didn't want him around when Al showed up. At least it was daylight. I'd have a few hours to make a new scrying mirror and try to explain before it all hit the fan.

Unless he jumps me to the ever-after, that is.

"Us," Trent said as the door shut behind us and I looked up in the cool emptiness of the hall. "Unless he jumps *us* to the ever-after. Get it right, Rachel. I said I would help."

"H-how . . ." I stammered, but he just smiled, his grip on my elbow never changing as he helped me to my chair.

Nineteen

My leg hurt, and I sat in my rolling chair, as I had done for much of the first part of my life, numb as someone else moved me around. Saying nothing, Trent smoothly pushed me through the downstairs labs until we were rising up to the first floors through a different elevator than we'd come down in. The humming, chill silence of the basement labs was replaced by the warmth of neutral carpet and soft conversation as he wove me through the front offices, skillfully evading or redirecting comments or requests from curious employees.

Almost without notice, the noise muted, then vanished. The warmth of the sun spilled in over my feet, and still I sat, doing nothing as the chair halted. I felt Trent slip around from behind me as he took a tray from someone coming in, then his beautiful voice rising and falling reassuringly as he ushered whoever it was out and shut the door with a soft and certain thump.

Then there was silence. Slowly the wonderful scent of coffee slipped into me.

My breath went in and out, and I looked up to see that we were in Trent's office. The fake sun was coming in the huge video screen showing this year's foals standing to take in the last of the warming rays, but it felt warm on my feet and looked real enough to me. Trent was sitting behind his desk, his feet up on his daily planner, his fingers steepled as he watched me, a curious tilt to his head, his fair hair almost in his eyes. Between us on a wooden tray was a pot of what had to be coffee and two empty cups with the Kalamack logo ghosted in silver.

"Are you okay? You kind of spaced out." He put his feet on the floor and leaned over the desk, an excitement I'd never seen before sparking in his eyes, making them almost . . . mischievous? "I've never said that before. Spaced out. But that's exactly what you did."

Still feeling numb, I looked at the carafe of coffee, then my silver bracelet, the Möbius strip with Latin etched into it wrapped around me, shining in the sun. "Did I?"

My voice trailed off as he got to his feet and came around to the front of the desk, his motions still having a quick edge. "You started to go into shock. I thought my office would be better than a roomful of helpful Ceri." He hesitated. "Unless you want her in on this, too?"

Having her here would be like asking someone else to take my bullet. No. I was done with that, and I shook my head as he poured two cups and offered me the first. It wasn't the shock of injury, but the realization that the bracelet was going to come off, that everything was going to change. I was going to be a demon for real, the power, the responsibility . . . If people were going to die from my decisions, it would no longer be because I was too afraid to act. *But to kill someone* . . . I didn't know if I could do that. I desperately didn't want to be that person.

The sound of the coffee chattering into the second cup was loud as I brought mine to my lips, my hands shaking. The mug was warm in my fingers, and the coffee slipped into me, both bitter and rich, shocking me awake. "Thank you," I said softly as he sat back on the edge of his desk with his own cup.

He inclined his head slightly, looking as fabulous as ever, more appealing than before because I had no idea what he was going to do, what he was capable of.

"Don't do that," I said, my gaze going everywhere but to him.

"Do what?" He sipped from his mug, one long leg draping to the floor, the other pulled up slightly.

"Sit on your desk and look sexy."

Trent hesitated. Clearing his throat, he slipped from the desk, fidgeting as he looked at his chair, behind his desk. It was obvious he didn't want to sit there, and looking somewhat sheepish, he used his foot to shift one of the leather chairs in front of his desk so that it faced me more fully. "I've never sat in one of my own chairs before," he said as he eased back into it, slowly, as if testing it out. His eyes roved over his desk, taking it in from a new point of view. He might not have any idea what it meant to me—that he wasn't behind his desk and in a position of power—but then again, he probably did.

More nervous yet, I held my coffee with two hands and sipped, afraid of what was coming.

"You're ready?" Trent said, and I flicked a glance at him.

Crap, he looked even sexier now, more relaxed, more accessible—more off-limits. I swallowed my coffee and rested the cup against me, warming my middle. "Yes." My voice didn't even quaver, but I was a wreck inside. Al was going to take me. He was going to take me and stick me in a little box. And that was if I was lucky. This was a dumb idea.

"Mmm." His foot was twitching, and he stilled it as he saw me notice. "I have a room set up. Lots of circles, protection. We should break the charm now before the sun goes down so we have a chance to prepare for him popping over."

My breath came fast. If we waited, Ceri would get involved. "No."

"No?" I felt his eyes land on me, his almost subliminal fidgeting stop as he probably weighed his chances of changing my mind. Sighing, he stretched for his phone. "Give me a moment, then. I'll get some charms sent up that might contain him for a few moments—"

Alarm was a wash of adrenaline, waking me up almost more than the coffee. *I might never see Ivy or Jenks again . . .*

"We're not going to trap him when he shows."

"You're joking."

We, I thought, my pulse quickening. I had said "we," and it had sounded right. Scooting my rolling chair back, I looked up at him, breathless. Trent had a ley line running through his office. I'd used it once to find the resting site of a murder victim in his stables. I could see and talk to Al through a ley line even if the sun was up—and duck out of it if he tried to abduct me. "Am I in it?" I asked him, knowing he understood when his frown turned severe.

"No. Rachel—"

"How about now?" I said, shifting backward. I could feel nothing from the line, and I suddenly wanted the bracelet off, knowing it for the manacle it was. How had I allowed this? Was I so thoroughly ruled by fear? *Oh God. My mom . . .*

"No." Trent stood, and I rocked him to a halt with a raised hand.

"I promised Al . . ." I said, my voice catching when it rose. Taking a steadying breath, I tried again. "I promised Al that I wouldn't ever summon him into a circle," I said, my voice low to keep it from breaking. "Trust is going to keep him calm long enough to listen."

Almost laughing in disbelief, Trent put all his weight on one foot. "I thought you were going to be smart about this," he said, calm but mocking as he stood before me in his thousand-dollar suit. "*Nothing* is going to keep him calm. He's a demon. You can't trust him."

"You're asking their entire species to trust you to give them a cure, not a death sentence," I said, then glanced at the closed door and the knock that Trent ignored. "I won't let you offer them a cure in a way that prevents them from accepting it." Trent was scowling, and I shrugged. "Look, I understand if you want to leave the room and let me handle it."

"I'm not chickening out," he said, affronted as he just about read my mind. "I'm pointing out that a little preparation will make the difference in walking or limping away from this. Why are you making this difficult?"

I extended my coffee to him, and he took the half-empty mug as if unsure of what it meant. "Even with the promise of a cure, you've grossly overestimated our chances," I said matter-of-factly, shaking inside. "I'd prefer to contact Al immediately after taking the charm off, but if you can take it off for me right now, I'll wait and call him when I get home. He'll probably sense me and be waiting for me in the line by then." *I'm never going to make this work. Never.*

Trent set both our mugs on the tray with twin sharp taps, his motions abrupt. My pulse pounded as he said nothing, moving behind me and, in swift motions, shifted my chair two feet back. My hair swung as he jerked the chair to a halt. "Now you're in the line," he said darkly.

"Thank you." I clenched my hands to hide their shaking.

Trent grumbled something I didn't hear, his head down as he went behind his desk and crouched. I heard a drawer open and close, and when he stood, he had a mirror in his hand. It was my scrying mirror. I could tell from here.

"Where did you get that?" I said, my eyes widening as I reached for it. "I thought it was lost in the quake!" My scrying mirror would make everything easier. How had he gotten it?

Trent shrugged, his eyes not meeting mine as he handed it over. "I asked the coven for it. I knew you were going to want it eventually."

The glass felt cold on my fingers, empty. The etched mirror still threw back the world in a wine-tinted wash, but it was pale and two-dimensional—dead. *God, what have I done to myself?* I suddenly realized Trent was standing over me, inches away, the scent of a green woods coming from him to ease my headache.

"Tell me how you plan on staying alive long enough to bargain with him if you don't use what I've prepared," he asked, his tone telling me he thought I was being stupid.

I looked up, feeling sick. "I don't really have a plan, but

hiding in a spell-proof room surrounded by an arsenal isn't going to help. He's got my summoning name."

His brow furrowed. "So do I," he said as he went to his desk.

True. My breath slipped from me in a long exhale. I was not going to be their dog toy. I'd seen dog toys, and they were eventually broken and covered in slobber, left in the rain to be forgotten. My faint smile faded as I saw Trent's worry, his concern . . . his fear under his professional veneer. He would do this with me, and he knew the danger.

Rummaging now in his top drawer, Trent said, "Can't I just—"

"Defense only. Promise me," I demanded. He hesitated, his eyes never shifting from mine. "Damn it, Trent, promise me," I said, not wanting him to lie to me. "You're all about my taking responsibility, well, this is my decision. I have to do it my way."

Grimacing, he slammed the drawer shut, a bit of colorful silk in his hand. "It's not that I don't trust *you,*" he said as he straightened, stressing it.

I shifted the heavy glass on my knees. It used to be alive, but now it felt dead. Or was I the one who was dead? "Trust me?" I mocked. "He might kill you. I'm not saying he won't. But if you raise one charm in anything other than defense, I will spell you down myself." I waited while he frowned at me, his desk between us. "Sure you want to stay?"

His grumble was enough for me, and I looked behind him at the door, feeling like two kids behind the barn playing show-and-tell. Ivy and Jenks were going to be mad. Ceri would be ticked that I didn't ask for her help. Quen would say I was foolish for not asking for his assistance. But I didn't want to endanger them. Ivy and Jenks were moving on without me, and that was good. Ceri had her life with her children before her, and I wouldn't risk that. Quen was a dragon, ready to swoop in and save me, but leaving me still afraid. Trent . . . Trent was good enough to help, and bad enough to not be a crutch. Perhaps more important, I *wanted* to do this on my own. Trent could help because I needed it and he'd gotten me into this. He was damn well going to be there when I got out.

Goose bumps tingled up my arms when I recognized the cap and ribbon in his hand. "Thank you," I whispered, remembering the vengeance of the lines running through me with no aura between me and the energy of creation. "Is it going to hurt?"

"No." His word crisp and short, he put his cap on with a quickness that dared me to say he looked funny. He seemed so different, I didn't know what to think anymore. The ribbon went around his neck, over his collar and down his front. It swung as he dragged his chair into the line to face me squarely. I should have been able to feel the line, see the ever-after with my second sight, but I was dead inside.

"Why am I even here if you won't let me do anything?" he grumbled as he settled himself, his knees inches from mine.

I was starting to shake hard enough for him to notice, but I couldn't stop, and I should be shaking. Why was he here? Because he was strong enough to watch my back, and weak enough that it would be me solving this, not him. But I couldn't tell him that.

"Give me your hands," he said, and my eyes jerked to his. His need to do this shone in them. He was itching to give something back to Al for his missing fingers, itching to prove to the demon that he wasn't a doormat, a familiar, a commodity, but someone the demon needed to take seriously. God, I knew how that felt. How was I going to keep him alive?

My fingers slipped into his, and we clasped hands, my knuckles resting on the cool glass of my scrying mirror. His hands were cool, mine were shaking, and he gave me a little squeeze, jerking my attention back up.

"Don't let go until I say," he said as I stared at him, startled. But he had closed his eyes, his lips moving in something that wasn't Latin, wasn't English. The syllables slipped through the folds of my brain like slushy ice, chilling and numbing, the musical rise and fall like unsung music, the wind in the trees, the growth of a tree to the sun. Mesmerizing.

Trent's eyes opened as if having felt it in me. *"Sha na tay, sha na tay,"* he intoned. *"Tunney metso, eva na calipto, ta sowen."*

My eyes widened as my fingers gripped his tighter. I suddenly realized something was stirring in my chi. I stiffened as the sensation of a painful lifting rose through me, the delicious hurt of the old being peeled back to expose new skin, hurting from the first breath of wind. Like liquid light sliding around corners, ley-line energy coursed into me, trickling enticingly slowly as it tripped every synapse one by one.

My breath came in a heave as I suddenly realized it tasted like Trent's soul, his energy spilling into me in ever-increasing waves. Frantic, I looked at Trent, his eyes shut, his lips moving as he chanted, his fingers starting to shake as they held mine. I could do nothing. He had told me not to let go.

My breath came in, and I held it. I could feel the charm he had bespelled me with begin to unravel, laying within me, still, like a knot that had been loosened and needed only to be pulled apart. His energies mixed with mine, gathered in my chi until there was enough for him to ease me back into alignment with the rest of the universe. It was colored from his soul, both light and dark, mixing without mixing, swirling with my natural energies until the two were one.

And finally it reached the tipping point. With a wrench, I felt a tug, and like two drops of water, my soul was realigned with reality.

Trent's eyes flashed open, wide and wondering as his chanting stopped. "My God," he whispered, suddenly tense and shocked. The heat of the charm lay in his eyes, the promise of what could be—what might be if I could trust another with my heart again. And it hurt me knowing it wasn't mine.

"Is it done?" I said, feeling the pain of unfulfilled passion. I ached for it to be gone.

Trent licked his lips, shaking his head. *"Tunney eva so Sa'han, esperometsa."*

I gasped, Trent's fingers tightening on mine as the sudden power of the lines flooded me, pure and untainted. They rang my soul like a bell, bathing us in sound inside and out. I gloried in it, my head flung back as I breathed it in, feeling it pool in me like gold, washing away my lingering headache and tingling all the way down to my toes. It was glorious, and I almost cried as I realized how deeply I'd cut myself off. Never. Never again.

Exhilarated, I looked at Trent. My eyes opened wide as I saw him sitting before me with his head down and his aura glowing about him like a second shadow, magnificent and beautiful, not a hint of demonic taint, the tragic streaks of red running through the brilliant haze of gold.

And then I realized he was clenched in pain.

My eyes went to our clasped hands. "I'm sorry!" I said, trying to pull away only to have his hands grip mine more tightly.

"Dampen it so I can think," he gasped, and I did, still able to feel the currents ebb and flow. My God, why had I done this to myself?

Trent looked up, a sheen of sweat on his brow. *"Sha na tay, euvacta,"* he whispered, and I sucked in air when his fingers spasmed, opening from mine and falling away. "Now it's done and sealed," he almost croaked, looking at his fingers as they cramped into claws.

Breathless, I sat up. Eyes wide, I looked at the bracelet. It still hung on my wrist, but the words were gone and the metal had turned black. The spell was broken. Frantic, I pushed it to my hand, wanting it off. The metal pinched my skin, and then with a wrench, I felt the metal seem to expand and it slipped over my folded fingers and was gone.

My heart pounded. I stared at the ring of black metal as it wobbled to a halt and sat on the carpet in a fake patch of sunlight. *It was done.*

"Better?"

Blinking away tears, I focused on Trent. He was easing back, looking wan. I nodded, unable to find the words. I could feel the lines—all of them—though the sensation was fading. They sang in me like the heartbeat of the sun, a thousand tones all harmonizing to one om of sound. And then they all slowly vanished with the sensation of sparkles, leaving only the soft hum of the line we were sitting inside.

"Thank you," I said, then grimaced. Now it would get difficult.

On my lap, the sparkling line of the scrying mirror glittered, caging the ruby image it was throwing back into reality. My fingers ached where they rested on the smooth surface, and I could feel the latent energy pressing into my legs. The bracelet was dead, the mirror was alive. Everything had shifted. Now all we had to do was convince Al to let me stay . . . and everything would be fine.

Trent was rubbing his hands, the white marks of where I'd gripped him too tightly obvious. "I'm sorry," I said, and a heavy weariness edged his grim expression.

"For this?" He held up his hand, the white pressure marks easing.

I shook my head, afraid to bring up my second sight to see Al waiting for me already. "For what happens next."

Silent, he got up to stand beside me. He avoided my eyes, and I wondered what he'd felt as his soul had crept into my own through the cracks and crevices, bursting the wall that he'd put around it. He was still looking at his hand, probably remembering Al taking his fingers off in an attempt to move him to the ever-after one ounce of flesh at a time. A pang of tension that had nothing to do with talking to Al went through me, and I took his hand and turned it over. "When this is over, can I fix that?" I asked him even as he stiffened, surprised that I'd touched him.

His posture eased. "If you like," he said as he pulled his hand away.

"Are you sure you can cure the demons?" I asked, and he nodded, shakily moving to take up a position behind me as

I put my free hand on the mirror. Al would listen. He'd give me anything for that. *If he believed me.* Fear made me jerk as my eyes closed, and, taking a breath, I drew the glory of the ever-after energies into me. My gut was a slurry of emotion—doubt, dread, the fear that I wouldn't be able to live up to my bold words that I could be the demon—hope, confidence, and elation from being connected to the lines again: all mixed together until I felt as if I was going to throw up. A quiver went through me when I found the collective, and I felt Trent shift his feet. *Al?* I called out in my mind before I lost my nerve. *He would listen. I'd make him.*

But there was nothing. No response, no echo. I frowned, worry joining everything else.

"Maybe he's dead or in jail," Trent said, knowing what was going on from my attitude.

"He might be sleeping," I said, having run into this before. Shoving my fear aside, I steadied myself to try again. *Al!* I shouted in my mind. *Ah, it's Rachel.*

This time there was a faint stirring, like a bat opening his beady little eyes, reflecting the world in a cold, uncaring light as his consciousness joined mine. It was him, and a spike of fear-based adrenaline was cold in me. *Um, Al?* I said again, wary at the rising hatred in me, a reflection of Al spilling into my psyche.

Goddamned mother pus buckets. His evil, cold thought slithered through mine, calculating, ancient, bitter—and utterly lacking his usual noble British accent. *Back already? Leave me the hell alone!*

A bare hint of intent warned me, and I yanked my hand off the glass. I jumped as a pop echoed both in my ears and thumped through my lap, and I looked down to see a tiny crack running through my mirror.

"What happened?" Trent asked, peering over my shoulder.

I could smell him, feel his breath on me, but my eyes were fixed on the glass. My lips parted and I ran a finger over the mark, feeling only the smooth, unblemished mirror. The break hadn't gone all the way through. The amount of mental force needed to crack it even this much had been immense, though. If I hadn't severed the connection in time, it could have been me.

"He cracked my mirror," I said, not sure if it was going to work anymore. "He doesn't think it's me. He thought I was one of his buddies, messing with him." Feeling reckless, I put my hand back on the calling glyph. "Give me a sec."

"Ah, Rachel?" Trent said, but I shrugged out from under his hand and focused on the mirror.

Hey, you sad excuse for a lousy-ass demon, I thought loudly. *You broke my friggin' mirror! It took me all day to make it, and I'm not going to make another! I'm trying to talk to you, so knock it off, moss wipe!* I was tired of being afraid. I'd be bitchy instead.

Again, I felt my consciousness expand, and I waited, ready to pull my hand back.

Rachel? Al's thought came with a hint of his noble British accent. *You're alive?*

So far so good. Now it would get tricky. *Yes, I'm alive, but if you keep throwing crap at me, I'm going to turn around and—*

You're alive! Al bellowed in anger, and I winced, my bravado vanishing.

Uh, yeah. Hey, um, Al . . .

And you're with that elf! The force of his thoughts arced through me like fire.

I pulled my hand from the mirror, certain he knew where I was. "Help me up?" I asked Trent. "He's coming. Get behind me."

"Where is behind you?" Trent grumbled, his hand warm and sturdy in mine as he cupped his second hand under my elbow and steadied me as I rose. "He could pop in anywhere in the line."

"Then just stay close," I said as he kicked the chair out of the way and I wavered on my feet, bringing my second sight into play. I wanted to sleep in my bed tonight, my bed in my church, and I wasn't going to let Al take me. But inside, doubt trickled and took hold as the red-sheened nightmare of the ever-after wavered into existence, the grass-covered, windblown desert that the imbalance from the elf/demon war had made of the original Eden overlaying the calm orderliness of Trent's office. If I concentrated, I could see the walls, but it was the horizon my eyes went to, the ever-blowing wind shifting the waves of dried grass that grew outside the broken city center. The scent of burnt amber tickled my nose, more from my imagination than the little bit of ever-after leaking through.

My hair shifted in the gritty wind, and Trent's grip tightened.

"Rachel Mariana Morgan," Al said softly, and I gasped, almost falling as I spun and pain stabbed through my leg.

The demon was standing not thirty feet away. He was in the ley line in the ever-after, we were in it in reality. It was a middle ground that bent all the rules, and if he wanted, he could drag me from reality and back down into the foul-smelling earth.

"Hi, Al," I said, my resolve shredded and leaving only the cold fear of self-preservation. "Hey, you look good," I offered lamely, and the demon tilted his head to eye me from over his blue-tinted glasses, taking in my bland black sweats. Red, goat-slitted eyes peered at me, his lips curling back in a snarl to show his thick, blocky teeth. His grip on his walking cane tightened, and I noticed he was wearing gloves again, their white starchiness bright against the velvet green of his coat and his brilliant vest and dark trousers. Shiny boots with buckles, and lace at his throat and cuffs, added to his vision of a noble British lord at the height of his glory. A tall hat finished the outfit, shading his eyes from the painful sun.

"I look good?" Al said, his voice dripping with sarcasm.

Trent's stance tightened as Al took three steps toward us.

"I look good?" he said louder, his pace quickening and his hand coming out. "I'm broke and living in squalor!"

"Hey!" I shouted as I felt the line seem to collapse into

Trent, sucked in as he drew a massive amount of energy into himself and threw it at Al. The demon never slowed, a quickly raised hand deflecting the energy. Behind me, Trent's fish tank exploded. Suddenly my feet were wet, heavy in thick socks.

"Stop it, Trent!" I exclaimed, pushing away from him and almost falling. "You promised." Oh God, he was going to ruin it. All I had going for me were daring and trust, and Trent was trying to prove how not strong we were?

"No, I didn't," Trent said grimly, and my skin prickled at the energy gathering in his palms.

"I'm paying Ku'Sox blackmail to keep him quiet about your leaking ley line," Al intoned, flinging the same hand out to block another spell thrown by Trent. It ricocheted to my right, exploding the video screen in a shower of sparks. Al's magic could not act on anything out of the line, but he didn't have to if Trent kept throwing stuff at him.

"The elves are breeding true, and everyone's blaming me!" the demon bellowed, his square face red. "And you think I look good!"

My eyes widened, and I took a deep breath. Al was three feet away, reaching for my shoulder, and I tensed, the shields in my mind down but ready to go up in an instant. "Yes, I do!" I said, face scrunched up, ready to take my lumps as long as he didn't try to jump me.

I gasped as I felt myself yanked backward, right out of the line.

"Hey!" I shouted again, the image of the ever-after and Al vanishing. I couldn't see him, but he could probably see me. "What are you doing!" I yelled at Trent, then did a double take. He had let go of me and was darting evil glances at me as he tried to catch his fish, flopping about on his wet carpet. People were pounding on his door, apparently locked. The broken shell of the video screen gaped blackly where once there was sun and a view of the pastures.

"Keeping you out of the ever-after," he almost snarled as he caught a blue damsel and tossed it into the shattered remnants of the fish tank and its two inches of remaining water. The fish darted behind a rock, unhurt.

"Well, stop it!" I said, feeling my leg ache and pushing the chair away. "If you want to help, give me my crutch."

He stood helplessly over his lionfish, knowing he couldn't touch it lest he get poisoned.

"Give me my crutch!" I demanded, hand outstretched. "I can't reach it from here."

With a last look at the gasping fish, Trent stomped to the back of my chair, little splashes coming up from his feet. He undid the clasps with unnecessary roughness, and then extended the crutch to me like a sword. From the hall came whispers. "Your crutch," he said dryly.

I took it, arm hurting as my weight landed on it. "Please help me," I whispered, my back to the line so Al couldn't see what I was saying. "I can't do this alone."

Trent's scowl softened. His eyes flicking behind me, he nodded. "I'm fine!" he shouted at the knocking on the door. "I want my old tank brought up out of storage." He hesitated, eyes on mine. "Please," he added as if it hurt.

Scared, I took a quick breath as his hand cupped my free elbow and we squished across the wet carpet. Whoever was at the door was probably calling Quen, not getting his old fish tank. We had to wrap this up fast.

The line was glowing before me through my second sight, little energies jumping from it to ping against my aura like static electricity. Trembling, Trent helped me back into the line. Al was here. Al was going to listen. And Trent had my back.

Al was waiting with the sureness of a lion having treed its prey, leaning against a rock with the ugly red sun beating down on him. His arms were aggressively across his chest and his angry look went right to my core, strangling my confidence in three seconds flat. He knew that I could step outside the line and be safe—until he summoned me. One way or the other, he thought he had me, and another tremble shook me, making him smile and show his teeth.

"I don't think I like this plan," Trent whispered.

"Promise me this time," I said, not looking at him. "Promise!" I shouted.

"I promise." He was angry, but Al's evil smile now had a hint of pride because I'd forced Trent to do something he clearly didn't want to do. I was alive. I was causing trouble. Al was intrigued. He'd listen, and that's all I wanted.

"Explain yourself . . . student," Al said. His attention flicked to the defunct bracelet on the carpet, and his eyes narrowed.

"I've been hiding," I said quickly.

"You're mistaken if you think your elf can save you," he said, pushing away from the rock. "He's less effective than that witch of yours, though Newt did pay me a handsome sum for him."

Pierce was alive? My breath came in fast, and I exhaled in relief. It didn't last long as Trent shifted backward, tugging at me. I refused to move, the pressure on my leg becoming almost unbearable. I cried out in pain, and Trent's hand fell away and he moved to stand in front of me instead.

"Her elf is going to do just that," he said, the red glow of the ever-after sun turning his hair auburn, almost as red as mine. "I did *not* work this hard at getting her to accept who she is to let you take your spoiled brat of a little-boy temper tantrum out on her. She stays on my side of the lines."

Lips parting, Al hesitated, and I saw another weight shift from anger to acceptance, one rock against thousands. "You put that putrid elf shackle on her?" he said, his boots whispering in the dry grass as he came forward. "You robbed her of the lines with your lies?"

"She needed to know what she would lose before she would ever accept its cost," Trent said, his chin level and his eyes unrepentant. "Now she knows."

My jaw tightened, but it was true. After feeling the lines in me again, I'd do anything to keep them, whereas before I would have let it go, oblivious, until it was too late.

Unaware of my thoughts, Al wreathed his hand in a dark

mist. "You will never enslave us again, and not through Rachel!" he said, and that fast, Trent doubled over, gasping in pain.

Shit. "Stop it! Stop it, both of you!" I exclaimed, my head reeling as I lurched to help Trent only to have my leg almost give way under me. "Al, he has the cure for the demons. You really want to kill him? I could have taken it off whenever I wanted. He was not enslaving me, he was trying to help, and I was not listening! I'm a demon, damn it! Knock it off!"

With a growl, Al dramatically snapped his fingers, turning sideways as if not wanting to see us. Trent grunted softly as the curse broke, stiffly finding his full height. Tugging his suit straight, he stood beside me smelling of ash fires. "You okay?" I asked, almost supporting him as he threw the last of the pain curse off.

"This is a stupid idea, Rachel," he said bitterly, his eyes a dark black in the red light. "Let's trust a demon to be reasonable. Brilliant!"

Al turned. "You lied to me. Ran away. Shacked up with an elf?"

The last was a question, and I think it was what he was most interested in. "I took a sick day," I said, letting him wonder. "I lost my aura in the lines while cursing Ku'Sox. If Trent hadn't put my soul in a bottle till it healed, I'd be dead. Sorry about sending Ku'Sox to you, by the way. Are you okay?"

Al pulled his suspicious eyes off Trent and leaned across the ten feet between us, his teeth bared in a nasty smile. "I'm broke and paying him blackmail. Now that you're alive to take the blame for unbalancing the ever-after, I'll give you the honor of paying him instead."

"Trent knows the cure for the demons' genome," I said quickly, heart pounding. "Al, you don't have to keep going on like this. You can move on if you want."

His steps slow and his hands behind his back, Al crossed the distance, the glint of hatred in his eyes for Trent, the snarl on his face for me. The scent of burnt amber flowed between us. It was as if he wasn't even listening to me—mistrust of the elves ran that deep. "You ask me to trust an elf," the demon growled, looking at his hands in his gloves, always apart, always alone. "You ask too much."

"Al, I think I know what you looked like," I said, not knowing why. "Originally, I mean."

Al turned back to me, his coattails furling and his red eyes finding mine over his glasses. Beside me, I felt Trent take notice. "This is why you came out of hiding? To tell me that?"

I wished I could bring myself to lean on Trent more, but I didn't want to look weak. "No."

Al's attention flicked between Trent and me. "You're in trouble?" he asked dryly. "I can fix that."

He reached out, and I backed into Trent, my leg protesting. "No! I'm not leaving with you. Listen to me."

But he came forward again, even as Trent put an arm around my waist and pulled me into him. *"So ma eva, shardona,"* Trent whispered, and I gasped as the line lifted through me, feeling like light as it flowed, my aura scintillating like dust in a sunbeam.

"What are you doing?" I breathed at the delicious sensation, feeling the stray strands of my hair floating and the warmth of Trent at my back.

"It's not a circle," Trent said, his words a breath on my ear. "I didn't break my promise."

Al, though, seemed to know what it was as his hand clenched and dropped, inches from touching me. He drew back, his expression both disgusted and amazed, and I breathlessly waited as the feeling of rising energy grew in me, a tantalizing zing of Trent's energy mixing with my own.

"Curious." Al's eyes flicked to Trent's, and he backed up another step. "I'm broke, Rachel," Al said in a monotone, as if it hurt to admit that in front of Trent, but his voice grew more animated as he continued. "Tales of an elven cure will get me *nothing*! You will come back to the ever-after and prove you're alive so you can tap into the funds that have been accruing in your name and I can buy some *damned groceries!*"

"No," I said firmly, and then said to Trent, far more nervously, "Can you stop that, please?"

Immediately the line in me fell to nothing and he let go. "Sorry. It's not supposed to hurt."

"It didn't," I said, not wanting to admit that it had felt pretty damn good.

Al snickered, and again I blushed, lifting my chin. "I'm a demon," I said. "I admit it, the world knows it, but I belong here, in reality. I'm not going back to the ever-after under duress."

Al's posture lost the brief glimpse of indulgent amusement. "I beg to differ, Rachel Mariana Morgan," he intoned, his eyes flicking from me to Trent, reassessing the situation.

"You can beg all you want," I said boldly, my heart pounding. "Trent's been working to get legislation through to make me a citizen again, with rights and responsibilities. If I'm lucky, I'm going to have to pay taxes next year, right, Trent?"

"Ah . . ." he faltered, inching back a bit more.

Thoughts were whirling behind Al's eyes, the possibility of a demon having rights in reality having distracted him. I think it bothered him that he wasn't accepted as a person, much as he'd deny it. Hands on his hips, he eyed me up and down, his gaze lingering on my hurt leg. "Why did you break that bracelet? To fix your leg?"

His tone was bitter, and I shook my head, the motion quick with nervousness. "I have to twist some charms."

"You mean curses," Al said, almost leering.

"Curses," I affirmed, wishing I hadn't shoved the chair out of the line. "I have to find HAPA or I'll get blamed for several murders. But I broke the charm so that I could fix Winona."

Al looked up from where he'd been analyzing his fingernails. Like magic, his glove ghosted back into existence. "Winona? A new friend of yours?"

I shook my head, remembering Winona's courage. She

was braver than I was. "They cursed her, Al, with my stolen blood. I can't hide behind what I *want* to be anymore. It's hurting too many people. I'm a demon, and I won't let fear keep me from being a demon anymore. She needs my help," I whispered. "It's my fault she's the way she is, and no one is going to fight my battles anymore." I looked up. "Even if it scares me."

Trent cupped a hand under my elbow, supporting me in such a way that Al wouldn't readily see. "HAPA has a vial of her blood," Trent said. "Once they get done analyzing it, they're going to try to duplicate it and use it to eliminate Inderland one species at a time."

Al turned to face us fully, his eyebrows high. "Let's all hope they start with the elves," he said drolly. "How very careless of you, Rachel, giving out free curses."

"It wasn't my idea."

Taking off his hat, Al wiped a gloved hand over his hair before replacing the hat and squinting into the sun. "Demon," he scoffed. "You may be a demon, but you don't have two curses to rub together to protect yourself. You're coming with me where you will be safe."

I shifted my weight, and we backed up a step, to the edge of the line. "No."

Al stepped forward, and Trent put a hand out between us, stopping him cold. "She doesn't want to go with you."

Al's eyes narrowed. "Rachel can't protect herself," he said as if I wasn't standing there. "You know it better than she does. If you truly care about her, let her go. I'll keep her safe. Fill her with curses until she can stand on her own."

I blinked. *Care about me?* Boy, did Al have it wrong.

Trent leaned forward over my shoulder, our heads almost touching, his front to my back. "Safe? The same way I kept her safe by hiding her? I nearly killed her trying that, and hiding with you will do the same. No. She will have the sun and shadow both."

Sun and shadow both? I'd heard that before. It was an elf thing, and I suddenly felt uneasy. Things were spiraling out of control. I pulled away from Trent to see him better. He looked grim, squinting in the bloodred light, his hair blowing in the fitful wind like the tall grass around us. His jaw was clenched. Determined. He looked determined, and something in me twisted. Not again. I didn't want his death on my soul.

Al smacked his walking cane against a large rock standing like an island in the sea of grass. "Sun and shadow. *Sun and shadow!*" he shouted, and Trent's grip on me tightened. "There is no both. There is one or the other, and you will come with me now!"

Al reached, and I pulled the line into me. Like a flood it burst into my soul, raging through the hard-won, already desensitized channels, and racing to my hands. Feeling it, Al jerked his hand away, and Trent got it instead. The man grunted as the full force of the line burned him, and I winced, dampening the flow immediately. "Oh, crap. I'm sorry, Trent!" I said, and he frowned as he straightened from his pain-instilled crouch.

"My fault," he said as he found his full height. "It's okay."

Al leaned forward, and Trent grasped my shoulder, ready to yank me away. "It's down to pride, Rachel," the demon said, so close that I could see myself reflected in his goat-slitted eyes. "Even if I could get the rest of them to accept that you are sun and shadow both, there's the undeniable fact that you broke the balance of the ever-after. I'm paying Ku'Sox through the ass to keep it quiet. I need a source of income, and you're it."

Pride. That I could fix. "What if I sign the income from my tulpa over to you? You can pay him from that until I fix the line," I said breathlessly.

Al jumped as if startled, and even Trent made a questioning noise. "Tulpa?" Trent breathed, his words tickling my ear.

"I'll tell you later," I said, distracted as Al frowned, a calculating squint to his eyes. "That might buy a few groceries until I can work out something with Trent in lifting that elven curse," I offered, and sure enough, he twirled his walking cane in wide circles as he thought about it. If I could satisfy him, give him something he wanted, he'd let me do what I wanted for a little longer.

"And you think you're not one of us," Al said, his tone flat but with a trace of pride.

"Oh, but I do," I said, my jaw clenching against the pain in my leg. I had taken off the bracelet. I had gotten Al to listen. I had Trent as an ally. Three impossible things before midnight. I began to shake, the limits of my flagging endurance reached.

For a long moment, Al eyed us. "Sun and shadow," he grumbled, and Trent jumped when the demon snapped his fingers dramatically and a piece of paper floated down, flashing into existence from a space three feet over Al's head. The demon reached for it as it fluttered, his gaze never leaving mine, a hint of a smile about his lips. "Sign it," he said, extending it.

I reached out, but Trent was faster, snatching it before I could. "She's not signing anything until my people look at it."

I was going to fall down if we didn't finish this soon. My feet were soggy, hidden by the dry grass, and I reached for the pen stuck in Trent's pocket, making him blink in surprise. "Why?" I said, taking the paper from him as Al smiled. "If it's not what I agreed to, I will burn Al's gonads off the first chance I get. Turn around. I need to use your back for a second."

"Ah, hold on a tick," Al said, snapping his fingers again and catching the new paper drifting down. "How silly of me. This is the one. Here."

I crumpled the first and dropped it. Al burst it into a quick flame that vanished before it could reach the dry grass, ashes melting into the gritty wind. "Mmm-hmm," I said, satisfied, as I slapped the paper on Trent's back and signed my name. Al would need it to get at my funds, and apparently there was a lot there if he wanted physical proof of our agreement.

The demon was smiling as Trent stood and I handed the signed paper across him. Al was standing a bare three feet away, his mood almost jovial as he took the paper and it vanished in a wash of black sparkles. "Thank you, Rachel," he said, carefully reaching for my hand as Trent stiffened. "Welcome back, my itchy witch."

I couldn't help my smile, feeling a wash of energy flowing from him to me as he kissed the top of my hand in an overdone show of flair. Trent was glowering, clearly unhappy, as he stood within yanking distance while Al flirted. I was ready to cry in relief. I was back, alive, with the line in me and on good terms with my teacher. Somehow we had done it.

"Bye, Al," I said as he eyed me from over his glasses.

"If I ever see you in sweats again, I swear by Bartholomew's balls I will flay you." Al dropped my hand. His smile faded as he looked at Trent, and then he was gone, the grass he had displaced whispering back into place.

I took a deep breath, exhaling the gritty wind and feeling my feet go cold. I'd done it. No, *we'd* done it.

"Signing an unread contract with a demon wasn't very smart," Trent said, and I dropped my second sight. The hum of the line fell to nothing in me as I dropped it, too, but I could feel it just within my reach, easing my headache away with the heartbeat of creation.

Reality superimposed itself over the red-sheened everafter. My hair settled, and I looked at the ruin of Trent's office. Smiling, I walked over to the desk to see how much of that coffee was left. "Oh, I beg to differ," I said smugly, dropping my crutch on the rolling chair in passing.

He looked mad, but I was in a great mood even if I had one hell of a night facing me.

"My office is trashed," he grumped as he squished across his damp carpet and took the coffee that I was holding out to him. "Why are you smiling? My fish are dead."

"Because Al and I are okay," I said, taking a sip from my cup and musing silently over the rim of it. "And that's important to me. But I'm sorry about the fish."

"You think *that* was okay?"

I sat back against Trent's desk, trying to look sexy in sweats. "Yup. Al fixed my leg." I smacked it to prove my point, and it made a dull *thwack* of sound. "He could have taken me any time he wanted, but he listened." I'd known it from the start but Trent wouldn't have believed me. "I told you not to do anything. That show you put on for him told him one thing, and one thing only."

Trent looked up, his eyes running from my dangling foot, up my curves, and finally to my face. "What's that?"

I smiled, taking a sip. "You're willing to risk death to help me."

Trent's eye twitched as he thought it over, realizing what he must have looked like to the demon. "Your hair is a tangled mess."

"Is it?" I couldn't stop smiling, my relief buoying me up. "You have ever-after dust all over your face." I slid from his desk, feeling frumpy in my black sweats but bursting with success. "Right here," I said as I set the coffee down on the low table beside him, leaning over him and brushing my thumb under his eye.

Trent jerked, his hand reaching up to grip my wrist.

"What are you doing?" he said, and I hesitated, not knowing.

We both turned as muttering voices grew loud outside the door, and the *snick* of a key sounded.

"Sa'han!" Quen said as he pushed open the door, stopping dead in his tracks as his feet squished into the soggy carpet and he saw the broken video screen and the busted fish tank. Behind him was David. Both men were looking at us, and Trent let go of my wrist. Slowly I straightened, confused. *What was I doing?*

"Ah, thank you. I couldn't have done it without you," I said as I dropped back, my feet damp and my enthusiasm fading.

What in hell was I doing, indeed?

Twenty

The foyer was dark, seeing that it still had no lights or windows, and I smiled blandly at David as I almost pushed him out the door, my band of defunct silver making a dull bump in my pocket. He'd been reluctant to leave since bringing me back from Trent's, and though having a self-assured, handsome man in the church was always a pleasure, I was just about at my wit's end trying to get my curses made with him hanging around sneaking glances at my recipes. I kept telling him everything was okay, but he knew it wasn't, even if a zing of excitement ran through me every time I reached for a ley line and found it waiting for me.

I'd known that breaking Trent's charm wasn't the magic pill that would make everything better, and indeed, now that the excitement had worn off, I found myself dealing with a moody vampire who was worried about keeping Nina out of jail, and Wayde sulking in his room because I'd gotten snagged a hundred feet from him. At least Jenks had forgiven me for having broken Trent's charm without him. And I still didn't know why I had touched Trent so . . . familiarly.

But what was bothering me the most was the demon texts open on my kitchen counter, making me wonder what I might have to do to keep my promise to myself. Was it okay to use a demon curse to catch a person committing a horrendous crime? What if the curse looked benign? Was using "dead-man's-toe" morally okay if the man's relatives had knowingly sold him for parts? Was it okay if they hadn't, but using it would keep a sick wacko organization from making more tragedies such as Winona? I didn't know, and I was too tired to figure it out. No wonder Trent always looked stressed under his facade of cool. Finding effective curses that didn't violate my moral code was getting harder, but I wasn't going to succumb to fast, easy, cheap, morally wrong magic. I was a demon, but I was not demonic.

"Thanks again for bringing me home, David," I said as I leaned into the early evening, one hand on the door frame. Cold air spilled in, holding the hint of rain yet to fall. The sun was near setting, and the sky was fabulous with pink and blue and white, the wind pushing the darkness before it. The street itself was gray and silent—expectant, maybe, and I was stuck in the church making curses while everyone was looking for HAPA. Maybe that's why David hadn't left sooner, wanting to make sure I wasn't headed out after them alone.

Sure enough, David eyed me in suspicion as he hesitated on the stoop, his long coat touching his toes and his hat on his head, looking yummy and delish in a lone-wolf kind of way.

"Really, we're all good here," I lied, wincing when the pixies flowed out of the church over us in a shrill wave to test their cold tolerance.

Shrugging his coat higher up his neck, David squinted at me. "Just don't go out alone," he said, glancing behind me and into the sanctuary, bright with electrical light. "Even with your magic, you need to be more careful, not less. That guy . . . Eloy. He's a sniper. You can't protect yourself against that. Bullets travel faster than sound."

I frowned at his sharp gray sports car, at the curb, wishing he'd get in it and go away so I could make my curses in peace. "You're right. I'll be careful."

He shifted his shoulders, uncomfortable. "Watch the I.S. and the FIB, too."

"Glenn?" I said, surprised, and he shook his head.

"Not Glenn. The I.S. and the FIB. They're watching you tighter than HAPA now that you have access to your full range of magic. They don't trust you, and probably for good reason. Why do you think they wanted that list of magic you could do?"

My gaze went down, hearing the truth of it.

"Promise me you'll stick with Ivy or Jenks," he said, touching my sleeve to bring my eyes back to his. "Outside your pack, you're vulnerable. Friends are there to watch your back."

Friends. Again my eyes couldn't meet his as I remembered why I'd faced down Al with Trent, not Ivy and Jenks. I hadn't wanted to risk my friends. Trent wasn't my friend. I didn't know what he was, but he wasn't my friend.

David squinted in distrust, and I plastered on a fake smile. "Rachel," he said, a small but sturdy hand landing on my shoulder. "I know you're capable, but perhaps you should let the I.S. and the FIB handle this from here on out. You've done your part for home and country."

"That's funny. I don't feel like I've done anything except get caught, get shot, and limp away with nothing to show for it." My jaw clenched when the pixies streamed back in, shouting about invaders coming. Must be the Were Scouts canvassing again for pop bottles. "The FIB is outclassed, and the I.S. keeps making stupid mistakes. I need to be at the next take—if only to prove they can trust me. That's what I'm aiming for. Trust."

His expression was just shy of pity, and I looked past David to the diesel truck, COOLE'S POOLS AND TABLES on the side, that was squeaking to a stop at the curb. I'd forgotten that I'd made the appointment, and I'd almost canceled when Ivy had reminded me of it. But the need to have something, *anything,* done and accomplished, even if it was nothing more than having Kisten's pool table fixed, had stayed my hand. David eyed the truck, then me, his hands in his pockets.

"I will not go out alone," I said as the truck's door slammed and three scruffy Weres got out. Apparently their numerous tattoos gave them protection against the cold as they had no coats. The tidiest had a clipboard, and the others a satchel of tools each.

Seeing them, David seemed to relax. "Promise?" he said dryly, and I winced.

From my shoulder came a tiny "Promise, promise!" as Jrixibell, one of Jenks's youngest daughters, mocked the serious Were. The curses to find HAPA were sitting on the kitchen counter waiting for Ivy to take them to Glenn. Apart from getting in a car and driving around the city, there wasn't much I could do until one pinged on HAPA. I could sit and watch nature documentaries with Jenks and the kids the rest of the night if I wanted. And trust me, watching a dozen pixies scream as a crocodile chomped on a zebra was something not to be missed. They invariably cheered for the crocodile, not the zebra.

"Promise," I said with a sigh, and Jrixibell squealed and took off, leaving a bright spot of sunshine that slowly faded from my shoulder.

"That's my girl," David said. Ducking his head at my puff of annoyance, he went out, turning back when he was only one step down. "The tattoo looks good. You like it?"

I couldn't help my smile as I remembered Trex from the bus. "Yes," I blurted out as I briefly covered it with my hand. "Thanks. For everything, David. You're too good to me."

He tugged his hat down over his eyes, but I could still see his smile. "I could say the same thing," he said softly as the three pool table repair guys started up the walk.

"See you later," I said, fidgeting as I breathed in the coming night, wanting only to be out in the pink and blue—hunting. *The FIB didn't trust me?*

David headed for his car, nodded to the Were with the clipboard in passing, sort of a nonthreatening threat that one Were gives to another entering his territory. The two behind the first slid to the side to give David lots of room on the sidewalk. I waited for them, leaning against the door frame when the Were with the clipboard hesitated, watching David get in his car. Turning to me, the rough man cleared his throat.

"Ah, Ms. Morgan?" He glanced at his clipboard. "I'm Chuck, from, ah, Coole's Pools and Tables. We're here for a table repair?"

He looked understandably confused. It was a church. "I'm Rachel." I slid backward into a cloud of pixies. "You've got the right place," I said, trying not to sneeze at the cloud of pixy dust. "Come on in. The table is just inside." I held my breath and stiffened as the pixies swirled and retreated deeper into the church. The light coming in was eclipsed as the Weres followed, shuffling. "Sorry about the pixies," I added as one shut the door.

Weres generally didn't like sanctified ground, and the three repair guys shifted their shoulders as if trying to fit into a new skin while they looked the space over. The pews had been removed long ago, leaving the worn oak floors, but you could still see where the shadow of a cross had once hung over the altar up front. Tall ceiling-to-knee-high windows of stained glass let in light when the sun was up. Ivy's baby grand piano was just inside the entrance, and my unused rolltop desk sat alone at the opposite far end where the pulpit used to be. Across from it was a coffee table, chairs, couch, and TV making up sort of a makeshift waiting room. In the middle of the high-ceilinged space was the pool table, under a long light, almost making an altar to Kisten's memory.

The three guys took it all in with their mouths hanging open. The pixies playing in the open rafters didn't help. There'd probably be a gargoyle up there when the sun went down. God, my life was weird.

"Shit, man," the dark-haired Were with the starburst tattoo said when he finally looked at the torn and battered pool table. "Who burned your table?"

"Shut up, Oscar," the Were with the clipboard growled.

"We had an incident," I said, looking at the ring of burnt felt and wishing I'd fixed it sooner. But stuff kept interfering.

Jenks dropped from the rafters, startling the crap out of Chuck. "Some nasty bitch of a woman from the coven of moral and ethical standards tried to fry Rache," the pixy said, apparently proud of it. "I pixed the Tink-blasted dildo, and Rache's black-arts boyfriend blew her right out the front door. Bam!"

I cringed as the Weres hesitated. "Ah, we had an incident," I insisted. "Can you fix it?"

Jenks laughed, then flew off, yelling at his kids to get out of their stuff.

Chuck was running his hand on the flat surface, picking the edges of the felt where it had been burned. "We can fill the gouges with a composite, sure. Level it. Wax the cracks. Put some new felt on it." He looked up, then blinked at the three pixies watching him from the overhead light. "Uh, it will take a couple of hours with that gouge. We might have to do two thin layers instead of one thick one."

"Whatever it takes." My fingertips brushed the nicked varnish. *Kisten, I still miss you.* "I'll tell Ivy you're here. She's probably going to want to watch to make sure you get it level."

"We guarantee it," Chuck said, then stiffened. Two giggling pixies rose up with a piece of equipment from one of the satchels. "Hey!" he shouted, then glared at Oscar, who was staring, transfixed, his hands spread wide but clearly at a loss as to what to do, afraid he might hurt them. "Bring that back!" Chuck yelled, staring at the ceiling where a cloud of pixies hung, screaming at the top of their lungs, fighting over it.

"Jenks!" I said, exasperated. "Will you get your kids under control!"

A piercing whistle just about split my head open, and the kids scattered. The instrument dropped, and I gasped as Jenks darted under it, catching it and falling a good three feet before getting his wings under him and halting his motion. Adrenaline made my head hurt, and I exhaled loudly as Jenks dropped the gadget in Oscar's hands.

"Sorry," he said, looking as frazzled as I felt. "They've been cooped up all day. I'll get them outside now that the rain's quit."

The three Weres had clustered, looking at the finger-size level as if the pixies might have damaged it. "Thanks," I breathed to Jenks. "I didn't mean to yell. I'm just . . ."

Jenks grinned as he dusted. "Don't worry 'bout it, Rache. I yell at my kids all the time."

Still, I felt guilty about the lapse, but he had already zipped to the top of the hallway to shout at his kids about getting their asses outside and cleaning their huts for winter before he bent their wings backward. Things had been different since Matalina died, but seeing him handle his fifty-plus children alone had granted him a new respect from me. He was a good dad, if a little unconventional.

I smiled hopefully at the suspicious Weres as the church emptied of pixies, Jenks included. "I'll be in the kitchen if you need anything," I said, wanting to make my exit before they decided we were too weird and left. "And thanks for coming out on such short notice. I really appreciate it."

"Yes, ma'am." Chuck had his eyes on the rafters and the single pixy Jenks had let stay.

Spinning on my heel, I stepped lightly down the hall and to the kitchen. Ivy was standing at the table, in her coat, fingering my prepped curses as if trying to figure out how they worked. Her purse was on her chair, and she looked as if she was ready to leave.

"Oh!" she said, flushing as she dropped the charm and it clanked back into the rest. "Ah, are they the pool table guys?"

I nodded and came farther in, still feeling like we were walking on eggshells. Jenks had told me she'd gone scary evil when she'd found out I'd been taken. It had been Nina—Nina, not Felix—who had kept Ivy from hurting herself or anyone else until she'd finally broken down and cried in frustration before focusing her soul on getting me back. I thought it telling that Ivy had been there trying to help Nina, but it was Nina who had helped her.

"Be nice," I suggested. "They aren't keen on being in a church, and Jenks maxed out their 'acceptable weirdness' levels already."

She smiled with her lips closed. "Not a problem. These are done then?" she asked, picking up the one she had dropped, holding it carefully between two fingers.

Nodding, I yanked a chair out and turned it before sitting in it backward. "Yup. Providing they aren't hiding in a ley line, they should work. I had a great focusing object." I frowned, remembering the HAPA knot I'd found while showering, snarled behind my ear. It was my hair, but their knot. It would work.

Tired, I put an elbow on the table, dropping my forehead into my hand and rubbing it. Ivy touched my shoulder, and I jerked my head up. "You're sure you're okay?" she asked, a hint of a smile for having surprised me.

"I'm fine," I said sourly. "Just . . . anxious." Winona was safe, but as soon as HAPA set up shop again somewhere, they'd mutilate someone else. I had to find them first.

My hand went to my middle, and Ivy began stacking the charms in a small sack with a spell-house logo on it. I felt ill, jittery from the Brimstone and queasy on self-awareness hitting me from all sides. Eyes flicking to the messy counter, I wondered if Trent would still accept a curse from me to give him his fingers back. And why had I touched his face?

Ivy carefully creased the bag closed, the folding paper sounding loud. Her attention went to my jiggling foot. "I wanted to stay while they fixed the table, but if I go now, the amulets can be on the streets at the next shift change. Mind if I take your car?"

"No, go ahead," I said, stopping my foot's motion.

"Thanks. I'm going to see if Nina will talk to me after I drop them off. I'll have my cell on in case Glenn calls."

My gaze flicking to her, I nodded, absently biting a finger-nail. The image of Nina choking that man to death flashed through me, and I stifled a shiver. The FIB had been there, making it hard for the I.S. to cover up the incident—and they would cover it up if they could. "Is the FIB prosecuting?" I cautiously asked, and Ivy put the bag in her purse.

"If it's proved that the man she killed is HAPA, then no. That's not what I'm worried about." Ivy looked at my shoulder bag on the table, and I pulled it closer to get my keys for her. "Nina's in trouble," Ivy said as she caught the jingling keys. "Felix, too, and not because they killed a HAPA member. He severely misjudged his impact on her, and she doesn't have the ability to handle alone what he's been pumping into her the last couple of days. He can't simply leave anymore. She'd kill the first person who touched her the wrong way. The longer he's in her trying to give her control, the worse it gets." Ivy's eyes were haunted. "They're both severely unbalanced. I don't see how—"

Ivy's words broke off, and she looked at me, more grief in her eyes than I'd seen in a long time. "They aren't going to make it, are they?" I said, and Ivy closed her eyes as she shook her head. They were bright when they opened back up.

"Felix doesn't have a clue about what to do. Rachel, she's too good to die like that."

"You can help her," I said, and she dropped her head, her long hair hiding her face.

"I can," she said softly. "Rachel . . ."

Chest tight, I shook my head. Ivy had a huge need to give, to nurture. Some of it was her vampiric nature, but most was her heart. She grieved for her own lost innocence, reviling the monster that Piscary had made her into, unable to love without hurting what she most desired. She'd been getting better, but if she could help Nina, it might allow her to see the beauty in her own soul. "If you can help her, you should," I said, both scared for her and loving her for her sacrifices. "You know how to cope with the power and passion. I mean . . . if you want to."

She pulled her head up, refusing to look at me. "I was exactly like her once," she whispered. "It was so hard. I don't know if I can help her without becoming her again."

"I know you can," I said confidently. "You survived. Nina will, too, with your help."

"Yes, but . . ." She hesitated, her gaze finally coming to me. "I survived because I fell in love." *With you* was unspoken.

My heart hurt, but I kept smiling. This was a good thing. Ivy needed to feel good about herself, and this might finally prove to her that she deserved positive things in her life. "Go," I said, and she looked down at her hands.

"I'll be with Nina if you need me," she said, and I blinked in surprise as she bent down and gave me a chaste peck on the cheek, like you might see any two friends give each other in parting. In a swirl of vampire incense, she was gone, her boot heels click-clacking in the hall.

"Thank you," I whispered, touching my cheek. There hadn't been a twinge of reaction from my scar. I didn't know if that was a good thing or not. Demons couldn't be bound, so it stood to reason that I couldn't, either. Were the toxins finally wearing off, or had she truly let me go?

I sat where I was, listening to her speak to the Weres for a moment, and then the door shut, leaving only the Weres talking among themselves. My heart ached, but it was an old feeling, one now laced with pride in her. The revving of my car was a faint hint, and then even that faded, leaving the soft rumble of Weres talking and the rising scent of curing polymer.

The kitchen was a mess, as disorganized and jumbled as my thoughts because I hadn't cleaned anything while I spelled, as I usually did. Throat tight, I lurched to my feet. If I hustled, I could get this tidy in ten minutes. Sighing, I looked over the clutter. Maybe twenty.

From the front, I could hear the guys going in and out, bringing in more tools. I was glad Ivy was moving on. Really. I just wished I wasn't quite so alone.

One of the Weres yelled back, "Red or green, ma'am?"

"Green!" I shouted as I looked down at the open demon texts, my fingers cramping as they skated across the dark, perhaps blood-based print. I'd had a surprising amount of luck with finding a curse to thwart a memory charm. Demons apparently didn't like to forget. It was a communal curse. Say the words and pay the cost, and you were good to go. And since I'd gotten rid of the damn bracelet . . .

Was it easy, like a wish? Or was it using my resources to their fullest potential?

I didn't know anymore. But I did know that I didn't want to be ignorant and oblivious of what happened when all was said and done. The I.S. didn't have a problem using illegal memory charms, and I wanted to remember.

Running a finger under the print, I whispered the words, trying to practice the cadence before I actually tapped a line and did it. I hadn't accessed the collective since taking off the bracelet, and the last thing I needed was to do it wrong and attract attention. *Certo idem sum qui semper fui.* I am the same as I was before—or something like that. My Latin sucked.

Settling myself at the center counter, I took a deep breath and tapped the line out back in the garden. I couldn't help but close my eyes and smile as it spilled into me, seeming to bring with it the shiny, clean sensation of a thin, new ice. It was different every time, and yet the same. I let the line course through me, humming like the pulse of the universe. *Thank you, Trent,* I thought. Thank you for taking this away so I would know it for the gift it is.

Slowly my pleased smile faded and my eyes opened. Faint, at the edge of my awareness, something wasn't resonating right, not in this line, but somewhere. The tear, I thought, and my gut clenched. I'd fix it. Somehow.

I looked back down at the words, feeling guilty not for the tear, but that this curse wouldn't work on anyone but a demon. "Stop it," I whispered, head bowed over the print and the energies of the line building in me, demanding action. Guilt. Was I going to feel guilty about everything? I was a demon, damn it. I wouldn't even need this curse if I was a normal witch.

Head up, I shoved the guilt down deep. If the I.S. wiped Jenks's and Ivy's memories, I'd find a way to fix them. The important thing was that *someone* remembered.

"Certo idem sum qui semper fui," I said softly, shivering as I felt a sliver of my awareness dart from me, arrowing through the theoretical collective of whispering demons' thoughts, down to the dark annexes where no one went. I shivered, my fingers sliding over the textured paper as the sensation of my soul melting around a stored curse shook me. And then, like folding space, my splinter of awareness and my soul merged like water drops, bringing the curse within me forever.

"I accept the cost," I whispered, blinking fast as I felt the curse spread through me with the sensation of burning warmth, tingling through my skin and recoiling at the edges of my aura. It was done. I would never forget again.

Maybe that's why Newt went crazy, I thought as I severed my connection to the line with abrupt haste. Someone had felt me tapping into the collective and had come to investigate.

The soft scuff of shoes in the hallway was like sandpaper over my awareness, and I shut the book, my fingers trembling. Nothing had changed, but I felt different. I'd used curses before, but it had always been with too much soul searching. Now . . . I just used them.

It was Wayde, and I didn't look up as I dropped down to shelve the demon book in with my regular cookbooks. I didn't know if I was going to tell Ivy or Jenks about this. More choices. More guilt.

Wayde had halted in the threshold, and I rose when he cleared his throat. He had been in a snit all afternoon up in the belfry, and I wasn't going to feed his pity party. Yes, I'd gotten snatched, but it hadn't been his fault. It had been mine. Sure enough, he looked irate, his stance stiff. "Done sulking?" I said as I went back to the table and the rest of my demon library.

"It would've been different if I'd been with you," he said, still in the doorway.

"Absolutely." I couldn't make an antimemory charm for Trent, but I had promised to get him his fingers back. I was on a roll, baby. "You might have stopped them completely." I looked up, seeing his surprise. "Did Ivy tell you that their security guy was across the street with a sniper rifle, ready to take out his own people if he couldn't kill everyone holding them?"

Wayde silently rubbed his beard. There were reasons he hadn't been on the scene, and that was just one of them. Uncrossing his arms, he straightened to his full height. "The finding charms are gone?"

"Mmm-hmm." I didn't see the need to tell him they'd been curses, and I pulled the top book onto my lap and started turning pages. A standard transformation curse ought to do it, as it would return Trent to a pristine state, fingers and all. The question was, turn him into what? A fox, maybe?

Clearly uncomfortable, Wayde picked up a dirty bowl. My head snapped up, and he shrugged. "I'm hungry. Mind if I clean up while you read?"

He's learning, I thought, smiling. Mixing food with spell prep was a *bad* idea. "Thanks," I said as I shifted pages in earnest. "I'd really appreciate that."

"Cool." His eyes roved over the kitchen, and I could almost see him prioritizing. He really was a smart man, good with his hands and figuring things out. Feeling guilty, he wanted to do something for me, and my expression became weary as he set the largest bowl by the sink.

"My sister was a royal bitch if the bus's kitchen was ever left dirty," he said, and I flashed him another smile before he caught me thinking about him.

Propping an elbow on the table, I dropped my head in my hand. His sister was Ripley, Takata's drummer. I'd found that out just last month. "That must have been a fun way to grow up," I said. "On a bus. Every day being somewhere different. All that creativity around you."

I looked up as the bowls clanked at the sink. "The band?" he said, his back to me as the taps started. "No, not really. It was a bitch in its own special way."

"How could it have been that bad?" I said, trying to imagine it, then blinking as he bent to get the soap from under the sink. Damn, he looked good in tight jeans.

Coming up, he squirted too much soap into the pan and smacked the bottle closed. "People get careless when they lack stability," he said as he set the bowls in the sink to fill. "If you're somewhere new every day, you feel no accountability. You don't care who you hurt. You do what you want and damn the rest because you won't be there for the fallout."

My focus blurred as I thought of the demons. They never moved but had the same attitude. Maybe they were fleeing their past?

"Too many drugs, too much meaningless sex." Wayde leaned against the sink as the bubbles became mounds. "The demands of the music sort of suck everything out of a person unless he or she is tapped into something bigger." His eyes touched on mine, and he smiled. "Like your dad. He's like the ass end of a black hole, spewing the universe's guts to the world."

I couldn't help my chuckle. "Still," I said, not believing that it could be all bad. "You got to see things. Be a part of something that touches people. The music alone . . ."

Wayde turned the water off. Taking a dishcloth, he wrung it out and started wiping down the center counter. "Takata was cool," Wayde said as he pushed everything to the floor instead of into his hand. "He treated me like a little brother. Watched out for me. Everyone knew my sister would jam her drumsticks up their, uh, noses if they messed with me. But the music?" Wayde lifted a shoulder and let it fall. "Not really. The shine . . . It's fake, you know?" He dropped back to lean against the counter as if it bothered him. "By the time it's been corralled by mixers and synthesizers, packaged into plastic, it's dead. The magic that Takata gave it is mostly gone, even when he's riding the high of a thousand people. His best gigs were always when he was so stoned he forgot there was an audience and just spilled his soul out to the gods as he looked for an answer and happened to take the rest of us along."

Wayde turned away, his back to me as he dunked the rag in the mounds of bubbles. "But mostly it's just a job," he said to the evening-darkened window. "A hard job that left him emotionally and physically drained after every performance."

"I wonder why he didn't quit," I said, thinking of the years between my dad's death and finding out just recently that Takata was my birth father. Having a second parental figure might have been nice. But then, remembering Takata's orange jumpsuits, I questioned my own logic.

Wayde was back at the counter, wiping it down a second time. "The money was a sure thing. Sometimes, the crowd would bring the soul back, make it alive. For a minute or two, the universe made sense. A year of hell is worth three minutes in heaven. Or so they say."

He smiled deviously at me from under his reddish-blond eyebrows and turned away. Rolling up his sleeves, he plunged his hands into the suds and started to clean up my mess. I was silent, the book on my lap forgotten as I thought about what he'd said. My mind started to wander, straying back to him. He looked good there with his hair all over and that sexy butt of his. His sleeves were up to show some of the tattoos I normally didn't get to see.

Stop it, Rachel, I thought, and I put my eyes back on the book in my lap. "So, ah, why did you leave?" I asked. "Tired of spending a year in hell for three minutes in heaven?"

Wayde was digging in the drawers for a dry dish towel, pulling out a gold one that was torn but really soaked up the water. "Takata asked me to," he said as he began to dry the largest bowl. "He said his daughter needed someone to yank her back from the edge of the stage before she fell off."

I frowned, wondering if Trent would mind being the size of a fairy for a day. He could talk to the newest tenants in his garden. "Gee, thanks," I said sourly.

"Well, what about you?" Wayde leaned over to set the bowl between us on the counter. "Growing up to be a bad-ass runner must have had its perks."

"Right," I said dryly as I rubbed my forehead. "I was in and out of hospitals until I was almost eighteen, or didn't Takata tell you that? Home-schooled most of the time, but with enough public school to know what it's like to get beat up."

Wayde winced, the cloth slowing on the next bowl. "Growing up sucks."

I reached for one of Ivy's sticky notes and started making a list. Ceri knew this curse. She would help make sure I got it right. Me trying out curses on myself was one thing. On Trent, it was completely different. "I would've given a lot to be somewhere new every day where no one knew who I was, that my dad was dead and my mom nuts."

"That bad, huh?"

Suddenly I wished I hadn't said so much. "Not really," I said, trying to back out of my mini pity party. "I'm a drama queen tonight. Ford, the FIB's psych, would say my child-hood gave me trust issues, but hiding from my mom that I was getting beaten up and fighting off boys with sticky hands gave me a better perspective of what's really impor-tant. I wouldn't change it." *Much.* I hadn't talked to Ford in ages, and I wondered how he was getting on with Holly. I suddenly realized that a bunch of my friends needed baby-sitters and vowed to start screening my calls. All I needed was someone else's kid on my hip as I took down a surprise assassin.

Wayde set a third pot inside the stack and dropped down to put them exactly where they belonged on the bottom shelf. "And what is important, Rachel Morgan?" he asked, and I looked at him through the open shelves.

"Friends you can trust." I tapped the pencil against the book. "Maybe Ford was right."

Wayde silently dropped the cloth and returned to the suds to wash the smaller stuff.

"I want these guys, Wayde," I said into the silence, thinking about Chris dancing in delight as Winona withered in agony and turned into a monstrosity. "I want them to know they can't do what they did to Winona with impunity." My hands gripped the demon texts, and I forced them to open. The pages were beginning to glow. Responding to my anger, perhaps, even though I was not tapping a line right now? Damn, I'd missed the weird stuff like this. Everything was connected. I'd forgotten how that felt.

"You'll get them," Wayde said, his back to me and the metal stuff clanking.

"I'm not so sure." Something always seemed to break their way. HAPA was like mint. You could rip it up, and six months later, it was back, healthier than ever. Mint smelled better, though, and you could make juleps out of it. I don't know what I could make out of HAPA. Compost, maybe.

"You want these rinsed in saltwater?" he asked as he held up my spoons.

"Yes, but not until you get the suds off them," I said, looking at the dripping bubbles.

Wayde silently ran the tap, letting the spoons sit on the drying cloth for a moment as he washed the mortar and pestle, actually taking a scrub pad to them. "At least I can tap a line again," I said, rubbing my leg and circling in to where there should be a bullet scar but wasn't. "Trent doesn't think he did anything, but he did."

Why am I telling him this? I asked myself, but I couldn't talk to Ivy or Jenks. They would jump to the wrong conclusion. Fidgeting, I looked past Wayde to the dark night, wanting nothing more than to be out in it.

"I trust him," I said, thinking Ford would be proud of me. "He let me handle Al my way." I chuckled, remembering Trent's ball of magic ricocheting into his fish tank. "Mostly."

"Sex changes people more than wars," Wayde said as he dried his hands, then dunked the spoons in the saltwater.

I blinked. "Where does sex come into this?"

His back to me, Wayde pulled himself to his full height, hesitating, as if to collect his thoughts. From the front of the church, the big farm bell we used as a doorbell gonged.

"Jenks!" I shouted, still wondering where Wayde had been headed with his thoughts. "You want to get that?"

There was a brief silence, and then Jenks exclaimed, "It's Trent! What the hell does he want?"

My eyes widened, and I froze, Wayde grunting as he turned around with a handful of dripping spoons. *Trent? Here? Why?*

Twenty-One

The doorbell gonged again, the big farm bell echoing through the church like, well, a church bell. I looked down at my jeans and white T-shirt, glad I wasn't still sporting the sweatpants I'd come home in. My clothes were probably a far cry from what he had on, but this was my church, damn it. I shouldn't have to dress up.

"What's he doing here?" I muttered as I shut the demon book and tucked my shirt in.

Jenks hovered up and down, a bright silver dust lighting the hallway. "You want me to let him in or go out and swear at him?"

Distracted, I bunched my hair up into a ponytail, then let it go. "Yes. Let him in, I mean," I said, and he darted off. "At least the kitchen is clean." I flashed Wayde a smile. "Thank you. You have no idea how much I appreciate that."

The Were ducked his head, a hand raised. "No worries. Ah, I'll be across the hall. Unless you want me with you?"

Jenks had worked the series of pulleys and weights we had so he could open the front door, and I heard Trent's voice mixing with that of the Weres up front. Jenks was yelling at his kids, and it was noisy. "No, no thanks," I said, answering Wayde. My thoughts went back to having touched Trent this morning, and I winced. Why on earth was that more embarrassing than when we had kissed?

Wayde scuffed his way to the back living room, hesitating when Trent appeared at the archway, Jenks on his shoulder and a black craft bag in his hand. He was in a suit, but it was more casual than usual, and his shoes looked comfortable and not shiny.

"Rachel, if you have a moment?" Trent said as he halted before Wayde and me. "I can't stay. I've got a meeting downtown in fifteen minutes, but I wanted to give you these since I was in the area."

The memory of Trent, calm and collected in a black thief suit, flashed before me, and then the sight of him angry and belligerent, his shirt off as he stood at the back of my mom's car and changed. Jenks snickered at the silence, and Wayde came forward, his hand extended to fill the obvious gap. "Mr. Kalamack. You probably don't remember me. I'm Wayde Benson."

Trent glanced at me warily, his hand going out to the Were. "Mr. Benson. Of course. Last year's Halloween concert. Good to see you again. Rachel tells me you're keeping her out of trouble lately. Sorry about that spell."

I shook myself out of my funk as Jenks landed on my shoulder, laughing at me.

"When she lets me," Wayde said, seeing that I still hadn't said anything. "Thank you for getting Rachel's ass out of a sling yesterday."

Trent thought for a moment, gaze distant. "The observatory? It was a lucky guess."

"Lucky guess," Jenks scoffed from my shoulder. "Piss on my daisies, he had three spells going when I broke into his spell hut and caught him trying to—"

"Can I talk to you for a moment?" Trent interrupted, his twitching eye belying his cool exterior, the bag in his hand crackling in his grip. "I promise it won't take long."

Wayde dropped back a step. "If you'll excuse me, I was going to talk to Jenks and Bis about how we're going to arrange security now that HAPA might make a go for Rachel."

"Say what?" Jenks blurted out. "You think those moss wipes are coming back?"

"I wish," I muttered. "I've got some serious hurt with their name on it."

Trent stifled a sigh, and Wayde shifted to his back foot. "It was nice talking with you, Mr. Kalamack."

"Likewise."

Catching Jenks's eye, the Were nodded to the back living room, and the two of them headed for the porch and the dusky evening. Jenks's complaining was cut off when the screen door slammed, and I turned my back on Trent. "Do you want some coffee?" I asked over my shoulder as I headed into the kitchen, but what I really wanted was to know what was in the bag.

"No thanks. I can't stay."

It was the second time he'd said it, but he didn't seem to be in a hurry. His steps were soft behind me, and I turned to see him looking around the brightly lit kitchen, giving me a bland smile when he brought his attention down from the top of the fridge where Bis usually lurked when he wasn't on the steeple.

I need to do something with my hands, I thought, forcing my arms down from around my middle. "Well, I want some coffee," I said as I reached for the coffeepot. "I, ah, haven't had time to wash the sweats yet. Do you need them back right away?"

Oh my God, what am I doing? He doesn't care about a pair of sweats!

"No need." Trent looked from the demon text on the table and set the black craft bag on the center counter between us. "I made something . . . if you want it."

I turned from the darkening garden, the clean coffeepot in my hands. "Really?" I looked at the bag. I didn't think it had a Statue of Liberty made out of macaroni in it.

Head down, he carefully upended the bag and a dozen or so ley-line charms slid out. "I made them for helping to confine Al, but since you wouldn't let me use them on him, you might want them for HAPA." The rims of his ears were red, and I squinted, trying to read his tells. He looked up, and I forced my expression to become neutral. "Spelling has become sort of a hobby of mine. Something to take my mind off business. I've no use for them now," he said, folding the bag up and dropping it on the counter.

I set down the coffeepot and leaned over the charms, my head inches from his. "Curses?"

"No."

I touched one, noticing that he hadn't said *what* they were. A tiny pricking in my thumb sparked through me, and I dropped it, hearing it ping metallically on the counter. Wild magic.

"Trent," I said, suddenly feeling uneasy. "You're not my familiar. Did Al talk to you? Did he put you up to this?"

Grimacing, Trent rocked back a step from the counter. "No, but he's right. You're a demon, but you don't have the stored spells they do. You need these more than I do." He looked at the charms, his expression becoming almost irate. "I've been going through my mother's library the last couple of years, trying things out just to see if they work. Modifying them if necessary. Things change in five hundred years. Sometimes it's not the flour that weaves the spell properly, but the flakes of calcite in the stone used to grind it. Ceri—" He frowned, then finished. "Ceri thinks it's a waste of time, but it's important to me to regain what we can of our heritage. If you don't take them, I'm just going to throw them in a drawer."

It was an interesting story, but I wasn't buying it. I stared at him. "Quen is outside in the car?"

"Yes . . ." he said warily.

I pushed myself into motion. "I'll be right back."

"Rachel, wait."

My breath caught as Trent snatched my elbow when I passed him, his light touch stopping me dead in my tracks. I stared at his fingers wrapped around my arm, and he let go.

"Okay, the ring I made specifically for you after you left

today," he said, and my heart thumped. "But I really am working on modernizing my spell library, and you might as well get some use out of the results. Your church was on the way to my meeting tonight, and . . ." His words cut off as I eyed him. "You should see the closet I've got. Boxes of charms that will never be used—"

"He's at the curb, right?" I asked, pointing into the dark hall.

Trent's head drooped, and I hesitated as the guys up front hammered at something. He knew I wasn't going out there, but maybe just the threat of it would get him to tell me more. Sure enough, he ran a hand over his hair, leaving it mussed, and shifting his weight to one foot, looking almost angry when he finally met my eyes. "Can I have some of that coffee?" he asked shortly, and I stifled a smile.

"Sure." Feeling confident and sassy though I had no right to, I turned my back on him and went to make a fresh pot, running the taps slowly so I could hear him better.

"My father was a businessman," Trent said, and I turned the taps off. "A good one."

I turned, reaching for the cloth Wayde had left out, wiping the bottom of the pot dry. "So are you."

Trent grimaced. "So I hear. Did you hear how my mother died? Not the official story, but what really happened?"

My smile faded. "No."

He was silent. I recognized his distant expression as he tried to figure out how much to say, and I got the coffee out of the fridge. The bag was cold in my fingers, and the grounds smelled wonderful as I opened it up: bitter as burnt amber, and rich as the sunrise.

"I have tons of memories of her pressed and beautiful, as only mothers can be to their children," he said, inches away and miles distant. "Her hair arranged and smelling like perfume, diamonds glittering in the night-light." He smiled, but not at me. "She was the perfect politician's wife at official functions, but I remember her best from when she'd look in on me while I was sleeping, checking on me when she got back from wherever she'd been. I don't think she ever knew I woke up. It's funny how things stick with you the best when you're half awake."

Not meeting his eyes, I measured out the coffee. My mother had never worn diamonds when she tucked me in.

"The days I didn't see her leave, she always came back smelling like oil, metal, and sweat. Like a sword, Rachel," he said, and my breath caught at his earnest expression. "That's how I remember her best. Until the day she . . . never came back at all. Quen won't tell me, but I think she was with your father the night she died."

My God, no wonder he had hated me. "I'm sorry. That had to be hard."

A shoulder lifted and fell. "No harder than you holding your father's hand while he breathed his last, I'm sure. My dad was business, my mother . . . She was a lot of things."

I stayed where I was with the center counter between us, feeling ill. His mother and my dad? Then my dad and his father? All dead, all gone. Leaving us to . . . what?

"I was asked to become my father when he died," he said, dividing the charms into three piles. "I was expected to be him. I'm good at it."

"It's not what you want to be," I whispered with sudden insight, remembering bits of conversation here and there, his quick conversion from businessman to child thief on our three days out West.

He never looked up, arranging the spells he'd made for me, wild magic woven with the power of the moon and sun, shadow and light both. "I'm good at it," he said again, as if convincing himself.

But I knew that wasn't what he wanted to be, and I remembered the cap and ribbon he kept stuffed in a pocket, probably in his suit even now. I recognized in his silence the pain of wanting something and being told that it's not for you—that you should be something else that was easier, not so hard to become. "You were pretty good when we went after that elven sample in the ever-after."

Trent put his hands on the counter, still at last. "You called me a businessman. You were right. I should have sent Quen to get the sample." His expression became empty. "Quen wouldn't have gotten caught."

"I was mad," I said. "It was the worst insult I could think of. Jenks says you weren't a slouch when you, ah, reacquired Lucy."

His eyes darted to mine, then away, but I saw the pride and love for his daughter. "I had fun with that. Jenks is quite the operative."

I gazed at the charms between us, wondering how long he had worked on them. Fun. He had called it fun. The Withons would have killed him had they caught him. That had been the agreement. He'd been confident enough of his success that it had been *fun*.

"I'll leave these with you, then," he said, his voice low, almost a monotone. "Throw them out if you don't want them. It's all the same to me. The ones with the blue pins temporarily paralyze your opponents, the ones with the gold pins temporarily blind them. Maintain eye contact when you pull the pin so the charm acts on who you want." Trent looked at his watch. "Sorry about the coffee. I have to go. Maybe next time."

He was leaving, and for some reason I couldn't fathom, I didn't want him to. I hadn't known he relaxed by rescuing elven charm recipes. Or that he was stuck in a life he didn't want. "Trent, about this morning."

He hesitated, now eyeing his phone. "Don't worry about it. The carpet has been replaced and most of the fish survived."

"No," I said, coming around the corner of the counter. "I didn't mean that . . ." Trent looked up, waiting, and I swallowed hard. "I didn't really thank you. For helping with Al."

"You're welcome." He hesitated, his eyes going to my empty wrist, tossing his hair from his eyes. "Is that all?"

"No." He snapped his phone closed and tucked it back in an inner pocket of his jacket, and I fidgeted, remembering his face when he'd opened up to me, just that little bit. "Ah, I'm sorry you can't be what you want . . . to be."

His professional mask back in place, he put his hands behind his back. "I never said that."

"I know." The silence stretched until it became awkward. "Thank you for the charms."

Finally he smiled, but it was faint and it faded fast. Even so, I exhaled as if it meant something. "You're welcome," he said, tugging his jacket sleeves down. "Good luck finding HAPA. My guess is they're downtown somewhere."

Downtown? They couldn't be downtown. We'd find them in an hour if they were downtown, and they knew it.

But he was leaving, and I just stood there, feeling inadequate. Trent glanced at my hands, then gave me a sharp nod. "I'll see myself out," he said as he turned away. "Good choice on the fabric color for the table. Red is tacky."

Red is tacky echoed in my mind as I slumped back against the counter as his steps grew faint. He made a comment to the Weres working on the table, and then he was gone.

"You are pathetic, Rache," Jenks said, and my eyes darted to the top of the rack and I saw him standing there, hands on his hips and frowning at me, his wings a silver blur. "Rachel and Trent, sitting in a tree, K-I-S-S-I-N-G. No wait, it was a hospital room, and he had his hands on your ass and you had your tongue down his throat. I can see why you might be confused."

"Grow up, Jenks. He's helping me to help myself. You watch. In three months, he's going to be knocking on my door with some problem that only I can solve, and I'm going to do it because I owe him. He's a businessman. Period. I am a commodity he has been working toward for two years."

Damn it, why had I fallen for that poor-me crap? Ticked, I went to the demon texts, piling them up in my arms before going behind the counter and shelving them.

"Yeah, okay." Clearly not believing me, Jenks landed next to Trent's charms and kicked one, sending it rocking. "Except for one thing."

I came up from shelving my books, catching the charm he had kicked as it rocked off the counter. The tingle of wild magic pricked, and I shivered, remembering it flowing through me and the charms he'd been making for the last year or so. Wild magic. "What," I said flatly.

"This," he said, kicking at the ring, and I took it up, turning it in my fingers to study it. It really was pretty, made of three individual metallic bands, interwoven to make one solid piece—sort of like a puzzle ring but able to hold together off a finger. "He didn't tell what it does," Jenks said, rising up as his kids started screaming from the front room, arguing over the chalk again. The Weres began laughing, and I didn't think it was because they were almost done.

I'd noticed that myself, and I set it down in mistrust. "So? He was in a hurry."

"Knock it off or I'm going to come in there and turn your wings backward!" Jenks shouted down the dark hall, then came back, grinning. "So I've seen my boys do that a hundred times with the neighboring pixy girls. Give her their favorite seed and be too flustered to tell her what it was." He rose up again, the screams from the front becoming louder. "I gotta take care of this. 'Scuse me."

He darted out, leaving me blinking as I stared at the ring, among the rest of the charms. A cold feeling was trickling through me. Jenks was wrong. Trent had simply forgotten.

Right?

Twenty-Two

The pool cue slid between my fingers in a steady motion that Kisten had taught me. Squinting in the sun, I pulled back, staring at the one ball perched at the top of a very tight rack. I'd watched Wayde set them up, and he knew what he was doing, jamming everything to the front of the rack before carefully lifting up and away. A tight rack was crucial for a good break. With that you didn't need a lot of power, just a wee bit of accuracy.

Sending the cue stick forward, I hit the ball, sending it into the others with a satisfying crack. Pixies squealed and scattered, making a rainbow of dust over the sunlit table as I slowly straightened, my smile satisfied but a bit melancholy. The balls rolled and bounced, but none went in. I stepped to the side, my fingertips trailing across the smooth varnish of the bumper. It was cold and hard, not like Kisten's skin—but I still felt like he was here somehow. Sort of.

"Nice break." Wayde's eyebrows were high, his estimation of me rising by the looks of it. Smiling my thanks, I extended the cue to him. It was the only decent one we had, but now that the table was again usable, we might invest in a stick or two.

"Jenks, get your kids off the table," I said as I dropped back about four feet to give Wayde some mental as well as physical space. "They're getting their dust all over it."

Jenks's wings hummed at a higher pitch, and the three or four pixy bucks watching rose up into the lights. "You never worried about their dust before," Jenks said, darting over to snag his daughter before she got in the way of Wayde's shot.

His motions quick and sharp, Wayde took aim at the two ball. With a short tap, the ball plunked in, and the cue ball rolled backward a good two feet. I exhaled, recognizing his skill. It wasn't hard to make a ball back up, but to get it to stop right where you wanted it to line it up for the next shot wasn't easy.

"You want to play the winner?" I called out to Ivy, lounging on a chair with her back to the wall as she pretended to read a magazine and watch us without being obvious about it. She'd put herself right in the sun, which told me she'd had a rough morning. She sat in the sun only when she was frustrated.

"No."

She didn't look up, but the pages of her magazine crackled as she turned them. Ivy was casual this afternoon: jeans and a baggy sweater, her hair down and her phone on the table. Though she looked comfortable, there was a quickness to her motions and a slight widening of her pupils that told of a rising excitement. It could have been from her morning with Nina, but it had been almost twenty-four hours since my curses had hit the street, and I was betting it was that. The sun was streaming into the westernmost windows, but it would be dark in a few hours. We could bring in a bunch of bad-behaving humans in the dark, but I'd much rather do this *before* the dead people came out to play. Especially Felix. I was starting not to like him. His lack of ability was starting to impact Ivy, and I didn't like it.

From behind me, I heard another ball thunk into a pocket. Spinning, I looked quickly at the table, seeing the nine ball gone and Wayde lining up a bank shot with the five. "You're good," I said as I sat on the back of the couch and waited my turn.

"I think he's been sandbagging the last month, Rache,"

Jenks said as he sifted a gold sunbeam right onto the cue ball.

Wayde stood from where he'd been bending over the felt, stoically waiting for the ball to stop glowing. "The table was crap," he said, eyes meeting mine from under his shaggy bangs. "Pool is a game of absolutes. You can't play well on a crappy table." With a smooth, unhurried motion, he pulled back and sank the five. "And it *was* a crappy table."

I couldn't argue with him, but I had just gotten used to having to compensate for that dip by the far pocket. Sighing, I got up from the back of the couch and went to press my forehead to the cold stained glass, seeing the blurry world through a rose tint. He might clear the table before it was my turn. It made for a lousy evening of play, but I was too antsy to play anyway. The longer it took for my amulets to find HAPA, the more likely they were going to mutilate another innocent. My fingers twitched. Was I a demon, or was I a *demon?*

The crack of the balls broke the stillness, and I turned around when there was no accompanying thwap of a ball hitting the bottom of a pocket. "Nice of you to get your balls off the table so I have some room to play," I said as I took the offered cue. Wayde smiled at the innuendo, Jenks snorted, and Ivy gave me a one-raised-eyebrow look. I shrugged, refusing to acknowledge the sexual banter that just seemed to flow out of my mouth when I got a cue stick in my hand. I knew it was from Kisten, and it sort of hurt.

Wayde, though, took it in stride, looking cocky as he dropped back a few steps to watch. Nervous, I lined up an easy angle shot to a far corner pocket with the ten. I always had trouble with the ten ball. I didn't know why. Sure enough, I hit it wrong, and the ball bounced off the tip of the pocket and rolled to the rail. "The Turn take it," I swore softly, frowning as I held the stick out. I was going to get in three shots this game, max.

Wayde ignored the stick, instead moving both the ten and the cue ball back to their original places. "Try it again," he said as the light over the table glistened like gold in his stubbly beard when he pulled back and smiled. "And angle it a little more."

My eyes narrowed at the show of chivalry. "I don't need your pity handicap," I said, and Jenks flew to Ivy, his wings clattering loudly.

"This isn't pity," Wayde said as Ivy rattled a page to cover Jenks's badly whispered comment. "You're a good shot. You just need to slow down, pay attention."

My hand closed around the cue ball, and I set it down hard where it had come to rest earlier. "Your turn."

"Hey! Watch the slate!" Ivy exclaimed, and the slant to my shoulders shifted.

"Sorry," I said, then turned to tell Wayde to take the stick before I jammed it somewhere, but my jaw dropped when I realized he had moved the cue ball again. "I said, it's your turn!"

"Line it up." Wayde's eyes were on the table, not me. "Exhale on the down stroke."

"Yeah, stroke it, baby!" Jenks said, his hips gyrating as he hovered over Ivy.

"Oh my God," I muttered, but then, because I really should have made that shot, I tugged down my T-shirt and bent over the table. I exhaled, sending all the tension out of me, my thoughts about Kisten, my anger at HAPA, my worry over Winona—my new doubt that Trent was simply trying to get me to work for him . . . With a smooth motion, I hit the ball. It hummed over the felt as if pulling my aura with it, barely tapping the ten, shifting the momentum to it and sending it into the pocket with a satisfying little thump.

Pleasure sifted through me as I straightened and smiled while I handed the cue stick to him. "Nice, but it's your turn," he said, even as he took it.

"Nah, you gave me that one," I said, appreciating the gesture. "Your go."

Wayde nodded. Moving gracefully around the table, he lined up a shot that should have been easy—until he muffed it, sending the cue ball bouncing around to miss everything and come to a halt inches from where it had started.

Jenks whistled, impressed. I was, too, even if my smile had gone a little dry. He'd done it intentionally, but what could I do? Cry foul and not play anymore? "That was tighter than Tink's . . . ah, he's good," Jenks said to Ivy, then darted up to rescue the chalk from where his kids had snatched it again.

I held my hand up, and the chalk dropped into it. *He is good,* I thought as I chalked my cue. Maybe a little too good. Feeling centered, I lined up the thirteen and easily tapped it in.

Wayde's teeth showed and he ran a hand over his beard. "Anyone want some chips?" he asked as he headed for the kitchen, mistakenly thinking I would sink a few more before it was his turn again. Yeah, that was likely.

Ivy winced when Jenks's kids began a high-pitched, shrilling demand. I knew they were speaking English, but it was so fast I couldn't keep up. Wayde, too, looked pained, and in a noisy cloud of blue-faced pixies, they vanished into the hallway, Jenks trailing along behind. There was a crash from the hanging rack, and Wayde yelled that nothing broke.

I sighed, leaning on the stick as I looked over the sunlit table. From behind me came Ivy's somewhat threatening "They're going to get grease on everything."

I sashayed to the table, deciding to try the trickier bank shot if Wayde wasn't here to tell me how to do it. "You weren't worried about it last week."

"Last week, it was a crappy table."

Her magazine rustled, and I took my shot and missed. Standing, I looked over the table again, deciding to take another. It wasn't a serious game, and if he said anything, I'd just play stupid. My lips curled up in a smile as I bent over the table.

"Jenks tells me the charms on the counter are Trent's," Ivy said, her tone rising in question. I could understand why. I hadn't touched them: him making me a macaroni statue would have been better. If I used them, I'd feel like I owed him a favor. But to leave them there would be stupid if they would help. Damn it, why did I see ulterior motives in everything?

Disconcerted, I ignored her question, exhaling as I sent my cue gently forward. The balls cracked together, and one dropped in. It was Wayde's. Sloppy. "Yup," I said, avoiding her eyes as I maneuvered around the table. She was silent, and I looked up from where I was leaning over the table. Ivy was waiting for more. "He made them. In his spare time. Wild magic." Which was another reason not to use them. Who knew how the magic had to be broken?

"Mmm," she said, attention returning to her magazine.

"'Mmm'?" I held the cue stick with both hands, hip cocked. "What does that mean?"

Ivy didn't look up, still reading as she said, "Maybe I misjudged the little cookie maker. Most of your ex-boyfriends would have told you not to do it. He gave you a weapon."

"Trent's not my boyfriend," I said quickly, and her eyes widened.

"Good God, no," she said just as fast. "That's not what I meant. I meant Nick would've told you to summon a demon to solve your problem. Marshal would've told you to not go at all. Pierce would probably have demanded to go with you, then gotten in the way and screwed it up. Trent, though, gave you a weapon. One you might use."

I couldn't help but notice that she'd left Kisten off the list. Lips pressed, I reached for the chalk. "Of course he gave me a weapon," I said as I chalked the tip and blew the excess off. "He's a murdering bastard, and he's protecting his investment." But it hadn't looked like he was worried about money when he'd told Al I was going to be of sun and shadow both. What in hell did that mean anyway? Sun and shadow both.

"Turn-blasted businessman," she said lightly, mockingly.

I leaned against the table, my focus becoming vacant. I was never going to call him that again.

"So are you going to use them?" she said, and shifted uncomfortably.

"The charms?" I thought about the Pandora charm he'd made that almost killed me, him freeing Ku'Sox with the singular intent of giving the world something worse than me to deal with and to make me look harmless, and then the finesse he'd needed to first weave a charm that cut me off from the universe, and second bring me back into it as well. "I don't think so."

"Mmm."

"Mmm" again? What is it with her and these one-word answers? "Thanks for taking my finding curses out to Glenn," I said. "What area are they concentrating on?"

Ivy played with the ends of her hair as she turned a magazine page. "He didn't tell me."

Her attitude was stiff, and I frowned as I smacked the balls around, not paying attention. "Is it Nina?" I carefully asked as the balls bounced, most of them ending up on the bumper.

Ivy's brow furrowed. "No. She's coping. Felix is taking the situation seriously, and with the three of us together, we might all make it out alive."

But her jaw was still tense, and I flicked a glance at the empty hallway, listening to pixies arguing over barbecue or ranch. "Daryl?" I asked, not knowing how much leeway I had when it came to her relationships—now that I wasn't one of them.

"No." She grimaced at her magazine. "Yes. But that's not what's bothering me."

Tension furrowed my brow, and I forced it smooth as I took a shot and missed. I'd asked. She knew I wanted to know. If I pushed now, she'd shut down.

"Glenn's not telling me something," she said softly, and I turned, sitting against the edge of the table to give her my full attention.

"You think he wants to break up?" I asked, fishing for an answer.

Ivy let her magazine fall forward on her lap. "Rachel,

listen to me. It's this HAPA thing. He knows something, and he's not telling me."

"Oh." Moving around the table, I pushed half the striped balls to the center for better play. I was relieved that it wasn't anything to do with her, Daryl, and Glenn, but I didn't like the idea that he was withholding information. I didn't want to chalk it up to human/Inderland tensions, but what else could it be? David's warning drifted through me, and I shoved it away—but still the thought lingered.

"I think it seriously bothered him that we knew Nick was alive and didn't tell him," Ivy said, chewing on her bottom lip, her gaze distant.

"That was my decision, not yours," I said, and she shrugged. "I'll talk to him," I said, giving the cue ball a smack and sending the balls bouncing around the table.

Ivy was wincing when I looked up. "Don't. Please?" she asked, and I hesitated in my anger. "I'll talk to him myself. I don't know how long this is going to last anyway."

I stood up, leaning against the table. "Oh, man. I'm sorry. Is it his dad?"

Her expression twisting into one of doubt and heartache, Ivy shrugged. "Glenn is having a hard time keeping up, and it's starting to bother him." Her gaze became distant, and I wondered if she was thinking of Nina as she played with the collar of her baggy sweater.

"Oh." I looked at the table, not sure I liked the sound of this.

Ivy's head shifted, and I heard the hum of Jenks's wings. Half a second later, he darted into the room, his youngest daughter on his hip as she cried about the chips. Wayde followed him in with a bowl of chips and a garden of pixies wreathing him.

Wayde was eyeing the table as he set the bowl in front of Ivy, clearly oblivious to the fact that I'd been taking shots at his balls as well as generally moving things around. Sure it was illegal, but it wasn't as if we were playing a serious game. "Cool," he said as he noticed that a few of my balls had been sunk. "See? You just have to slow down." Then he frowned, and I watched his lips move as he counted his own set and came up short.

"And exhale on the downstroke, baby. Nice and slow," Jenks said, gyrating.

Ignoring Jenks, I handed the stick to Wayde. Ivy took a single chip, placing it between her teeth with a careful precision and crunching down. Jenks's kids shrieked, and my eyes widened as Ivy snatched up her phone an instant later. Seemed as if she had it on ultrasonic instead of her usual vibrate. Vamps and pixies could hear it, but not witches.

I watched her listen, and Jenks went to eavesdrop, hovering when she waved her hand at him to stay off her shoulder. I found I was holding my breath, taking the stick without looking when Wayde missed his shot and handed it to me.

"Got it," Ivy said, her voice tight, and her eyes went to the door. My gut tightened, and sweet adrenaline poured into me. The soft ache in my head from the lingering epoxy fumes vanished, and I smiled. We were on.

Saying nothing more, Ivy clicked her phone closed. She brought her attention from the door, smiled, and stood—all in a fluid motion that sent Jenks back-winging to get out of her way.

"Here," I said, handing Wayde the cue stick without looking at him. "You win."

"What?" he said, mystified for only an instant, and then his brow furrowed. "Hey, I've been meaning to talk to you about this."

Oh, for Pete squeaks. This was why I didn't have a boyfriend. Never, never, never.

Jenks rose up with a war whoop, whistling for his kids. From the belfry, Rex padded in with Belle on her shoulder, the gaunt fairy riding the cat like a horse, partly to stay warm, I think, in the drafty church. Things were going to move fast from here on out.

"Rachel?" came Ivy's voice from her room. "Where's my sword?"

The gray dimness of the hallway was soothing as I headed to the kitchen and my charms. "In the foyer where you left it last week when the evangelists were canvassing the neighborhood," I said as I passed her open door. Boots and leather jackets were strewn on her bed, and what looked like a new knife set. She'd taken a class last winter and was dying to try them out legally on someone.

I eyed Wayde when he paced into the kitchen behind me. "Have you given any thought to the fact that HAPA doesn't know your bracelet is gone?" he said, and I flung open my charm cupboard, intentionally almost hitting him.

"Yes, I have, actually. If they make a try for me, they'll be in for a surprise." *And I hope they do go for me.* "Ivy, where are we going?" I shouted, hands on my hips as I looked over my stash. *Pain amulets, yeah. I always needed one of those.*

Jenks zipped through the kitchen, Rex and Belle under him, the cat watching him with her tail up straight. "I've got some of that new nectar crap in the fridge," he said. "If it gets late and I'm not back, just warm it up. And you have to warm it, or it drops their core temp."

"I got this!" the irate fairy said. "I spent three years tending younglings before I became a warrior. That they're pixy brats instead of fairy fry don't mean troll turds."

Ivy walked in, intent on reaching the blade oil she kept in the pantry. She was in her working leathers, and I suddenly felt underdressed. "Damn, you look good," I said, ignoring Wayde beside the archway with his arms crossed over his chest.

Ivy looked down at herself, an oil-soaked rag in her hand. "Thanks. You wearing that? You're going to leave skin on the pavement if you have to run."

Jittery, I grabbed three pain amulets by their cords, then a couple of disguise charms just in case. I wanted them to recognize me, but someone else might want to use them. My gaze slid to Trent's charms on the table, and in a surge of decision, I shoved them in there, too. "If we have three minutes, I can get my leather on." *I should have called Trent about that ring. Too late now.*

She nodded. "We can wait that long. Glenn is sending a car. Jenks, get your kids to shut up, will you? I can't think with them yammering like that!"

He rose, his wings a bright silver I'd not seen in almost a year. "Where we going?" he demanded. "Cold? Warm?"

Wayde cleared his throat, and I stiffened. "I don't think you should go," he said, and the kitchen became silent.

A pixy giggled. Belle made a weird lisping whistle, and the kids followed her out, teasing Rex by flitting almost in front of the cat's nose. Ivy gave Wayde a look, then turned on her heel, leaving the kitchen and shouting over her shoulder, "Five minutes!" Jenks trailed behind her, still wanting to know if he needed his cold-weather gear.

Alone in the kitchen with Wayde, I closed my charm cupboard. Amulets clanking as I dropped them into my shoulder bag on the table, I turned to face Wayde. "You're not my alpha," I said, then brushed by him headed for my room. Five minutes would give me just enough time. I could even put on some makeup.

"If David was here, he'd tell you to stay," Wayde said from behind me.

"All David said was for me not to be alone," I said, then stopped on the threshold to my room. I was never going to have another boyfriend. Ever. "Look, if you want to come along, come along. But I can tell you right now that Glenn won't let you on-site."

Ivy brushed past us on her way to the back living room, her unsheathed katana in her hand, and Wayde pressed back to get out of her way. "Ivy? Where we going?" I called, my thoughts on my closet, not the questionable smarts about going after a militant hate group again. This time, though, I had my magic. I had Ivy and Jenks with me, too—as well as a bunch of I.S. and FIB guys.

"Library" came from the back room, and then Wayde

pressed back again when she came out. "Downtown Cincy. The one you broke into a few years ago."

My eyes widened, and I took a step back into my room. "No way!" I said, remembering the locked rooms down in the seldom-visited basement. Trent had said they were downtown. How had he known?

"Yes way," Jenks said in passing as he zipped over us, a whining preteen following him.

Ivy sent her gaze into the kitchen, shocking the hell out of me when she asked, "Can I have one of your pain amulets? Just in case?"

My mouth literally dropped open and I nodded. It was the first time she'd ever asked for my magic, and I wondered what it meant. "Sure," I said, and she vanished into the kitchen.

"Two minutes!" she shouted from the kitchen, and the pixies squealed from the sanctuary. She brushed past me in a swirl of vampire incense, and I looked at Wayde.

"I gotta go," I said, hand on my door to shut it in his face. "If you're coming, you might want to change."

"This is not a good idea!" he said loudly, and I closed the door.

No, riding behind you on a bike wasn't a good idea, I thought sourly. God! You show one tiny slip of softness, and they think you're a damsel in distress. At least Pierce let me fight my own battles, even if he did mess them up royally. Man, I hoped he was okay. Being Newt's familiar was not a good thing. At least he was alive. And probably having the time of his life trying to kill her, now that I thought about it.

From the other side of my door came Wayde's exasperated voice, saying, "You've already been targeted by them once. You think Glenn is going to let you out of the car?"

I stripped down to my sports bra and socks, then dropped to my hands and knees to look under my bed for my running boots. Low heel, good traction, supple leather. Ivy had gotten them for me for my birthday last year.

"Rachel?"

Grimacing, I threw the boots onto the bed and rose, snatching up my leather pants and shoving my feet into them. My fingertips touched the mended part where the bullet had gone through, and I sobered. "If I'm not there," I said loudly, "they'll get away. I know it!" I said, believing it to my core. "They're just too lucky to be believed."

A sparkle of dust slipped under my door, and I gasped. "Jenks, get out of here!" I shouted, grabbing my shirt and covering myself.

"Hurry up, Rache! Let's go!" he said, not caring I was still half naked.

"Get out!" I shrieked, and he blinked, wings becoming red when he saw me.

"Oh, crap," he murmured. "Sorry. The car is here . . ."

"I still have one minute," I said, adrenaline making my motions jerky as I gave up on modesty and put my shirt on. What could he see around a sports bra anyway? I felt like Cinderella as I jammed my boots on and opened the door to find Wayde still there, fidgeting.

My boots were still unzipped as I shoved Wayde out of my way and clomped through a cloud of cheerful pixies. Ivy was waiting at the front door, looking like a sexy predator with her leather jacket and sword, and she handed me my shoulder bag, already stocked with my charms, splat gun, and a slew of sleepy-time potions.

"You got your phone?" she said as I looped the bag over my shoulder.

"Yes." I patted my back pocket and hopped on one foot to get my boot fastened.

"Got minutes on it?" Jenks asked snidely.

"Yes!" I exclaimed, getting the other boot zipped. "Let's go!"

Ivy reached for the door, took a breath, and opened it. The late sun spilled in around me, and I headed out after her, waving to the pixies that wreathed us, thinning to nothing as we reached the curb. A black FIB van waited, and I looked up when Wayde ran down the steps and reached for the door's handle. "I'm coming," he said, and he shoved the wide sliding door open.

"'Bout time he figured it out," Jenks said as he zipped in ahead of me, and accepting Wayde's help, I got in, settling myself on the far end. Ivy was already sitting next to Glenn, and I smiled at the FIB guy driving us.

Downtown, I thought as Wayde got in and slid the door to a firm, definite shut. *How had Trent known?*

Twenty-Three

The van was one of those big ones, with half the seats turned to look backward. Glenn and Ivy were sitting next to each other with their backs to the front of the vehicle. There was a faint tension between them, a hesitation that hadn't been there before, and I wondered if my capture had been the straw that tripped the camel. Or whatever. Wayde sat at my left, currently gripping the chicken strap and looking ill. I couldn't blame him. The revolving lights were on and we were running red lights and swerving a lot.

A blueprint of the subbasement at the library was spread across our collective laps. It was laid out like a fortress with nested rings connected by the occasional passageway. Not what you'd expect under a city library, but Cincy was one of the oldest cities in the U.S., and she had more than a few surprises under her skirts. The money for the failed subway had gone somewhere after all.

Jenks hovered over it all as if nailed to the air as we bounced and swerved. "I didn't know that was there," he said, his hands on his hips and lighting a small circle of schematic.

The paper rattled as we took a turn and Glenn's grip on it tightened. "It's an abandoned military post from the Turn," he said, leaning so close I could smell his aftershave. "They mothballed it shortly after, but if you know your history or think to look for it, you can find it."

He looked up when Ivy bumped his knee, and she said, "That was good thinking, Glenn."

"Thanks." He didn't look at her, and she met my eyes and shrugged, her expression sad. Jenks's wings hummed as he noticed our exchange, and I made a mental note to ask his opinion of Glenn's attitude when this was over. He was better than a lie detector in finding discrepancies between words and body language. I knew he liked Glenn, but he had liked Pierce, too. Man, I was glad I didn't need to feel guilty about the man's death.

The car began slowing, and I looked out the front window as the driver stiffened. "Sir?" the man said without turning around. "We're at the outside perimeter. I was going to go straight to the drop point, but we're being flagged down." His voice shifted, and he added, "It appears to be I.S. personnel bumming a ride."

Glenn looked over his shoulder, and Jenks darted to the front, stopping just short of hitting the windshield. "It's Nina," he said, his wings turning a particular shade of orange that meant he had mixed emotions. Ivy, too, looked uncomfortable.

"Pull over," Glenn said, sounding tired. "We have room."

"You're taking her in?" Wayde said loudly, and I winced as Ivy's jaw clenched. "She killed a man. Why isn't she in custody?"

Ivy took the map and folded it smaller as the car rocked to a stop. "The vampire she was channeling at the time is high up in the I.S. If he wants to go, she's going. I doubt very much he's going to let her take the fall for his error in judgment."

"Besides," Glenn said as he leaned over to open the door, "if we don't pick her up, Felix will commandeer another car. The fewer outside the library, the better."

I was unable to find fault with his argument even though I was sort of agreeing with Wayde for a different reason. Nina was in over her head, and Felix was dragging her into deeper water. Nina would be a detriment in a fight, but as Glenn had said, if she wanted to be there, she was going to be there. Might as well try to have a say in where she'd be.

The wind from the river was brisk as the door slid noisily open. Nina stood waiting with her hands behind her back, looking professional in her elegant, sharp dress suit, her haunted eyes and posture telling me that it was she alone. Ivy's words lifted through me, and I hoped we weren't making a mistake. Both Felix and Nina had failed by murdering that suspect, but that's probably not how Nina saw it. Behind her was a slew of I.S. and FIB vehicles, officers yammering as last-minute details were hammered out. We were about a mile from the library, and it was still too close for me for the level of activity.

"Mind if I ride with you?" she asked meekly, and Ivy pushed Glenn over to make room.

Nina hesitated, looking for recrimination in everyone's faces, and from the front of the car, Jenks shouted, "Get in, will you? Were you born in a stump? It's cold out!"

The light was eclipsed as Nina gracefully entered in a wash of nervous vampire and expensive perfume. My mood worsened as she shunned the space beside Ivy, sitting beside me instead. I found out why when Nina shivered, pulled herself straighter, and turned to beam toothily at me, Felix firmly in control once more.

"Good afternoon," she said, her voice smoother than before, and now holding the cloying richness of caramel. "What a wonderful day for a procurement."

My welcoming smile faded, and I said nothing, not happy with the man behind the woman. Slowly Nina's smile vanished. Ivy wasn't happy, either, and when the door shut, the car smoothly reentered traffic. The lights were off, and I inched away from her, trying not to look like I was.

"Mmm, is that a schematic?" Nina extended her hand, and Ivy gave it to her. "This is a much better copy than we have," the vampire admitted, spreading it open on her lap, her knees spaced apart far more than I'm sure Nina normally would allow.

Glenn leaned back into the seat, clearly not liking her on the run, much less in the car with us, even if it was his idea. "It's the original," he said.

"The detail is exquisite," Nina breathed, her finger tracing the circular defenses. "We have nothing like this. You say it was in the FIB files? Ah, here's the secondary entrance. That's where I will be."

"I have a team there, but you're welcome to observe," Glenn said stiffly.

Nina looked up from the map as we rocked to a halt at a stoplight. "Observe. Yes," she said, smiling in a way that said she'd be doing a little more than that if he/she got her way. Glenn was frowning, but I thought it was a good place for an unreliable vampire. She'd be out of temptation's path unless the excitement came to her, whereupon she'd be justified in letting loose and doing some damage to fleeing felons.

Glenn stiffly took the map up and refolded it. "Your people have a net sink in place?"

A shadow of annoyance crossed Nina as the map slipped from her, but she stifled it and smiled at the FIB detective. "It took me all morning, but I found three witches in the tower with the skill to set one and the ability to work together." Her eyes came to me. "Witches are a funny lot, picky about whom they share their minds with. If anyone tries to jump out using a line, they'll find themselves in a cell."

I stifled a shiver, and feeling it, Nina said, "How are you doing, Ms. Morgan? I'll admit I'm surprised to see you after your capture and injury."

Jenks snickered from the rearview mirror, and Glenn shoved the folded map into his jacket pocket. "I'm not," the detective said sarcastically.

Jenks flew into the backseat. "You thought she'd stay home and watch my kids?"

Nina ignored the pixy yo-yoing up and down, instead looking at me with a worrisome intentness. "I understood you were shot at close range," she said, her gaze flicking to the patch job on my pants and back again.

I shrugged, wishing she wasn't sitting so close. "It was a small rifle," I said, trying to downplay it. "Algaliarept ran a healing charm. I'm better than before." My lips pressed, and I didn't care if my anger pushed her buttons. "Don't you think it's odd, how HAPA always seems to get away?"

Nina glanced sidelong at Glenn. "Yes, I do, actually. But very well," she said as if she had a say in the matter. "If you say you're a hundred percent, you're a hundred percent. What concerns me the most is your reputation, Detective Glenn."

Ivy stiffened, and I wondered if I should ask the driver to crack the window. It was starting to smell really good in here. Which wasn't good at all. What was Felix playing at? There was no reason he needed to be in Nina right now. He was making matters worse.

"There's nothing wrong with Glenn's reputation," Jenks said for the rest of us as he came to land on the headrest of the empty front-passenger seat.

Nina shifted the hem of her dress coat and smiled, showing no teeth. "I'm starting to wonder if HAPA is even there," she said, and Jenks made a rude sound, his wings folding, and turning his back on the vampire. "My amulet has failed to ping, and we're right on top of them. There's no line to interfere. From all appearances, we are descending upon an empty bunker."

I felt a stab of worry. I looked at Ivy, who was looking at Glenn. Glenn wasn't looking at anyone, his jaw set and his focus distant. Crap on toast. Were we out here when my amulets hadn't worked?

"They are there," the FIB detective said defensively as the car eased to a halt at a light and I braced myself. "We didn't find HAPA with Rachel's magic. We found them through careful detective work." Glenn finally met my gaze, and my heart seemed to skip a beat in worry. "Not to say your amulets weren't helpful, but if HAPA chose their last base knowing they'd have to circumvent magic, their next would be the same. Kalamack told us his intel pointed at the city center. I sent a few people that way in the archives."

"He told me that, too," I said, glad now that I had his charms with me.

"I simply matched up city-owned buildings with abandoned medical sites. It wasn't until I threw in military posts developed during the Turn that I found the lower levels to the library."

Jenks strutted across the headrest, walking right off it with his wings going full tilt. "You don't think Glenn would get us out here unless he checked it out first, do you?"

The knot of worry in me eased, and I leaned back into the seat. "I didn't know anything like that even existed."

Glenn nodded, reaching out when the van took a corner tight. "You don't build a library that spans two blocks for no reason. It was set to hide a military base, right in downtown Cincinnati." His attention going to Nina, he added, "I'm surprised you don't know of it. It was built under your nose. It's perfect for HAPA's needs."

HAPA's needs, I thought, frowning. Their need to hold people against their will. A place with electricity and solitude, one with quick access to people and escape.

"The bunker is too deep for magic to easily penetrate," Glenn was saying, "but your amulet will light up as soon as we get deep enough. We sent a team in this morning. Someone from HAPA is down there. I guarantee it."

My eyes narrowed, and my gaze shot past Glenn and out through the front window as the van's brakes squeaked. "Approaching the drop-off zone, sir," the driver said, and my shot of adrenaline made Ivy's and Nina's pupils dilate. Crap, I had to get out from between these two before someone got bitten. Like me.

I tugged my bag onto my lap to check that my splat gun was in there, hesitating when I saw Trent's charms in a haphazard pile. Nerves were starting to hit me hard. This was the best part except for the takedown. Jenks was feeling it, too, wiping his wings and checking for tears. I reached to turn off my own cell phone, accidentally hitting Wayde. "Sorry," I said, but he was fidgeting, trying to find a way to tell Glenn he was coming with me. *Good luck there, Wayde.*

Oblivious to Wayde's distress, Glenn had slid closer to the door, his entire mien shifting to hard-assed FIB officer. "Get out, cross the road, get into the library," he said tersely. "There's an FIB officer behind the main desk in the back. Jenks is going to loop the cameras, but no sense in pushing our luck. They belong to the library, but Jenks assures me that someone has tapped into them for their own use."

Own use? I looked at Jenks, surprised. "When did you have time to scope out the library?" I said, and his dust shifted an embarrassed red.

"Give me a break, Rache," he muttered, landing on the headrest. "Ivy and I knew about the library this morning. We didn't know if we were going to let you come or lock you in the bathroom until an hour before Glenn called."

My eyes narrowed and my grip on my bag tightened. *Lock me in the bathroom?*

"There are FIB and I.S. people on-site," Glenn was saying, and I turned my glare to Ivy, "so if you spot them, ignore them. We've been bringing them in all afternoon, undercover. Rachel, if you're sure you want to risk yourself again?" Glenn prompted as the van rocked to a halt.

I scowled, not liking having been so far out of the loop. "Ask me again, you won't have to think about your family planning. Ever."

"I was hoping you'd say that," Glenn said; then his smile faltered. "That you're ready, not the family-planning part."

"What about you?" I asked Wayde as Glenn pushed the rolling door open and the smells and sights of the city streets flowed in. "You're staying, right?"

Glenn got out and stood on the sidewalk, his stance loose and easy. "He's staying," he said as he helped Ivy out. "Wayde, do I have to cuff you to the van, or will you be good?"

His disappointment obvious, Wayde settled back. "I'm

good. Just keep her alive, Detective Glenn, or you'll find out what a pissed Were who doesn't care if he goes to jail is like."

"Thank you, boys, for that overwhelming boost of confidence," I said, impatient, as Nina still hadn't gotten out, and getting nervous. Damn it, if they shut the door and drove off with me still inside, I was going to be ticked. "Will you get your vamp ass out of this van!" I shouted, and someone on the sidewalk turned to look.

Nina stepped gracefully from the van, and I followed, quick on her heels. My grip on Glenn's hand extended to help me was more than a little too heavy, and he eyed me until I let go, my feet securely on the sidewalk. Reaching behind me, Nina shut the door, and the van drove off. Before us was the library, traffic moving slowly between it and us.

Arms swinging, I crossed in the middle of the street, sure they'd follow. Jenks zipped over my head to go fix the cameras. Head down, I paced quickly, Ivy meeting me stride for stride. "I can't believe you didn't tell me," I muttered. "What were you planning on doing? Saying you were going out for ice cream and not coming back?"

Ivy glanced askance at me. "You were always going," she said. "The question was, and still is, just how close to the action you're going to get."

"I don't need a babysitter," I grumbled.

"No, but I'm not going to let you mess up Glenn's run because you're too much of a carrot for HAPA." She glanced behind us to Nina and Glenn. "Nina is going to be enough of a loose cannon. We don't need another one."

I frowned as she opened the library door, and I proceeded her in. She was right, but I didn't have to like it. My gaze went up, and I felt myself relax despite the reason we were here. I like libraries, and I breathed in the smell of the books, the quiet, and the reverent feel to the air. My gaze dropped to the tiled floor, and I smiled, remembering having fallen here, swearing loudly enough to make the head librarian frown at me from across the large room.

My smile vanished, and I started for the front desk, everyone following at their own pace, trying not to look like an invasion. The lady behind the desk didn't look like your average librarian—not with that bulge under her sweater that said pistol. "Back and to the left," she said, glancing once at the camera on the ceiling as she lifted the counter gate and invited us in.

I glanced up at the camera, seeing Jenks's tiny slip of silver dust sifting from it. Satisfied that HAPA wouldn't know we were here that way, I headed for the back offices.

I'd been here before, and the desks with their stacks of books and light-starved plants were familiar, but I stopped short when I saw Dr. Cordova bent over a cluttered table, giving directions to two FIB officers. Behind her, another officer manned a portable radio switchboard. The woman looked up as Nina cleared her throat. A flash of irritation crossed her face, then vanished.

"I didn't know you would be here," I said, and Glenn pushed past me, telling me to mind my manners with a slight shoulder knock.

"I could say the same for you," the woman said, her gaze lingering on my shot leg, then rising to my empty wrist. Slowly her smile faded. "How is your leg?"

"Fine," I said, smacking it. "It wasn't a very big bullet."

She stared at me, her expression bland. "I'm so pleased to hear that. A human would still be in the hospital."

It sounded like an accusation, and my tension spiked. "It went in and out, no big deal," I lied. "If humans would try witch medicine, they'd be on the streets a lot faster, too."

"Teresa!" Nina strode forward with the fading scent of copy paper and vampiric incense. "How pleasant to see you again. I must commend Detective Glenn on finding this place. Marvelous blending of both our respective strong points, don't you think?"

By her sour expression, "marvelous" was probably the last adjective on her mind. "Splendid," the woman said flatly. One of the men with her had a question, and she turned away.

I leaned against a vacant desk and crossed my arms over my chest. I didn't care if it made me look pensive. It was better than looking mad. The last time Dr. Cordova was on a run, everything went to hell and I ended up captured and then shot. She didn't like me, and the feeling was mutual.

The growing wing clatter of a pixy was a welcome distraction, and I brushed my hair from my shoulder an instant before Jenks landed on it. "I don't trust her," the pixy whispered.

"Why is she even here?" I said, gesturing with one hand. Apparently my voice was too loud, because Dr. Cordova turned, her expression ugly.

Jenks snickered, and in the near distance, Glenn smirked as he picked up three radio sets. They looked very polished and professional, far beyond what the FIB usually had. "We need to get downstairs," he said, and she turned away.

Nina eased up to me, breathing deep of the anger I'd given off, her eyes dilating. "Ms. Morgan?" she said as she extended an arm for me in a decidedly masculine gesture. "I'd be delighted if you'd walk with me."

I just bet. The memory of her losing control rose in my mind, the snarl she'd worn, her strength that had overpowered Ivy. She *had* killed a man. Ivy had tried to stop her and failed. We might have gotten all of them if not for her/him. My eyes went to Ivy's, and Nina slowly dropped her arm. "Uh, I don't know if this is such a good idea," I said, adding, "You going down there, I mean."

Glenn winced at the delay, but Nina was undeterred, and she gracefully took my arm and pulled me into motion. "I'm in control," she said, her gaze fixed on a point somewhere ahead of us as we began to walk. "I have spent two days breaking Nina of her . . . innocence."

Two days? No wonder Ivy was worried. Two days of practice against a thousand years of evolution meant nothing.

Jenks's wings hummed, and I jerked away, not because I didn't want a woman to escort me, but because the vampire controlling her was an ass. His breaking Nina was not a good thing, and I glanced at Ivy, seeing her anger. She had probably spent yesterday putting the woman back together again. Being a vampire was hard enough, but add in the depravity of a master and the demands they made on their favorites, and it was akin to legalized abuse. *And Ivy thought there was a chance neither was going to survive . . .*

Accepting my refusal with a fake hurt expression, Nina gallantly gestured for me to go before her. Ivy fell into place beside me, smiling falsely as she cheerfully said, "Relax, Rachel. If Nina so much as twitches in a direction I don't like, I'm taking her down and Felix with her." She smiled and patted Nina's face. "Nina and I have it all worked out. Felix."

Nina's smile grew thinner, showing both gratitude for Ivy's helping Nina and irritation that it gave Ivy a whisper of control over him. My mood worsening, I followed Glenn to the elevator. "Why is Dr. Cordova even here?" I groused, not really expecting an answer.

Nina leaned toward me, making me shiver when she whispered, "Probably for the same reason I am. We don't trust you, Ms. Morgan."

Swell. Just peachy damn keen. But I got in the elevator with all of them, and an uncomfortable silence grew as we descended. I said nothing, stewing over what David had said yesterday about them not trusting me. Maybe I was why Glenn was being closed with Ivy. Great. Now I was screwing up her relationships as well as mine.

"Rache, did I ever tell you the one about the pixy and the druggist?"

"Here are your radios," Glenn interrupted, and I turned from the blank silver doors in relief. "Please wear them," he said as he handed me one, then Ivy another. "I don't want a repeat of what happened with Mia. I never heard the end of it, you running off like that and leaving your nylons to show us where you'd gone."

"Thanks," I said dryly, fingering the tiny earpiece. There was a mic on the battery pack. This was very high tech, far more than usual. Someone had finally given Glenn some funds, by the look of it. I'd be able to hear everything, and it made me feel professional as I dropped the battery down my shirt. Nina had already put hers on, and was making faces as the plastic warmed up in her ear.

"You just slip it, sort of . . ." Glenn was saying, his hands moving in pantomime.

"I think I can figure it out. Thanks." My head went down, and I turned my back on them as I wiggled the wire to a more comfortable spot and clipped the battery to my waistband. A quick toss of my hair, and the wire was hidden. Not that it needed to be, but if I was going to do this, I was going to do it right.

"Test," I said softly, and Glenn held up three fingers to me. "This is radio three. Test."

From my ear came a soft, "Radio three, acknowledged. Please maintain silence."

I smiled, feeling like a part of something big, and I stood straighter. Ivy was doing the same with her radio. Nina was looking at her radio as if wondering why the I.S. didn't have anything this high tech, and I smiled a bit smugly, even if I'd never seen anything this elaborate, either.

"Turn it down, Rache!" Jenks complained. "It's going right through my head."

I fiddled with the control until he lost his pained expression, then looked at Glenn when he leaned close, his map rattling. "Rachel, I've put you on the outer ring at one of the surface shafts," he said, pointing, and I sighed at the distant location. "If they get past us, you and Jenks will have to stop them if they come your way. Okay?"

"Yeah, okay," I said, but I felt as if I was being gotten rid of. I suppose it was better than being in the car, but just. At least Jenks would be with me. Or maybe they were getting rid of him, too.

"I'll be with the main force," Glenn said, his eyes on the map. "With any luck, we'll get them before they know we're here, but if not, they'll likely head for the back door.

That's where I've got you," he said, turning to Ivy and Nina. "You'll be with a contingent of officers, since that's where we expect them to go. It leads to the Fountain Square parking structure, if you can believe it."

"I believe it," I whispered as the elevator dinged, but a warning flag snapped in a cold breath of realization. There'd be no Inderlander on-site at the actual capture zone.

The doors opened onto a dusty, dim hallway, lit by a cluster of flashlights aimed at the low ceiling. Three men looked up from another radio station, clearly temporary by the toilet-paper box they had it sitting on. Soft radio chatter was coming from it, obviously a different channel from ours. One of the men snapped to attention, but the other two simply acknowledged Glenn's presence and dismissed him. "Sir!" the one barked, and I squinted at the unfamiliar uniforms of the two at the radio. Clearly we weren't in the hot zone yet, but the new uniforms and attitudes bothered me.

I hung back, a question rising to pop against the top of my head, sending little tendrils of thought sparking through me. Expensive new equipment, unfamiliar personnel with a whatever attitude toward Glenn, only humans at the take zone . . . Glenn withholding something from Ivy.

The silver doors shut, sealing off the last of the clean, bright light, and I shivered as I felt the underground take me. I took a deep breath, sending a thought out to make sure I could still touch a line. The energy tasted like books, and I imagined we were still in the semipublic areas.

"What's up, Rache?" Jenks said as he landed on my shoulder, and I smiled as if nothing was wrong.

"Ask me later," I whispered, squinting in challenge at the two radio guys before they turned away as one, heads close together as they discussed something. They weren't FIB. I'd stake my life on it. I'd also stake my life on the fact that Glenn knew they weren't FIB. So who were they and why were they here, the-men-who-don't-belong?

"Rachel," Glenn said softly, and I jerked. "Do you want night goggles?"

Shaking my head, I hitched my bag higher. "I'm good," I said, my thoughts on that special flashlight of Trent's. I had to get one of those.

Glenn started down the hallway. "The stairs are this way."

Ivy and Nina pushed past me, clearly eager to bust some heads. Jenks had gone ahead to light the way, and the scent of vampire incense rolled over me as I followed, last in line. Nina was excited, and I breathed her in, enjoying it. It was a good thing I'd sworn off vampires or I'd be in trouble right now, walking in the dark with two of them. Nina smelled as delicious as Ivy.

As if hearing my thoughts, Nina looked over her shoulder. A stab of fear slid to my middle, and her black eyes darkened. "Rachel?" she said in warning, and Ivy took her arm.

"Isn't she fun?" Ivy said lightly, trying to distract both Nina and Felix.

My tension eased when Nina looked away. "I honestly don't know how you do it, Ms. Tamwood. Most of my people would have succumbed years ago."

Jenks dropped back, lighting them with his silver dust. He'd heard everything with his exquisite hearing. "Ivy defines herself with her denial."

Nina looked at him in question. "Do tell," she said, and I wondered how old Felix was if he was using one of Pierce's phrases. "Nina tells me that Rynn Cormel has given you your blood freedom?" she asked. "Is that so?"

Glenn had reached a fire door, the lock clearly having been broken recently. His face was troubled when we came to a halt before him, and I didn't wonder why. I knew Ivy was holding Nina's arm and flirting to distance Felix's thoughts from me, but he might not. "We have to be quiet from this level down," he said needlessly. "Rachel, can you still tap a line?"

"So far," I said, but one more stairway might put me below the easy reach of one. Good thing I still had my splat gun. And, ah, Trent's charms.

Glenn worked the latch, and the fire door opened, show-ing a dark stairway leading down. The air shifting the strands of my hair smelled of oil and canned meat. Jenks hovered uncertainly, finally moving forward to light the path as I followed Ivy down.

The stairway was tight, more like an escape hatch than anything else, and I wondered if this was really a way out. I could understand it if this was a last-stand kind of bunker, but it would be a death trap if there was a real catastrophe—such as an invading force knocking at your door.

We reached the end in silence, and Nina gently pushed open the second fire door. She looked too eager for my liking, but Ivy was nearby. Maybe the pain amulet she'd asked for earlier was for Nina after Ivy cracked her head open.

"Saints alive, I've missed this," Nina said as she slipped into an even darker hallway.

"Easy, Felix," Ivy whispered, her hand on Nina's arm.

"Dim the light, Jenks," Glenn whispered as he followed me into the hallway, and I got a quick glimpse of a cylindri-cal passageway before Jenks landed on Ivy's shoulder and his dust settled and went out. It looked as if the builders had simply set huge sewer lines and poured a flat floor in the bottom of them. Thick cords of electrical wiring snaked along the curved walls at head height. I knew there were possibly more than fifty men down here scattered about, but I felt alone, and I shivered.

"This way," Glenn said as he brushed past me. "We have twenty minutes to get in place. Rachel, we find your service shaft first."

Jenks couldn't dampen his glow and still fly, and Glenn cracked a glow stick, the pasty green light making enough glow to see by as I followed him. The hair on the back of my neck prickled as Ivy and Nina whispered behind me in the dark. I couldn't hear their footsteps, but my gut knew they were there, and I tried to slow my pulse before I set the vampires off.

Fingers fumbling, I turned my radio up, and my shoulders eased at the sound of people. Almost before I knew it, Glenn stopped, looking first down, then up. It was my air shaft, bisecting the tube we were in. One pipe went straight down, the other up. A grate covered the lower shaft, and I looked down it as Jenks went to check it out, noticing that the tube made a sharp right turn about three feet down. Jenks's wings sounded unreal down here, reminding me of summer and dragonflies. "This is it?" I whispered, and Glenn nodded.

"Radio?" he asked, and I gave him a thumbs-up. "Ley line?" he asked next, and I hesitated, reaching out, finding the barest whisper. It would be enough.

"I'm good," I said, and Ivy's eyes tightened at my word choice. I still had my splat gun, for the Turn's sake, and I wasn't going to hide upstairs with Dr. Cordova. "Don't hang around on my account," I said, and he peered down the dark hallway as Jenks rose to check out the upper shaft, flying right through his previous light trail. He really was amazing, when you got right down to it, and I wondered why they'd stuck him with me.

Glenn snapped another glow stick, and a cold, sickly green light joined Jenks's pure glow. Glenn handed it to me, and then checked his watch. Wings clattering, Jenks dropped back down from the upper shaft.

"What are you still here for?" he said snarkily as he hovered at my shoulder. "We've got this. Go on!"

"Jenks, if you want to go with Ivy, I'm good with that," I said, thinking he'd be of better use with her than sitting at an air shaft with me.

"Hell no!" he said, landing on my shoulder. His wings stopped, and it grew darker. "I'm staying here. You never know. They might come this way."

Glenn nodded sharply, checking his watch again. "Okay. Sing out if you see something. Channel seven puts you through to me alone. You know where the dial is?"

I bobbed my head, and Jenks swore at me when my hair hit him. "Thanks, Uncle Glenn," I said sarcastically, wanting to know why he'd arranged for no Inderlanders at the take zone. He'd be griping about it if it was Dr. Cordova's idea, so clearly it was his own—and a faint feeling of mistrust slipped into me.

Behind him, Nina was beginning to look impatient. "I can hear them," Nina whispered. "Little men, like mice in the walls. We need to go."

"Yeah, go," Jenks said, as clearly unnerved by her comment as much as I was.

With a last nod, Glenn turned away. Ivy and Nina followed, and in three seconds, the sound of their steps faded. In another three, they turned a corner and the light from Glenn's glow stick was gone.

I exhaled and leaned against the wall, listening to the silence and breathing in the scent of fear that was more than forty years old. Slowly I recognized the draft pulling my hair up. Tilting my head, I turned the earpiece down and slid to the floor. "How long till they move on them?" I breathed.

"Fifteen minutes, sixteen seconds," Jenks said from my shoulder.

I was silent, then crossed my arms and shifted my weight to my other hipbone. "We're not going to see any action, are we?"

"If you go by Glenn's prediction, not a fairy's chance in a pixy garden," Jenks said. "But I wouldn't be here if I didn't think they were going to screw it up and send them our way. The bastards are going to run, and it won't be for the back door."

"That's what I think, too." I smiled in the dark and waited.

Twenty-Four

The green glow stick that Glenn had left me made Jenks look like a tiny, sickly wraith as he sat on my knee with his legs pulled up, mirroring me. It seemed colder now that I wasn't moving, and my back was to the curved wall as I sat beside the ventilation shaft, my shoulder bag next to me. The draft was pulling the stray strands of my hair up and back. I rolled the glow stick between my palms as I listened to the sporadic radio chatter. I had the speaker cranked since it wasn't in my ear, dangling down my front so Jenks could hear it, too. The conversations revolved around HAPA: who they were, what they were capable of, how many times they'd evaded arrest. I should've been listening, but I was thinking about Trent's charms.

"You okay?" Jenks asked, his wings glittering like they held water drops.

I smiled, remembering how beautiful his wings were close up when I'd shrunk down to help him through the first difficult day after his wife died. "Thinking about Trent's charms," I admitted.

Jenks scowled, his angular features pinching as he picked at his boots. "Yeah? That Pandora charm he made you almost killed you. You should've let me bury them in the garden."

I dragged my shoulder bag closer, peering down at the blue and gold pins. It was hard to tell the difference in the dim light, but I shoved two paralyzing charms in my right boot, two blinding charms in my left.

"Oh God. You're going to use them!" Jenks moaned, and I moved my knee wildly until he took off.

"I'll look pretty stupid if I need them and I don't have them," I said, wiggling my foot until the cool metal warmed and their pinch vanished. I wasn't one for organization, but even I knew that leaving loose charms rattling in a bag wasn't a good idea, and as Jenks pantomimed hanging himself, I gathered the rest, slipping them into a zippered inner pocket of my shoulder bag where they wouldn't interfere with my reach for the splat gun. I still didn't know what the tiny ring Trent had left me did, and I looked at it, remembering what Jenks had said about his boys. Trent had simply forgotten. That's all.

"Do I have time to make a call?" I asked, leaning over to get my phone out of my bag.

"What? *Right now?*" Jenks dropped back down to my knee, his expression disgusted. "Seriously, Rachel, it was sweet and all that he made you charms, but are you willing to trust your life to Trent's maybe skills?"

The memory of watching him preparing to break into the Withons' high-security compound and steal his own daughter filled my thoughts. It wasn't how good he had looked in that black thief outfit, every line of muscle showing, or the obvious preparations he'd made, all the way down to getting me to help him get there alive. It was his confidence, his desire. I'd seen it under the arch before it fell, in the Arizona desert when he summoned Ku'Sox, and in a stupid little bar in Las Vegas when he didn't want to leave to get our car. I'd seen it yesterday afternoon when he helped me with Al. He was trying to be what he wanted, and he really . . . wasn't half bad. For some weird reason, I trusted him. *God help me.*

If he got me killed, I was going to be pissed.

"How much time do we have?" I asked Jenks again, my pulse hammering as I turned my phone on, praying I'd get a signal. One bar. It might be enough, and Jenks was silent as I scrolled through my recently called numbers and hit Trent's.

"Enough if you're quick about it," Jenks said, his expression worried. His wings moved fitfully as he stood, his back almost to me as a show of his ambivalence.

"I just want to know," I said as I tossed my hair from my ear and put the phone to it.

It rang three times before it was picked up, and I fidgeted while Jenks pouted. I didn't know what I was going to say, a feeling that was compounded when the line clicked open and Trent's very muzzy voice murmured, "Rachel? Mmm, hi."

My eyes met Jenks's, and he sniggered at me. Hi? He sounded half asleep. Elves usually napped around noon, but Trent had been taking a lot of flack since coming out of the closet as an elf, and I'd be willing to bet that he was trying to stretch his natural sleep schedule to at least finish out a human workday before crashing. "Um, you got a minute?" I said, warming.

"I didn't think about this before I installed that switchboard," he said, his voice sounding more like his own. "What can I do for you? Since I'm awake."

Embarrassed, I winced. "Sorry," I said, meaning it. "Ah, about those charms you gave me?" I should have called him earlier, and my scuffing feet made echoes as I turned the radio down all the way. Jenks could probably still hear it.

"Charms." Trent's voice smoothed, his polish returning, and I heard the sliding sound of fabric as he got out of bed, presumably. His voice was normal, meaning he didn't have anyone in there with him, and I don't know why the thought occurred to me even as he added, "What about them?"

"You, ah, didn't tell me what the ring does."

"Oh. Sorry," Trent said, and I heard a click and an echo as he put me on speakerphone. "It's a line jump," he added, and I almost dropped the phone.

"I didn't know you could do that," I said, my wide eyes

touching on Jenks's to find he was as mystified as me. "Who did you buy it from?" *Don't say Al. Please don't say Al.*

I heard the smooth shutting of a drawer, and Trent's easy voice saying, "No one. Elves can jump the lines with enough prep work. Ah, I've never actually tried that one out. It's supposed to bring the two rings together. It was originally a way for star-crossed lovers to meet against fate, but when you break it down to bare tacks, it's simply a line jump. A come-to-me kind of thing. Just turn the ring, tap a line, think of me, and say *ta na shay*. I've already got mine on."

Ta na shay. I'd heard that before somewhere. Holding the ring up in the faint pixy light, I slipped it on my ring finger, then moved it to my pinky when it was too tight. Jenks made kissing sounds as he stood on the rim of my bag, and I flicked a finger at him. The ring fit my pinky perfectly, which threw me until recalling that Trent had stolen my pinky ring once.

"I thought you could use it if you ever got trapped in someone's circle," Trent said. "That has got to be . . . frustrating."

It was. *Every time.* "Thank you," I said softly. "I can't ever repay you for this."

"You could come work with me," he said, and I made a fist of my hand, the ring glinting. "Is that all you wanted?"

I heard in his voice his desire to be gone and about his day, but something in me hesitated. "No," I said, and Jenks's wings stilled and drooped. "Since I've got you on the phone, do you know anything about the FIB taking on new people? A new division, maybe?"

Immediately Jenks's attention sharpened, his wings clattering to dust silver into my bag. A chill dropped down my spine, magnified by the dark nothing we were surrounded by. Jenks had noticed the-men-who-don't-belong, too, it wasn't my imagination.

"I don't generally follow the FIB's hiring and firing practices unless it impacts my interests." Trent's voice was somewhat concerned but not really. He was dissing me, and I didn't like it.

I grimaced, finding the words to explain hard in coming. It wasn't as if I could tell Trent that my roommate's boyfriend was acting distant and that I thought something hinky was going on at the FIB. Jenks gestured for me to say something, and encouraged, I said, "Glenn's been acting funny since I got nabbed by HAPA."

Jenks smacked his head with his palm. From the phone, Trent said, "I'm sure he simply blames himself for your capture—"

"Trent, listen to me," I said quickly, cutting him off. "I wouldn't come to you with something unless I thought it was important. I don't know what it means, but you are *going* to take me seriously or I'm never going to come to you again. Don't assume that because you didn't see the dragon first that it doesn't exist."

I heard him sigh, then the squeak of a chair. "I'm listening."

My pulse hammered. He was listening. I was going to him with a concern, and he was listening. Like a business associate, or like a friend? *Did it matter?*

"Something is wrong. Glenn has Ivy, Jenks, and me out at the outskirts of the run."

"You're on a run?" Trent said, his voice rising in disbelief. "Right now? And you just thought to call me about the ring?"

Irritation flooded me, but I pressed on whereas I might normally have just hung up. "He has us on the outskirts. Everyone with Inderland blood in them is on the fringe. It's humans only at the take site. Last time, it was an even mix."

"Perhaps he wants this to be recorded as a human effort," he said, but Jenks was shaking his head right along with me.

Fiddling with the zipper on my boot, I said, "I'd go with that except that there's an entirely different unit of people down here. I've never seen them before. They're like . . . men in black. They almost ignore Glenn, even as they seem to be helping. I'm sure they're the source of the new equipment, the really top-of-the-line stuff. It feels like they're running the take and letting him have the credit if he stays out of the way."

Jenks hummed his wings. "Tell him the guys with the tech stuff smell like the desert."

I looked at Jenks, surprised, and he shrugged.

"The tech people smell like the desert?" Trent repeated.

"The FIB doesn't fund Glenn enough to have doughnuts at his weekly meetings," I said as I flicked my earpiece, hanging down my front. "He's hiding something from Ivy, too. He's never been secretive, well, not when it comes to business."

"New people running the take . . ." The faint scratching of a pencil came through the phone, sounding alien in the chill dark. "Allowing Glenn apparent free movement in terms of personnel and sharing their equipment. I'll look into it," he said, and I heard something clunk. Shoes maybe?

I frowned. He was brushing me off. "Hey."

"I said I'll look into it," he said, his voice a tad harsh. "I'm not brushing you off, but I'd like to show at my office, and I'm not dressed."

Jenks snickered, and I felt myself warm. "Oh. Sorry."

From the earpiece dangling across my front, a tiny voice shouted, "Down! Down!"

Shit, it had started. "Trent, I gotta go."

"My God, you really are on a run," Trent said, and I stood, flustered.

"Thanks for the charms," I said, then closed the phone, cutting him off. Jenks rose up, his dust lighting a good bit of tunnel.

"Holy crap, that was gunfire!" Jenks exclaimed, landing on my shoulder to hear better. I grabbed the earpiece and held it before us like a candle. If I put it in my ear, Jenks wouldn't be able to hear.

"Give me an excuse!" Glenn shouted. "Everyone down! Fingers laced. One twitch of magic, and you will be shot!"

Chris's voice was shrill, swearing at Eloy, at Glenn, at me. *Why is she swearing at me?*

"Chris! Help!" Jennifer cried, and then she shrieked. There was a masculine grunt, and I tensed, leaning forward. It was a weird feeling, knowing what was going on and not being a part of it. Jenks, too, looked frustrated.

"Cease and desist!" Glenn shouted. "You are wanted for questioning in the—"

"Corrumpro!" Chris exclaimed harshly. Gasps of fear rose, and then a cry of pain.

"Put that out," Glenn directed calmly, and I heard another crash. "Someone cuff her! I don't know, shove a sock in her mouth! Use the zip strips!"

I looked at Jenks. He was itching to fly. "They should have had someone who can do magic there," I said, and he nodded.

"Lock her down! Lock her down!" someone yelled. "Gimmie a strap. Shit, she's wiggly. Ow!"

Chris screamed, and then her voice became muffled. My lips curled in a half smile. That was one way to stop a curse, but they needed to strap her, and fast.

There was a quick, three-beat thump in the background. Then Gerald groaned, and I heard him slide to the floor.

"Strap them! Do it now!" someone shouted, and a crash made me wince. If they didn't get control in thirty seconds, I was sending in Jenks.

The sound was muffled for a moment, and then a shuffling scrape turned into heavy breathing. Jennifer was crying in the background, and finally the sound of someone hitting the floor came, loud, followed by a soft grunt.

"I think that was Eloy," I said, and Jenks nodded.

"Get him *down*!" Glenn shouted, and then a thump again.

For a moment, silence, and then I heard Glenn swear under his breath. "Don't move."

There was an *oof* of breath, then Glenn laughed. It wasn't a pleasant sound. "Go ahead, Eloy. I don't care if you're alive or dead at this point." I held my breath, imagining it, and then Glenn whispered, "Good choice."

A masculine voice called for Glenn, and I heard Eloy swear, his voice muffled. "I've got this," Glenn said, his tone telling me it was over—if Jennifer sobbing quietly was any indication. "Put the fire out. Someone put the fire out! I need another zip strip over here. Now! Can we have some lights?"

In the near distance, I heard Chris snarl, "Shut up!" and Jennifer's sobs subsided.

There was a scuffle as I think Glenn yanked Eloy up, and I heard the familiar ratcheting of a zip strip. "You sure it's him?" someone asked. "He might be disguised."

I fumbled to flick on the mic, whispering, "Check with the amulet, Glenn."

"Holy crap, Rachel!" Glenn exclaimed. "You startled me. I forgot you were listening."

I shifted my feet and grinned at Jenks. His dust was an excited silver. I was glad they'd gotten them. Score one for the FIB. Jennifer was pleading in the background, but no one was listening. It looked like it was all over, but I wasn't moving. Not yet.

"Yep, it's him," a new, low voice drawled, and Jenks's wings clattered. "Thank God we got them before they abducted anyone else."

"Damn, Rache," the pixy swore as he made the jump back to my knee. "They did it!"

"And they did it without us," I said softly, feeling left out. I could hear the Miranda being recited, ignored. Jennifer was crying, Chris was swearing, and I think Gerald was knocked out. Eloy had yet to say anything, which wasn't unusual, but I could imagine the scene well enough. He'd be standing with his arms cuffed behind his back and his shoulders hunched. His hair would be messed up, and he'd likely be sporting a new scrape from hitting the floor. He'd be silently thinking up a way to escape, his eyes darting about. I didn't know Eloy, but I knew his type—my type. There was always a way out.

Calls were going over the airways to bring the vans in. And still I sat. Waiting. My tension began to build. Eloy wasn't talking. Eloy had a way out. I knew it.

"Get up, Eloy," Glenn said suddenly, cutting through the radio noise. "Arms out. Assume the position."

Okay, so he wasn't standing yet, but I could see him in my mind's eye: slowly getting up, assessing everything, looking for a hole as he got patted down for whatever they could find. He was going to run.

"Hey!" someone said. "Lookie what I found on him! What do you think it is?"

A second man laughed. "A can of deodorant?" he said, then shouted, "Don't point it at me, jerk-off! It might be magic!"

I reached to toggle the mic to ask Glenn to describe it to me, then settled back when a deep, almost bland voice I didn't recognize said, "Excuse me," and presumably took it, muttering, "Damn fools. No wonder they can't catch their asses in a windstorm."

They, I thought, my eyes meeting Jenks's. He had heard it, too. Just who was down there with Glenn if it wasn't his usual men? But as long as Eloy didn't have it, whatever it was could wait. It was probably a can of sticky silk to ward off Jenks.

Not yet ready to leave, I sank to the floor. There was a soft pop as someone clapped their hands, and Glenn shouted, "Okay. We got 'em. Area is secure. Everyone can come in. Nicely done, people."

A soft cheering, both from the room and from the distant sites by way of the radio, filtered into the dark. And still I sat. Waiting.

"HAPA isn't so happy now, huh?" Jenks said, his dust several shades brighter as he lit the tunnel with a healthy glow.

"Yes," I said softly, thinking as I spun Trent's ring on my pinkie.

Seeing me not moving, he landed on my knee, his dust

feeling like snow as it sifted over me. "I know the way back," he said, looking worried.

I tucked the glow stick in my bag so my eyes could readjust to the dark. "Not yet."

Jenks's wings stopped moving, laying flat on his back, and it grew dark. "I know what you mean. It's kind of anticlimactic, listening to it happen. I'm surprised you stayed put, Rache. You knew you weren't going to see any action. I'm proud of you."

No action. Right . . .

Dr. Cordova's voice slowly became audible, and in a confusing mix of about three separate conversations, I heard her come into the room with a bevy of aides, and my pulse quickened. "Congratulations, Detective Glenn, on a well-implemented run," she said loudly, and the radio chatter almost doubled.

"Thank you, ma'am. I'll be sure to let everyone know you're pleased," Glenn said, his annoyance that she was down here obvious even over the radio.

"Let's move them out," she said decisively. "Get them to the FIB lockup."

My jaw clenched, and I looked at Jenks. That hadn't been the plan. Catching them was one thing. Holding them was another. That's where the vulnerability was, and it would take an I.S. cell to hold a magic-using human. "What the hell is she doing?" Jenks whispered, his wings lifting as he prepared to take flight.

That deep voice, faint from being whispered, came again. "Don't let her move them, Detective. If she does, they're gone. I promise you."

"You tell me how I can overrule her, and I will," Glenn said, his voice tight, and then louder, with a sliver of false respect, "I'd rather wait for the I.S. containment people, ma'am. It was arranged that they'd hold them, not us."

"Allow humans into I.S. custody?" Dr. Cordova snapped. "We have them. They're strapped. They can't do any magic." The voices in the room died away, leaving only the background chatter of independent conversations revolving around traffic and where to park.

Again that deep voice began arguing with Glenn, even as Glenn tried to do everything he could to no avail. "Don't do it . . ." I whispered, the sound of my feet scraping on the cement loud as I began walking in circles, trying to wake up my cold, stiff muscles.

"Ma'am," Glenn started, but was immediately cut off.

"You, and you," Dr. Cordova demanded. "Take them out."

"Ma'am, I protest," Glenn said. The unnamed man in the background swore, then began barking out orders and clearing the room.

Jenks was hovering beside me, his expression worried. "Glenn is more pissed than a foreclosed troll," he said, and I nodded, balancing on one foot to pull a knee to my chest to stretch my cramped leg.

"Do you recognize that man with the deep voice?" I asked, and Jenks shook his head.

"Noted," Dr. Cordova said sarcastically. "Excuse me, you're in the way, Detective."

Glenn make a low sound deep in his throat, and I winced at the sharp clatter and pop as he took his earpiece off and set it on some counter. Dr. Cordova's voice rang out loudly, "I want them out of here in separate vans in five minutes. Move!"

Jenks had landed on the opening to the ventilation shaft, his silver dust lighting the corridor, when Ivy's voice, smooth and silky, came faintly. "Hey, good tag, Glenn." She hesitated, and then asked, "What's the matter? You okay?" His answer was hardly more than a growl, and Ivy exclaimed, "She's retaining custody? Is she fried?"

I carefully stretched the other leg as I turned the speaker up as far as it would go. "I thought you were going to put them in our custody," Nina said.

"Apparently not," Glenn muttered.

"Look out!" a voice cried, and there were several exclamations and the soft pop of gunfire. "Fire in the hole!" someone else shouted. "Loose gun!"

My pulse quickened, and I quietly wedged the lower grate aside, dropping my shoulder bag into the lower shaft and out of sight. Jenks's tiny features creased. Wings going full tilt, he said, "Oh, this isn't good."

"Shhh."

"Stop!" Glenn shouted. "Someone get him!"

"Son of a fairy!" Jenks said, rising up to light a six-foot circle. "They're escaping! Right under their fairy-wiped noses!"

I took a deep breath. Faint, so faint I almost didn't hear it, the man with the deep voice said. "Alpha unit, prep beaters. Beta, stand by to receive game. Keep it tight, people. Reassemble at bird nest."

Put me in the dark by myself, will they? I thought as I carefully swung myself over the side and stretched to find the bend, four feet down. A shiver went through me as I hung my feet over the edge of the hole and stretched until my toes brushed the curve of the pipe. If I hadn't guessed right and he was actually headed for the back door, he was going to get away.

A cry of surprise went up, and someone shouted, "Get the lights! Get the lights!"

"Eloy! You son of a bitch!" Chris's shrill voice rang out. "I'll kill you for this! I swear, I'll kill you if you leave me behind!"

I couldn't help my grim smile as I settled inside the pipe below the level of the floor. Apparently we were all having a great day. As Jenks hovered, I dragged the grate closer. I could tell when the lights came back on in the distant room because everything got quiet, then the noise started back up again with demands for information. I didn't hear the man with the deep voice. He was gone. I think the men at the radio station were, too.

"Spread out! Find him!" Glenn shouted, and I knelt in the shaft with my feet running down it, my head poking above the level of the floor. I fumbled for my splat gun, the cold metal making me shiver as it met the small of my back.

"Is anyone still at the back door?" someone yelled.

A faint voice called out, "Not enough," and Ivy swore.

"Nina, give me your finding amulet," she demanded, and then I heard her run. For an instant, I considered telling her where I thought he was heading, but then didn't; what if I was wrong? This way, both bases would be covered.

Nina was laughing. It seemed to be the right response, as all hell was breaking loose.

"There is nothing funny here," Dr. Cordova snarled, barely heard over the back-and-forth chatter on the radios.

"Teresa, you are funny," Nina said, sounding sourly amused. "You should've listened to your detective. Knowing your limits is a strength, not a weakness."

"This is not my fault!" Dr. Cordova shouted. "I hadn't taken custody of them yet. Detective Glenn, I'm holding you responsible for this! That man wasn't searched properly! He had a weapon!"

"Of course you are, ma'am," he said, and I exchanged a wide-eyed look with Jenks, who was now standing on the grate, hands on his hips and wings silent.

"You think he's coming this way?" Jenks asked, and I nodded. From the radio burst a shouted realization that the can of spray was gone, too. Fingers fumbling, I turned the radio off. Grabbing a couple of zip strips from my shoulder bag, I stuffed them in the tops of my boots. No wonder Ivy wore a waist pack when she was on a run. I had more stuff jammed in my boots than toes.

"What are you doing?" Jenks hissed. "You should call for help!"

"Go get help if you want," I said, and he darted up as I repositioned the grate so I could poke my head out. "He's coming this way, and I'm going to stop him. Douse the light, will you? It takes forever for your dust to settle."

He frowned, hands still on his hips. I made a questioning, waiting face at him, and slowly his look changed to one of amusement. There was a faint glow from the floor, but it might just have been a memory on my retina. "I get first crack at him," Jenks said as he landed on my shoulder.

"And I'll get the last," I said, my heart pounding as the faint sound of running feet broke the stillness, the sound as old as the savannas.

Twenty-Five

Heart thudding, I reached back for my splat gun, bringing it forward and peering into the blackness of the tunnel. If I couldn't bring him down with the gun, then I'd consider the charms. Reaching for the line, I filled my chi with a bright, scintillating glow of power, letting it leak over my soul and spindling a wad of it in my head just in case. Satisfaction was almost as warm as the line in me, and again I wondered how I could ever have willingly cut myself off from this. It was like bathing in light.

I heard Eloy slide to a stop, and I peeked up through the opening I'd left in the grate. There was a faint glow from a cell phone being used as a flashlight—he was looking for the air shaft, running his hand along the ceiling. It was hard to see, but his face was still bruised from Winona's beating. Breath held, I watched him. Grinning, I took aim. This was going to be easy.

The gun clicked . . . and Eloy dropped and rolled, right out of my line of sight, his faint light extinguishing. The blue ball burst open against the far wall of the shaft, useless. Damn!

Jenks flew through the grate, his sword out. "I told you I get first hit," he said, and the ping of pixy steel rang followed by the hiss of propellant.

"You have got to be shitting me," Eloy said, and I poked

my head out of the hole in the floor, fear for Jenks making me careless. "A bug?" His shadow tensed. "Morgan? Is that you?"

"Give it up, Eloy!" I shouted, shooting at his voice. The light was gone, and I heard him swear. Crouched in the shaft, I waited for a sound, not wanting to get sticky silk in my eyes. At point-blank range, it would glue them shut. I had only so many sleepy-time balls left, or I would have peppered the hallway. Jenks was probably down, staying silent to keep from being stepped on. I wanted to keep Eloy busy until he was up again.

"When this is done, I'm going to come for you," Eloy said, and I shot at his voice, hearing him scramble back with another half-heard oath. "I know where you live. I'm bringing you in."

"Everyone knows where I live," I said from inside the lower air shaft. "I've got a sign out front with my name on it, moss wipe!"

"I'm going to find you," he whispered, and I shivered at the hatred in his voice, his sureness. "I'm going to sever your spinal cord in your sleep. You're going to wake up with me bending over you, unable to move. And then I'm going to milk your blood for the next one hundred and sixty years like the animal you are. I'll use you to wipe your species from the earth."

His threats were not going to happen, but I shivered anyway.

He was too far down the corridor. I needed a better angle. Heart pounding, I quietly wedged myself out past the grate and rolled onto the floor. Flat on my stomach, I closed my eyes and whispered, "You're going to have a hard time with that from jail."

"I could do it from jail." His voice was introspective, casual. "I'd rather do it myself, though. The pleasure. You know."

"Rache!" Jenks shouted, and I rolled, invoking a circle as the shot echoed in the tunnel. The gold of my aura glowed in the dark. Smut crawled over it like a living patina, dimpled where the bullet had ricocheted off. Through the haze, I saw Eloy by the faint light of my circle. He was crouched with his gun pointed at me, a young man overflowing with fear, hate, and misplaced zeal. The smell of gunpowder hit me. Behind him, Jenks was white faced and struggling, stuck to the floor.

"Son of a bastard," I breathed, scared for Jenks. Arms out, I shifted the angle of my gun and pulled the trigger. I rolled as the pellet hit my circle and broke the amber wash. My heart pounded in the new darkness, but I heard only a disgusted grunt.

"*Noli me tangere,* bitch," Eloy said, and my teeth clenched. *Don't touch me? Had I missed?* "Anticharm gear. You think I'd do this without it? Your magic is useless."

"You know some Latin," I said, my eyes searching for the barest hint of a glow, a glint. Anticharm gear wouldn't stand up to repeated abuse. "I'm surprised they teach you that in the bunkers."

Eloy chuckled, and I shifted my aim higher. If I hit his face or hands, he'd go down for sure. "I didn't grow up in a camp," he said, and I adjusted my grip on my gun, beginning to sweat. "I'm from a very well-respected family. Most of us are. I went to the best schools, better than you. That's why you're going to fail. We're smarter than you. You can't help it."

His shoes scuffed, and I shot at the sound, rolling as his gun popped again. Little bits of concrete peppered me, and I clenched my teeth, not wanting to set a circle and light the tunnel again. Jenks was still down and vulnerable. Where the hell was everyone? Weren't they looking for Eloy? Fingers moving, I reached to turn the radio back on to call for help. There was nothing. It was dead, and I thought of the two men running the radio. Had they been beaters or receivers? Had they left Glenn now that Eloy was on the run, planning on acquiring him themselves? They weren't HAPA, were they? Damn it back to the Turn, it would explain a lot.

"We are everywhere, at every level," Eloy gloated, cementing the idea in my head.

"You know what they say. Book smart, street stupid," I said, one hand letting go of the gun, my fingers reaching inside my boot for the charm to paralyze someone. "How's your elven?"

"Jenks! Light him up!" I yelled, then put the butt of the pin between my teeth.

It was a huge risk, but Jenks dusted, and in the faint glow, I found Eloy's eyes. "Look at me, you bastard!" I said between my clenched teeth—then yanked the amulet to pull the pin.

I was still connected to the line, and I sucked in my breath as something alien reached through me, pulling the line like a wind-whipped ribbon over my synapses with the sound of wicked, chiming laughter. It coated me in fear, and I fixed on Eloy's eyes, hoping, praying, that Trent had done this right and I hadn't just given Jenks's location away.

Eloy blinked, his expression going slack. And then he slowly collapsed, falling facedown on the cold cement.

It worked! Adrenaline washed through me, and I waited, hardly breathing, my gun pointed at him, afraid to look away to see how Jenks was. Hot damn, it had worked, and he was down!

I took a tense step forward, intentionally scuffing my shoes. Eloy didn't move, slumped on the floor with his arm twisted at an awkward angle half under him. "Jenks?"

"I'm okay! He's down," he said in disgust, and I flicked my gaze to him then back to Eloy. "His aura went passive. God-blessed mother moss wipe of a pixy. Flew right into it. It's not sticky silk, Rache. It's worse. I'm stuck to the floor like a troll booger on the underside of a bridge."

Gun pointed at Eloy, I edged closer, bending to reach for a zip strip from my boot. "You need some help?"

"I need half a fairy farting brain!" he snarled. "No. You'll rip my wings off. I've almost got it. Zip-strip him before he wakes up, will you?"

He subsided into half-heard swearing as the glow from his fitfully moving wings lit the slumped shape of Eloy, his back rising and falling as he breathed. Trent's charm had worked.

In the distance, I could hear voices echoing in the dark. They could be thirty feet, or three hundred with the way sound traveled. "We're over here!" I shouted and, gun pointed, I wedged a foot under Eloy to roll him over.

"Rache! No!" Jenks shouted, still stuck to the floor.

His eyes were open. The spell had played itself out that fast.

"Crap!" I exclaimed, pulling the trigger, but he was faster, and his foot swung out, connecting with my ankle. I fell, my foot going numb. My arms flailed, and my head hit the side of the cement tube as he shoved me.

Stars were born and died underground, and I felt myself falling, my side scraping on the rough walls of the tunnel. Idiot! I should have double-tapped him!

"You are one tough bitch," Eloy was saying as he stood over me, and I groaned when he kicked my middle, my air huffing out as I clenched in pain. "Anyone else I'd kill right now, but I'll be back for you in about a week. Count on it." Crouching, he pulled my head up by my hair. "A lifetime of rest and relaxation wait for you, madam cow. Your blood is going to wipe the scourge from the world and make it clean again."

"You bastard . . ." I gasped, still clenched over my middle. "This is our world, too."

"And the monkeys and the donkeys, but we don't let them live in penthouse suites." He dropped my head, and my face hit the cement. My head throbbed, and my ankle felt like it was on fire as he yanked my arms behind my back and zip-stripped me with my own zip strip. The line energy I had stored washed out of me and my connection to it died. I was on my own.

"Cute," he said as he picked up my splat gun. I clenched my eyes shut, expecting him to shoot me, but they flashed open when I heard him run for the air shaft instead. Wiggling, I rolled over, finally getting a good breath of air. Voices echoed in my head, real or imagined, I couldn't tell.

"You chickenshit fairy flop!" Jenks shouted, his wings going like mad as he tried to unstick himself from the floor, finally taking his boot off and darting almost to the ceiling before dropping back down and trying to free his sword. "You're the one who's going to get the lobotomy. I'll find you. I swear I'll find you!"

By the light of Jenks's dust, I blearily watched Eloy standing under the upper air shaft, shooting up into it with that can of spray. It looked like silly string, spreading out to make a thick net falling out of the ceiling. Tucking the can in his back pocket, he quickly gathered the strands into a thicker rope. The smell of propellant drifted to me, and I hoped I wouldn't sneeze. My head hurt, and I was afraid I was going to vomit.

My fingers pushed against the cold floor and, panting, I levered my upper body up. "Eloy!" I croaked, but he didn't even look as he reached over his head and started climbing. His feet swung wildly until finding the walls, and he was gone, my splat gun shoved at the small of his back.

"This is exactly why I don't like weapons," I whispered, licking my lip to find it swollen. "They can always be used against you." Pissed, I sat, my back to the wall, cursing myself as I felt my ribs, and Eloy's noise diminished.

"Rache. You okay?"

"Yes." I went to rise, but my ankle gave way and I fell back, my breath hissing out. "No."

"Maybe we're getting too old for this," he said, and I leaned forward so he could reach the zip strip.

"Just break it, will you?" There was a thump from the tunnel, and I grimaced.

"So call Glenn already," he said, and I felt a light pressure on my wrists as he wedged his sword into the fastening clamp. "No shame in asking for help."

"Radio is dead," I said, and Jenks swore.

"Those mother moss wipes with the fancy equipment are not working for the FIB," he said, then swore again, blaming Tink, the sun, and the stars all in one long breath.

My hands were suddenly free, and ·I pulled my arms to my front. I reached for a line, relishing the scintillating energy as it ran like a chattering stream through my neural network, washing away my slight headache. "Oh, that feels good. Thanks, Jenks."

"I broke my Tink-blasted sword!" he said in disgust, and I realized why the elaborate swearing as he came around front. "Look at it! Snapped it clean through."

"I think I sprained my ankle," I said, nauseated as I put a hand to the wall and slowly stood. "He's got my gun, too."

Jenks hovered before me, a green tint to his dust as he looked at his best garden sword, the pixy steel snapped at the hilt. I eased my weight to my injured ankle, and hissed, jerking it up again. "You want to call it?" Jenks said, and I glanced at the mouth of the tunnel.

The memory surfaced of Winona fighting Gerald as he stripped her, and Chris dancing in delight as the curse made with my blood twisted her into a monstrosity. Eloy's slurs and misplaced superiority made my eyes crinkle in renewed anger. My pulse hammered. I wanted him. I wanted him bad.

"Hell no," I said, and Jenks threw his broken sword at the wall. It made a sliding ting as it hit and fell, and I felt bad for him even as he darted to the mouth of the upward-facing tunnel, more determined yet. Hobbling, I managed the few steps to the shaft and looked up into the dark. The end of Eloy's makeshift rope dangled, looking too thin to support my weight. "He climbed that?" I said, and Jenks went up and down like an impatient yo-yo.

"It's only five feet. Then it goes at an angle."

Five feet. Straight up. My upper-body strength wasn't that bad, and I reached for the makeshift rope. The sticky lace-work clung to me, and I started to feel a little better. The slimy rat had kicked me when I was down. Took my gun.

Tied me up with my own zip strip. Made Jenks break his sword. It was enough to make me wish that Trent had given me a charm to turn people inside out.

I could hear thumps from the shaft, and knowing no one—not even the mysterious alpha or beta teams—would be guarding the other end of the air shaft, I tensed my arms and started up. "Move it, witch!" Jenks shouted, and I swung my body weight, trying to get my good leg up to help support my mass.

Jenks was right, and I found the other end of the weird rope stuck to the wall of the shaft where it made a sixty-degree angle and sloped upward. My ankle wasn't hurting as badly, and panting, I wiggled my way up, hitting my shoulder on the wall as I struggled.

"Good God, Rache," Jenks swore, hovering an inch before my nose as I lay in the shaft and tried to catch my breath. "Think you can make any more noise?"

"He knows I'm coming," I wheezed. "Get out of my way," I added as I got my arms in front of me and started dragging myself forward on the flats of them. I didn't know what I was going to do without my gun, but I drank in the line as I went, filling my chi again with the line tasting of earth and ice-rimmed moss. Jenks hovered for a moment, then darted ahead. Slowly the shaft grew dark, but it didn't matter. There was only one way to go.

The shaft was only two feet tall, and about as wide, made of dark metal, and claustrophobic. The edges where it was soldered together were thick, looking like someone had been in a hurry as I dragged myself over them. If this was a Turn-instigated shelter, then it had probably been constructed in a matter of months. The shaft could come out anywhere, but I bet Eloy had a car waiting already. He was that kind of planner. *Who had given him the gun when he escaped from Glenn? Who had cut his zip strip?*

A sudden commotion ahead of me brought my head up, and I waited a breathless moment as I heard Eloy shouting, thumps, and Jenks's laughter. I gathered myself to surge forward, and the pixy was back, grinning. "What did you do?" I said, and he landed before me, dust spilling from him bright enough to read by.

"I got your gun back," he said. "He had it stuck in his waistband in the back, and he couldn't do anything when I shoved it out and dragged it off him. Dumb place to put it, if you ask me. It's up about twenty feet, waiting for you. He might scoot backward to get it, but I doubt it. He knows you're coming. He still has his pistol."

And maybe four bullets. "Thanks," I wheezed, feeling renewed hope as I resumed inching forward, dragging my lower body along. My ankle throbbed, and I ignored it. I wanted my gun. The shaft was rising at a steeper angle, and I could smell cold cement. Slowly the sounds of Eloy's passage faded, and I pushed myself into moving faster. The shadow of my gun slowly appeared, and I grabbed it, my knuckles scraping as I crawled forward with it in my hand.

Frustrated by my pace, Jenks walked before me to light his way. There was a crash from somewhere ahead, and I froze, feeling the weight of the earth press on me. "Hold on a sec," Jenks said, and he darted ahead again.

The tunnel grew dark. My ankle still throbbed, but I pushed on, arms aching. I heard Jenks before I saw him, an excited red to his dust as he slid to a stop, inches before my nose. "He's out!" he said, and I blew the hair from my eyes. "That was a grate popping off. It opens up into a sewer line or something. You're almost there. Hurry your little witch ass up!"

"Swell," I breathed, thinking someone had made a mistake. You don't have an air shaft empty into a sewer, even if there was negative airflow. "You think you could slow him down?" I panted as I tried to move faster.

He gave me a thumbs-up and darted ahead. The air suddenly smelled a lot fresher, and I thought I saw a patch of lighter darkness ahead. I could hear cars, and I wondered how far I'd crawled. A city block? "I'm going to smack you so hard you won't wake up until next week," I whispered as I pushed myself the last few feet. "Making me crawl through a pipe. God!"

Heart pounding, I managed the final span, carefully poking my head out past the broken grate hanging from one twisted chunk of metal. I was about five feet above the floor of what looked like a subway tunnel, lit by a thin strip of streetlight coming in through a grate, almost even with me on the other side of the wide cement tube. Eloy was nowhere to be seen.

"Holy crap," I whispered, looking up at the rumbling sound of traffic overhead. We were under Central Parkway. This wasn't a sewer line, but the old subway system, or what was left of it. It figured they'd use it for a bioshelter during the Turn.

I looked down at the five-foot drop. I had to take it head-first, but if Eloy could do it, so could I, and hearing Eloy's sudden oath and Jenks's laugh, I slowly wiggled into the lighter darkness, reaching for the ground. My hips started to slide out, and I tossed my gun to the cement an instant before I fell.

The ground rushed up, and I stifled a gasp, palms and arms taking most of the impact. My shoulder hit, and I rolled, tucking my head so I wouldn't crack my nose open. The stink of wet cement hit me as I sucked in my breath and tried not to cry out. Everything hurt, and holding my elbow, I tossed my hair from my eyes and looked for my gun.

"Hurry!" Jenks said, looking frazzled as he hovered before me. "If he gets out onto Central Ave., he's gone!"

I reached for my gun. Jaw clenched, I staggered to my feet, trying not to put too much weight on my foot. At least I could stand now. My boots were tight enough to give some support, but it still hurt like hell.

Jenks flew beside me, braver than I was for doing the same thing with no sword to back up his words. The street noise grew louder, the sunlight leaking through dimmer. The tunnel ended in a wide stairway, and the quick flash of sunlight followed by a thump of metal on metal made me lurch forward.

"Wait!" Jenks whispered, almost in my ear, and I hesitated. That slow, rasping noise started again. Eloy was still down here, and I put my back to the wall beside the stairway, trying to catch my breath and regroup. He had a pistol. Trent's charms didn't last very long and could be circumvented by simply avoiding eye contact when they were invoked. Frowning, I pulled my remaining zip strip from my boot and left it in the dirt. I'd have to bludgeon Eloy into unconsciousness and sit on him until Jenks could get help.

I smiled, liking the idea.

Heart pounding, I peeked around the wall and saw Eloy at the top of the stairway. The man had his back hunched as he stood under a door set flush with the ground, like a root cellar, pushing it up with his back to make a crack big enough to get his hand through, but little else. It was hard to see with only the dim sunlight leaking in, but it looked like he was trying to saw through a chain. *Where in hell had he gotten the saw?*

I ducked back and met Jenks's eyes. He grinned at me, and I grinned back. "I take the high ground, you take the low," he said, and I shook my head.

"You're compromised without your sword," I whispered, and he scowled. "I need help. The radio is off. We're fighting HAPA. Go get Glenn. Tell him where we are. I'll keep Eloy busy until you get back."

"I'm not going to leave you. You're compromised, too, you stupid-ass witch."

God, I loved hearing him call me that. "Get Glenn!" I insisted, awkwardly shifting my weight. "Even with my gun, I can't bring him down by myself. As you say, I'm compromised."

Jenks's face tightened, but he nodded. "Can you just stay alive for the next five minutes?" he said, and lifted up and away, his wings a bright flash as he found the sunbeam and followed it out.

My pulse hammered. Moving slowly, I tightened the grip on the butt of my weapon and I came around the wall, gun pointed.

"Shit!" Eloy exclaimed as my bad foot scuffed and he spun. The heavy metal door slammed down again, sealing us in a room with only a thin, dusty thread of sunlight. Jaw clenched, I fired, aiming for his smug face.

Eloy dove off the steps and into the shadows. His metal saw clattered, abandoned, and my shot broke harmlessly on the stairs. Frowning, I realigned my sights. "Give it up!" I shouted, my voice echoing in the shadows. "The FIB knows where we are!"

The pop of his pistol going off shocked through me. Jumping, I dove for cover. My ankle gave way, and I fell, my splat gun skittering away from me even as I found a broken pillar to hide behind and flashed a protection bubble into place. *Damn it!* I'd lost my gun, and my head pounded with the remnants of the sudden flow of energy I'd used to make an undrawn circle strong enough to deflect a bullet. Three hearts pounded, one in my ankle, one in my head, one in my chest. But I'd gotten it up in time, and I was safe.

Bubble holding, I peeked up over the broken rubble and saw my gun in a spot of sun just to my left. If my ankle wasn't throbbing, I might chance making a run for it, but he had three bullets left, and I was sure my gun was in Eloy's view. I could hide in a bubble until help arrived, but if I did that, he could simply walk away. Suddenly I realized how deep in the crapper I was, and I dropped my inner circle to set a wider one, one that encompassed both of us and would keep him from reaching the door.

"Maybe I should have shot you," Eloy said as he came out from behind his pillar, satisfaction oozing from him, his gun pointed at me. "Where's your bug?"

"He's a pixy, dumbass. Get it right." I got to my feet, agony stabbing up through me. Damn it, I had lost my stealth as well as my gun. "I'm not letting you leave," I mocked, hands on my hips as I tried not to look at my gun, glinting in the sun. "I can hold that bubble all day. You're stuck until the I.S. gets here. If you jump a line, you'll end up in a cell."

Eloy smiled as he looked at my gun, then came forward a few steps. "I wanted you alive," he said, his voice soft, echoing in the hard space. "Which is why I only strapped you before, but I need to get out of here more, and Kalamack's records say there's another one of you, a male. What was he trying to do, rebuild the species that killed his own?"

My satisfied expression faltered. I glanced at my gun, wanting it.

Eloy took a few steps closer, his gun pointed down. "I'm all for conservation, but when I see a snake, I kill it. I'm just going to shoot you. A demon can't hold a circle if she's dead."

Crap on toast, he didn't want me alive anymore. Weapon held casually, he glanced behind himself and saw my bubble glowing between him and the door. "I'm curious," he said lightly as he brought his pistol up. "Are you faster than my bullet?"

With no warning, he shot at me again. Gasping, I flinched, dropping the large circle and slamming a new one into existence between us. The bullet hit with a thump of sound that echoed through me, followed by a tiny ping as it sank into the ceiling. Dust trickled down. I could hear cars overhead, but no pixy wings. *Damn it, Jenks, where are you?*

Seeing me behind my circle, Eloy started backing to the door.

Panicked, I flashed a new barrier up between him and the door, stopping him in his tracks. He was still farther from the door than before, closer to me, two bullets in his gun.

Eloy put his weight on one foot and looked at the chamber of his pistol. "We have a problem, you and me. Drop your circle."

My lip curled. "Right." I squinted at him, listening for the sound of pixy wings but only hearing the *shush* of traffic.

In a sudden show of anger, Eloy slammed his foot against the inside of my circle in a back kick and found it solid. Then his flush vanished, replaced with a smile that chilled me. Eyes darting, he took several steps closer. My breath came fast as he pulled his gun up, squinting.

"How about . . . now?" he said, pulling the trigger.

I sucked in my air. The line was already running through me, and I wavered on my feet as I forced it into a new circle, sweating with the effort. My head was humming, and my foot felt like it was on fire. The bullet thunked into my barrier and went zinging into the dark. One. He had one bullet left.

The man nodded, as if congratulating me. "Not bad, not bad," he said, and I dropped my circle, enticing him nearer. If I could touch him, I could drop him with a blast of everafter. The thing was, he probably knew it and wouldn't get that close—unless I made it irresistible.

My pulse pounded as he edged forward, tense and eager. The sheen of sweat glistened on his brow, red where Jenks had pixed him, black and blue where Winona's feet had pounded him. His blue eyes glinted as he stepped in and out of the sun leaking through the pavement grates. Lips a hard line, he pulled his gun up, smiling, showing his teeth. The gun was FIB issue, and I felt myself pale. No one was coming, and as I remembered the bells that didn't ring in San Francisco, I reached deep into myself and found a sliver of courage. I had survived then. I would survive now.

"Feeling lucky?" I said, and he inched closer, his arms stiff and his aim unwavering. "Well, do you?" I mocked, and his finger moved.

The gun sounded like a cannon as it fired. Energy pulled through me, leaving me gasping as I fell to one knee. I felt the bullet hit my bubble and twang off. I lunged forward for my spell pistol as cement cracked under the bullet. My circle fell as I hit it, and my eyes closed at the sudden pain as I found the cement floor, front first. My hands scrabbled, reached, and found the butt of my splat gun. Elated, I turned, still on the ground, and brought my gun up.

Eloy was there, and I cried out when his foot slammed

into my raised hands, knocking the pistol free and probably breaking a finger.

"You son of a bitch!" I shouted, trying to sit up with my hands clenched to my chest. Trent's ring burned on my finger, and I panted, feeling the pain where Eloy's foot had jammed it into my skin, cutting me.

"Some demon," Eloy said, swooping down to pick up my splat gun. "You're going to be downed by your own spells. Pathetic."

"It wouldn't be the first time," I said, reeling from the pain in my hand. What in hell kind of demon was I? But then I stared at the ring, glinting with my own blood, and had a sudden idea. It would jump me to Trent, but with that net sink in place . . . it would jump me—and anyone I was touching—into a jail cell.

Hope pulled my head up, and Eloy stared at my grim smile as I clutched my bruised hand and spun the ring on my finger to prime it. Slowly Eloy's own smile failed as he realized I wasn't giving up.

He began to raise my gun.

Screaming, I lunged at his knees. He cried out in surprise, and we went down together, me on top.

The world spun as he shoved me off, and I took the foot he was swinging at me right in the ribs. Grabbing it, I tapped a line, thought of Trent, and shouted, *"Ta na shay!"*

"Let *go!*" he shouted, kicking until my fingers gave way and he danced back, shaking in anger. "Don't you ever touch me again, you putrid animal!" he shouted, and I curled into a ball as he drew his foot back and kicked me, lifting me from the concrete. Agony thumped into my middle, and I cowered, holding my bruised arms over my head. I didn't understand. The charm was supposed to jump me to Trent! It hadn't worked! I had spun the ring, I had said the words, and I had thought of Trent—seeing him in my mind not as the businessman he showed the world, but as he had been in the woods, a shadow crouched on a tree, wild and ephemeral. Maybe he was the businessman after all . . .

Gasping for air, I looked up, my lank hair falling into my eyes. Eloy stood before me in a patch of sun, my gun in his hand. "Was that supposed to have done something?" he shouted.

My lips parted as my eyes went to the taut form standing behind him. *Trent?*

"Something did," Trent said, and Eloy spun.

Sweet and golden as honey, Trent pulled back and rabbit-punched the man square in the jaw. Eloy's head snapped back, and he dropped like a stone. I stared as his body hit the ground, the displaced air shifting my hair from my eyes for a second. *Trent is here?* The charm *had* worked—sort of.

"Ow, ow, ow!" Trent whispered, hunched over his hand, his expensive suit and perfect hair looking wrong against the dull concrete walls. "Is it supposed to hurt that much, or did I do it wrong?"

Still clenched over my bruised ribs, I managed to sit up. "That's why I always use my foot. I thought I was supposed to go to you!"

Sidestepping Eloy, Trent picked his way to me, his nose wrinkled as he glanced up at the ceiling and the obvious street noise. "You were trying to bring him to me?" he said, incredulous, and I shook my head as he extended his hand to help me stand. He had a ring, twin to my own. "I was in a meeting. *Oh my God.* I was in a meeting. I vanished right in front of them." He slapped his pants pockets. "I don't have my phone. My wallet."

"Welcome to the club," I said, then groaned as I got to my feet, waving off his help since my hands were swollen and bruised. "No, I wasn't trying to bring him to you. The I.S. has a net sink up," I said as I bent over my knees and tried to stand up straight. I think I had a bruised rib—I couldn't even breathe right. "I was going to jump us to you and land in a cell. I didn't expect you to show up." Still hunched over, I tilted my head and found his eyes. "Thank you."

His lips twitched. "You're welcome."

I looked at Eloy, resisting the urge to kick him, but only

just. "I think you saved my life again. They know about Lee. You need to warn him. Eloy was going to come back for me."

"I will." Trent met my eyes as I tried to straighten up, making it only halfway. His gaze held pity, and I looked away, unable to stomach it. "He beat you?" he said, his voice holding unexpected anger.

Like I'd do this to myself? "I'm fine. It's part of the job," I whispered, still unable to breathe right. My fingers searched my ribs, and I winced.

The smell of clean laundry grew stronger, and I went to shove his hands off me as he tried to help me, but he was determined and my hands hurt. My jaw clenched, and when I had to sniff back a tear, I got mad. Damn it, I was not going to cry! "I said I'm fine!" I exclaimed, and he fell back at the sound of pixy wings.

"Jenks, what took you so long!" I said, then winced when my chest ached. Yep, at the very least they were bruised.

"Oh, for sweet mother-loving Tink!" he exclaimed in disgust. "I leave for five minutes, and you ask *Trent* to help you? Damn, girl, why didn't you just ask me to leave if you wanted some alone time to beat up the bad guy? Ah, his aura is brightening, by the way."

The grit ground under Trent's thousand-dollar shoes as he crouched at Eloy's head, lifted it up by his hair, and slammed it back down. Eloy groaned, his entire body becoming slack.

"Yeah, that did it." Jenks tried to land on my shoulder until I waved him away.

"Not bad, Trent. Not bad," I said as I began limping to the stairway. I could hear people, blessed people, coming to help me. "Hey! We're down here!" I shouted, then almost passed out when I began to cough.

"I'm okay. I'm okay!" I said, thankful there was no blood as Trent's arm went around me, holding my ribs so I wouldn't fall apart.

With a clatter and a boom of sound, the twin metal doors at the top of the stairway were flung back. The late-afternoon sunlight poured in, blinding me. "It's us! We're good!" I tried to shout, but Trent had swung me up in his arms and the clean smell of his silk suit poured over me. I couldn't see through my squint, but I heard men shouting and feet stomping down the stairs.

"He's over there," Trent said, then, "No, I've got her. Is there an ambulance on-site? She's banged up pretty bad. I don't know. Jenks?"

"How the hell should I know what happened?" the pixy said, and I shut my eyes against his sparkles; they were giving me a migraine. "I was out looking for the FIB!"

"I'm okay," I insisted, squinting. "I just need a pain amulet. Does anyone have a pain amulet?" Ivy had a pain amulet. Ivy was somewhere else.

"I'll get you to an ambulance," Trent said softly, the obvious cost of his clothes granting him passage to the surface as he went up the stairs against a tide of uniformed people flowing underground.

"Rachel?" came Glenn's voice as our heads broke the surface and the wind blew my tangled hair into Trent's face. "Jenks said . . . My God! What did he do to you?"

"I'm fine," I said, feeling dizzy as Trent stopped and the two tall black men peering at me coalesced into one. "We played chicken with his bullets, and I won. You mind getting that light out of my eyes? I can't see crap."

Glenn and Trent exchanged uneasy glances, and I realized it wasn't a light in my face, but the sun. "Close your eyes, Rachel," Trent said, and I did, a faint feeling of fear sliding to the back of my head and making me shut my mouth, too. Some of those blows had been to my head.

"Is she okay?" Glenn whispered. "How did you get down there, Mr. Kalamack?"

"She tried to jump out and jumped me in instead," he said simply. "She just needs some shade. I've got her okay. Can you get those reporters out of here?"

"Lord have mercy, they found us already," Glenn said, and I cracked an eye, almost smiling at the phrase and the hint of his southern background showing. "Ah, the ambulances are over there. You got her?"

"Yeah, we got her," Jenks said, and I winced as his dust hit my face.

"No ambulance," I whispered. "Trent, no. I want to see Eloy put in a car and leave. If you put me in an ambulance, they'll take me to a hospital. Promise me."

"No ambulance," he said, and I relaxed—until I realized I was still in his arms as he marched through the stopped traffic to a bus bench and set me down. His arms slid from me, and I shivered in the heat of the afternoon.

Slowly, bleary and blinded by the sun, I started to notice things. Traffic was stopped both ways, and Trent slowly sat down beside me, propping me upright without appearing to. Jenks was between us on the back of the bench, dusting in worry. FIB guys were everywhere, their successful mood making it feel like the Festival of Honking Horns. I could see the opening into the tunnels and the official vehicles arriving on the scene. Numb, I sat and shallowly breathed the good Cincy air, the late afternoon thick with the scents of a million people. The delicate scent of cinnamon and wine laced with green sherbet seemed to grow stronger.

"Ah, Trent? I think she needs an ambulance," Jenks said suddenly, and I sighed, my eyes closing.

"She's fine," Trent muttered, propping me back up. "Can you point out any of those men you saw earlier? The ones that weren't FIB or I.S.?"

Jenks's wings clattered, and I touched my cheek, warm where Eloy had smacked me. "Ow," I murmured, and Jenks rose up, his dust falling on me a worried black.

"I'm going to find Ivy." Jenks darted off.

Trent shifted uneasily, squinting even though we were in the shade. The wind moved his fair hair fitfully, and I started to reach for it, to brush it out of his eyes, but he beat me to it. My chest hurt, but I smiled, wondering if he missed his pointy little ears. They would hold his hair back better than what he had now.

"Rachel, I don't see anyone here not FIB or I.S.," he said, oblivious to the fact that I was slowly starting to slide into shock, the pain from my ribs making it hard to breathe. "How confident are you in your assessment?"

"That's because the guys with the radios bugged out when Eloy got free," I said as I flipped the useless radio earbud hanging down my front, and he reached for it, his gaze sharp on its construction. "You want it?" I said, and he nodded, reaching back for the battery pack as I dropped the bud down my shirt and he pulled it through, scraping my skin. "Alpha and beta teams are meeting up at the bird nest," I said, almost slurring. "Beaters and receivers. Personally, I would think they were HAPA's extraction team. If HAPA had any money, that is." I pulled my head up. "Look, Glenn isn't having a very good day, either."

The unlucky man had clearly been hijacked by Dr. Cordova in his quest to dissuade the newspeople. She looked pissed as she chewed him out in front of an FIB van, her arms pointing wildly. We had recaptured Eloy, so I don't know what her problem was. The sound of Ivy's footsteps drew my attention, and Jenks flew in to make nervous circles around me.

"What are you doing?" she hissed at Trent as she reached for me. "Look at her. She's going into shock. And you have her sitting on a bench? What are you doing here anyway?"

"He's saving my ass," I said, smiling up at her until my face hurt. "Hi, Ivy," I added, then hissed in pain when she tried to slide her shoulder under my arm and lift me. "Ow! Ow!" I cried out, and Jenks let a burst of yellow dust slip from him.

"Watch it!" he shouted, but Ivy had jumped back, her eyes going black as she pulled her hands from me.

Trent had gotten to his feet, and as I listed sideways, he propped me back up with a single, obvious finger as I tried to breathe, my ribs hurting. "Her ankle is broken," Trent said as he held my shoulder, and Ivy's eyes went even wider. "Her ribs are bruised, and her hand has suffered major damage. She'll be fine, but—"

"She needs an ambulance!" Ivy hissed, dropping her pain amulet around my neck and carefully scooping me up. My shoulders slumped at the quick relief. It didn't get rid of everything, but it at least took the edge off.

"She didn't *want* one!" Trent said loudly.

"When does Rachel ever know what she wants?" Ivy said, her pace jarring as she walked away with me. I looked back, giving him a painful bunny-eared kiss-kiss as Ivy toted me away. The last I saw of him, he was standing beside that bench looking disgusted, his suit askew and the radio in his hand, probably wondering how he was going to get home. I almost felt sorry for him. Almost.

"Thanks for watching her, cupcake," Ivy said dryly to Jenks, and he clattered his wings aggressively.

"Hey! I got you as soon as I could!" Jenks exclaimed as he flew alongside. "You were the ones who let him get away."

"No ambulance," I protested as she carried me, wincing when she took the curb hard. "I want to see Eloy get in a van, and then go home. My gun is still down there, too. And my bag."

"You can get your gun later," she said, glancing over her shoulder. "I've already got your bag in one of the FIB cruisers. Do you think you could work with these guys just once without finishing a run needing stitches?"

Jenks laughed, and Ivy started in with unusually cheerful chatter as she led me to the waiting ambulance, her topics ranging from the celebration pizza party Glenn had invited us to, all the way to Dr. Cordova's unique vocabulary that she'd shared with everyone when Eloy had gotten away. I let her words wash over me, soaking them in and thinking they were better than a bubble bath. She'd been worried on finding the shaft empty except for my shoulder bag, and I couldn't help but feel loved.

The ambulance guys were great, patching me up and making me feel less like a battered woman and more like a battle-weary warrior. They even let me keep the door open as they gave me a shot for infection and wrapped my ribs—

fortunately not broken, and my ankle—which was. I wanted to watch and make sure the van that Jenks told me Eloy was in left with no incidents. I wasn't the only one.

Dr. Cordova stood by her car and watched, too, getting in and slamming her door before she drove off in the opposite direction.

We had gotten him, but I felt empty. It wasn't the victory I had wanted.

It looked like it wasn't the victory Dr. Cordova had wanted, either.

Twenty-Six

*S*ilvers, grays, blacks, and browns had taken over Glenn's apartment, Daryl's touch turning the open floor plan from a rather sterile place of uncomfortably mixed styles to something pleasantly relaxed. *It was masculine, calming and powerful,* I mused as I sat on the overindulgent, black leather couch with my ribs taped and my ankle propped up, smiling as I took with my left hand the plate of pizza Wayde handed me. It had just come out of the oven and was too hot to eat, but the hamburger, tomatoes, and bacon set my mouth watering.

In the few months that Daryl had been living with Glenn, she had completely redecorated his space. If I had to choose, I'd say it was soft modern, having simple lines and clean surfaces, but mixing in plush and lavish textures. The couch I was drowning in was about the only thing left from his original furnishings. I'd be worried that the unemployed woman was taking over his life, but in all honesty, the place looked so great that I'd let the warrior dryad redecorate any time she wanted.

Seeing that I had a can of pop beside me, Wayde went back into the kitchen. Ivy was already in there, Daryl was on the far end of the couch with me, and Jenks was buzzing about, waiting for the vegetarian pizza to come out since too much animal fat gave him the Hershey squirts. His words, not mine. Glenn was fiddling with the TV, jumping among stations to find the evening news and the official explanation of what had happened at the library. So far it had been sports scores, pig prices, and the latest Cincy scandal. I'd been sitting here with my foot up for almost two hours while Glenn and Ivy made the pizza and decompressed. I wanted to get up, but I didn't think I could, the couch was so plush and I'd had enough time to stiffen up. Besides, my ribs hurt, and it was easier to do nothing.

The soft hum of Jenks's wings brought my attention up from the TV, and I took the napkin he held. "Here, Rache," he said, landing on the arm of the opulent couch. "Big FIB detective had a royal hissy fit last time he found pizza sauce on his leather."

"Hey, that wasn't me," I said, turning to Glenn.

"You were the one in the chair," Glenn said as he stood and ambled into the kitchen. Ivy was just taking the veggie pizza out, setting the hot pizza stone on a thick pad stuffed with thyme, and it smelled wonderful.

Plate on my lap, I tried to lever myself up with my good hand and shift my back to the arm of the couch so I didn't have to twist so much to see the kitchen. It was harder than it should have been, but I managed. "It was game night," I said, catching my pizza before it slid off the plate. "It could have been anyone."

Glenn didn't say anything, and I watched the play of emotions as Ivy took a slice of vegetarian pizza and left the kitchen, her napkin dramatically waving as she handed the plate to Daryl, sitting on the edge of the couch, before going to her own chair and waiting pizza. We'd been coming over for game night for a few weeks now as Ivy and Glenn tried to get Daryl more socialized. The woman wasn't healthy, and even the excitement of Jenga could set off her asthma. My thoughts went to her, Ivy, and Glenn, and then I wished they hadn't. I wanted them to be okay, but still . . . there was a new space that hadn't been there before.

Most of Daryl's species had been wiped out in the industrial revolution, though there were some signs that they were coming back in the mountains—now that we weren't cutting down hundred-year-old trees anymore. Frail, pale, and sensitive to pollution, the woman didn't get out much. She was a warrior, though, and for all her delicate beauty and flowing clothes, I'd seen her pin Glenn with a cheese knife to his throat when she thought he was cheating.

My eyes went to the ozonator Glenn had put in last month, the machine purifying the air and leaving it with the smell of a thunderstorm. It seemed to help, and now that I noticed, all the new furnishings were eco oriented, with no petroleum or synthetic anything to make her condition worse. Method to her redecorating madness, perhaps?

Jenks spilled a silver dust and rose an inch before dropping back down. "Daryl, turn it up!" he exclaimed as BRIMSTONE BUST AT LIBRARY flashed up on the screen and the lady announcer in her lavender suit began talking. The pretty, petite warrior woman licked her fingers and snatched up the remote, knowing how to work it as if she'd been born with one in her hand. Magic, technology—sometimes I failed to see the difference.

The announcer's voice became loud and I leaned forward, straining over the hum of Jenks's wings. "If you tried to use the downtown branch of the library this afternoon, chances are good that you were turned away as the FIB and the I.S. took part in a rare combined effort to catch one of the country's slipperiest Brimstone distributors."

"Brimstone?" Jenks shouted, and I shushed him.

"In a late hour of action, officials stormed the lower levels of the downtown branch of the Cincinnati library. The chase ultimately covered almost two city blocks through some of Cincinnati's old bioshelters, created during the Turn, until Eloy Orin was apprehended trying to emerge from Central Ave.'s access doors." The woman turned to the attractive, gray-tinged man sitting beside her and smiled. "Brimstone in the library? It gives new meaning to the phrase 'hooked on reading.' Right, Bob?"

The TV changed to a shot of Central Ave., bright under

a low sun. The picture was blurry, clearly taken from some distance. "Look!" Jenks exclaimed, hovering to block the TV. "Rache! That's you!"

I leaned forward to see a figure in a red shirt being carried out by a man in a suit, Trent, obviously. "Good God, I look Brimstoned," I said, hoping this wouldn't be syndicated out to the West Coast. My mom would pee her pants, then call her neighbors to brag.

"Which is why you're sitting," Ivy said. "Eat your pizza. You've hardly touched it."

"Quiet," Wayde muttered from the kitchen. "I didn't get a chance to see this."

"You didn't miss anything," I said as I lifted my wedge of pizza while the announcer gave a brief history lesson on the tunnels and how there was no record that they connected with the library.

Again Wayde shushed me, his eyes bright. "She's talking about you!"

I chewed quietly, not excited. Most times my name made the news, I had to hide in the church for two weeks.

"Though sources haven't verified it, witnesses claim that Cincinnati's very own demon witch Rachel Morgan was on the scene. Phone calls to the firm she calls one-third her own have gone unanswered—"

"Because I'm eating," I muttered, shushed by both Daryl and Wayde.

"But Vampiric Charms is known to have worked with the FIB in the past."

"Oh, crap!" I exclaimed as the thirty-second video of me wearing nothing but an FIB coat flashed up on the screen. I didn't care if the important bits were being blocked out. I looked awful, my hair wild and the coat riding up to show my fuzzed ass.

"Whoa! I didn't know the station had that," Glenn said, and I flushed.

"Trent's in the background," Jenks said, and horrified, I looked to see the elf, his eyes averted.

"Oh God. Can we please turn this off?" I pleaded, and Daryl worked the remote to turn the volume down, her little mouth drawn up as she laughed at me.

Glenn stood behind Ivy, a beer in one hand, smiling at last. "Thank you, Rachel, Ivy, and Jenks," he said, raising the bottle in salute. "You were the difference between success and failure. Good tag."

Ivy shifted in her chair and raised her glass above her head, clinking with him. "I wish I'd been there at the end. I would've enjoyed smacking Eloy under the flag of justice."

I would have enjoyed smacking Eloy a little more, too, and as the announcer flirted with her male counterpart, I set my pizza aside. *Caught not once but twice with my own magic,* I thought as I spun Trent's ring on my pinkie. But at least we'd gotten him. My smile faded as the memory of the-men-who-don't-belong surfaced. If their radio had been working, things might have turned out differently. I might not be so banged up, for instance. They had left, and that was just . . . wrong.

Focus blurring, I remembered Trent's casual acceptance of everything, his matter-of-fact recitation of all the things wrong with me before the ambulance personnel had their look and confirmed it. He hadn't panicked when finding me beat up and broken. Instead, he quietly sat beside me and looked for the-men-who-don't-belong. A part of me thought I should be mad that he let me sit there in pain, but I wasn't. He'd known what was wrong with me before the ambulance personnel had. Nothing had been life threatening, but finding the-men-who-don't-belong had been then or never. Besides, I *had* told him no ambulance.

Head down, I spun the ring on my finger, squinting as I noticed that one of the three bands had turned black. *It was a three-charm spell,* I thought in surprise. It still had some power.

Wayde wandered out of the kitchen with a plate of pizza in one hand, pop in the other, and looked over the seating arrangements. Seeing the Were at a loss, I shifted my legs so he could sit between me and Daryl. "Thanks," he said as he sank and a puff of vampire- and dryad-scented air rose. "I still don't believe that you eat pizza," he said to Glenn as he inched himself forward and out of the cushion trap to set his plate on the coffee table. "You're okay, FIB man. You can run with me anytime."

Glenn gave him a look, his expression one of wondering mistrust. "Thanks."

Ivy picked a pepperoni off her pizza and gave it to Glenn. He was still standing over her, watching his bust through the newscaster's eyes. "You should tell everyone at the FIB you eat pizza," Ivy said. "It will do wonders for your street cred."

"My street cred is fine," he said. "And they already think I'm insane. Seeing that I like working with witches and vampires."

Jenks hummed over my pizza, and I gestured that he could have it. "But it's a good kind of insane," the pixy said as he sat on the crust and used his chopsticks to nibble the tomato sauce.

Glenn made a noise deep in his throat, then headed back into the kitchen, clearly not convinced. Ivy stood with her empty plate and followed him. She was looking a little sultry, and I'd be surprised if she came back to the church with me tonight. Good thing Wayde was here to get me home. It'd be hard to drive with my ankle and wrist messed up.

Wayde choked, and I looked up from my bruised hand when he shouted, "Turn it up!"

Daryl was already reaching for the remote, but Jenks beat her to it, stomping on the button until the announcer's voice blared, " . . . tonight when Orin escaped, while being moved to a more secure FIB facility."

"What?" Ivy exclaimed from the kitchen, and suddenly her scent poured over me as she stood at my shoulder, mouth agape.

"Son of Tink!" Jenks said, and Glenn bellowed for everyone to shut up. *He had escaped? How?*

"Authorities are asking for your help if you see this man,"

the woman in lavender said as her face was replaced by a shot of Eloy, recent by the apparent bruise from where Trent had hit him and the swollen bump on his head from where he'd further slammed his head on the floor. Eloy's head was cocked and he looked determined, angry, and disdainful. Anger stirred in me. He hadn't escaped. Someone had broken him out. Eloy had said they were everywhere. The-men-who-don't-belong, maybe?

"Orin is considered highly dangerous and should not be approached," she was saying as another picture of him popped up, this time a full-body shot. "Please call one of the numbers below if you see him."

Two numbers: one for the FIB, the other for the I.S. "Call the I.S.," Jenks said, hovering before the TV with his hands on his hips. "The FIB can't even hold their farts."

"You're in the way!" Wayde leaned to see around him, but they'd gone back to a wide angle of the studio showing the newscasters sitting side by side.

"Sounds like a dangerous man," the guy was saying, "evading both the I.S. and the FIB. Let's hope they get this one soon."

The woman smiled brightly. "If it were me, I'd be half-way to Brazil. You know how I like my sun. And speaking of sun, is there any sun in our forecast for tomorrow, Susan?"

I stared at the map of the East Coast, with the low pressure dropping down from the Canadian wilds, stunned. *Nice segue.*

"Glenn?" Ivy said, and I twisted in the couch and saw her staring at an empty kitchen.

Jenks rose on a column of silver sparkles. "He's in the bedroom, on the phone. Oh, he's pissed."

I grabbed the arm of the couch and tried to get up, failing. Daryl was already halfway across the room. Ivy joined her at the locked door, hammering on it when a polite knock got no result. Her jaw clenched. "Glenn?" she shouted, and Jenks hummed by her ear, telling her to be quiet so he could hear.

I sank back into the cushions, stymied. I could *not* get up out of this damned couch. Wayde was looking at me, and I stared back. "You going to help me, or just sit there?" I asked, and he sighed and set his pizza down.

Wayde hauled me up, my ribs protesting. My foot was numb from human medicine, and I grabbed the crutch he handed me, hobbling to Glenn's bedroom door. "What's he saying?"

"Just a lot of swearing so far," Jenks said. "He wants to know who approved the move."

"Dr. Cordova," Ivy whispered.

"You heard that?" Jenks said, impressed, and she shook her head.

"She was bitching about it under the library," Ivy said, then frowned, brow furrowed as she listened to Glenn.

"I didn't approve a transfer!" His voice came clear through the thin walls of the apartment. "I don't care if Cordova told you to, she's not your boss, I am!" There was a hesitation, and he growled, "Cordova has been trying to close my division ever since its inception. I think she *wanted* him to escape."

At Glenn's words, I blinked. A sudden thought stabbed through my head, and I staggered, almost falling when my crutch snagged on the rug. Ivy glanced back when Wayde caught me, and I waved her off, stunned as the new thought circled. *I think she wanted him to escape.*

"Rache?" Jenks said, concern in his features as, within me, old thoughts rearranged themselves into a new reality: the I.S. trying to catch HAPA without involving the FIB; Cordova being hands-on at a run she had no business attending; Jennifer gaining her freedom as Cordova reamed out the entire team; Cordova's insistence that the FIB retain custody; Eloy's boast that his people were everywhere; and the fact that when we did catch him, he escaped not once, but twice—the FIB-issued pistol in Eloy's hand as he shot at me.

"Rache?" Jenks asked again, and I shook my head.

"I need to sit down," I said, and Wayde took my elbow,

helping me move to one of the bar stools instead of that couch made for entrapment. Seeing me there, he waffled between staying and going back to the door. I waved him off, and he retreated, leaving me to my awful thoughts. The FIB didn't want HAPA caught. That's what Felix had said. That's what Felix had known.

I had a very bad feeling that Dr. Cordova was a member of HAPA. Glenn didn't have a clue. No wonder he couldn't catch them.

The memory of Cordova's angry expression when Eloy was snared intruded. And her anger again when Glenn tagged him on Central Ave., how she'd driven off amid a media circus, not toward the FIB or the I.S., but somewhere else. Somewhere else to arrange a breakout?

"Oh my God," I whispered, one hand gripping my crutch, the other holding my ribs. The FIB had access to every blueprint in the city. They'd know the best places to hide, and with a whisper, HAPA would know when to move. *HAPA had infiltrated the FIB.* It was the only answer that made sense.

My gaze rose to the closed door with the Inderlanders clustered before it, all of them hearing every word Glenn was saying, and as my ankle throbbed through the pain amulet, my phone, stuck in my back pocket, began to hum. If HAPA had infested the FIB, who were the-men-who-don't-belong?

Mouth dry, I fumbled for the phone, seeing a text from Trent. *Trent texts?* I thought, thinking it odd, and then my expression blanked. RADIO IS ACTIVE. MEET ME DOWNSTAIRS. JUST U.

Crap on toast, it wasn't over yet.

Feeling unreal, I slid from the bar stool, my ankle jarring all the way up my spine. Jenks turned, sympathy showing on his face. I froze, my hand still shoving my phone away. Alone. He had said alone. That wasn't even considering how he knew where I was and who I was with. Trent knew something and wasn't sure who he could trust—except for me.

"We'll get him, Rachel. I promise," Jenks vowed as he took in my cold face, but I didn't have the heart to tell him we wouldn't. Even if I told them my awful thoughts and we brought Dr. Cordova in, something would get fouled up. Human error, Eloy had called it.

"I'm going to take a walk," I said, and Ivy turned. Wayde and Daryl were next, and I flinched under their combined looks.

"With your ankle like that?" Ivy said.

"A drive then," I said, my eyes flicking to Glenn's door and back as I made a barely perceptible head shake. If Jenks or Ivy came, then Glenn would follow. He'd call the FIB's home office. It'd be the tunnels all over again.

Ivy's face paled, and her breath eased out slowly as she gained understanding. She knew I didn't want Glenn to know. Something had broken between her and Glenn, and trust came too hard to the vampire. She'd keep them all here for me, and I was proud of her and me both as I hobbled to the chair by the door where my coat and shoulder bag were.

"I've got . . . my phone," I said, to tell her I wouldn't be alone, and she nodded, lower lip between her teeth. *All I need now is a really big stick to hit Eloy with. I bet Trent would hold him down for me.*

"Give me a minute to get into my cold-weather gear," Jenks said, darting to the light fixture where he'd left it.

"She'll be fine, Jenks," Ivy said softly, and the pixy jerked to a stop, mistrusting it.

Wayde crossed the room as I dug my coat out from the bottom of the stack. "Sit down," Wayde said, and I shoved my crutch at him to hold while I shrugged into my coat. "I know it's a shock, but if you caught him once, you can do it again."

Coat on, I reached for my crutch, and Wayde tightened his grip, not letting me take it. Behind him, Ivy shook her head at Jenks, telling him to leave off.

"Let go of my crutch," I said, giving it a yank. "I'm going to take a walk. Clear my head." *Find Eloy. Smack his head into a wall, dance on his guts . . . I'd get creative. Spontaneous like.*

"By myself, thanks anyway, Jenks," I said as I slipped my shoulder bag up, and the pixy hovered at the ceiling in uncertainty, looking ticked but trusting Ivy. "I'll be back in an hour!" I exclaimed, not liking the helpless feeling they were filling me with. "Save me a slice of pizza. Does anyone want anything while I'm out?"

Wayde was standing in front of the door as if he couldn't believe they were going to let me leave, but there was no reason I shouldn't apart from maybe having trouble driving. I thought of Winona and the wreck they had made of her body, and my eyes narrowed. I'd improvise, overcome . . . adapt.

"You sure you have everything you need?" Ivy said, and I almost smiled.

"Yes," I said, and I pushed Wayde out of my way with a gentle pressure.

"You're going to let her just walk out?" the Were said as I opened the door. Hobbling past him, I headed for the lift. "She can't drive with a broken ankle."

The hallway was empty, and my arm hurt from the crutch. God, I hated it.

"So she'll sit in the parking lot until she gets cold," Ivy said with false indifference.

"Besides, we're good at putting the pieces back together," Jenks said, and the door closed behind me.

Yes, they were good at putting me back together, and I felt like Humpty Dumpty as I made my scuff-thumping way to the elevator. My ankle hurt and my ribs ached as I waited for it. I got in when the doors finally opened, punching the lobby button with a vengeance, hard enough to make my bruised hand complain. I should have made a healing curse, but the honest truth was that I was afraid I might get it wrong and end up worse off.

HAPA was deep in the FIB. How long, I wondered, had this arrangement been in force? Had they evolved together? Or had HAPA only recently infiltrated the nationwide organization? And how did the-men-who-don't-belong fit in? Trent said the radio was active. Were they after Eloy themselves, or helping him escape? I was going to find out.

The doors opened, and the cooler air of the deserted lobby brushed my anger-warmed face. I got across the tiny divide and started for the twin glass doors, looking for Trent's car and not seeing it. Hesitating, I heard the lift close and immediately start back up.

My eyes narrowed. *Wayde,* I thought, then frowned as I looked over the scantily decorated entryway. Three days ago, I hadn't been able to bring myself to hurt him. Today, with a broken ankle, bruised ribs, a damaged hand, and a new outlook, I felt different.

I stood and watched as the light held steady on Glenn's floor, then began to drop again. "Stupid, tenacious Were," I muttered as the elevator dinged and I hobbled to stand next to it, out of sight. I dropped my bag as the doors slid open, pulled back my crutch . . . and as he walked out of the elevator, I swung it at him.

"Holy mother!" Wayde shouted, falling back into the elevator as my crutch hit the doors and splintered. I'd moved too soon.

"Don't follow me, Wayde!" I said as I got in front of the elevator and stopped the doors from shutting with my broken crutch. Wayde was pressed flat against the back of the car, his eyes wide as he stared. "I'm telling you, *don't follow me*! I need some time alone right now, okay?"

Part of me wanted to tap a line and smack him a good one, but I didn't. Restraint. That was going to be my new watchword. That I'd given myself permission to do demon magic scared the shit out of me. I didn't want to become Al. I'd use my magic only if necessary. Wayde was a reasonable person. We could settle this without violence.

I turned for the doors, angry but trying not to be. It was harder to walk without my crutch, but I managed, my pulse fast as I snatched my bag from the floor and lurched for the handle of the glass doors. Beyond them in the glow of a streetlight was Trent's car, the lights aimed at the front of the building. There was a tiny scuff behind me, and I turned, ticked.

"Hey!" I yelped, scrambling to stay upright when Wayde plowed into me, pinning me to the glass wall beside the door. "What in hell are you doing?" I wheezed, my back to the door and squirming as he felt in my coat pockets.

"Looking for your keys," he said, and my hand met his cheek in a loud smack.

"Get off!" I yelled, and I heard the jingle of keys as he backed up. "What in hell is wrong with you!"

His head lowered, Wayde backed off, my keys in his hand. His face was red where I'd hit him, but he didn't seem bothered about it. "You'll thank me for this later," he said, looking as if he'd won. "I know you're mad about Eloy, but running out and trying to find him isn't going to help anyone, least of all you." He jiggled my keys as if he had the world by the nads, and I frowned, tugging my coat straight. *Now?* I wondered. *Can I use my demon magic now?*

Trent hadn't come in yet. I knew he was watching this, and my thoughts whispered *restraint.* I could walk away, but if I did, he'd just follow me in my car. I needed my keys. "You," I said as I limped toward Wayde and he backed up, blinking, "haven't known me long enough to give me advice that I'm not going to take. Give me my keys."

"No." He raised them high over his head as if it were a game. "Let's go upstairs, have some pizza, beer, and burn HAPA in effigy. Tomorrow when we're done with our pity party, you'll make some charms and we'll find out where they went. We don't have to tell the FIB or the I.S. We can take care of this ourselves."

Taking care of this myself was exactly what I intended to do. Adrenaline seeped through me, erasing every hurt, making me alive. "Keys," I said, backing him up until we were at the elevators again. "Give me my keys!" I demanded, my hand out, and he held them in the air like a school bully. "Wayde, I'm not afraid anymore to hurt you!"

He shook his head. "My God, you're a bitch when you're on pain meds."

"That's alpha bitch, buddy," I said, shaking, "of an honest-to-God pack. And you will respect that. Give me my keys, get in that elevator, and go away, or I'll pin you to the ground and rip off your ear."

Face grim, he shook his head. Pity had slipped into his eyes, and he slid the keys into his pocket. "He hurt you, Rachel, and I know what that does to you. My sister is the same way, and she hurts herself worse trying to get back at them. It doesn't make anything better."

I looked at him for a good three seconds, feeling my impatience grow. Trent was waiting, and Wayde wasn't listening. My ankle was starting to hurt again. Maybe I shouldn't have busted my crutch. I had tried. My idea of no violence wasn't working. "Maybe you're right," I said, relaxing my body as if I had given up.

Wayde smiled. "Good," he said as he looked away to push the up button.

I lunged forward, grabbing his shoulders and slamming his head into the wall. "Sorry," I breathed as he howled, reaching behind to get me.

"Son of a whore!" he swore, and I hooked my good leg behind his and pulled. We both went down, but I was expecting it. Arms pinwheeling, he fell headfirst into the ashtray beside the elevator. Kneeling beside him, I grabbed the heavy metal bowl and slammed it on his head.

Wayde yelled, and I hit him again, adrenaline pulling a scream of outrage from me. He went quiet, and I held my breath to make sure I could hear him breathing. I suppose I could have used my magic on him, but this was a lot more satisfying.

"I never should have helped her off the couch," he whispered, and I hit him again, the ashtray bonging with hard certainty.

He groaned, and this time, he really was out. There were three lumps on his head, and I shoved him over so I could pull his eyelids back to make sure that his pupils were dilated properly. "I told you I wasn't afraid anymore," I said as I slowly got up, shaking. Good God, my mother would laugh her pants off. I'd beaten up my bodyguard.

I gave a moment's thought to taking his belt off and tying him up, but Trent was flashing his lights at me. Not wanting Wayde to follow, I felt his pockets for my keys and fished them out. Still shaking, I got up, made a salute to the camera in the corner, and hobbled out.

The cool night air was like a balm, and I headed for Trent's car with my thoughts swirling. I'd hurt Wayde, but he'd be okay, not dead like if he followed and ended up shot. "You could have helped me out there," I said as I yanked the handle up and slid into the sharp little black two-seater, finding the seat warm from the electronic heater. The windows were down, but with all the vents wide open and aimed at me, it was comfortable even in the chill autumn night.

Trent revved the engine, giving me a sideways grin. "I told you to come alone. You think I want to be on a security camera?"

I eyed his black attire as I put my belt on and he jammed the car in first and headed smoothly for the exit. "Besides," he said as he paused at the entryway to the apartment complex, then gunned it, "If you couldn't get rid of your bodyguard, you aren't fit enough to tag Eloy. How come you didn't make up a healing curse?"

"I haven't had the time. Besides, I'm okay," I said, and he nodded. Adrenaline spiked, and I couldn't help my smile. The car was fast, Trent looked good, and we both knew more than the I.S. and the FIB combined. "Do you know who the-men-who-don't-belong are yet?"

He shook his head and tossed my battery pack and earbud to me. "Not yet, but they're human, and they're targeting HAPA, not helping them. They have one of their men with Eloy and Dr. Cordova at the 'watering hole.' Take a listen."

I fumbled for the earpiece and put it in. The sound of

light chatter and the clinking of a spoon met me. It could be anywhere.

"You know what the watering hole is?" Trent asked, slowing at a stop sign.

I shook my head, then hesitated, smiling as the distinctive sound of ice being crushed nearly blew my ear out. "Grand latte! Italian blend! Easy on the syrup, light on the froth! Ready for pickup!" Mark shouted.

"You're not going to believe this," I said, thinking Trent looked a shade too devilish to be good backup, but he'd do. "They're at Junior's."

Trent grinned across the car at me, and something in me fluttered. "You're right. I don't believe you."

Twenty-Seven

Ribs aching, I sat next to Trent in his snazzy car as he pulled into Junior's and parked, lights off, engine running. My fingers looked silver in the dash's blue light, and all my bruises were invisible but aching. The earbud lay on the console between us, the volume cranked as terse commands went back and forth in a busy, well-organized flow. Inside Junior's it was peaceful. *I can change that,* I thought dryly, knowing that the next ten minutes were really going to mess up the new understanding that Mark and I seemed to have.

It was nearing three in the morning according to the clock on Trent's dash, and if the coffeehouse had been in the Hollows it would be jumping. As it was, it felt much later, the brightly lit eatery sending its glow through the plate-glass windows onto an almost deserted parking lot. Junior, or Mark, as his name really was, was stocking shelves from a pallet of boxes beside him. There were no other employees that I could see.

In the corner, two customers argued over their to-go cups—Eloy and Dr. Cordova. Eloy had a jeans coat on over his white prison jumpsuit. Dr. Cordova was going more casual than usual in black pants and a knit top—comfortable to travel in should she need to jump a plane. In the corner, an athletic-looking man in a jogging outfit sat with his back to them, but I'd sell my best panties online if he wasn't one of the-men-who-don't-belong watching everything going on behind him with some sort of electronic gizmo.

Trent hit the seat warmer again as it went out. "Here," he said, reaching into his belt pack and handing me a tiny vial. "You look like you're hurting."

I took it, my eyebrows high. "And this is?"

"Numbs the pain. I could really use your assistance, but not if I have to help you in the door. It masks pain better than your amulet. But it won't heal you." He grimaced, needlessly flicking his fair hair back out of his eyes. "I'm not that good, either."

"I *said* I didn't have the *time*," I said, and he looked at me.

"And I wasn't going to ask for Ceri's help," he added as if I hadn't said anything. "All you have to do is swallow it."

"Oh thank God," I said, slugging the tiny vial of amber liquid back. My lips curled as the bitter concoction slipped down, tasting of ash and willow. Trent's lips parted, clearly surprised, and I shrugged. He was right. I wasn't much good if I couldn't move fast.

Inside, Eloy and Dr. Cordova continued to discuss something, her arms waving in her dramatic fashion, Eloy leaning back, letting her rage, his disdain obvious. Breath held, I waited for something to happen, but nothing did. My wrist still hurt, my ankle still throbbed, and I still couldn't take a deep breath. "It's not working," I said, my estimation of Trent's abilities fading.

In a quick, irate motion, he took the empty vial. "I haven't invoked it yet. *Ta na ruego*," he said as our fingers touched.

Starting, I shivered as I felt a filmy sheet of numbing gray slither over me, working from my aura in, muffling the pain and storing it up for later. Wild magic tingled along my muscles, and I took a deep, painless breath. "Dude. That's good stuff. Thanks."

Trent cracked his neck, and I filed the motion away as him trying to hide his pleasure. The chatter from the earbud was getting intense. Inside, the man at the table was stirring his coffee, the sound of his spoon hitting the table a bare in-

stant after he did it. My heart pounded as he turned halfway
to the window, noticing us. His eyes almost black in the dim
light, Trent adjusted his rearview mirror to see the Laundro-
mat down the street. "Ready to go?"

I gave my ankle a wiggle and took a cleansing breath. I
was going to pay for this in spades later, but for now, I didn't
hurt. "Yes, thank you."

"I have another when we're done if you want it. You've
got an hour until it wears off."

An hour? Jeez, not much of a spell. "Thanks again," I
said, meaning it.

Trent reached for the door handle, and from between us,
that low, deep voice drawled in a smooth, even tone that ri-
valed Trent's, "Blockades in place. Beater, approach at personal discretion. All units stand by for cleanup. This is going
to be a messy one, people."

"Wait," I said, reaching out to touch his knee, and Trent
hesitated. "I don't like the sound of this," I said as I barely
resisted the urge to flip the visor mirror down and look
behind us. "They're going to trash Mark's place."

"Negative, that's a negative," a sharp voice with a New
York accent said. "Black car in the parking lot. Two civil-
ians. Ninety-eight percent confident that it's the demon and
the elf."

My pulse jumped, and I grabbed the battery pack to flip
on the mic. "What are you doing?" Trent said.

"These guys are good, and a joint venture might be the
start of a beautiful friendship," I said. "Besides, they're here,
and we could use the help."

Trent looked at the expensive toy in my hand, then
nodded. Pleased, I brought the battery closer to my mouth.
"Hey, hi, guys. Your plan sounds good and all, but there's
one problem. Eloy knows that's your man in there pretending to be a jogger slamming down a six-hundred-calorie
drink. He's going to make a bloodbath of the place, and I
can't let that happen. I like Mark, and he's too nice to get
shot."

"Morgan!" the deep voice barked, then faintly, "Who counted the equipment?"

"I did, Captain," a faint voice said. "The discrepancy was noted."

"You failed to inform me that the radio was still active!" There was a slight hesitation, and then, very clearly, hitting every vowel hard, "Morgan, leave the watering hole."

I could resist no longer. I flipped the visor mirror down, but there was nothing behind us. "Its code name is Junior's, captain of the-men-who-don't-belong. Get it right." Handing the battery pack to Trent, I pulled my bag onto my lap and started looking for a piece of paper. "I've been listening to your plans for the last fifteen minutes, and they suck. Eloy is going to shoot your men, *if* you're lucky. He's going to start throwing curses if you're not. He's got a vial of my blood, a demon textbook, and fewer morals than the most depraved demon I've ever partied with." Receipt in hand, I shuffled around for a pen. Exasperated, I looked up. "You got a pen?"

Disbelieving, Trent pulled a slim black-gold pen from the console and handed it to me, his fingers not shaking like mine were.

"Thanks." Clicking it open, I jotted a note. "You've been after him for months and failed to catch him. I propose we try together."

"Drive away, Morgan," the captain said. "This is your last warning."

"Don't get your jockstrap in a knot," I said, grimacing when the tip of the pen broke through the paper I was using my leg to write on. "He kicked my ass a couple of times, too. He and Cordova are a potent team. Apart, neither of us is effective, but together?" Nervous, I clicked the pen closed. DON'T CALL I.S. OR FIB. GET OUT ASAP. SORRY ABOUT THE MESS. R.

The radio was silent, and I added, "I propose we work together on this. What do you say? Frankly, I'd like to prove to you that I'm a team player. My demon magic, your guns. Work with me, gentlemen. I could be your new best friend."

Again, a long silence. Fidgeting, I handed Trent his pen

back. Sure, I'd said we needed to work together to get him, but the truth was, I was more interested in showing this very dangerous underground group of well-funded humans that I was not the enemy. Once they took care of HAPA, I might be next on their list.

"What do you propose?" the captain's voice said, and my eyes closed briefly in relief. Beside me, Trent made a small sound, as if he only now realized what I had been doing. *Not as oblivious as you thought, eh, little cookie maker?*

"Eloy wants me, Captain, above all others," I said. "With us distracting him, you can get your men in there without him and Dr. Cordova killing everyone. I suggest you do it."

Breath held, I waited. Beside me, the scent of mulled wine became stronger. Trent's foot was twitching, and he stilled it.

"You may approach the suspects," the captain said, and I exhaled loudly, meeting Trent's eyes and smiling eagerly. "Engage at will. You will stand down when we take the premises or you will be shot. Is that clear?"

"Crystal," I said, and Trent clicked the mic off.

"I see what you're trying to do," he said as he dropped the battery into his belt pack and affixed the earbud to his left ear. "I'm not sure it's a good idea."

My tension heightened, and I opened the door. "They know I exist. Better this than trying to be mysterious and threatening. I tried that and landed in Alcatraz." Relishing the lack of pain, I got out. It was a false sense of well-being, but I'd take it. The thump of the door shutting echoed, and I realized I hadn't seen another car since we'd pulled in. The-men-who-don't-belong had cleared the street. Even the I.S. had trouble with that.

My boots were nearly silent as I quickly moved to the front of the car, wanting to get in fast. The man in the corner in his jogging outfit was watching us, his lips moving.

"Please tell me you're not trusting this?" Trent said mildly, meeting me step for step.

"Not for a second."

His hand dipping into his jacket pocket, he pointed a fob at his car and locked it. The shiny vehicle beeped, and I looked at him. We were on a run, and he was worried about his car?

"Seriously?" I said, and he half smiled at me as he reached in front of me to grab the door handle. Adrenaline scoured through me as I was forced to hesitate while the glass door opened and Trent gestured for me to go first. The chimes rang, and I boldly walked in, my tight shoulders not relaxing at all as the coffee-scented air enveloped me. Eloy's eyes landed on us, and he cut Dr. Cordova's harangue off short.

I gave the man in the jogging suit a bunny-eared kiss-kiss, and Trent chuckled at something coming in over the earbud. "We never did decide how we were going to do this," Trent said as he took my arm when Mark looked up, his first enthusiastic hail dying away when he saw it was me. "What do you have in that bag of yours?"

"My phone, a hair pick. My keys." I slipped my note into Trent's hand and smiled at Mark. "Can you get this to Mark for me?"

Trent's grip on my arm tightened as the note slipped into his fingers. "You don't have any charms at all?" he whispered through his clenched teeth, leaning in so his breath tickled my ear even as he smiled confidently at Dr. Cordova, spinning in her chair to look at us like we were stupid. "What do you plan to do? Spill coffee on them?"

I kept smiling. "I was having *pizza* at Detective Glenn's *house*," I said tightly, my lips hardly moving. "I didn't think I needed any charms. I've got my usual. Splat gun, magnetic chalk, plus the charms you gave me. What have you got?"

"Nothing you're going to like. You lead, I'll follow."

That surprised me, and I gave him a sideways smile that he mirrored before I focused on the two people at the table. Plan A it was. Go in brash and come out bashed. "Hello, Cordova, Eloy," I said, refusing to address her as doctor. "Nothing like a good caffeine buzz before kidnapping and mutilating more people, eh?"

"Well, if it's not Daddy Warbucks and Little Orphan Annie." Eloy leaned his chair back on two legs, the picture of confidence and contempt. My eyes narrowed.

"By the Turn, you really are stupid," Dr. Cordova said, and both Trent and the guy in the corner tensed as she reached into her bag. My pulse hammered and I felt Trent tap a line as she pulled out a big-ass, honking pistol the length of my arm. The thing could probably stop a vampire. My hold on the line strengthened. Maybe this hadn't been such a good idea.

"You cost me my job," she said, sighting down it. "I'm going to kill you dead."

"No, Doctor, you're not." It was Eloy, the demand in his voice jerking her attention to him in annoyance. "There's room in my truck for three."

Dr. Cordova's eyes flicked to Mark, then the guy in the corner, his hands out of sight. "I'm not going to jail," she said, her aim shifting from me to the jogger.

I edged closer, pulling in enough energy off the line to make Trent wince. "Oh, I can guarantee that, Cordova," I said.

White faced, Mark edged back behind the counter. I gave a quick shake of my head when he pantomimed having a phone to his ear. Maybe we were all stronger than we thought.

I jumped when Eloy's chair thunked forward, back on four legs. "You can shoot her in the leg, though."

Dr. Cordova smiled, the gun coming up again. *"Rhombus!"* I shouted, and Trent swore, hunching as I stood tall, my hand outstretched toward Dr. Cordova and the bullet headed for us. It twanged off my circle and a light in the corner shattered.

Dr. Cordova's gun boomed again, her face ugly as she shot at the jogger. The-man-who-didn't-belong had vaulted over the counter at the first shot, and she screamed as her gun went off a third time, leaving a splintered hole the size of a squash in the wall of the counter. I could see Mark through it, his face white as he skittered out of sight.

"Get the operative!" Eloy was shouting, shoving Cordova

at the front counter where the-man-who-didn't-belong had gone.

"Get your circle up!" I shouted at Trent, then dove through mine, feeling his energies licking my heels as I rolled to a stop, my hand deep in my bag as I looked for my magnetic chalk. I'd circle them like every other demon.

"Crap!" I exclaimed as I saw Eloy aiming at me. I fell onto a table, knocking it down to hide behind. A sharp ping of sound and the chimes hanging on the door behind me rang with a weird, choking peal, hit by the ricochet.

I pulled the line into me, my hands aching and my wrist throbbing with the pain Trent's charm had dulled. Energy roiled beneath my skin, gold and black mixing in darkness and light. I heard Trent struggling, and I looked over the table. He was behind the counter. A burst of energy hit the ceiling like a cloudburst, and someone grunted. Eloy was taking aim at me again, and I threw my ball of energy at him, flashing a circle up with hardly a second to spare.

Eloy dove for cover as the black-and-gold ball hissed toward him. It hit the wall, spreading out in an ugly, almost electrical storm before subsiding. I kicked the overturned table out of the way, teeth clenched as my broken ankle twinged through Trent's charm. *Not yet. Give me a little more time.* Eloy looked up from the floor, and I started to scribe a circle, my eyes never leaving his.

"Chubi whore," he snarled, and I flashed a bubble in place. Expression ugly, he raised his gun at the ceiling. It went off in a series of three pops. Dust sifted down on my bubble, and I looked up.

"Look out!" Trent shouted, and I cowered as the light fixture fell on me, bouncing off my bubble and sliding to the floor. Seeing me unhurt, Eloy bared his teeth and shot at me again.

I'd had about enough.

I stood, pulling in the line like it was a ribbon from a spool, gathering it in my soul until my hair started to float. My palms burned as I forced it into my hands and shoved it at Eloy like a beach ball. His lips parted as the head-size ball of energy broke through my circle and added my barrier's energy to its own. I was vulnerable, and he took aim. *"Dilatare!"* I shouted, then dropped, covering my head.

The ball of energy exploded in midair, rocking the light fixtures and making the tempered-glass windows shake. I looked past my arms and saw Eloy sprawled on the floor. Heart pounding, I scrabbled to reach him, eager to do some personal damage.

"Stop!" Dr. Cordova shouted. "Stop right there, demon!"

I dove for Eloy as he moved to sit up. Sliding, I kicked the gun from him, then continued my foot's arch to smack his head. Grunting, he slid back, before I connected, hatred in his eyes. I grinned savagely, and he smiled back.

"I said stop!" Dr. Cordova shouted again. "Or I kill the kid. Right here. Right now."

Shit.

I stopped.

My sour expression turned to fear as Dr. Cordova dragged Mark out from behind the counter, her arm around his neck and that honking huge pistol pressed into his temple. Shit, shit, shit! I'd really messed this up. Trent limped out from behind the counter from the opposite side and joined me. His hair was wild, and his eyes were dark with anger. Tense and jerky, he helped me to my feet, and I palmed my chalk to him in the process. "Where's the jogger?" I said breathily as I watched Dr. Cordova yank Mark closer to Eloy and the back door.

Touching his lip and finding it swollen, Trent shook his head. "He pulled out. I think we're on our own."

At least he isn't dead behind the counter. "Aren't we always?" I said bitterly, scraping my resolve together. So we had to bring them in ourselves now. Damn it, they had Mark. The kid looked terrified. The memory of Winona surfaced, and my heart clenched. *Not Mark. Not him.*

"You want to take his place?" Eloy looked far too confident.

"Rachel, no."

I shook Trent's hand off me. "Finish that circle. Get them into it. Invoke it. That's the plan," I breathed, my heart pounding. I had to buy Trent some time. This was the only way.

Hands up, I stepped in front of Trent. "You've been a bad boy, Eloy," I said. "Murdering what scares you. That's not how grown-ups solve problems. And, Cordova? I'd like to have five minutes alone with you. Maybe show you up close and personal what that bastard did to Winona. You know Winona, right? Cloven feet, horns, red pelt? Can't miss her."

Mark was frozen in her grip, too scared to move. His eyes were on mine, terrified. "Charms on the table," she said, the strain obvious in her voice, and I took another step forward.

"Here's the sitch," I said, locking my knees so they wouldn't see them shake. I wasn't afraid, I was mad. "The guy in the corner just stepped out to get his buddies. He's got lots of friends with really cool toys, and if you don't let Mark go *this instant,* I'm going to get mad enough to do something I'm going to regret. I'm a demon, Cordova. Don't push me."

Cordova jammed her weapon into Mark a little harder. "Charms on the table. Now!"

Eloy was touching the back of his head where he'd hit the floor. His gun was again pointed at Trent. Mark's eyes were clenched closed, and his lips were moving. In a charm? I wondered, my heart pounding hard. Probably a prayer.

A part of me said the hell with it. Take a chance. But the fear of becoming careless with other people's lives was stronger. I had to be more careful now, not less, and I angled an arm down to let my bag hit the floor. Trent's charms spilled everywhere, and my phone slipped out.

"Rachel, wait."

It was Trent, and Dr. Cordova jammed the mouth of her weapon harder into Mark's head, making him gasp. Eloy's aim shifted to me, and I strengthened my hold on the line, ready to make a circle.

"Not now, Trent," I said. "It's me they want."

"No, it isn't."

Mark opened an eye slightly, and I risked a quick look at Trent, standing beside me in his loose-fitting, head-to-toe black, smelling of wine and broken wood as he lifted his chin and dared me to protest. He looked ticked, but not at me. "What are you doing?"

He shook his head, looking far too calm and in control. "This is not utilizing our skills to their fullest extent," he said softly, his hand on my shoulder, and then he sent his gaze past me to them. "I know how to stabilize the Rosewood enzymes," he said loudly, and I stiffened. "I'm the one you want. Not her."

"Trent!" I exclaimed, a thread of panic coming from out of nowhere to tighten around my heart, and he pushed me behind him, surreptitiously handing my magnetic chalk back. "What are you doing?"

"Something you won't," he said, and then his eyes touched on mine. "You're a good person. Don't change because I'm a bastard." Anger and frustration filled him, and then . . . as he turned so they couldn't see . . . I saw a thread of excitement running behind his thoughts, a desire to find justice, a need to prove to himself that he was not just his father, but that his mother lived in him, too. He had an idea—one he really liked and I probably wouldn't.

Someday, you're going to be glad I have that particular skill.

God save us. He was going to do something bad. Seeing my understanding, he leaned back, breaking eye contact as if it hurt. "Trent . . ." I whispered, and he handed me the battery pack and earbud.

"Improvise."

And then he turned away.

"Take me," he said boldly, his hands at his sides, his fingers spread wide, making his missing digits obvious. "I can cut your research down to days."

For three seconds, Eloy considered it. Dr. Cordova tightened her grip on her pistol, clearly reluctant to let Mark go. "He's not a witch," the woman said, and Mark's eyes met mine, looking for direction. I had none to give.

A slow smile began to spread across Eloy's face, and my heart pounded. He had his gun again, and he motioned for me to move. "Back up, Rachel," he demanded, his voice dripping scorn, and Dr. Cordova shifted her feet, which made Mark stumble.

"He's not a witch!" she said louder, and Eloy gave her a look that told her she was being stupid. "If we take him, the entire country is going to be on us!"

"Exactly right." Satisfaction in his every motion, Eloy gestured for Trent to put his hands on his head and come closer. "It will be on every news station in every U.S. city. Everyone will know that HAPA has struck back. They will know that we are no longer going to sit and hide, but that the animals that have enslaved and murdered us will again be hunted and slaughtered." He shouted at me, righteous anger slamming into me like a wall, "You will *back up!*"

Mouth dry, I retreated, slipping when my foot hit the charms spilling out of my bag. Was that why Trent had taken my place? Did he know my magic was faster? Was he going to distract them so I could do something? Improvise? Damn it, I wish I knew what he was doing!

Dr. Cordova shifted from foot to foot. A gap of air showed between Mark's head and the gun in her hand. I found my balance, spooling line energy until my skin hurt. There was nothing from the earbud dangling down my front.

"Get rid of that useless witch," Eloy barked, and Dr. Cordova shoved Mark at me.

I reached out and caught him, keeping us upright as our feet scrabbled for purchase amid the spilled charms. He was a tad overweight, and we almost went down, even as he turned to face them, sweating and stinking of redwood.

I crouched to grab a charm, pulling to a stop when Eloy made a negative sound.

Hand reaching, I froze as I saw Dr. Cordova's gun aimed

at Trent's middle. A shot there wouldn't kill him right away, but it would kill him.

Trent just stood there, his lips pulled back from his teeth slightly, that same wild look I'd seen on him once before as Cordova's arm wrapped around his neck, her gun pointed into his side. "I would have preferred Eloy, but this is acceptable," he said, and then I stiffened when I felt a circle go up. It wasn't me. It wasn't Mark. It was Trent.

"No!" I shouted, reaching out helplessly as the gold shimmer wove a net around all three of them. Behind the haze, Trent became boneless, his dead weight making Dr. Cordova tighten her grip on him. The gun went off, and Eloy cried out, the shot ricocheting off the inside of Trent's circle and slamming into Eloy's shoulder.

Swearing, the man fell back against the inside of Trent's circle, one hand on his shoulder, the other pointing his gun at Dr. Cordova.

"Ta na nevo doe tena!" Trent shouted, Dr. Cordova's arms holding him to her.

Dr. Cordova screamed as Trent's magic hit her. I backed up, horrified as I recognized the curse, the same one that had mutilated Winona. *Where did he get the blood?* I wondered when Cordova let go and fell, pawing at herself as her body contorted, her shoes falling off as hooves formed. Her head hit the floor, her brow heavy and misshapen. Small horns scraped the tile as she screamed, her voice cut off in a strangled gurgle of terror as she looked at her hands, now thick and short fingered. Terrified, her voice came in high-pitched squeals as a curly red pelt wormed its way out of her skin.

Blood seeping from around his fingers, Eloy pressed against the wall of Trent's circle. Gun forgotten, he stared in horror as Dr. Cordova turned into the mirror image of Winona. The woman's thin tail lashed wildly, and he recoiled when it touched him. It worked on humans. The curse worked on humans . . .

"On the floor. Now," Trent said to Eloy. "Or I'll turn you into what you really are, too."

His voice was cool and dispassionate, hard and unforgiving. I stared at him, seeing not a businessman out of place playing at something he was not, but the same man who'd perched atop a horse in the sunset, the world at his fingertips and justice waiting to be meted out—calmly, surely, and satisfyingly. Eloy dropped his gun, terrified.

I jumped when Mark accidentally bumped my shoulder. He was watching, wide eyed. "Wow," he breathed as Trent's circle dropped and Dr. Cordova mewled weakly, her little hooves scrabbling at the tile. "I almost didn't come in tonight."

Eloy lowered himself to the floor, his eyes never leaving Dr. Cordova. The woman was crying, dark streaks running down her black face. Her breath rasped in and out, and she cried out pitifully. Eloy jumped when Trent kicked his gun to me, then Cordova's to a corner.

Cold steel slid across the tiles, and I stopped Eloy's gun with my foot, not bothering to pick it up. "I thought you said I wouldn't like your charms," I said, and Trent grinned, reminding me, for some reason, of seeing him perched in a tree, crouched and dangerous. He hadn't killed anyone, and a part of me was undeniably glad.

An unexpected burst of radio noise came from out of nowhere, and I twisted, finding the earbud on the floor. Something was happening.

In a surge of motion, Dr. Cordova scrambled to her feet, her hooves skittering on the smooth tile. Goat-slit eyes wide in panic, she tried to run only to reach for a table and miss, her jaw cracking on the flat of it. She slid to the floor and started to crawl, crying.

"Get her!" I cried, and Eloy lifted his head. In a fast crab walk, he lunged for Cordova's gun, six feet away under a table.

"Look out!" Mark shouted, and I turned to the front windows—just in time to see six men boil in the front door. The-men-who-don't-belong screamed at us to freeze as they surrounded all of us. Though dressed unalike and in street clothes, it was obvious they were professionals. It wasn't the wicked-looking guns pointed at us, or the boots designed for running. It wasn't the short haircuts, or that every single one of them looked like he could do a six-minute mile. It was their faces, as uncaring as if they'd have no problem shooting us even if it was a mistake.

"Gun! Gun!" I shouted, pointing at Eloy, but it didn't matter. They already had him down, and as I watched, someone snapped his wrist when he refused to let go of his pistol. Eloy screamed, and I felt myself pale.

Remembering what the captain had said, I put my hands in the air. "Whoa, whoa, whoa!" I shouted as a very large black man walked in, his cap saying "captain" more than his confident walk. "I got nothing on me but chalk. Splat gun is in the purse. Where in the *hell* have you been?"

Trent started to kneel with his hands behind his neck, and one of the men grabbed him, shoving him into a booth. "Hey," I started, affronted, and then shouted, "Hey!" again when the captain grabbed my biceps and roughly propelled me onto the same bench as Trent. "I thought we were working together!" I exclaimed, but my sudden pull on the ley line sputtered to nothing and my knees gave way.

Smiling as if having expected it, the captain hauled me back to my feet, a silver amulet in the shape of an eagle suddenly glowing brightly. Dazed, I wondered if that was where my attempted blast of ever-after had gone. "Did you just . . ." I started, reaching for it, and he shoved me farther into the booth.

I hit Trent's shoulder, and the elf grinned at me as he scooted over to make room, his hands carefully atop the table where everyone could see them. "You enjoying this?" I said, in a bad temper, and he smiled even wider, the scent of woods and wine spilling from him.

"It's better than studying portfolios with Quen," he said as Mark landed on the bench across from us, looking scared but relieved. My shoulder bag was next, sliding to a stop at the end of the table. The charms, I noticed, were being swept up with a huge, very quiet vacuum cleaner that was taking everything not nailed down: chunks of plaster, broken glass from the pictures, Dr. Cordova's shoe . . .

People were still pouring in, some of them in street clothes, but most in nondescript blue work coveralls. *Hats and clipboards,* I thought, thinking they could walk anywhere at any time and get into anyplace, never seen, never noticed. And what was with that ley-line drain? I'd never felt anything like it. Watching the captain, I started to slowly spindle the line, taking it in a trickle.

"Knock it off, Morgan, or I'll show you how we take down dead vampires," the big man said without looking at me, and I let go of the line. *Damn! Who had I just invited into my parlor?*

"They're fixing the damage," Trent said as the dusty scent of wall spackle pricked my nose and a metal ladder clanked upward.

"You okay?" I asked him, and he nodded, his enthusiasm undimmed but getting harder to see as his usual calm control exerted itself. I could see it there, though, simmering.

"Yeah!" Mark said, leaning over the table toward us since we appeared to have been forgotten for the moment. "What just happened? What is she?" he said as Eloy and Dr. Cordova were literally dragged out the back door.

"Justice," Trent said, and the big man standing at the end of the table turned.

"Better you don't know," I said as the captain's eyes squinted. He had his arms over his chest, his biceps bulging from under his polo shirt. "I thought we were doing this together?" I complained. "Nice of you to come back, but if all you're going to do is abuse us, you can just go away and we'll take Cordova and Eloy in ourselves."

"Relax, Rachel. I'm sure this will even itself out," Trent said as he scooted a bit farther from me and relaxed his shoulders. In an eyeblink, the businessman was back, but I could see through it. I think the captain could, too.

"Truer words have never been spoken," the man said, his

voice the same one from my earbud. His eyes never leaving mine, he shifted a lapel mic closer to his mouth. "Cleaners."

My gut tightened as the captain's satisfaction that they had HAPA was tempered by my feeling of a new uncertainty. We'd given them their take, but I didn't like how they were treating us. Mark hiccupped and slid to the back of the booth when the captain eased his well-muscled bulk onto the bench across from me. Past our little corner of quiet, a dozen people silently worked washing Eloy's blood and Dr. Cordova's spit from the floor, spackling, painting, replacing pictures of babies dressed up as flowers. From the ceiling, the whine of a battery-powered drill intruded, and I blinked as they replaced the broken fixture with an identical one.

"Thanks for the help," he said, and I brought my gaze back to the captain, startled to see him sitting quietly with his hands laced on the table.

"Really? You're appreciative?" I said tartly. "You could have fooled me. Here I am trying to get to know you, and you get nasty."

The captain inclined his head. "I wanted to evaluate your performance in a controlled setting. You did good. He did better. Interesting."

Trent? I thought, following the captain's attention to him, and Trent frowned, clearly angry with himself. He had thought this might happen. I'd known it was a possibility, but I had so badly wanted a working relationship with someone who had guns that I'd ignored it. My heart pounded, remembering both the ley-line sink and his comment about taking down dead vampires. And now they were interested in Trent? Great.

Trent cleared his throat, the sound attention-getting, confident. "We just saved you—"

"Nothing," the man interrupted as he leaned back, sourly eyeing us all. "You got in the way. Made a mess of things. Jeopardized six weeks of work—not just this acquirement, but the entire week. The last ten minutes proved to me that you're a menace, Morgan, not only to yourself, but to everyone around you."

I'd been told that before, and it still didn't bother me. "We can work together, you know. It works with Glenn pretty good. Inderlanders and humans." I wasn't going to give this up. I wanted *someone* on my side.

The captain's focus sharpened, his mind clearly on something else. "Tell me about Mathew Glenn."

Beside me, Trent stiffened. "Don't."

"He's one of the most honest, upright people I know," I said hotly. "You think he's HAPA? You think he's working with that nutcase you just carted out of here? He's dating my roommate and he eats pizza. There's no one except maybe Jenks and Ivy I would trust more with my life."

Trent's foot touched mine. "You're making a mistake."

"That's exactly what I'm telling them!" I said, then frowned as a man in a lab coat came in, a little tackle box in his hand.

"No," Trent said patiently. "*You're* making a mistake."

I shut my mouth. I didn't like men in lab coats. The big man across from me sighed, his arms back over his chest as he flicked a glance at the doctor, then back to me. "I think so, too. Just wanted your opinion."

My chest hurt as he stood up and gestured for the man in the lab coat. "You leave him alone. You hear me?" I all but hissed. "If you touch him, I swear I'll . . . I'll . . ."

The man in the lab coat stopped at the table beside ours, opening up his little box and bringing out a glass vial and three syringes. The glass vial hit the table with a clear and certain clunk, and I stared at it, my pulse hammering. Seeing what was happening, Trent sighed. Mark's eyes were huge, but he didn't move, trusting us—trusting me.

"Roll up your sleeves, please," the doc said, and I stared up at him, scared out of my mind. Beside me, Trent was undoing his cuff button, his motions having a quick sharpness that told of his anger.

"I'm sorry. Do what he says, Rachel," Trent said, and

I shook my head, shrinking back and holding my arms to myself.

"No. You can't do—hey!" I shouted as someone grabbed me from behind and another yanked my arm out, pinning it to the table. I tried to rise, the line singing in me. The captain pinned my wrist to the table, and the line washed out of me. I tried to stand, but someone behind me had grabbed my feet from under the bench.

"Rachel!" Trent shouted, and I caught my panic. The captain was watching me sharply. Mark was frightened, his arm out as the doctor finished injecting him with something. Trent offered his arm next, and I felt a moment of helplessness. I couldn't fight them all alone.

"It's a memory blocker," Trent said, his eye twitching as the doctor tied his arm off. "I recognize the label. I'm sorry. I should have . . . done something."

Memory blockers? I hesitated in my panic, and then a new fear slid into place behind it. I would be fine, but Trent. Damn it, I didn't want him forgetting the last three days! I'd had fun!

"You lied to me!" I said, and the captain smiled.

"Not at all. I haven't shot you—yet," he said, and I struggled until the man holding my arm hurt me. Wanting to fight back, I looked around the coffeehouse. Everything was back where it belonged, right down to a cup of coffee steaming at the pickup window. Most of the-men-who-don't-belong were gone. It was just us—and whatever they had injected into Trent.

Trent grimaced as he bent his arm up to prevent any blood leaking out. His motions jerky, he pulled his sleeve back down and buttoned it.

"You're all going to pay for this," I said and the doctor gingerly tied a rubber hose around my arm. "You're all bullies," I said, wincing as the needle slipped in. "Bullies and weenies. You know what happens to weenies?" The needle pulled out without a pinch, and the doctor turned to put his stuff away. Someone let go of my feet, and I kicked at them.

"They get roasted!" I shouted as the man behind me let go of my shoulders. Panting, I sat there as they all left and the door shut behind them. Damn it to the Turn and back. As soon as it took hold, Trent was going to forget—the curses he gave me, helping me with Eloy under the streets, our conversation in my kitchen.

And then it was just us three, the doctor, and the captain.

Trent's car keys hit the table, dusty from the vacuum and apparently lost in the fight. Or maybe they had lifted them to search his car. I was betting it was the latter as Trent dragged them off the table and into his hand with a sour expression. This sucked. This sucked royally.

Mark was pale, and he pulled himself away from the wall. "Are we going to die now?" he said, his voice quavering.

The captain put his hands on the table and looked down at us. They were huge and covered with scars. "No. You're going to forget the last two hours happened."

I looked up from rubbing my arm as the doctor snapped his bag shut and glanced at his watch. I wasn't. I was going to remember. I wasn't going to let this go. Ever.

"You will not notice anything out of the ordinary when we are gone," the captain continued, "and you, Mark, will change your entrance code at the back door to 0101 like I told you the last time. Got it?"

Mark bobbed his head. "Yes, sir."

I could feel the demon curse hazing through me, spilling along my muscles like slow tequila as it neutralized the toxins. "And maybe repaint the floor with some metallic circles so I can catch people easier," I added, making the captain of the-men-who-don't-belong frown.

"Yes, ma'am," Mark said obediently, and the captain turned to Trent and me.

"You're not going to get away with this," I said, frustrated anger filling me. "I hate memory charms! They don't last. We will remember." I'd make sure of that. It might take me a week in Al's library, but I'd find a way to return Trent's memory. I didn't want to be the only one to remember this—

the way he looked, what he did to see the run through. How dare they take that away, a moment when he was exactly who he wanted to be? It was only two hours, but it was the stuff that made us who we were.

I jerked back as the captain reached for me, finding his hand behind my neck as his other hand pulled my lower eyelid down to see how my pupils were dilated. "Which is precisely why we don't use them, Ms. Morgan," he said softly as he gauged my state. "I prefer old-fashioned drugs."

"Get off," I snarled, and he jerked his hand back as I tried to hit him.

Eyes narrowed, the captain leaned away. "You both will forget the entire evening," he said, and I glared at him. "Including the realization that HAPA has infiltrated the FIB. We're getting them one by one, and your interference is sending them deeper. HAPA does not exist anymore as far as you're concerned."

Bullshit. But I forced myself to relax like Trent and Mark were, pretending. I let my hands unclench, and my shoulders slumped. Beside me, Trent breathed, slow and relaxed. *I'm sorry, Trent. I will get your memory back for you. I promise.*

Head bobbing, I watched the captain huff as if satisfied, then glance up at the doctor, standing at the end of the table. "Well?" the captain said, and the doctor looked at his watch.

"They won't remember a thing," the man said, his European accent harsh. "Not even how they got here."

"Good. Let's go. Lady. Gentlemen," he said, hands on the table as he rose. Without a backward glance, they headed for the door. Just as they reached it, the captain hesitated, turning with one hand raised in question. "Oh, and if you ever interfere with another one of my actions, I will put both of you in the cells next to those cretins we just caught. I have lots of room in my facility, and unlike Alcatraz, I've never had anyone break out. Elf. Vampire. Were, *or* witch."

Touching his forehead in salute, he turned to leave, holding the door for the laughing couple coming in. Depressed, I sat for a moment as the bells jingled against the door.

That's a different chime, I thought as I looked up. My eyes were damp, and I wiped them. How was I going to explain to Trent why he was here dressed in thief black and with his lip swollen? He'd never believe me.

Something hit my foot, and I jerked my attention to Mark as he slid out from the bench, confusion pinching his eyes. "Ah, I'll have your coffee in a sec," he said, glancing at the seat as if wondering why he had been in it. "What was it you wanted?"

I swallowed hard, my hands shaking. "I'd like a grand latte, double espresso, Italian blend—"

"Light on the froth, heavy on the cinnamon, with a pump of raspberry in it?" he finished, starting to smile. "I remember. And for you . . ." He looked at Trent. "It was a grand latte, hazelnut, with two pumps, right? You were in here last week."

"If you would," Trent said, his low voice sounding as depressed as I felt.

Mark strode briskly away, his pace jerking to a pained slowness after three steps. Rubbing his shoulder as if confused, he went behind the counter, pulling his sleeve up to look at the new bruise in the making.

"I'm sorry, Rachel," Trent whispered as if to himself. "I should have worked harder to find a memory charm that worked on demons."

My head jerked up. "You remember?"

Trent's jaw dropped. "B-but . . ." he stammered, his eyes going to my arm where they had injected me.

"You remember!" I said, elated, then lowered my voice, almost dancing as I moved around to sit across from Trent, taking my shoulder bag from the table and sliding it next to me. "Oh my God! Trent! How?"

Looking delighted but confused, he leaned in until our heads almost touched. "My father owns the patent on those drugs. You don't think I know how to circumvent them?" He shook his head, amazed. "But you. Rachel . . . I didn't have time . . . It was either the pain charm or the memory charm, and I thought you'd rather be alive without your memory than dead with it."

I leaned back, then forward again, not knowing what to do with myself. He remembered. "The I.S. was wiping the memories of witnesses, and since I didn't want to solve these crimes for them and wind up with nothing in my bank account . . ." My words trailed off, and suddenly I couldn't look at him anymore. His ring glinted on my pinkie, and I turned it over and over, a weird feeling coursing through me as I avoided his eyes. "It doesn't work for anyone but demons. I would have found something for you, but there wasn't time to do that and everything else."

He was silent, and I looked up. "I'm glad you didn't forget," he said, and I froze when he reached across the table, put his hand on mine for a bare second, and gave it a squeeze. I blinked, startled, and he jerked away, the rims of his cropped ears turning red.

"You okay?" I said, a new tension starting to build as he hid his hand under the table. There was a group of highly trained, well-funded humans who could take down Inderlanders and keep them incarcerated. We had helped them capture two HAPA members, one deeply entrenched in the FIB. I was having coffee with Trent. It was the third thing that I was worried about.

As if appreciating the change in topic, he shifted uncomfortably on the hard seat. "I'm finding it very hard to believe that there's been a group of humans policing HAPA and Inderland without my knowledge." Crossing his arms, he looked over the repaired coffeehouse. "I wonder who funds them. I've got some toys they might be interested in."

I snorted, my arms draped over the table in contrast to his upright decorum. "They just tried to wipe your mind and you want to sell them stuff?"

Shrugging, he flicked his eyes to mine, looking embarrassed. "I need to make a call."

In the background, Mark was staring in confusion at the note in his pocket. I bit my lip, feeling the sweet relaxation of burnt-out adrenaline. I didn't want this to end yet. We had gotten HAPA, survived the-men-who-don't-belong, and my coffee was on the counter waiting for me. "Can it wait? I need a moment to catch my breath," I said, and his attention jumped to me.

"Sure." His gaze going to the dessert shelves, he tilted his head. "How about a piece of cherry pie to go with that coffee? Bringing down bad men makes me hungry."

"Perfect," I said as I stood. *Pie? Trent liked cherry pie?* I'd have to remember that.

"My treat," Trent said, and I hesitated, waiting as he reached behind him for his wallet. His breath caught and he blinked up at me. "Ah, I didn't bring my wallet," he said, and I laughed.

"I got it this time, Daddy Warbucks," I said, and I ambled to the counter, happy and content with the world.

Twenty-Eight

My pace was fast as I hustled through the cold, sunset gloom toward the DMV office. They were about to close, but if I could get in the door before it was locked I was going to try an old-fashioned sit-in to get them to cough up a permanent registration; the one that Nina had gotten me was ready to expire. I'd been trying all week. I would have asked for Nina's help, but she was on extended sick leave. She was in bad shape, but Ivy was making a difference. It must be hard to adjust when a dead vampire suddenly isn't in you anymore. Like a crash from riding the high of a drug.

Someone was coming out of the bland-looking building, and I ran the last few steps, reaching out with my gloved hand to catch the door and missing. The man looked up from buttoning his coat, his eyes going over my shoulder and widening. Behind me reflected in the door's glass was a ruddy square face, a hunter-green top hat, and a wicked, smiling grin.

"Al!" I shouted, spinning to put my back to the door, heart pounding. I hadn't realized the sun was so close to setting. "What are you doing here? I've got to finish this before they close. I'll meet you in the garden in twenty minutes."

"Twenty minutes," the demon scoffed, peering over my shoulder at the line still stretched to the door. "Not likely. Let me have a go," he said petulantly. "Scaring civil servants is beyond all but the most depraved demons, and you, itchy witch, are not nearly nasty enough."

He was reaching around behind me to the door handle, and I put a hand on his chest. "No. I'm trying to be a part of society, not get my way out of fear."

Startled, he looked down at my hand and Trent's ring still glinting on my pinkie. Behind me came the *snick* of the lock being slid into place, and I slumped. Damn . . .

Smiling over his glasses, he reached for my hand and I slid out from his reach. "Same difference," he said lightly, swinging his walking cane as he looped his arm in mine and escorted me back to the parking lot. It was cold enough to snow, and I jammed my free hand in my pocket, depressed, as Al walked jauntily at my side with a walking cane and a hat. Not much had changed in the month since putting HAPA away, but then not many people remembered that HAPA had been responsible for the murders.

"Anyway, we don't have time for you to practice scaring civil servants," he said as we made our way back through the cars. "I want you to try that curse. The marvelously complex one rife with risk that you've been avoiding. We have a party to attend later tonight."

Swell. Head down, I reclaimed my hand and dug through my shoulder bag for my keys as we neared my car. "Al, I'm not ready to fix Winona. What if I get it wrong?"

But he had put a heavy, white-gloved hand on my shoulder, and even as I reached for my car door, my outsides seemed to pull inward with a rush of ever-after, and I snapped a bubble of protection around me as I felt the line take me. It held the icy sensation of frost, and my mind seemed to relax into an om of a hum. I had missed this.

They're going to impound my car if it's still here in the morning, I thought at Al flatly, but the world was already materializing around us, damp and green. I had no idea where we were. It was cold and snowy outside in Cincinnati.

Al's hand slipped away, and I looked up to see a plate-glass ceiling. Tired ferns edged the slate path we were standing on, and moss. Benches lined the way, most having clay pots on them with even more ferns and flowerless orchids. I peered through the vegetation, deciding that we were in a huge hothouse, the ground cold and gray beyond the glass and the heaters that I could now hear humming. The greenhouse was large enough for trees, and it smelled like vermiculite.

Ahead were more trees, and behind us was a small table and two wire chairs with comfortable, plush cushions. It was vaguely familiar, and I looked up into the dark, silent canopy high overhead.

"Where are we?" I asked. "Trent's interior gardens?"

The demon tilted his head, giving himself a devilish mien. "Of course. Popping right into Trenton Aloysius Kalamack's house would be rude."

It must be something else, because Al had never before been interested in what was rude.

"Mmm, where is my little bitch?" he murmured, his buckled boot grinding into the slate as he turned.

"Winona?" I asked, my anxiety swelling.

"Not Winona. Ceri." Al breathed deeply. "Bloody-hell wench was easier to deal with when I had control of her soul. She's gotten positively uppity. Wait here. I'll fetch her." He hesitated, his head spinning to look down the trail. "That way, I think. I can smell baby shit."

"Al!" I called, not wanting to be caught in Trent's hothouse alone, but he had vanished in a cascading wash of black ever-after.

I slumped. I was probably on-camera, somewhere. "Hello?" I called, going to sit in one of the chairs. A rustling at the edge of the ferns caught my attention, and I looked down expecting to see a rodent or maybe a bird, but my lips curved up in a smile when I found a gaunt fairy, silver and pale, standing guard with a hand-carved spear pointed at me. She didn't have any wings, telling me she was one of the fairies who had attacked me last summer.

"Hi," I said, my eyes widening when the fairy made a

stabbing motion at me, snarling. "Um, I know your sister Belle. I'll take her something if you like."

Immediately the fairy straightened and stood her spear up to point at the sky. Giving me a long-toothed, scary smile, she ran into the brush. I watched the slowly swaying vegetation grow still, wondering what Trent felt about having become the first year-round landlord of a clan of fairies. They couldn't migrate, and this was far better than inviting them inside the house. Maybe I should set up a little hothouse of my own. Nah, I liked the pixies too much.

I dropped my keys into my bag, and seeing my phone, I pulled it out to text Ivy that I was at Trent's with Al and that my car was parked at the DMV. There were soft steps on the slate walk, and I looked up, dampening down an unexpected wash of feeling at the sight of Trent. He was moving at a confident pace, but his stance was wary as he came forward, unbuttoning his suit's jacket to show a soft linen shirt and a gray tie. I had no doubt that I'd tripped some sort of alarm, but the fact that it was Trent coming to see me, not Quen or a faceless security guard, did a lot to ease my mind.

The memory of tagging HAPA at Junior's swam up, and I flushed. It wasn't that I was embarrassed, but I had felt so free with him, talking about memory charms while having pie, and now everything was awkward again. I didn't know why.

"Rachel?" he said as he came to a stop beside the table, a long, narrow hand coming to rest atop the tiled surface. "When did you get here? Is Ceri with you?"

I pulled my eyes from his hand, still bare of any ring save the one, twin to my own, on his index finger. "Uh, hi. No. Hey, I'm sorry, but Al is wandering around, looking for her."

Trent's face lost its expression, a ribbon of fear sliding behind his eyes before he mastered it. "You're joking, right?" he said, his hand with the missing fingers going behind his back.

Wincing, I pulled my shoulder bag closer to me on my lap. "I wish I was. I'm sorry about this. He thinks that charm, uh, curse for Winona is ready. Trent, I'm sorry. If I'd had any warning, I would've called. He snagged me from the DMV parking lot thirty seconds ago."

His eyes narrowed, and he sighed, looking up into the vegetation. I followed his eyes and saw a camera blinking. "Really!" I insisted, scooting to the back of my chair. "He's been like this lately. Popping into my kitchen like it's his closet and he's looking for his slippers. I think the other demons are giving him a hard time, and he's using me as an excuse to leave. He keeps taking my spelling equipment and whipped cream."

Trent reached for an insanely thin phone from the inside of his suit's jacket, flipping it open and beginning to tap fast with his thumbs, like an adolescent girl. "If there's a *demon* wandering around, Quen should know," he muttered.

"Sorry." It was the third time I'd said it, and my gaze lingered on his mutilated hand.

"It happens around you," he added sourly, eyes on his tiny keyboard.

"You're taking it rather well."

Trent snapped his phone closed and tucked it away, his remaining fingers curling, hiding the fact that some were missing. "If he so much as touches my girls, I will hold you responsible."

I stiffened. Taking my bag from my lap, I set it on the slate floor, leaned back in the chair, and crossed my legs to look more confident. "Al is not my responsibility," I said lightly, even as I felt a new tension begin to take hold. *If he touched Ray or Lucy . . .*

Pulling the other chair out, Trent sat, angled away from me but not enough to be rude. "He's here because of you. Take responsibility."

I frowned, pulling my thoughts back from the curse I'd found to put maggots into food stocks. "Can we wait to see how bad he is before we start burning me in effigy?" I said sourly, and he cracked a smile.

Relief spilled into me, and he shifted to put the flat of

an arm on the table as he looked into his garden, his mind clearly on other things as we waited. "Have you seen any more evidence of HAPA?" he asked, and I uncrossed my legs, surprised.

"Yes and no." I forced my teeth to unclench. "Glenn is quitting the FIB."

Trent's eyes flicked to mine and held. "Really?"

I nodded. "As far as anyone knows, you took me out for coffee so I could blow off steam. I think Ivy and Jenks suspect something, since no one seems to care that Dr. Cordova is gone and I'm not hell-bent on finding HAPA, but Ivy tells me Glenn is quitting the FIB, packing up Daryl, and moving to Flagstaff where the air is cleaner." Ivy was pissed, to say the least, which made living with her difficult. Well, more difficult than usual.

"I think the-men-who-don't-belong asked him to work with them," I whispered, and Trent's foot stopped moving. I looked up to find him watching me with an I-told-you-so expression, and I picked at the stone table. "It's either that, or he figured out that Dr. Cordova was a member of HAPA and he wanted out."

"Felix won't return my calls." Trent was reaching for his phone again. "Damn," he swore softly when he changed his mind and left it where it was. "I don't like the closed hearings they're conducting with the three HAPA members they have, either. It smacks of the old days."

It was one of the few times I'd ever heard him swear, and it made me smile even if the news wasn't good. "Does Ceri know what we did on our coffee date yet?" I asked, and he jerked his attention to me.

"God no." He shifted uncomfortably. "I think she suspects something, though. We've had cherry pie for dessert five nights in a row."

His voice drawled, and my smile deepened. We both settled back, content to wait as events shifted around us. I kind of liked having secrets with Trent, and I glanced sidelong at him in the growing darkness as snow started to fall, a soft hush on the glass ceiling. His profile was clean and young, his smile at our last words fading into a slight frown at some private thought.

He had turned Dr. Cordova into a monster, and I didn't care. What made it so different from what Chris had done? Was it because his justice was an eye for an eye, brutal but satisfying in a horrible way? Was it because Cordova wanted to wipe out Inderland, and he was protecting it? Or maybe that I knew he'd never do anything like that to me?

Someday, you'll thank me for that skill echoed in my mind. *Don't change because I'm a bastard* quickly followed it, and I dropped my eyes, confused.

"There she is," Trent said softly, his gaze on the path as he stood. I still didn't see anything, but a second later, I heard Ceri's voice. Another moment, and she made a turn on the path and was there. She had both Lucy and Ray, the smaller baby, over her shoulder, looking back at Al. I stiffened and rose to my feet, even if the demon was following at an obvious ten-foot distance. He was making funny faces and turning his hair different colors to entertain the little dark-haired girl, and I didn't like it.

"Ceri! What are you doing?" Trent exclaimed, almost panicking as he strode forward to take Ray from Ceri's shoulder. The little girl fussed, clearly wanting to watch the funny man with the nose drooping down to his chin, waving like an elephant's trunk.

"Relax, Trenton." Ceri shifted Lucy out of the way and gave Trent a chaste kiss on the cheek before she came to me. "The girls need to see what a demon is. They're safe. Al wouldn't dream of abducting them. I'd follow him into the ever-after and turn evidence on him for every shady deal he has made in the last thousand years."

Smiling at me, she touched me on the shoulder, and I stood to give her and Lucy a hug, still not sure about having the girls so close to Al. "Isn't that right, Aunt Rachel?" Ceri said wryly as I drew back.

"Aunt Ra-a-achel?" Al drawled.

I ignored him, busy arranging Lucy's fair hair to show off her pointed ears. "Not to mention that I will be very unhappy if he does."

Al made a rude sound, and Ray gazed at him, quiet now that she could see him. "Happy, happy," Al said sourly as he rocked to a halt when Trent pointed where he should stand, ten feet back from the table. "How did my life spiral down to making one person happy?"

Watching Al suspiciously, Trent pulled out a chair for Ceri, and she sat. "It happens when you become a parent," she said, arranging herself with small motions of grace. Her eyes went to Ray, resting in Trent's arms, the baby fixated on Al. "Stop trying to charm her."

"But she is such a *darling*!" he cooed. "I think I shall take you anyway. Such beautiful hair you have."

My face went cold, and my head jerked up.

Ceri's eyes narrowed, her aura almost flashing into the visible spectrum as she tapped a line hard enough to make my teeth ache. "Al. Leave. Now."

I tensed, but Al wasn't moving, instead pouting like a forgotten uncle as Lucy and Ray kicked and fussed. "I didn't mean *now*," he protested. "I'm not going to *raise* the child. I'm having enough trouble with Rachel." Smiling at Lucy, he whispered, and with a sparkling explosion of lights, two dozen tiny horses with butterfly wings burst into existence. Both Lucy and Ray squealed in delight, Lucy almost squirming off Ceri's lap to chase them.

"Al!" Ceri shouted, and with a flash of burnt amber, the beautiful horses fell to the earth and turned into squirming maggots. I recoiled, and Lucy howled her outrage. Ray simply looked surprised, the emotion appearing far too mature for her tiny features. Ceri's lips were a hard line as she stood, Lucy struggling in her arms.

"If you *touch* my children," Ceri threatened, and Al threw a hand dramatically into the air.

"Tish tosh. I do not want your babies. What is a demon for if not to scare?"

Lucy tight in her arms, Ceri stalked forward, her hair starting to float. "You aren't scaring them, you are *charming* them!"

Al grinned, showing his flat, blocky teeth. "I am scaring you, love," he said, reaching out to tickle Lucy.

The little girl squealed in delight. Ceri yanked her back, and Trent sucked in his breath, clearly furious. I wasn't all that happy, either, and I understood their dilemma. Putting the babies down might only make them more vulnerable. Taking them from the room might have the same result. There was no safe place if a demon wanted you and was free to roam about. The only way to fight a demon was to not look away. Not even to blink. The only thing keeping Al civilized was . . . what? I didn't know, and it made me uneasy.

"Perhaps we should leave, Rachel," the demon said, his voice having a mocking lilt, and Ceri's frustration flashed over her. "I don't think we're welcome here."

"You said you could help Winona," Ceri said as she jiggled Lucy, trying to get her to stop reaching for Al, and Al's smile grew wicked.

"Perhaps."

Al was looking at me, and a wave of worry made my stomach clench. "I think I can. I've been working on it," I said as I looked at Ceri, glad when she moved Lucy farther from Al. "I have a curse prepped, but I don't know if it will make things worse or better. I've never tried mixing curses before."

Ceri took my hand and gave it a squeeze. "It's an honest answer."

Ray cried out to get Al's attention, and Trent frowned, holding her closer when the demon blew bubbles at her like kisses, each one a different color. "I can help Winona," Trent said darkly. "We don't need a curse. Or you, demon."

Surprised, I turned to look at him, seeing his slight flush. That wasn't what he had said before.

Al, too, huffed, his back to us as he stared up into the foliage. It was starting to get dark, and there were little lights up there where the fairies were, tiny fires in the trees. "It was a curse that changed her," he said as if he didn't care. "Only a curse can reverse it, not wild elf magic, and it will be Rachel's curse," he said, turning to me as I made a noise of protest. "I *know* I can do it," he said, his hands behind his back as he looked up to the snow collecting on the ceiling. "I want to know if *you* can. Besides, you're the only one who knows what she looked like before."

I fidgeted in the chair. "What if I make her worse?" I asked, and Al shrugged as if he didn't care. His hands, though, were still clasped behind his back. It was one of his few tells, and as I looked at Ceri, she raised an eyebrow in question, recognizing it as well.

"Should I get her?" Ceri asked, bouncing Lucy on her lap to distract her.

Al pulled a watch from a tiny pocket by way of a gold fob. "I wish you would," he said distantly. "She sounds fascinating."

"It isn't fascinating, it's horrible," I said sourly, but looking at Ceri, I saw her hope, her confidence. "I'll try it if she wants to risk it," I said, and Al threw up his hands in a small exclamation.

I suddenly found myself holding a slightly squishy Lucy as Ceri stood, plopping the babbling baby in my lap. "I'll get her," Ceri said breathlessly, then ran down the path, her soft shoes almost silent.

"Ceri," I called as I held the baby out from me, but it was too late.

Lucy was craning her neck to watch her mom, a sound of dismay coming from her. Her little face screwed up, and she started to cry. "Trent, some help here?" I said, but it wasn't until Al strode forward saying, "Let me," that Trent got to his feet and intercepted him, taking both babies and moving to a bench just down the way.

I exhaled in relief as he put space between the girls and Al. They'd grown another month older since I'd seen them last, and Lucy was standing now, holding Trent's knee and wobbling as she fussed for her mother. Ray wasn't happy, either, looking more mad than anything else, her little face squished up in annoyance as Lucy filled the air with her noise.

"Al—" I whispered, wanting him to do the curse instead, but he shook his head.

"No," he said, his head down as he examined the tiny spear now sticking out of his arm. Apparently the fairies didn't like him. "Your curse seems fine. The last thing I want is you embarrassing me."

"Liar," I said, and he turned to me, shocked.

He plucked the spear out and dropped it, clearly wanting to protest, then seemed to collapse in on himself. Expression bothered, he glanced at Trent, trying to wrangle the two babies into some semblance of quiet, then came close to me, his boots with the silver buckles rapping smartly. I leaned back in my garden chair, and he put a hand on the table, almost pinning me there. "Hell, Rachel," he breathed into my ear, and I stifled a shiver at his dusky form around me. "I don't know what I'm doing, either. If you screw it up, it looks like another stupid-Rachel moment. If I screw it up, it looks as if I don't know what I'm doing, and while the first is embarrassing, the second is *intolerable*."

He pulled back at the sound of hooves on stone, his red eyes wide. "Chin up, chest out, stand up straight," he said as he yanked me to my feet, smacking my gut and shoulder in quick succession until I stood before the table, scowling at him. "Don't say anything. Ceri thinks I'm a god."

I knew that wasn't true, and I edged away from him as he waited with one arm behind him, one before, as if he was meeting royalty. Somehow he'd gotten from the outskirts to the center of the patio, looking as if he belonged among the ferns and Victorian garden furniture. Ceri and Winona were dusky shadows as they came around the bend, a small garden lamp lighting their path. Trent pointed them out to the girls, and Lucy's wail turned plaintive with little mmmmum-mums and half bounces for Ceri to come and pick her up.

Winona looked up as I said hi. She was in a comfortable, long-sleeved sweater and floor-length skirt, but her gray-skinned, ugly face with its curling horns and abnormally pointed chin put her far from normal. Her head made her top heavy, and her goat-slitted eyes reflected the light like a cat's.

"Hi, Rachel," she said, her smile fading as she looked from me to Al, standing beside me at the table. Clutching Ceri's arm, she whispered, "Is that him?"

"Yes!" Al exclaimed as Ceri disentangled herself from Winona, gave him a dry look, and physically pushed him out of the way so she could set the lamp on the table. "I am Al!" he continued, looking almost hurt, but upon bending closer to Winona, still standing at the edge of the light, his goat-slitted eyes widened. "My God, what did that bitch do to you?"

Winona lifted her chin as Ceri hissed at him to behave, and I smacked his shoulder with the back of my hand. But I had to agree that she looked monstrous, especially in the early dark of a snowy evening. "My apologies," Al said, sincere enough, I suppose. "Winona, to better gauge my student's possible success, may I . . . inspect you?"

Winona looked fearfully at Ceri for advice, but she'd gone to pick up Ray. Standing beside Trent, she gestured for Winona to approach Al. "It's okay," I added, and Al gave me a sidelong look.

"Oh, I doubt that," he said, but Winona had been brutalized so badly that Al held little threat. At the bench, Trent and Ceri had a hushed argument. Clearly they hadn't united entirely on their child-rearing guidelines when it came to demons. Trent wanted to take the girls into the vault, and Ceri wanted to use it as a learning experience. Me, I was leaning toward the vault.

"You may look," Winona said softly, her feet tapping the slate as she came forward into the light. I watched Al's face, not hers, as he leaned closer to her, breathing in her scent. His hand came out, and she stiffened.

490 • Kim Harrison

"I won't harm you," he said formally. "May I touch you?"

I thought it was weird how careful he was being, like she was important or fragile, and after a moment's hesitation, she nodded. He took her hand with an almost painful care, turning her stubby fingers over to trace the lines of her gray-skinned palm, studying it carefully. I remembered waking up in Al's kitchen once feeling that fragile, seeing him with curly red hair and a thinner body, one quickly hidden once he knew I was awake.

I backed up to the edge of the light, watching as Al turned her hand over to study the top. It looked tiny in his, and Winona's lips parted when he rubbed his thumb over it gauging the thickness of her pelt. Worry came from nowhere. I could fix this, couldn't I? What if I made it worse?

"You have a pouch." He made it a statement.

"You're not seeing that."

Her fear was obvious, the lantern's light making her look even uglier as she pulled her hand away. Al's brow furrowed, and his fingers twitched. He wanted to touch her again, but was afraid of what it might look like. "I thought so," he finally said. "Wings?"

Winona blinked, looking at me like I had the answers. "No. Should I?" she said, and I remembered the ruin of the woman under the museum floor.

Taking a step back, Al straightened to his full height, seeming to tower over her. "I'm not sure," he said in a rare bit of honesty. "There are schools of thought that say we had wings once. I occasionally have dreams of being able to fly. It could be . . . nothing."

"You don't remember what you used to look like?" Winona said, and Al made a face, clearly uncomfortable.

"No," he admitted, taking her hand again and lifting it as if showing her off. "I don't believe that we looked like this—entirely. But you're in a unique position to help us remember."

Ceri's breath hissed in as she jiggled Ray. "Winona is not going into the ever-after to help *you*!"

Winona backed up, arms around herself as she pulled out of Al's touch. His hand fell to his side, and he looked disappointed even as he studied her, how she moved, how she clearly could hear things we couldn't, her ears flicking everywhere.

I licked my lips. "Chris's data said she was producing more demon enzymes. How can she be that far off from being a demon?"

Al walked around Winona, his eyes never leaving her. "You, Rachel, are producing more demon enzymes than Winona, and you look nothing like her. True, much of Winona's appearance is closely tied to several genomes that are responsible for the expression of the proper enzymes, but this?" Again he took her hand and pulled her into taking a clicking step forward with him into the light. "No. Every witch has the capacity to look like this if the right genes are turned on at the proper time, but as a species, you *never* looked like this, no matter how far back in the genetic history you go." He hesitated, dropping her hand. "Still, Winona, you are very intriguing as you are. I offer you a choice."

Ceri patted Ray's back as she came forward to stand with me. "She's not going to help you."

"I'm not talking to you," Al said to Ceri, his eyes on Winona. His gaze was so intense, she blushed.

"No!" Ceri insisted, and he sighed, looking away from the troubled woman. "She would be poked and prodded as you tried to figure out what was turned on correctly and what was a mistake. No. You fix her, or you leave her alone."

Al lost his serious air, again becoming his customary shallow, self-centered self. "I can't guarantee my student's magic will leave you any better," he said, distancing himself. "At least now you can breathe, eat, and take a shit without help."

I stiffened. "That's not what you said a minute ago!"

"Yes, it is." Al turned to Winona. "Well?"

Ceri dramatically threw a hand into the air and turned her back on all of us, and Ray fussed when her view of Al was eclipsed. It hadn't been the resounding encouragement that I was hoping for, and my gut clenched as I exchanged a look with Trent. There was a faint hint of excitement in him, a desire to know if I could do it, and I felt my heart thump. Lucy had finally quieted, her little face determined as she wobbled at her dad's knee.

"I want to be normal again," Winona said as she gazed down at herself. "I trust you, Rachel. Whatever happens. I want to do this. Please."

Oh God. She wanted to do it. The butterflies in my stomach turned to lead and hit bottom. I'd been working up this curse for a good three weeks. It was mostly cosmetic, and ninety percent of it was concerned with her face. She might end up being forced to be a vegetarian, or the horns might grow back. But at least I now knew how to do a transformation curse and end up with body hair only where I wanted it.

"Okay," I said, and Al's breath exploded out of him in impatience. "Winona, it shouldn't hurt. I've already twisted the curse and stored it in the collective. I just have to touch you and say the magic words. If it gets too unbearable or you think it's going wrong, say the invocation word again, and it will reverse."

What if I kill her?

Ceri went to Winona, tears in her eyes as she gave her a hug. "I'm going to miss you," she said as she pulled back, disentangling Ray's grip from her horn. "After you're normal, you're going to leave!"

"I'll come back for visits," she assured her, tears welling and spilling over and making dark tracks on her cheeks. "Ceri, you've been so kind to me. I'm going to miss the girls. Trent, thank you!"

Al sat back against the table and checked his watch again. His eyes met mine, and he made a "get on with it" gesture.

"I need some space," I said, and Ceri wiped her eyes. Giving Winona a last hug, she whispered something in her ear, and backed off, coming to stand beside Al, looking beautiful next to him, Ray on the hip farthest from him.

"Isn't this marvelously exciting!" Al said, and Ceri gave him a dry look.

I was starting to shake, and I forced my jaw to unclench. Smiling sickly, I put my hand on Winona's shoulder and closed my eyes. I didn't need to shut them to work the curse, but I didn't want to see her pain if I did it wrong.

I renewed my grip on the ever-after, letting it pour into me. I could feel it pushing on Winona, and I whispered, "Touch the line. Let it flow through us both."

She took a shaky breath, and then the blockage eased and the energies between us balanced. "Don't pull back," I said, and when I felt her nod, I yanked more of the line into me.

She gasped at the increased flow, and when I felt her soul tremble, I touched the demon collective. *"Uno homo nobis restituted rem,"* I said, praying that I hadn't forgotten anything and that Winona wouldn't be paying the price for my stupidity. I'd picked out the trigger words myself, and though they didn't need to make sense grammatically, I hoped they did—or I'd be the laughingstock of the ever-after.

Winona made a gasping gurgle, and my eyes flew open. A wash of expected ever-after covered her, a bright gold from my aura stained with demon smut. She began to crumple, and when I felt the magic start to backwash into me, I let go, whispering that I took the price for this before the imbalance could even rise.

"Al?" I said, backing up as I watched her convulse on the slate. "Al! I did it wrong!"

"Wait!" He grasped my shoulder and pulled me back when I went to help her. His eyes were fixed greedily on her. "Wait," he echoed himself, softer. "You did it right."

It didn't look like that as she jerked and gagged, covered in my aura and a reflection of my smut crawling over her slumped form. Ceri had retreated to stand by Trent; they both looked worried. Ceri was holding her breath, and she let it out in a gasp when the ever-after shimmered a pure gold . . . and ran down from Winona, back into the ground like rain.

My heart thudded. She wasn't moving. Al's grip on my arm tightened, and he wouldn't let go as the woman took a deep breath. Winona had fallen with her back to us, and she slowly sat up. My shoulders slumped in relief and I exhaled. I couldn't see her face, but it had worked.

Her back to us, she looked at her arms, running her normal hands down her faultless skin. They were smooth, not covered in fur. Her bare feet poking out from under her skirt were white, with ten toes. Tugging her sweater straight, she turned to us, elated, and my mouth dropped open. "How do I look?" she said, then put a hand to her throat, recognizing that her voice was higher. "Did it work?"

Sort of? Swallowing, I looked at Ceri, then Al. His hand fell from me, and he shrugged.

Lightly curling brown hair framed her normal-looking face. Her chin might have been a shade more pointy than I remembered, but it was still normal. She had high cheekbones, a beautiful complexion, and a turned-up nose. Though subtly different from the young woman I'd first seen in the cage under the observatory, she looked human. Except that her eyes behind her long eyelashes were still slitted like a goat's.

"Well?" she said, feeling her face and thinking that it had been a success.

"Um, it's close," I said, and then, at a loss, I scrambled for my shoulder bag, digging until I handed her the small compact mirror.

Winona scrambled to her feet, wobbling as she came closer to the light, her attention on the mirror. Her eyes widened as she saw herself, and she put a hand to her face, feeling the new outline of her jaw. Al grunted when she stuck her tongue out, and Winona smiled when she saw it was normal.

"Close enough," she said as she felt behind herself. "Thank God that tail is gone."

"Are you sure?" Al purred. "Should we check?"

"Stop it," Ceri muttered, her jaw clenched in the dim light.

Close enough? "What about your eyes!" I exclaimed. "I don't understand. They should have changed. Why didn't they change?"

She looked at me and burst into tears.

"Oh, Winona," I said, reaching out for her and starting to cry myself. "I'm so sorry. I'll try again. I'm sure I can fix them."

"No," she sobbed, stepping back. "It's okay. I'm crying because I'm happy. I don't care about my eyes." She looked at Al fearfully, then back to me, starting to cry even harder. "Thank you. Thank you, Rachel. I never thought I'd have feet again. I don't care what my eyes look like!"

I patted her back, glad she was happy with the results and horribly relieved that I did the curse right—mostly—but I was still puzzled about the eyes. "Are you sure?" I asked again, and she pulled back, taking the linen handkerchief that Ceri handed her and wiping her nose.

"Absolutely," she said and sniffed, her face glistening in the dim light from the lantern. "I kind of like them."

"I thought you might," Al grumped, checking his watch again as he sat down at one of the chairs before the table. "You women are all demons in disguise."

Ceri gave Al a long look, up and down, reading the tells a thousand years of servitude had given her. "He didn't know how to do it, either, did he?" she said, and Al frowned.

"No." I felt good, and I began to smile, feeling the fear of the last month finally start to dissolve. I'd been hiding from myself for a long time, thinking that by ignoring the parts I didn't like and couldn't change, I could deny them. Even when I'd admitted they were there, I hadn't accepted them. Only now, when I understood who I was and took responsibility for my mistakes, did it all feel balanced, and as I looked at the faces around me, I felt a kinship that I'd never felt before—even if I didn't trust Al.

I had stopped a human hate group from gaining demon magic and the potential threat that had been. I'd found a way to work with the I.S. and the FIB both, though they were still yammering about that stupid list. I had saved Winona. With Trent's help, I'd even found the courage to tell Al I was alive and that I would fix the damage I'd made in the ever-after. Hell, I'd even discovered a new secret force and gotten on their watch list. Ivy and Jenks were slipping from me, but we had right now and I was going to hold on to that as long as I could. But perhaps what made me smile was the simple pleasure of having had pie with Trent—it felt good knowing that there would always be someone ready to do risky things with me, right down to taking on HAPA or the-men-who-don't-belong.

There was a slight tug on my jeans, and I looked down to see a fairy holding up a small bit of cloth. I carefully bent to take it, smiling at her as she backed up and vanished into the ferns.

Al's eyes were on mine, a pleased smile on his face, not knowing that I was happy for a lifetime of no's turning into yes. He took in my mood, and then his expression shifted as he turned to Trent, still sitting at that bench with Lucy.

Lucy, though, wasn't with him, and I tensed as I saw the little girl wobbling her first steps toward her mother. Trent was on his knees behind her, ready to catch her if she should fall. His face was a curious mix of delight and pride as he stretched his hands out. Fatherhood was sitting well on him.

"Ah, little girls," Al said as he tucked his watch away and bent to see her better. "All the best things wrapped up in sweet innocence and a will of iron. Escaping her father to play with the demon."

"You!" Ceri said, and then her face became alarmed when Lucy shrieked in delight, her pace bobbling as her path became clearer. She was headed for Al, not Ceri.

Trent's hands spread wide in dismay as he hovered behind her, not wanting to ruin her first steps, but not wanting her to touch Al, either.

"Me," Al said. "The big bad demon."

"Begone, demon," Ceri said, her expression holding fear as well as delight at Lucy's success. "Your work here is done."

Al smiled, the dim light making shadows where there should be none as he leaned toward Lucy while she squealed in delight and tipped forward. Trent lunged, but it was too late, and Al calmly reached forward and caught her as if he'd been doing it all his life.

"Done? No," Al said as Trent snatched her back, but the damage had been wrought, and the girls were clearly not afraid of him. "I do believe that it is just the beginning."

I'd often wondered what the Hollows would be like if I'd chosen a more flexible third-person point of view instead of the more intimate first-person to tell Rachel's story, and though I will never rewrite the Hollows to show what others are thinking when Rachel stubbornly pushes her way through life, the chance to see Trent's inner thoughts at this, a surprisingly pivotal scene in *A Perfect Blood*, was irresistible. Enjoy!

Kim Harrison

*F*inally, Trent thought, hand raised to forestall any questions from his employees as he wheeled a silent Rachel through the front of the main building on his way to his office. The mercurial woman hadn't said a word, but he knew more than telling as she had stared across the lab at him that she finally understood that the bracelet blocking her access to the ley lines had to come off. He'd only meant it to give her the time she needed to accept who she was. He hadn't counted on her hiding behind it. Perhaps she was more traumatized than he realized.

"Sir?" his secretary called as he passed her desk, and he smiled as if everything was fine, not balanced to swing them all into ruin.

"Candice, could you bring in a pot of coffee for two," he said lightly as she stood, and the woman checked her motion, going to the small employee kitchen just down the hall.

His office enfolded him like a warm blanket. The salt water fish tank he kept as much for the charm-breaking qualities of the water as for the colorful fish took up a large part of the wall behind his desk, and he frowned, not wanting to put her in the back of the room. The vid screen with a live-action feed from his yearling pasture was bright, the lights incorporated behind it casting a credible illusion of sun across his floor. Hearing Candace in the hall, he shifted Rachel—still worrisomely silent—so that her feet were in the artificial beam. He rocked away, then came back to move her so she couldn't see the corner where the rat cage had once stood.

"Sir . . ."

He spun to Candace. He didn't flaunt his millions but it tended to show even when he didn't try, and it bothered him when Rachel noticed. "Wonderful," he said, taking the tray before the curious woman could come into the room. "Candace, I'd like to not be disturbed please. Can you see to that?"

Nodding, the woman reluctantly backed up, her eyes lingering on Rachel. "Is she okay?"

Trent's pointed reply hesitated. Office gossip had Rachel half dead of a demon attack when the reality was she'd spent the night getting a slug taken out of her thigh. She had every right to be in shock. The way he'd felt after finding her, suffering and struggling at the end of her endurance, had been a surprise. The idea that their antagonistic better-than-you relationship they'd had since kids was slipping into dangerous territory had him questioning his own actions.

And here I am, secluding her away so she has only me to thank for what happens, he thought. *Bloody hell and damnation. I don't have time for this.*

Candace was still waiting for an answer. He wasn't going to give her one. "On second thought, take the day off," he said, and the woman's eyes brightened. Hooking his foot on the door, he swung it shut, right into the suddenly startled woman's face.

"Thank you, Mr. Kalamack," echoed briefly, and then nothing. If his secretary was out, everyone would assume he was too—at least until Quen found him.

The tray clattering on his desk failed to rouse Rachel. Concerned he sat in his chair. He'd swear she was okay, but maybe this was too soon. She was peaked in her borrowed sweats, but Rachel was tougher than she looked, a trait he remembered from camp when finding her refusing to submit to fatigue. It was one of the first things that attracted him to her. Still did.

Taking the top file from his IN box, he waved the scent of coffee at her.

Like magic, Rachel took a deep breath and pulled herself out of her funk. Head lifting, she looked at the vid screen, then him, her expression unreadable.

His heart gave a thump. She was ready to take that damned bracelet off. He'd been preparing for weeks: charms, circles, invocations. Finally he would be able to show her he was more than just a checkbook. *Why does that bother me so much?*

"Are you okay? You kind of spaced out." Setting the folder down, he leaned over the desk. "I've never said that before. Spaced out. But that's exactly what you did."

A strand of hair slipped between them as her head dropped and she looked at her hands, unmoving in her lap. "Did I?"

The soft hint of fear in her voice pulled him up and he came around to the front of the desk, not liking the position of authority that came from sitting behind it. "You started to go into shock. I thought my office would be better than a room full of helpful Ceri. Unless you want her help with this, too?" Back to her, he poured out a cup of coffee.

She seemed improved as she reached for it, shaking her head at his suggestion that Ceri join them. A spike of something went through him. She wanted him here with her. Not Ceri, not Quen, but him. *Why me?* His fingers fumbled as he poured his own coffee.

"Thank you."

Inclining his head, he sat back against the edge of his desk. *Maybe she just doesn't want Ceri's or Quen's death on her hands.*

"Don't do that," she said, and he eyed her from over his cup as he took a sip.

"Do what?"

504 • Kim Harrison

Her eyes traveled over him, making him freeze. "Sit on your desk and look sexy."

Okay, that's not what I expected. More surprised than embarrassed, Trent stood, hesitating at his indulgent chair behind his desk. Sitting there wasn't going to happen, and setting his coffee down, he shifted one of the smaller leather chairs before his desk to face her. "I've never sat in one of my own chairs before," he said as he eased down, leaning to take his coffee as he saw his office from a new angle.

Rachel silently hid behind her own cup, and a pang of worry struck him. "We can wait if you're not sure," he said reluctantly, thinking she looked scared under her thin bravado. His charms would help; he'd worked on them every morning for the last three weeks, and he was eager to try them.

"I'm sure."

Relieved, he stopped his shifting foot when she noticed it. "I have a room set up," he said, wanting to do this before Quen interfered. "Lots of circles, protection. We should break the charm before the sun goes down so we have a chance to prepare for him popping over."

"No."

"No?" he echoed, and then realigned his thinking. She wanted to do it here, in his office. "Okay, give me a moment, then," he said as he stretched to reach his phone from the wrong side of his desk. "I'll get some charms that might contain him for a few moments sent up—"

"No, as in we're not going to trap him when he shows," she said, and he fell back into his chair, staring at her.

Talk to a demon with no preparations? His hand ached, and he made a fist, hiding his missing fingers, fingers that her demon, Algaliarept had taken. "You're joking," he said, and Rachel's distant mien sharpened to an irate defiance as she unlocked the wheels and rolled her wheelchair back two lengths.

"Am I in it?" she asked somewhat breathless.

The ley line that runs through my office? Trent wondered.

If she was in the line while standing in reality, and a demon was in the line while in the ever-after . . . It was the middle ground that broke all the rules and made all things possible. "No. Rachel—"

Jaw clenched, she moved back a foot. "How about now?"

"No." She frowned at him, waiting. His eyes narrowed, and when she made an exasperated face, he stood, his arms crossed over his chest. She wasn't the only stubborn person in the room, and it rankled that she had a simple, viable option he hadn't considered. If she contacted Algaliarept within a line, all she'd need to do was step out of it to be safe from him. At least until the sun went down.

Seeing his indecision, Rachel raised a hand to explain. "I promised Al . . ." she said, then caught her breath at an unknown emotion. "I promised Al that I wouldn't ever summon him into a circle," she said, her voice low. "Trust is going to keep him calm long enough to listen."

"I thought you were going to be smart about this," Trent said sharply, and she glared at him. What was wrong with her? Trust? It was a demon, for the Goddess's sake. "*Nothing* is going to keep him calm. He's a demon. You can't trust him."

Still she sat there tapping her fingers on the arm of the chair. "You're asking their entire species to trust you to give them a cure, not a death sentence," she said, glancing at the knock on the door. "I won't let you offer them a cure in a way that prevents them from accepting it."

Is that so? Arms over his chest, he ignored the knock as well.

"Look," she said with that infuriating tone she had when handing out ultimatums. "I understand if you want to leave the room and let me handle it."

"I'm not chickening out," he said, and whoever was at the door left. "I'm pointing out a little preparation will make the difference in walking away from this or limping. Why are you making this difficult?"

Rachel extended her cup of coffee toward him, and

he took it, not sure why she'd given it to him. "Even with the promise of a cure, you've grossly overestimated our chances," she said, pale as she looked over his office as if trying to remember where the line ran. She couldn't see it with that bracelet on. "I'd prefer to contact Al immediately after taking the charm off, but if you can take it off for me right now, I'll wait and call him when I get home. He'll probably sense me and be waiting for me in the line by then."

Trent's pride stung. He'd gotten her into this. He'd get her out. Motions abrupt, he moved her two feet back and her hair swung with the momentum. "Now you're in the line," he said darkly. This was a foolish idea, but he had a few charms he knew by heart.

"Thank you.

Her soft voice stopped him cold. *Her hands are shaking.* Frustrated, he went to get her scrying mirror out of his desk. If they were going to do this, they'd do it right.

Rachel's shock was obvious when she saw it. "Where did you get that?" she said, reaching for it. "I thought it was lost in the quake!"

"I asked the coven for it," he said, pleased. "I knew you'd want it eventually."

His smile faded as she took it with a proprietary reverence. The thing was decorated with ley line symbols that made his fingertips ache and the rims of his ears hurt. "Tell me how you plan on staying alive long enough to bargain with him if you don't use what I've prepared."

Her new fragility was unexpected. "I don't really have a plan, but hiding in a spell-proof room surrounded by an arsenal isn't going to help. He's got my summoning name."

No plan? How does this woman survive? "I have your summoning name, too," he said, trying not to make it into a threat. She didn't say anything, and he finally returned to his desk, rummaging in his top drawer for his ribbon and cap. He'd be damned if he faced Algaliarept again without them. "Can't I just—"

"Defense only," she demanded. "Promise me."

He hesitated, weighing her anger against simply lying to her to get that bracelet off.

"Damn it, Trent, promise me," she said, and he turned to keep her from seeing his flush. "You're all about me taking responsibility, well this is my decision. I have to do it my way."

He slammed the drawer shut, his cap and ribbon in hand. "It's not that I don't trust *you*."

Rachel snorted. "Trust me? He might kill you. I'm not saying he won't. But if you raise one charm in anything other than defense, I will spell you down you myself." She hesitated. "Sure you want to stay?"

This wasn't how he'd wanted to do this, but he nodded. Rachel slumped into her rolling chair. "Thank you," she said. "Is it going to hurt when you take the bracelet off?"

"No." Frustrated, he shifted his chair to face her. He'd never hurt her again. It had been agony when his spell had hit her instead of Winona. Unable to meet her eyes, he draped his ribbon over his neck and fixed the cap on his head. The line hummed about him, and he shuddered as he opened his second sight to make sure there were no demons ready to snag them.

"Why am I even here if you won't let me do anything?" he grumbled as the image of the red-smeared ever-after wavered over the reality of his office, the knee-tall grasses waving in the gritty wind and the broken city shining in the red light.

But then he noticed she was shaking again. Fear iced through him. *He* had to be the one to break the spell bound into the bracelet, but Ceri should be here to protect her from Algaliarept, not him. Or Quen. Either of them were experienced in dealing with demons. But she had asked him, and he wasn't going to fail her. Never again.

"Give me your hands," he said, calm though he was fighting the shakes as well.

Her fingers were cold as they slipped into his, and they clasped hands, their joined knuckles resting on the tingling sensation of the scrying mirror. She looked frightened, and he gave her fingers a tiny squeeze to make her look up. "Don't let go until I say," he warned her, and when she nodded, he closed his eyes to begin the spell. It was in Elvish, and he shoved his feeling of embarrassment away.

"*Sha na tay, sha na tay,*" he said, his voice becoming more sure as he chanted it, seeking the attention of the Goddess that he was reluctantly beginning to believe in. He'd seen too much not to. His pulse quickened, an awareness seemed to touch on him—one eye among thousands idly turning his way. The line was all around him, and dizzy with it, he let it fill his chi. And when he was sure he had the Goddess's attention, he reached for Rachel's chi.

His eyes flashed open as he found it empty, utterly and desolate, dead where once it had been bright with life. And Rachel herself? He mused, seeing her with his eyes closed waiting breathlessly for him to break the charm. She couldn't feel him there, his soul twining about hers. *My God, what have I done to her?* He had to rekindle her chi before breaking the spell, and the only way to safely manage it would be to use his own energy.

"*Tunney metso, eva na calipto, ta sowen,*" he whispered, changing his chant as he allowed the energy of his chi to spill into her, and her aura seemed to pulse with it.

Rachel's fingers gripped tighter. She was feeling something; he was doing it right, and he forced himself to calm. It was indescribably intimate, as if he was touching her face, running his fingers through her wild untamed hair, caring for her when she was helpless.

But then again, she was.

His chanting bobbled as her eyes opened, clearly feeling a change. A shimmer of moisture glistened, and he closed his eyes, unable to bear seeing her realize what he'd done to her. Her chi swam with his energy, alive once more, but the charm still prevented her from connecting with the lines as it looped forever. He slowed his chanting to pick the spell apart, widening the syllables, spacing them, and therefore

their intent, farther and farther apart until at last the spell
was frayed enough that the cadence lost its meaning and . . .
disintegrated.

For an instant, it was as if their souls stood at the same
place, their energies the same. Rachel gasped, and they
stared at each other in wonder. "My God," he whispered.
What have I done to her? He thought, humbled. The spell
was broken, but it wasn't sealed, and her soul was bare to
him, the scars of her tragic past and her triumphs over pain
and her aching need to find her place. He just wanted to
hold her to him and tell her it would be okay, that she had
survived and was beautiful.

But he couldn't. She'd never believe him.

"Is it done?" she whispered.

Shaking his head, Trent licked his lips. *"Tunney eva so
Sa'han, esperometsa."*

Rachel gasped as the line flooded her through him, and
he bowed his head, holding her fingers as it burned, the energies shifting between them and growing stronger. He was
hurting her again, but he couldn't stop it. The line raced
through them both, stronger than any he'd ever felt. But then
he realized she was glorying in it, this force that had him
gritting his teeth in pain.

"I'm sorry!" she said as she realized it, too, and he tightened his grip before she could pull away.

"Dampen it so I can think," he said, and he looked up
when she did, longing to touch her face in reassurance—she
was shamed that she hurt him. She was shamed that she had
hurt him. "Sha na tay, euvacta," he whispered, sealing the
curse so it would never act again.

Rachel gasped when he pulled his hand away. Head
down, he let go of the line, feeling overly full, tingly, as if
he'd run through a lightning storm naked in the rain. His
hand cramped up, and he hid it, trying to rub the ache away.
"Now it's done and sealed," he said, but he wasn't sure she
heard him, frantically pushing at the bracelet on her wrist.

The silver metal had gone black, and with a final wrench,

the circlet slipped from her, hitting the floor to roll to a halt in the fake sun. Eyes wide, she stared at it, then him. He was an idiot. She didn't need his help. The woman could channel enough ever-after to down an elephant. "Better?" he said, and then cringed when he realized she was crying.

"Thank you," she said, her hand was on the mirror to call Algaliarept. "I'm sorry," she added, and he flushed as he realized he was rubbing his hand where her fingers had gripped him.

"For this?" he said, dismissing it, and she shook her head.

"For what happens next."

She wanted to summon Algaliarept. Into his office. With no protection whatsoever. Panic hit him, and he shoved it away. Adrenaline demanded he move, and he pushed his chair out of the line to make more room for whatever might happen. Though they were inside, the gritty wind from the ever-after pushed on him, and the cloying, rank scent of burnt amber. He stood beside her, gazing at the red sun and dry grassland superimposed on his office. Rachel's touch on his hand shocked through him, and he jerked.

She was trying to open his fist, and his fingers sprang open.

"When this is over, can I fix that?"

My fingers, he realized, shivering when she brushed his palm. *She's talking about fixing my missing fingers.* "If you like," he said with a false calm, then pulled away, stifling a spun-sugar feeling as her hand slipped from his. *It's the adrenaline,* he thought, not meeting her eyes.

"Are you sure you can cure the demons?"

Nodding, he stood behind her, not sure what had brought that up. She waited for more, and when he remained silent, she set her hand on the calling glyph and closed her eyes. Trent's hair seemed to prickle, and he drew his fingers away before they could touch her shoulder.

"Maybe he's dead or in jail," he offered when there was no response, and she pressed her fingers into the mirror harder.

"He might be sleeping," she said, making him wonder at the concern in her voice. She was worried? About her demon master?

She twitched, shifting subtly in the chair as if listening to voices he couldn't hear, and an eerie feeling stole over him. She was talking to her demon, and again he fought the urge to put his hands on her shoulders. Head up, he scanned the ever-after, the reality of his office almost disappearing.

Gasping, Rachel pulled her fingers back. A dull crack echoed through the room, and his attention jumped to the mirror. A silver line now marred its perfection. "What happened?" he asked, a hand on her armrest as he leaned over her shoulder to see it. He froze as the scent of her hair met him. It was touching his cheek, tickling him.

I can't afford this, he thought, but he didn't move, watching her finger trace the new line. "He cracked my mirror," she said, clearly angry. "He doesn't think it's me. He thought I was one of his buddies, messing with him." He froze when she glanced at him, accepting his nearness—or not noticing it. "Give me a sec," she added, bending her attention down.

Trent straightened. She'd gone flippant. Not good. Nervous, he touched her shoulder to caution her, but his words died at the pressure imbalance between them. Good God, the woman was packing! "Ah, Rachel?"

She shrugged his hand away in annoyance. Peeved, he came around the chair. She was talking to Algaliarept. He could tell. The emotions were cascading over her, so clear he could almost hear her in his thoughts.

And then her bravado vanished, chilling him.

"Help me up?" she said as she lifted her fingers and set the mirror beside her in the chair. "He's coming. Get behind me."

Excitement and alarm sifted through him as he cupped her elbow. His charms. He had almost nothing. The woman was crazy. Trust? Trust was going to keep Algaliarept calm? "Where's behind you?" he said as he scanned the ever-after. "He could come in anywhere."

Rachel bobbled in his grip as she kicked her chair out of the line. "Then just stay close."

The texture of the line seemed to richen about him as her hair began to float; she'd only now just brought her second sight into play. What had he been thinking? The woman was recovering from a gunshot, and he agrees to a demon parlay? In his office?

"Rachel Mariana Morgan . . ." intoned a hard, elegant voice, and Rachel gasped, both of them spinning to look behind them. It was Algaliarept, and Trent stiffened, his hatred and fear crashing over him at the sight of the ruddy-faced, dark-haired man leaning against a rock in the ever-after. Trent's mutilated hand twitched, and he made a fist.

The scent of burnt amber grew, then vanished under the meadow scent that he identified with Rachel. She was worried. She only smelled like that when she thought she was in trouble. "Hi, Al," she said, her voice quavering as she fussed with her sweats—the demon was frowning at them in disapproval.

Hi? Trent thought. *Had she really said hi?* He should have insisted they make a circle. He should have called to have his charms brought up.

"Hey, you look good," she added when Algaliarept remained silent.

The demon didn't move, accessing them standing together to make Trent nervous. Algaliarept had blue-tinted glasses to counter the red sun and hide his goat-slitted eyes. His crushed velvet coat with tails was taking on an orange haze in the gritty wind. The hat made him look overdone and stuffy. If it was anyone other than a demon, Trent would've believed the finery was to hide an insecurity complex that needed constant reassurance. The knit gloves cinched his opinion. Gloves were for sissies.

"I look good?" Algaliarept said, his voice dripping sarcasm as he stood up from the rock.

Trent's eye twitched, agreeing that had been a stupid thing to have said.

"I look good!" he shouted, taking three steps toward them, his hand coming out as if to grab Rachel. "I'm broke and living in squalor!"

Rachel's face was creased as she begged for clemency, but the demon was coming at them. Was she going to do nothing? Alarmed, Trent pulled hard on the line, collecting it in his fist. He didn't have time to harness it with a spell, and he threw it raw at the demon. It wouldn't down him, but it might slow him up.

"Hey!" Rachel shouted, and snarling, Algaliarept flung out a hand, deflecting Trent's gold and red tinted energy. Trent ducked as it pinged into a new direction, cringing when it hit his fish tank. With a sharp crack, it exploded. Water flowed out in an awe-inspiring sight, carrying everything with it.

"Stop it, Trent!" Rachel exclaimed, and Trent stumbled when she shoved him. "You promised!"

Stunned, Trent stared at his fish flopping on the floor. "No, I didn't," he said grimly, as he gathered up the force of the line again. The demon had stopped, not because of the energy, but to stare at the fish dying on his carpet. Blast it to the Turn and back, he'd had some of them for over a decade. Ticked, Trent threw another ball of energy while the demon was distracted.

His eyes never lifting from the gasping fish, Algaliarept casually deflected it as well. It ricocheted into the vid screen, exploding it in a shower of sparks. Damn it all to hell, he was destroying his office with his own magic!

The demon was looking at them when they turned back around. "I'm paying Ku'Sox blackmail to keep him quiet about your leaking ley line," Algaliarept said, his anger obvious. "The elves are breeding true, and everyone's blaming me!" he added, his square face red. "And you think I *look good!*"

Rachel took a deep breath. "Yes, I do!" she shouted right back, and the demon reached for her. Panicked, Trent yanked Rachel backward, stepping them both out of the line. Reality flashed entirely back into existence, and his feet suddenly felt twice as soggy. His fish flopped, making little splashing sounds. Damn it all to hell, his fish.

"Hey! What are you doing!" Rachel barked at him, and Trent ran for the nearest, scooping it up and tossing it into the few inches of remaining water.

"Keeping you out of the ever-after," he almost snarled as he caught another. *Not the tang. Maybe I'm in time.* He ran to his lionfish, stymied as he hovered over it, watching it die. He couldn't touch it. The thing had toxic spines.

"Well, stop it!" Rachel said as she pushed her chair in anger, then winced as all her weight hit her bad leg. "If you want to help, give me my crutch."

Trent looked up from the gasping, colorful fish. He couldn't save it. Maybe he couldn't save Rachel, either.

"Give me my crutch!" she demanded, her gaze darting to the line and the waiting demon. "I can't reach it from here."

With a last look at the doomed fish, Trent stomped to her chair, little splashes coming from the soggy carpet. Fingers fumbling, he undid the clasps and stomped back to her. Water had reached the hall, and there were whispers behind the door. "Your crutch," he said dryly as he extended it to her.

His fingers burned as she snatched it away in anger. How could he help her if she was not willing to even listen to him, accept his help? Frustrated, he debated if he should walk out the door and leave her to her fate when she wedged the crutch under her arm, pulling him to look at her. Her back was to the line, to her demon.

"Please help me," she whispered, her eyes frightened. "I can't do this alone."

Understanding crashed over him, and he forced his expression to remain unchanged as he flicked a look at the line behind her. God, he was a fool! Her anger and bluster were a front. If she showed weakness in front of Algaliarept, he would take her. Maybe she did need him.

Shamed for his misunderstanding, he gave her a nod,

then turned to the door. Someone was pounding on it. "I'm fine! I want my old tank brought up out of storage!" he shouted, and then his eyes came back to Rachel's. "Please," he added, and her eyes welled up in relief. In that poised moment, something in him shifted, a possibility cascading over him so new that it hurt. *What am I doing? I . . . I can't allow myself to . . . to even think it!*

Heart pounding, he shoved his feelings away with a measured practice. He could not fall in love, and not with a demon, and not in the middle of a conflict! This was adrenaline. This was the excitement of playing with fire. She was able to do the things he wanted to. He was projecting. That's it. It was nothing real.

But his heart pounded as he took her elbow to help her hide her weakness. Together they squished across the wet carpet. They stepped into the line without pause, and the tingle of their shared magics went through him as they both brought up their second sights. Trent scanned the line, surprised to find Algaliarept simply waiting. Listening. Maybe she was right. Or maybe he knew once the sun went down, all the magic in the world wouldn't save her. "I don't think I like this plan," he whispered, his lips among her hair, and he breathed her in, taunting himself.

"Promise me this time," she said, her breath quick from the pain. "Promise!"

"I promise," he said immediately, and then frowned at the demon laughing at him.

With a slow motion, Algaliarept shifted his posture, becoming sly and weighty. "Explain yourself . . . student," he muttered, his eyes on the defunct bracelet on the carpet. Perhaps they could reason with him after all.

"I've been hiding," she said quickly, and they both stiffened when Algaliarept pushed up from the rock he'd been leaning against.

"You're mistaken if you think your elf can save you. He's less effective than that witch of yours, though Newt did pay me a handsome sum for him."

He was getting close, and Trent tugged at Rachel's elbow to get her closer to the edge of the line. She wouldn't move, and when she grunted in pain, his hand sprang from her elbow. Damn it, if the woman wouldn't take steps to protect herself, then he'd have to do it for her.

"Her elf is going to do just that," he said as he moved to stand between Rachel and the demon. "I did *not* work this hard at getting her to accept who she is to let you take your spoiled brat of a little boy temper tantrum out on her. She stays on my side of the lines."

Head tilting, Algaliarept sent the full force of his attention to Trent. Maybe he should have kept his mouth shut. "You put that putrid *elf shackle* on her?" Algaliarept said, his anger returning. "You robbed her of the lines with your lies!"

Resolute, he lifted his chin. He hadn't wanted to say this in front of her, but maybe Rachel needed to hear it as well. "She needed to know what she would lose before she would ever accept their cost. Now she does."

The demon's expression became ugly. "You will never enslave us again, and not through Rachel!" he said. In a blindingly fast motion, something sped from him.

Agony stabbed through Trent, and he dropped to a knee before her demon, unable to breathe. It was as if his spine was being pulled from him, and he stifled a scream, eyes wide.

"Stop it! Stop it, both of you!" Rachel shouted, but it sounded far away and distant. Her hand on him was shaking, sending sparkles of more pain through him. Oh God, he was a fool.

"Al, he has the cure for the demons!" Rachel said, and he managed to look up, see her panic, panic for him. "You really want to kill him? I could have taken it off whenever I wanted. He's not enslaving me, he's trying to help, and I was not listening! I'm a demon, damn it! Knock it off!"

Suddenly, the pain was gone. Gasping, he almost fell prostrate. His hands gripping the soggy carpet eased, and he took another breath, then a third. Slowly he stood, his knees wet and his hands shaking. Algaliarept was standing a distance away, the knee-high grass waving about his feet. What had saved him? That she'd admitted she was a demon? Did he still breathe because he'd gotten her to admit that she was a demon when all of Algaliarept's attempts had failed? He could work from that. Perhaps survive.

"You okay?" she said as she bent over him. Her voice trembled, and the demon's eyes narrowed at her concern.

Realizing she was holding him up, he pulled himself straight. "This is a stupid idea, Rachel," he said sourly. "Let's trust a demon to be reasonable. Brilliant!"

The demon's chuckle was not pleasant, but it was clear he agreed. "You lied to me," Algaliarept said, and Rachel lifted her chin defiantly. "Ran away. Shacked up with . . . an elf?"

Startled, Trent pulled himself up. The demon was concerned they'd become close?

"I took a sick day," Rachel said boldly. "I lost my aura in the lines while cursing Ku'Sox. If Trent hadn't put my soul in a bottle till it healed, I'd be dead. Sorry about sending Ku'Sox to you, by the way. Are you okay?"

My God, she's really concerned about him, he decided. What the devil had been going on during those weekly lessons of hers in the ever-after? But what truly shook him was when Algaliarept's angry smile faltered at her question, as if what she felt about him mattered. By all that was holy, the demon *liked* her?

Stunned, Trent's thinking radically shifting to one of fear. What had Rachel become that a demon cared whether she lived or died, that he would suffer on her behalf, that he would . . . Damn it, Rachel had done it to himself as well. She had them both dancing to keep her safe. No wonder she'd made him promise not to hurt Algaliarept.

"I'm broke and paying him blackmail!" the demon raged, but it was obvious now to Trent that he'd never hurt her, and if she'd been right about that, she was probably right about a lot of things. He'd been working with bad information.

No, just not believing what he'd been given. There was a difference.

"Now that you're alive to take the blame for unbalancing the ever-after, I'll give you the honor of paying him instead," Algaliarept finished, and Rachel gripping his arm. Trent felt himself pale. With that breathless look on her face, anything could come out of her mouth.

"Trent knows the cure for the demons' genome," she said, and panic iced through him.

But she'd turned away, pleading with the demon. "Al, you don't have to keep going on like this. You can move on if you let it."

Stop! But another part of him wondered what he was willing to sacrifice to save her, and it scared him he didn't know the answer.

Goat-slitted eyes met his when he looked up, the quirk to the demon's lips making him wonder if the demon knew exactly what was going through his mind. "You ask me to trust an elf," the demon said as if testing the waters. "You ask too much."

Licking her lips, Rachel stepped forward, pulling Trent along with her. "Al, I think I know what you looked like. Originally, I mean."

"This is why you came out of hiding? To tell me that?" Algaliarept nearly snarled, but his anger was a front to hide his desire to know. Truth after truth was falling on Trent, changing his entire world. Algaliarept was hurt that she'd left him. Hell's bells.

"No," she said, and Algaliarept's glare became suspicious.

"You're in trouble?" he asked dryly, looking at her leg. "I can fix that."

Again a white glove reached, and Trent drew Rachel away, pulling her back to his front. He hadn't liked the possessive glint to Algaliarept's eye. The demon's expression became ugly, and Rachel took an annoyed sounding breath. But she didn't push from Trent, and his hold became more decisive.

"No! I'm not leaving with you," she said, annoyed when Algaliarept came even closer. "Listen to me."

Once more the demon reached, and Trent circled her middle with his arm. Breathing in the scent of her hair, he exhaled as he tapped a line and whispered, "*So ma eva, shardona.*" Rachel made a small sound as the spell took hold, and his face warmed. He had joined their auras was all, a simple task when knowing her neural pattern so intimately, first when he'd protected her soul when her aura had been scraped off battling Ku'Sox, and then today, feeling hers chime through him when he kindled her chi back to life. The demon would see it, know it for what it meant. Algaliarept wasn't the only one who would see Rachel safe.

"What are you doing?" Rachel breathed, clearly feeling something.

"It's not a circle," Trent said, his breath in her hair. "I didn't break my promise." No, it wasn't a circle, but the demon would understand that he'd have to fight to take her, and with their auras blended, it would be messy and probably make Rachel mad at him.

Sure enough, Algaliarept's eyes narrowed and his white-gloved hand dropped, inches from touching her. Trent exhaled as he drew back. "Curious," was all that the demon said, but he backed up another, and then a third. Rachel had become positively pliant in his arms, and he wondered if perhaps he should stop.

Flicking a look at Trent, the demon slumped. "I'm broke, Rachel," he said, clearly embarrassed to be admitting it. "Tales of an elven cure will get me *nothing!* You will come back to the ever-after and prove you're alive so you can tap into the funds that have been accruing in your name and I can buy some *damned groceries!*"

He was playing on her sympathy, and Trent's hold on her strengthened until her breath came in a gasp.

"No," she said, and then to Trent, "Can you stop that, please?"

Immediately he let go of both the line and her. "Sorry. It's not supposed to hurt."

"It didn't," she said, her face reddening when Algaliarept sniggered.

The air was chill between them where there'd just been warmth, and Trent flushed when she edged away from him. "I'm a demon," she said, and Algaliarept flicked a sour look at him. "I admit it, the world knows it, but I belong here, in reality. I'm not going back to the ever-after under duress."

"I beg to differ, Rachel Mariana Morgan," the demon said.

"You can beg all you want," she said matter-of-factly. "Trent's been working to get legislation through to make me a citizen again with rights and responsibilities. If I'm lucky, I'm going to have to pay taxes next year, right Trent?"

"Ah . . ." he hedged, but clearly that had piqued the demon's interest.

Algaliarept ran his gaze up and down her, his attention lingering on her leg. "Why did you break that bracelet? To fix your leg?"

"I have to twist some charms," she said, her apparent confidence ringing false.

"You mean curses," Algaliarept all but leered.

Trent glanced at his watch, then the hall. It was quiet out there, too quiet.

"Curses," she affirmed. "I have to find HAPA or I'll get blamed for several murders. But I broke the charm so that I could fix Winona."

Al looked at the door as well. "Winona? A new friend of yours?"

Rachel nervously took a step forward. "They cursed her, Al, with my stolen blood. I can't hide behind what I *want* to be anymore. It's hurting too many people. I'm a demon, and I won't let fear keep me from being a demon anymore."

Perhaps she listens to me after all, he thought, amazed, but she'd taken another half-step forward, and he inched up to stay with her.

"She needs my help," Rachel said as if asking Algaliarept for understanding. "It's my fault she's the way she is, and no one is going to fight my battles anymore. Even if it scares me."

Trent stood ready to grab her at the first hint of provocation. "HAPA has a vial of her blood," he said. "Once they get done analyzing it, they're going to try to duplicate it and use it to eliminate Inderland one species at a time."

One thick eyebrow rose over a goat-slitted eye. "Let's all hope they start with the elves," the demon said drolly. "How very careless of you, Rachel, giving out free curses."

Rachel stiffened, clearly hurting. "It wasn't my idea."

Squinting up at the red sun, Algaliarept seemed to soften. "Demon," he scoffed. "You may be a demon, but you don't have two curses to rub together to protect yourself. You're coming with me where you will be safe."

Alarmed, Trent backed them to the edge of the line, Rachel pliant under his hand.

"No," Rachel warned the demon, and Trent put a hand out.

"She doesn't want to go with you," Trent said. It wasn't a threat. No, it was more of a promise. She wouldn't leave unwillingly while he breathed. It was that simple.

And wonders of wonders, the demon stopped, brow furrowed as he thought that over. "Rachel can't protect herself," Algaliarept said, and Trent shivered as he spoke to him alone. She had been right. Trust, though foolish, made the demon listen. "You know it better than she does. If you truly care about her, let her go. I'll keep her safe. Fill her with curses until she can stand on her own."

Shaking, he leaned over Rachel's shoulder. "Safe? The same way I kept her safe by hiding her? I nearly killed her trying that, and hiding with you will do the same. No. She will have the sun and shadow both."

Algaliarept's eyes narrowed, and Trent shrugged when Rachel pulled away from him to stare at him. Nervous, he shifted his soggy feet on the soggy carpet.

With a fast motion, the demon smacked his cane against a rock. It wasn't aimed at him, but Trent jumped anyway. "Sun and shadow. *Sun and shadow!*" the demon shouted. But it felt like a tantrum, not an ultimatum. "There is no both. There is one or the other, and you will come with me now!"

Algaliarept reached, but it was Rachel who pulled the line first, flooding Trent with the strength of it since he still held her shoulder. Grunting in pain, he held his breath to ride it out. "Oh, crap. I'm sorry, Trent!" she exclaimed.

"My fault," he almost gasped. "It's okay."

Algaliarept was eyeing them both, his hands behind his back. He was stymied, and hope spun through Trent like a sunbeam. "It's down to pride, Rachel," the demon said. "Even if I could get the rest of them to accept that you are sun and shadow both, there's the undeniable fact that you broke the balance of ever-after. I'm paying Ku'Sox through the ass to keep it quiet. I need a source of income, and you're it."

Rachel's smile made Trent sourly wonder if she was enjoying herself. "What if I sign my income from my tulpa over to you?" she said, and the demon grunted in surprise. "You can pay him from that until I fix it."

"Tulpa?" Trent questioned, and she beamed at him.

"I'll tell you later," she said brightly. "That might buy a few groceries until I can work out something with Trent in lifting that elven curse."

Twirling his walking cane in wide circles, Al eyed her, more than a hint of satisfaction in him. "And you think you're not one of us."

"Oh, but I do," she shot back at him, but she was starting to shake, and Trent held her up to help her hide it.

"Sun and shadow," the demon grumbled, but both of them heard his defeat, and Rachel exhaled, her tension leaving her. "Sign it," Algaliarept demanded as he snapped his fingers and snagged the piece of paper that had appeared, drifting down to them.

Trent reached to take it before Rachel could. "She's not signing anything until my people look at it."

But Rachel snatched it, a gleam in her eye. "Why? If it's not what I agreed to, I will burn Al's gonads off the first chance I get. Turn around. I need to use your back for a second."

Was she serious? He thought, but Algaliarept had cleared his throat, nervously shifting as he held out a new contract.

"Ah, hold on a tick. How silly of me. This is the one. Here."

Rachel smugly crumpled the first, and Trent felt a tweak on the lines as she dropped it and it burst into flame. "Mmmm, hum," she said, making a spinning motion at Trent to get him to turn around.

Nervous, he did, jumping when the paper slapped on his back, and then the light, sure pressure of a pen. He turned back when the paper slid from him, and with a shocking suddenness, he realized he was three feet from the same demon who had mauled him twice. Not only that, but the demon was smiling at him.

"Thank you, Rachel," Algaliarept said, the paper vanishing in a wash of black sparkles, and Trent stiffened when he reached for her hand. The picture of elegance, the demon brought it to his lips, flicking a look at Trent to not interfere. "Welcome back, my itchy witch."

Rachel squirmed in pleasure to make Trent frown, but Rachel was safe. For the moment.

"Bye, Al," she said happily, and Algaliarept stepped back, eyeing her over his glasses.

"If I ever see you in sweats again, I swear by Bartholomew's balls I will flay you," he said, and in a wash of burnt-amber tainted air, the demon vanished.

Rachel's sigh jerked through him. "Signing an unread contract with a demon wasn't very smart," he said, dropping his second sight and shifting is damp feet in the soggy carpet. His lion fish was dead, his vid screen a gray empty hole. The lack of the fake spot of sun seemed to make the room dark.

"Oh, I beg to differ." Clearly in a good mood, Rachel

dropped her crutch on the rolling chair and walked to his desk. She set her feet gracefully into the wet carpet, mesmerizing him.

He looked away before she could notice, frowning at remains of his fish tank. "My office is trashed," he grumped as he squished across his damp carpet and took his coffee that Rachel was holding out to him. "Why are you smiling? My fish are dead."

"Because Al and I are okay," she said as she eyed him over her mug and took a sip, becoming shockingly sexy when she licked the coffee from her lips. "That's important to me."

The fading adrenaline made him shaky, and he dropped into his chair before his desk. "You think *that* was okay?"

Shifting her shoulders, she leaned against his desk to look even more sexier, sweats and all. "Yup. He fixed my leg."

Trent's eyes widened as she gave it a smack, and he looked at the chair where she'd dropped her crutch. *When did he do that? When he kissed her hand?*

"He could have taken me anytime he wanted, but he listened. I told you not to do anything. That show you put on for him told him one thing, and one thing only."

Bothered, Trent set his cup down. He let his eyes travel up her curves, and he swore he saw her shiver. "What's that?" he said flatly.

She took a sip, and again his attention was captured by her mouth. "You're willing to risk death to help me."

"Your hair is a tangled mess," he said, thinking he liked it that way, like a lion's mane.

"Is it? You have ever-after dust all over your face."

He couldn't move as she slid from his desk. Setting her coffee down, she leaned over him and brushed her thumb under his eye.

Passion spiked through him. Almost without his volition, he reached up and grabbed her wrist, wanting to pull her down to him and kiss her soundly. But he stopped, unable to draw her down that last few inches. "What are you doing?" he whispered, wishing she would tilt her head in invitation.

The clatter at the door pulled their attention to the door, and his heart pounded at the snick of a key.

"Sa'han!" Quen said as the door swung, stopping dead in his tracks as his feet squished into the soggy carpet and he saw the broken vid screen and the busted fish tank. Behind him was David. Rachel straightened, her hand that had touched him hidden behind her back.

"Ah, thank you. I couldn't have done it without you," she said, three steps away, her head down and her face a bright red.

The want for that kiss had shocked him more than the interruption, and he fell back into the chair, cool and nonchalant as Quen came in with his questions and demands. He wasn't sure if he believed he'd really helped, but one thing was very clear. He wanted that again, that feeling of standing with her against all odds and succeeding. He wanted it so bad, he was going to risk destroying everything he and his father had worked for. He should walk away. Right now. But as she was ushered out the door under David's arm, all he wanted to do was follow her.

What the hell was he doing, falling in love with a demon?

Don't miss the continuing
Hollows adventures of Rachel Morgan with
EVER AFTER
Coming February 2013

This is close enough. Thanks," I said to the cab driver, and he swerved to park at the curb, a block down from Carew Tower's drop-off zone. It was Sunday night, and the trendy shops in the lower levels of the Cincinnati high-rise were busy—the revolving door never stopped as laughing couples and groups went in and out. The kids-on-art exhibit had probably brought in a few, but I'd be willing to bet that the stoic pair in the suit and sequined dress getting out of the black car ahead of me were going up into the revolving restaurant, as I was.

I fumbled for a twenty in my ridiculously small clutch purse, then handed it over the front seat. "Keep the change," I said, distracted as I tugged my shawl closer, breathing in a faint lilac scent. "And I'm going to need a receipt, please."

The cabby shot me a thankful glance at the tip, high maybe, but he'd come all the way out to the Hollows to pick me up. Nervous, I readjusted my shawl again and slid to the door. I could have taken my car, but parking was a hassle downtown on the weekends, and tawny silk and lace lost a lot of sparkle while getting out of a mini-cooper. Not to mention the wind off the river would wreck havoc with my carefully styled hair if I had to walk more than a block.

I doubted that tonight's meeting with Quen was going to lead to a job, but I needed all the tax deductions I could get right now, even if it was just cab fare. Having skipped filing a year while they decided if I was a citizen or not had not turned out to be the boon I had originally thought it was.

"Thanks," I said as the man handed me the receipt, and I tucked it away. Taking a steadying breath, I sat with my hands in my lap, debating if I should change my mind and go home. It wasn't that I didn't like Quen, but he was Trent's number one security guy. I was sure it was a job offer, but probably not one I wanted to take.

Curiosity, though, had always been stronger in me than common sense, and when the cabby's eyes met mine through his rearview mirror, I reached for the handle. "Whatever it is, I'm saying no," I muttered as I got out, and the driver, a Were by the rough look of him, chuckled, having heard me even over the sound of traffic. The thump of the door barely beat the three loud teenagers dressed in Goth descending upon him.

My low heels clicked on the sidewalk, and I held my tiny clutch bag under my arm, the other hand on my hair. The bag was tiny, yes, but it was big enough to hold my street-legal splat gun stocked with sleepy-time charms. If Quen didn't take no for an answer, I was going to shoot him and leave him facedown in his twelve-dollar-a-bowl soup.

Squinting through the wind, I dodged the people loitering for their rides. Quen had asked me to dinner, not Trent. I didn't like that he felt the need to talk to me at a five-star restaurant instead of a coffee shop, but maybe the man liked his whisky old.

One last gust pushed me into the revolving door, and a whisper of impending danger tightened my gut as the scent of old brass and dog urine rose in the sudden dead air. It expanded into the echoing noise of a wide lobby done in marble, and I shivered as I made for the elevators. It was more than the March chill.

The couple I'd seen at the curb were long gone by the time I got there, and I had to wait for the dedicated restaurant lift. Hands making a fig leaf with my purse, I watched the foot traffic, feeling out of place in my long sheath dress. It had looked so fabulous on me in the store that I'd bought it even though I couldn't run in it. That I could wear it tonight was half the reason I had said yes to Quen. I often dressed up for work, but always with the assumption that I'd probably end the evening having to run from banshees or after vampires. *Maybe Quen just wanted to catch up?* But I doubted it.

The elevator dinged, and I forced a smile for whoever might be in it. It faded fast when the doors opened to show only more brass, velvet, and mahogany. Taking a steadying breath, I stepped inside and hit the R button at the top of the panel. Maybe my unease was simply because I was alone. I'd been alone a lot this week while Jenks tried to do the work of five pixies in the garden and Ivy was in Flagstaff helping Glenn and Daryl move.

The lobby noise vanished as the doors closed, and I looked at myself in the mirrors, tucking away a strand that had escaped the elaborate braid Jenks's youngest kids had put it in tonight. If Jenks were here, he'd tell me to snap out of it, and I pulled myself straighter when my ears popped. There were ley line symbols carved into the railing like a pattern but were really a mild euphoric charm, and I leaned backward into them. I could use all the euphoria I could get tonight.

My shoulders had eased by the time the doors opened and the light strains of live chamber music filtered in. It was just dinner, for God's sake, and in a better mood thanks to the charms, I stepped to the reception desk, smiling at the young host, his hair slicked back and wearing his uniform well. Behind him, Cincinnati spread out in the dark, the lights glinting like souls in the night. The stink and noise of the city were far away, and only the beauty showed. Maybe that's why Quen chose here.

"I'm meeting Quen Hanson," I said, forcing my attention away from the view and back to the host. The few tables I could see were all full.

"Your booth isn't ready yet, but he's waiting for you at the bar," the man said, and my eyes flicked up at the unexpected sound of respect in his voice. "May I take your shawl?"

Better and better, I thought as I turned to let him slip the thin silk from my shoulders. I felt him hesitate at my pack tattoo, and I straightened to my full height, proud of it.

"This way, please?" he said as he handed it to a woman and took the little plastic tag, handing it to me in turn.

I let a little sway into my hips as I fell into step behind him, making the shift to the revolving circle without pause. I'd been up here a couple of times; the bar was on the far side of the entry, and we strode through tables of upscale, wining-and-dining people. The couple that had come up ahead of me were already seated, wine being poured as they sat close together and enjoyed each other more than the view. It had been a while since I'd felt that, and a pang went through me. Shoving it down, I stepped again to the center, unmoving portion and the brass and mahogany bar.

Quen was the only one there apart from the bartender, his stance hinting at unease as he stood with a ramrod straightness in his suit coat and tie. He had the build to wear it well, but it probably hampered his movement more than he liked, and I smiled as he frowned and tugged at his sleeve, clearly not seeing me yet. The reflection in the glass behind the mirror showed the lights on the river and beyond it, the Hollows. Seeing him against them, I decided he looked tired— alert, but tired.

His eyes were everywhere, and his head cocked as he listened to the muted TV in the upper corner behind him. Catching the movement of our approach, he turned, smiling. Last year, I might have felt out of place and uncomfortable, but now, I smiled back, genuinely glad to see him. Somehow, he'd taken on the shades of a father figure in my mind. That we kept butting heads the first year we'd known each other might have something to do with it. That he could still lay me flat out on the floor with his magic was another. Saving his life once when I had failed saving my dad probably figured into it, too.

"Quen," I said as he needlessly tugged his dress slacks and suit coat straight. "I have to say this is better than meeting you *on* the roof."

He smiled, the hint of weariness in his eyes shifting to warmth as he took my offered hand in a firm grip to help me onto the perch of the bar stool. Tired or not, he looked good in a mature, trim, security sort of way. He was a little short for an elf, being dark where most were light, but it worked well for him, and I wondered if that was gray about his temples or a trick of the light. A new sensation of contentment and peace flowed from him, one I'd not seen before. Family life was agreeing with him, even if it was probably why he was tired. Lucy and Ray were thirteen and ten months respectively. As Trent's security advisor, he was powerful in his magic, strong in his convictions . . . and he loved Ceri with all his soul.

Quen made a sour, amused face at the reminder of our first meeting at Carew Tower. "Thank you for agreeing to see me," he said, his low, melodious voice reminding me of Trent's. It wasn't an accent as much as his controlled grace extending even to his speech. He looked up as the bartender approached and topped off his glass of white wine. "Rachel, what would you like while we wait?"

The TV was just over his head behind him, and I looked away from the stock prices scrolling under the latest national scandal. My back was to the city, and I could see a hint of the Hollows beyond the river through the bar's mirror. "Anything with bubbles in it," I said, and Quen's eyes widened. "It doesn't have to be champagne," I said, warming. "A sparkling wine won't have sulfates."

The bartender nodded knowingly, and I smiled. It was nice when I didn't have to explain.

Quen leaned in close, and I caught my breath at the scent of cinnamon, dark and laced with moss. "I thought you were going to order a soft drink," he said, and I set my purse on the bar beside me.

"Pop? No way. You dragged me all the way into Cincy for a meeting at a five-star restaurant; I'm getting the quail."

He chuckled, but it faded too fast for my liking. "Usually," I said slowly, fishing for why I was here, "when a man invites me somewhere nice, it's because he wants to break up with me and doesn't want me to make a scene."

Silent, he tightened his jaw. My pulse quickened. The bartender came back with my drink, and I pushed it around in a little circle waiting. Quen just sat there. "What does Trent want me to do that I'm not going to like?" I finally prompted, and he actually winced.

"He doesn't know I'm here," he said, and the slight unease he had been hiding took on an entirely new meaning.

Dude . . . The last time I'd met Quen without Trent knowing about it . . . "Holy crap, did you get Ceri pregnant again? Congratulations! You old dog! But what do you need me for? Babies are good things!" Unless you happen to be a demon, that is.

He frowned, hunching over the bar to sip his drink and shooting me a look to lower my voice. "Ceri is not pregnant, but the children do touch on what I wanted to talk to you about."

Suddenly concerned, I leaned closer. "What is it?" I said, a flicker of anger passing through me. Trent could be a dick sometimes, taking his "saving his race" quest to unfair extremes. "Is it about the girls? Is he pressuring you about something? Ray is your daughter!" I said hotly. "She and Lucy being raised together as sisters is a great idea, but if he thinks I'm going to sit here while he shoves you out of their life—"

"No, that's far from the truth of it." Quen set his drink aside to put his hand on mine in warning, imprisoning it on the bar. My words cut off as he gave my hand a squeeze, and when I grimaced, he pulled away. I could knock him flat on his ass with a curse, but I wouldn't. It had nothing to do with the fancy restaurant and everything to do with respect. If I knocked him down, he'd knock me down, and Quen made up for his lack of power with a spell lexicon that put mine to shame.

"Ray and Lucy are being raised with two fathers and one mother. It's working beautifully, but that's what I wanted to discuss," he said, confusing me even more.

I drew my hands back to my lap, slightly huffy for him trying to manhandle me. So I jumped to conclusions. I knew Trent too well, and pushing Quen out of the picture to further the professional image of a happy, *traditional* family wasn't beyond him. "So discuss. I'm listening."

Avoiding me, Quen downed a swallow of wine as if needing the support. "Trent is a fine young man," he said, watching the remaining wine swirl.

"Yes . . ." I drawled, cautiously. "If you can call a drug lord and outlawed-medicine manufacturer a fine young man." Both were true, but I'd lost any fire behind the accusations awhile ago. I think it was when Trent slugged the man trying to abduct me into a lifetime of degradation.

Quen's flash of irritation vanished when he realized I was joking—sort of. "I have no issue in taking a secondary public roll in the girls' lives," he said defensively. "Trent takes great pains to see that I have sufficient time with them."

Midnight rides on horseback and reading before bed, I imagined, but not a public show of parenthood. Still, I managed not to say anything but a tart, "He gives you time to be a dad. Bully for Trent." I took a sip of bubbly wine, blinking the fizz away before it made me sneeze.

"You are the devil to talk to, Rachel," he said curtly. "Will you shut up and listen?"

The unusual, sharp rebuke brought me up short. Yes, I was being rude, but Trent irritated me. "Sorry," I said as I focused on him. The TV behind him was distracting.

Seeing my attention, he dropped his head. "Trent is conscientiously making sure I have time to be with both Ray and Lucy, but it's becoming increasingly evident that it's caused an unwise reduction to his own personal safety."

Reduction to his own personal safety? I snorted and reached for my wine. "He's not getting his fair share of daddy time?"

"No, he's scheduling things when I'm not available and using the excuse to go out alone. It has to stop."

"Ohhhh!" I said in understanding. Quen had been keeping Trent safe since his father had died, leaving him alone in the world. Quen practically raised him, and letting the billionaire idiot savant out of his sight to chat with businessmen on the golf course probably didn't sit well. Especially with Trent's new mindset that he could do magic, too.

Then I followed that thought as to why I might be sitting here, and my eyes got even wider. "Oh, hell no!" I said, grabbing my purse and shifting forward to get off the stool. "I am not going to do your job, Quen. There isn't enough money in the world. Not in two worlds."

Well, maybe in two worlds, but that wasn't the point.

"Rachel, please," he pleaded, taking my shoulder before I could find the floor. It wasn't the strength of his grip that stopped me cold, but the worry in his voice. "I'm not asking you to do my job."

"Good, because I won't!" I said, my voice hushed but intense. "I will *not* work for Trent. Ever. He's a . . . a . . ." I hesitated, finding all my usual insults no longer holding force. "He never listens to me," I said instead, and Quen's hand fell from my shoulder, a faint smile on his face. "And gets himself in trouble because of it. I got him to the West Coast for you, and look what happened!"

Quen turned to the bar, his voice flat as he said, "His actions resulted in a bar burning down and the collapse of a U.S. monument."

"It wasn't *just* a bar, it was Margaretville, and I'm still getting hate mail. It was his fault, and I got blamed for it. And let's not forget San Francisco getting toasted. Oh! And how about *me* ending up in a *baby bottle* waiting for my aura to solidify up enough that I could survive? You think I enjoyed that?"

Okay, the kiss needed to break the elven spell had been nice, but I still felt tricked.

Upset, I turned back to the bar's mirror. My face was

red, and I forced myself to relax. Maybe Quen was right to bring me here. If we had been at Juniors, I probably would be halfway out the door looking for my car. Angry as I was, I looked like I belonged here with my hair up and my elegant dress that made me look svelte not skinny. But it was all show. I didn't belong here. I was not wealthy, especially smart, or talented. I was good at staying alive—that's it—and every last person up here save Quen would be the first to go if there was trouble. Except maybe the cook. Cooks were good with knives.

Quen lifted his head, the wrinkle line in his forehead deeper. "That's exactly what I'm saying," he said softly. "The man needs someone to watch him. Someone who can survive what he gets himself into and is sensitive to his particular . . . quirks."

"Quirks?" Frustrated, I let go of my clutch purse and downed another swallow of wine. "Dude, I hear you. I understand," I said, and Quen blinked at my word choice. "I even sympathize, but I can't do it. I'd end up killing him. He's too pigheaded and unwilling to consider anyone else's opinion, especially in a tight situation."

Quen chuckled, relaxing his tight grip on his emotions. "Sounds familiar."

"We are talking about Trent, not me. And besides, the man does not need a babysitter. He's all grown up, and you—" I pointed at Quen, " . . . don't give him enough credit. He stole Lucy okay, and they were waiting for him." I turned back to the bar and the reflection of the Hollows. "He can handle whatever Cincinnati can dish out," I said softly, going over my short list of trouble. "It's been quiet lately."

Quen sighed, slumping aside with both arms around his drink to look depressed. I wasn't going to fall for it. "I will admit that Trent has a knack for devising a plan and following through with it. But he's lousy at improvisation, and that's where you excel. I wish you would reconsider."

Hearing the truth of it, I looked up and Quen lifted his drink in salute. Trent could plan his way out of a demon's contract, but that wouldn't keep him alive against a sniper spell, and that's where the real danger was. My jaw clenched and I shoved the thought away. What did I care?

"I left the I.S. because I couldn't stomach working for anyone," I grumbled. "That hasn't changed."

"That's not entirely true," he said, and I frowned at him. "You work with Ivy and Jenks all the time."

My eyebrows rose in disbelief. "That's just it. I work *with* Jenks and Ivy. Not *for* them. They don't always do what I think is best, either, but they always at least listen to me." I didn't do what they thought was best, either, so we got along tolerably well. Trent, though, was another story. He *needed* to listen—the business man made more mistakes than . . . me.

"He's doing much better," Quen said, and I couldn't stop my chuckle.

"He is not."

"He worked with Jenks," Quen offered, but I could hear the doubt in his voice.

"Yes, he worked with Jenks," I said, the wine bitter as it slipped down. "And Jenks said it was like pulling the wings off a fairy to get Trent to include him on even the smallest detail of his plan. No."

Quen's jaw was clenched again, and the worry line in his brow was deepening. "Quen, I understand your concern," I said, reaching out to put a hand on his arm. It was tense, and I pulled back, feeling like I shouldn't have touched him. "I'm sorry, but I just can't do it."

"Could you maybe just try?" he said, shocking me. "There's an elven heritage exhibit at the museum next Friday. Trent has a few items on display and will be putting in an appearance. You'll love it."

"No." I faced the mirror and watched myself take a drink.

"Free food," he said, and I eyed him in disbelief through the reflection. I wasn't that desperate. "Lots of contacts with people with too much money," he added. "You need to get out and network. Let Cincy know you're the same Rachel

Morgan who captured a banshee and saved San Francisco, and not just the witch who was really a demon."

I flushed, setting the glass down and looking around for a clock. I usually didn't wear a watch because Jenks was more accurate than one. I finally found one on the TV. Jeez, had I only been here ten minutes?

"I bet you would pick up a few legit jobs," he said, and I stiffened. I wasn't out of money, but the only people who wanted to hire me wanted me because I could twist demon curses. I wasn't that kind of a girl, even if I had the potential to be, and it bothered me that Quen knew who had been knocking on my door. Working a couple of easy chaperoning jobs for Cincinnati's elite would do wonders for my esteem.

Isn't that what Quen is offering me?

"There would be a clothing allowance," Quen wielded. My pulse quickened, not at the thought of a new pair of boots but me being dumb enough to consider this. "Rachel, I'm asking this as a personal favor for me," he added, sensing me waver. "And Ceri."

Groaning, I dropped my head into my hand, and my dress pinched as I shifted to turn away from him. Ceri. Though she had agreed to having a public image with Trent, she loved Quen. Quen loved her back with all the fierceness of someone who never expected to find anything beautiful in the world. Hell, if it was nothing more than being a security escort I could stomach Trent's demands for a few hours. How much trouble could the man get into at the museum, anyway?

"You fight dirty," I said sourly to his reflection, and he toasted me, smiling wickedly.

"It's my nature. So will you do it?"

I rubbed the back of my neck as I turned to him, guilt and duty pulling at me. Avoiding him, I sent my eyes to the TV. It was showing the Cincy skyline, which was odd since it was a national station. The banner THIRD INFANT ABDUCTED flashed up, then vanished behind an insurance commercial.

Act as Trent's security? I thought, remembering his savage, protective expression under the city when he downed that man trying to abduct me. And then how he looked on my front steps when he found Wayde carting me out of the church over his shoulder. Trent had spun a charm to knock the Were out cold with the ease of picking a flower, his coat furling and his hand outstretched in wide-eyed demand. True, it hadn't been needed, but Trent hadn't known that.

My fingers spinning the footing of my glass slowed as I recalled Trent opening up to me and telling me about the person he wanted to be. It was as if I was the only person who might really understand. *And Quen wanted me to be the one to deny him it?*

"No," I whispered, knowing that Trent would count my presence as his failure. He didn't deserve that. "I'm not going to be his babysitter."

"Rachel, you need to put your petty grudge aside and—"

"No!" I said louder, angry now, and his words cut off. "This isn't about me. Trent can stand on his own. He's better than you give him credit for. You asked me, I said no. Find someone else to spit in his eye."

Quen pulled back from me, his face creased in anger. "That's not what I'm doing," he said, but there was a whisper of concern in his denial. "I simply don't want him out there alone. There's nothing wrong with someone having your back. He can stand on his own without having to be alone."

Behind him, the TV was showing the front of Cincy's hospital, lit up with lights and security vehicles. *Have his back?*

"I won't bring it up again," he said, shifting away from me and suddenly closed. "I think our table is ready."

Confused, I slid from the stool, shimming until my dress fell right. If I was there, Trent wouldn't see it as me watching his back. He'd say I was babysitting him. Quen had it wrong. *Didn't he?*

"After you," Quen said sourly, gesturing for me to follow the man standing before us with two huge menus in his hand.

God, save me from myself, maybe Quen was right. "Quen . . ."

But then my gaze jerked up to the TV over the bar as I caught a familiar phrase, and my thoughts of Trent vanished. With a sudden flash, I recognized the new Rosewood wing behind the newscaster on the scene. The Rosewood wing was simply a fancy name for the three comfortable houselike facilities they'd built for the terminally ill babies suffering from Rosewood syndrome. The cul-de-sac was damp from the earlier rain, and lights from the I.S. cruisers and news vans made everything shiny. The thought of THIRD ABDUCTION echoed through me, and I jerked to a halt. Behind me, Quen grunted in surprise.

"Turn it up!" I exclaimed, turning back to the bar and shoving past Quen to get closer.

" . . . apparently abducted by a kidnapper posing as a night nurse," the woman was saying, and I felt myself pale. "I.S. officials are investigating, but so far they have no leads as to who is taking the failing infants, and why."

"Turn it up!" I said again, and this time, the bartender heard me, aiming a remote and upping the volume. I felt myself pale as Quen rocked to a halt beside me, both of us looking up. A phone buzzed, and Quen jumped, his hand fumbling to a back pocket.

"Because of baby Benjamin's miraculous progress in fighting the largely lethal disease, officials are not hopeful for a ransom demand—they fear that he was taken by unscrupulous biogenetic engineers trying to find and sell a cure."

"Oh my God," I whispered, fumbling in my clutch bag for my phone. They'd killed all the bioengineers during the Turn. It was a tradition both humans and Inderlanders alike gleefully continued to this day. That I was alive because of illegal tinkering didn't make me feel any better.

"Let's hope they find them soon," the woman was saying, and then the headlines shifted to the latest Washington scandal.

Head down over my phone, I punched in Trent's number. It would go right to his private quarters, bypassing the switchboard. I felt hot, then cold, my grip on my phone shaking. He wouldn't have abducted the baby, but he'd have a short list of who might have. HAPA maybe, now that they couldn't have me. Trent had once promised that he'd give the demons the cure to their infertility, but after suffering through the chaos wrought by his father saving me, I couldn't believe that Trent was looking to increase the number of survivors just yet.

The busy signal shocked through me, and I glanced up at the shadow of a man standing too close: Quen, his brow furrowed as he looked at his phone's screen. Blinking, I remembered where I was. Quen's lips twitched, and he held out his phone. It was smaller and shinier than mine. "He's on my line," he said with a thin, distant voice. "You talk to him."

Fingers shaking, I took the phone. "He'll know we're together, that we talked." Oh God, I didn't want Trent to know that Quen doubted him. He looked to him as his father despite the monthly stipend.

Quen shrugged. "He'll find that out, anyway."

Mouth suddenly dry, I answered the phone and put it to my ear. "Trent?"

The hesitation was telling, but he caught his balance quickly. "Rachel?" Trent said, clearly surprised. "I'm sorry. I must have hit the wrong button. I was trying to reach Quen."

I held the phone tighter, my pulse pounding. His voice was beautiful, and I felt glad for having turned Quen down. "Ahh," I said, glancing up at a stoic Quen. "You hit the right number."

Again Trent hesitated. "O-o-o-o-okay?"

"We were having dinner," I said, explaining nothing, and Quen's face went even more bland. "Quen and I. You saw the news? Do you know who did it?"

My worry came rushing back, crowding out my brief flash of pleasure for having caught Trent off-guard. It happened so seldom. The host was still waiting, and when Quen shook his head, he smiled ingratiatingly and walked away, dropping the menus on the bar with a loud smack.

"No, but I'm going out there right now." Trent's tone was tight, and my idea that he was fixing Rosewood babies died. "Since you're with *Quen*, would you both meet me there?"

My lips parted, even as I heard the accusation in his tone. He wanted me there? With him?

"Rachel, are you there?" Trent asked, and I flushed, glancing at Quen before pushing the phone tighter to my ear.

"Yes. The hospital, right?" *Where all the news vans were? Swell.* I couldn't help but wonder if his invitation was because he wanted my professional opinion or simply to find out what Quen and I were doing.

"Rosewood wing," he said, his tone grim. "I doubt there will be any indication as to who took the infant, but I don't want evidence to be buried if the I.S. doesn't like what they find. If one of us is there, we will at least have the truth, uncomfortable or not."

I nodded as Quen exchanged a few words with the bartender and slipped him a bill. The I.S. was an offshoot of the original FBI and local police force before the Turn, responsible for hiding Inderland crimes before humans could find evidence witches, werewolves, and vampires existed. Covering up the uncomfortable or unprofitable was in their blood.

"Rachel, may I talk to Quen?" Trent asked, shaking me out of my thoughts.

"Um, sure. I'll see you there." My stomach was in knots, and I held the phone out. "He wants to talk to you."

Quen looked at the phone, his stance never shifting as he reluctantly reached out. Turning sideways to me, he drew himself up. "Sa'han?" He hesitated. "Having dinner." Another pause. "Of course Ceri knows. It was her idea."

Ceri was in on this, too? Frowning, I forced my arms from my middle. Trent would be pissed. I knew I'd been when my mom and dad rented me a live-in personal security guy for a few months.

"No," Quen said firmly, and then again, "No. I'll see you there."

I could hear Trent complaining as Quen closed the phone, cutting him off mid-protest. That wasn't going to go over very well, I decided, and when Quen gestured for me to head out before him, I meekly fell into place, my thoughts turning to the hospital.

Behind us people laughed and clinked glasses. Below, Cincinnati moved with her people, uncaring and unaware. It felt wrong now. Someone was stealing Rosewood babies. The "why" was ugly.

Quen was silent all the way to the elevator. He avoided my eyes as I handed him my ticket to give to the coat-check woman. I could have given it to her myself, but high-society came with weird rules, and it was no skin off my nose. "You're not going to tell him?" I said, hoping he wanted to use the time it would take to get to the hospital to come up with some story other than Quen wanting to hire me to babysit Trent.

Gaze distant in thought, Quen shook out my shawl and I turned around, my head lowered. "You might be right," he said, and I shivered as the silk settled over my bare skin. "I may have acted without thought."

It was an honest answer, but Quen might be right as well. Trent didn't need a babysitter, but everyone needed someone to watch their back.

RETURN TO THE HOLLOWS WITH
NEW YORK TIMES BESTSELLING AUTHOR

KIM
HARRISON

WHITE WITCH, BLACK CURSE
978-0-06-113802-7

Kick-ass bounty hunter and witch Rachel Morgan has crossed
forbidden lines, taken demonic hits, and still stands. But a new
predator is moving to the apex of the *Inderlander* food chain—
and now Rachel's past is coming back to haunt her . . . literally.

BLACK MAGIC SANCTION
978-0-06-113804-1

Denounced and shunned by her own kind for dealing with
demons and black magic, Rachel Morgan's best hope is life
imprisonment—her worst, a forced lobotomy and genetic
slavery. And only her enemies are strong enough to help her
win her freedom.

PALE DEMON
978-0-06-113807-2

After centuries of torment, a fearsome creature walks free,
craving innocent blood and souls—especially Rachel Morgan's,
who'll need to embrace her demonic nature to survive.